"What is the meaning of it, Watson?" said Holmes, solemnly, as he laid down the paper. "What object is served by this circle of misery and violence and fear? It must tend to some end, or else our universe is ruled by chance, which is unthinkable. But what end? There is the great standing perennial problem to which human reason is as far from an answer as ever."

—From The Adventure of the Cardboard Box

"There is nothing in which deduction is as necessary as in religion," said he, leaning with his back against the shutters. "It can be built up as an exact science by the reasoner. Our highest assurance of the goodness of providence seems to me to rest in the flowers. All other things, our powers, our desires, our food, are really necessary for our existence in the first instance. But this rose is an extra. Its smell and its color are an embellishment of life, not a condition of it. It is only goodness which gives such extras, and so I say again that we have much to hope from the flowers."

—From The Adventure of the Naval Treaty

"The greatest schemer of all time, the organizer of every deviltry, the controlling brain of the underworld, a brain which might have made or marred the destiny of nations – that's the man!"

"Barker beat his head with his clenched fist in his impotent anger. 'Do not tell me that we have to sit down under this? Do you say that no one can ever get level with this king devil?' 'No, I don't say that,' said Holmes, and his eyes seemed to be looking far into the future. 'I don't say that he can't be beat. But you must give me time—you must give me time.' We all sat in silence for some minutes while those fateful eyes still strained to pierce the veil."

—From The Valley of Fear

The Confessions of Sherlock Holmes

The Theological Odyssey of the Great Detective

Volume 7

The Curtain Falls

Thomas Mengert

Blue Forge Press

Port Orchard, Washington

The Curtain Falls
Copyright 2024
by Thomas Mengert

First eBook Edition August 2025
First Print Edition August 2025

ISBN 979-8-89439-056-7

For information about film, reprint or other subsidiary rights, contact: blueforgegroup@gmail.com

Blue Forge Press is the print division of the volunteer-run, federal 501(c)3 nonprofit company, Blue Forge Group, founded in 1989 and dedicated to bringing light to the shadows and voice to the silence. We strive to empower storytellers across all walks of life with our four divisions: Blue Forge Press, Blue Forge Films, Blue Forge Gaming, and Blue Forge Records. Find out more at www.BlueForgeGroup.org

Blue Forge Press
7419 Ebbert Drive Southeast
Port Orchard, Washington 98367
blueforgepress@gmail.com
360-550-2071 ph.txt

Introduction by Dr. Watson

The philosopher Pascal was right when he proclaimed that the heart has reasons that reason knows not of. The engagement in mental gymnastics between Sherlock Holmes and Professor Moriarty lie along the spectrum of doubts and misalignments where different questions are posed to existence by intelligent minds. Human existence as encountered over the course of a single lifetime can never exhaust all points of view, but our feelings whether mediated by language or portrayed in music or the visual arts are often far more instructive because they engage the emotions. The search for a definitive answer to the great questions has always left a remainder, a residue of the inexplicable until we wonder if our problem lies in our questions not in the answers that we fail to achieve. Closure would bring human development to an end. Our Original Sin would appear to be our inability to be satisfied with something less than the infinite. If God cannot be defined and confined by our conceptions we are thrown back upon ourselves in our search for meaning. This is bound to lead to dissatisfaction so that the religious sense will always return with an imperious demand that we open ourselves to that which exceeds our grasp.

It is the peculiar intimacy of the God revealed in Holy Scripture that makes it less than a mere instance of cultural imperialism for the Gospels to record Jesus as commanding his disciples to carry the news of redemption to the very ends of the earth. It is this need to correct the errors and atrocities of history that all nations and people feel. Even those who are impervious to the effects of their own sins have little doubt regarding the sins of others against them. Not the least of these sins is the great social uprising that is called war. It is no accident then that among the greatest titles appended to Jesus is Prince of Peace.

As my great task nears its end I feel it to be incumbent upon me to refer to the intersection between faith and national policy. Each of these has played their role in this composition. The moral instinct is such that even the most blatant exercise of national self-interest demands that moral criteria come into play at some level to justify human actions and to create an orderly image of history as an ongoing process. Every nation would like to imagine that it is in the vanguard of human progress and that what benefits the nation will somehow advance the evolution of the entire human race. At the same time past experience has revealed that a principle of racial or class superiority is repeatedly brought forth as the only way that social and international order can be maintained.

Even my own religion of Roman Catholicism rests securely on a spiritual distinction between the ordained clergy and the mass of lay persons whose theological role is to listen, to learn, and to obey rather than to discern, to define, and to teach. In this sense theology can never be a science that is theoretically open to universal inquiry because by its nature eternal truths are conceived as a matter of divine commission conveyed by sacramental ordination to the priesthood. Even sacred scripture is held to be such because the Catholic Church through its ordained clergy has chosen to recognize it as such and simultaneously to rest its own institutional competence upon a commission contained within those very writings. The circularity of this process will always be troubling to those who entertain a skeptical attitude to any organization, even one that claims to speak directly from God. This has led since the Protestant Reformation of the 16th century to a universal skepticism even towards the Catholic Church. This skepticism has become now so pervasive and familiar that it now has set the tone for how we perceive history. The search for some overriding principle to guide thought and action is now focused upon certain natural forces whether they are conceived as the blind adaptation of living forms to evolution as posited by Charles Darwin, to the battle between the erotic energies and death instinct of Sigmund Freud, to the collective unconscious of Carl Jung, to the phenomenology of spirit of Georg Hegel, to the *elan vital* of Emile Bergson, or to the will to power of Friedrich Nietzsche.

These forces or energies do not require the posited deity traceable to the Hebrew scripture for validation. The result has been a creeping atheism and a certain attitude in world affairs that still maintains the cast-off shell of a religious faith for whatever pageantry or personal solace it may provide while allowing national aspirations a free expanse in practice to pursue their own business or territorial interests relatively unhindered by moral considerations. The place of religion in public life in consequence has changed substantially in the new century

The ultimate sign of aging is the realization that everything of significance in one's own life is behind one. It is too late to make a newer world. Any illusion that one may have had that one was riding securely on the crest of history is followed by the dawning certainty that the better days were years ago and what will follow is only the mockery of our hopes. As the list of our dead friends grows longer year by year the lights along the shore that assured us of our position become confused. Everything grows more disoriented and our conscious mind more aware that we are part of an age now existing only in memory. The great structures of faith and of nation are both revealed as only passing reflections in a pool of stagnant water. Too many things have come and gone, too much has happened that required all one's power to face and to emerge again intact, but not unscathed. It will require new dreamers to arise and to face the long trek towards the distant mountains of their own aspirations.

Clarity only comes with retrospection. The race for profits and colonial rule could not have ended well unless we are to assume that greed and exploitation will always be rewarded without consequences. When does the tide begin to shift? When does yesterday's slave become tomorrow's master? There does appear to be a balance in the created universe. No social order long endures without some cataclysm to reset matters. This is true even in the animal kingdom. The great predators that keep the African herds in balance prevent the overgrazing of the herbivores. But can we claim an equal function for the predatory instincts in the economy of nations? Does mankind prosper when the masses are reduced to whatever degree of subjugation they are powerless to resist? Is this great war an example of some moral nemesis or does it merely serve to winnow the excess male population and thereby reduce fertility in the exploitive European nations so that the colonized nations can reassert their long subjugated sovereignty.

If India possessed a great civilization when what is now the British Isles was mired in the Bronze Age, why should it be subject to us now? Does this mean that civilization and charity toward exterior foes is a mere luxury between periods of armed conflict? Is it possible that religion and culture are merely the vanguard of conquest and control? A mind subdued is less resistant to subjugation. Would the natives of Peru for instance have gone submissively into the silver mines of their Spanish conquerors if they had not been first baptized and told that the meek would inherit the earth by the well-armed conquistadores? It took until 1821 for Peru to secure independence from Spain. By then the silver was gone.

We civilize the natives by first destroying whatever once made life meaningful to them. We have them grow whatever will fetch the highest price in our own markets, tea, coffee, cotton, and tobacco rather than rice, squashes and beans. What is it to us if our diseases or malnutrition reduce their numbers and capacity to resist our rule? All of this proceeds unhindered until we turn our eyes of conquest toward each other. What was the Boer War but a rehearsal in arms for what was soon to come? I cannot face the daily news from France. Each day the promised armistice seems more distant, more impossible to achieve. Even the fresh

American troops are dying now like the soldiers before them in the trenches. They shall not return from France with tales to tell of the Old World with all its grandeur but rather blind and lame with their memories of their dead comrades. I devote myself now to this account of those last years of the Victorian Age and of the dawning years of the new century when disarmament seemed for brief time to be a real possibility.

I begin this penultimate volume of my final reminiscences of the later career of Sherlock Holmes with an account of what befell Rodger Baskerville in his attempt to enlist the American government in the great enterprise of spanning the two great oceans of the world by building a canal through Costa Rica. In this volume I will also turn my attention to presenting the matter in the journal that will explain at last the manner of my ultimate reunion with Sherlock Holmes after his great hiatus of 1891-1894. I do not believe that I can do so by any better means than by following the account of that period as recorded in Holmes' own voice as recorded in his journal entries.

I must however apologize to my faithful readers for misleading them by publishing an account of that reunion in a tale entitled, *The Adventure of the Empty House.* I did so at Holmes' request in order to provide a cover for Colonel Sebastian Moran who for various reasons wished to withdraw from England and to cover his exit by convincing the public to believe that he was under indictment and in police custody. Meanwhile he made a quiet exit aboard a tramp steamer to his plantation in the East Indies. The memory of the public for various crimes is remarkably short-lived, because there is always some new set of atrocities to stimulate its appetite for the startling and the sensational. Then there are always the far greater crimes committed between nations where thousands die in a single day as on the Western Front. After the Americans declared war on Germany and her allies the Great War finally turned a decisive corner as the balance shifted.

Unfortunately there were soon reports that Russia had undergone a revolution of sorts and that a separate peace treaty was to be signed in March of 1918 at Brest-Litovsk. Battles still lay ahead, but some final settlement is in sight at last. From the perspective of 1918 the course most likely to be followed by rest of the century is hazy indeed. After 1903 when Sherlock Holmes retired from private practice our old association entered a new period that this volume will explain. Some of my readers may have concluded without any evidence that either Holmes or I had died or perhaps worse that we were mere relics of a dead era and with no relevance to a rapidly mechanizing era of science and engineering feats. The skills that Holmes possessed might then have been seen as little more than parlor tricks and Holmes himself viewed as a harmless eccentric.

Some might have seen me in the role of one who acts as an impresario of a traveling sideshow of feats and marvels. Sherlock Holmes might even have acquiesced to that appalling characterization the better to pursue a course of renewed anonymity that would allow him to effectively vanish from the public eye. He would be tempted to do nothing to contradict this fallacious and unjust assessment although as his erstwhile biographer it would be painful to me. I was still jealous of his reputation and felt the need to celebrate him long after the parade of public acclaim had passed him by. Holmes however swore me to silence and I have obeyed that request leaving only this immense record as a final testament to be published when he or his executors sees fit to do so. Meanwhile Holmes began a new career after 1903 at the urging of his brother Mycroft, one involving the fate of nations that I fear that either another hand or his own must record for posterity, perhaps in a volume to be set as a sequel to this present account. I confess to be being weary at last. I have endured a long illness, hoping to survive long enough to finish this immense task, fearful always that I might die before it was completed to my satisfaction.

I still take my daily walks by the sea although they are shorter now than they once were. I have learned at last the value of new friends as old acquaintances perish. I have come to realize that old age comes on quite suddenly. It seems only yesterday that new schemes for my life sprouted up like weeds alongside my cottage; now it takes only a quick calculation for me to realize that I have neither the time nor the energy to launch some new mission or project for reformation into the stream of life, one able to advance even one of the possibilities that seem to me still to augur a new world. I must be content to do what the elderly always do: lament the many wasted opportunities of their youth and at the same time to condemn the folly of the present age where they have become strangers even to themselves. I used to enjoy sea tales of adventure and romance imagining far vistas and all manner of strange sights and customs. When did that fire disappear? Now it is like attempting to kindle a fire with wet wood where no amount of initial heat can elicit a bright glow blossoming into a self-sustaining flame. If I came upon some city of ruins I would no longer seek to reconstruct the vanished lives of the inhabitants. It is enough that they lived there once and have moved on. The village graveyard once so picturesque is now a reminder of the utter desolation of the dead. I don't know when it dawned on me that the aged are not merely an encumbrance; they represent while still living an embarrassment, a mockery of youth, and a delayed distribution of assets. I don't know which age of man is most deserving of pity. The first lines of Tithonus by Tennyson haunt me...

The woods decay, the woods decay and fall. The vapors weep their burden to the ground. Man comes and tills the field and lies beneath. And after many a summer dies the swan.

We live in a historical era where all former truths and institutions appear to be failing simultaneously. It is becoming impossible to step outside of the force lines that draw us back into the currents of exploitation. A subtle claim or lien appears to have been levied upon us while we slept a debt that we can neither escape nor defer. History envelops us in its tentacles and draws us into the realm of its inscrutable purposes. We are enlisted in games, subscribed to mailing lists, diffused among a social order that exceeds our grasp. Even if we choose to resign, our petition for release is not accepted. Each day the horizon of our security draws ever closer and should we choose to bolt for cover the unnamed predator comes out of hiding to track us and bring us down. Every place that we choose to stand has a prior claim upon it and even if we should purchase it outright, covenants are already in place to curtail our uses. But to be without property is barely to exist at all. We are urged to make our will for we might die tomorrow. Property must be neatly transferred as there are already hungry claimants.

If hiding is ineffective and a frontal assault is ill-advised, then what is left for us? Shall we shout in indignation or attempt some distracting maneuver so that we may vanish before pursuit is contemplated. We hope that our very insignificance will save us but to little avail, for then we may cease utterly to exist; better far to balance along that treacherous axis that separates insignificance from being a potential threat to the powers that be if we are to survive. To be old might be thought an advantage; memory is at least impervious to assault. But no even here the present impinges on the past and we see that we have been moving nearer each day to the abyss while we congratulated ourselves on our wisdom and progressive views. Disquieting artists like Franz Kafka and Andre Gide seem to catch the sound of the distant tremors of the earth beneath our feet, the scent of noxious sulfurous waters. Disaster is the order of the day. Disquiet the substance of our uneasy slumber.

When the Great European War began in 1914 every nation used the same formula; it was to be "a war to save civilization." Industrialism and colonial exploitation had at first sustained peace and trade relations even while they had provided the surplus wherewith to fight a war of untold dimensions. Years of national introspection combined with collective pride had managed to convince each citizen that the portals of darkness began as soon as a border was crossed. It was time for one great supreme effort to enlighten the ignorant denizens of other nations and to allow the surplus energies of one's home nation to break forth to the wonderment and eventual praise of the degenerate hordes that were still enthralled with trophies of their lost glories. So entrenched (and I use that term advisedly) was this perception that the mounting carnage of the following years did not call this absurd faith into question; it only raised the stakes of the contest further and proved to those still at home that no price of blood and suffering was too great to ask in order to prevent the settling down of a new Dark Ages that might last for centuries if final victory was not achieved.

During the writing of this immense work of many volumes I have also been engaged in that final task of every human life – to come to a final position towards one's own decisions and the pattern formed by those choices that is called one's character as an individual. It is hard enough to do this when the outer world provides a serene setting for contemplation, but when the world itself seems uncertain of the parameters of virtue and the purpose for human life and culture by descending into war this task is well-nigh impossible. The length of this manuscript and its diverse paths and scope reflect the difficulties placed before me by fate, or by choice, for I might have remained silent and allowed whatever sad *dénouement* that follows to assume its own form without the aid of my commentary and attempt at a synthesis. Still, I have pressed onwards to the end and at times considered that together Holmes and I, in our twin narratives, have gone a considerable way in our respective commentaries to say something of the historical period that coincided with our life on earth.

I find lately that I must write any insights I may have down quickly before they are forgotten and lost forever. Only then do I reflect that the world is no longer really mine. My generation is passing. The stage is being cleared for a new play and I must retire to the wings and finally leave the darkened theater behind me to seek repose and a quiet dinner before returning to my humble quarters and entering that land of dreams from which I will soon have passed over to the long anticipated, but equally feared, abode of the shades. So in leaving I will echo the words of one who I claim as my Savior by saying simply of my life and work, "It is finished; into your hands, Father, I commend my spirit."

Adieu, dear reader…

The Curtain Falls

Thomas Mengert

Book Seventeen

Holmes and Watson Reunited

The worst crimes are not those that go unsolved but rather those that do not even scruple to go undetected because society has long since grown accustomed to them so as to see them as inevitable. Among these crimes are the oppression of the weak, the degradation of woman for gain, the loss of innocence of children, and the final abandonment of the elderly. These have so long existed among us that we have grown accustomed to their presence. Some even see their practice not as crimes but as virtuous and as proof of a fallen world or part of the inscrutable will of God to separate the wheat from the chaff. I do not share their opinion.

—Sherlock Holmes

Dr. Watson's Narrative Continues

Some preliminary words upon the course of history are necessary in order to fully comprehend the events that follow. The life course that Sherlock Holmes and I had followed and that eventually brought us to America manifested, as does every age, a certain underlying pattern of events and assumptions that to a large extent determine both our circumstances and even that inner configuration that we term our personal identity. The Victorian Age in England with its great expansion in transportation and communication made it possible for huge expansion to occur in industrial production and in trade. At the same time the source of national wealth and power shifted from the great agrarian landed-estate holders to the newly rising bourgeoisie and the rise of the lower middle-class householders that filled the offices of the great metropolis of London.

England did not experience the convulsions that gripped France during the revolution of 1789 or the outburst of liberalism that convulsed the continental powers in 1848. The closest that England came to revolution was the Chartist Movement and the resistance to mechanization mounted by the Luddites. Craftsmanship still existed and the commons still managed to survive enclosure in some rural districts. The ultimate political logic of domination of the many by the few had yet to take hold as it soon would and the political atmosphere could still be influenced by various mass-movements from Irish Home Rule to the formation of craft unions and industrial syndicalism. There were even those who advocated socialism in its many guises and even anarchism had its appeal for many. But all in all it was a period of social stability and peace.

The wars of religion of other centuries now seemed extremely foolish and ill-advised. People had learned to confine their animosities to the conviction of their own salvation and a corresponding confidence that those who did not believe correctly would recognize their errors of belief when they were plunged into hell, without first undergoing some form of earthly torture by an ardent inquisitor anxious to please some reigning prince in Germany. In fact England preferred nothing more than to be left alone and not be drawn into some continental fracas. After the Franco-Prussian War of 1871 the alliances of England were designed to keep things going as they were with a united empire and administrative efficiency, both guaranteed by British maritime superiority. All of this was soon to change.

It may be hard to realize or to admit, but history reveals this truth that most of the human species exists in order to fulfill the needs of a minority ruling-class that tolerates governments but considers itself to be superior to them. Even democracies that give lip-service to popular rule are soon subverted by the existing power structure. In fact the very nature of so-called populism is to place its hopes in some demagogue who can raise the level of fear, envy, and desperation first to a fever pitch and then to direct these emotions to attain some end that will ultimately betray the hopes and aspirations of the ignorant hordes for social advancement.

All power rests upon the control of space and time and for this reason nothing is more important than the task of the map-maker and the time-keeper: one divides the land or the factory floor into worksites and the other determines how long the laborer is to be confined to serve industrial production and the profits of the few. The great American philosopher and naturalist, Henry David Thoreau, was correct when he said that "most men live lives of quiet desperation." But it is actually far worse than he ever supposed, because the real truth is that history reveals that the majority of humankind ceases to be of any value when they can no longer be reduced to some level of willing servitude. The position of the female sex when considered in region after region around the world bears out the truth of this observation. She is valued according to her ability to carry heavy loads and her time is seldom at her own disposal. Property laws even in supposedly advanced civilizations keep her discretion over property at a minimum and consider her opinions to be either quaint or impertinent in directing world affairs. Her social position even at the higher levels is determined and constrained and it is hard to know who is most to be pitied, the young woman of fashion and wealth or the maid-servant who waits upon her when both positions are already determined by social needs that exceed her own plans or aspirations.

I realized before we left Washington D.C. that the nation-state is not the true center of sovereignty but is a means to the great end of maintaining social peace and directing individuals to their assigned roles in the overall economic structure that benefits those who can reap a disproportionate share of the befits conferred. Our mission in America was now accomplished, even if not to our complete satisfaction, and I agreed with Irene Adler that we must both combine our efforts to get Sherlock Holmes away from Washington as soon as possible before his continued efforts undermined his health.

Already I did not like the late hours that he was keeping at the time. He would return each day exhausted from his investigations and I would listen from my room as he slept for any sign his old deathly cough, the one that I so dreaded lest it return and sign his death warrant. But the nights remained silent and I would find a note in the sitting room the next morning when I awoke to inform me that he needed to leave early with Inspector Hopkins and requesting that I would again make every effort to amuse Irene Adler for the day.

This routine was at last broken upon the morning following our discussion of which I have just given an account. Irene and I went down together to the hotel dining room where we found Holmes and Inspector Hopkins had preceded us. They had engaged a table in the corner, far from the other guests of the hotel. Holmes had taken to the strange American custom of morning coffee in preference to a civilized cup of tea and he was enjoying this beverage as we arrived. Both men stood up to greet us and we were soon made comfortable. A steaming teapot stood before us and I poured a cup of tea with fresh cream for Miss Adler and then one for myself as well.

I was surprised and gratified to see that Holmes did not seem as depressed as he had been of late. But he did not have about him that air of easy triumph with which he would treat the conclusion of some of his most difficult cases, problems that were as he would say, elementary in nature. On this occasion he showed only an air of quiet satisfaction not triumph so that I began to hope that we might indeed manage to pull him away from the city of Washington with its pestilential and swampy air. I was certain that the dry air of the American West combined with a healthy sea voyage home to England by way of Yokohama and Hong Kong would finally allow him to conquer that disease of the lungs that had cast a shadow upon him throughout the course of his life. In answer to our questioning glances Holmes at last condescended to speak.

"I must begin by telling you that Rodger Baskerville has returned to Costa Rica," he announced. "It is not the end that I had in view, but when I tell you all of the circumstances I believe that you will agree with me that it was the best and only course, because no other alternatives would meet with success. Even I had not imagined that this man could bring to bear such influence in a land that boasts that it is a country of laws and not of men. I am afraid that no government has ever evolved in which personalities may not trump principle when it comes to the skilful application of money and influence."

"From the beginning a great wave of fog descended upon our investigation. Doubts were raised; procedural and diplomatic considerations were suggested to us. We were asked to recall the complexity and inconvenience of probing too deeply. Through it all Inspector Hopkins attempted to interject normal police procedure and to call attention to the primary fact, which seemed simple enough: a girl was dead! But still, a margin of doubt remained, or so we were told. We could not tie Baskerville's movements to the crime and any motive that he possessed, however convincing it might be do us, could not carry the day without further evidence of a connection. I even appealed to the President, warning him that if he placed the fate of the nation's ambition to build a canal in the hands of this man, the nation would be subject to constant delays, demands, and difficulties. President McKinley smiled when I said this and assured me that there were other plans in view which might make the Costa Rica connection unimportant in the end."

Holmes continued after a significant pause, "I immediately thought of Baron Maupertuis and wondered if some joint financial arrangement had been reached with that man and the government of the United States. After all, the cost of the canal might require some source of private financing from international investors. There would be barges, excavations, dredging, and road building. Could we doubt that many private parties could anticipate making a fortune in the contracts that would be awarded? They in turn would need to borrow heavily to mount so grim an advance upon the obstacles set by nature. I tell you, the world is growing not merely too large for us, but too large for any prior conception of world affairs. It is more inter-connected and thus more complex; the locus of responsibility is too diffuse. The problems with international evils are that they are becoming so intermeshed with national policy that no nation may chart a course that does not involve at least some dealings with the devil."

"I believe that President McKinley is a good man at heart, but his policies are limited by a view to enhance prosperity alone, which has become, as Shakespeare once said in a different context, the god of his idolatry. He is a man who enjoys comfort and what he is seeking is 'a comfortable solution.' He does not relish military conflict for its own sake or to prove the national mettle like that man Roosevelt. He would avoid wars if he can manage it, but he will undertake any means if he may justify it later with what he believes is the greater good of the nation's prosperity. He assumes that his public office may justify compromise with his private morality. He has come to assume that it is alright to proclaim Christian principles in their purity to maiden aunts and old members of the congregation who are readying themselves for eternity, but that real moral choices in a real world must consult first the oracle of the politically expedient. In politics compromise with evil means is the order of the day and the man of conscience must withhold final judgment on the course that events have taken until like President Grant he is engaged in writing his memoirs."

Holmes spoke dejectedly, "I can see his point of course.

What is history but the justification of the actual decisions that determine the fate of nations by calling their course inevitable? We believe that we are the victims of history, but it is we who make it by our collective actions. Thus it is that good men and women add their silent voices to atrocities by consent, which speaks by way of acquiescence to advance the greatest evils of the age. The people bow to power and the powerful claim to speak in the name of the people. The whole matter is circular. I am afraid that that is the way things are and I fear it shall always be so."

Inspector Hopkins spoke up here, "In spite of Mr. Holmes' grim assessment we were not entirely without success. We did manage to get the fellow pressured to leave the country by ship and I personally made sure that he met the sailing hour of his vessel. You are quite safe now, Miss Adler, and may rejoin your acting company at any time. I believe that they have concluded their engagement in Baltimore and are moving on to Charleston and from there to Savannah. I have here a letter to you from the management of the company, which contains I am told a remittance of money still owed to you. The decision to join them of course is up to you."

Our eyes then turned to Irene who reached out her lace-cuffed hand for the letter that she read carefully. She also gazed with some satisfaction at the monetary draft contained with the letter.

The Inspector cleared his throat before speaking again. "There is included as you see a sum that represents an insurance settlement covering your back wages had you been able to work during these last few weeks and an additional sum to cover any restorative period of convalescence you may require due to any pain and inconvenience you may have suffered as a result of witnessing the attack and its fatal aftermath."

Irene Adler gazed down at the draft with an amused expression on her face before evidently reaching a decision. She folded it and placed it back in its envelope before secreting it in her bosom.

She looked up at once brightly and announced to us all, "I believe that I will take this funded opportunity to pursue a long held ambition of mine. I have always wanted to see the American west, particularly San Francisco. Perhaps I may persuade you to accompany me, Sherlock? I am afraid that my nerves are not yet quite what they were and it would be a great comfort for me to know that I am being escorted across those desolate regions of prairie and mountain by you and Doctor Watson; oh and by you also, Inspector Hopkins."

Inspector Hopkins spoke up at once, "I am afraid that I must return to London, dear lady. My superiors insist that the termination of our diplomatic mission here to America, also terminates my duty to accompany Mr. Holmes and Dr. Watson. I was instructed to guard them on the Atlantic crossing back to England, but I of course have no control over any decision that these gentlemen may now make, for they are both private agents and may do as they will. I can report anything of consequence that we have learned here to Scotland Yard and to Mr. Mycroft Holmes and the other men at White Hall when I return to London."

Irene then turned her appealing eyes to my companion. They were such eyes as no man may refuse and yet call himself a gentleman. Holmes smiled. "Ah well, so it must be. We shall accompany you where so ever you may lead us my lady, Dulcinea," he said.

Our return destination was thus changed to one by way of San Francisco rather than taking the direct Atlantic route home to England. It was set by the woman whose memory had long haunted Sherlock Holmes so that in the still watches of the night I would often hear his violin playing melancholy airs that he had first heard when they were sung in a darkened opera houses by Irene.

To Sherlock Holmes she would always be, "the woman." Our trip to America had showed me how just that appellation was when applied to her for in it was contained not only his profound respect but something more, a secret marriage of hearts based upon a friendship that though it might never be that of man and wife was yet a manifestation of how close two souls might be when consecrated to a common goal. Their virtue was that each recognized the need of the other to remain subject to their unique vocation and talent. Their roles were in a sense greater than themselves and each had denied the demands of love to pursue different ends. They had elected to forego the privilege of the common lot of humanity, which must find in marriage the best path to heaven. It was a great relief to me to know that the remaining burden of care for her welfare among strangers had been lifted from Holmes' shoulders. Our great foe had returned to his lair in Costa Rica where I could not doubt that he would remain. If he was no longer welcome in America, then he would be forced to negotiate by proxy through his American associates. He had evidently committed himself completely to the inter-ocean canal project of the Americas.

Still much was unsettled in my mind. To assume that the canal would be built in Costa Rica rather than Nicaragua or further south across the Panama region of Columbia would be to assume also that Baron Maupertuis would assume a secondary role and merge his efforts with that of the Americans. I could not imagine the Baron accepting such a subsidiary role because he had already staked his European reputation on building an independent European canal. There were indications that he had placed his future loyalties with Germany.

There were other reasons why he might oppose an American bid to build a canal. For the present his control of the railroad in Costa Rica had given him the best means for rapid transit of goods across the Americas. He would not surrender this advantage readily. In fact I could only imagine his doing so under the condition that a canal, if in his control, would make the existence of the railroad superfluous. I could see that a great struggle between two alliances was emerging. America would prefer England as an ally rather than Germany and England in turn would be willing to countenance an American canal over one controlled by any continental interest, whether of Germany or of France.

A canal controlled by Dutch interests alone was also unacceptable for England because should a continental war break out, an invading army could occupy the Netherlands within weeks and by doing so gain control of the canal. It is true that the Belgians might resist for a time, but however gallant their defense of their own small nation might be they could not hope to oppose the French or German armies in case of an invasion and violation of their neutrality. Indeed Belgium had become what no nation wishes ever to be, a strategic zone for exterior conflicts, a natural site for battle, a fulcrum upon which the larger nations might decide the future fate of Europe. Thus far my own reflections had progressed during that festive breakfast with Holmes and Inspector Hopkins. Irene was looking joyous that morning at the prospect of our leaving Washington. She was no doubt looking forward to being busily engaged at last in arranging matters for our imminent departure. When the breakfast ended, Inspector Hopkins volunteered to go with Irene to engage railroad accommodations for the following day while Holmes beckoned me aside for a private conversation. It was my first time in weeks to share his full confidence. It was only after the Inspector and Irene had left that he allowed his face to assume that grave air that the situation entailed. His first words showed me how deep the waters that surrounded us still were.

"I put a good face on the matter, Watson, for the sake of Irene. It is true that Baskerville is gone, but the man has shown a remarkable persistence and a tendency to return when I least expect him. It would have been a comfort to me to know that he was languishing in some American prison under lock and key instead of escaping us once again."

"You fear another encounter then, Holmes?" I enquired.

He thought about this for a moment before replying, "No, in fact I doubt that the man will live out the year. His plan was to make himself an essential go-between for all of the parties in the affair, but that position is I am afraid a two-edged sword. Events are moving swiftly. I believe that the real parties of interest will begin to see that one obscure man has become more of an obstacle to direct negotiation than an aid to its resolution. We have come to the point where sheer power exceeds the ability of even the central figures to control it. It is part of the vanity of Rodger Baskerville that he cannot imagine a conclusion, unless he plays a central role. Who can say what he will do in the case of ultimate failure or what price may be exacted from him?"

"You just said that he has powerful friends in America who have managed to shield him from a murder charge. Surely they will protect him no matter what course events may follow," I commented.

Holmes answered, "If they really desired to protect him in all cases then he would still be here daring the authorities to arrest him. Instead he has sent back into exile in Costa Rica. I doubt that many visas will be forthcoming for him from England or even America in the future. No doubt even the embassies of Columbia, Brazil, and Venezuela have been informed that he is a person to be watched. He will never have more power than he possesses at present in Costa Rica, but even there he has played loosely with many men who may still recall his former role in the old regime of the Tiger of San Pedro. He has, unfortunately for him, resigned his stable position with the British government in order to act as a free agent with the Americans and by doing so forfeited the protection that the British government might have offered him. Meanwhile the great barons of American industry now need not rely upon him, an obscure adventurer, when they have President McKinley and his likely successors at their beck and call. The entire nation has been fanned to fever-pitch with the desire for American expansion."

"I tell you that under the joint effects of his disappointment in his mission here and his poor health Rodger Baskerville will not live out the year. He has become tangled in his own web of stratagems at last. He has overreached himself and nemesis is at hand. I caught a glimpse of his face as he stood on the deck of the ship that was to carry him back into exile in the land of his former triumphs. From where I stood on the pier with Inspector Hopkins at my side he looked a defeated man. He did not know of course that he was watched, though I saw his eyes dart over the crowd from time to time. At last he gave up the search and his face turned towards the bow from time to time as the last passengers boarded. I could see the baffled fury in that face and the dread of his destination. I believe that his quick mind had already realized that his hour in the sun has passed. His friends in America were allowing him to be deported and yet there is nothing of substance to which he can return. Even now an agent of Baron Maupertuis may be awaiting him in Costa Rica to settle accounts."

"It is also possible that men like Lady Beryl's brother may

have used his absence to strengthen their own coven of revenge. I tell you, Watson, I would not care to be in his position. The ship began to move and the last I saw of him was the vision of his white face at the rail. He has quite lost his tropical coloring during these last weeks. It was a horrible sight that visage so filled with despair. It was the same face that I could imagine he would have thrown upwards in his expiring moments to the implacable night sky of Devonshire had he succumbed, as we supposed so many years ago, to the quicksand clutches of the Great Grimpen Mire."

As I listened to these confident words of Holmes I thought of my own last glimpse of Rodger Baskerville. I thought of the desperation in the eyes, the flushed countenance, the trembling fingers, each speaking in their way of a man in the last stages of addiction to cocaine, the very fate that I had once feared for Holmes. Rodger Baskerville was a man caught in that most deadly of webs, that of his own twisted soul, warped by ambition, hungry for sensation, passionate and single-minded, but directed only towards ends produced out of the delirium of his particular aspirations for personal glory. Such men burn themselves out from within like a stump soaked in saltpeter and set ablaze. There comes a point in such men where they begin to realize the horror of their position, yet are unable to change. They go on and on heaping ruin upon ruin until at last they take that last plunge that invites destruction. For all men there is an equivalent of the Falls of Reichenbach, a point where they begin to glimpse the irrevocable nature of the life that they have led and to understand the person that they have become through the course of their own actions. Woe to the man who finds in that dread hour, which may be even the hour of his death, that he is bound and unable to repent for the sovereign goodness and mercy of God now repels him. Such a man desires only a refuge from the brutal clarity that reveals him as he is. He scorns the hope of forgiveness and wishes only that he might again begin his life, the very life that he has led heretofore, but without the knowledge of its ultimate end. He dreams of the days when he imagined himself to be a god with all of the world open to his desires and appetites. Such men desire eternal youth, but without youth's innocence. What terror encompasses them when they look upon their withered visage in the glass and know it to be their own image that they see! These men cannot relinquish with grace as time passes the remnants of their strength and beauty. They do not know that finally these traits of youth and power were never really theirs at all, but were only in trust and that a final accounting must be made at last. Our lives are lent to us for a sum of days and nights, but that sum must finally be calculated and the result must be visible for all to see, for there is finally nothing secret, nothing hidden, but all will be revealed upon the last day.

Men like Rodger Baskerville have stood all their lives upon the very brink of hell. Can such men ever turn back? Is there some fragmentary truth in the grim teachings of John Calvin on predestination? John Calvin was one, who saw about him the manifold evils of men and women, but he had despaired of the efficacy of the human efforts of sinners; even a feeble effort, which at the final hour might invoke the mercy of God. Had John Calvin retained his Catholic faith and not desired certainty about salvation even to the point of heresy, had hope not long since died within him (and all who today follow the teachings of his heresy) he might have trusted the promise of Jesus, who has sworn to be with his Church until the end of time.

The efficacy of the cross of Christ promises salvation to all who are led to that test that lies beyond death when alone in full knowledge we may invoke His Holy Name and ask to be forgiven, even if it be at the price of an entrance into the condition of Purgatory. Perhaps there may be some even then who will prefer the fires of hell, there to burn as a tributary candle to their own glory rather than to be consumed in the fire of the love that God has for all of His creation.

Universal salvation may not be assumed, but in the individual case we may still piously exercise hope even for the most wicked among us. Our daily prayer must be that we will not be led into temptation and that we will be spared the final test, in the name of the One who was sorely tested, yet was obedient in all things to the will of the Father.

In the end Holmes' assessment of Rodger Baskerville's state of mind proved to be correct. It may be as well to resolve all doubts and to frankly state here that weeks later in San Francisco we received a wire from Washington to inform us that a passenger of the vessel Nemesis, one Rodger Baskerville, was reported lost at sea two days before the ship docked in Costa Rica. Whether the man was a victim of a long delayed providence, or whether his own bitterness and despair had caused him to procure his own end by jumping overboard, I may not say. In any case, with the death of Rodger Baskerville, the curse of the Baskerville family was finally lifted. The male heirs of Sir Hugo Baskerville were free again to pursue their lives untainted by ancestral guilt. The case we had begun so many years ago had finally reached its successful conclusion. However, before I leave this question of ancestral guilt behind I must direct the attention of my readers to the whole question of memory and its role in the preservation of grievances. Anyone who has ever visited the site of a dreadful accident or spent time on an ancient battlefield must wonder whether time alone can ever erase and expunge what once took place there. The whole idea of forgiveness and atonement seems to imply a sort of law of conservation of events even when time intervenes. Certainly the pattern of possibilities of the present moment is conditioned by all that went before.

Some assume that the debt of sin is owed to God directly and only the infinite merits of the God/Man Jesus could ontologically change events by way of redemption. Redemption in turn implies a restoration to a prior state of being. That restoration however seems to be contingent upon procuring a substitute victim to take the punishment due upon itself; but due to whom? Is it the justice of God that demands retribution, even if it is shifted from the evil-doer to the innocent substitute? Or perhaps it is the case that human nature itself anchored as we are in causality cannot contemplate any forgiveness that does not rest upon some sort of payment in kind? Only by assuming that God demands vengeance can we be persuaded not to exact that retribution ourselves. Prayers of reparation then represent our desire to participate after the fact in the propitiatory offering of Jesus on the Cross. Perhaps it is best to frame this act as an instance of love towards God motivated not from necessity, for surely the sacrifice of Christ was complete in itself, but as an example of love's largess, its supreme foolishness that gives even when that gift is not required.

Seen in this way the justice of God, at least in the New

Testament, is groping towards the idea that in eternity our own strict accounting methods are seen as superfluous in light of the abundance of God's mercy. Our penances in this way are better framed as the proof that we offer to ourselves that love is possible for us, freely given even when it is not strictly required of us. We demand this of ourselves and God is pleased to indulge us in this effort; not that it is trivial for love never is, but that the God who accomplishes all things acts through grace within us so that the result is more attributable to God than to ourselves. The curse in any case is lifted and the demands of justice satisfied.

From the Journal of Sherlock Holmes

December 24, 1893
London

The passing of the generations and the legacies left for good or ill whether recorded in history or in the short and soon to be effaced memory of one's immediate offspring provide no small portion of the material recorded in my case files. My own family is no exception to this process. My comparative freedom was purchased by the sacrifices and ingenuity of father and mother and the line of generation that produced them. The mixing of two strains of blood even when initiated by love and sanctioned by the church in marriage often produces strange cross-currents of antagonism and misunderstandings. The final settlements usually happen after death when any real clarification is impossible to achieve. As a result the property left that the principals were unable to consume or to liquidate in their own lifetimes passes to their heirs as a final remembrance or at least as compensatory damages for the wounds inflicted between parents and offspring.

No sisters graced the household premises of Sigurd and Violet so no gentle touch bestowed on my father after my mother's death could ameliorate his pain and isolation or cause him to view with a gentle and paternal tolerance the eccentricities of at least two of his sons and the stern demeanor of the first who emulated but could not surpass his sire. It is no small matter to make yield a brutal landscape in the north of England so as to exalt a family into the ranks of the minor gentry who need not look to wages for a living but instead rely upon a property sufficiently large that it can support its owners. Some degree of fractiousness is bound to remain though with the result that the one case that still eludes my full elucidation is the one of my own character and of those closest to me by early experience and a common parentage.

The snow was falling yet again this morning as I left for the train station to meet my brother Sherringford. Still there has been no word from Watson. But I must not show a disconsolate face to Sherringford. After all, this is a most happy season, one that will see the brothers Holmes reunited once again at the Christmas season. I trust that all will go well. I arrived early and waited on the chilly platform in my greatcoat with the Inverness Cape and my old deerstalker hat. At last the Scottish Express train pulled into the station with great plumes of steam and coal smoke. Doors sprang open and loads of people began to disembark to mingle with the crowds of merry people awaiting them. My height was an advantage here as I looked about anxiously for my brother. Sherringford was the last man off of the train. He emerged finally like Jonah from the belly of the whale all bundled up in his great Yorkshire woolen coat and top-hat and carrying a rug to cover his knees and keep him warm during his journey. His head emerged like a turtle blinking about and looking for me from his many scarves. A porter was busy gathering his luggage and Sherringford was soon directing the fellow with his walking stick raised above his head in a gesture of admonishment.

"Careful my good man," said he, "If I wanted a roustabout I would go to a circus, please handle those items carefully! Ah Sherlock, here to meet me and in good time too, perhaps you can deal with this fellow. Where's Mycroft, tucked up in his stuffy club no doubt on such a cold day as this. It would do him good to walk about a bit if he can still manage to rise from his chair. Shall we be off? Where am I staying, the Northumberland Hotel? Yes, the rooms there will be quite adequate."

As we walked toward the street entrance to catch a cab he continued with unusual animation. "Have you moved back yet to your rooms in Baker Street? No? That is not good, Sherlock, waste of money this living at hotels. What? You have engaged other rooms? Well I will have to see them. Blasted and unnecessary indulgence though if you ask me, this business of retaining two domiciles, one a sort of museum in Baker Street dedicated to the memory of the great detective and now you say that you are keeping new rooms as well! Thank God the estate is doing rather better of late. We had a good harvest and you shall receive some of the usual proceeds as will Mycroft. That will undoubtedly be good news to his grocer."

We soon left the station and joined the busy street traffic where we succeeded before we were quite soaked by the snowfall in engaging a hansom cab to take us to the Northumberland Hotel. I saw that Sherringford was made comfortable in a suite with a sitting room before leaving him to return to my own rooms above the bookstore. We are to meet at eight at Simpsons where I have reserved my usual table. The bookstore had not yet closed when I arrived, but the hour was pressing when all good folk shut up their shutters so that the Christmas Holiday may begin. The Church bells were ringing in the streets and a light snow was still falling as I entered the door and shook the snow from my hat and shoulders in the vestibule. A few late shoppers were making their final Christmas purchases. I crossed the well-lighted main room and was about to take the stairs at the rear of the shop that led to the upper rooms when our clerk, who had just rung up the last sale of the day, called out to me.

"Oh Mr. Holmes, you had a caller while you were out." I turned back immediately to find that the young man was smiling at me. He continued, "I gave him the package that you left with me and he took it with him ... Oh wait; he left a note as well."

I walked over to him in high anticipation and took the note from him but with trepidation as well before turning away to read it privately. Its contents were as follows:

Honored Sir:

I am sorry to have missed you, but I wished to thank you for your gift to me this Christmas, not for the parcel alone, which I am taking with me, but for the first hope that I have had in years that my good friend, Sherlock Holmes, may still be alive. I had planned to delay the publication of his final adventure for an indefinite time after my return from Switzerland, but as the public began to speculate and as unfortunate rumors were going about that he had died during one of his unfortunate experiments with cocaine, I can keep silent no longer. I cannot allow the name of the man whom I respect above all others to be bandied about in this fashion. I have long been determined to share with the public the facts such as they appeared to me on that dreadful day. I reached at that time the only conclusion that seemed possible, which was that he had indeed perished in seeking to rid the world of an arch-foe that had become the focus of his efforts to engage with and to subdue one of the primary agents of the criminal underworld of England. But my conversation with you a few days ago has opened for me a door that I fear to enter but must if I am to find peace at last. I may be mistaken but I believe you may have some secret knowledge to impart to me. I wish to speak with you before the New Year, if you would be so kind as to meet with me. You may reach me at my enclosed address in Kensington.

As for the nature of my suppositions, daring as they may be after so many years, your conversation reminded me of one of Holmes' sayings that when the impossible has been eliminated then whatever remains, however improbable, must be the truth. As I reflected upon this dictum in conjunction with your own observations made to me, I began to realize that my conclusions made upon the scene of the tragedy appeared to me now to be highly improbable and for the first time a light began to dawn upon me. I realize the fantastic nature of my speculations, but I ask you to humor me in this. I still cannot account for the absence and for my friend's long silence. However, if he is indeed still alive, such is my faith in him that I trust that he has had good reasons for keeping his long silence. If I should be so fortunate as to see him again in this life, no matter how or for what reasons that meeting may still be delayed, I trust that he in turn will know that the years have not dimmed my affection for him, and that I can imagine no greater happiness than to see him once again.

I remain, my dear sir, your humble and obedient servant,
Dr. John H. Watson

I took the note and walked upstairs in silence. For perhaps the first time since my mother's death, I found myself quite overcome with emotion. I sought refuge in my rooms where I wept freely still clutching the note to my heart.

Dr. Watson's Narrative Continues

I am afraid that I also was quite overcome after reading the last journal entry for I remembered clearly the impression made upon me at the time of meeting the man whom I fully believed to be an old bookseller. It was not the first time that Holmes' remarkable ability to assume a character in every detail had fooled even me who knew him so well, for he could assume not merely the voice and aspect, but as it were the very soul of the person he was impersonating.

That meeting had left me troubled. It is not an easy thing to switch from despair to hope. I had long since mourned Holmes and accepted the fact of his loss, but now it seemed to me that I had accepted Moriarty prematurely at the valuation assigned to him by Holmes. The man had grown to appear invincible in my eyes as all evil tends to do. It was only now that I came to reflect that the man was little better than crippled with his stooped back and poor eyesight so that the notion of him grappling with a man in the full vigor of his strength, a man almost a foot taller than him, suddenly seemed absurd. Was the coldly reasoning and resourceful Professor Moriarty a man who could think of no better plan than to rush impulsively like a madman and grapple with Holmes on a cliff-face above a seething waterfall, particularly since he had given Holmes time to write a final note to me before engaging in that final tussle?

No and again no! How could I have been so blind? If I had been wrong in my reconstruction of what had happened then Sherlock Holmes must be alive! Even had such a physical match taken place, Holmes must have emerged the winner when faced with such a feeble physical opponent. I could still not fully imagine though what had actually taken place and since it was a delicate subject, I was content to dismiss it from pointless speculation. I cared for only one thing, that Sherlock Holmes might still be alive! It was then that I began to apply his methods in earnest during the subsequent days to the case at hand, to discover the whereabouts of my friend.

Holmes had always been suspicious of the fortuitous happening or the chance meeting. What appears to be accidental is often the product of design. I therefore reflected that to meet so soon after my return from America with an elderly bookseller who had given me my first hope in years was too fortunate to be merely accidental. If it may not be thought blasphemous by comparison, it was rather like the meeting of the disappointed disciples with the resurrected Jesus in the guise of the stranger on the road to Emmaus.

I thought back upon the manner of the old gentleman that I had met and seemed to discern in his manner precisely that strange humor with which Holmes liked to tweak others upon occasion and against which I had learned finally to develop my own version of a bland and understated humor that Holmes chose to call "pawky." The more I considered this the more convinced I became that the man I had met was Holmes himself!

I could not imagine the reason for his long absence, but so great was my joy at the possibility, which was now assuming the guise of conviction, that I forgot then and forever after whatever resentment I might ever have entertained towards him had I known for certain of his deception. It occurred to me that it might not yet be possible for him to appear as himself on the streets of London for dangers of which I had no knowledge might still threaten him. I determined therefore to sustain the conceit of his ruse while letting him know in case he doubted it that I still held him in the very highest regard and would be happy to see him, if circumstances known to him alone, would allow it. In addition, I must confess to taking pleasure in my own "pawky" way at turning the tables upon him and leading him to suspect that I was still fooled by his disguise. It was part of my own enjoyment of Holmes to assume a role of ignorance at times simply because he always took such delight in the process of enlightening me.

So it was that I left that note for him on Christmas Eve. I had visited the old bookshop (and hearing definitively that it was under new management) for the first time since returning from Louisiana. I entered it that day with hope in my heart that I might encounter the old bookseller there. I felt pleased and at peace to be

in London again, for it now contained, I was certain, the elusive
Sherlock Holmes.

$\mathfrak{J}$f I may take this occasion to reflect further upon my feelings
as I read the journal entries, I will do so now. As I read the
secret journal entries I sensed a shift of tone from those that
had preceded them. The new entries had about them a note of
resignation, but not of discouragement. It was rather as if my
friend had begun to realize the limitations inherent in all human
activity. It began to dawn upon me as well that the man of good
will must learn to accept failure by all the standards by which this
world defines success. There is no greater desire within us than
that of making progress, for it is progress that augurs final
triumph.

Ours is after all an age of unparalleled progress. The
methods of science are now being applied even to the sources of
revealed truth itself. Perhaps (says these new theories) Christianity
may be reduced to a quaint historical or even textual gloss on
events of which their final actual truth or falsity may never be
objectively ascertained. We are able to view the life of Christ only
through the filter of the evangelists and the traditions of the early
community of believers. Can such witnesses be said to have been
unbiased? Perhaps they shared the illusions subsequent to many
dreadful events. Perhaps the early faith served only the cause of
wishful thinking, adding balm to disappointed hopes. What were
the events of which I speak?

Well, certainly the primary question (one that still haunts
us today) is the question of whether the tomb containing the body
of Jesus was really empty. Did Thomas indeed probe the wounds
of Christ, so as to know that it was truly He who stood before them
in the upper room? How can the fate of one man be dispositive for
the redemption of all of mankind? Yet I find speculation on these
questions to be both unanswerable and unimportant because the
truth cannot be discovered by deciphering a text. Either the Holy
Spirit is alive within the Church or it is not. Surely, if the Holy
Spirit is a co-equal and actual Person and member of the Blessed
Trinity, then that witness should be an adequate one for us of the
truth about God and about humankind. A facile skepticism merely

plunges us back into the primal isolation that is expressed by the take in Genesis of the fall of man and of woman in Eden.

I do not here attempt to legislate for all of the denizens of the earth. I have not the power to do so. In any case, of what relevance is all of this for those who are now satisfied that human ingenuity seems so close to achieving at least a temporary happiness for increasing numbers of people in this present life? For these people is not the span of a human life long enough? A man with any wisdom is soon bored and disgusted with the course of things long before his natural demise. Should not a man with any detachment at all then choose to relinquish the burdens of our flesh long before they assume the intolerable bondage of old age with its inevitable decline into foolishness and the period of pain and petulant complaints?

I seemed to sense though in Holmes' journal, as I have said, a resignation that was not discouraged, but rather seemed to imply a more daring hope: that it is precisely by failing that man achieves a reunion with his God, for it is only when a man accepts that even his greatest efforts at virtue are compromised by his very nature as man that he may turn to God in true contrition and accept the forgiveness that was so dearly purchased for him by the way of the cross. Christianity begins in defeat; for Jesus of Nazareth was truly dead and all seemed to be lost. So do all earthly desires for vindication by our own power come to an end in the vision of the feebleness of Jesus who fell three times on the way to Calvary, a path not to his glory but to His humiliation and death, stripped of even his garments and bleeding to the final drop of his blood.

For this reason it should not surprise us when the Catholic Church itself seems to falter on the way to the Second Coming of Christ. Nothing is as dangerous to Christianity as a desire for a premature victory over evil. We are born to struggle with evil, not to triumph over it. The triumph when it comes must be the gift of God and not of our own achievement, lest the suffering of Christ be a mere vanity among vanities. Age brings the dawning of awareness that life is always incomplete and unfinished. As Robert Browning once said, *"Man's reach must exceed his grasp, else what's a heaven for."*

This reflection began to illuminate for me the peculiar way in which Holmes had chosen to engage in dialog with Professor Moriarty. The process had been more protracted than I had imagined it would be. The stakes were as high as ever and neither party had as yet conceded; but in the struggle with Moriarty Holmes appeared to realize that Moriarty must find his own way in the end. An entire Weltanschauung is not altered in a short period of time. For that reason Holmes had returned to London and taken up again his former station in life, to do what he could with those remarkable gifts that he possess and as for me, I determined then and there to take my place again at his side as his friend and colleague.

I recall as though it was yesterday how we finally met again in our own proper personae. It was just after Christmas when I called again at the old bookshop. This time I found him present. I was led upstairs by the clerk whom I had recognized from the early days when as a lad, all dirty like his chimney-sweep father, he had aided Holmes as one among the group of rag-tag urchins that Holmes had dignified by the name of the Baker Street Irregulars. On this occasion he smiled and pointed to the stairway to the upper rooms as I entered the shop. I nodded and passed on. I climbed the stairs, not seventeen steps as in Baker Street, but only eight in number. I had long ago learned to observe such things.

I paused just outside the door. From within there came suddenly the sound as of old of Holmes' violin as he played a selection from Paganini's First Violin Concerto. It was played with all the charm and passion that now seemed to me to recall my own youthful days in Baker Street before my marriage. I seemed to feel my former vigor return to my step and the years themselves to fall away. Had I changed really? Was I not inside still the young chap, just back from the slaughter of war in Afghanistan, seeking again some way to adjust to being at home in England once again? Holmes was still in many ways a mystery to me. Perhaps he would always be so. We are each of us mysteries to one another, because who can walk in our steps and who may observe the soul's inner workings but only God. I waited outside the door until the piece of music was finished and I heard the soft sound as he lay the instrument down upon a table before I knocked on the door and heard as of old the incisive voice of Sherlock Holmes as he invited me to enter. I hesitated no longer but pushed the door slowly open and stepped inside...

28

From the Journal of Sherlock Holmes

December 28, 1893
London

The past three days have been extraordinarily eventful ones. It was after Christmas but still within the Octave of Christmas that I was to have the incomparable joy of seeing my old friend John Watson again. I had already determined in my heart to accept any condemnation of my actions that he might care to make. I was determined to bare my neck to the blade. I had begun to fully appreciate that in attempting the universal I had quite forgotten the burden of the particular where alone moral virtues must demonstrate their presence or absence. Charity in all truth does begin at home.

I had failed again and yet again to show John Watson the irreplaceable and unique position that he occupies in my affections. It is not the smallest of our habitual sins to take for granted those upon whose affection and esteem we may habitually rely. I was determined that I should hereafter value him as more than my colleague, but as a brother. After receiving his note to me I was able to entertain the hope that he would indeed forgive me when we met. It was this hope that made Christmas Day a day of great joy for me because the mists seemed to be clearing at last. I was to join Sherringford and Mycroft for Christmas dinner.

The snow had ceased to fall sometime during the night. As I left mass and passed the merry people on the steps of the Church I knew that this Christmas at least I would not be alone in foreign lands with only the saturnine face of Colonel Sebastian Moran and the complaining sound of the camels to greet the Christmas dawn.

My desert days were now finished. I was again in England, my England, for better or for worse. The streets of London wore an unaccustomed hush and the faces of the people were brighter for the grace of the day. I had filled my pockets with schillings that I distributed to the carol singers, many of them from south of the river or even from the east-end regions. This Christmas largess to strangers was some small repayment for my years of absence. I even took the extraordinary measure of returning about noon to Baker Street and sent Mrs. Hudson into hysterics by my unannounced return. When she had quite recovered her composure I told her that I had been abroad in most desolate regions engaged on a mission of great importance to the nation, but that I now planned on returning to Baker Street and to occupy again the old rooms that had been maintained for me in my absence by Mycroft.

She was gracious enough to accept again her old and untidy tenant, although she made it a condition of my return that I must give up target practice with pistols in my rooms. I left her with a bottle of sherry as a gift, to fight as she said "the rheumatism" before wishing her the compliments of the season and departing for my current residence to rest and get ready for dinner later at the Diogenes Club.

The men of the Diogenes are not renowned for their sociability to say the least, so it came as no surprise to me that Sherringford was one of the few guests present. We were allowed admittance for the annual Christmas dinner only because the by-laws of the club admit family members for the dinner. It is one of the few concessions to festivity in honor of the season. As one member put it to me, "We are grim and gruff but we are not un-Christian after all." The long habit of silence is not easy to break however, so what passes for festivity at the Diogenes Club would be termed a rather stiff and stoic dinner elsewhere in the world of lights and laughter. Still I did hear that evening an occasional rusty wheeze that might by some stretch of the imagination be termed laughter and there were many toasts offered which gradually thawed the chill of the company to at least a mild degree of warmth. Mankind is so constructed that we all require some degree of fellowship in order to maintain sanity. Even the members of the Diogenes are not immune to this common human need, but being men who have witnessed much of life, many have concluded that any human intercourse is an occasion for conflict and competition. So it is that they have purchased some degree of peace and good-feeling by limiting the social dimension to a mere proximity of men who think exactly like themselves and even then they but seldom express their opinions and only in the dining room. Many monks would envy this degree of discipline.

On the night of Christmas however the entire club is open ground. Extra tables are brought in so that food is eaten even in the august domain of the great library. The food is cooked by an army of extra cooks at a restaurant just down the street which closes its doors to all others so that it can add its labors to the cooks in the usual kitchen, located in the basement of the Diogenes club. The dining room is on the first floor while the library and other rooms are on the second and third floors. There is even a fourth floor which houses a few well-appointed bedrooms where members or guests may avoid the clamor of even the most sedate of hotels.

So it was that I was to spend my Christmas, the first real one in many years, with my two brothers and I could think of no better place than the Diogenes to do so. We need not fear any constraint that might still exist between us there, since we would be quite at home in that region of reticent solemnity provided by the rest of the company at hand. Dusk had settled down upon London when my cab pulled up before the Northumberland Hotel. Sherringford was already in the lobby awaiting me. I think he was surprised to see me at the very stroke of the hour that we had arranged earlier. I was determined to give him no cause for complaint. He greeted me, not effusively but with a courtly courtesy, and we were soon off through the wintry streets with the sound of the horse's hoofs muffled by the recently fallen snow. Our progress was slow so that our cab might not skid or overturn as we wended our way through the streets. I was able to observe everywhere signs of festivity in the houses and clubs that we passed along our way. It seemed as though holly wreaths were upon every door and even our horse sported a collar of bells that rang merrily in the frosty air. My spirits were lightened by Watson's missive. It was the lifting of a great burden from my soul. I was even happy to be with Sherringford. There is no greater threat to happiness than misunderstandings among family members and I hoped that this evening might resolve forever any remaining differences that lay between us.

At last we pulled up before the Diogenes Club. It was as well-lit as any club that we had passed along the way to our destination. We were soon admitted to the sacred precincts, checked our cloaks and hats, and were ushered into the library where great bowls of punch and eggnog awaited us on a long table. There were light triangular salmon and cucumber sandwiches galore as well and several cold custards, crumpets, scones, and cheeses. Standing by the fire was brother Mycroft with his immense bulk like a moon set to eclipse the sun. He nodded to us at our entrance and crossing over to us shook hands with Sherringford and with me and formally welcomed us to the Annual Christmas Fete of the Diogenes Club.

It was a proper fete indeed! As the meal progressed I could see that even Sherringford was warming to the spirit of the occasion. We were first served with chilled oysters served with fresh limes from Madeira, a standing tradition of the club. This was followed immediately by an excellent leek soup ala crème. Then we were served a fish course of flounder dipped in a marvelous egg batter and seasoned with fresh tarragon. The main course was roast leg of lamb with mint jelly or alternatively a thick cut of rib roast served with a fluffy Yorkshire pudding. The wines offered from the club's cellar were many and various.

The conversation during the meal was genial and general in nature and there was even an occasional jest or witticism offered so that the company was soon as mellow as the grand feast before us was generous. It caused me to reflect that abundance when shared may cheer the coldest of hearts. The men of the Diogenes Club had all contributed to the annual Christmas fund according to their means and a hall had been rented in Whitechapel, which was serving a Christmas feast of roast goose to many of the denizens of the East End on that very night. Though dour, the men of the Diogenes were not so cynical about the nature of humankind that they were strangers to charity which alone alleviates the human condition. After dinner we were all allowed to stand up and stretch a bit before being served with the Christmas Plum Pudding topped with brandy and a dollop of clotted cream and a sprig of mint.

It was after dinner over our glasses of port that Sherringford broached the first serious topic of the evening; that of my pending return to London practice.

"So then you are quite determined to remain a detective, Sherlock? Ah well, so be it, though I had hoped that your travels might have caused you to consider a proper government position. I am sure that Mycroft could procure an appointment for you as an ambassador in a nation with a climate more congenial for your lungs. On the other hand what country can compare to parts of our own England for fresh sea air? Have you met up yet with your old friend, Dr. Watson? No? Well I should do so if I were you. The man is solid and reliable. I admit to always feeling easier in my mind knowing that he was at your side. Just the sort of capital fellow to come to your aid should violence threaten. I warn you Sherlock, that if you continue in your present line of endeavor you may eventually come up against a fellow who may be too much for you. Oh you may smile, but you are not the young boxer or fencer that you once were in your university days. These new fellows do not play by the rules. They are just the sort who might sneak up behind you in an alley when your guard is down. Help me Mycroft. Do you not agree that our younger brother might find a safer line of work?"

Mycroft smiled as he answered, "Well we all have tended towards our own ideas of a mission in life have we not, Sherringford? I recall that you have even had occasion in the past to question my own choice of a vocation."

Sherringford started at this but kept his good humor. "I have indeed! But in your case it was because I could never figure out what precisely it is that you do? I believe that you are a consultant of sorts for the government, though where your expertise may have come from I cannot say, for the life of a hermit has been your only life as far as I can see. At least Sherlock gets about and sees things. It takes experience of life to give valid advice to the men who control this empire of ours."

I spoke up for Mycroft. "I believe that brother Mycroft's primary skill lies in his memory and his ability to weigh facts and to give them their proper weight and order. In this way he is a master of policy. Many decisions in government are based upon what may be called the one-sided view. Mycroft is able to show that statesmen possess alternatives and in this way to avoid taking precipitate action. He might even be called 'the conscience of the nation;' his advice is never severed from the ends of the moral order, which must condition all actions and preserve them from the seductive attraction of immediate expediency. He is the keel of the ship of state, to see that all goes straight and true."

I could see that Sherringford was impressed by my summation of the duties of Mycroft's anomalous position. "You would have made a fine barrister, Sherlock. Is this true Mycroft? Ah, I see that you cannot speak in your own behalf; secrets of state and all that. Very well then, I beg your pardon for my past aspersions. Indeed, tonight I would overlook much because I see that if nothing else you have found a most congenial place here at the Diogenes. I don't know when I have had a finer feast. You must both come up to the estate more often so that I can show you some of Yorkshire's bounty. No mutton tripe or haggis I promise you! The fortunes of the estate are in fact doing better; I am happy to say. I was even able to give the miners an increase in wages and I am establishing a hospital and a home for aged miners. I was sure that you would both approve the expenditure. As I grow older I realize that the men and women who work the mines and weave the woolen goods on our estate are in a sense our family and that we prosper together or we do not prosper at all. Give a man a chance I say and he will repay your confidence nine times out of ten. I have brought along a draft for each of you of your share of this year's profits from the estate. Please accept them on this Christmas night in the name of our dear father and mother. Gentlemen, shall we toast them now?"

We all rose to our feet. Sherringford turned towards us and said, "I propose to you then our dear parents and the estate of Sigerside, a Merry Christmas to us all!"

o it was that we drank to the memory of our parents and sealed our own brotherhood by drinking to one another's good health as well. Though much had long divided us, we were brothers still. It is age that often heals the wounds of youth. So many years had passed, years during which we might have shared each others joys and trials, but a common blood as often unites families as well as divides them. But on this evening as I gazed upon both my brothers with affection, as they conversed with each other genially before me, I felt that the past had been put in its place and that a new understanding beckoned us onwards to the years ahead, whatever they might bring.

It was all too soon that we were all summoned back to our places at table so that the flaming Christmas pudding might be served and the annual Christmas celebration might be brought to an end. We were among the last to leave, having remained for cigars and brandy until after the midnight hour had struck. Sherringford and I left the club then and entered the cold of the December streets from the warm air of the club. The snow had begun to fall again, but our cab was waiting for us in front as pre-arranged. We dropped Mycroft off first at his lodgings in Pall Mall before continuing on to the Northumberland Hotel. I helped Sherringford to the door and was surprised when he turned briefly to embrace me before turning away and entering the lobby. I stood for a moment and watched his back as he walked over to the lift before going back to the cab that carried me through the still and empty streets of London to my own temporary lodgings above the bookstore where I was soon peacefully asleep.

n the following morning I picked up Sherringford again and we had breakfast together across from St. Pancras station. Sherringford was not a man to tarry long away from the estate when he had duties to perform. It was a custom on the estate to open the courtyard to the tenants on the last day of the year and to toast in the New Year around a bonfire. Punch was served and fireworks were set off at midnight. A great fire was lit in the entry hall's fireplace and there was music played in the gallery above while the local gentry mingled below.

Outside tents were set up and the local Anglican Church

supplied a group of madrigal singers and fiddlers to entertain. Sweet cakes were served all round and rum punch was provided so that the New Year always began with all and sundry asking for a blessing for the coming year. Sherringford considered this to be one of his more pleasant duties as master of Sigerside and as magistrate. He usually worked for days upon his annual address, which the vicar as usual advised him should be a brief one. He was already muttering phrases to himself and reaching into the various pockets of his cloak for his notebook and pencil.

Mycroft was not able to join us for breakfast due to an urgent cabinet meeting, but he had wired the hotel with his good wishes and Sherringford had wired back his thanks for the hospitality shown him at the Diogenes Club. I saw him to his railway carriage and gave the conductor a tip and requested that he would see especially to my brother's comfort on the way back to Yorkshire. Sherringford was well supplied with scones leftover from our morning repast and carefully bagged for him by our waiter, so I did not doubt that he would be comfortable and well-fed on the snowy journey homeward. I saw the train off before turning and making my way through the crowds and back to the bookstore, which was open once again now that the holiday was past. Within an hour of my arrival, as I sat in my old dressing gown with my pipe charged as in former days with the Latakia mixture favored in Persia, that our clerk came to the door to announce the arrival of, as he delicately put it, "an old friend." I knew at once that he could only be referring to Watson.

The fatal hour had come round at last. I seemed to see again his dark form walking swiftly down the mountainside in Switzerland after receiving the message that an English woman was sick and needed immediate aid, never dreaming at the time that he had just said farewell to his friend, Sherlock Holmes, for three long years. Once again there came a pang to my heart. I did not know at first how to receive him, so it was that I grasped my old violin and began to play an old air that I knew he loved well.

Ever the soul of courtesy and decorum, he allowed me to finish and to place my violin upon the table before me before knocking on my door. I summoned up my courage at last and asked him to enter. He stood for a moment in the empty doorway and gazed at me before turning and closing the door behind him quietly. An instant later he had crossed the space between us and grasped my hands in both of his and then forgetting all decorum embracing me warmly.

"Holmes, can it really be you! I could barely hope, but then I could come up with no other solution after meeting you the other day. How did you ever manage to climb out of that dreadful pit?" He was quite overcome with emotion and for a moment he swayed and had I not caught him and led him to a chair, I believe that he would have fainted. In a few minutes he was quite himself again after I had poured him some whisky.

He explained his momentary weakness by saying, "It is no small matter you know to have what one has deemed an impossible benefice bestowed upon one. If you could know how many nights I prayed in those first days that by some miracle you might have survived. I stayed three days in the inn before I concluded that you were indeed lost. I returned to England thinking how I had failed you by being absent from your side at the critical hour. Only as the weeks turned to months did I give up the last vestiges of hope that you were still somehow alive."

His brave words cut me to the heart. "Watson, my very dear fellow, I am so sorry. It is entirely my fault and that of my own assumption that over time you would draw the proper conclusion on your own. I instructed Mycroft to preserve my rooms exactly as they had been, but to allow no one to enter there but you. Knowing how unsentimental Mycroft is, I thought that you would eventually conclude that I was still alive from this fact alone. You know how I am about my things. It was only when I heard that you had penned an account of our final adventure together and delivered a copy to Mycroft that I was sure that I had played a part in the creation of a problem that you found insoluble. By then years had passed and I was residing in the South of France. It was too late then I felt to simply write and tell you that I was alive. I could not yet return to England because I knew that I was still in danger here and would only endanger you also by returning prematurely. Even now events are still unfolding that place, not only you and me, but all of

England in danger. There are events of which at present I may not speak. I have entered as it were a pact with an evil force in an effort to defeat it by giving it its own freedom. It is an experiment, the most deadly one of my career, to pose no resistance to a known evil in order to defeat it from within itself. I will not tempt your patriotism by asking you to be a party to that experiment until it is concluded. So you see my dear fellow, even now after all my wanderings I am still not a completely free agent. How then could I have communicated to you that I was alive? Still it is only your own noble nature that encourages me to believe that I have your forgiveness at last."

Another warm embrace assured me that this was indeed so and in what seemed no time at all we were seated next to my small coal fire whisky in hand while he questioned me further.

"But where have you been, Holmes?" he enquired. "But no, do not tell me if it would place you in danger."

I attempted to put my thoughts in order; so much had occurred that it was difficult to know where to begin. At last I said, "You have perhaps read of the explorations of a Norwegian named Sigerson. Well then, you could hardly have guessed it, but you were reading an account of your old friend, Sherlock Holmes. I took you for my example and silent mentor as I took up a pen into my own hand. It was only then that I realized the full demands of literary art and of how well your own accounts were written, of how you often minimized your own abilities so that my own insights might shine all the brighter before the reader."

Watson answered with enthusiasm, "But those accounts were marvelous! I read them of course, along with half the female population of London. I must tell you that you have become a sort of Count of Monte Cristo figure among the fair sex, Holmes," he chided me.

I smiled. "Well I did embellish my little adventures a bit I must admit. I needed to pay for my bread and cheese and I thought that a boring travel account would hardly sell among the masses. I did not speak of the real hardships though, which were attributable to the camels and my own rather bony posterior. The combination brought me pain that I can feel even now. In any case I did indeed visit those regions spoken of by my *nom de plume,*

Sigerson. I traveled in India and Tibet where I met with the head Lama at a Tibetan monastery. I also visited Persia and your old place of Nemesis, Afghanistan. I looked in at Mecca and then proceeded to the Sudan where I had a most profitable interview with the Khalifa at Khartoum. From there I traveled northwards along the Nile to Egypt and then to Montpellier, France where I was engaged for some time in research into the coal tar derivatives. But then I hear that you have also been traveling yourself, Watson."

"Great heavens man you proceed too quickly; I have a thousand questions to ask you; but yes; I am but lately returned from the leprosarium being established in Louisiana," he replied. "I actually did not intend to return to England. The loss within two years of the two people who meant more to me than any other people on earth was more than I could initially endure. It would not be too much to say that I felt at the very edge of my reason. I took therefore a course that I would not have had the courage to take had my life brought me the happiness that I had anticipated. The two people I speak of are of course you and my wife, Mary. To lose the first was painful beyond repair, but the loss of the second was to deprive me of all private joy in life."

He caught my expression of pain and continued.

"I mean this in no way as a reproach, Holmes. My only desire is to explain my frame of mind at the time. Since I had no longer any joy in myself and since I could not anticipate seeking again in the vast anonymous crowds for two souls whose very nature was such that I could imagine no replacement for them, I determined to seek out for company the only souls whose circumstances might be more desolate and disconsolate than I felt mine to be. I thought to give them some degree of solace in their isolation and their pain."

"I had heard of the efforts to establish a hospital to treat leprosy in Louisiana from a colleague and since I had some experience in the treatment of the illness while in India, I thought that I might find a position on the staff there. I wrote at once in application and was accepted. So it was that I leased my medical practice to a young graduate of the London School of Medicine and departed for Louisiana. As my months there passed I found in the courage of the patients an antidote to my own despair. There is as you know no known cure for the disease at the present time. The task of treatment then is to prevent the loss of functioning that comes with the disease. The tissues of the fingers and hand in particular are subject to injury and loss with the resulting disfigurement so characteristic of the course of the disease. The nerves are deadened so that the patient unwittingly tends to be the proximate cause of his own injuries. I came to reflect that my own nerves had been injured and that just as I advised my patients to exercise extraordinary care to prevent further damage, so must I take care, as I was doing, to stay distant from those places that contained associations for me that I could not face at the present time."

He continued as though re-living those bleak and hopeless days, "But unlike my patients, time began to heal me. The habit of thinking first of others allows our own pain, which is only exacerbated by self-concern, to diminish with time. At the conclusion of the year I heard from my young surgeon in England that he wished to continue his professional studies and could no longer keep my own practice here going. Rather than seek a replacement for him from so far away, I decided to return and see if I might now face an England empty of Mary and of you. And now I find that a generous providence, which could not restore Mary to my arms, has at least restored to me my dearest friend. In the face of such an unanticipated gift I can ask for nothing more."

Tears had come to my eyes in the course of his frank and gallant speech. It was indeed the Watson I had always known, a man of honesty, courage, and loyalty, the one whom I value above all others. I clasped his hand again in mine with wordless gratitude and I believe that he saw in my aspect what no words might express, my sorrow for being so long without him, and my joy in his presence once again by my side... I can write no more tonight.

3 was quite overcome once again as I penned my last entry. I feel more my own cool analytical self today so that I may continue from where I left off my account of our remarkable reunion. I could not tell Watson yet about Moriarty. My relations with that man involve, at least at the present time, a degree of trust. I may not make his plans known and he in turn will not act upon them for some years to come. I felt at our last meeting that Moriarty has begun to yield. In any case, I can do no more at the present time. Our situation must then be resolved for good or ill over the next several years.

I owe a similar duty to Colonel Sebastian Moran. My duty to him is not one of silence, but rather to protect him from his own nature in return for his services during my long hiatus. His habit of gambling is indeed lamentable and I fear that he may be incurring debts that will exhaust his present funds and will force him to return to his plantation on an island in the Malay archipelago without the stake he had hoped to obtain from the wealthy men of England. No doubt matters will reach a crisis by the spring of this coming year of 1894.

The result of these considerations has been that I have not even now told Watson the full story of my journey beyond what he has read in the accounts published by me under the name of Sigerson. Until matters become clearer then I must keep my own counsel out of a duty to men who were once my greatest foes. How strange are the twisted circumstances of life that demands that we must do injury to our friends and protect our enemies!

But to return to the circumstances of my meeting with Watson, I thought it only proper that we celebrate the season and our reunion by going out to our old place of celebration, Simpsons. So it was that we were soon seated at our old favorite table with a splendid meal ordered and with full tumblers of ale at our sides and the warmth and delightful smell of the finest cooking in London all about us. We spoke freely and without the constraint that too often makes even the discourse of intimates a performance rather than an opening of the heart.

I used the occasion to begin an explanation of the motives that lay behind my long pilgrimage insofar as I might safely disclose them. I told Watson that as the years passed I had lost that genial attitude of easy and resigned acceptance that takes life's many absurdities and injustices at face value because they seem inevitable. I began over the years to feel that everything that I saw about me was a product of inertia in the conscience of mankind. If it is true that man is redeemed and has an eternal destiny, then it would seem that some evidence should be forthcoming that we do indeed desire that God's will be done on earth as it is in heaven. Instead it seems that man was creating even through progress in the technical arts an ever more elaborate hell for his fellow man. The mass of humanity was still enslaved to crude modes of production and distribution. The present industrial order served only to enrich the few. The rigid class structure of England preserved an aura surrounding unjust privilege so that what should have been condemned as an un-Christian discrimination, among souls that were equally valued by God, had become a strict and unquestioned hierarchy, just as the legions of hell are presumed to be. It seemed to me that egalitarianism should not be the province of free-thinking socialists alone, but rather the inevitable course of the working out of practical Christian charity among believers.

The English had failed even in the home country to share the benefits of human progress. The past century had witnessed a decline in the acreage freely available for common grazing in the Home Counties of England. The daily necessities of life were increasingly tied to a trade and currency-based economy rather than on the simple barter and sharing economy formerly prevalent among neighbors that had formerly been the basis for survival if not prosperity in rural England. In contrast to this a market-based economy generates by its nature mistrust, fear, and inequity that breed laws to constrain conduct. Laws in turn breed excessive government. When government grows it becomes itself ungovernable. Finally the citizen becomes a mere adjunct to processes that constrain his life from all sides so that the freedom and dignity, which should be the heritage of all men and women, become privileges purchased from the state. States in turn become the vassals of great fortunes that can elect or even appoint rulers. The result is always the same: a new serfdom descends again upon the mass of humankind. But this wage servitude is one that is exercised in a more subtle but still obtrusive way than in the old feudalism. The lords may bear other names, but lords they are and serfdom may now be called employment in great factories or shops, but it is a form of serfdom still. If the religions of the world are indeed the custodians of society's ultimate values, then it is to the religions of the world that we must look if we are to find a common set of values that may ennoble human nature and provide for the best opportunity for each soul to best serve the benevolent dictates of God. I explained to Watson that I had gone forth to clarify my own values as well as to escape danger so that when I returned I might use my remaining years as productively as possible in the service of the good.

Watson heard me out and I saw with pleasure that he approved of my sentiments. "You speak in the voice of my own conscience, Holmes. The death of my wife Mary only served to reinforce for me the vanity of human life that I witnessed in the slaughter of soldiers, those of England and of the rebels as well, in the bleak wilds of Afghanistan. The people there are the best example that I know of the state of nature described by Hobbes in his book, 'The Leviathan;' what that state would be like if it could be compressed into one place. Afghanistan combines desert bleakness, cold, and violence. The land itself seems to manifest the denial of all human hopes and aspirations. Scarcity is the rule there so that mere survival requires daily vigilance. The result is an inbred brutality among the competing tribes that makes them unmanageable. They are free in the way that only the truly desperate ever are, for they have nothing to preserve, not even their own lives. To die in battle is often the summit of their hopes. For this reason the region is ungovernable and will always remain so."

"During the years of my marriage I forgot the message that I had learned in that desolate region. I began to hope again for what every man desires: security, comfort, and love. Mary provided these for me in abundance and so completely that I even forgot at times the stimulation of adventure at your side. My trip with you to the continent in flight from Professor Moriarty in 1891 was our first lengthy excursion together in years. Only the threat of death to you could tear me from my fireside and the comforting routine of my medical practice and domestic bliss. I could not know then that the occasion of that journey to Europe at your side was to be the last time in years when my life would in any way resemble the template of happiness that I had plotted out for the remainder of my life."

"Within two years my life as I had known it ended. My wife and you, my dearest friend, were both lost to me and I was plunged again into that barren frame of mind that had been mine when I returned as a wounded soldier from the campaign in Afghanistan. So it was that I also set out upon my own pilgrimage, no longer flying from dread and despair, but meeting it head-on in the loathsomeness of leprosy, that ancient scourge of humanity that makes its victim an outcast. Even by the ancient law of Israel the leper must deem himself unclean. The leper is dreaded because it is he who manifests what we all in fact are, unclean. The leper becomes for those not similarly afflicted a sort of living corpse, a ghost walking among the living, to remind them of their own mortal nature. We dread the leper because he seems to decay before our very eyes and to manifest in his physical condition the manifestation of our secret sins. The leper is driven forth from the company of his fellows then, not because he is the exception, but because he proves the rule! He reminds us of our state before God absent redemption. We are each of us mirrors to one another and what we condemn most in others is what calls to mind that we ourselves are mortal beings."

"So it was that when Mary died I felt as alien in England as if I were a Pashtun soldier in Afghanistan and not an Englishman at all. Every man's happiness seemed to mock my misery until I found myself hating every incident of felicity to which I must now forever after remain a stranger. I sought out the lepers then, not so much from a motive of charity, as out of loneliness and a need for community again with my fellow human beings. Their desolate condition restored me to life. I realized with surprise that many of them had been fortunate and even wealthy before the advent of the disease that now severed them from the lives that they had known.”

“The region around the leprosarium is a dusty place. The incessant southern sun bakes the soil in the fields where the patients labor to meet their meager needs. The wooden dwellings seem dry just as leprosy is dry. It is as though the ancient admonition, *‘Remember man that thou art dust and unto dust thou shalt return,’* was engraved upon the gateposts there. The lepers are walking parables and my yearlong study of them brought not dread of them but acceptance. I tell you, Holmes, that until a man accepts the inevitability of his own death, he is unworthy and incapable of a proper appreciation of life!”

Watson searched my eyes to see if I understood what he was attempting to convey. I encouraged him to go on with his account, fearing any interruption by any comment of my own. He continued as though he was speaking from the very depths of his soul.

“What we flee from is the realization that it is only through the narrow gate of death that we will find all that we sought by such strenuous means on this green side of existence. It is not that we should ever put God to the test by demanding proofs for eternity before we believe, but rather it is God who puts us to the test by asking us what we desire in the end by first allowing us space and time to ask ourselves wherein we find good and evil. Shall we put God first and find that in his love we possess all things or shall we pursue all things, only to find at last that we have somehow lost God in the sheer multiplicity and magnitude of creation?”

“For this reason God has given us death as a sign of His mercy. God does not desire death, but it is we who require it in order to curtail an endless pursuit of the gifts while forgetting the source of those very gifts! If we, greedy as we are and knowing that we shall someday die and must render an account for all that is entrusted to our care, can lose sight of God, then how evil might we be if we were immune from death so that every advantage purchased through the enslavement of others was not temporary but eternal?”

“If our days, evil and short as they are, are an inadequate

corrective to our desires, then why would we ever turn to God if our lives were uninterrupted and full of ease? Knowing the inevitability of our own death brings us up short and restores equality among men and women, the equality unrealized in the course of earthly life. Human beings would be very devils if they were granted a premature eternity. Death is God's mercy upon us then in that it takes from us everything so that we know that all remains God's alone. We are nothing in ourselves and everything that we possess must find its place according to God's will or else it would be better that it not exist at all."

It was strange for me to hear in Watson's words a formulation of my own conclusions after all my travels and to think that by two separate paths we had both arrived at the same destination. I also had grown impatient with what I saw all about me of plenty existing side by side with destitution. I saw that poverty and greed are interrelated and the existence of disparity is only made to seem inevitable because of the systems of ownership and wealth creation as procured through the ever more attenuated and abstract constructions of the human intellect. But what man creates, man may change. Charity it seems to me takes the most direct route. It unites men face to face in the nakedness of our mutual need and the grace-inspired response. The reason that this simple interchange is so often prevented is largely due to fear that we may share the fate of the man who needs our aid. If we part completely with our own meager share of this world's goods, we must wonder what benefactor will come to our aid in our own time of need. It is for this reason that we desire a surplus in order to preserve some measure of protection from a world that may not come to our aid when we need it. There is a direct proportion between the abject penury that we witness and our fear that if we attempt to fill that need that we ourselves will share the same fate.

Yet the truth is that we already do share that fate, or at least shall do so with time. Death is not mocked. It will demand in time our very bodies from us and we shall become as insensate as the things that we now possess. Their endurance beyond our death is the rule of the servant over the master: the more that we possess then the louder becomes the laughter of material creation at we who claim dominion over it. It is God who creates all things and all things subsist in God, so that in the end unless we also subsist in God then we are nothing, not even ourselves, for we are created for God and can only really be said to exist in Him. This relationship is the central insight of all religion, but most especially of Christianity. We are born in bondage with the debt of Original Sin, a sin not our own, but yet a sin that makes our very nature hungry and dependent.

Man is naked! This was the first discovery of our primal parents after their sin, that they were dependent creatures. Created in union with God they could not imagine, prior to their sin, that to be like God knowing good and evil would bring about their ruin and for that reason alone was forbidden to them by God. They had thus far in their existence known only goodness and love. God intended that only goodness was to be visited upon them. A contingent being, one that has been created good, cannot imagine a state alien to itself until that condition encounters evil. Therefore, to primal innocence the malice of evil cannot appear until it has already been experienced though sin. But the supreme goodness of God must be such that it must bond to itself any being seeking its own best interest as a creature. God alone can heal this primal wound of our nature.

December 30, 1893
London

The conclusion that each of us had reached regarding the problem of evil still left unsolved the question of why if all of our legitimate needs were once fulfilled in God we would ever desire to possess a power and authority beyond our means to tolerate let alone profit by the responsibility that only an absolute being such as God could endure? How then could primal human evil ever have come about? Is evil a mere misperception or is it a desire for evil per se?

It is my considered opinion that Original Sin is less a matter of literal content than of the desire of our first parents (and hence of ourselves as well) to change their own ontological status from contingent to absolute, to experience all things not in God and as a gift but for themselves as objects, received as our due and with no mention or reference back to God; with no sense of obligation or of love and without the natural worship and gratitude owed to God. This attitude represents a fundamental ontological stupidity when assessed in retrospect, rather than merely being an ill-advised investment in human emancipation from parental rule.

If the narrative of a garden is taken too literally we mistake its full meaning. To a desert people the image of a garden is the ultimate symbol of plentitude and ease, just as labor and death are the ultimate symbols of our present human condition. The story of the Garden of Eden bridges this gap. Metaphysical evil is best explained to the initial recipients of this narrative in just such visceral terms. There was a reason that the fertile river region of Mesopotamia provided the site for the cradle of civilization. Water is more than merely the symbol of life; it is life itself. The religion of desert regions where tribal conflict over fertile land is everywhere the basis of social reality would naturally require an origin story that incorporated a garden. No greater message of ingratitude and duplicity could be conveyed than to show metaphysical evil reduced to eating a forbidden fruit. The inspiration implied in Holy Scripture requires an awareness of how the initial audience would have understood the moral truth conveyed by the perceptive image. Only thereafter could other evil choices be mistaken as proximate goods by our inherited, changed, and degraded nature. Original Sin then consists in this: not to choose evil for itself, but simply to desire that things should take the place of the perfect love of God. From this Original Sin all other sins flow. Once divorced from God and the gratitude owed to God a principle of mindless utility takes its place. Evil has about it a quality of stickiness and of multiplicity so that the very lord of evil says of himself that his name is legion, "for we are many."

In contrast to this orientation goodness is always found in unity and in the realization of a proper order. Unity is the mark of charity, because charity calls us back to God and God is one. Warfare and murder are the primarily manifestations of evil. In war adverse interests and conflict are made most manifest as we compete rather than cooperate with each other. The Holy Trinity in contrast shows that one may unite three Divine Persons into one single essence that is so close that the three are in fact one.

The primary purpose of the doctrine of The Holy Trinity is to show to us how the individual will can merge into the will of the many, each one of which forms by consent one common belief as one universal Church. Within this One Body of Christ there is no distinction of what is mine and what is thine. This ideal communitarian structure is impossible without love and without the worship of a higher principle with no reference to utility as such, but rather to a personified and loving God. This ontological order is both symbolized and actualized by the sacramental order. The real meaning of sacramental communion in the Catholic Church is to make manifest that unity which is both symbol and the very means by which the symbolic becomes actuated, so that the world is transformed indeed and evil is defeated.

For this reason the Sacramental Body of Christ is what evil most hates and fears. By the simple means of the Holy Mass all of the glamour of evil is revealed as shadow and not substance. The ordinary is used defeat the extraordinary. Poverty is used to shame wealth. The sacrificial suffering of Jesus on the cross is used to purify and to concentrate our mind so that it may turn the awareness of each of us to our need for God alone and of all other things only in Him. The death of Jesus is meant to encompass in one time and place and in One Person, Jesus who is God, a common redemption for all humankind and of creation itself—all things made new. So it is that death is used by God to give us life.

All of this mocks the world as we know it under the guardianship of the Prince of this World who laughs at anchorites and tempts the hermits of the desert who have sought the desert, precisely because it is desert, and can give them what they most need, a re-orientation of our perceptions and assessment of all things—the very process of conversion of heart. Just as the early martyrs sang as they went to their deaths, for love of the chance to witness to the faith, this gospel message was first received more in the heart and than in the understanding. Any theology will therefore fail to the degree that it approaches human certitude in other domains. Theology must retain its sense of mystery. To desire most what man least desires naturally, that is the way of sainthood! Jesus told St. Peter that when he was young he might do as he pleased, but that when he grew older he would be bound and led by another to go whither he would not wish to go. So it is for all men and women. We are led at last into the valley of the shadow of death.

The final proof then of Original Sin is that we incline first to evil and only later come to the good; when what is evil lies in ashes about us, when our very flesh becomes mere rags hanging from our bones, when we can look at the leper and recognize ourselves. From our present fallen-point-of-view then the truth of Christianity is not found to be self-evident. Rather, Christianity is true and persuasive in proportion to its absurdity, in its manifold contradiction to our expectations and desires, in the startling reversals made manifest in Christ, who desires not to be ministered to but to minister, and who in the end gives His one life so that the many may live, whose actual Body and Blood received in Holy Communion are the material sources through which (under the species of bread and wine that are among the most common things) God brings about the salvation of the world. That God desires to act as the servant of creation rather than its arbitrary master is a scandal to evil, but entirely at one with the revelation that as the gospel proclaims, *"God is love and he who abides in love abides in God and God in him."*

December 31, 1893
London

After discussing our past experiences during the years when we had been separated, our conversation merged into a discussion of the present and future for each of us.

Watson began, "So Holmes, I take it that your travels are for the present at an end. May I assume that you intend to resume your practice as a consulting detective or will you continue to live here as a gentleman antiquarian and bookseller?"

I smiled at this new image conjured up regarding my future endeavors. "You should know, Watson, that an old hound such as I can never give up the chase. My plans are to return to Baker Street when the New Year commences and I had hoped that you might care to resume again your old residence there also. There are advantages in living in the very heart of Westminster. After all,

London is still the very hub of the civilized world. If like me you wish to exercise influence for the good on the course of human events, then you will need to reside where that influence may best be brought to bear upon the men who are forming the policies that govern international affairs."

The good Doctor did not answer me at once. I feared for a moment that he had not yet completely forgiven me after all, but his words soon reassured me that such was not the case.

His observation showed remarkable insight into my character, "Your practice of old was fortuitous in nature, Holmes. You would take on any case that promised to raise unique issues. Am I to understand that you now intend to address only those problems that present larger issues of state?"

I put him off at first, "All problems are large that trouble the human heart. I will never turn aside from solving the purely personal cases presented to me, but I have served my apprenticeship as it were and I hope, having once disposed of the matter of Professor Moriarty at Reichenbach, that I may now devote the energies that I once used to keep track of his various crimes to other malefactors whose field of endeavor have a more international scope."

"So Mycroft has succeeded at last in turning you into a diplomat!" he chided me.

"Not at all," I demurred. "I am afraid that my recent experience with the Khalifa in Sudan has turned me away from pursuing a life in that direction. I saw during my time there that the scope for diplomacy is quite limited. Men of great affairs believe that they may turn history by their decisions, which sooner or later take the form of the exercise of force. War is the black ensign of great ambitions. No, Watson, my international practice shall be devoted to the search for peace. It is not that I believe that men of diverse views, particularly when those views have their source in religion with its absolute claims, will ever be brothers in legal terms, although we are in fact all children of God; my hope is of a more humble sort that men may at least refrain from killing each other to spread and enforce their diverse views and advance their perceived material interests. "

"The freedom of man of course must include the freedom to

embrace the dictates of conscience and no conscience may be called free that must turn to arms in order to repulse physical attack. To do so is to become evil because we fear evil in others. Over the years I have become convinced that the Christian must be as disarmed as Jesus was. On the occasion of His betrayal Jesus assured us that whoever takes up the sword will perish by the sword. The beginning of a worthy life for all of humankind will come when we resolve not to take a human life under any circumstances. What person does not feel that it is he who is the victim in any conflict?"

"In the last analysis no war is defensive in nature. The very tactics of warfare demand aggression! No army has ever existed that fails to press an advantage home when once opportunity to do so is offered. The dogs of war bite in all directions. It is for this reason that the nations of the world should resolve, if only out of mere self-preservation, to forswear all arms and to allow for the less biased judgment of the entire community of nations to govern the resolution of disputes between nations. It is then that the common conscience of mankind may best assert itself."

"We know that God desires peace and unity among his children. He has said that blessed are the peacemakers. Yet all nations consider it their first duty to build up great stores of arms which they claim are only to be used in defense. I ask, 'in defense of what?' The force of arms always serves their own secret ambitions. What nation does not excuse any atrocity when it serves its own interests and material aspirations? The capacity of nations for self-deception seems infinite. For this reason I believe that there must be a willingness to face even an undeserved martyrdom rather than to take up arms. Christianity conquered the force of Rome through the sheer number of its victims. The slaughter of our enemies is finally its own condemnation."

I fell silent then, wondering whether Watson, the old soldier of Afghanistan, would share my present pacifist views. He had seen what I had not, actual battles in that bleak and cold land where nature itself seems to be conscripted into the service of war. After some time spent in reflection he spoke up at last. "I have spent my life as you know, Holmes, as a physician. No man who has seen how our poor bodies are beset around by the invisible enemies of disease may see the health of any man or woman menaced by the hand of man with equanimity.

I have always thought that diplomats should be forced to tour the rounds of a surgical ward, or for that matter to attend births and see with what labor life is brought forth into the world. Why should a bullet bring to nothing what it has been the burden of a lifetime to foster and preserve? The worst of war lies in its vast disproportion of human effort. Man's ultimate efforts should be directed against the common human enemies of hunger and disease. Only when these have been defeated should mankind have the luxury to consider aggression. War is a luxury that all should promptly forswear. My late tenancy among the lepers has taught me that even the most intolerable of fates may be accepted with grace. I saw how it is precisely when some men are deprived of even the integrity of their very flesh that their souls may best shine forth with greater brightness out of that wasted garment. These souls accept death as the price of life, thanking God for their temporary tenancy in this glorious world of frost and sun. So, Holmes, if that is your intent as you resume your practice, to use your great gifts to rid mankind of war, then I shall be willingly at your side."

We clasped hands then as we had once done so many years ago when young Stamford had first introduced us and we had first taken up our lodgings at 221B Baker Street. We were older now and life had shown us, what it shows all young men, that the strength that we once thought would move both earth and heaven, that we assumed would reside in us forever undiminished, that these will fail us in turn. Each of us was now aware that the sun of our lives had passed its zenith and that the coming seasons of our lives would soon make but winter arches. We had each been sorely wounded by life and watched as our dearest ones were taken from us. Watson still carried the pain of his wounded leg and I the uncertainty of my afflicted lungs. But resolution may ever supplement any inadequacy of resource. Who may say what adventures might still lie before ones who like us are resolved to face them determined and unafraid?

Book Eighteen

Sherlock Holmes in London

Dr. Watson's Narrative Continues

When he had once made a decision Sherlock Holmes was always swift to act upon it. By the first full week of the New Year of 1894 he was again a resident in Baker Street. He did not make a general announcement of his homecoming, for he was loath to give the public an explanation of his long absence at this time. He entrusted that task to me. The result was two stories, which I now see contained several inaccuracies some of which I now confess. I knew at the time of writing them that certain elements seemed far-fetched, but as always I placed my first loyalty to Holmes' wishes and trusted my readers to know that when dealing with a man's private affairs some items must be held back through the exercise of proper discretion.

In any case I decided to respect Holmes' wishes at the time. It was only with reluctance that he had ever consented to my efforts to gain for him a proper public appreciation and to share with the world a record of the astonishing gifts that he possessed. He had always insisted that his methods if studiously pursued might be applied by anyone, but it was my belief then as it is now that Sherlock Holmes underrated his own unique artistic nature.

The products of art are unique to the artist. So it was that I always saw Holmes, not so much as a detective, but rather as a man who was penetrating into human existence itself to probe for those ultimate truths of our inner essence insofar as it could be discovered and recorded. For many years he had engaged in an active correspondence with William James, the great American philosopher and psychologist. He had met him through the agency of his brother, the novelist Henry James, who was no mean psychologist himself. Indeed, Holmes was of the opinion that art alone may fully encompass human reality. Human nature is in a sense always re-making itself and by doing so changing the definition of any pre-conceived notion of human nature. It is this creative element that produces culture and it is not too much to say that culture is as determinative of our choices as biology.

Moreover it was Holmes' theory that man's place in the scheme of creation is not a fixed point but rather more like a scale and that human nature may partake of either the animal or the angelic at will. Humans may even come to see themselves as a mere reflection of the machines that they create and use. Repeated human behaviors may produce over time a being similar to those mindless automatons whose motion is driven by a coiled spring. For this reason Holmes was obsessed at times with questions of anthropology as inseparable from theology. Any transcendent end reserved for the soul must build upon our present actions and character. Great leaps in human development and mental capacity must be accounted for in some fashion. Among other questions he found it startling that the extant writings of antiquity showed such an immediate grasp of complex concepts and had the words to express them. Where were the texts displaying an intermediate stage of mental growth? Ideas drive the human race and no idea is more influential than those through which man defines his own nature and governs his own life accordingly. We divide the approaches to knowledge into arts and sciences.

Artists extend our conception of the possible, while not losing track of the perennial character present in the nature of any created being. The balance in human development between nature and nurture will perhaps never be definitively resolved. Not the least among the traits presumed to indicate innate human qualities are those pertaining to the differences between the sexes, the qualities and demeanor deemed appropriate to each sex. The Catholic Church has deduced or constructed certain definitive ideas on the morality implicated by these questions to the extent of using them as a foundation for two of the seven sacraments, Marriage and Holy Orders. The belief that certain aspects of social behavior are innate lends stability to the social order and safeguards certain primal emotional tendencies in human beings.

In spite of this obvious benefit, empirical observation shows that consistent adherence to natural law is not uniform between cultures or religions. Even the Ten Commandments implicate questions and complexities not capable of resolution without some parallel commentary on the bare text. In this process a wider vision is required so as to grasp the context of the whole. Even then the difference of method makes theology more akin to art than to science. This conclusion alone implies that theology will never be a simple science, if it is to be considered a science at all.

The Jewish scriptures present God in the context of relationships: covenant, faithfulness, restoration, reassurance in time of trouble, renewed confidence after periods of exile or desolation; the focus is upon the action of God upon the both the individual and the community. Science in contrast attempts to minimize the role of the observer and to deal with exterior reality as it is in itself. The ideal language of science is one bereft of metaphor and analogy beyond what is necessary for measurement to be made and correlated through mathematics. Even when insight plays a role in various conceptual leaps the results can hardly be accepted unless they are capable of some form of universal transcription into a formula that can later be verified by empirical testing. Until then only a hypothesis may be said to exist.

Art has no similar need to be verified because truth is not its aim in the first place. Even in cases of mimesis the similarity is best understood as a transcription from one form into another form rather than a direct copy of the original. This means that artistic productions obey their own conventional rules. Proper interpretation requires advance consent to understand, abide by, and to play by those rules if the artistic communication is to take place. There is no way to eliminate the need for proper interpretive methods to guide that understanding. Philosophy may be conceived of as the source of just that critique of understanding that can provide a wider context for the various assertive modes of human discourse.

Any review of the extensive variety of pursuits that Holmes pursued would reveal that no one mode of inquiry is apposite to all uses. The ultimate philosophy is that which studies methodologies as such. I enjoyed observing his efforts in this direction. The scope of his inquiries seemed destined to grow by the year. His latest fascination I was soon to discover lay in the area of theoretical physics and its relation to theology. At what point did the supernatural find a nexus with observed reality in its multiple dimensions? The materialists are obsessed with a need to locate God spatially, so that as our awareness of the size and inanimate character of the cosmos grows, faith is proportionately diminished.

This ignores the fact the only real access or reference point that we have in regard to God is through our subjectivity as living beings. There is far more wonder in beholding the perception and responsiveness of the simplest life-forms than in the most majestic whirling galaxy in far-off regions of space with no immediate reference or importance to us. Nor may God be considered to be a mere projection of our own desires. Instead, we look to God as a handy way of positing the reality of an all-embracing consciousness that can validate and preserve us by acting as a grounding agent for our highest and most essential convictions. Human consciousness then is not a primary phenomenon, but rather a reflection of something higher than itself from which it takes its origins. Religious observances are a way of celebrating and communicating with the over-arching reality of a divine order of things that relates to us, but is not co-extensive with any conception that we may ever form or entertain of it.

A week after Holmes returned to Baker Street, I was able to join him there in residence. I moved again into that comfortable bedroom that had been mine for so many years. It was on the opposite side of our cluttered sitting-room from Holmes' own bedroom. Indeed, he had given me the larger room, preferring for his own use a more den-like abode. We also had a third room that had become over the years a sort of storage room for the odd items and records from his many cases. It served as well as an actor's dressing room. It was there that he stored his many elaborate disguises with which he occasionally penetrated London's underworld. He could assume the manners of any social class or occupation at will and his mastery of various obscure dialects showed that he had a ready tongue. He could think himself into a role until I would often roar with laughter at the accuracy of his portrayals. He could even imitate the voice of our landlady, Mrs. Hudson, which he would do for her now and again.

"Well I never!" she would say. "If I didn't know as how I'm a standing here with my mouth closed, I'd be sure I was over there where you be Mr. Holmes, a looking out of the window. Fair gives me the chills it does to hear you carry on so!"

The year 1894 began slowly for us but soon the cases began to come in and before long Holmes was as busy as he had been before departing on his long excursion to the east. I in turn resumed my medical practice. I commuted daily to Kensington. My practice had grown during my absence, but the young doctor who had taken over from me was soon to leave for Australia after taking a supplementary course of study in his specialty. I was forced to take up most of the load myself and to manage as best I could. It was some months before I was again directly engaged in a case with Sherlock Holmes of any great moment. That case was the one of the murder of that young man-about-town, Ronald Adair. It was in the course of that case that I was given my first hint that Holmes' relations with his old enemies, Professor Moriarty and Colonel Sebastian Moran, were not what I had always supposed them to be. Even then, Holmes kept back many facts that were only made clear to me in the year 1897.

It has been no easy task to assemble such a vast series of events as I have done here, but I am happy to have been able to finally set down the entire record of these complex events in his later career. I close this account by including the last entries in Holmes' journal which explained as much as will ever be known of the gradual process by which Professor Moriarty came to accept those arguments made by Holmes and came finally to wish to aid him to apprehend the ship carrying a virulent plague to England, the plan that had been advanced by the fantastic schemes of Baron Maupertuis. I may not close this long manuscript and consign it to my strongbox maintained for me at Cox and Company Bankers without recording here the strange circumstances of our final trip across the great western lands of America and our pilgrimage to the site of the last massacre of the American Indians at Wounded Knee in the Dakotas.

ith our business in Washington concluded at last, we were able to begin our new journey to the south and west with light hearts. We parted with Inspector Stanley Hopkins at the train station, entrusting to his care a letter to Mycroft explaining the details of what Holmes had been able to accomplish during his mission to America and explaining that he would be returning to England by way of the orient and a much deserved rest. My last glimpse of Washington was of a city that had clothed itself in white monuments in simulation of its own belief in the unaided ability of man to proudly determine his own happiness and to veil its increasingly ill intentions beneath a veneer of purity.

I had once read with all the enthusiasm of youth the works of Voltaire, Rousseau, Locke, and Emerson and had once dreamed that a nation might be devised that would marshal the enlightened minds of great men of all races advancing to achieve noble ends. I had even dreamed that America was that nation. Perhaps a time had existed before the age of venality and excess manifested in the 1880's and 1890's when a way lay open before the citizens of that great land in all of the purity of possibility that goes with youth; but that time had passed by the time that Holmes and I visited America.

All my careful observations revealed as the last year of the nineteenth century dawned were that America was not so different after all from the European empires. The disparity between master and slave had survived even a civil war and indeed had grown in the last decades of the century. The growth of the land-mass to which Americans now lay claim was the fruit of treachery and slaughter. Even as our train sped southwards and then on toward those lands beyond the Mississippi that we desired to visit it passed over the lands once trod by the Cherokee and the other tribes from the Iroquois to the Seminoles.

After visiting the great estate of Biltmore in Asheville, North Carolina where we were now bound in answer to an invitation we returned to the northern states where the heart of the great Indian leader, Tecumseh, was broken. I recall that I reflected at the time that the Americans were dying in the Philippines in order to wrest freedom from the people of those islands so that the American empire might now have a stepping-stone to engage in the pillage of China. I could not know then as I do now as I write these words that over one hundred thousand of the native inhabitants of those islands were to die before the Americans brought them into submission.

By then, our great friend, Thomas Brackett Reed, was dead. He had retired from government, as he had foretold to us, just as the nation that he had loved took its fatal turn toward the greed of the European nations for colonial possessions. Even President McKinley was soon to die, as we learned after our return to England, a victim of the hatred of a deranged and deluded man who was as hungry for fame as to be a liberator. He was ignorant of the universal loathing that his act would soon unleash upon him; thus violent designs beget further violence and he who takes up the sword will surely perish by it. We heard before we left Washington that we must not assume that our first impressions of American values would be encountered or sustained as we continued south into a conquered and bitter land, the former Confederacy. Even the amendments to the Federal Constitution after the Civil War of the 1860's had failed to penetrate a culture of adamant fundamentalism and its loyalty and belief in the institution of slavery or its nearest equivalent. Latent violence simmered just beneath the surface of assumed gentility of the people no matter how threadbare their circumstances. Religious hysteria stoked by fears of damnation and an equal confidence in their own rectitude as the chosen people of God could easily tolerate murder and theft, greed and the darkest forms of racial oppression. The beauty and fertility of the mountains could not counteract the hostility to learning and culture and the poverty that these always engender.

The dream of national unity at the time was already doubtful. I had of course seen much of this already in Louisiana, but I could not be sure what effect might be produced in Holmes. There was much of the rationalist in my friend. His reading of Montesquieu and Locke inclined him to view religious dogma with the same suspicion that he would apply to the facts of any case presented before him in Baker Street. Intense religious emotionality was as likely to elicit scorn and mistrust as it was an answering response. This did not mean that the dry as dust presentation of theology in the average seminary was more congenial to his tastes because he detected in this certainty merely the opposing disposition of theological force directed to control any misplaced leniency that was more indicative of concessions made to sinful human nature than to God. The primary problem in this strictness however was the view or attribution of any conclusion of the Church as being co-extensive with God-in-Himself rather than being merely an approximation or religious intuition.

Even Sacred Scripture seemed to Holmes at times to betray certain indications of a distorting human element projected backwards into events that better mirrored a later epoch of the communal needs of the early church and what it needed to believe in order to maintain its authority and structure. He saw the task of theology as more about the acquisition of an adequate method of interpretation than of rote memorization and verbatim application of an obvious and unchangeable content to be reinforced by various anathemas.

In recent years such a categorical approach to theological truth became historically less sustainable as the Catholic Church began to feel its loss of political power and decisive influence on European affairs. A review of history appeared to reveal a less than adequate set of alliances between the Church and the powers of the age as mediated first by the feudal order and later by the great Renaissance families. By the 19th century great moral questions as they touched society in general seemed to be more aligned with questions of order and efficiency arrived at by a pragmatic calculus than from recourse to doctrinal sources. The idea that God took an active and providential role at any more general level of discourse existing between nations seemed lacking in empirical proof so that to all intents and purposes religious dictates no longer directly guided let alone determined most national policy choices.

Even at the internal ecclesiastical level of organization material matters and career imperatives often appeared to predominate and the personal style and mental habits of successive Popes resonated throughout the entire structure and set a tone for how the Holy Roman Catholic Church was to address the challenges posed by secular thought. Increasingly there was something inherently suspect and even unbalanced in attempting to be overtly engaged in the pursuit of holiness. The Church had always been able to point to the saints as examples that a high degree of moral excellence was in fact obtainable by cooperating with Divine Grace. At the same time the Church did not court ridicule from various skeptics; mystics might as easily be channeling the dark forces as manifesting extraordinary grace.

Then there was the matter of maintaining independence from the great empires that was to some extent guaranteed by possessing the Papal States under the direct governance of the Church. Their loss was a critical blow to a model where even the nations, at least insofar as they were Christian, were presumed to be answerable to the Popes as Vicars of Christ on earth. This loss of political power in turn led to a loss of esteem towards the head of the Church governing as appointed by Jesus Christ.

Instead of the belief and subservience of former ages, by the latter decades of the 19th century a critical spirit entered into theological speculations. The former generally accepted theological model derived primarily from St. Thomas Aquinas and the other scholastics such as St. Bonaventure had seemed entirely adequate to answer any questions. Novelties of any kind savored of an effort to apply the human imagination to reconcile any and all sharp edges in the magisterial teachings. A good Christian life was best conceived as a combination of good conduct and frequent recourse to sacramental confession as signs and evidence of the hope for "final perseverance."

This always left some residual doubt as to the ultimate eternal fate of even the most outwardly virtuous soul. The early days of martyrdom had this advantage: to actually die for the faith was the best evidence of supreme and adequate faith and virtue. When less is asked for from the believer; less is achieved. Catholic writers chose to avoid moral laxness and presumption by supposing that the worse outcome was always the most likely. God's holiness appeared higher to the degree that it was more remote and unlikely to elicit a sufficient response in the sinner. No definitive judgment was offered as to the eternal fate of any individual soul, but it seemed at least probable after external observation that most souls went to hell. As one grows older and more jaded in one's opinion of one's fellow men and women this assessment grows more understandable.

The position of Queen Victoria as the head of the Church of England exercising her control through the Archbishop of Canterbury had the advantage of making anything that benefited the British Empire automatically moral in nature. America in contrast manifested an uneasy alliance between fractured Christianity in its many guises and the optimism bred of conquest and expansion as the motley assemblage of many nations that constituted its population profited by the economic subjugation n and utilization of the many resources offered by a virgin land once its former inhabitants were pushed aside.

Catholicism had been fighting a rear-guard action to make the vision set forth by Jesus and entrusted to his Church a reality pending the return of Christ throughout its existence. The path of history was the best evidence of the degree of the success of this program in any era. My own weariness at times threatened the faith that I had embraced without causing me to abandon it. I needed time to put all of these many thoughts into some sense of order. This account when considered in its entirety represents my best effort in this regard. The synthesis represents my own limited effort to find a single thread and to trace its ramifications through my one individual life as we each must do if we are to avoid a state of *mauvaise foi* as the French say. Religious protestations or even convictions when they are maintained with neither passion nor love for God do not demonstrate true faith.

I recall as our locomotive climbed along the course of the lovely scene of autumnal pageantry in the Appalachian Mountains toward Asheville and the great estate of The Biltmore Mansion that I sought refuge from my troubled thoughts once again in the journal that now went on to describe the events of the years after our reunion in 1894...

From the Journal of Sherlock Holmes

January 1, 1894
New Years Day in London

My meeting with Watson finally brought my great circle to completion. How thankful I am that this year at least may end with a proper conclusion, so that the period that lies before me may include as little as possible of the doubts and fears of the past and begin on a new note.

Already my time spent in Devonshire seems distant to me. My premature retirement is at an end and I am forced once more into the thick of life to do battle and no doubt at times to fail. Carrying one's particular cross is always a messy business. If our religion was one that met all of our immediate desires, then the atheist might have a point and religion might be considered to be only a mythological construct made up of those parts of our own nature that we cannot contain within ourselves but must project like magic lantern slides upon the world outside. But Christianity and before it Judaism is not of natural religion. These religions make endless demands upon us even while withholding perfect clarity in both doctrines and in the nature of the ultimate fulfillment of our aspirations, so that even St. Paul himself admitted that at present *"we see through a glass darkly."*

Everything appears distorted by the lens of our present position in this troubled world. We are nagged by the doubt that if Jesus Christ was not arisen from the dead, then Christians and all of humankind remain in their sin and moreover are most to be pitied, because of the obstacles of their lives and their determination to meet them in a loving manner. St. Paul said this because he realized that in pursuit of the way, the truth, and the life Christians are asked to set aside their own comfort and to abandon all of those partial formulations and loyalties that many people negotiate with the ways of this world in order to achieve a purely natural order of happiness.

The Christian concept of heaven is in the last analysis devoid of the sensual elements celebrated by Islam. No earthly harem is allowed him. The Christian husband must accept the fact that age comes upon even her whom he loves above all others as his wife and he must face her eventual loss as Watson had done and yet find the courage to move on alone. The Christian knows that his neighbor has a claim in the order of charity to make upon his wealth and substance, a debt so great that Jesus tells us, not to give merely out of our abundance and superfluities, but even from our very substance as well if we would be perfect as our heavenly Father is perfect.

Are not most Christians rather like the rich young man in the gospel who went away sad because he could not bring himself to give away everything and come to follow the shortest way to salvation at the invitation of Jesus? The logic of Christianity is such that it does not advise that the Christian should act in this world as an ordinarily prudent man or woman would do, but rather that he should act as God would, without God's immunity from the ills that flesh is heir to except in the case of Jesus. Our charity must exceed a mere pittance then to be effective and deserve the exalted name of charity. Did not Jesus give everything, including his very body and blood to the end of life? What Christian actually desires to imitate their Savior to this degree? Is our professed faith then mere folly so that few today wish to follow the actual Way of the Cross?

The example of Jesus Christ has led many throughout history to renounce what all men desire, pleasure combined with peace of mind in its ruthless pursuit. The way of pleasure, of wealth, of power, and of honor is soon revealed to be a path that man must tread without Jesus at his side. At the very moment of his triumph a man is snatched away by death to the devil's laughter. The devil wishes above all to show that man can in fact live by bread alone and the words that come from the mouth of God will never be enough to satisfy our inordinate hunger and thirst for more!

God in turn asks everything from us so that He may give everything to us in return, but transformed through love into a new order of creation. Yet this is no *quid pro quo* because God gives His life to us as the only recompense appropriate to love. Even when we fail it is God who will make up that which is still wanting. If Christianity asks more than we may supply out of our own fallen nature, it also assures us that through the infinite merits of Christ and the gifts of the Holy Spirit the suffrages of the Church will supply what is lacking in us but not provide us with an excuse for lethargy. Instead the Church comforts us in our affliction at having needlessly withheld so much of what we were given into our own custody and use by allowing us to appeal to Christ in the wretchedness and despair of our final hour for a misspent life.

This means of course that Christianity is a religion that convicts its members of sin. If we are at peace then it is not because we have prevailed in the great test, but because even having failed it we have not lost the faith. The entire Church lies beneath the brooding care of the Blessed Virgin Mary who pleads our case before the Holy Trinity that is only too willing to hear in her pleas once again the words, *"They have no wine."* How stale and paltry is our solitary harvest. Our only claim to salvation is the sign of the bread and wine given to us by Jesus Christ, wine that is not of our pressing and such that it is was once flavored with gall! Yet Jesus drinks our drugged wine and then goes on to be pressed by the weight of his final hour on the cross so that from him might flow forth both blood and water: the blood of the Sacrament of Holy Communion and the water of the Sacrament of Baptism.

Every doctrine of the Catholic Church clothes some metaphysical reality. Dogmatic statements assert that behind every appearance there is an ineffable reality the complete experience of which is reserved for heaven. What the Christian believes is so daring and daunting that human nature quails before the task. Christianity does not accept our fallen human nature as it is, but rather aims to transform it and by doing so to show us what human nature might have been had the fall of man and of woman in Eden not taken place.

Jesus Christ in his human nature reveals what God intended for us from the beginning. St. John assured the early Christian community that as adopted children of God they would one day see and be seen with new clarity and even be granted a vision of God—they would know even as they were known. Images of light and of darkness are contrasted. To become a Christian was to escape blindness and to see things correctly. The story of Eden in Genesis has always been read historically and as an origin account. It seems equally probable that the story of the Garden of Eden is an explanatory wisdom tale of contrast that focuses on our present condition of metaphysical exile where the same fallacious reasoning of Adam and Eve are revealed. Just as in the prophetic literature the message is less a historical account than it is a comment on our present ontological condition and its moral causes.

Eden was perhaps never what we have long supposed it to be, a place of unearned and unalloyed delights, but was rather a condition where man and woman might have walked in familiar company with God, not as His equal knowing good and evil, for God alone burdens himself with the full knowledge of the consequences of evil, since He alone can bear that knowledge, but as creatures knowing only good and that good as always derived from God as its source.

God alone knows what it is that we truly need. The devil offers to supply other gifts as "the Prince of this World," but those gifts absent God are finally revealed as wanting and as empty and illusory. To possess all things and to lose God as the price of attaining hell is to lose our divine capacity to enjoy all things in love and gratitude, which we may only do in and through God.

Ontologically speaking then, the fires of hell are to receive all things, but not in God, so that what we desire is to be our own ultimate end, which of course as a finite being we cannot be. St. Augustine knew this well and no truer words were ever spoken than these words from his Confessions spoken in prayer to God, *"You have made us for yourself and our hearts are restless until they rest in you."*

New Year begins in my life today, one that will prove no doubt as inadequate as the others, but one that may at least encompass the surety that I have sought for so long in my faith and this as well to have Doctor John H. Watson, one who has followed a parallel path, once again at my side. This is the first New Year's Day in many years that has found me in England. Tonight I will spend in my old lodgings in Baker Street. Watson will be joining me later for dinner. I have reserved a table at Simpsons and Mycroft will join us there.

I was up early to attend Mass today in honor of the feast dedicated to Our Lady and to the acceptance of Jesus into the Jewish community through circumcision. I have reflected often during my travels about the strange position of the Jewish people in the Christian era. It is no easy matter to be accused of missing the very God whose existence and nature was first announced by the Jewish writings and whose worship once was confined to the careful observance of the Torah. The worship of the Christian is contrast is to create a world community of mutual charity through the sacramental grace of God. The strictures of the old law are seen as bearing a prophetic function that was fulfilled by the one sacrifice of Jesus Christ upon the cross for all men and all women.

The wisdom literature in the Jewish scriptures is completed in the teachings, both moral and ethical, of Jesus. Jesus of Nazareth is seen as the fulfillment of the promises made to Israel and to embody in Himself the perfect adherence to the will of God that fulfills the law at the same time that it makes the law itself only a scaffold destined to fall away with the advent of Christ and the mysterious gift of the Holy Spirit that makes us heirs of more than the promises that were made to Israel as a community. Salvation now entails a degree of closeness with God the Father that restores what was lost by the first sin in Eden.

Christianity returns Jewish history to the primal beginning of all things and perhaps it is this that is such a scandal to the Jewish way of thinking by providing a new beginning to the human race. Jewish thought is oriented towards exclusivity and to the end rather than to the beginning of history and the second chance for humanity as a whole that Christ provides as the new Adam. To the

Jewish mind what was lost in Eden was relinquished forever. The ultimate extent of the Jewish blessing, according to the Sadducees, was merely the attainment of a long life and the creation of a fruitful line of descendants in an intact and someday to be victorious Israel. Only in the latter ages of Jewish history did some sects such as that of the Pharisees discern a hidden message in the ancient writings that might indicate that death itself would be defeated and that the dead still lived on in some measure in the bosom of Abraham who himself was held in the embrace of God.

But the advent of Jesus Christ changed all such worldly expectations as the expectation of a political Messiah. No longer was the sinner or the unclean leper to be scorned by having their misfortune made attributable to personal sin. The message that had once been consigned to the Levite priesthood and its functions was now made simple and general and extended through the very Flesh and Blood of Christ to all men and women, but with this difference that God has chosen to absorb into His own Infinite Being the logical consequences of sin. This was not to deny the essential function of the Jewish people, but it was an enlargement of the significance of Jewish history until it embraced all of humankind and indeed all of creation. But to achieve this end, Jesus embraced the complete rejection of a generation of His own people, a rejection that in form at least has been renewed and reaffirmed until the present day within the Jewish community, which still awaits the Messiah and an earthly rule in a restored Israel.

There are elements of this hope for a terrestrial Kingdom of God on earth even in Christian thought. It is not impossible that the Christian doctrine of the Resurrection of the Body is representative to some degree of this desire for a restoration of the mundane joys of life. But present at the same time within it is a vision of human destiny which encompasses a different end for humankind in which all will be wedded to God through the person of Jesus so that the Holy Trinity may be said to have been joined by creation itself, but now in a redeemed state.

In the end it is said that *"God will be all in all."* The fate of the angels as created beings, no longer subservient to physical creation, will be similarly embraced in some fashion into God. This raises the metaphysical question: what if anything will remain outside of the Kingdom of God. If God is someday to be all in all then what will be the fate of the remnant of both visible and invisible beings that has chosen a different course in the created world? What will become of the Tree of Life now dry of the sap of the Divine Life that once sustained it? How dry and barren must creation be if it is no longer in possession of even the least hope of reunion with God! What then will be its final state of being?

Perhaps it will be like that of a man who returns to where a dwelling once stood after a great fire to find that all has been swept away and where even the ashes no longer bear testimony to the house that once was there with all of its many memories. I often think of the stars and planets and the great void that contains them to be similarly afflicted by emptiness. Stars are only lovely when filtered through the atmosphere of life that surrounds us here and which is in a manner of speaking the very breath of God.

Even if by some unknown means men should make a machine that might allow them to venture beyond the veil of our planet what would they encounter but a realm of silence and astral motion, one that is alien to humankind. Of what use would there be of our senses in worlds that can never minister to our physical needs with air and water? We would be snuffed out on the instant like a candle. In a similar way the advent of Jesus as pure love into our fallen world must have been suffocating to His divinity. For Jesus to accept the mandates of the Jewish law was to enter into the restrictions of that community even when those very restrictions led at last to His death on a cross as the ultimate symbol of exile and rejection.

Similarly, to accept our own nature as human beings should be to reject any artificial immortality attained by our own means and to lie down in ashes at last when our time comes, with only Baptism, the Sign of the Faith, traced over us one last time on the occasion of our death and burial. We must surrender our very flesh then to the slowly burning ministry of decay. Not for the Christian soul are the glories of the pyramids. Not bound in cloths with sacred oils and myrrh as were the ancients, we repose only in the mind of God and the intercession of the living community of the Catholic Church.

The Catholic Church itself asks only that it fulfill its apostolic functions as the good servant, and to lie in patient waiting and anticipation of what St. John assures us, *"has yet to be revealed."* The true Christian is content to be among the sheep of the one fold and asks for nothing more than to be a child of God who accepts what is to come as a little child, for unless he does so he shall not enter the Kingdom of Heaven. For this reason even the wisest of the Saints knew when to bow their heads and to say to themselves that they have guarded what was revealed and turned aside from all of the higher branches on the tree of the knowledge of good and evil. There is much that can never be known, but only revealed by God in due season. For this reason a complete, as opposed to a merely adequate theology, is impossible for us to attain by our own efforts. If this is so then my own efforts to enlighten Professor Moriarty may have been a presumptuous enterprise. Each day I realize more and more that any final conversion of heart must be mediated by God to the individual soul.

It may be at precisely this point that I should point out that theology as such does not have as its proximate end, a conversion of soul. One might equally maintain an atheistic or agnostic position and still function as a theologian, just as one could be a zoologist but never do field-work or travel to the Galapagos Islands on an expedition. Theology is the application of human reason and critical methods to the claim of transcendent revelation. It is one of many possible discursive rhetorical practices. As such the primary duty of the theologian as such is not to God but to his fellow theologians and their shared enterprise. One must learn to play the game in order to take the field.

Similarly the task of the Bishop is not to be a theologian, at least not primarily, but to be a pastor, a guider of souls towards adopting the official teachings of the Catholic Church and applying those teachings in prayer and in a believing community to the tasks of daily life with the ultimate end of conversion and progressive sanctification of souls through the Sacramental Grace of God. He achieves this task with the aid of the ordained priesthood. My own particular vocation as a detective is to uncover facts and to draw conclusions about what occurred in any problematic fact pattern that presents a client with loss or physical harm such as murder. A review of my cases will indicate that potential clients come to me with problems and it is my task first to solve the mystery, but secondarily to decide how that knowledge should be applied when set against a wider ethical perspective. Knowledge is a dangerous thing even for the client.

But to return to theology, the primary question posed to the theologian is the degree of reliance to be placed on any given reading of an authoritative text such as the Bible so as to harmonize it with an intuitive sense of whether that particular reading is compatible with the synthesis reached by the Catholic Church through its magisterial teaching. This leads to the possibility that the theologian may act in a critical capacity by placing that tradition as an object of independent study rather than of the automatic assent of the believer.

The tension and hazards in this enterprise will be immediately apparent. The theologian will by his very nature be seen by a Bishop as an interloper if not as a possible danger to the souls that have been entrusted to him. The theologian as such may view the Bishop as well-intentioned but as one who talks about what he does not really understand. Recitation and repetition will seem boring and irrelevant to the insights of the theologian and the dull business of savings souls will appear a pointless exercise considering that most people remain sinners until they draw their last breath, hopefully with an act of contrition on their lips and a priest handy to give final absolution so that the grieving relatives will not go away with the thought that the man or woman before them has just plunged into immediate and unending punishment. Catholicism as an institution is constrained by the documents entrusted to its care and that provide its foundation and justification as the presumptive ultimate source of God speaking to humankind in word and action. How the Catholic Church understands and formulates that task of preservation and apostolic action and the conclusions that it reaches raise the very questions that theology attempts to solve.

ondon has just concluded its Twelfth Night celebrations in which mummery and masquerade plays a part which reminded me of one of my strangest cases, the one involving the Amateur Mendicant Society, for such I must describe it although it had no official existence. As with so many of my cases this one involved no commission of an actual crime although, it inconvenienced many people.

The Amateur Mendicant Society had no actual formal identity as an entity but consisted of men and women from the upper strata of society who desired to experience first-hand the contempt and negligence with which London's paupers must deal on a daily basis. The prospect of stripping away the layers of social protection conferred by their actual upper-class status proved to be so eye-opening that they rented a warehouse in the east-end of the city where they might manage the transformation from young men and women of fashion and then to re-emerge in the guise of various unsightly beggars. If this experiment was at first undertaken as a mere lark it might have been considered reprehensible, but its serious purpose was later acknowledged by all concerned in the matter who petitioned the court for leniency. That youthful and idealistic purpose was to unmask the many forms of cruelty that is meted out to the poor in a supposedly Christian nation by supposedly civil persons.

I will give an example here of what they experienced. A young woman of fashion who will here remain nameless was in the process of selecting a hotel, which would host her elaborate debut in one of the first excursions before the warehouse was acquired. The choice came down to two hotels of equal attraction and suitability. A friend suggested that rather than simply to toss a coin that the decision might be guided by how a young working-class woman applying for employment would be treated by the management of the two establishments. She had already met with the head waiter and the chef in company with her mother while maintaining a demure and retiring role with her face hidden by a veil. She appeared a few days later before these same individuals;

but now as a young cockney girl who desired scullery work. That she was immediately subjected to both insult and callous treatment of the worst sort as a condition of obtaining employment is the best that may be said. Her eyes were immediately opened and she had the pleasure on the following afternoon to return to both establishments in the company of an older brother who desired to place various pointed inquiries to those who had dared to insult his sister.

To the lubricious and fawning apologies of the managers of the hotels both brother and sister turned a cold eye and enough of the previous day's conversation was repeated when the staff was summoned to give an explanation to cause a pallor to overspread the faces of the employees. In parting the brother explained that the profits expected by a grand fete planned by the family would be reaped by a more civil hostelry of his choice and the promise that he would gladly horsewhip the two primary agents of the offensive comments rendered to his sister if done to any other young woman regardless of her place and position in society if he should hear of it. Both of these individuals declined to accept his offer and afterwards were summarily dismissed after the owners received a further letter from the young woman's father who happened to be well-placed in the government and belonged to various clubs of which he was a member. Other member of the society were apprehended and charged with various offenses on the most flimsy evidence. Others were charged as vagrants or under various obscure statutes and ordinances forbidding impersonation. These charges were later dropped and various high-priced barristers became involved in the matter. At last, after assurances were made that the "society" had been officially dissolved, the final troupe of young scamps was released.

I became involved when I was asked to trace a young gentleman who had been pressed into involuntary servitude to the British navy by a brutal press gang operating in the east-end. I managed to find his whereabouts and a small sum exchanged with a villain accomplished his release. The sum might have been larger but I convinced the head of the press gang that he should release the young man at once and at the price offered by mentioning a certain name known by many in that region of London and feared to this very day. Even after the sum was paid over I was obliged however to parry a sudden move with my walking stick and I left the offender sprawled in a most awkward manner upon the dock.

Many similar instances could be recounted here but the key point is that these young people gained an invaluable insight into the workings of the world that no amount of time spent at school or at Bath could have ever taught them and they were each and all better for it. It is astonishing that the differences imposed by monetary capital and social class can bestow various immunities from the full brunt of the human condition and how swiftly innocence and grace if left unprotected can be snuffed out by cruelty and oppression.

As I near the median point of my life (assuming that I will manage to attain and perhaps surpass the three-score and ten year allotment, while still retaining my faculties and strength, some sort of assessment seems in order. If I have anything to regret in life it is the time that I have wasted in seeking to adapt to various expectations of the outer world, always under the assumption that others knew better the secrets that I was only beginning to discern. It did not occur to me until I was away at school that duplicity and venality rule the world and that power in any form that it manifests should be regarded with the utmost suspicion, particularly if it appears to be utterly respectable and benevolent.

If this sounds cynical it is because the contrary state of affairs is so often presumed. One need only look about one at the masses of distressed persons of all ages whose legitimate needs play no part in the social equation to know that something is dreadfully wrong and that our most revered institutions are powerless or at least unwilling to change it. If even the redemptive sacrifice of Christ has left history for the most part unaltered, then where are we to look for succor and relief but to ourselves by drawing upon an inner moral instinct that may or may not be seconded and reinforced by doctrinaire theocrats. I am not entirely out of sympathy with Moriarty at times in this regard and it is well that I should admit it if only here and to myself.

I am startled at heroic virtue when I find it and appalled when I witness the mute suffering of women and of children. These reactions were particularly present when I was in the Arabic lands and beheld the spectacle of the overburdened and stooped figures in dark robes where only their sorrowful eyes gazed out of the prison of their sequestered existence upon a brightly lit world of sand and desert soil. If they once possessed beauty it was swiftly lost under such conditions and in any case was held in such suspicion by the men that they were never allowed to forget that their fate had been decided by the prophet.

How do these structures become established among us while retaining the supposed sanction of the will of God? The Christian lands are no better. There the duplicity is less evident but as deeply rooted. Perhaps that is why I find more true morality along certain men branded as heretics as much because of their challenging insights as their technical variance from revealed truth. In fact Jesus at times resembled the unorthodox in his own era more than the most religious figures of His time. The response was as swift and decisive as it always is.

January 6, 1894
Epiphany and My Birthday

Today is my fortieth birthday. I feel as though I have left behind that first flush of youth with all its follies and to have entered that season of maturity that is middle age. I am installed comfortably again at Baker Street. I have hung out my shingle as of old and no doubt clients will soon begin to climb the seventeen steps to consult me. Perhaps the coming years will see my practice grow to what it was before or I may be entering upon the most fruitful season of my life in some new dimension for I know at last who I am and wherein I have placed my trust.

It would have been more to my liking if I had managed to definitively succeed with Professor Moriarty by coming to an understanding so that I might close forever that volume of my life and embark upon truly virgin soil, but we are never any of us entirely free of the past. Moriarty will continue to haunt me for years to come, which is all very well and good as long as in return what I have tried to share with him may haunt him as well.

As for my birthday I have always taken great joy in being born on the Feast of the Epiphany for what has been my life if not an effort to reveal what is hidden? The detective is the one who searches out that which was lost. Is it any wonder then that I have joined my mission to that of Jesus who announced that he came to seek out that which was lost so that there would be in the end but one flock and one shepherd? I may never know the full purpose of my three-year hiatus. All that remains to me now is this journal of disjointed thoughts, which may never be read by anyone but me. Still I am glad that I have kept some record lest I forget what I have learned and why I now believe as I do. Still, my own personal Epiphany is but the advent of another dreary year in London, that "city of the dreadful night."

I have read with sympathy but not approval the testimony of those desolate poets of recent years who have tried to make a sort of desperate music from their attitude of despair. They have no charm for me. I prefer those who maintain a desperate faith such as Robert Browning and Francis Thompson to Ernest Dowson and to Edward Fitzgerald, the translator of *The Rubaiyat of Omar Khayyam*. Best of all is the Jesuit Gerard Manley Hopkins whose words seek to burn through the very page that has recorded his poems.

Not for me is the languor of darkness in the poems of Algernon Swinburne or even the high melancholy of Alfred Lord Tennyson. Such things may be uttered in elevated language and composed to a seductive rhythm, but still be foolish and empty for all of that. But still the poet must be allowed his day in which to sing. Nor am I among those whose religion hides a subtle hatred of mankind. I can laugh with Rabelais or shake my head with Thackeray, Dickens, and Shakespeare at the foibles of man, yet still love those occasional moments of nobility in our flawed humanity. These represent the best parts of our history. All of which is to say that I have not taken the path of the easy solution of despair, nor have I adopted a religion in which I claim to find every question answered to my present satisfaction. I leave to the Catholic Church those tasks that exceed the grasp of any one man or woman and I believe and follow where I must trust the larger apostolic community to know more than I. There is a dialectical relationship between the individual conscience and the demands of religious dogma that may never be completely resolved, although God asks that we honor both. Prayer brings about that openness to experience that mere will-power is inadequate to obtain.

It is no small part of maintaining the Christian life to listen to what is announced. The first step of conversion is always first to hear what is being proclaimed. The second step is reflection, so that the call of truth may elicit a response from the depths of the soul. The third step is to act upon what has been heard and believed so that its wisdom may become the very atmosphere in which one abides and so that every action and thought consults first the depths of God that are now living within the very heart and conscience, both of which have now been elevated above our mundane cares and self-preoccupations so that God has become, not a mere outward possibility for us but an actuality and the standard against which is measured all aspects of one's life.

As long as religion is simply an area of speculation, of one truth among many, it will only be a hypothetical explanation or a vague possibility open to the few. But if, as it proclaims itself to be, Christianity is the very essence of why there is any existence at all, if all things truly exist in Christ and for Christ and through Christ, then everything, even the most distant facts of space and time become insignificant unless they exist within the realm of the Holy. Existence then is not something that stands against God and of which God is the mere cause and existence mere effect. Existence comes forth from God as a directional entity, directed towards its source and with God alone as its final end. The Cross of Christ reduces evil then to an epiphenomenon that serves the good ends of God and is allowed to persist only so that the good may be defined and refined in the cauldron of events.

Just so far metaphysical insight may take us, but God has so willed it that even the vast sweep of metaphysics should be reduced to one man, to Jesus the Christ, and to one place, Golgotha at Jerusalem, and to one set of men as witnesses, the Apostles and their successors, and one Church, the Roman Catholic and Apostolic Church, to carry to all men and women the truth of Christ.

When time shall cease there will be one end, at a time that God the Father has reserved to Himself, when all events will cease and thereafter have a new beginning. So it is that Christianity does not exist as mere metaphysics alone but exists above all as a collective body, the body of the Catholic Church in which Christ dwells, Body, Blood, Soul, and Divinity incarnate in each day and in each place where the Holy Mass is offered. Each Mass participates in the one Sacrifice at Golgotha, an actual event that took place in space and in time: particular, unique, and everlasting in its significance. Around that event each man and woman (indeed all of creation) gathers, so that existence itself weeps that it should have come to this after all - that evil should demand that such reparation be made by God and to God for fallen creation. No act stemming from within creation itself would ever have been adequate to achieve this salvation of all things. Yet now all is reconciled, all is healed from within by the infused life of God, back into what had once been lost, the very Holy Spirit of God pregnant within creation. Created being could never regain salvation from within itself, but only through a free action of the Holy Trinity that willed it so to be from the beginning.

God requests only that we ask for this gift so that the treasury of His love that is already open and waiting may be ours. God entrusts the Keys of the Kingdom of Heaven to the Church, not so that the Church may lock it up again, but so that the Church may announce to all ages and to all men and women that Christ is dead, Christ is arisen, and Christ will come again.

So it is that I try and keep my ears open for the voice of God within the Catholic Church and to overlook the vague and transient failings of history (as these afflict all men, even those most called to manifest holiness in their personal conduct). But I believe that I hear Watson's familiar tread upon the stair. No doubt he wishes to summon me to set off in a hansom cab to join Mycroft so that we three may dine together at the Diogenes Club in honor of the day when I was born at Sigerside in Yorkshire, forty years ago to this very day.

have made no entry here since my birthday which was indeed a joyous day. The fare at the Diogenes Club was excellent as always and it was good to open a new decade of my life with my brother Mycroft and my dear friend, John Watson at hand. But all such celebrations must end eventually and the path of mortality formerly of little concern lies open now before me. But I am again in harness and have already been consulted on several cases of note. I am about to set my pen aside as a journalist. Watson must hereafter be the source for any public notice that I may receive in the future.

My last words as the explorer Sigerson have been dispatched to my publisher who has informed my readers that the good Norwegian has retired to a farm in Lapland, an undisclosed location with his dogs and reindeer his only companions. There have been requests to the wanderer for various speaking engagements as well as other inducements accompanied by scented handkerchiefs; these no doubt seeking engagements of another sort. All such inducements have been firmly declined by the publisher at my request. I am afraid that my Norwegian persona is a solitary, as after all so am I. No doubt he will be swiftly forgotten as the legend of his travels fades away. My days as a wanderer and philosopher have passed. I am now only "that detective fellow" who is consulted from time to time by the official police. I suppose that I am at heart a strange, lazy chap after all, one who prefers meditatively to play his violin, to smoke his unsavory tobacco, and to try his landlady's patience with malodorous chemical experiments.

It is a relief at last to be able to reside again in blessed obscurity. To be a public figure or a man of power is to stand alongside oneself as a shadow, to be a stranger to one's own limited personality and resources. For this reason even Mycroft who in many respects simply *IS* the British government prefers to be an unknown denizen of the Diogenes Club. No, I shall leave it to Watson to comfort himself, if he so wishes, by writing up any further cases of mine. But here is a knock upon my door even as I write. No doubt it is Mrs. Hudson with another client. Away then journal! Yes, enter Mrs. Hudson!

February 3, 1894
London

A false alarm, Mrs. Hudson merely brought me my lunch. She insists upon fattening me up evidently under the impression that if I am substantial enough I will not melt away again. I am touched by her motherly solicitude and I am put to great efforts to explain to her that she may put aside her worries in that regard. I am home to stay. Every region of the world has its own difficulties. There are no treasures to be found in Samarkand, in Madagascar, or on the road to Mandalay. Human venality and cruelty are constants even as human kindness and generosity are. These factors emerge unbidden in all times and places. Whether they are to be traced backwards to God's misplaced grace or to its absence, it is enough that they are present. I am impatient lately with the delicate weavings of armchair theologians who speak of the mysteries of God as though He was as easy to comprehensively describe as any other article of commerce.

This fundamental inadequacy is no easier to contemplate when it is encountered in the documents issuing from Rome. The aura of certitude seems to mirror the grandeur and scope of its object rather than to elicit a proper reticence. Who has measured God? I have often told Watson that a detective must have imagination in order to understand human motives and to trace human events. I think this faculty is even more necessary in churchmen who must act as intermediaries between the soul and its creator. Imagination should remind us of what we do not know of God and alert us to the inadequacy of formulae that are all too redolent of the times in which they were written. Even the words of absolution and assurance that one's sins have been forgiven must be uttered and clothed in some way with a prior understanding and human compassion to be really convincing. What man deserves to hear another confess without reminding the penitent that the priest is a man as well and subject to sin?

As for the sins of woman, what man can ever understand

the parameters of that hidden sea, the conscience of woman? The female sex is too close to the mysteries of life and death to be judged as though nature had no existence within her. She is part of the tides and seasons and as complete within herself as the sun and moon. What man lonely observes, she experiences in the depth of her being. She is subject to influences that we can barely grasp tied as she is to the outer world that man can manipulate but never truly conquer.

February 5, 1894
London

I took a walk today through the busy London streets simply to break out of the enforced solitude of this most bitter season of the year. The recent snowfall has ceased but the legacy of mire and slush is everywhere to be seen. At last I was forced to take a cab and from its shelter peer about as I directed the driver eastward along the embankment. The city of London reposes now against a background of leaden skies and fog. I feel trapped by the particular surroundings that now encase me as does my own particular history. More and more it occurs to me that the aspirations of all mankind are for the universal. Which of us does not finally grow weary of the unique pattern of experience and interpretation that we term our identity? We are encased by our own personalities. Year after weary year reveals the same struggles with the same set of intractable problems and the people who embody them. In fact if it were not for morality, the sanctions of the law, and our fear of ghosts, wholesale murder of that list of enemies that each of us keeps would be an attractive concept. How many wrongs still rankle within us, how many insults lie like an infected splinter along our memory's way?

In an idle hour I have compiled a list of toxic agents, any one of which would readily dispatch a human life and most are absolutely untraceable. There is for instance a frog that lives in Columbia of a rich golden color whose skin is so toxic that it goes about in broad daylight and no predator from the jaguar to the anaconda will touch it. Then there is the Taipan of central Australia the poison of which is a hundred times more powerful than that of the cobra. A thin needle could easily be the conduit for this venom and might be fired from a small tube affixed to an umbrella tip with a small powder charge as a propellant.

Some noxious agents are even poisons where any contact is sufficient to produce death such as aconite derived from wolf bane or the agent derived from the colorful but deadly castor bean. Then there is the Egyptian scorpion whose sting is so painful that victims have been reported to seek a speedy death to escape the agony of the resultant contraction and spasm of the limbs after being stung. The list of such agents, each a development from within nature itself, raises the question of whether such horrors are mere amoral phenomena or whether nature has within itself its own inherent malice extended towards life. The life of one life-form is ensured by the death of other life-forms, but where is the source of balance between them beyond mere chance? Is Original Sin adequate to explain this imbalance and disproportion? The various religions of the world seek to escape the particular and to find some way of transcending our temporal condition by finding some point of transcendent unity that resolves all such conflicts.

Yet morality for the Christian is always incarnational. The entire concept of atonement implies that the concrete act of the Crucifixion of Christ has universal efficacy. Christianity does not seek to attain God by direct manipulative means. God must come to us. Even the heretical Gnostics recognized the unique significance of the life and death of Jesus, but whereas they emphasized the appearance as somehow less important than the mysterious underlying reality of the godhead, orthodox belief insists upon the flesh and blood reality of the act by which we are saved.

God therefore evidently does not spurn the particular and the fleshly. Our soul is not some appending Platonic essence set in opposition to the body; it is the living form of the body itself. That this form can survive death without the matter that it formerly organized is the essence of Christian hope. Similarly our actions during our lives cannot be seen as mere physical phenomena. Each is caught up in some mysterious way into the history of the universal salvation of the world. Nothing is morally indifferent when seen from this perspective. The material universe, even that part of which lies beyond the very possibility of observation, reflects the action and agency of God in our regard by the mere fact of existing. Holiness pervades all things while not interfering with their fallen nature but rather enacting redemption from within them through grace.

If evil sprang forth from an initially good creation, redemption and reconciliation emerge under the will of God from within exiled creation. Again it is the particular that realizes through the action of grace the universal. This is a great mystery, the ultimate mystery, but to deny it is exist in a state of perennial frustration with the seeming trivia of an unfolding universe that will end in maximum disorder and the dispersal of all elements. Time itself is the conduit for that dispersal and time flows in only one direction. Redemption then must by its very nature reverse time or transit over it to attain that initial condition from whence all else flows. Certainly if all things may be as it were re-constituted by God, the soul must be the first of these elements to be thus re-embodied in a now perfect flesh. This the Church proclaims in the doctrine of the Resurrection of the Body as affirmed in the Apostle's Creed. How this is to be accomplished is not the business of the Church to define. The doctrine bears witness to the promise, not to the means by which God will achieve this miracle. The significance of the doctrine of the Resurrection of the Body is to teach us not to despise the temporal and the material but to see in all things and within every action the realization that creation is somehow advancing the realization of the Kingdom of God among us.

The universal is always achieved by the realization of the particular and is not to be advanced by mere esoteric magic but rather by our everyday actions. Christianity is the exact opposite of the so-called mystery religions of Mithraism or Pythagoreanism. Even the Holy Sacrifice of the Mass is not a mere re-enactment of the sacrifice of Calvary but is the thing itself; just as the Body and Blood of Christ are really present upon the altar. Christianity is a religion of the concrete and the particular, not of the merely symbolic and the universal. The underlying principle is dynamic and efficacious because imbued with grace. Grace in turn is the universal action of God in the world. God is present in all things in some manner and all things work together for the fulfillment of the divine intent and the final good of all to whom salvation has been promised.

This affirmation of providential design raises the question of how so much that appears to be accidental and unfortunate, particularly when the accidental is out of proportion to mere failures of human foresight, can ever work for the greater good. It does not seem to me that providence minutely attunes the happening of all events. To believe so would be to transform our contingent universe into the mere working out of a mechanical device like some great clock that is gradually unwinding. There is instead a spontaneity and freedom of sorts in all events—a principle of indeterminacy that at the same time does not gainsay providential design. How the two are balanced is unfathomable. This means that history in the broadest possible connotation is not ascertainable until it happens. Any pattern to be discerned is always an afterthought.

God's foreknowledge of events does not equal their proximate causation by divine means. Creation operates under its own power and accident is the evidence of this process in action. We are asked to respond to events beyond our control with compassion and moral direction even when we encounter manifest evil. These failures do not call into question the meta-destination of providential design or intent. These failures are a scandal though to mere unobstructed human reason. Any effort to reconcile the two is a mere exercise of fancy. Such a view of providence was nevertheless devised in the philosophy of the German philosopher Leibnitz in his theory of monads.

There is no simple closure to the universe of even physical events, let alone moral events. The paradox instead is the simultaneous existence of a metaphysically finite universe occupying a field that appears to be infinite. There is no expanding edge to being; rather all is contained and subsistent within its own set of rules. Beyond those rules there exists nothing imaginable from within our own perspective. Neither language nor thought can ascertain what may exist beyond the being of which we are a part; therefore even speculation is useless in this regard. We take the world as we find it and do the best that we can with it.

solid wall of fog has moved into the city today so that even to walk abroad is to invite pick-pockets and minor assassins to make one their victim. So it was that Watson and I after a breakfast of raspberry scones brought our chairs close up to the fire as we used to do on such days in the past and engaged in a bracing discussion touching upon long forgotten cases that have yet to be revealed, and if I may so, somewhat elaborated into romance by Watson's inveterate pen.

"You have perhaps heard me speak before of the Treppoff Murder and my summons to Odessa by no less a person than Tsar Alexander," I began. "It was an affair not without interest, not only in itself, for as usual the crimes that touch the nobility are usually the most obvious in respect of motive, some palace intrigue or vulgar act of revenge for a stolen mistress. The real interest in this case lay entirely in the insight that I was able to obtain into a man who may preside over the very last of the old feudal order in a 19th century empire."

"Still a murder of anyone highly placed in government is bound to resonate throughout the body politic by bringing such a figure within the ambit of crime from which his class is usually immune by virtue of its protected station in life," Watson opined.

"Ah, you must have your penny-dreadful horrors old fellow. Very well, we shall descend into the details. It was a case of poisoning of course. I knew that before I even left London. The question resolved itself into the usual one of motive and opportunity. In this case I had the advantage that Count Treppoff was not, as is so often the case among the nobility, universally hated by his serfs. He was a follower of Tolstoy's doctrines of Christian ethics deprived of the supernatural motive that alone can be the basis for so demanding a set of principles. The Christian you see does not, as is so often supposed, act out of a delight in virtue for its own sake as Kant taught, but rather from the personal motive of love of God. Take that love away and one may still find good manners and civility (for these remain intact and undisturbed) but the sacrifices demanded of the true Christian may even involve the risk of martyrdom and thus require a higher motive than any mere ethical considerations may ever provide. But I forget: you always desire that a story should not be reduced to its mere essentials like a geometric proof but rather it should be spun out with all of its drama and atmosphere intact." I settled back in my chair and watched as the smoke from my pipe eddied about the dim recesses of the high ceiling of our sitting room.

"Well then to begin, I was happy to escape the confines of London and to find myself on the continental orient express. My train had soon left Vienna behind and was crossing the vast Hungarian plain. I do not have your love of landscape, my dear Watson, but even I was impressed by the loveliness of the hilly region that lies at the base of the Carpathians as we crossed into Wallachia on the border of Bukovina. It is a region that produces a marvelous plum brandy called slivovitz and the sweet Muscat wine that is served with every meal. I could have enjoyed a week in the villages that we passed spent among the Szegeny and the Slovaks but it is always a capital mistake to allow the ground to settle after a crime has been committed for then few clues will ever be found.

So it was that I took the Black Sea boat for Odessa from Galatz and found myself among the Romanoff's. No autopsy had yet been performed due to the heat with the result that I could not seek the usual clues for arsenic or cyanide. I was forced thereby to rely upon only the observations of the servants who were quite distressed because they were fond of their benevolent master. The symptoms of his end had come upon him suddenly and were alarming in the extreme, which suggested poison. I recall wandering to the window and looking down into the garden where I observed the distinctive blossoms of monkshood or as it is also called in this region, wolfbane. I inquired whether the Count had any vices. His only indulgence it seems was his love of an infused floral tea. Well it was a small matter to test the samovar for lingering traces of aconite and the rest was merely a matter of looking for one who had access to the samovar on the afternoon in question. You will recall that the vegetable alkaloids are among the most virulent of poisons."

"Who then committed the murder, an anarchist?" Watson inquired.

"Well the young heir to the throne Nicholas had assumed so at first, but in reality it was a servant girl who had long wished to consummate an impossible alliance with her master. She eventually broke down and confessed of course; but by then some fourteen local revolutionaries were already on their way to Siberia after being beaten to get them to confess to the crime. I pointed out to the young sovereign that he had hardly given my methods a chance to reveal the true culprit, but he is a man of fixed ideas and direct methods and I fear that someday he will pay a great price for his impetuosity. He is a most romantic young man and one lacking in all imagination. These are the worst possible qualities in a leader, because it makes him inflexible and unable to adapt to changing conditions. History is the product of personal characteristics projected like light from a magic lantern slide upon a wall. Why it is that mere individual psychology and personal foibles can turn the tide of nations? This all is part of the legacy of another era when democracy was but a dream. We may now be witnessing the end of the era of anointed monarchs though it may take some great cataclysm before one era definitively yields to another."

"Unless even democracy is only a passing phase..." Watson said quietly.

"The fateful day must come Watson; it is a matter of prophesy and the desire for justice that burns in the human heart. Christianity is essentially democratic because it sees each man and woman, each slave and free-man, as finally an equal child of God. It was only early Christianity that was non-political and then only because the return of Christ was expected momentarily and earthly existence proportionately discounted. Ever since, the virtues have been reaching out towards the day when the will of God, as expressed in the mandate of charity, will recognize the full measure of human dignity for every man and woman on the earth. Any sovereignty that does not recognize this trend must finally yield sway so that God's will may be done on earth as it is done in heaven, as the Paternoster expresses it so well. Russia is a land to whose fate is tied the destiny of many nations and perhaps the world," I concluded. "It may never know democracy, but any progress from the present autocratic rule would seem to be an improvement. My only prayer is that change when it comes does not come as the result of a cataclysm."

Later—

As the evening drew down and the gas lamps were lit in the streets we were still discussing some of my more obscure cases. Among these was the strange case of the Paradol Chamber. It represents for me still an axiomatic case of human folly and the strange desire present among many for an easy regeneration of our corporal faculties by some obscure or arcane methodology that goes about garbed in the accoutrements of science. In this case a gentleman came to England from Hungary who claimed to be a physician who had discovered a South American herb called "Paradol." This herb was one of those odiferous plants that awaken associations to various pleasant aromas, but is just sufficiently distinct as to be unique. Even now I hesitate to name the fellow because he still has friends in high places that swear by his treatments. These consisted of having the patient lie down in a metal chamber while an infusion of the smoke of burning blossoms of Paradol was introduced by a mechanical fan. After some fifteen minutes of this exposure (and no doubt just before the patient succumbed to asphyxiation from smoke inhalation) the fumes were blown away and the patient usually reported feeling purified of excess bodily humors or toxins as a result. A skeptical mind of course might suggest that receiving again an unobstructed access to oxygen might have accounted for the feelings reported. Be that as it may, the man in question here, who possessed a high social reputation, began to recover his former health and soon every other great lady and society hostess in London had been at one time or other subjected to the rigors of the Paradol Chamber. The reputed "doctor" meanwhile was free to suggest the very feelings later reported by asking the patient whether she was feeling various sensations. The force of suggestion or Mesmerism can be quite effective in some persons. Such minor frauds have always existed and in most cases do no real harm, but this fellow managed in addition to worm out information during the sessions that was used later by a confederate for blackmail purposes."

"The connection was never made by his victims to the seemingly innocuous talk of the doctor during the treatment sessions. The matter was finally brought to my attention by an irate husband and I brought a certain amount of pressure to bear upon the fellow who seemingly overnight decided that one of the more obscure Baltic nations needed to receive his unique ministrations. He has not returned to London since then but his place has been filled by other purveyors of cures for various hysterical ailments. Women are the believing sex; perhaps they need to be because the future of the life of every generation lies in their hands. When the women of the earth lose faith, then faith is lost indeed!"

"The mind-body connection of course is quite complex and it is not impossible that certain stimuli may cause the body to generate its own healing from within its own resources. It may even be that the body may summon through concentration certain latent energies as some Indian fakirs are said to do through the postures of yoga. The mechanisms of such things may exceed our present knowledge and yet be valid for all of that. Premature conclusions have always been the bane of science and of the science of detection as well. I try to keep an open mind where no imposture or imposition works definite harm. After all in a world that finds hope such a rare occurrence and disillusionment so ready to hand it may be better to err on the side of optimism."

February 8, 1894
London

I am often startled at the source of the fascination accorded to the tales of my cases as brought forth by Watson and cunningly placed in the Strand Magazine by the man acting as Watson's go-between with the publishing media. Certain habits of mind and domestic foibles evidently have lent color to those tales that they would not otherwise have possessed if the same deeds were accomplished by another personality type. I have even imagined at times that my appeal in these tales is such that it is I who make the stories interesting and not the crimes themselves.

The avid reader as a result finds himself a familiar witness to the natural setting provided by what amounts to a closet drama where Baker Street has become a Mecca for persons seeking solace in various untoward circumstances.

What for me is a labor is for the reader a sort of magic realm of reassurance that restores an emotional sense that justice has been done and the moral order reinforced by being refracted through my own values and habits of thinking. It is not my desire to serve the function of a general arbiter of social justice or moral truth for the simple reason that I have yet to turn my convictions into anything more than general guidelines in the onrushing tide of events. Any system existing by itself comes with time to lose the thread back into human experience where the conditions for decision are altered by the very circumstances that accompany any life-in-process. Only a post-hoc analysis can reveal later whether any decision was adequate to restore the equilibrium that the reader imagines that I possess a key. Nothing is ever restored that has not been somewhat altered by the process that brought the problem to my door in the first place and I have been changed as well by each encounter.

Sometimes the personal situation revealed is such that the forces must simply work themselves out and any intervention on my part comes too late to prevent the inevitable harm of events already in motion. Only in retrospect can we discover the point at which things began to go awry, often due to some minor mistake or misinterpretation that as in Shakespeare's King Lear leaves utter desolation in its wake. Often the most innocent must bear the cost of other's wrongs while the one most responsible or in the best position to have intervened at the critical hour finally sees the ultimate result of his former negligence or hardness of heart. Even when I am consulted I have found that clarity often has come too late. On these occasions I blame myself severely and only Watson is able, with his deep wisdom born of seeing much human suffering, to help me to release my grip on the tiller of events. Forces come swiftly about that exceed our capacity to grasp and to avoid before they become hardened into the granite permanence of the past. It is then that the jackals of regret gather and we come to mourn what we now cannot alter or redeem.

My thoughts yesterday were personal but what if they could be extended to the course of historical development not simply of nations but even of religion. The pretense that religion shows no development and is in fact ahistorical and firmly based in an accurate and complete knowledge of God lies behind every fundamentalism. Adherents to this manner of belief find within it a sense of personal power that is easily interpreted as the will of God. St. Ignatius of Loyola insisted upon the importance of the discernment of spirits precisely in order to combat and counteract temptations masquerading as acts of virtue. Even good deeds can be swiftly turned into dangerous channels by the craftiness of the evil one, the personified evil that the Catholic Church includes among its articles of belief.

Christianity is not a mere ethical system. As an heir to Judaism it always displays a relational tone and quality that exceeds any merely legalistic basis. In fact absent a relationship with God the demands made of the Christian believer far exceed the most challenging aspects of Judaic belief because good actions must now be accompanied by a proper disposition of being done with love. On the occasion of the institution of the Holy Eucharist at the Last Supper and knowing that He would soon be betrayed and abandoned Jesus told his apostles that he had eagerly anticipated sharing this Passover Meal with them and even as He prepared to distribute the bread and wine He have thanks that His body and blood were about to be shed for the salvation of the world. This visceral and personal event is not a mere theological pronouncement; it is a drama wherein the apostles and Jesus attain a unity that is the fundamental nature of that same universal sharing that it is the mission of the Catholic Church to preserve ever since.

Theological truths however sound like mere abstractions until they are translated back into individual acts of love and compassion. The sacrament as sign must be incorporated into a way of life that validates formal belief by giving evidence that what is professed with the lips is believed with the heart and demonstrated in acts of charity. Anything less is only an empty gesture. For the same reason religious belief cannot be imposed under duress. Far too many conversions were procured by overzealous proselytism dedicated to stamping out the cultural practices of newly encountered lands and the formal imposition of imperfectly comprehended beliefs seen as a form of magic by conquered peoples. The power of the gospel is one of attraction rather than compulsion.

However, the urgency to "save souls" led to any number of atrocious acts committed by Europeans toward the conquered nations. Even at home the assurance of Jesus that the poor would be always with us did not imply that the rich could use this as a means to reconcile the impoverished to their natural condition of penury. As the Second Coming of Christ was first deferred generation after generation the early enthusiasm for equality was replaced by an easy acceptance of social gradations so that with time the downtrodden masses have learned to turn to secular remedies for relief rather than to depend upon the goodwill of the Christian community. No small measure of indignation towards religion takes its origin in this contradiction between belief and practice. It seems fairly obvious that no person should be richer in a monetary sense for being a Christian. Jesus advised that one's treasure should be in heaven where no thief can break in and steal and where no rust or moth may devour.

February 10, 1894
London

I used to tell Watson that a general text on the art of detection would make a huge difference in the effectiveness of law enforcement at the official level. Thus far I have confined my own efforts to writing an occasional monograph for private circulation and providing occasional hints to Scotland Yard when they are baffled and decide to climb the seventeen steps to my lair and solicit my assistance in some particularly thorny case. If I have not done more in this area it is not due to laziness but to an insight they I arrived at only by questioning what I am actually doing when I am asked to intervene in some affair where a manifest injustice appears to have occurred.

I am guided at such moments not by some outside institutional loyalty but by my own internal sense of what is right in the circumstances presented to me. Lawyers in contrast are for the most part guided by the demands of their profession and their identity as officers of the court. The client must be represented with zeal but only within the bounds of the law. Of course there is sufficient law available on demand for a skilled advocate to cobble together some support for virtually any claim or defense no matter how absurd they may appear if stated in plain language.

The law is its own world. For this reason I prefer my own conscience to whatever is peddled about by Scotland Yard. The actual function of the legal system as a whole is to preserve established social norms and to allow change when it must occur to benefit those who are in positions of power. The lower orders of society provide the gage of any social pressure building up below before it can take effective political action and dislodge the legal system and re-allocate resources between the social classes. I have tried on repeated occasions to point this out to my brother Sherringford but he always rolls his eyes and tells me to stop spouting what he calls "more French Nonsense." Sherringford has never forgiven the French for their revolution in 1789. His answer to social indignation is to tell the masses to work harder and they will have less time to be discontented. He points out that any superfluity of resources possessed by the lower orders of society will be swiftly dissipated in vulgar and unseemly ways. He looks to religion and to fear of reprisals now or hereafter as the only things that will keep them quiescent with "shoulder to the wheel."

This attitude also makes Sherringford sympathetic to what he calls the beneficent effect of British rule in India and in Ireland let alone in Africa. His vision for mankind as a whole is to preserve the British Empire at whatever cost because if left to their own resources the colonized parts of the world would sink again into savagery. If I try to point out the achievements in other cultures that once possessed their own empire status he will remind me that they were even more sanguinary than we have been. Mildness and toleration are the luxury of armchair thinkers from his point of view. The rise of the lower orders in economic power even in England would lead to the triumph of intellectual mediocrity and vulgarity in matters requiring taste and sophistication.

In his view if even pick-pockets can be executed for their offenses then shopkeepers and householders need not fear any incursion from more audacious forms of theft. For Sherringford property is the basis for all civilization—an intact estate carefully administered is worth any amount of labor. Therefore social mobility is as unnatural as to invite breeding between species. If I point out that this is hardly a very Christian attitude he counters with the observation that a sufficiently well-endowed parish or bishopric settles any theological niceties among Churchmen and that the local vicar has never refused to come to tea when invited on the grounds that his host is less Christian for being wealthy.

My personal approach may be less finely attuned theologically than one might expect from a good Catholic but the same innate skepticism and habit of seeing facts from an oblique angle that has made for success as a detective makes me impatient with any moral system that applies hard and fast categories to the complexity of human existence and the strange currents that seem to divide disproportionately the results flowing from the great institutions of church and state alike. If I seek to play a small role in remedying what I call manifest injustices I can only hope that God will value my intent over my performance when my life lies before the august throne of the Divine Judge.

February 11, 1894
London

It has always amazed me how the various social systems of which religion is one deal with the realities of human life. In spite of the startling news of the resurrection of Jesus and the even more intimate indwelling of the Holy Spirit at Pentecost the course of Church history has been one of unending contention. The pattern has been from surprise to certainty and the question at the present day is how and by what means Catholicism has answered questions that were so unclear at the time of the death of Jesus that the news of the resurrection was first met with wonder if not with incredulity.

As the initial apostolic period became a distant memory the momentum of belief became self-sustaining just as an object in motion will tend to stay in motion unless acted upon by an outside force. That outside force at the present day is the friction encountered by confronting the increasing effectiveness of survival techniques and the increased productivity of the secular state. The comprehensive services once provided by the Church are now delegated to the secular realm for definition and fulfillment. Even the concept of a soul as a floating Platonic essence somehow imprisoned in a visible body has disappeared and with it the internalized consequences of dying without the absolution that only the Catholic Church can bestow.

This in turn means that the general civilizing function formerly achieved by Christian belief must now flow through some internalized sense of social duty. To say that the average man or woman can be attracted to virtue per se and that wisdom has the same appeal as folly is to deny human history. Sherringford, the ultimate social realist has a unique approach to the betterment of humankind. I will try and put his position in his own words, a summation of many discussions that we have had.

"I detect at times a certain Wordsworth quality in your Romantic views, Sherlock. If I may say so it disables you for life and I fear at times for your safety. You seem to think that all classes of society are equally capable of reason and that sufficient education will awaken the philosopher who sleeps within the rustic breast. I have even succumbed to some of your views to the extent of opening a small infirmary for the aged on the estate and also a lying-in hospital for tenant women about to give birth. I have ensured that the theories of Lister are applied so that maternal deaths from sepsis are remarkably reduced. A small school here has bestowed the rudiments of literacy. But beyond these small contributions I prefer to not spread the seeds of social discontent by implying that all persons should be judged by a standard that they are unable to attain. It is cruel to awaken false hopes under the guise of democratic sentiments. Each element in society should circulate within its own proper orbit. Where would we be if the planets were suddenly to go roaming about the solar system? How long before a ghastly collision would occur?"

"The only reason that the American system has prospered is that the more fractious members of society are urged to move westward and exhaust their violent emotions by taking land from the Indian tribes that already inhabit those regions. Someday the plains will be settled and the predatory spirit of the Americans will be turned about upon their fellow citizens. It is then that the new American dark ages will begin. Mark my words Sherlock, the human species demands limits and social distinctions so as to provide an orderly means of ascent in evolutionary development. Freedom granted without limits or conditions will always lead to social chaos and criminality and if the leaders manifest these same characteristics of vulgarity and lack of culture then anything is possible. The ape in man is never completely subdued."

February 12, 1894
London

I was thinking today of the advantages that my brothers and I enjoyed in our youth growing up in Yorkshire. We were granted the space and time at Sigerside in which to form our own sense of who were, to choose from our father's library those books that best awoke within us a path, a destiny. My own passion was for the Waverly novels of Sir Walter Scott. I can still recall stormy evenings when the Yorkshire winds howled beyond the casements as I read. The immense crashing of the ivy against the leaded panes of the windows were for me as the crash of the horses hoofs as they brought together the lances of the plumbed knights. The ringing of sword and the clash of armor was present in each new gust of wind.

Mycroft meanwhile pursued history and was particularly well-versed in the writings of Thomas Carlyle. This was excellent preparation for his later dealings with Bismarck, the Iron Chancellor of Germany. I recall him reading the letters of Talleyrand and a biography of Cardinal Richelieu during one long vacation from Oxford. His vocation to statecraft was already evident. Meanwhile Sherringford was obsessed with practical accounting and the output from the various tenant farmers on the estate. I can still recall his distain for his younger brothers, neither of whom had joined the local hunt as young men. It is not that I cannot sit a horse, but I make it a point never to trust my welfare to a beast that may take it upon itself to toss me head over heels into the nearest ditch should anything alarm it. Horses seem to delight in taking fright at the slightest thing and I value my head too much to risk it so callously. Nor do I bear any particular animosity to foxes. The spirit of hunting is within me of course, but I seek out my foxes among the human species, and my wolves and hyenas as well.

Each of us brothers manifested in our youth what we would later become in time. We parceled out between us our father's own complex character as landowner, social reformer, and parliamentarian. Few families pursue a linear course or long retain preeminence in public life; yet there is often a central problem or preoccupation that often takes more than a single lifetime or individual to resolve.

Each of us has in his own way attempted a synthesis of the efforts of our forebears. We each felt in our own way the urgency of the times in which we live in this busy nineteenth century with its manifold changes. The desire to have some impact upon the stream of events may not have met our father's own precise desires but his spirit is alive within us. The visions of our adulthood owe much to the dreams of our youth when fancy weaves about us a sense that our lives will be such lives as the world has not yet known. In youth is where the roots of the tree of our whole lives are planted. May these roots be planted deep, for life alas soon dampens the ardor of our wishes with the reality that we are but one of many and the life that we imagined in the guise of legend is all too soon summed up by an obituary that few will care to take the time to read.

The realm of the personal seems to shrink to nothing when we confront the sheer extent of the world as it presents itself to us; yet religion has its base precisely within that private realm that we call the soul. My readings in astronomical science are singularly unhelpful in this regard. It appears that the true extent of the universe exceeds our units of ordinary measurement to such a degree that any talk of human significance is meaningless unless we locate that meaning along a scale that is not dependent upon observations of celestial bodies in space. The smell of a rose is of no consequence upon Jupiter and Saturn, planets consisting of a coalescence of frozen gas crystals. Moral actions or aesthetic values only achieve significance within human beings. For this reason the earth is big enough for my conceptions and I feel no need to pursue a God existing somewhere beyond the stars.

The figure of the crucified Christ focuses the eye and the mind as well. Any assessments of human life by the adherent to the Christian faith must take their origin here because it subsumes all of human suffering into a single person whose voluntary submission to death forms the primary element in the three-fold confession:

Christ has died; Christ is risen; Christ will come again

It is this faith that has sustained countless lives for two thousand years when all else seemed meaningless. This confession is our only bridge to the unified simplicity that the philosophers posit and the scientists pursue.

Professor Moriarty, whose publications I have read, indicates that the goal of physics to reduce all phenomena to a single formula that will explain how entropy proceeds from a hypothetical point of absolute unity and perfection into the decayed and decaying universe that we now inhabit. Such a state of perfection and unity, if it ever existed, must have preceded all subsequent events so that both space and time must take their origins from that primal seed. Everything since is a mere repercussion of some primary aberration of what should have remained unmoved unless perfection itself can be conceived of as an unstable state of being.

Does the impetus of reality emerge from within such a structure or does some projected and yet to be realized project act as a strange attractive influence to call time and space into being in order to pursue some end beyond what we can imagine? In either case we as thinking human beings occupy an intermediate position in the great dispersal of events. What we call history is only a momentary observation that is no sooner glimpsed than it is superseded by larger happenings. Yet we see significance within our limited range of causality by speaking of good and evil. These categories we ignore at our peril because upon them all claims to human dignity rest.

February 14, 1894
London

An odd circumstance occurred the other day. I stopped in for an early dinner at Simpsons and while finishing my custard a small commotion ensued and I looked to the entrance to discover that a noisy but not boisterous party had entered including Oscar Wilde and his youthful, but not to my mind prepossessing companion, Lord Alfred Douglas. As he was being shown to his table Oscar turned aside and came over to my table alone to greet me. He was courteous as always and expressed surprise that I had returned. It had been his vague understanding that I was on the continent recovering from an unspecified illness. I did not say much to disabuse him of that belief since I knew that what is said to Oscar in confidence would undoubtedly be repeated at some fashionable dinner-table in London and possibly with a novel and mysterious embroidery suggestive of some vague scandal.

Oscar meanwhile appears to court all manner of suppositions as to his own life by his flamboyant insistence that what is obvious should be disregarded. It is a dangerous game he is playing and I would have told him so in more private circumstances. It has not been my practice however to intervene before I am consulted, but I fear that someday I will need to intervene in some manner in the case of the celebrated wit and playwright. It troubles me that society finds exciting what it so fervently denies. Should that membrane of denial be pierced it is anyone's guess what noxious effusion may be emitted, to condemn as unheard of conduct that which occurs in fact in every public school of the land.

To upset the pretences upon which society is based is to court the revenge that such social tension restrains. It is this misdirected energy that explains the scapegoat phenomenon that sees evil in the most prosaic faults attendant upon human nature while ignoring far greater evils because they are traceable to faceless institutional structures considered to be essential to commerce and to government. In his physical aspect Oscar is beginning to show the results of indulgence. He is wined and dined everywhere and his plays have become the jewel of the London season. His wit, though as amusing as ever, has developed a somewhat predictable quality so that what was formerly surprising is now little more than a predictable inversion of expectations. He has yet to graduate to high tragedy in his art and my fear is that he may be reserving it for his actual life.

February 15, 1894
London

In order to be all-embracing Catholicism like a net cast into the sea must make room for all of humanity. The call to conversion however has all too often presumed that we must manifest an equal sanctity to Jesus in order to merit salvation. A swift review of humanity would then conclude that the majority of the human race would be damned if held to this standard. This of course would breed despair at the prospect of a human life and some might conclude that if most of the human race is to be damned for one reason or another, either through some deficiency of belief or of conduct so that a only a select few might possibly be saved, then the more prudent course to minimize human suffering and eliminate sin now and hereafter would be for the human race to simply die out completely.

God apparently does not take equal exception to the

animals except in the sense that they participated in the fall in Eden so that in a sense all of the created order is to be redeemed along with humanity on the last day. If this is indeed God's will as the more universalist theologians have advocated, then the redemptive drama on Golgotha and the mercy of God is far more extensive and inclusive than the teaching of the Church has often supposed it to be. Even at the present day anathemas are preferred to general absolutions and catechesis prefers to error if it must on the side that presumes hell to be the most likely final destination regardless of the sufferings of Christ that are as a result believed to be only of marginal effectiveness leaving a substantial remainder to our own devices and overarching metaphysic of Christianity still places the onus of evil squarely upon the human race but has yet to be entirely clear regarding the actual scope and means of effective realization of the redemptive plan of God. St. Paul's epistles urge the early Christian community to conform their conduct to the dignity of their calling and St. John assures those who he addressed to know that they are "God's beloved children" now but what they shall be has yet to be revealed. This latter approach leaves room for some degree of uncertainty by keeping some open ground as does the promise of Jesus in John's Gospel that "in my house there are many mansions."

Perhaps heaven provides us with a sort and manner of environment that is appropriate to our particular capacities. God's judgment may be finer adjusted than any strict binary division of heaven and hell can provide. Perhaps a time will come when Catholic doctrine may take a closer look at its traditional approach to salvation, its extent and character in order to resolve the difficulties that I only point out here. Loyalty to the Church mandates proper respect and deference to the *Ordinary Magisterium* and to the Pope. No perfect synthesis can eliminate every doubt or satisfy every reservation over what still lies veiled in mystery. To err in either direction is to encounter risk. For this reason some discipline must be maintained here as in so many other areas of human life.

Of course every pronouncement no matter how solemn must, it seems to me, be understood against the data available at the time of the pronouncement. Many factors must be weighed into the balance. Change or elucidation of latent meanings and intentions are in this sense possible as new perspectives emerge so that deeper insights can prevail. If the Holy Spirit was capable in an instant to make all things clear as they are for God our minds darkened as they are would be unable to receive such knowledge. All is adapted to our capacities. This is just one more mercy of God.

February 16, 1894
London

atson and I are still actively engaged in our discussions of several other interesting past cases. Among them is that of the Grice-Pattersons and the Island of Uffa off the coast of Sweden where that estimable couple retired after a distinguished career spent at one of England's foremost universities where the husband was a Professor of history. I was consulted by the wife of the Professor when she noticed certain symptoms of an alarming nature in her husband.

These symptoms were indicative of what the French term an *idée fixe* or obsession. In her husband's case it was related to a felt need to discern an overarching pattern in history. Professor Grice-Patterson was once (for he is now dead) the foremost authority upon the Italian theoretician Giambattista Vico whose theory of the fourfold cycle of history has intrigued many. I recall that I was much intrigued at the time by the Professor's mania because in many ways it mirrored my own speculations. My conviction of course is that history is irrelevant to the average lifespan because great cycles take decades or centuries to resolve themselves. The best that can be hoped for is that one may not find oneself straddling one of those fissures that appear now and again between historical epochs. What more unfortunate generations can be conceived for instance than those which straddled The Thirty Years War of the 17th Century? Vast regions were of Europe were so depopulated by the ravaging troops that provender was non-existent and the raided civil population was faced with the usual result of starvation and even cannibalism.

If there has ever been proof of Original Sin, human history

is that proof. The educated man must finally reach the conclusion that for the majority of the human race in all eras of human history life has not only been nasty, brutish, and short but quite often not short enough. It seems rather the blind striving of the genes rather than any prospect for amelioration that causes generation to follow generation. What is the blind force that causes inanimate matter to evolve life-forms each in competition with the others for a limited supply of available essential nutrients? Why do lethal organisms exist and perhaps even originate out of the primal ooze of protoplasm to decimate entire populations of higher order phyla? A mere microbe can fell an elephant, the brain of a genius be consumed by a one-celled parasite. Is all the earth but one great culture medium for the vile swarms of infesting agents of disease and decay?

There would appear at times to be a malign intentionality at work in the agents of human destruction to destroy our dignity as an image and likeness of God. In the face of this what sense does it make to seek overarching patterns to history amidst the onward sweeping scythe of wars and revolutions? What use is it to a dying individual man or woman to contemplate the progress of the race unless it may relieve his present intense distress? But Professor Grice-Patterson was one of those men who seek to escape his own mortality by charting immense symphonic dances of events that bury thousands. He would step out of his own life onto an imaginary safety platform from which he could observe these cycles or vibrations of history seeking an underlying basal note or core around which he could construct a theory that would outlive him. He had retired to the remote Island of Uffa with his personal library of many volumes in several languages intending in his declining years to trace out of the data contained within them the supreme pattern of events that would unite all events into one tapestry. This man's wife had heard that I was a man who often found a thread of sense in the unfathomable facts brought before me so she urged her husband to consult me while the couple was on a short visit to London. I responded to her letter of solicitation by agreeing to meet her husband before his return to Uffa for the waning summer days of the short Swedish summer.

I recall his unique appearance well to this very day. He was a little shrunken individual as though his substance was made up of the ephemeral dust of fractured book-bindings and stale leather. There was something almost mummy-like about the fellow as though he had just been unwrapped in a backroom of the British Museum. I half expected to see a scarab escape from his topcoat and scurry up the walls. He deposited his bony hindquarters on the chair that I proffered to him while regarding me as though cataloguing an exhibit in a display case. In the course of the discussion that ensued he kept referring to his watch as though time itself was escaping him, minutes which might have been better spent elsewhere than in speaking with an ex-chemist in a humble flat in Baker Street. A reconstruction of our discussion that day follows.

My boat sails tomorrow for Stockholm, Mr. Holmes and none too soon for me since I have already consulted the authorities on the question that needed to be answered."

"And what was that question pray?" I asked him.

"It was a mere detail, hardly worth mentioning, but since you ask it involved a question of certain bronze age axes which bear a remarkable similarity to those found in Lapland."

"You resolved the issue to your satisfaction?" I inquired.

"Without question sir; it does nothing to disturb my previous conclusions, but only makes my case stronger. You are not perhaps aware that I am about to publish in a single volume a comprehensive theory regarding the evolution of arms in the Nordic regions that will prove that the invaders of Rome were part of a cyclic pattern that pre-dated the Vandals and the Huns."

"You are to be congratulated."

"That is beside the point. I am nothing but a conduit of history."

"Oh surely more than that, to your dear wife for instance..."

He appeared puzzled for a moment as though this thought had not occurred to him.

"Oh I suppose strictly speaking you are correct sir."

"You were speaking in some other capacity before?" I asked with a smile.

"I don't understand you."

"Well then, I make it a habit in my practice to assume that words do not simply materialize out of thin air, they must be uttered by a thinking agent."

"That is surely obvious."

"Not as obvious as you may think. Have you heard the phrase that out of the fullness of the heart the mouth speaks? Surely a corollary of this is that the heart must be consulted before any real speech occurs. Our words proceed not as mere sound but as embodiments of our very self. The detached observer must therefore take care lest he be so detached that he might simply float away like a balloon from his own self. I am continually forced to observe that caveat in my own practice as a consulting detective. I mention it to you because your wife has been concerned about your health of late."

He looked somewhat taken aback. "I had thought to consult you today on certain historical questions. My personal life is of no consequence."

"Ah, I must correct you there. It is not possible to obtain a state of complete objectivity. You also have a history which is all that any man has."

"Yes as a source of bias and deception."

"On the contrary, our history is what gives us any existence at all. We are constituted by it into the miracle of individuality. This alone is the substratum out of which any meaning must emerge. There is no meaning without the resistance of the individual will to mere circumstantialities. If even insensate rocks resist the movement of the glacier that slides over them; even so must each of us take a stance to the history that passes over us and through our days and nights; to do anything less is not to be a man but a mere unconscious tracing of events. We are not mere disembodied observers. Our assessments make our observations possible. The fact of human existence alters the universe in some essential way."

His reaction was sudden and significant. It is not too much to say that my words found their mark. I was happy to hear that the solvent of my brief ministration proved adequate to cure his longstanding monomania and that he returned home to that lovely island of Sweden where he resided a changed man. Just as there is nothing like stubbing one's toe on a mahogany table to convince one of one's own physicality or an illness that consigns us to our knees to remind us that we are not as the gods of Olympus; so can a remembrance of love return us to a sense of our own unique significance. In a later correspondence I was gratified to hear that the insight I had done my best to convey sufficed for the Professor and that he returned to Uffa in time to enjoy by his wife's side the waning summer sun of that brief season that remained to him as it passed over the Baltic Sea.

February 17, 1894
London

It is delightful to be back in my own domicile with Watson at my side in the old accustomed chair reading his sea stories. The weather continues cold and foggy although we both take a constitutional once a day along the Thames embankment. Today we were discussing the remarkable case of Ricoletti of the club-foot and his abominable wife of some years ago. It was on a day similar to this that our door burst open and a strangely garbed man literally threw himself in at our feet.

"I have killed her, Mr. Holmes; Lord help me I have killed her," he groaned.

I have grown accustomed over the years to strange entrances at our sitting room, but this last was as strange as any. Watson and I helped the man up and into a chair, which was made more difficult because of his disabled foot which made all forward movement awkward in the extreme.

After helping him to a more comfortable position I gave him the usual disclaimer. "Before you say another word sir I must tell you that although I am not an agent of the official police I am at least bound to see justice done if a crime has been committed." Our strange client sat in his chair in evidently great distress of mind before beginning his tale.

"I care nothing for what shall happen to me now for she is dead, oh she is dead!" he cried.

"Nevertheless, you must bethink yourself before you give us any details, for we may later be called upon to attest to your confession before a court of law," I answered. "As a mere consulting detective I have no privilege of immunity in my communications with a client who may have committed a criminal offense." He was silent for a time breathing heavily. At last he spoke.

"Forgive me sir; it is kind of you to have my welfare in mind when I at least hold myself in utter contempt. Who would have thought that after all of her harsh words to me through the years that these last should have caused me to raise my hand against her and even then more in protest than with any desire to do her harm. But you can know nothing of this. You cannot know how my wife has cost me first my patrimony, then my business, and finally my self-respect. If God created her beauty it was the devil himself that created her tongue and the words that she has spoken to me year in and year out. How often have I heard her call me an abhorrent cripple, a deformed monster, and heard her cruel laughter echoing in my very dreams. Who would have thought that I was storing up within me a murderous anger, I who have never killed so much as a bird? Yet I am a murderer!"

He paused here to wipe his fevered brow. After he had regained his composure he continued his strange tale, "I tell you honestly sir that if she had always abused me to that final fatal degree I would have left her long ago. Who would not? But she wore me down by degrees until I could bear no more. Each effort to please her was at first met with smiles and seeming approbation, but in no time her fancy would roam and her demands increased. At last my judgment fled and I became prey to a recklessness of mind and spirit that have plunged me into financial ruin. I watched as my friends fell away one by one unable as they were to witness the spectacle of my folly and degradation at her hands. What they could never see was that some unaccountable fate had ordained that my soul was irrevocably joined with hers. Our very spirits seemed to meld so that I felt that I could not exist without her. Even her abuse became over time a stimulus to ever greater effort. I began to inhabit a realm of higher ideas to match her particular ambitions. I felt like a mountain-climber in the high Alps, one who wishes to scale the barren rock face of the Matterhorn. You can have no idea of the charm of such a woman, one who seems herself driven by some dreadful urgency to grow, to expand her influence, to control. I tell you gentlemen she was once to me like a goddess, one who like the Indian Kali demanded blood sacrifices. Now that sacrifice has been made at last, but it is she who has become the immolated victim not me."

He paused before continuing, "I wonder, if that is what she desired all along? Am I finally only the dumb instrument of her willed destruction? Why was she never happy? The fortune of my youth has been spent upon her. What woman of her class in London was ever better appareled or rode about in a finer coach? We would have traveled more, but there was always the business to maintain and ever-increasing debts to pay. At last the business itself foundered and there was only debt and more debt. At last I was forced to do what I had never dared to do hitherto, I refused to consent to a crime and to sign my name to bank drafts with insufficient funds and why, merely to add to the arsenal of trinkets and fripperies that were for her what meat and drink are to a starving man! It was then that she spoke the words that I had long dreaded to hear: 'I am leaving you abhorrent cripple, you are at last an empty husk.' I do not know whether these words were merely one more of her ill-considered utterances, but be that as it may they were her last. In spite of my club-foot I crossed the space between us in an instant like a leopard and her throat was in my hands. I can still see the contempt in her eyes in all their black beauty as my hands tightened about her. She put up little resistance and a moment later she fell from my grasp to the floor and lay still. It was only then that I realized what I had done and in horror I ran from the house clothed as I am to you, a man of whom I had been told, a man who knows what to do when all others do not. That is my lamentable tale sir; do with me as you wish."

I could not tell him this, but his tale was a common one. I remember telling Watson at the time not to add it to his annals because after all there was no crime to solve. Its point of instructiveness was not for the investigator, much less for the police, but for the alienist. There are bonds that can unite a man and a woman in a fatal *idée fixe* or *folie a deux* from which neither can extricate himself. Each recognizes in the other some unclaimed aspect of himself. At last the roles are exchanged at the last minute and the persecutor becomes the victim as perhaps she has all along wished to be. What a strange suicide is this that uses another's hand to do the slaying! Such women are as old as Eve and woe to the man whose own dark star leads his vessel to her siren isle.

Such women often hold their own sex in contempt because the freedom of the man is denied to her. She seeks always that lost part of herself that was never hers because each sex must finally reconcile itself to its incompleteness. A woman who hates her sex will hate the other sex as well and with double the hatred because his very masculinity is a daily reminder that she is a woman and will always be one. She wears a badge of shame imposed by her own vain desires, for to be a woman is in reality no dishonor. She imagines that a man possesses infinite power and freedom and judges each actual man against the standard of her own imagination. This would be harmless if it were only an error of judgment, but she acts upon it by destroying all that will not live up to the demands of her illusion. Even if such a supreme man could be found she would hate him still as a reminder of her own deficiencies. For such women as these there is but one answer: to flee them swiftly for they breed first unhappiness and finally desperation and despair. But there will always be found men who will attempt the impossible and seek to rescue them. Such a man stood before us that day.

I recall still my parting advice to him: to regain his self-respect by going directly to Scotland Yard confessing the murder and to obtain counsel for his defense. I refused to take from him the one chance that he still possessed to act the part of a man and to unify his life under the guise of one deliberate decision that was his alone. I must record here that he did not take my advice. I read in *The London Times* the next day that his body had been found floating in the Thames.

At first I reproached myself for not having done enough to spare him the full measure of his despair and his loss. He had over the years so entwined his every breathing hour with that of his persecutor that he could not imagine life without her. The poet Baudelaire, a victim of an exaggerated love for his mother and a later obsessive devotion to the sometime actress Jeanne Duval is a case in point. Between these two obsessions he fell prey to various addictions and to disease and finally died a helpless paralytic.

This is why a relationship to the father is so essential to particularly those men who possess a literary or an artistic nature. Woman was never meant to be the source of our salvation. I agree with the philosopher, Arthur Schopenhauer, who sees in woman the embodiment of the will to existence to perpetuate itself, not for any purpose beyond mere life itself. The higher functions whether of art or of science are the means by which mankind escapes fatality, a fatality that woman already accepts by her mere existence.

What woman would risk death in bringing forth life if she were not already condemned by her very nature to such an inevitable sacrifice? What man ever can be as self-effacing as a woman or more heroic when tragedy rears its head? It is the fate of mankind to dream of immortality, to build the city of their dreams, to perpetuate themselves in pale versions, in faulty imitations of themselves. Woman seeks no such individuality, it is enough that she is united to the great cosmic forces that being already immortal need no added engineering from her in order to endure. This keeps her immune from male folly, which she looks upon with a blend of amusement and contempt. He is to her both a child and a man at once, her consort and her conqueror, but finally only a means to an end that life may continue on its untrammeled way.

I must pose this question to Professor Moriarty when we meet someday. Does the universe in his opinion simply spring forth by some causeless aberration of non-being, some whim of metaphysical possibility? Or does some outside force with some desperate end in view create a world of open-ended possibility that entails the possibility of evil without actually recognizing it until it is too late to reverse course and to reconsider? Or perhaps love when it is found is so precious that it is worth the risk even of all the evils of the world.

February 18, 1894
London

Once the springs of memory are tapped the result is a flood. I remarked as much to Watson today as we sat once again on either side of our homely fire with the smell of a pungent mixture of Latakia and Turkish tobaccos in the air between us.

"No doubt you recall the case of the old Russian woman I commented…"

"Well there were several," he replied.

"But surely they were not all Countesses and surely they did not offer to place me on retainer to locate God for them."

"She was seeking spiritual guidance of a sort as I recall," Watson muttered absently looking up from his book.

"Oh much more than that; it was her intention to be quite certain about the most direct route to God so that she could dispose of her husband's fortune. Perhaps if I make an effort to recreate the scene you will better recall the extraordinary impression that she made at the time upon us both. I can still recall that squat but energetic figure composed of equal parts of sable fur and a great hat bursting with pheasant feathers and lace…"

Which of you is Mr. Sherlock Holmes?" she inquired looking from one to the other of us.

"My name Madam; and this is my intimate friend and associate, Dr. Watson, before whom you may speak as freely as before me."

She hesitated but a moment after a short and apparently satisfactory appraisal of the good doctor before pressing on.

"I am the Countess Sonia Alexandrovna Kapushinski and I have come expressly from Moscow to consult you on a matter of unparalleled importance."

"A long journey Countess; I trust that I shall not disappoint you."

"Your reward will justify all of your efforts, sir," she replied and opening her purse she reached within it and deposited ten one hundred pound banknotes upon the low table that stood before her. These are yours from this moment, for I have heard of your reputation and I desire that you may set aside any other matters until you have solved my problem for me."

"It is not my custom to charge fees in advance of performance Madam. Perhaps if you stated your case I could better advise you as to whether your problem is one that comes within my peculiar talents."

"It is because your talents are as you phrase it 'peculiar' that I have come so far. You would oblige me if you would accept my little gift; it will bring me the first assurance that I have had since my husband died."

"Let us leave this matter aside for a bit. If you trust me as you say than you must believe me when I tell you that my art is best exercised according to my own sense of what is proper and money in advance has been known to bias judgment in the case of better men than me. Look about you Madam; my lodgings testify to my desire to retain a certain degree of abstemiousness in all my affairs. The mind works best in the bracing climate of moderate need."

"Very well Mr. Holmes," she replied. "Your words only increase my confidence based upon the reports I have received from others in Russia. Yes, your reputation is not unknown even in my far-off country. But I must delay no further...I wish you Mr. Holmes to tell me how I may find God."

I recall looking over at Watson with amusement.

"Is that all Madam?" I said making an effort to suppress a smile.

"I am quite serious Mr. Holmes; my dead husband's soul is at stake!"

"Perhaps if you told me something about your late husband, I could better advise you."

She hesitated and dabbed at her eyes with a handkerchief secreted in her cuff before continuing, "He was a violent man sir to all who knew him but most of all to his serfs. His children have only the bitterest memories of him. I alone loved him. I loved him for the sake of the memory of the gallant young officer that he once was. I met him in the Crimea. My father was a Colonel in the light infantry there and I was not as you see me now, heavy with age and too much good Russian cooking but was a spry young thing and much courted by the officers of the regiment. My father desired that I should marry into the nobility and I followed his wishes with the greater alacrity because they corresponded with my own inclinations. After our marriage my husband was mustered out and he returned to the land where he desired to set up as a specialist in forestry. The family holdings in the Caucasus Mountains are much wooded but cold and forbidding in their aspect. My married life was spent in those mountains and if I travel now it is because I desire the expansiveness of far horizons. Our estate looked more like a Polish hunting lodge than a nobleman's manor house. I have known hard times and my hands beneath my gloves resemble those of a peasant woman."

"Yet you loved your husband," I interjected quietly.

"I did and do love him, because no other woman ever could," she replied in a soft voice that still resembled that of the young girl she had once been.

"And now you wish me to reassure you that he is with God in heaven?" I inquired.

She answered passionately, "I wish you to find me the means to purchase his salvation if it costs every ruble that I possess!"

I hesitated before replying with open hands, "I fear that God is not subject to purchase by the ordinary means."

"Then you must find for me some extraordinary means!" she cried.

I thought for some time before answering the woman who sat before me twisting her gloved hands in distress. How could I reassure her yet still stay within the bounds of orthodox belief?

At last I began, "I need not tell you of the all-encompassing mercy of God and that He will not turn aside from the final penitence of even wicked men."

She nodded.

"Was your husband penitent at the end?" I inquired.

"I cannot say. He was stricken by sudden failure of the heart and brought back to the house in a wagon already dead."

I paused before continuing. "Your husband's case is indeed

a hard one, but not beyond all hope. Who can say what fleeting perception in the twilight realm of the near embrace of death may still be possible. Our consciousness may only widen as we take leave of our ordinary senses. He may have repented then."

"But I require assurances!" she cried again.

"We have only one assurance, the character of God's love for us, which may overcome all things," I replied. "The faith that you need Madam is not your husband's but your own. You must seek your own trust of God and then apply it to your husband's case."

"But what if I do good deeds and by the most direct means, can I not then bestow any resultant merit upon him?"

"What you are seeking is vicarious reparation for the sins of others. Such reparation already exists and is being made daily for the sins of the world by the collective Body of Christ the in the Church and by the souls of many whose merits exceed their own needs. But more than this, the merits of Christ are infinite and may well be best applied where the need is greatest as in your husband's case. It is not a matter, my dear Countess, of your finding God but of God finding you and I assure you that He is always seeking. You must have confidence."

"But is that confidence not presumptuous?"

"It is only presumption when one proceeds under the false assumption of the efficacy of one's own efforts to bridge the gap that exists between even the highest of human virtue and the holiness of God. The direction of grace is always from above to below; it does not reverse itself. We do not grace God by our belief or by our virtues; even our most strenuous efforts are inadequate to bridge so insuperable a gap as exists between all created natures and God. This was the mistake that the devil made: to attribute his own holiness to himself only to find all of his great attributes reduced to the ashes of evil through a false attribution and reliance on his own exalted nature. You cannot purchase salvation for your husband from God, still less from me. That salvation exists only as a gift and one purchased for us by the One who takes upon Himself all sin. This, my dear lady, is the mystery of faith that the Catholic Church possesses as her only treasure."

For the first time since her entrance I saw a sense of peace come into her face.

At last she said, "Very well Mr. Holmes. Is there nothing that I can do though?"

I told her, "Live a good life. See to the welfare of your children and urge them to forgive their father and I will see that this thousand pounds is donated to the Oratory of Our Lady of Lambeth whose fathers will say daily masses for the repose of your husband's soul and for your intentions as a family. Their mission in East London will also benefit many of your countrymen and other poor and elderly men of the sea. It is never too late for charity to work its miracles among us. Your husband's labors were not in vain."

"But what of me? I would like to find God also; but how am I to do so? Where shall I go to find my place with God?" she asked with a touching appeal in her voice.

I answered her, "It is not the believer who must go to God although the tradition of the pilgrimage has brought comfort to many. The task of the believer is so to prepare the conditions within his soul that God may come to him. Jesus assures us that both He and his Father will come and make their dwelling place in the heart that purifies itself to receive this gift."

"But how am I to purify myself?" She persisted.

"Ah there you exceed my poor capacity as a consulting detective, Madame. You must go to a spiritual director. The way is neither complex nor hidden though, as he will no doubt impress upon you. The evangelical counsels as well as the traditions of ascetic spiritual disciplines advise a purging of worldly attachments."

She pondered this for awhile before replying, "I control a great estate in Russia. Many people depend upon me. What should I do?"

I answered, "Your obligations to others may foreclose a closer severance from all worldly ties for the present, but you may still devote yourself to a life of prayer and lead others on your estate to embrace a holy life and to practice mutual charity towards one another. If you fulfil your present duties in the state of life in which God has seen fit to place you, then I have no doubt that God will find His way to you in due season, my dear lady. I wish you peace."

She left shortly afterwards and Watson and I listened as her carriage entered the busy late afternoon traffic below in the street. We did not hear of her again.

"Yes I do recall the case, but it is was hardly a case presenting a real mystery," Watson commented.

"Ah but perhaps your sense of mystery is too exclusive, old fellow," I replied. "I should say that it is in just such cases as these that we see manifested the only real mystery that exists among us, the mystery of love in God and in His people."

To this Watson silently assented with a nod and shortly afterwards we set off for dinner at a Russian bistro where we dined on borscht and Ukrainian dumplings down on Oxford Street after stopping first for a quick prayer on the way at a chapel round the corner from our lodgings for her intentions and for her peace.

February 19, 1894
London

In thinking back on the case of the Old Russian Woman and the approach that I took in dealing with her I reflected upon the central problem of how religions come to arise among us. In the case of Judaism, from which Christianity appears as a later development, that origin is five-fold.

The first is through a direct encounter of Abraham with a God who promises a specific, exclusive, and enduring relationship with him and with his descendants. The second is through various prophetic writings that using this initial covenant as their support carry on the "word of God" in greater specificity but not relying upon the directness of an actual theophany. Third, at an even greater distance are the historical accounts and the wisdom literature that elaborate on the way that God's promises affected the chosen people over time and directed them to return to the covenant when their conduct had brought calamity upon them. Fourth are the various legal texts and the liturgical texts of worship that were meant to cover the day-to-day conduct of the Jewish people in pursuance of the covenantal relationship. Fifth and last of all there are the various books that seek to go back in time to the ultimate origins of the human race and forward to explain in detail the final achievement of the purposes of God. It is the completeness of this literature combined with its evidently world-wide significance that accounts for the role that the literature of this particular people has had throughout world history to this point. There is an appeal and universality in the themes of Holy Scripture that makes such universal claims tenable.

Christianity goes a step further though and brings God down to earth and within the human species through the Incarnation of Jesus as the Christ in a way that completely transforms religion beyond any mere functional goals it may have hitherto possessed. The former phrases such as chosen people, covenant, and law become somehow incorporated and transformed in a miraculous fashion by being caught up in the life and death of Jesus of Nazareth. The paradoxes of His existence are such that even the earthly Christological searches for a definition are finally brought up short because they cannot encompass how Jesus can be both God and Man simultaneously and in all the fullness of those terms. The more carefully we seek to define what we mean by these attributions the more incomprehensible these terms become. Formulas with no experiential referent drift insensibly into meaninglessness. This in turn forces the would-be believer into various difficulties in strenuously seeking to categorically affirm what he or she does not understand and then to bet his or her eternal life on the outcome of that theoretical struggle.

For this reason faith is spoken of as a gift. Jesus says that "no one can come to me unless the Father draws him." This phrase would indicate that any debate about various religious claims, but particularly with regard to Christianity, in the ordinary sense of those terms is futile. The human mind is constantly thrown back on itself and into the dilemma from which it tries to extricate itself: who am I, what am I, and what purpose if any does my life possess? It is not too much to say that Christian history up to the present time indicates that various premature solutions to these questions, even after receiving divine revelation, have either been slightly off the mark or at least ineffective to harmonize human actions into anything that could self-evidently claim to be worthy of the promises of somehow living on intimate terms with God after death. Salvation properly understood is living in relationship with others and with God in an intimacy and comprehensiveness that cannot be understood or expressed at the level where we now exist. Rather than realize the level of discourse towards which Sacred Scripture is directed, the human mind in its search for certainty has deformed the texts so that they will provide a closed circuit of self-affirmation to the concrete believing community while exiling all others into the outer darkness. This territorial mindset is precisely what has been responsible for most of the evils committed in the world.

Even the elaborate efforts of Islam to finely adjust human conduct according to the revelations of Mohammed by restoring the Godhead back to its former distance from human affairs have proven to be inadequate. If Jesus is the Son of God, whatever that phrase means in the actual lived experience of Jesus, then any effort to remove our concept of the deity back into its former distance is bound to be an exercise in futility. Evidently, God in His very essence is a tri-part community of Divine Persons united by a love that exceeds even our highest conceptions of what such a quality would entail.

Instead we are left with the three cardinal virtues of faith, hope, and charity the exercise of which combined with the gifts of the Holy Spirit dwelling within the baptized believer as a child of God will ensure our salvation. This is as close to closure as we are likely to get. The desire of the Old Russian Woman to save her husband and herself, even if that gift could be procured by proxy after death, merely demonstrates our human need to both find love and to give love by virtue of our own efforts.

My words to her indicated that what she asked of me was not mine to give but her faith would be adequate if combined with a trust in God that must by its very nature be absolute. If the primary purpose of God is merely to refine a small subset of humanity and to punish the rest forever, then we as mere human beings are in no position to forestall the deity from achieving its purpose; but there is evidence in Christianity that in spite of whatever obstacles we may raise to any automatic supposition of universal salvation, God's love is such that indeed with God all things are possible.

I took that affirmation as my justification to renew her hope and to send her back into life with an assurance that can never be reduced to perfect conviction because conviction demands absolute proof and that is simply not forthcoming in transcendent matters. We as Catholics are not without aid from worship, from the sacraments, and from community, but the rest lies precisely at the discretion of the God we claim to worship and adore.

The memory of other cases cascaded down to us both each day as we discussed times long gone by. "Perhaps you may recall the singular affair of the aluminum crutch, Watson?" I said across our hearth this morning over tea.

"Yes, I have even referred to it in one of my own narratives," he replied.

"You have acquired a habit if I may say so of teasing your public with brief references to cases that were as I recall mere fragmentary occurrences and not demonstrative of the more useful gifts of the practical detective," I remarked.

"You may say so, but then you have always tended to underestimate your own gifts, Holmes. I need only give as an example the way that you misled me as to the full extent of your education at the time when I first shared these rooms with you."

I smiled at this. "I must admit the truth of your observation, but you may recall that you were afflicted at the time with a lamentable earnestness having just been invalided out of the army. I could not resist pulling your leg a bit when I would look across the room and see you studying me as though I were some sort of prime exhibit in a museum."

"Yet you must admit to having possessed certain eccentricities at the time," he answered in a vaguely nettled tone.

"Ah, those were merely the result of acquired habit, Doctor. You must recall that the inveterate bachelor need only consult his own preferences in keeping a household, whereas you have had the advantage of the tutelage that only living with a woman may provide for the male of the species. In any case I apologize now for misleading you. But speaking of eccentricities it is surely rather strange to carry about an aluminum crutch long after one's recovery, yet our client did so on that morning when he sat before us."

"He was an American as I recall," Watson observed.

"Yes, a veteran of the American Civil War. He had come that morning to upbraid me about a monograph that I had written for Punch about the former issue of slavery in America. You may recall that I have expressed on occasion an opinion that the south had a right to secede from the union."

"Then how would the appalling institution of African slavery have been brought to an end?" Watson objected.

"By changing hearts and minds Watson; what you and so many others tend to forget is that the granting of nominal freedom to the former slaves only plunged them into a period of economic marginalization from which they have yet to recover. The south was an entirely agrarian sub-nation as dependent upon a subject people as Ireland was dependent upon a supine labor force provided by the native Irish and as Russia was dependent upon its serfs. Even England is dependent upon a numerous working class whose conditions considering our lamentable climate are little better than slavery."

"It was in just such terms that I defended myself that morning to our ardent abolitionist. Slavery alas is only one of those residual institutions that destroy human dignity through selective deprivation. I defended the right of secession because only the threat of secession can prevent the national government from erecting a tyranny in which all individual rights disappear. The states alone provide some link with the private and local base communities where alone democracy can hope to thrive. If nothing else you must admit that those soldiers who died in that appalling conflict lost all of their rights. Was such a sacrifice worth it?"

Watson still seemed unconvinced, so I continued as follows, "Life itself is the first prerequisite to the exercise of liberty. This is why all loss of freedom is essentially an attack upon the vital processes. Far more men and women are killed by the selective exposure to disease through the maintenance of unwholesome living conditions than are ever formally enslaved, imprisoned, or willfully executed. In essence then I was not defending the southern right to possess slaves but rather to take the broader view so that those northern states that congratulated themselves for their superior enlightenment should turn the torch of inquiry inward to their own society and recognize its inveterate ills that are the functional equivalent of slavery. The ex-soldier in question carried his crutch as a badge of his own heroism. The crutch only kept him buried upon the same field of conflict as those dead who never left it. Freedom requires first of all the ability to shake off the past no matter how appalling our experiences may have been. Life must constantly reinvent itself or we sink into an abyss deeper than the Great Grimpen Mire. Each of us is haunted by past events and the often terrible injustices meted out by those who go unpunished in this life. Revenge once begun is a fire that is never quenched.

My discussion on that morning with our client was designed to restore him to an identity not mediated by cannon-shot and the cries of dying men. I fear that America was so marred by that conflict that it has become addicted to the obsequies of the crypt. No more fatal destiny can befall a people than to reserve its greatest accolades for the military-caste forgetting in the process those who enhance life by invention, by the arts, and by the healing craft of medicine."

"Yet he left the room as I recall somewhat chastened still not wholly convinced," Watson concluded having heard my explanation patiently as always.

I replied, "We can but plant seeds, old fellow. What is education but a scattering into the winds of the thoughts of those who have preceded us upon this bewildering sphere? Now and then a phrase may be recalled that sums up the human condition for those who must face the ever new challenges of living and perhaps they will persevere more readily due to our efforts."

February 20, 1894
London

onight Watson and I have plans to go to the Albert Hall to hear Dvorak's *New World Symphony* followed by a late supper at the Diogenes Club. It is the height of the winter season and the boxes will be filled with bejeweled dowagers and the young and blushing debutantes scanning the other boxes for potential suitors among the elegant young men and even some older gentlemen as possible candidates for their hands in marriage. Among such a crowd old fellows like Watson and me will be quite invisible and I can concentrate on the soaring notes of Dvorak. The largo section is such as can break the human heart, yet withal the total effect is to bestow such vigor that my very being tends to expand in listening to it.

One hears in Dvorak that "still sad music of humanity" that as Wordsworth said is "neither harsh nor grating but of ample power to chasten and subdue." Music it seems to me is the one essential language of the spirit in that though wordless it allows us to fill-in the emotion evoked with our own unique joys, tragedies, and triumphs and by doing so to make the music our own. The thread of personal associations is stimulated so that under the influence of music we can discover our more noble selves and imagine that our lives have an immortal significance beyond the trivial happenings of the day. But better still we can look at our fellows with that universal sympathy that restores beauty and dignity to the often sallow faces and dim eyes haunted by doubt and disappointment that we encounter. It seems as we grow older that the fantasy of childhood becomes like a distant country visited once in a dream but from which we have long been exiled. So it is that we must turn to music to restore us to what we once were in all truth.

As I settle once again into professional harness the adventures of these past years seem as illusory as if I had only read of them last night in some geographic journal. Already my own *nom de plume* Sigerson has passed into the oblivion of last year's sensations and new heroes have gripped the public mind. There is nothing more fickle than public acclaim. I tried to explain as much to Oscar Wilde the other night. He stopped by my table at Simpsons and introduced me to young Lord Alfred Douglas. It may have been my imagination but he struck me as a petulant little tart and I needed constantly to remind myself that he is a young man not a mistress but no doubt a mere protégé and nothing more. Oscar's too generous nature might do well to be curbed in his regard. I did not like the fellow on sight and Watson gave me a significant look that bore only one interpretation. I hope that we are both wrong for Oscar's sake and for his dear wife, Constance.

On another matter, I sent off a remittance yesterday to the Monastery in Ireland that had made me so feel so at home during my recent visit there. It was a bale of scotch-tweed blankets and five hundred-weight of steel-cut oats for their morning gruel as well as fifty pounds sterling to allay any expenses incurred during my residence there. After living among the monks the triviality of London society is more evident to me than ever and I am hard pressed to suppress a scornful attitude to even harmless pursuits. What I require most is to be in harness once again. I trust that a case worthy of my mettle will soon present itself.

February 21, 1894
London

Well Holmes," Watson began today, "Perhaps I can at last fill-in my notes regarding some of your other more obscure cases."

"Of course my dear fellow," I answered, "If that is I am not boring you in recounting them."

The fog continued as before and neither of us felt up to being jostled about in the streets and squares of Westminster. So it was that I summoned Mrs. Hudson and ordered up some roasted chestnuts, a sharp cheddar cheese, and enough brandy to see two middle-aged gentlemen through a long afternoon. With that I gave my attention to Watson.

"I think we are now proof to interruption and well supplied with necessaries. It is a habit acquired from my journeys to see that no campaign is begun that neglects logistical support from an able quartermaster and Mrs. Hudson is a most redoubtable supplier of the troops. Ask away old friend!"

"Well then to begin with I ask you to fill in some of the details of the service that you once performed for the Royal Family of Holland."

"Well behind these closed doors we may discuss it for it was a matter some delicacy. It involved a case of madness in a distant relative who became convinced that she was the Queen of the

Netherlands and kept insisting that the palace designation and address be changed to her somewhat more humble address. Her neighbors had accustomed themselves to her particular delusion, but matters reached a head when she made a public proclamation that a delegation of Chinese officials including the Emperor of China planned a state visit to her and the school children of Holland were to be given an official holiday so that they could cheer the passing entourage. The newspapers picked up the story and such was the amusement of the populace at her delusion that a sort of unofficial holiday began to seize upon the public mind. The problem of course was where to find the required Chinamen to play their roles for the occasion. London as you know abounds in Chinese as well as in representatives of other eastern nations. I possess some useful contacts in theatrical circles so I was approached by a delegation to interview people for parts in the charade and to select a proper suite of oriental servants and principals.

The royal family very wisely decided that what could not be prevented could be turned into a gala. So it was that a day was decreed for the great event. A great dinner was prepared with no end of noodles and soy and hundreds were fed from beribboned tables set along the harbor. The 'queen' followed an impressive caravan of bowing Chinese 'ministers of state' and the 'Emperor' graciously doffed his top-hat that reposed above his red and gold robes. The whole thing was a complete success, so much so that the 'queen' decided afterwards to abdicate in favor of her daughter who planned on immigrating to America in a month where such titles are not recognized. Thus was the spurious title given a quiet burial at sea and the lady in question, though she was as eccentric as ever, was able to feel that her life's ambition had been satisfied. If only each of us could in a similar fashion find a way to be, if only for a single day, what in our own eyes we are!"

As we settled down once again by the fire after an excellent lunch Watson brought up another case.

"What of the case of Vamberry the Wine Merchant?"

"Ah a painful case that was. Vamberry had joined one of the more obscure anarchist groups and had taken it upon himself to secretly poison some of his more expensive vintages so as to quietly weed out the aristocracy of England."

"But surely the poison could be tasted by those with sufficient funds to afford the more expensive wines," Watson objected. "Would that not have awakened suspicion?"

"A good palate is not to be purchased, Watson. Many vain persons drink wines constantly that might with impunity be substituted with the most wretched swill and no questions would be asked. In any case Vamberry used only small amounts of poisons with a tendency to accumulate in the body over time."

"Then how did you catch him?"

"Well I had my suspicions from the first, but it was a servant girl at the London townhouse of the Earl of G———— who was responsible in the end for ending his nefarious career. She had made it a habit of finishing the remainder of her mistress's various friends' glasses and was substantially discomposed by taking more than her usual indulgence on multiple occasions. The remainder in the case was tested and traced back to Vamberry who promptly ran out of the back of his shop and under the wheels of a passing hansom cab. It was reported thereafter that German and French Wines from foreign firms replaced that sold from British vintners for the rest of that season, which was unfortunate for those who had been quite innocent of any wrongdoing."

Watson still appeared interested in my reminiscences so I continued with the tale of the peculiar persecution of the young tobacco millionaire who came to me one sunny day in July to explain that he was contemplating suicide and that I was his last hope; that he would throw himself into the Thames at precisely midnight in expiation for his own sins and those of his fathers before him. As I recall he was a most sensitive fellow, more the poet than the businessman. It has not been a rare occurrence in my professional career to observe that families occasionally produce individuals who react against type. Clearly the man before me was neither an agronomist nor a commercial type. He had been cast in a role for which he was profoundly unsuited and in his attempt to fill that role he had lost whatever initial personality had once been his own. He had in addition been subjected to the contempt that one type of mind often feels for the personality and talents that it does not share. Of what use is a poetic sensibility to the increase of sales of tobacco-leaf? The sad result was that this young man resented and held in contempt the very fortune that ensured his own present station in life. He felt compromised in his essential dignity as a human being by being a beneficiary. He had yet to emerge from the eclipsing shadow of his progenitors and to stand upon his own ground of being.

My task therefore was a simple one: I must, I reflected, recall the man to his own inherent worth and expunge the constant reiteration in his mind of self-accusation and disgust. He was a man of extreme wealth and responsibilities to others so that I could not council mere retirement from the firm. He must at the very least find a way of shifting his tobacco empire to one more suited to govern it. This would set him free at least externally, but I feared that the resultant leisure might only add more time for the uninterrupted persecution wrought by his own memories of the past.

It is unfortunate that the mind of man can not be purged at once and forever of the past so that the mind, concentrated upon the task of the next moment may cease to brood on that which will forever remain cast in the stone of unalterable memory. We must all live with our past. The diminishing years ahead may allow less time though for a new self to develop, one proof to accusation and regret. Thus it is that the aged are most likely to despair. The healing of age must come from surrender to the limited role of each life in the world of history and by surrendering to the coming ages and generations the unfulfilled tasks of the day come to accept what is. Life pushes us off of the stage still gesticulating and muttering our last lines while the audience's attention has already turned to those fresh players just making their entrance.

I tried to explain this to the victim of this obsession and to tell him that he was not alone and that all men and women live beneath the burden of the past, both individual and collective. The Christian faith is one of expiation, not through our own efforts, but by our Jesus on our behalf. No man saves himself alone but only enmasse with all of mankind, united in the Holy Spirit, who is our advocate and only solace. I suggested that he might pray the Confiteor prayer, which begins the mass and ask for the intercession of the entire people of God in these words:

I confess to you my brothers and sister that I have greatly sinned in my thoughts and in my words, in what I have done and in what I have failed to do - through my fault, through my fault, through my most grievous fault—Therefore I ask Blessed Mary, ever virgin, all the angels and saints, and you my brothers and sisters, to pray for me to the Lord Our God.

It may be the greatest paradox of the Christian faith that the confession of guilt and inadequacy and the dropping of all postures of defense will ensure one's own dignity and stature before God. True self-respect can never be attained by accumulation, for the simple reason that all contingent being is subject to change, to decay, and to loss. We are insubstantial events in an immense universe of other lives to whom even our memory must be a futile effort at preservation. Our very substance is only lent to us and the lease is of no long duration. I told Watson that I was happy to report that my young friend entered upon a religious retreat with the Jesuits and that at the end of thirty days he emerged with a new direction in life and the humility to cease acting as the prosecutor and judge in his own case.

Watson though, as insistent as Boswell was over every bit of minusciae touching upon Dr. Samuel Johnson, still persisted in his desire for more reminiscences. "And what of the repulsive story of the Red Leech Holmes," Watson inquired.

"Well, perhaps we can enter into that story on another occasion, old fellow, since we have just finished a most excellent lunch which deserves more respect than to be followed by a tale that may upset the stomach."

February 22, 1894
London

Each day I expect a flood of clients at my door and each day I listen in vain for the grating sound of a hansom cab's wheel against the curb. Still, this enforced idleness provides an opportunity to discuss many past cases of interest with the one man best entitled to share these recollections with me. Today these recollections involved the case of the Atkinson Brothers of Trincomalee.

As with so many of my cases this one did not involve a case of crime but rather a misunderstanding. Old Thaddeus Atkinson had built up quite a fleet of trading vessels that plied their way between the island of Ceylon and markets in Hong Kong. The eldest son had followed his father into the shipping trade while his younger son had gone out on his own and become a sheep farmer in Australia. When it came time for the father to leave this world he had at first contemplated leaving the ships and the plantation in Trincomalee to his eldest son in return for his eldest son's efforts to sustain the shipping business. The younger son did not object to the passing of the trading fleet to his brother but felt that he should share in the family plantation where he and his brother had been raised, a place that still had many pleasant associations in his mind. He had hopes that either he or his children would someday be able to leave the dry and barren pasture land of the Australian sheep farm and enjoy the lush and Monsoon-watered gardens of the family estate in Ceylon. Old Thaddeus relented in the face of this objection and passed the plantation to each of his sons in equal measure.

Years passed and the younger Atkinson brother passed his share of the plantation to his children in due course. Meanwhile the children of the elder brother continued to work the land so that both the plantation and the trading company prospered. In Australia the demands of the sheep farm kept all members of the younger Atkinson brother's family too busy to consider travel to their place of origin. At last the gap between the branches of the family grew to assume an aura of permanence although correspondence and occasional remittances of rents continued.

It was at this time that the younger son wrote a hasty letter that promised that though he had passed his share of the plantation to his children it was his wish that should the plantation ever need to be sold that the proceeds would remain with those who had worked the land for years i.e., the children of his elder brother. This communication was received by the branch of the family in Ceylon as one that set right an ancient inequity, for they had always felt that the land was theirs by right and that the younger brother and his issue had no valid claim because he had left the family business to strike out on his own years earlier. The entire matter therefore was based upon unexpressed expectations and long held resentments. The father, Thaddeus, had maintained an equal love for both of his sons and on that basis had divided the estate equally while any profit accruing to the plantation through direct labor was naturally set aside for the elder son. The only rent to be paid was on land that the elder son was unable to farm directly.

This case was brought before me by a solicitor in London who was evidently under the impression that my idea of justice might prove superior to his own as he was to advise the family what course to follow. Of course the strict legalities of the matter were quite clear as is so often the case. Any attempted conveyance of a future interest in land that would only be triggered by a future contingent event (the sale of the plantation) after that property had already been passed as a gift to the younger son's progeny in fee simple absolute was completely void for lack of ownership. The younger brother no longer had any estate in the land to convey. Well I am no Solomon to be dividing babies and I explained this to the representative of the family who called upon me seeking guidance as to whether a conveyance prior to sale might restore the goodwill of the branches of the family and if so should he advise the heirs of the younger son to convey the property to their cousins. I thought long and hard on the problem. Many elements presented themselves. The younger son had gone off on his own to make his way in the world through his own efforts without the paternal aid that a present job on the plantation might have provided and that only the elder son had enjoyed. Also the fact that the property had passed to his children meant that their separate needs must be considered.

It is not uncommon for elderly patriarchs to behave in a high-handed manner in these instances and presume to plan for their children's lives even after they have reached maturity, not fully realizing that each generation in a sense inhabits a different world due to the march of events and the exigencies of the economies to which they are exposed; where symbolic gifts of goodwill are made their meaning must be derived less from law or equity than from trying to meet the legitimate expectations of all parties. If these cannot be met then compromise is the order of the day.

The case was interesting because it shows how swiftly divergent interests and intermarriage with outside parties dilute shared loyalty and love within a family. Recognizing this I proposed that since there were no plans to sell the plantation and that therefore the contingency in the younger brother's attempted belated conveyance was purely speculative in nature that the status quo should be preserved but a cordial invitation to visit should be made so that any of the Australian branch might visit and that a permanent guest house could be established to receive them if they should care to return. Proximity possesses its own healing qualities. The new generation may prefer to return to the old way of life and the two branches of the family may as a consequence meld again into one. Time is the great separator, but it is also the great healer. Nothing stays the same and the need for adaptation is the spur to evolution.

My suggestion was accepted and a lamentable family fissure was avoided. The case was successful and a problem was resolved but my investigation was confined to simply making a prudent suggestion that would allow each side to act generously rather than seeking to remedy the bitterness of heart by taking a firm line in a murky set of circumstances. I was glad to have done some good of course but a clergyman might have done as much and I am a detective after all. Halloa, what is this? I hear the music again of a wheel scraping the curb and...yes there is a ring at the bell. I am again to be in proper harness. "Come in sir and let us have a clear statement as to what brings you here today."

April 30, 1894
London

Months of work and no recording made here of my labors, but so I have wished it. My commonplace books are now the source for any records of my cases. It is there that I record the minutia of fact and evidence in my own coded script. Yet I write here today because I have heard from my old shikari friend, Colonel Sebastian Moran. I am afraid that he has gotten himself ejected from one of his card clubs and has gone so far as to write a draft on his bank without sufficient funds to pay it! In other words the fellow is temporarily insolvent until a remittance comes from his plantation near the island of Sumatra. He might of course appeal to the Professor, but he is embarrassed to do so, and has come to me whom he still treats somewhat as a private banker as I was during our travels together. No doubt I am still only that lean and awkward fellow precariously balanced upon a camel.

He called upon me here in Baker Street and I am afraid that I was forced to take a rather stern line with the fellow. But at last we came to an understanding. I pointed out that he simply could not go on as he has done and that gambling would certainly be his undoing in the end. I am afraid that months of late hours, strong drink, and dallying with various bar maids and chorus girls has wrought great changes in his formerly robust constitution. I therefore advised a change of air and that he return to his Malayan plantation at the first opportunity. I would pay for his ticket on a first-class boat. I did request though that he aid me in a case that is before me at present in return. It is a matter requiring some discretion.

I have been consulted by the wealthy Adair family. It appears that young Ronald Adair, after being sent down from Oxford for misbehavior, has rather gone to seed of late. He has become involved with a most unsavory person who is now writing letters demanding funds. She will no doubt desist if young Adair is pronounced dead, as she has thank heaven no real proof of an indiscretion committed. She has relied thus far on threats of making strident and embarrassing scenes at the door of the young fellow's club. I have advised the family that the young chap should be "absent from felicity awhile" and that he be sent out of the country and employed on the family's sheep farm in Australia. He will require a guardian of sorts to see that he not, as they say, jump-ship at an early port, but shall continue on to Adelaide. I believe that Colonel Moran is the perfect man for this job. I shall rely upon Watson to complete the ruse and bury both Ronald Adair and the good Colonel Moran, even as he has buried Professor Moriarty in his account entitled, *The Final Problem*.

Watson may do this by means of a tale to be called, "*The*

Adventure of the Empty House." I have prevailed upon Watson to use it as the occasion to also explain my return from the dreaded Falls of Reichenbach. It will include a reference to the supposed murder of young Ronald Adair and an audacious attempt upon my own life by Colonel Sebastian Moran with an airgun. I dislike having to request that Watson deceive his public readers in this fashion, but it is all for a good end. Perhaps the Colonel may be of use to me in the far-east someday. In any case, he does no good for himself in London. I do owe the fellow something after all for acting as my guardian across the desert wastes of Asia. If I may aid him to shake off his gambling creditors, I may also provide an incentive for those very gentlemen to take up a more productive occupation with their leisure time once the bird has flown and I may enable young Adair to take up the wholesome business of wool production in a far-off land. I trust that all will proceed as I have planned. I am afraid that I must enlist the aid of Scotland Yard in this charade, but Lestrade owes me a favor or two and perhaps now is the time to collect.

May 7, 1894
Dover

atson and I arrived in Dover last night for a bit of a holiday. Dover is one of those comfortable towns without the pretensions of Deauville, Biarritz, or Cannes or the hectic crowds of Brighton where one can settle in for a few days of rest and restoration, walk about above the chalk cliffs or visit the castle above the town, and in the evenings find a pub with a goodly fire and quaff there a pint of stout and feast on fish and chips or a steak and kidney pie to one's heart's content. Sherringford would be appalled at my plebian tastes. I have noticed though that discontent flourishes most where excess money coagulates like a clot in a vein. The ones who enjoy life best are those who knowing that times of trouble must come do not neglect the simple pleasures of the day. To what end are the vast surpluses of empire? Do these not lead first to the coveting of power and from power wars later take their origin. What poor man has ever rushed to war when fields must be tilled, horses shod, or fish brought to market. Christianity takes its origin in the Carpenter of Nazareth and his fisherman friends. Where are the soldiers or brokers, the money-lenders or officials among the apostles? These are the ones who in the name of future bliss cause present misery. So it is that I rejoice in the laughter of yeoman farmers over English ale or cider and am even willing to overlook the ribald pleasantries of an honest bar-maid whose ample bosom adorns a heart of compassion for those whose evenings are brightened in some manner by her charms as she serves their simple meals. Where ideas blind one to life the human touch is destroyed and in vast abstractions much evil hides its grim visage.

Our walk today was lovely. Wild flowers adorned the downs along the sea-path and the air filled my tired lungs, weary of the heavy London damps of winter. Even the blood is purged in such an atmosphere and the gulls and cormorants make a music that says England to the weary traveler long exiled from home. It was of just such scenes that I dreamed as we traversed the vast Asiatic plains. What joy can exceed the homely delights of one's native land? We brought along a bottle of claret and some honest English bread and bramble jam. Later as we walked by the harbor we passed a fishmonger's shop and found there cups of whelks and cockles which carried yet about them the sweet scent of the channel waters from whence they had just been harvested. We arrived back at the Whitehorse Inn in time for tea and crumpets that I much prefer to cucumber sandwiches and cake. There is an art to crumpets. They should be lightly toasted but not hard and only butter, honey, or marmalade should fill the airy cells of which they are composed. The art of living is best seen in the value placed on what seem incidentals. It is these simplest of joys that will flit through our consciousness when our powers fail and life's retreating tide leaves us like so much sea-wrack along the beach. I believe it was the Roman poet Catullus who said, "While we are living, let us live." It may be the one sentiment that I share with Colonel Sebastian Moran.

May 18, 1894
London

I received a letter today from Colonel Sebastian Moran which I transcribe here:

My Dear Mr. Sherlock Holmes,

I appreciate your aid in my recent fracas with one of London's more exclusive card clubs. I am afraid that I must plead guilty to fleecing some of the bankers and brokers by levying what I am pleased to call my little Malayan Tax upon them. It has always been my opinion that my little incursion upon the private sphere of these well-heeled predators is at least as justified as most public levies which are soon wasted by incompetent officialdom. I fear though that I have as they say already been banned for life from my favorite clubs in the far eastern regions so that I must seek out some other means to finance my occasional trip home to the motherland of England.

I am writing this aboard ship where my skills at the evening game of whist has surprised but not scandalized my fellow passengers. I shall arrive back at the plantation with enough funds to sustain me for some years to come so my trip to London was not in vain. I must say that I miss our little talks regarding metaphysics but now that you are back in harness with Dr. Watson by your side I doubt that we shall meet often again. I shall of course follow with great interest your subsequent career.

Speaking of public officials and taxation, you no doubt have read in 'The London Times' of the recent death of Merridew of abominable memory. He always represented for me the perfect example of that petty despot who ruins the lives of others and goes away unpunished. A more perfect example of the coward and the sneak cannot be imagined. I must confess that I planned to seek him out on this most recent trip and thrash him with a proper horsewhip but I am happy to say that providence intervened by his timely demise in which I may as well say here and now I had no hand. Thus I leave England pure and unsullied by any private vengeance, which must please you.

I do not know if you have read 'Justine' or 'Juliette' by the

Marquis de Sade but since you once confessed to having read the 'Song of Maldoror' by Lautreamont and 'Les Fleur du Mal' by Baudelaire you may have taken a brief excursus into France's greatest rebel. Justine represents a sort of nightmare inversion of 'Clarissa' by Richardson but dare I say that Richardson dwells a bit too longingly over his villain Lovelace to avoid the suspicion that he too was tainted by a certain envy of vice.

Similarly it has always been my private opinion that the Marquis may have been one of the greatest satirists of all time and that beneath his cynical voluptuaries there exists a secret desire that virtue might triumph after all. Perhaps disillusionment and despair had more to do with his peculiar tastes in sexual congress than either innate desire or madness. If he despised mankind he despised himself no less but he despised the cold Deist God of the Encyclopedists most of all. What creator God can exist if He is not finally answerable before His creation? Should any immoral or negligent God be impervious to a summons before the court of humankind for what we see about us?

De Sade is Job with a weapon: not satisfied to simply indict the deity but to oppose him. I have often noticed that the devils may act as our adversaries but that they forbear to accuse God to His face, whereas man does accuse God whenever he implies that God has made an evil world. So it is that I propose for your earnest consideration that your God of compassion, your distant God who hides behind his creation, is one with nature red in tooth and claw as I have always maintained.

There must be a part of you who agrees with me for I call to mind your occasional ethical suspension when dealing with particularly obnoxious individuals. I once read of your dealings with Dr. Grimsby Roylott of Stoke Moran under the title of "The Adventure of the Speckled Band." Now be honest Holmes. Surely you must have known that beating that cord with a stick would drive the snake back through the air vent where it might attack its principal agent, the evil doctor. I also call to your mind the case of "The Adventure of the Copper Beeches." Was it not fortuitous that the great dog chewed up the master of the house who had exercised such tyrannous control over his poor daughter?

The stories of your cases are filled with private retribution to which you make no objection; yet when Moriarty and Moran avenge those who cannot avenge themselves you call it crime. What were the knights of the Crusades but just such avengers? Your mild counsel has always seemed to me to be selective in its application and I have always believed that it was your secret approbation of many of our actions that explained why it took so long to bring our little organization to justice at last.

The vast majority of the human race is like sheep and it is precisely the civic order that keeps them such even in the so-called democracies. The armed force of the state suppresses anarchy by sustaining the systematic bleeding of the populace to feed the governors and their venal minions. Surely you realize that, Holmes. If you had joined us what a combined force we might have made! As it is I must now return to the east where I have organized the natives to keep imperial rule at bay. The same imperial rule which you and I both know will finally force a confrontation between the great European powers. Only force will restrain the rule of force between nations and that force can only be the will to preserve the multitudes who are always sacrificed on the altar of the few. Anarchy is not chaos but the preservation of the many by seeing each as sovereign so that he or she may not be trampled underfoot to sustain the very system that exploits their labor and renders their lives a misery. It is ideas that render some men superior to others and those ideas always promise salvation by ensuring the preservation of some form of slavery by the social order. What is property and capital to those who shall never possess it? It is a premature civility finally that preserves every injustice that the world has ever known. Better far if every man's hand was raised in arms against all others for then at least some of those who enslave the multitude would die and die they must for they will never relinquish their strangling grasp upon the common man until they do die.

Even the French revolution although it finally led to Napoleon brought many a despot from the vile aristocracy to the guillotine. Is chaos so much to be avoided that even partial vengeance for such great and sustained crimes (which could only be remedied at such a high cost) should have been foregone? In the name of what should such deferral be allowed? Why delay the hour of the scimitar? How many have died with only the dim assurance of the everlasting progress of mankind to comfort them? Better far to see my particular enemy bleeding at my feet and know that he at least is dead and that his career of any particular and homegrown despotism is ended at last. I fear though that we shall never agree on this but you must allow me the particular morality of my impatience. I have long since surrendered the illusions of hope. Democracy is none other than the same deferral of justice that Christianity represents. At least the Old Testament God sanctioned the fall of Jericho at the hands of the Jews. Do you blame me for seeking justice in my time and at my own hands? Power is for those who grasp it and make of themselves God's regent. It is these who will see in the bloody red of the setting sun their own Armageddon. I am proud to be one of them. Farewell Holmes.

> *Your friend and sometime adversary,*
> *Colonel Sebastian Moran*

June 1, 1894
London

The Feast of Pentecost has come and gone and life has returned to busy London. I am again in harness and new cases come in daily. Watson is again at my side to offer his own unique but invaluable assistance. I fear that the leisure that has allowed me to follow the habits of a regular journalist will now and hereafter be in short supply. Already this year is almost at the mid-point. Time has seemed to accelerate with my return to London. I am no sooner waking when I seem to look at my watch and see that the hours have raced by and another night is about to fall upon the sultry paving stones of the great metropolis with all of its seething activity. I no longer need chide fate for withholding the little problems whose solution gives me such delight. The great constants of human life play themselves out again and again before me. The actors change but the parts stay the same. Perhaps it is only life that is eternal while we poor temporary manifestations are only part of the eternal succession of events.

The Holy Trinity of the Godhead will always be a mystery to the mind of man. The Nicean Creed is remarkable less for its assertions than for what remains undefined. The Holy Spirit is spoken of in it as the Lord and the Giver of Life. The Holy Spirit appears to be the active and distributive principle of God, the principle that penetrates most deeply into creation so that even mortal life would not be life at all if it did not manifest the vitality of God. The Holy Spirit is no less personified for all of that but it is no mere non-personified force emanating from the union of the Father and the Son. But to think of the Holy Spirit in splendid isolation and divorced from the humble ministration of giving life is impossible. For this reason we contemplate the Holy Spirit best when we revel in the diversity of His gifts.

This need not lead to the excesses of polytheism though since the principle of life is one in spite of the variety of forms and degrees of its realization. Each instance of life, rather than being as Plato would have it, a mere shadow of an eternal idea is instead a concrete summation of the idea and hence a fully realized and yet unique being. The action of the Holy Spirit is one though contained in various vessels. It is only a small leap from this conclusion to state that in the case of Sanctifying Grace God has intermingled His particular essence with human beings. The baptized soul is not only immortal but in immanent possession of eternal life through the Tree of Life, which is the Mystical Body of Christ within the Church.

Yet this world that we know is passing away and what is to come has not yet been revealed. It is this which creates divided loyalties in the heart of man. We desire that all that we know of good be preserved and ourselves with it, yet all that we know and are eventually passes away. We exist in the first planting before the first pale green sprouts arise from the soil under the light of a new heaven and a new earth.

Where have the dead gone who were once our daily familiars? In how short a time will we join them in their vast secrecy as to what is to come? If it is true that we are even now working out our salvation, surely the sun has long since passed its equinox and as Sir Thomas Brown says so well shows us now but winter arches. For this reason I labor daily in what seems to be the unique path set aside for me by my minor talents and dispositions. It is best to labor now for an hour is coming when no one can work, when all shall be gathered up or definitively left in that self-defined state that will not admit God into its life and by doing so carve out of being itself some dark corner of everlasting regret. I know nothing of this anymore than I know yet the fullness of life in the promises of Christ. So it is that I pick up the tasks of each day and hope that they shall all lead to something good in God's own time.

July 1, 1894
London

was going over some of my papers today and stumbled upon the letter which first introduced me to the peculiar set of facts of some years ago to which after Watson's fashion I have assigned a case name "The Adventure of the Tired Captain."
 His letter read as follows...

Dear Sir:
 I am Captain Josiah Hawthorne late of Her Majesty's merchant trade. I have been retired for the past three years and though a man whose good health might give him grounds to hope for some years yet with which to complete a proper human life I have developed a disposition of late of such melancholy that it is only with difficulty that I manage to leave my lodgings. I find this strange because when at sea I have always been a man of decision and resource. How is it then that I wake each day to such a sense of inner emptiness and destitution that my bed might just as well be my grave.
 When I am able to force myself abroad into the busy London Streets the faces that I meet, though I study them for some sign or degree of fellow-feeling seem as bleak and empty as the grey of the sea when a gale threatens. My life appears to have no story. My retirement income is adequate to meet my frugal needs so that I have no cause for complaint yet I am among the least happy of mortal beings. So it is that I desire to consult you. I

realize that you are not an alienist although your associate Dr. Watson is at least a medical man. Yet I trust that you may be able to help me because I hear that you are a man who sees the light where all is darkness.

I will call upon you then on Wednesday and trust that you will spare some time to hear from my own lips the dark forebodings of a distracted man,

Captain Josiah Hawthorne

I have often spoken to Watson about the lessons that may be communicated by physiognomy. I have made it a practice to learn to follow the nature of a conversation from across a crowded room by simply observing the changes in posture and facial expression among the interlocutors. This practice is least difficult when the subjects are women. Women have the capacity, or perhaps it is merely the practice, to create a private space even in a public arena. Various subjects are thrown about as it were from one to the other much as an object might be variously formed by lathes and milling machines only to emerge in a finished condition, smoothed and jointed. All the while each feminine face is responding with that angular detail of eye that shows approval, humor, or condemnation. Often one member of their group will assume a confessional mode and the others offer various advice or sympathy. An engineer of human emotions would note that among any group of four women the lines of influence are such that six one-on-one influences exist and in addition each one of the group can be impacted by three dyads, one triad, and that the four together in consensus make another relation so that a total of eleven primary relations are possible. These in turn do not occur in order but may take on various combinations and sequences. Such is even the most elementary social gathering among women.

In contrast the male of the species when deprived of the basic hierarchy of command and obedience is often at a loss of how to proceed. It occurred to me that the Captain's affliction might be simply that he wanted a wife who often supplies her spouse with a center about which he may orbit as a planet circles the sun. Still it is a capital mistake to theorize without data and the captain's plight might be due to other causes.

When he first arrived at Baker Street I noticed at once the signs of depression of spirits that his letter had referenced. He seemed like a man about to vanish into the dark corners of the room as though the very walls might absorb him. There was a tragedy to this because he had obviously once been a man of some stamina. To escape the ego is often held forth as the task of the virtuous man, but nature abhors a vacuum and to empty out the ego of particulars without substituting something else, such as the inner light of grace, is to open oneself to that surrounding darkness to which Pope Leo has referred in his great prayer by referencing, the evil spirits who prowl about the world seeking the ruin of souls.

It was with this background of thought that I received the Captain that day. I heard again his recital of his complaints and Watson as well applied his clinical attention to seek a physical cause for the man's all too evident anguish. As he continued to speak it became clear to me that here before us was a man whose entire career as a captain had accustomed him to solitude, for to seek out confirming consultation prior to action aboard ship could only undermine his own authority in command. A captain must appear omniscient in the face of changing wind and weather. He must appear solid though the very timbers of his ship are groaning and the seas about to rush in to the common ruin of all aboard. To take such a man and to plunge him into another sea of unaccustomed humanity stripped of all that had once defined his very soul could well account for his present state of anomie. Danger itself was meat and drink to such a man and dire contingency a stimulus to preserve the lives that might be momently overwhelmed by the great forces of nature. Safety was for him a strangling of his vital forces. Now the man before us was as becalmed as a ship in the doldrums beneath a glaring tropical sun.

My diagnosis complete I advised my client to seek out danger by any means at his disposal and to find some way that others would look to him for safety. So it was that the tired Captain became a sort of unofficial constable in the worst sections of Whitechapel late at night. Many a woman was spared being accosted or attacked because she sailed like an unarmed merchant ship in the wake of our client who like a man-of-war went from tack to tack all night in the dark waters of the east-end of London. I am happy to be able to report that his weariness soon vanished and that a year later he returned to report that he had found his place on land and that as Captain Hawthorne of Whitechapel he was well-known, well-liked, and universally respected.

The case is significant not merely in itself but in its general applicability to diverse personality types. If it is true that the Christian life is an emptying out of self-will and of too preeminent self-regard, it is also true that we should not seek to exceed the measure of grace granted to us by God and that many a heretic has begun with a too ardent abstemiousness and purging of the natural affections by adopting an asceticism to which his own abilities were inadequate. True humility does not spurn the human but allows it to be nourished by what God alone can accomplish within us and according to a time and sequence that God alone knows. It is in the small hints and opportunities of life that we grow morally so that in the end nothing is trivial where our conversion of heart is in question.

Editorial Note Dr. Watson

There follows a significant gap of months in the journal entries. The next entries appear in 1895, 1896, and 1897. I will now provide selected extracts from the very last entries of the Journal in my possession so that the record may be complete. The entries deal with matters of the heart and conscience and with the workings of grace in two equally complex men and such matters will always remain somewhat shrouded in mystery to others who do not share that complexity. But through reading of them I at least was at last able to see how it was that Sherlock Holmes, by the most gentle of means, completed what he had begun on the brink of the Falls of Reichenbach so many years ago when the beckoning prospect of death given and received had been so close to both men. That was the time when Sherlock Holmes and his great foe, Professor Moriarty, had both stood above the fearful abyss. I now saw that it was not a physical abyss only, but one that lies in its many forms of evil and despair always close at hand for us all.

From the Journal of Sherlock Holmes

January 6, 1895
London

There is an advantage to having one's birthday at the beginning of the year before time has sullied our natural sense that with the New Year there will come some sudden improvement in the moral condition of mankind. Unfortunately there is already news from France of the condemnation to Devil's Island of a young Jewish officer, one Alfred Dreyfus, on a charge of treason. One can only hope that this is not one more instance where a person lower in the command structure has been set aside as a handy scapegoat for some malfeasance or oversight of someone else. There is an undercurrent of violence and satisfaction in such cases that awakens my instincts as a detective. The matter may need a second look.

February 1, 1895
London

News has reached England of the abdication of Queen Lili'uokalani in favor of a Hawaiian Republic. There was a short-lived rebellion to restore her to rule but it was swiftly defeated and her abdication, however unjust it may be under the pressure of outside interests, will prevent further violence. How long the republic will endure of course is an open question at this time. The United States sugar interests will undoubtedly play a major role in the ultimate disposition of those lovely islands. On another matter, the steady growth of the

American economy has made money less available. A nation without adequate gold reserves will be tempted to supply the lack by instituting bank-notes not backed with precious metal. Such a practice is likely to weaken a nation's posture in international affairs because credit is a poor substitute for ready assets. Something will undoubtedly need to be done and I have heard from Mycroft that a loan from one of the great European banking houses is being contemplated in order to prevent a currency collapse and a resulting economic contraction. The Italians have gone to war with Ethiopia in a futile effort to secure a foothold in Africa, too late and too little to be of much use. The victory will probably be short-lived.

April 7, 1895
London

xtensive business as a detective has precluded my keeping entries here as of old. Most of my theological conclusions have already been recorded and my meetings with Professor Moriarty have been much attenuated of late. He works his work and I mine. I have resumed my old habit of writing here merely to get my emotions under control. A dreadful thing has happened. Oscar Wilde was arrested yesterday and charged with acts of gross indecency. The man has acted the fool of course, but to be pilloried in this fashion merely because he has some sort of need or compulsion to be martyred while ignoring the advice of his friends to flee to France is a national tragedy. Meanwhile the French are amused at us and the Germans are contemptuous toward us. They ask themselves, "How does this puerile probity serve England?" It is merely one more instance of the English need to pretend to possess a degree of virtue that we as a nation do not possess.

Oscar has been quite mad of course, but his madness has a certain quality of nobility about it. "Bosie," like some remote Lady of Shalott, has of course emerged untouched and un-regarded by the press and public alike as such highly-born tarts usually are, while a great man of English letters shall be pilloried and brought low to answer for malfeasances that are common practice in the

British School System and an occasional recreation thereafter to many. Far greater sins go unpunished daily; not least among them those cruelties that are practiced towards students whose cruelty to each other in turn is learned at the hands of wicked schoolmasters.

I dropped a line to Mycroft to see if some sort of fortunate mishap could still be arranged so that Oscar could be spirited across the channel, but Mycroft said that matters had proceeded too far at this point and the law must take its course. I have thought much upon the matter. The denial of the facts of human anthropology does no great service to religion. Any pretence to the contrary merely allows for greater aberrations to occur as we project our appetites upon others and then destroy in them what we cannot eliminate in ourselves.

The matter of a trial of course is a *fait accompli*. The enraged and aroused public anger must now be assuaged. Many Englishmen of high standing however have suddenly decided to take a vacation of undetermined length to the continent for their health this spring. Meanwhile people who once avidly claimed Oscar as a close acquaintance and friend now deny ever having supped with him and enjoyed his wit. The ladies whose hearth and board he once frequented are now suddenly "not receiving visitors." It is a nasty business all round and more a commentary on England than on the one man who told the English more about themselves than they care to know. There is a fine-line between wit and a rapier; slice too deep and the blood gushes forth.

Oscar, I call him by this familiar name because his own geniality invites informal address, always combined vice with innocence. The impression that he always made upon me was that of a man who feels compelled to press matters to the limits inherent in any idea or behavior as though through mere persistence he could get down to some essential and overriding truth about human nature. There was always a fatality in his experimentations.

In a sense he invited the fates to work their will upon him, all the while believing that by some fortunate change in the wind he would emerge unscathed. I believe that he assumed that the great limitations set by nemesis would spare him or that everything on earth was only a representation and not the thing itself. By assuming that everything is as unsubstantial and ungrounded as a fashion or decorative taste he lost respect for the eternal verities and as a result he will now be reduced to that most basic tutelage of the underlying brutality that awaits all those who lose sight of the hatred and bitterness that contradicts and sets a final limit to our more humane sensibilities.

Satirists play a dangerous game. Daniel Defoe was once imprisoned for publishing his witty essay, *The Shortest Way with Dissenters.* It is always a risky matter to point out to a Pharisee that he is in fact a Pharisee. But I would wish to point out that *une personne debauchee,* whose sexual tastes are inverted, at least leaves no unacknowledged *batard* behind to bear testimony to his unrestrained impulses. Whose sin is the greater and which most mocks the fidelity upon which the Church models its own sexual ideal and self-image as a spotless bride. To confuse what the Church is called to be with what it is in fact explains much of Christian history. I must stop here lest I become irreverent when my intention is merely to be truthful.

May 26, 1895
London

The verdict in the Wilde case is in and Oscar has been condemned to two years at hard labor for acts of gross indecency. He is neither physically prepared nor mentally adapted to such a sudden alteration in his life. If it doesn't kill him outright it bids fair at least to destroy one of England's foremost literary figures. The whole matter is as unnecessary as it is absurd. A pardon of sorts might be sought but no one has the courage to request it for fear of moral contagion through association. Any anthropologist could explain that sexual expression is one of the few constants in human behavior and one likely to take any number of forms and permutations. To seek to contain it is like seeking to place walls around the sea. The best that can be hoped for is that persons will be true to their vows if they have the strength to enter into them in the first place and that children will be raised without exploitation, abuse, or ridicule in a supportive environment that is both loving and stable so that their developmental needs and security can be assured. Since these most basic elements have yet to be attained in society any further efforts seem to me to be both ineffective and hypocritical.

July 4, 1895
London

Thomas Henry Huxley, the great promoter of evolution, was buried today in St. Marylebone Cemetery in Finchley. The affair was meant to be quiet and unofficial, but many of the great minds of England attended. I was never in sympathy with the fellow but I felt obliged to join the crowd of onlookers and to pay my respects. I found in him one of the great populizers of an idea taken beyond its proper limits. Evolution is the biological parallel of the idea of economic progress through technology. It presumes that change is always towards greater adaptation to an environment that is also changing. The callous dismissal of inefficient species that lag behind or are unable to adapt sufficiently has come to justify ruthless behavior in business affairs.

Huxley presided over one of the first blows delivered to a naïve approach to Holy Scripture along with Friedrich Schleiermacher's contribution to hermeneutics. The prior assumption that the Bible is a supernatural text and thus beyond historical infusions precluded any approach to the text beyond a literal one. If instead Holy Scripture is approached as a human document, one reflecting the inspired author's experience of God, a gap emerges that will allow for critique and interpretation. But carry this too far and another problem emerges.

If religion and particularly Christianity is conceived as the philosopher Ludwig Feuerbach has done as a mere evolutionary stage of the human mind derived entirely from our own projections or as a primitive substitute for empirical science, then the religious stage of mankind must be followed by something else. Christianity does not allow for such a substitution because it holds itself out to be both absolutely truthful and in accord with all that can be learned from nature about how things are and what their ultimate purpose is. The God of the Jews is not merely an example from a wider class of deities but the origin and end of all existence. Another problem is that the work of men like Huxley blurs the differentiating factor of human life with other life-forms and by doing so seems to compromise the existence of the soul, the transit vehicle into eternal life. Whether any of these threats are fatal to belief depends upon how one approaches them. Fear would imply a lack of faith while mere blind assertion would raise a question of denial or deliberate mendacity engaged in because of our self-interest or dependence upon a fragile and superseded worldview.

In any case Huxley bore his share of abuse for his views and his determination to face the truth deserves respect if it was not motivated by a similar zeal to promote an alternative to religion. Self-interest takes many forms. The inverse of faith is often as blind and compromised by self-interest as a fundamentalist approach is to authentic faith, one that has been tested by experience and by intellectual challenge.

While I was there I saw Joseph Lister and other men of science and for a moment I thought I caught a glimpse of Professor Moriarty although I might have been mistaken. The professor finds zoology to be a mundane pursuit and prefers the more abstract science of physics. I am sure that if I brought the matter up, particularly that the great apes and man having had a common ancestor, he would point to a portrait of Huxley and opine that the best proof of such a relation was the man's visage there for all to see. In any case one can conclude too much from comparative anatomy. I am of the opinion that the animals recognize in us our superiority and simultaneously feel a bond with us, particularly if we treat them kindly. I am also well acquainted with human savagery that often throws the most bestial attributes of brute nature into the shade along a comparative scale of malice and cruelty.

This same search for alliance moves in both directions and I take it as an article of faith that God experiences dismay and sorrow at human sinfulness. The definition of God as "the unmoved mover" is so bleached of any approachable attributes that it is almost blasphemous. When God walks though the Garden of Eden and plaintively asks Adam, "Where are you?" I imagine a great sorrow and disappointment when he learns that Adam hid himself from his creator and benefactor out of shame. The drama of mistake and misfortune that is the problem of evil evidently inflicts itself on God just as it does us. To create is to be vulnerable. The incarnation was implicit in God before the first primal command was given, "Let there be light!" God must be approached through our experience of life and not as if we can abstract ourselves outside of the human condition and imagine how things might have been had we never existed.

October 5, 1895
Paris
The Cathedral of Notre Dame

The great scientist and researcher into the most dreadful diseases, Louis Pasteur, died on September 28th. The moment that I heard of his death I determined to attend his funeral. Along with Robert Koch who discovered the tubercle bacillus on March 24, 1882 and the bacterial agent of cholera in 1883 Louis Pasteur has saved more lives and prevented more dreadful human suffering than any man in history. Medicine is emerging out of the dark ages of humors and bleeding at last. It is to men such as these that we must look for a rational application of knowledge to remedy what nature inflicts upon us.

We are taught by religion to bear patiently with the ills that we cannot prevent or cure, but there is no virtue in cherishing pain for its own sake or reconciling ourselves to what must be opposed with every effort of human courage and ingenuity. It is only by pushing the frontiers of knowledge forward that we can hold our place in the evolutionary chain of development and advance towards longevity and progress over time.

Pasteur is to be buried in Notre Dame along with the other great benefactors to France and to humanity. Doctor Watson stood at my side during mass and together we were privileged as so often before to be witnesses of the great events that have coincided with our brief sojourn on earth. It is a blessing to be contemporaneous with men whose memory will span the centuries and be honored long after the names of generals and admirals have been forgotten.

The New Year begins! Watson and I managed to escape the confines of London this year for a ceremonial fete at Baskerville Hall. Sherringford had the grippe and felt unable to undertake the visit down this year to London, but I did manage to get Mycroft to accompany us to Devonshire. We went down several days before Christmas and tramped about the open fields as part of a hunting party to obtain birds for the feast. It was a grand time, one made all the more pleasant by the company of old friends. Doctor Mortimer was there and as usual full of tales of strange discoveries in the border region of Cornwall and Devonshire where his strange excavations are still proceeding. He inquired when I might again be in residence at my cottage, but I had to tell him once again that the wide world now has called me back to itself. Indeed the year of 1896 bids fare to be one of great endeavors for me.

Doctor Mortimer of course responded that as far as he was concerned "the modern world could go to blazes." He pointed out that the only source of fascination lies in what has already happened as left in the remaining traces of our bygone ancestors. The tears had already been shed and the blood of ancient battles had dried. I told him that Watson's friend, Dr. Arthur Conan Doyle, was just the man to share his antiquarian interests. His novel, *The White Company,* had been published in 1891, the very year when I set out on my ambitious search for religious testimonies drawn from the eastern regions of the earth, seeking parallels, when they could be found, in order to frame a general theory of the religious instinct of mankind and at the same time to turn Professor Moriarty from his malign purpose of revenge upon the very country that had granted him refuge after the potato famine drove him from his Irish home.

Doctor Mortimer sniffed at my proposal but he still jotted down the address. His opinion is that religion can never be transposed from place to place and that all religion is an indigenous production. He is quite the naturalist at heart and higher theological speculation will never have any appeal for him.

There is nothing as fixed as religious prejudice and one's choice of religion is often as dictated by inner personal drives as by any claim that a transcendent reality may exert upon our search for ultimate truth. The desire to dictate to God is evidently as deeply rooted as our propensity to sin. In any case it was a lovely Christmas and it was with some reluctance that our small party of three took leave of our old friends and arrived back in the great city of London to greet the New Year.

January 6, 1896
London

My birthday has come round again and its joy has been tempered by word that the Jameson Raid that occurred on the last day of the year of 1895 ended in ignominious defeat. This vain effort to stir up some sort of dust-up in the South Africa at the behest of Cecil Rhodes was immediately communicated to Mycroft. My brother is getting tired of seeing national policy determined by strident provincial voices and the personal greed of various powerful investors. I don't know how long Mycroft will tolerate having his wise counsels set aside by persons who enjoy setting fires in the sagebrush and seeing what will happen. Isn't it enough that we are involved in Egypt and the Sudan without trying to dominate the bottom of the continent as well? The Zulu people are constrained to work in the mines under appalling conditions. Gone are the proud days of military defense under King Shaka in the first quarter of this century.

Why has systemic pillaging become the sign of civilization rather than the badge of our dishonor? I would like to take a hand in these matters so as to oppose the lies and insinuations that leverage British national pride and turn it to nefarious ends, but I have no appointment or official commission to intervene except in those cases when in sheer desperation I am consulted as a sort of novelty, just as one consults a gypsy fortune teller. My fee and my right to exact one seems to shrink once a solution is provided. It all seems so obvious in retrospect just as good sense always does. In any case I tried to celebrate as best I could at the Diogenes Club and to turn from Christmastide to the long succession of days that this year holds for me and

The shadow of the plot set by Professor Moriarty has not passed though I hear little from him. Has he forgotten his promise to refrain or have my prior efforts to bring him round born fruit at last? My patience is tempered by my fears.

June 28, 1896
London

It took me some time to locate this old journal of mine again. I am afraid that I am still a rather untidy fellow, but I knew it was somewhere upon my cluttered and dusty shelves. Who can say how a habit of longstanding can be so easily broken? This journal which was once so essential to my thought processes in years gone by has been too long abandoned to readily begin with it again. I may only plead as excuse the many cases that came my way after my return to active practice in London. These have continued to the present day. It is only appropriate however that I should make some entry now and that I record here and nowhere else that I have heard at last from Professor Moriarty. He is coming up to town to see me and has requested that I meet his train from Devonshire. The whole thing is most extraordinary. Dare I hope that he will have some good news for me? I confess that as the date for Her Majesty's Diamond Jubilee has grown closer, I have become increasingly nervous. The date will mark the promised completion of the Professor's announced plan to destroy England through the means of some unspecified agent in 1897. I have made no progress in what must remain idle speculations as to his method of doing so. It is always a capital mistake to theorize without data. Perhaps today my fears may be set to rest at last. At least some clue may be given me to enable me to avert the catastrophe.

Ⅰ met the Professor at a prearranged time at a small inn by the embankment with a view of the river. I was familiar with the place because it is frequented by students from the University of London. The proprietor is accustomed to unusual academic types and he and his staff have grown accustomed to the far-ranging and analytical discussions upon obscure and minute topics that are the favored fare of scholars. Much in academic discussion is hypothetical. The human mind proceeds by contemplating the unattainable and the improbable. So it was that I had no fear that our discussion, even if it was overheard, would cause anything but passing interest by the staff and the other patrons, who would no doubt be caught up in the thread of their own particular arguments. These would pay us scant attention.

The Professor was waiting for me when I arrived with a book propped up before him and a glass of claret at his side. He nodded to me in greeting as I entered and took a seat, feeling rather like I once did as a young chemist when summoned to the office of my tutor for a review of my progress. It took all of my effort to remind myself that we each had an equal stake in the topics before us and that as the one who had posed the thesis of a universe governed by providence it was I who was attempting to instruct the Professor and as such I was the tutor and he the pupil. I knew that such a role must be an unaccustomed one to a man who believed himself to be in possession of the truth, a truth that consists in the unattached phenomena of appearances that the senses may observe but with no fundamental basis in an absolute order from which it derives rather than emanates.

The distinction is critical. Derivation has an aura of inevitability about it, a closeness of causation to effect, or the sudden change of state as from a liquid to a gas. Emanation in contrast is a flow or causation by degrees so that the source hangs onto elements of its creation and only relinquishes them to an independent existence gradually as though the bond between the two was stretched rather than abruptly broken.

I have based my position upon traditional Thomist metaphysics and the idea that God is more that a mere moral agent in the universe. God is the ultimate source and final end of all observable phenomena, even those phenomena that appear to have no relation to the human condition and are unobserved by us. I know that this position is a scandal to materialist thought, as it is to pantheist thought also. What was Plotinus but a pantheist who believed that the universe is filled with God through a natural process of identification? Christianity on the other hand teaches that God as He is in himself is beyond all human comprehension and stands against creation as the absolute other; but not as an alienated and uncaring being but one the essence of which is not compromised or diminished as might be the case in emanation.

It is only through revelation and only to the extent of revelation that we may posit anything about God directly. Yet Jesus taught that we should see God as Father and relate to Him with the same filial trust that we apply to any human father. Jesus further assured the Apostle Phillip that to see Him was to see the Father! How then may we reconcile such remoteness and such closeness to human aspirations in one divine and triune God?

Yet that is what faith demands of us and I have made a similar demand upon the Professor, not that he simply enter into any alternate faith, but that he govern his actions by truth as taught by the One Holy Roman Catholic and Apostolic Church. I have placed all of my chips upon the board with but one spin of the wheel! But, is that not what we are called upon to do in our lives? We have only this one life and then we shall be only what we have made of this life and what we will inherit is predicated upon what we have dared to believe and act upon. God asks everything from us in order to give everything to us!

But that is of little comfort at times to those who live on the shadow side of the cross. Which of us does not feel abandoned in that bitter hour of thirst that is our present life? If we did not see the figure of Jesus in his struggle towards Golgotha, falling to the ground before us, then we who follow him could not proceed to take even one more step on our own way of the cross. I have determined that since I must risk all for my faith with my one single life, so must I also rest any argument that I would make to the Professor on that same conviction: that he abandon his final enterprise, the intention of a lifetime to destroy the England that he loathes, upon the self-same ground of Christian faith.

True Christianity excludes the comfortable middle-ground that the lethargic Christian hopes may exist, where he may have heaven, yet avoid the cross. For this reason, it takes an affirmative action of the will to turn ever and again, not to the celestial courts for comfort, but to find God where God chooses to be found, among the poor, the suffering, and among the sinful, those above all who need the grace that God alone may provide.

I know instinctively that it is this very aspect that most scandalizes and intrigues the Professor. What a paradox it is! That what is so remote that even creation in its totality is created out of nothingness would pay attention and care about the one tiny and insignificant being that is the single soul. It is the ultimate in disproportion! But the mind of man is ordained towards harmony; in what does this harmony lie but in the agreement of contradictory propositions and the desire for a perfect simplicity and order in our formulations?

Christianity proposes for our belief that God becomes man, suffers, and dies and then rises again; not as before but in the full panoply of glory. We are asked to assume that incompatible metaphysical categories may co-exist at the same time in the hypostatic union of the nature of Jesus as the Christ. We are even asked to believe that a visible sign possesses an absolute reality and efficacy such that our communion with Christ and with each other in the Holy Sacrament of the Altar is the means towards and the consummation of the very Kingdom of God here in our present life and the promise of everlasting life with God and in God when all that we now see has passed away to be replaced by a new heaven and a new earth.

Yet that is our faith, the faith of the Church, and we claim to be proud to profess it, even as were the martyrs in the shadow of their death. To believe all of this is to make an absolute choice in a world of contingent choices. But is this ever possible? Which of us does not drown daily in a sea of alternate and mutually exclusive possibilities? I have often thought that man or woman lucky who is not burdened by an excess of imagination. As our capacities increase so does the difficulty of separating the essential from the trivial and inconsequential aspects of our lives. Too much of an entertainment of contrasting and ill-assorted alternatives can paralyze the will. The result is a series of half-begun projects, gestures of compliance to forces that exist outside of us, while we seethe inwardly with rebellion or regret.

It can even become impossible under these conditions to discover that essential core of identity out of which we move into the world. This can create in us a terror of all things that are not within our ability to influence or better still to command. For this reason it is often well-advised to temper our will with a radical acceptance of all adversity, to exist in loving surrender to the minute elements that surround us each day, without passing any definitive judgment upon them or seeking to remedy them when that very effort may multiply ills for ourselves and others.

The desire for completeness is the enemy of at least a partial realization of any project. We are born to the tentative and the fragmentary results which haunt us all our days. This alone would be bad enough to endure, but the prospect of death threatens to destroy and reduce to insignificance even the most complete and certain of our victories over time and circumstance. I have lived my entire life in the shadow of death. I know that within me lies and festers that very microbe that brought my mother to an early grave that she caught from the miners to whom she tried to minister in the Yorkshire and Northumberland coal mines. My father never forgave her for what he felt was the abandonment of him and of his three sons. Even we, as his sons, were a source of constant reminder that half of our being proceeded from her.

The result was that he turned from that part of her that lay embedded in our being, in our French blood. So it was that our father turned to August Compte, to Herbert Spencer, and to Jeremy Bentham for his own faith. The furthest that his mind was allowed to proceed in a more Romantic direction was his reading of Thomas Carlyle and Ralph Waldo Emerson. If I might characterize him, I would say that he was a Philosophical Vitalist, a man who valued above all things the sheer power of his body and his mind. I have no doubt that my love of Richard Wagner is a legacy of that part of him that lies within me. He despised the delicate suggestiveness of the music of Claude Debussy. Yet he could appreciate the fire of a mind deeply banked as it was in the young Moriarty, who despite his meager and twisted body had within him a mind that could grasp the outermost suggestions of the most daring modern physicists and mathematicians.

So it was that my father endowed young Moriarty, with his dark Irish blood, with the respect and esteem that he denied to his own offspring whom he yet could not abandon for they did after all possess his own blood and were the heirs to the Holmes estate. As his own great vitality waned he struggled to accept his growing weakness and infirmities. But he would not abandon his walks across the moors, even in the course of what was to be his last illness. One day he simply did not return from a ride and we three found him on a high tor where he could just manage a last glimpse of Sigerside. He had struggled with his last remaining strength to an indentation in the rock, an out-cropping that was rather like a natural stone chair or throne. It was there that we found him, sitting up with his dead eyes focused on the home to which as a young man he had brought his bride from France believing that every happiness lay before him.

We buried him on that high tor and there he remains to this day. He did not wish to lie in consecrated ground amidst the humble dead of the parish. Did he have faith at the end? Did perhaps my ghostly mother's hand rest upon his shoulder in that last hour? Or was his love of solitude and his essential pride so great that it blotted out any desire other than to embrace his fate without faltering into what he had often called superstition. I shall never know. But I pray for his soul daily and trust that we shall meet again in the embrace of our God.

June 30, 1896
London

It had been two long years since I had last seen the Professor. I could see at once that he had aged, yet his voice and manner were as clear and incisive as ever. The climate of Devonshire seemed to have agreed with him. He was tanned and had even gained a few pounds, no doubt from indulgence in the hearty local fare and the Devonshire cream that is famous in the region. But we did not meet to discuss issues of health or agriculture. I was already aware that his stables had prospered under his care. Sir Henry had kept me informed of this. So it was that I knew of the dominant role that the Professor's contingent of horses was playing in the turf clubs of the southwest of England and that one of his entries had come first in a prestigious horserace in Lyon only last week.

I congratulated him upon this win as we settled down to our discussion. He acknowledged my compliment but swiftly moved on to the matter at hand. "No doubt you are surprised to see me in London," said he. "It is not my first trip here since my retirement. I have found that I do not need to even adopt disguises when I come. I always exercised the strictest control over my organization of specialists. I prefer to call them by that appellation. I exercised my control through agents so that my name was not known to the general criminal underworld. And now due largely to your efforts my chief lieutenants are all residing at present in the prison colonies of Australia. Still, it is no easy matter for a man of my years to interrupt his usual schedule and return to the vile air of London from his chosen abode. I must say that I am surprised that you can endure remaining here having once escaped its confines."

I thanked him for his effort in coming down to London to see me in person, but told him that a letter might have been quite sufficient, if it contained the news that he had abandoned his former intentions. The Professor shook his head at this off-hand suggestion. "No, I am afraid that would hardly do. This matter between us is personal and I must look into your eyes if I am to believe you. Each of us, Holmes, has spent his life testing the parameters of human reason, I through my science of mathematics and you through your own science of observation and deduction. Between the two of us we encompass a large part of the knowledge of human nature and of science. You are a competent chemist and I a competent physicist. Yet I venture to say that succeeding centuries will discover new areas of knowledge that will make any confident claims that either of us might care to make now, appear both premature and even primitive when set against what is to come."

I bowed my head to acknowledge his observation. The

larger paradigm shifts when they occur indeed make the certainties of the past appear not merely inadequate but obvious in retrospect.

He continued, "I have spent some considerable time in research since our last discussion and I may even claim to be rather an authority now on Church doctrine. Have you read the early Canons of the first Church Councils of Nicaea and Chalcedon or the more obscure Gnostic writings? Perhaps you are aware that for a time, the Arian bishops seemed about to carry the day over that of Athanasius. The search for a universally acceptable Orthodox formulation on many questions was not a matter for the first century alone but for the first four centuries. Indeed were it not for the Emperor Constantine, I have my doubts whether Christianity might not be reduced today in numerical parity to a series of smaller parallel religious sects, each as divergent from each other as Catholicism is from Islam.."

"The point that I wish to make is that if Orthodox doctrine was arrived at by a series of quite frankly political compromises, how may it claim to be divine revelation? The growth of the Christian religion seems to me to be preeminently the product of historical events rather than of divine revelation. But if this is so, then all of the claims of the Christian religion to be accepted on faith rather than on knowledge are vitiated. An absolute position cannot be grounded on historical accident; either it is absolutely certain and inevitable or it is only another example of contingent truth and as such no final claim can be made demanding complete and absolute assent to Christian doctrines."

This was indeed a formidable objection, but one that I thought I could answer. "You move right to the heart of the matter, Professor; I believe that you have put my king in check."

He smiled. "Well, I believe that both of us have seen that a mere exchange of pawns is a waste of time, Holmes. We are both too old not to wish for a decisive victory for one or the other of us without needless peripheral skirmishes."

I cleared my throat before proceeding, "Allow me to alter your metaphor, Professor. The search for truth is not a contest, both of us will benefit if we can arrive at agreement. It is my contention that if we both come down on the side of Christian doctrine we both win, for it is the path that leads us directly to God."

"Let us not speculate as to the odds of achieving that, Holmes. You forget that I am accustomed to your wiles. You are still in check as you have just admitted. What is your next move?"

"Very well Professor. Let us consider this matter of doctrine in Christianity, more particularly as it is formulated in the ancient canons of the early Church councils and as it exists at the present time in its fullness in the One Holy Catholic and Apostolic Church of which I am a member. The essence of your objection evidently lies in what appears to be the contingency of dogmatic claims. But surely your argument begs the question. The question is whether dogmatic language can, within the limits inherent of any verbal formulation, be accurate within the limits of language to define eternal truths? I would immediately point out that statements that cannot by their nature be reached or confined by ordinary empirical means must therefore be accepted on the authority of faith alone. The question of validity is not dependent on the means by which doctrine is generated. Truth in theology as in science may be discovered by gradual accretions and ever more accurate formulations. The difference of religious truth is that the assertions of faith, although incomplete and inadequate when seen *subspecies aeternitatis*, are at least accurate from the point of view of the earthly realm where they will be applied adequate for present use. Theological truth is accurate but numinous."

"In order to make this point clearer, please allow me to use an analogy here. You have no doubt heard of black light or ultraviolet light and have perhaps seen a device that can create such light. It is a peculiarity of this device that it also creates in the process some of the highest range of visible violet light that the human eye may perceive. The result is a curious blurred optical effect whereby the eye is made aware of its limits at precisely the point where the visible transitions into the invisible. That, my dear Professor Moriarty, is the very effect, again by order of analogy, that dogma is meant to have upon the human intellect. We exist on the border where human reason, perfectly accurate within its own province, touches upon the divine reality, which it cannot see clearly, yet it intuits it in a sort of blur. Human reason has come into contact with the numinous. Dogmatic language is therefore by its very nature suggestive and not definitive because it is not limited to the perfect clarity of the mundane world. For this reason there is an element of process that is part of all dogmatic assertions of faith. They are definitive, yet at the same time mysterious, for they cannot comprehend in the full reality of which they speak. Human reason has its limits, even as human sight. Faith takes over where the visible spectrum of human thought ceases. The development of dogma then is not a sign of the contingency of the truths to which it refers, but only a statement about the human knowing apparatus the limits of which become clearer as the language of faith becomes more refined over time."

"This process was announced beforehand by Jesus when He told his disciples that the Holy Spirit would recall to their minds the words that he had spoken among them and that the Holy Spirit would in time reveal all things to them when they were ready to receive it. So it is that the secrets of the hearts of men will someday be revealed as well. We proceed as far as we can within the present obscurity. It is God who enlightens the hearts of men ... and now I believe, my dear Professor, that it is you in turn who are in check," I added with a smile.

"I believe you are the very devil, Sherlock Holmes," Professor Moriarty replied.

"Oh let us hope not Professor, for a house divided against itself cannot stand as Jesus once said. In any case in our proselytism we are advised to be as gentle as doves, but to remain as wise as serpents. However, if as you say you have read extensively in dogmatic pronouncements, then I need not act as a catechist towards you but as a practitioner of apologetics. As a first principle we might agree that the matter that we are discussing would appear to lie outside mere earthly knowledge and pertain less to the mind than to the faculty of the will. It appears that faith is a matter of invitation and decision rather than of proposition and agreement.

The gospel expresses this best when Jesus says, 'I stand at the door and knock.' It is perhaps the most startling aspect of God's dealings with humankind that God does not overwhelm us with His presence but rather settles over us with all the gentleness of dawning light on a freshening morning in spring. The mists begin to rise from the meadows and the dew begins to melt slowly away. Birds sing from the distant trees and at last the entire earth seems to awaken into the clarity of day. After all we dwell within time and thus all of our perceptions are conditioned by the temporal order. This was no doubt true from the beginning. Perhaps the last moment of perfect coherence and order in creation was at the precise moment when God said, "Let there be light!"

Everything since then has been predicated upon succession and dispersal so that we cannot even imagine eternity except as unending time. We are time's prisoners. Even if by some unknown means God could slow time down in some obscure sector of the universe until it virtually stood still, it could not invalidate or cancel what had already occurred. It is as though all happenings are engraved into some marble surface never to be erased. But eternity is not the same as time. It does not simply continue or even stand still in an endless suspension of the moment. Instead eternity is more analogous to the joy that one might experience were one to be drawn forth on a rope to the heaving deck of a vessel after having been lost at sea. Eternity is as beyond our comprehension as is the grace of God that offers its possession to us. Salvation exceeds any question we may pose to it."

"Pain and evil are more self-evident than salvation and thus less in need of faith for affirmation. Pain after all is always more insistent to obtain our attention than pleasure so that it has always been easier even for Christians to speak of hell than of heaven when describing eternity. Hell might be best described as what it would be like to remain imprisoned exactly as we are in those moments where through our own decision we turn away from love and all of the light of being seems to fade into the night of our unmediated self as origin and as end as though we were absolute and not completely naked and dependent as we are."

"I tell you, Professor, that much is veiled behind the words in Genesis when after their sin Adam and Eve found that they were naked. What they realized was that they were suddenly calling to God across a great abyss that had opened between them and their creator. The tiny gap of freedom and knowledge that they had

168

attempted to procure so that they might live independently from God came to define their human nature and not just for them but for the entire human race. Being like God by knowing both good and evil had instead plunged them into what no human-being could ever endure: the absolute freedom to define the terms of the moral equation and not merely to be free to pursue an answer to that equation within the parameters first set by God for our protection and solace. Neither man nor woman may ever be their own definition. We exist by our very nature as complementary aspects of humanity, so that no human being can ever be totally complete in himself without love. We are born in need and in hunger for others people, which is God's mercy to us, for what a horror it would be if we, being deprived of God's nature, which is to love without limit, were possessed of only His supreme power. What evils might we not then devise if unhindered; history reveals to us."

"I often think that our cruelty to the poor animals that surround us is only a sign of how we would be had we greater powers than we do. We would be all tooth and claw! Each man would be a tyrant, loathing every other man and woman whose prerogatives impinged upon his own absolute claims. The problem of hell then is that it could only be filled with many self-proclaimed gods, each claiming supremacy over the others. What a devils' brew would that be, what pandemonium! Each would be subservient to his or her own evil nature, but one that would be deprived of the love that comes from God alone.

In order to diminish the incessant warfare the inhabitants of hell would consent to the rule of only one tyrant, the devil, whose hatred and promises of revenge against God would be the only point of agreement among them, not giving anything in return for such devotion and worship let alone gratuitously the devil bears no resemblance to God. There you have the parameters of the story of good and evil in Genesis in the best way that I can conceive of them, the origin of the problem of metaphysical evil. Such absolute evil is always a deprivation of a prior state and a pointless deprivation at that, a turning away from a good once known to an end that is endless frustration of our true purpose as created beings. I shudder at the thought and to my surprise I see that you also are visibly affected."

After a minute spent in contemplation Professor Moriarty looked up at me. "I believe that I have seen something of the reality that you describe, Holmes. I believe that so must any man who has attended the councils of nations or encountered men of power in this world. You see I may be more humble than you think I am. In any case we have not spoken yet of my plan."

He paused again before continuing, "It was conceived from a desire to humble the evil colossus of our age, this England to which you are so devoted."

I felt that now was a propitious time, so I urged him to continue, "I know that, Professor; but I think that providence in allowing evils to work their course shows the vanity of power and of its pursuit through unjust riches and through the exercise of force. The lesson to be learned must be learned less by individuals than by the extended groupings and organizations of mankind. I believe that both of us know that a great European war is coming, one that will shake the foundations of the kingdoms of this world. Whether it will be the final conflict foretold in Revelation I cannot say, but it should prove to any man who will observe it when it comes that folly is the common lot of man and demonstrate once and for all how mad is the road of domination and dominion."

I then went on to add this proviso, "But prophesy is not our province, you and I. We are not equal to the task, to solve problems that exceed the discretion and control of any single human life. The role of the Saints was not to change history, but to illumine it by showing forth the humble way of Christ. Through the centuries, men have sought for the True Cross and for the Holy Grail forgetting that the True Cross hangs in every Church where Holy Mass is offered and celebrated. The Holy Grail similarly is in every chalice that contains the Precious Blood of Christ in sacramental form. God always clothes Himself in the ordinary and the humble. The mystery of the Incarnation has really never ceased. God is present in the least of the brethren of the Son of Man. By this chosen appellation Jesus claimed to be the son of all men, the universal man, one who has not abandoned us although we have often abandoned Him."

The Professor looked then at me with a most peculiar

expression. "You speak of a great future war Holmes, but surely Mycroft is in the best position to pronounce upon that possibility. The current of the present age seems to be setting in a contrary direction. Asia is the rising star. Trade is tending to the east, away from Europe, towards China and Japan."

"You are forgetting Africa, Professor. During my recent journey I was instructed to see what conditions were like in the Sudan. Though Mycroft has not said as much to me, I feel certain that England is planning on assembling an expeditionary force to drive the Khalifa from Khartoum. It is more than simply the legacy of General Gordon and the national pride of England that are at stake. Sudan presses hard upon the Congo region with its immense riches. Then there is the matter of the Boers in southern Africa. That hitherto unexplored continent is being divided up between the great powers. As Africa goes so will the fate of China be determined, unless the Americans intervene to keep the Chinese trade open to all nations. The next years will be a scramble and sooner or later some event will occur to force a general European confrontation. It is then that I fear a general European War will break out. The results will be costly because nothing less than complete victory will be contemplated by each contending force."

"I would have thought that you would have anticipated such a conflict so that England can finally emerge supreme," commented the Professor. "Britain still rules the waves. But then again perhaps, if my little plan puts England in her place, then the arms race that you fear may be prevented."

"Are you such a friend of Germany then Professor?" I inquired.

He answered at once, "I am a friend of no nation. I see governments as only a ruse to bewilder men and blind them to their own interests. They are rather like religions in this respect. Both promise the loyal believer a better world and a happier life to distract them from their present misery. Both demand everything from the masses while favoring a privileged caste who survive on the labors of the multitude. It is all smoke and mirrors, my dear fellow, smoke and mirrors, patriotism and the pride of being a true believer. We are only wretched beings born in pain and dying in agony with only an illusory period between where we might at least exert our efforts to procure some measure of justice upon the few who batten off of their fellow men.”

“You always return to your atavistic theory of mankind, Professor,” I pointed out. “Yet you yourself are proof of the nobility of human effort and the grandeur of the human mind. If you truly believed as you do, then you would join Colonel Moran in his brothels rather than pursuing science and wisdom. How do you explain men like Aquinas and Confucius and Newton? Were they all only monkeys with a bit of mirror? If the stars are no more than superheated gases, why study their motions and why seek the eternal laws which govern them? Is it not because you seek behind the laws of motion for a single source, and more; you seek for an ultimate purpose to be deduced from the celestial regularities that you observe. You are progressing towards that final question that the mind must always ask itself, not the question of what, but rather the question of why. Why and to what end do all things exist?”

“Which is an unanswerable question that proceeds from the mind of man alone, purpose does not exist in the mindless vacuum of dead matter,” shouted the Professor.

Evidently my last accusation had gone home to him like an arrow to its target. “But you are not dead Professor. You are alive and more than that, you are a man, made in the image and likeness of God and oriented to just those questions that will reveal that God in fact does exist! Your very being proclaims it. But to reduce your own questioning you shift your gaze to the bubbling of matter in the skull although to minimize thought in this manner belies your own experience. If you doubt God, then you must doubt yourself as well. You may be more humble than I have believed you to be Professor, but you are not as humble as to crawl about with the worms or chatter like a monkey in a tree. You are a man and as man you must seek God.”

“But I thought we were speaking of nations Holmes.” He smiled at me, but I could see he was on guard.

“We were speaking of all that demands loyalty of men. The sovereign claims of the state are but a reflection of the greater loyalty that we owe to God. There is idolatry in all national pride and it leads at last to war. What is a nation but the sum of the aspirations of its citizens, of their collective ambition, greed, and fear? Until universal justice is applied to all persons irrespective of their national allegiance, fear will persist among men, even as it does within nations, despite whatever partial legal order subsists within them. Men fear other men for the very qualities that they possess themselves. Therefore only charity may extinguish that universal fear. Nothing can be taken from a man who loves his neighbor as himself. If he loves in this way, then all that he has is already given into his neighbor's keeping."

"Is that your practical conclusion, do you think that such a rule of life will ever prevail among men?" asked the Professor.

"Perhaps not, but it is the logical consequence of the command of charity that alone may save men from themselves. Besides, what is the alternative if it is carried to its extreme? Will it not be the endless multiplication of arms? Every advance of science or mechanics is first turned to the elaboration of ever more deadly means toward our own destruction? The fears of man far exceed the peace that is found only in God. Reason will always council and reassure us that our motives are always defensive in nature and hence justifiable. History is rather like a dance that once begun makes it finally irrelevant which partner leads. The dance will continue until the music stops; but the music is becoming a dirge for the hope of the continuance of human life upon the earth. It is said that in the end there will be wars and rumors of wars until the final day."

We both paused to consider the problem that stood squarely before us—that of the fate of the species, and perhaps more, the fate of the entire earth alone of all the planets and stars that we could see teaming with life!

At last Professor Moriarty spoke up. "If that is to be so, Holmes, then why do you as a good Christian oppose me? Are you so loyal to England after all? Or are you rather a man of universal sympathies as you have just led me to believe you are? Allow me to destroy England as a grim warning to the wider imperialist world and I will be satisfied. Capital centralization will make slaves of the majority of the world's population given sufficient time; why not stop it now? Colonialism will only cease when it meets determined resistance. Wars always occur on colonized soil while at home all things go on as usual. I plan on reversing that process.”

“You are displacing upon me a question that you must answer for yourself, Professor. You see, it is actually personal with you and because it is personal, you must ask yourself how it is that you, as a single man, may justify making war upon, not just the English nation alone, but upon individual men and women, each one of whom is equal to yourself in possessing human dignity. The very abstraction that you deplore in the colonialist mentality you will be practicing in opposing it.”

He answered at once, “Why is it that the nations of the world may declare war, but not individuals? Who are these leaders of nations that we can devolve upon them the power to act for us? Is it not more honest for us to take the responsibility for what we believe? Why it moral for them to kill in our name while we remain unsullied by the powers that we grant to them? They are not gods after all but simply men like us. Is their declaration of war then any less personal? Must I be clothed with the insignia of office to secure immunity from your condemnation?”

I answered, “No, for what I say to you, I say of them also. These men shall be held accountable before God for the trust that their fellow citizens have placed in their care when they lead their nations into war. It is always personal because the commands of God are addressed, not to nations but to each individual soul regardless of his office. The command of charity alone may save, not just individuals, but even nations from self-imposed slaughter.”

“But you have averred, Holmes, that there will be wars until the end of time, by the moral dilemmas posed to us whether individually or collectively. My plan seems then to be in accord with the very words of God himself in the Old Testament. Perhaps I am advancing the will of providence by my little device and you with your idealist presumptions oppose it.”

“On the contrary, Professor, for Jesus said that scandals will come, but woe to the man through whom they come. War is surely the worst scandal of them all. It degrades the very nature of man. For that very reason it is covered in the panoply of honors and of anthems, of decorations and colorful uniforms with their various insignia. Wars are made into legends and are pursued as though they were games, but war is always the harbinger of death and mourning, of famine and destruction. In the end it is said that God will be forced to undertake a final intervention to defeat the anti-Christ in a battle waged upon the plain of Armageddon, but shall good men advance the date of the coming of the Prince of Peace by favoring war? Isn't that temping God and using His own word against Him?"

I brought this point forward because it has always troubled me that warfare plays such a role in Sacred Scripture and how easily passages have been cited to further aggressive ends by nominal Christians.

Professor Moriarty had also notice this. "You seem to forget your Old Testament. Was it not the God of Israel who was always a God of war?" the Professor sneered. "Or is it that that you believe that Christianity is indeed a new faith, so new in fact that God's own nature appears to change with the advent of Jesus Christ. How do you get from the early God of Israel to the Father who we are asked to call Abba? It always comes down to the question of how fathers are to be regarded in the Judeo-Christian writings, does it not? The sins of the fathers for instance are said to be visited upon the sons through generations! Why then do you demand that I should be better than the man who was my own father? You know what a brute he was and what I suffered at his hands. But he was an Irishman still plain and simple, and a Moriarty, a man driven into exile to the very country that he loathed, with a dead wife left behind and a crippled son in tow as a reminder of what he had lost? You ask me to forgive England, to allow it to grow fat upon the substance of its colonies of which Ireland was the first. Do you ask me to have mercy now because you are a Christian or because you are an Englishman after all and my enemy?"

"It is not I who ask this of you," I said to him while fixing him with a level gaze. "It is your God and mine who commands it. Thou shalt not kill! I know that what you contemplate is the death of the innocent for a plan that will be as far-reaching as the one you claim as yours must by its very nature be indiscriminate in its effects. I do not know the means that you have devised to wreak havoc among us, perhaps it is some new device or new type of weapon. But this I know, it will only work if it causes death or interferes with the commerce upon which life depends. In either case it will no doubt bring great suffering and starvation in its wake."

"And disease as well. Just as the famine in Ireland did," said the Professor quietly but with an expression of grim satisfaction on his face.

"Yes and disease, for what war does not bring in its train the scourge of all mankind's ancient physical enemies?" I replied.

He objected at once to my tone, "And was there no starvation and disease in Ireland in 1845 and the years following? Would you now take the sword of vindication from my hand? With what will you replace it? It has kept me alive, lo these many years! How many new victims must continue to perish simply so that the mythology of English supremacy that you find so comforting may continue? Religion brings peace of mind to the complacent and the well fed, but does little to aid the truly suffering beyond blessing their obsequies when they die! They had a right to live! My mother had a right to live! I vowed, before I abandoned her forever to come to England, that I would avenge her death. The prospect of doing so has sustained me through many bitter years. It was the reason for what you would call my crimes and it is the reason for this last great effort that I shall make on her behalf!"

With this he burst into heavy sobs of anger and regret. I saw at last the full measure of the man who stood before me trembling with passion. I saw at last how truly each of us two was brother to the other, for each of us had lost a mother in his youth to the ravages of disease and to an early death. Physical and moral evils tend to finally merge and complement each other. For this reason Jesus healed those who alike were afflicted by illness or by demons, for both arise from our common condition in a fallen world, one menaced by powers that we can neither understand or can control.

"You do have it in your power to vindicate your mother's death, Professor. But you mistake how it is that you may accomplish that end. The cycle of revenge is endless you see. Someone needed finally to step forward and take the blame upon Himself, one who was himself blameless. You know of whom I speak, our Savior; and it has already been done. The price has been paid in every lash of the whip and in every drop of blood shed upon His cross. Your revenge and vindication has already taken place, Professor, two thousand years before the crime that you would avenge was ever committed. The One who has paid the full debt and accepted the wages of your anger is the one who bids you to cease now. Proceed no further with your design! Abandon your machinations! Let all cease now, for the good of your own soul, so that you may see again after your death the one whom you loved and lost as a child."

This was not my usual manner of speaking to the Professor. Instead it was as though I was speaking to client who had come to me for aid. I regarded him then as my words flew home to his heart like an arrow to its mark. He dropped into the chair from which he had risen in the flood of his words and tears coursed down his aged face, tears that he did not attempt to hide even from me. I reached out and grasped for a moment his dry and withered hand before leaving him at our table in its obscure nook and assuring the landlord, who had come over to see if all was well, that the gentleman was quite alright. I waited for another few minutes at a discreet distance, but the Professor did not ask me to return to the table. So it was that I left him there, in that place where all men reside alone with their God within the silence of their own souls.

July 1, 1896
London

Professor Moriarty has departed with the same speed and unexpectedness as his announcement of his arrival had been sudden and unanticipated. He has always been a man who has kept his own counsel. Even Colonel Moran once confessed to me that his relations with the Professor had been confined to the receiving of summary orders that he never questioned. In a normal fencing match the victor must press his advantage because opportunity is often as swiftly eclipsed as it is revealed; but one can never be sure if a seeming weakness in the opponent is merely an enticement to lead one to overstep the mark and close too soon. In any case this matter between the Professor and me cannot be resolved by mere argument. The Buddhists are correct in their insight that Enlightment must be sought; it cannot be forced. The workings of divine grace are so subtle and so conditioned by unique experience that it may truly be said that God woos the soul as does a suitor.

How strange that God must be put to such labors in our regard, particularly when it is for our own good that God acts. But it is part of the legacy of Original Sin that we prefer to test the limits of mercy rather than to ask at once for the grace to follow the will of God without question, which is always the shortest route to attaining our ultimate good. I have therefore determined not to apply pressure to the Professor now but rather to await any subsequent opportunity as it may present itself and only then to advance and convey as much information or insight as I may while trusting to the Professor to assimilate and to incorporate any suggestions that I possess in his own good time and manner.

This manner of patient and piecemeal proselytism seemed to be a luxury that the Church could ill afford to exercise in prior eras. Salvation was a desperate matter and to hesitate was to lose a soul. Theology after the writings of St. Augustine came to dominate ran aground on the question of how grace could be reconciled with human freedom. Hesitation in accepting Baptism as well as anything less than heroic sanctity after conversion was interpreted in the most fatal terms. The Christian community was so small and exclusive and the times were so brutal and crude that desperation ruled the day. There was little sense in imagining any more generous dispensation than the narrowest parameters consistent with a benevolent image of God would tolerate. Even un-baptized infants were seen as so likely to manifest in later life the evils of un-converted mankind that they deserved hell if they had yet to experience those cleansing waters before death.

The times are little more tolerant now and I question at times the latitude that I have given myself here in my own theological suppositions. I certainly have no commission to interpret Church Doctrine in a more lenient fashion than the hierarchy; but within the scope of this journal I have attempted a synthesis that I would willingly submit to higher authority even if it is only in many respects the product of an amateur. I find a need to escape now and then to other regions in order to orient my thoughts. I have not returned to Devonshire since my departure from there two years ago. My practice as a detective has grown and it allows me little time for the leisure and freedom necessary for travel that was once mine. The entire period of my spiritual quest seems now as distant and alien to me as if it had never been. I am once again the old Sherlock Holmes of Baker Street.

Though I am happy to say that the worst of my old vices have not returned thanks to the ever vigilant Watson, I must admit that I have been using myself up rather too freely of late. Watson insists from time to time that we take an excursion down to Brighton or some similar seaside resort. His old love for the sea is still undiminished. How wonderful it would be if he could retire to some homely place down in Cornwall so that he might be near to my own retreat in Devonshire during our years of retirement. I am sure that even now he would be willing to retire if it was not for the need to maintain his medical practice.

My own labors are more demanding now than ever. I have as a result managed to obtain for the first time in years what might be termed a sufficiency of funds, which if not a fortune are at least enough that I might arrange for a young doctor from France who is a cousin of mine on my mother's side of the family to purchase Watson's practice. I could advance the purchase price to young Vernet so that he could purchase the practice outright and set Watson free. I would ask that he keep my name out of it of course and Vernet could repay me gradually when he is able to do so. I have no son of my own and I rather like the fellow. He is just the sort to keep up the good works among the lower middle-class pensioners who always made up the majority of Watson's patients, old soldiers from India, widows, and small shopkeepers. I intend to telegraph the proposal this very day and we shall see if the young doctor will leave the fields of Brittany for the fogs of London. If so, then Watson may retire at last and have time to aid me by his presence. I find since I have resumed my practice that more than ever I cannot manage without him.

My written correspondence diminished during my travels to nearly zero and even now is usually confined to only highly personal matters. It may have seemed strange to many during my time of notoriety prior to 1891 that I was able to manage my consulting practice from a suite of rented rooms and conduct it in a dressing gown. This informality was only possible because my own laconic nature demanded it and I was not dependent upon its commercial success in order to survive.

It is not too much to claim that detection was more a hobby with me than it was a business. I often refused fees or took cases that brought only aesthetic satisfaction while spurning higher paying clients who sought to use my skills to further some private interest with which my own principles conflicted. Watson reported on more than one occasion that boredom or depression often afflicted me to such a degree that I was nearly incapacitated, while at other times I would be so engaged that I would forget to eat anything, much to the concern of Mrs. Hudson. All of this was made possible because a remittance paid regularly was deposited to my bank account in London from the Holmes Estate in Yorkshire under the direction of my saturnine elder brother.

I have not commented in this journal until now that certain changes have occurred in the tax structure of the government that has made it a costly matter to maintain large landed estates. The result has been a change of some magnitude, particularly in Ireland and Wales. The largest estates are gradually being sold off as a result and even the middle-sized holdings such as Sigerside are affected. For this reason I have been forced by economic circumstances to take cases from highly-placed families and even cases from the continent where my name has penetrated due to the constant efforts of Dr. Watson to make my name known beyond the confines of England. This could not come at a more unwelcome time for me because I notice a decided diminution of my energy that may be an early warning sign of a reversal in my health. I hesitate to bring the matter up to Watson, but when he visits me I see that his professional eye has not failed to notice my cough and that I have lost weight recently. As a result I may need to seek refuge again at my cottage in Devonshire this winter in order to recuperate. Until then I must seek "to make hay while the sun shines" as they say.

Sufficient funds are coming in that I can retire for a time if need be and I am taking the trouble to invest in certain railway shares in America that will no doubt increase in value as the extensive western regions are settled under pressure from the tides of emigration to those shores. I even have some investments in certain gold and silver explorations in Colorado that may as they say "pan-out." Of course such willy-nilly expansion in America will no doubt bring problems that we cannot imagine from our present frame of reference. I am not at all easy with the greedy energy of the Americans, but to invest in African holdings or any of our home industries or in India seems even more unconscionable. I can only hope that the Americans will use some of their characteristic optimism and latent foresight to think of the future in time to avoid the perils of a dawning empire.

July 11, 1896
London

My effort to personalize my approach to Professor Moriarty has forced me to reflect on the limitations of a consulting detective in any pronouncements of a theological nature. I am more aware each day that what is appropriate for general affirmation in a creed requires precisely skills that I do not possess.

My entire success as a detective has depended upon my ability to see matters from a refracted angle where facts can be set in new relations to each other and a new solution to a mystery may possibly emerge. This approach of what might be called "Socratic skepticism" has grown to be habitual with me and I am unable to shake it off when confronted by subject matter where its utilization may lead to results in excess of what my initial questioning habit may reveal. Certainly any approach to early Christian documentation and the gradual sedimentation of Catholic truth will open avenues of approach and the very sort of radical inquiry that may lead a person of faith to go astray. At the same time commitment that is so blind and immediate that it is not persuasive or even violates our innate sense of what could reasonably be predicated of God possesses its own danger to the believer.

It seems to me that it presumes too much to believe that error or imprecise conclusions have been suspended in the case of theology when these qualities appear again and again in other disciplines of thought. The complex interweaving of select individuals who have bequeathed a contribution and had a disproportionate weight in the formation or expression of orthodox conclusions that now demand universal assent in faith must be taken into account at some point, perhaps even years after their contributions have been so deeply assimilated that they appear to derive from God in a most direct manner. The venturesome insight of yesterday assumes a new function gradually as the fundamental basis for further theological elaboration until the entire structure of faith appears to be imperiled by suggesting a review of the very process by which the structure was constructed in the first place.

The questioning process involved in my disputation with Moriarty is thus not generally applicable beyond its specific context, but it seems even more necessary when one attempts to convince a person like Professor Moriarty whose entire life has been spent well beyond the gravitational attraction of even such a venerable institution as the Roman Catholic Church. The former superiority and authority of that institution is being challenged in these latter days of the 19th century in ways that would formerly have been seen as the height of temerity and insolence.

Meanwhile the secular world is spinning off in directions where any truth whatsoever is being held by schools of thought that share very little if anything in common. The result is that discourses from such separate galaxies of thought have become so incommensurable that communication between them is well-nigh impossible and certainly unwelcome to the contending parties. It is not my desire to add to this general confusion by my own speculations. Whatever value they possess must be weighed in the light of the communal discernment of the entire Church and by submission to the prudential care of those who must safeguard the faith in light of the times and circumstances present to them.

I am still dwelling on my thoughts of yesterday. The key element in the position of Professor Moriarty appears to be the idea of revenge and retribution, that evil can best be opposed by re-directing it to its source. Pain and punishment play a central role in Christianity as well. The whole idea of satisfaction for sin through atonement of a spotless victim has always appeared to me to be unduly redolent of the practices of the tribal regions of the Near-East to be universally applied in all times and places. Feuds and blood-guilt stem from this same basic need to equalize evil by duplicating its effects. To make the innocent suffer appears from this point of view to be even more unjust than to visit retribution on the malefactor; but what if these prescriptions and methods to restore social equilibrium are derivative from a particular mindset rather than indicative of the nature of God? Even the saints have emphasized the need to vindicate the honor and dignity of the God, who is therefore characterized as resembling an irate monarch rather than a benevolent father. It is as though even in Christianity it is essential to retain the exchange value or violence and the security derived from fear.

Is it possible that the darker aspects of the gospels represent a residue of the religions that preceded their composition so that any more generous presentation to the early converts would have been rejected out of hand? How are we to understand authorial intent in perusing these documents? Did the expectations of the first recipients play no discernible role in the style and content of their composition? To assume so is to believe that the gospels are truly so universal that their appeal is immediately self-evident and that no particular end was to be served that biased the form or manner of the presentation of elements either in the selection of facts and episodes in the life of Jesus or in the words attributed directly to Him. Of course questions of this nature were considered to be entirely inapposite to these writings if they proceeded directly and in an unmediated fashion from God. The New Testament writings were to be accepted not weighed for narrative coherence let alone critiqued in the manner of any other ancient text.

But rather than getting caught up in endless disputes around topics that exceed my competence I have taken the alternate course of showing the costs entailed in unbelief. Take away the transcendent and the other imperatives melt away as well. The morality of the common man is dictated by factors that emerge from the context of daily life. This was undoubtedly why Jesus spoke in parables and why He constantly re-directed the questions of the religious experts of His day into self-examination and away from comforting legalisms. I can do no better and Professor Moriarty for all his scientific acumen is still a man after all.

July 14, 1896
London

Each day that has passed since my meeting with Professor Moriarty has suggested to me new things that I might have said to him. As with most insights, which are so often the fruit of a moment in which one phrase seems to sum up and to conclude various lines of reflection, so is a phrase that I jotted down immediately in my notebook after it came to me.

It read as follows: *"All of human life may best be conceived as a struggle between the impulses of wonder and disgust at the prospect that lies before us."*

Certainly life contains enough of a stimulus to both attitudes, but it is the final attitude in the prospect of death that matters most. Wonder is the natural attitude of youth, for one is still young and at the height of one's powers. To maintain wonder as one grows in age though becomes ever more difficult after experience has taught us its inevitable lessons. But it is in prospect of death with its dissolution and decay that a final test is placed before us. To affirm life still in an attitude of wonder when it can neither remedy past deficiencies nor allow time to live life over again in the guise of a new character, when the changes in the world seem to offer possibilities that one's own unfortunate position in history did not allow; it is then that the greatest test of our courage and endurance begins!

The impulse to condemn youth for being as foolish as one forgets that we ourselves have been is always present. But there is also the impulse to look back at our own lives as the summit of pointlessness and folly from the perspective of whatever wisdom one has managed to acquire in life. One imagines that if one's youth and beauty were to be miraculously returned that one would do everything differently when it is far more likely that our renewed powers would combine the intelligence of age with the same impulses towards gratuitous idolatry of the self that were characteristic of our youth.

Who can anticipate with equanimity the gradual eclipse of our powers? What humility it takes to see in the poor withered beings that we will become (if we survive long enough) still some measure of wonder and of beauty and to allow that irreducible dignity of the human being to summon forth from others the services that we were formerly able to render to minister to our own most basic functions.

Age seems to me to be a primal occasion for the insinuation of evil to render us hateful in our own eyes and to desire to hide beneath the panoply of wealth, of sumptuous garments, and of extravagant domiciles the reality of our final condition. Age should have then as its foremost characteristic a desire for simplicity, to steal an advance upon inevitable dissolution by seeing what good we can provide for those who are still in the season to enjoy the goods of this world and to find wonder rather than envy in their doing so. Of what good are the unseasonable joys of the avaricious, those who instead hoard up unto themselves the riches of the earth while so many go about deprived of the very means of life and livelihood? Worst of all is a disgust that would draw all of life into that jaundiced view that their own prior dissipations has induced within them or the proud contumely of the philosophical pessimist who with a sour abstemiousness has refused in youth the pleasures that age now makes impossible for him to attain.

To all of these death is the ultimate test. Simply to contemplate the universal process of physical decay and to know

that one is no exception is to walk with the famed poet Thomas
Gray in his country churchyard. Only those who have lived a
country life and seen death and decay in the lesser animals may
take the stern but necessary view that the earth must reclaim what
it has lent to us of the ingredients of physical being and return
them to the soil. The spirit of wonder may then accompany our
poor clay in our last hours and even into the grave in sure and
steady hope of the resurrection from the dead.

July 20, 1896
London

My musing on death has recalled to my mind a case of
some years ago. It was in 1889 if my memory does not
deceive me that Watson and I encountered in our rooms
one morning one Colonel Warburton lately retired from India with
a medical discharge. Watson had encountered him on many
occasions at his club for retired officers and noticed the man's
downcast demeanor and habit of engaging in inaudible soliloquies
at a table in the corner. There had been talk among the senior
members of ejecting him on more than one occasion. As a milder
alternative Watson had suggested to one of these that he might
bring the man by to see me. Considering the man's rank and his
former excellent service to Queen and country this alternative was
readily embraced by the executive committee.

Our prospective client was an impressive sort of man at
first glance when he presented himself that morning in Baker
Street, just the sort of regimental field commander whose stern eye
and handsome carriage would call forth confidence in his men; but
my experienced eye soon detected the tremor in his hands and the
halting gait of a man at the furthest extremity of nervous
prostration. He attempted to hide this manfully, but it was not
until he had the full support of an armchair that the vertigo with
which he was apparently afflicted as well seemed to pass.

Upon my inquiring why he had called upon us that
morning, he recounted a most extraordinary narrative. I glanced
over at Watson as the man began and saw that his physician's eye
had detected the same symptoms that I had noticed.

"I have come to see you, Mr. Holmes, in order to obtain your opinion as to whether or not I am quite mad."

I attempted to reassure him, "Well as to that Sir you may have mistaken the nature of my practice. I am not an alienist; although my colleague is at least a physician. Perhaps if you explained your affliction to a professional who is an expert in such matters..."

He spoke up in a most spirited manner, "No Sir you are the man for me. I have heard of your extraordinary abilities and discretion and the tale that I must unfold is for your ears alone."

Then looking over at Dr. Watson he was about to demur when I said, "My friend and colleague is a former military man and his advice is essential to any opinion that I will render."

The man accepted my terms with a nod of his head and began his story as follows, "A few years ago young Major Owen Warburton was as daring a commander as ever commanded troops in the Khyber Pass. What am I now but a mere rabbit of a man trembling at each sound in the street? And what did it? Thought sir, thought alone has brought me low. To enter battle, let alone to command others, one must believe that one will survive the encounter and that one is immune or at least indifferent to contingencies; that will power alone can carry one to victory. For years this conviction sustained me and as a result I was promoted to the rank of Colonel after many engagements and sent home for a well-deserved leave. It was here, yes here in placid England that an experience occurred that has left me a broken man. I who had seen men with shattered skulls on the battlefield, I who had watched men dying to right and left of me yet taken the ridge where the enemy lay in wait, I return home and..."

He stood up in his excitement and the trembling in his legs immediately caused him to subside back into his chair.

"Calm yourself sir! Watson I think a brandy is called for here," I said quietly.

The poor fellow had attempted to rise from his chair had only succeeded in toppling over the whole affair with the result that he almost fell into the fire grate that was smoldering before him. Watson prepared him a stiff brandy and the Colonel resumed his chair with a grateful nod to the good doctor.

"I appreciate your letting me tell my tale in my own way for my powers of concentration are not what they once were. I must begin by telling you that as a youth I was given a most pious upbringing in the Reformed Church of Scotland. It is one of the tenets of that strict faith that all things are pre-ordained by God. No event occurs but God has already so conditioned it that ultimate goodness will be achieved. Nothing in this world is accidental and even so-called human freedom is really only an illusion caused by our own proximity to events. We imagine as would a drop of water in a fast-flowing stream that it is we who are determining events when it is the flow of circumstance as guided by providence that determines all things. Our so-called free decisions are only post-hoc rationalizations of what has already been pre-determined in the natural order of divine causality. God is both the cause and the end result of all things and to Him be the glory! Who are we as mere sinful mortals to protest the wise dictates and oppose the hand that guides us through every seeming contingency? Such at least was my belief and it gave me courage to face all events with an equanimity that I no longer possess. It is my religious belief still, but my entire body seems to protest against this natural and pious conviction. The result is the tremors that you have observed."

He looked from one to the other of us for confirmation that his best efforts to hide his condition had been to no avail.

He continued, "You need not speak for I see what my commanding General first observed upon my return to India after my leave; it is still the case. These recurrent spells come upon me. It was during that leave that I witnessed a most strange event on the street. I saw a child crushed to death by a cart carrying a heavy load, an event that no doubt happens in London with its congested population with some frequency. The child was a little girl, perhaps five years old, who was offering me a bunch of violets at that moment while her mother smiled at her side. Suddenly the horse tied to the cart from which the flowers had come shied at the noise made by some chance event in the street and it backed up crushing the child beneath the wheels. The child's dying moan rings still in my ears and the dreadful scream of her mother. Medical aid was summoned at once, but alas it came too late to save her. An hour later I was in my club with a whiskey and soda before me and all about me was quiet and civilized, but I was convinced that death had followed me home from the Khyber Pass and reached out to claim not me but instead the child standing at my side. It was from that hour that I began to doubt the providential design in which I had always believed. Why had she perished and not I was the question that began to haunt me nightly, I who had tempted death a thousand times yet remained unscathed and here at my very feet in the very act of bestowing her tiny gift upon me a child had died with all her life in front of her. How could such an event ever be said to work for the good of the greater cosmos? What plan of God could ever make such sacrifices part of the general debt owed for sin? What possible purpose could dictate this shadow- play of events if the pain of those events must be born by those who have had no real hand in their evolution? If God determines all things, then why does He grant us consciousness so as to witness them?"

He paused again and wiped his brow with a handkerchief before continuing, "Suddenly I began to grasp the sheer magnitude of pain that afflicts this best of all possible worlds. What has been the testimony of all life-forms but one unending wail of pain in all sentient beings since the planet first began to cool sufficiently to support life upon it? What manner of God would create such a scenario, let alone tolerate its continuance through endless millennia? And if we are really only like bare molecules jostling about in the vast soup of physical existence under a rule of mere blind causality, who can live in such a sea of insignificance? I tell you, gentlemen, it was from that grim hour of my doubt in what my prior faith had proposed that I date my current affliction that has now progressed to the edge of madness. The ordinary contingencies of life seem now to be utterly beyond my ability to bear. The result is that I tremble constantly. If an immense claw were to reach through that window behind you and draw forth one or the other of you two gentlemen I would not be surprised. The world is to me a mere chaotic jungle. I am the toy of a malicious and demonic force as are both of you. I fear that my every thought and word will bring that force to bear its wrath upon me. But worse still I begin to wonder if God is not simply dreaming this universe of ours and that it will vanish when He awakens from His dyspeptic dream of a world in which all must suffer until He wakes!"

Colonel Warburton was silent for a time and I could see in him the ruin of a noble mind and nature. Truly it is a great task for a thinking man to stumble about in this world.

After looking to us for an answer he went on, "Now Mr. Holmes," he began again when his voice had returned to him, "Am I mad?"

I recall that I did what I could out of the bare inner resources that I possessed at the time to reassure him that he was not mad. He rose then with a despairing cry and wrung his hands in his anguish.

He cried, "I was hoping that I was, for if I am not mad why then sir God is mad! I should far rather be a demented lunatic and know that I have misinterpreted events than to believe that my idea of the good must be so ruinously mocked by this stormy sea of contingency in which we all must live."

Watson interrupted at this point to make an observation, "Well there are certain regularities that make cause and effect relationships possible in time. How are they to be avoided? Certain unfortunate instances are bound to occur."

"Which only mock those of us who crave that an exception should be made when events have such tragic outcomes," our client interrupted. "You see the dilemma do you not? Either the course of strict causality must be changed to accommodate God's mercy in the particular case even if this may appear an arbitrary interference of the supernatural into worldly affairs or such exceptions are precluded by some divine decree and therefore the uninterrupted order of causality precludes the existence of a merciful deity because He would prefer sustaining His order over succoring our needs in times of peril. Neither position is tolerable to a man seeking a moral universe."

He paused once more evidently trapped in the web of his own dichotomy. After some thought I addressed him in this manner.

"I see the dilemma as you have posed it sir," I answered. "But by setting up the question in such a way that only two alternatives are offered you have surely biased the possible range of answers that may be offered to reassure you with the prospect of a less mechanized faith. It may be that your own military training which sees advance and retreat as the two main options for the movement of troops may have blinded you to a different way of seeing things. I commend to your reading the Chinese book, The I-Ching. It proposes no less than sixty-six alternative lenses with which to view any situation and within each of these another six possibilities exist, for each hexagram is a combination of six lines. If to this is added a consideration of the balance of the four internal trigrams even more variety is provided to break down the western penchant for binary thought of mutually exclusive alternatives. But when we consider God we must surely multiply the dimensions of thought even further still. Who can say how manifestly attuned accidents may be when viewed from a higher plane of reference?"

"The providence of God may be viewed as harmonious only when seen from a vantage that is denied us here. More than this we must consider that our present position is in no way a finished one and that every cause generates effects that ripple outwards like waves in a pond to the furthest borders of time. In this sense nothing is ever lost. Each past event is still announcing itself in some vast far-off region of the cosmos where it is being heard for the first time. Each pulse beat is part of some underlying harmony attuned by a primal baton wielded by the Great Conductor so that the symphony of the whole cannot be heard by a single section of the orchestra that produces it. I admire the sensitivity that has awoken within you compassion for this poor lost child but it is presumptuous of you to assume that you know her role in the final drama of universal salvation. It may be that her early loss is meant to remind you who have taken so many lives in battle that each soldier was once in turn a child no less than her whom you mourn so vehemently. Your former confidence that each action that you took as a soldier and each thing that you willed was also willed by God, though it may have bolstered your pride and enabled you to ignore the perils of battle, did little good for your soul."

"But I fought for England!" he cried with passion.

"And can England never do wrong?" I queried him. "The

man who surrenders his individual conscience to any political entity may be a better soldier but less of a human being for all of that. Each one of us is answerable for his single, particular, and unique soul. We do not storm heaven in battalions but as individuals by a passion and conviction that is ours alone. There is no distributive or associative property in the algebra of God; he allows us each to decide our ultimate fate. If you are to enter heaven it must be as a man and not as an Englishman.”

“So what you are telling me is that my experiences as a soldier are the source of my present affliction, am I correct in this supposition, Mr. Holmes?”

“Not entirely. Your dedication to your troops was to be expected and your confidence is essential to command. No soldier can enter into battle with the gnawing doubts that affect you now, but I wonder if you were always secretly a man whose moral sense made your choice of a career one that could not be reconciled with the religious convictions of your youth. A time was bound to come when the doubts that afflict you now would surface. The accident that you witnessed was merely the trigger that brought old memories of the horrors of battle to your mind and what you refused to feel then became your present reality.”

He listened to me attentively and I saw his eyes widen as though he had been transported back to northern India during the mutiny when he had been stationed to an obscure outpost on the frontier. No doubt the sounds of the battles from long ago echoed in his ears. At last he turned to me and said, “But if you are correct then all that has happened to me resides in some obscure corner of my soul. Where shall I seek relief?”

“You are fortunate in possessing a faith that squarely confronts the evils of this world. Who can behold a crucifix and see the pain depicted there and not see simultaneously not Jesus alone but all of humankind in their sorrow and abandonment. Your healing is not within my capacity to bestow and no mere insight will be adequate. Your life is a composite of all that has ever happened to you and it is only in prayer and in reliance upon God that healing will come to you, not all at once but in how you live your life from now on. You are not alone in this. Your life is unique but not different in kind from what others have endured and their presence will be a healing force to you because it is in others that we find the face of God."

He left us shortly after this. No doubt for the first time he felt the full weight of the souls he had ushered into a premature eternity as a commander in India. I might have been easier with him if I thought that a milder physic than the truth would cure him. He was not unlike many men of power who invoke God to justify the outrages upon life that human policies have brought about throughout history. We are all part of the contingencies of the world through commission and omission of our actions. What this earth might become if the full weight of the gospel teachings were brought to bear upon history not only through the agency of the canonized saints but by humankind at large we cannot say but it would surely be one less marred by violence, scarcity, and injustice than the one that we see all about us each day. God's desire is that we become holy and He has provided us with the world that we encounter. We do not have the leisure to wait for a better world to present itself to us before we act.

If even God in the person of Jesus Christ had to take His mission as it was in all of its disappointment, rejection, and apparent failure shall we await some propitious hour before we begin to address the vast sea laid out before us as a stage for our labors that remain to create a world worthy to welcome Jesus when He returns on the last day? Unfortunately I fear at times that the world grows worse every day and thus the Parousia is likely to be indefinitely deferred. Nor am I satisfied with my own actions in this regard. I fear that Watson's encomiums aside I do not always terminate my cases successfully. I was perhaps unable on that day to give our visitor an answer adequate to his need for congruity in his faith and I am haunted still by the sound of his stumbling feet upon our stair when he left that day and was lost a few moments later in the busy London streets.

I am still thinking of my client Colonel Warburton and the brief encounter that has no doubt been the last that I will see of him. There are many thoughts that I might have shared with him because I share many of his doubts and perplexities. I can only trust that I am not also a victim of madness. Here is an example among the many things that trouble me. It is one of the paradoxes of Christian history that with each decade and century the imminent return of Jesus has become less necessary because the stress has shifted from the General Judgment to be rendered to all of humanity on the Last Day to the Particular Judgment that each soul must face after death.

The enthusiasm of the early church communities and their nascent grasp of the faith had not yet been filtered through the brilliant later minds of a St. Augustine or a St. Thomas Aquinas. The intricate melodies of Gregorian-Chant and the rule of St. Benedict to be followed by the monastic communities were future gifts to the Church. Disputation over the role of Prevenient Grace and its interaction with human freedom of will had yet to divide the Western Church and its great religious orders. The various Protestant movements that styled themselves as a reformation had yet to divide Europe. Even the catacombs of Rome had yet to be filled with the crumbling flesh of the dead confessors to a forbidden faith. The Roman Empire still styled itself as the heir to all of human progress although whole regions of the world existed and knew nothing of Original Sin or that an obscure Mediterranean nation was to be the source of salvation to the world when the budding Christian communities would finally reach them or even imagine that they existed.

In the meantime theologians were busy weaving the web of certitudes regarding which souls and under what conditions they might hope for salvation without being guilty of presumption. Judaism, now dispersed and irrelevant other than its early role in foreshadowing the advent of Jesus Christ was about to begin its longest exile that continues to this very day. This is the faith that I wish to present to professor Moriarty and to men like the desperate man who came to me a few days ago as the source of not only immediate moral guidance but the answer to why anything exists at all.

Christianity is predicated on a new creation even while we have yet to successfully engage the present creation from with our native capacities. In contrast the various earthly religions that have grown up around the more grounded peoples of the earth ask less of humanity because they expect less in terms of a future existence as immortal Children of God. Even the complex recycling of souls in Hindu belief look to endless rebirths and only gradual improvement between lives, while in Christianity this process is foreshortened to a single lifetime during which the soul must fashion its eternal destiny and even then only by the inscrutable action of Divine Grace on the soul that in its workings inspires and strengthens while at the same time demanding maximum cooperation in order to avoid eternal damnation. I wonder at times if it has been the nexus or crossroads between conflicting modalities of thought that have made theological processes take the form that they have within the Catholic Church.

I have at times asked myself whether Christianity is historically explicable in secular terms or is it true that some initial supernatural visitation must first instigate the will to believe and only thereafter assemble a structure of assent to whatever is presented by the governing structures of the Church. Even to pose this question in solitude is to tread upon uneasy ground. I will not tarry upon it. Any process of review or self-reflection at an institutional level must be engaged in by those whose task it is to act as apostles to the rest of the human race. I claim no such commission. I have learned to be satisfied with far less from my fellow men and women and to be grateful for such evidence that they occasionally demonstrate that we are made for more than this world alone.

ontinuing with my thoughts from yesterday it has occurred
to me that the category of religious thought may best be
summarized as an effort to attain a unified answer across
various fields of human inquiry by referring to a hypothesized
source that stands ontologically speaking outside of direct human
experience. Even should such a unique world of being care to
contact us some manner of translation, most likely through the use
of analogy and metaphor, would be necessary to act as a bridge
between such separate levels of reality. Whatever communication
resulted might then be formalized into rigid structures that entail
actual consequences in the world in which we live, some of them
being questionable, for any such assertions to be derived from an
entirely transcendent world, objects, or relations would make only
the most marginal sense from within our present frame of
reference, one that is derived from worldly experience.

In this sense the composite of theological constructs are
vulnerable to being colored by the presuppositions or general
world-outlook, the weltanschauung in German, of the theologian.
This means that there is bound to be a certain level of distortion
caused by the personality structure of the theologian and those
who support his views. In speaking of God our own preconceptions
are often dispositive of the results to be obtained. If we add to this
observation the social imperatives of various groups and even of
entire nations it can readily be seen that a phenomenon of
theological drift and infusion of alien material is almost inevitable.
Now add-in the factor of prayer and of private religious experience
and the objective content of religion cannot be anything other than
one that has been severely compromised. This in turn leads to the
question of whether public policy is more likely to be effective if it
is divorced from any extraneous religious infusions.

The Danish philosopher, Soren Kierkegaard, recognized
this paradox; one that is caused by a radical separation of the
demands of religion and those of ethics when he spoke of "the
teleological suspension of the ethical" that was demanded by God
of Abraham when Abraham was asked to sacrifice His son as a sin-

offering. Can our trust in God ever be so absolute that we are willing to approve of conduct that departs from any rational ethical base in favor of one derived from revelation alone?

This problem is collective as well as individual. Any posited institutional competence in matters like faith may be even less reliable than that of individual saints because institutional behavioral norms follow their own inherent logic that can, absent extraordinary Divine guidance, bias and distort the results obtained. Matters pertaining to faith and eternal life then can only truly be judged from within the very structures and groups where these extraordinary truths are taught and practiced. Any outside principle of verification must be seen as an intruder and an unwelcome one at that. The effort to maintain unity is a challenge that only sacramental grace can achieve. For this we look to liturgical practices. The function of liturgical practices is to reify through a process of formal repetition a cohesive body of belief among those who profess those beliefs and to simultaneously reinforce a relationship between a transcendent reality and those who believe in it.

If this series of conclusions that I have reached is true, then I am unlikely to prevail in any efforts that I can make to convert Professor Moriarty. The best that I can manage is to lessen his resistance and to clear the way for God to act. No Christian witness has improved upon the means chosen by John the Baptist who summarized his own mission by pointing out that he was "like one crying out in the desert." Our only real capacity is to prepare for the coming of the Lord by making the way easier. It is pointless to argue about the reality of the very source of all reality! If God exists, then we must presume that He knows His own business better than we do and that He is unlikely to be deterred in achieving His chosen ends by any obstacles that we may erect.

oday I woke from restless dreams. A strange terror oppressed me, one seemingly without cause. I looked about me and nothing seemed altered. Everything was in its proper place. No deadly November wind blew yellowed leaves before me reminding me of the inhospitality and foreign quality that greets the stranger. I was surrounded by familiar things and friends were near. I was aware of my own resilience and resources demonstrated on countless occasions and yet the mere thought that others at that very moment were deprived of these very things made their pain and exile my own.

Colonel Warburton's Madness is not a unique phenomenon. I have felt something like it from time to time. It is not an easy thing to admit when one is out of one's depth. There is a basic trust it existence that each of us must maintain in order to function. Just as life itself can only be maintained within a very narrow range of temperature and the earth itself is dependent upon certain rhythmic contractions such as tides and seasons that mirror the beating of the heart, the mind has certain parameters of stress beyond which its essential functions break down.

I have made it a habit to keep a center-post or fixed compass of conceptions and values, those very axioms from which Professor Moriarty would gladly escape to which I may retreat when these spells of metaphysical vertigo threaten to overwhelm me. I have read various memoirs that express the limits of the mental apparatus. Sometimes the most trivial perturbation can send the mind reeling off towards an abyss of loneliness or despair that must have its roots in experiences that precede the formation of language. I must confess to feeling an overwhelming pity for the human race that sometimes reaches a point where the only prayer that I can offer to God is that of the Buddhist, a sort of cosmic pity for existence, the prayer that death may come swiftly and that consciousness once extinguished will never be renewed or followed by rebirth.

The human person is not a single entity in the last analysis but an entire lineage of selves united by memories that leave their structural deficits behind so that the present crisis is only a further iteration on a familiar theme. The tears shed today had their origin in an event or series of events at a time or place entirely forgotten until some haunting resemblance triggers them once again and all of the obstacles that we may have erected to contain their anguish are of no avail. Literature has provided a physic for me at such times and I turn for guidance to the writings of Friedrich Holderlin, who died in 1843; or to his predecessor in death, Georg von Hardenberg who wrote under the pen name of Novalis, who died in 1801. They were born only two years apart in 1770 and 1772. It is comforting to know that others have known and endured these strange mental states and that their genius is at least partially attributable to their affliction.

August 1, 1896
London

I have received no commitment yet from Dr. Vernet about offering to purchase Watson's medical practice. He has thanked me for my proposal though and has agreed to keep my name out of the matter. He has written to Watson to introduce himself as a relative of mine who has just completed his medical residency in Quimper and to inquire if Watson might know of any small medical practice that he might purchase in London. Watson came in quite bursting with the news. I pretended ignorance of course and acted preoccupied with an experiment that I was conducting.

Watson is a most earnest fellow and I cannot resist at times the temptation to test his toleration of my own whims and fancies. In this case I felt a need to test just how far his own need to escape London had progressed. Also I must admit that I am stalling for time before leaving London because I fear that my period of convalescence may be an extended one.

I looked up from my experiment and responded to his eager announcement of his meeting the young doctor. "Ah yes Watson, Vernet is a splendid young chap. He rather reminds me of you when I first met you at the urging of my friend Stamford. He is just the sort to make house-calls and to ramble about London to visit the ill or attend women during their laying-in period. No doubt one of your peers will take him on as an associate internist."

"Or perhaps, he might care to take over my own practice?" Watson said hesitantly.

I was watching him out of the corner of my eye and said absently, "How's that? What did you say?"

"I said that he might perhaps make me an offer for my practice," he replied. "After all the location is excellent and the rent not prohibitive and my collection of medical instruments is all that could be desired."

I appeared to have some reservations, "Oh I hardly think that would do, after all he is only an untried quantity, but I do seem to recall that he has an Aunt in Rouen who is rather well-fixed in funds. She might be willing to advance him a small sum. Perhaps in the meantime you should search elsewhere among your older medical acquaintances for a more tried and able prospect. Besides, an old horse like you would no doubt miss being in harness."

He went on insistently. "Well I could begin again elsewhere if my practice was taken over gradually by a younger man. I might take a turn in a village infirmary just to keep abreast of developments, perhaps somewhere on the Cornish seacoast. I am a bit tired of the typical run of cases that an urban milieu presents ... or perhaps I could treat the tin-miners for a time in Cornwall," he stated reflectively.

I looked up with an air of opposition to this plan. "Dreams Watson, these are mere idle dreams! I can hardly spare you to go pottering about Cornwall when I am strengthening daily. I have as you know several cases in hand that will require your presence. No, I am afraid I simply cannot manage without my Boswell at my side."

He was silent for a bit, then with a nervous clearing of his throat he announced, "Holmes, as your physician I must warn you that it is you who must potter about for a time in the provinces. I have seen your pallor lately in the morning and the hectic flush of fever when you return in the evenings. You simply must cut back on your labors."

"Nonsense Watson, I feel fine. One must make hay while

the sun shines as they say. Have I labored these last two years to get my detective practice up and running again only to be mollycoddled because of a slight cough?"

"You have been coughing also?" he cried with alarm. "Are you running an intermittent fever? I trust there are no signs of hemorrhaging."

"Oh nothing to speak of; it is only when I have been exerting myself unduly that I am troubled by a cough, such as that matter the other day out in Camden Town. I am afraid that I had to use my walking stick to subdue the fellow before putting him in charge of a constable. No doubt I need to eat a bit more as well, but my appetite has been off lately," I replied honestly.

I am afraid that I was not feigning these symptoms and I am not such a fool that I cannot read their import. In any case they alarmed Watson sufficiently that he got out his stethoscope upon the spot and had me breathe a bit while he listened to my chest and back.

"I don't like the sound, Holmes. There is a decided congestion in the right upper lobe," I think you should lay up for a bit."

I answered him at once, "Out of the question my dear fellow. There are certain matters which have reached a most critical stage in my investigation of the moment. I simply may not desist."

Then after looking again at his concerned face, I sought to reassure him, "Oh very well, I will consider taking a holiday, but not for some weeks at least. Let me just clear my blotter and I shall accompany you to a site of your choosing. Perhaps the Cornish air will do the trick if that would be agreeable to you. In the meantime, you may, if you are so determined to retire, write to young Vernet and request that he come over to London to meet with you about a future sale of your practice, though I must say that Kensington will be the poorer for your loss, should anything materialize."

We attended a Paganini concert afterwards and I am embarrassed to admit that I had to go out to the lobby twice when I was visited by a fit of coughing. I trust that it is just the remnants of a recent cold but my past experience with tuberculosis counsels caution. It would be really too bad to need to rein in just now. My mind seems honed to a razor edge. Success has lately crowned every case that I have undertaken to solve, so that I am finally developing a regular clientele drawn from among the great families of England, thanks to my delicate handling of the rather private affair posed by the case of young Ronald Adair.

I have even been recently made a member of the Legion of Honor in France thanks to my trifling efforts to deal with Hurat, the boulevard assassin, who instilled so much terror in Paris during the spring of this year. Then there was that matter of the Vatican Cameos in which I was able to aid His Holiness Pope Leo XIII. No, I simply cannot desist at this time. I must press on. Besides, it is only one year until the Diamond Jubilee of Queen Victoria will be celebrated. Next year, I may need to devote all of my efforts to Professor Moriarty again and give up all other cases, thus my desire to work now before that final struggle begins.

August 14, 1896
London

Today was one of those oppressive days in London where the heat seems to draw forth from the pavement every noxious odor and to sublimate these into one common element with which to oppress the spirits of man. Summer which seems to be the season of growth and fruition assaults us with a sense of all of our unused potential, which we know we must review when winter comes again upon us. What then of that perpetual autumn of our seniority when only regrets are our daily fare? What penance is sufficient even for a life that one deems to have been adequate when assessed within the average parameters of humanity?

Watson is busy again now with his professional calls and I alone am stranded here in Baker Street with diminishing prospects. The result is that I have excess time on my hands for introspection, which is always a dangerous business to engage in for me. I am forced back upon the strange emptiness that must infect any man whose personal attachments in life and whose affections have been minimal. I have found that my mind when unoccupied begins to feed upon itself as though the enzymes with which I solve problems for others are, when applied to my own case, effective only to dissolve the fragments of my being into a general soup of *ennui* and indecision. Is it possible to maintain an identity apart from passion and self-interested pursuits? A man without a family to support possesses leisure at his own peril. How shall he profitably exercise the immense surplus of forces at his disposal? Nature has designed him to be knocked about with the various small tragedies of the day in his domestic circle. The husband is meant to be the court of last resort between a tearful spouse and children clamoring for justice. In that small courtroom of paternal wisdom my docket is empty and without advocates seeking my considered judgment and I feel the vacuum most on such a day as this. Perhaps Watson is right and we both need a change of scene from London by retreating to the west of England to enjoy its unspoiled beauty.

Whatever charm I formerly found in the confines of the great city of London has been diminished by my travels in desolate places. Industrial development is a cancerous growth upon the land. It mirrors the mindset of that most peculiar variety of mankind, the investor of capital. Money when it is liberated from the intimate ownership of land can float about freely and cause no end of harm. The logic of capital is profit and the source of that profit becomes irrelevant to the savvy investor who merely meets quarterly with his accountant or manager to see how much his net worth has increased. Entire factories are closed and tenants are evicted from housing as business logic is applied without regard to the moral consequences of those actions no matter what havoc may ensue to dependent families. Any government that is colonized by capital interests must inevitably succumb to indifference towards the public weal and the aspect of the city will mirror that neglect. London has become a great octopus or leviathan that devours everything around it as whole villages are absorbed and the rural districts tremble at its approach. Eventually a sort of urban rot sets in and the spirit of art withers away. The soul of man must receive occasional stimulation by great and sublime scenes of majestic beauty such as Mont Blanc where great glaciers remind us of our true stature when measured against the great untamed forces of the earth. Great conceptions take their origin from nature and petty despots feed upon whatever can be easily purchased and subdued.

September 1, 1896
London

The general state of my health is still a matter of concern and my cough has worsened. I am even reduced to depending on surrogates to do much of my field work. This cannot continue. It has always been my ability to see what others do not that has been the basis of my craft. Deductive reasoning is an ability that is common to mankind and can be indulged in by any competent investigator. The real difficulty for the competent detective comes from those inductive methods by which the mental shelves are stocked, from which he may draw when presented with a new set of circumstances. The imagination of mankind is after all limited. Crimes, because they stem for the most part from ungoverned passions, show a remarkable similarity over time. It is to this fact that the mentally deficient agents of Scotland Yard owe their occasional successes. If I have a weakness as an investigator, it is that I often assume that a set of circumstances is complex when in fact it is not, merely because I desire that complexity may rescue me from *ennui*.

September is not a good month for consumptives because the rapid changes, from summer warmth to foggy mornings, capture the coal dust in the air so that outdoor activities, at least if undertaken within the suburbs of Westminster, are ill-advised. Nor do I have the energy to travel to the many places from which summons have lately come. The result is that I am thrown back too much upon my own society. I pace about my rooms and brood. I am forever going to the blinds and looking out upon the busy streets. At last I am driven to this journal to see if there is any circumstance of note that has not found some reflection in this correspondence with myself.

It occurs to me that I have not commented here on the career of the brother of Professor Moriarty. No doubt his age has been a factor in this regard combined with the fact that he did not take up the same profession as his brother. The younger brother of

Professor Moriarty is a stationmaster in the West of England on the border of Wales. I only discovered his existence by telegram. He consulted me, completely unaware that I was well acquainted with the brother whom he sought.

Life is filled with such strange cross-hatchings and synchronicities of fate. The younger Moriarty was brought up in America by his mother's brother who had fled Ireland at the time of the great famine. He grew up and fought in the American civil war and later was promoted to the rank of Colonel upon the American frontier in the eighteen-seventies. He took his pension early and returned to England, invalided out as they say. He was not able to be a mail-carrier but he was at least able to qualify and perform the duties of a country station master, a humble but a useful occupation.

When I met him I could see little resemblance between the two men. Genius is like a lightening bolt and seldom strikes twice within the same family. Still he was intelligent if not imaginative and showed no signs of his brother's criminal tendencies. He also knew nothing of his father's drinking and brutal ways. His case put me in something of a quandary. So innocent and earnest was the fellow that I could see little benefit in acquainting him with the dark side of his ancestry. He imagined that his father and mother had both perished in the famine, but hoped that some kind soul might have adopted his brother after the death of their parents. If it seems strange that the younger son was sent to America rather than the older son it was because he was the stronger and seemed most able to bear up and to survive the long sea journey to America. Perhaps the mother assumed that by choosing different avenues to escape from Ireland's famine, at least one of her sons would survive. In the event both did.

I did not wish to lie to him though, so I told him that I could not take his case, without explaining why, and doubted if anyone not privy to inside knowledge could find his brother, which was an indirect truth, for considering the chaos of Ireland at the time, death claimed many and left no traces behind. I left him disappointed, but with his illusions intact. He will die without the burden of his brother's guilt to stain his own conscience. He had let me know in passing that he had already seen his share of atrocities during the war and later in the course of the displacement of the American Indian tribes before he was discharged. This let me know that the course that I had chosen was the correct one. There are burdens that might submerge the general faith in humankind that makes our collective existence supportable. No man can be a complete realist in all respects. Illusion might therefore best be defined as "a deferred exposure to reality by degrees." A very wise man once told me that life is a process of disillusionment, but that you must keep a few or you will go mad. It was not a sanguine assessment of life, but it was eminently practical. I am not at all sure that my own determination to understand the ways of darkness has not put me in a vulnerable position in more ways than one. Perhaps my tubercular infection is a displacement, a secondary reaction, a localization of a generalized infection brought on by too much exposure to evil and disease in human life. Illusions once lost are impossible to regain and innocence it seems to me is the primal gift of the angels and should not be lost to obtain a mere gratuitous wisdom. No one life can sum up all things, therefore to keep some remnant of the child alive within us is not to be despised, even by the philosopher.

December 21, 1896
London

I have become a stranger to this journal again, but since it is being kept for my eyes alone I need make no apologies. Perhaps it has already served its greater purpose. It has been my workbook, a place to try out ideas, many still only partially formulated in my mind. In it I have revealed those secrets that are harbored within every heart. Have they been tedious secrets after all? Is any life worthy of so intent a perusal? Does the recording angel of heaven sometimes grow weary and sleep at his task? I pray that he may do so in my case. So much of the course of my life has been only a mere repetition of a few central themes. How often has the same chorus been sung! It is now the nadir of the year and my energies have withered with the shortening days of autumn. Daily I have hoped for a word from Professor Moriarty so that I might relinquish the burden of responsibility that I feel. I know that all of England may be in ruins by this time next year if he should carry out his plan. I have never doubted that Professor Moriarty might use the great mind that he possesses to accomplish the end that he has long had in view. Still, I am determined to celebrate this Christmas with the same joy that I knew two years ago when I first returned to Baker Street. Since then Watson has always been at my side. If he chooses to write-up my recent cases, his readers will find the granary to be full indeed. But my labors have been at a great personal cost to me. I may not deceive myself any more. I am again plagued by consumption of the lungs.

Later—

Watson spoke to me sternly only last night. He says I must take an extended holiday at once and relinquish my practice or he will not be responsible for the result. I no longer have any choice in the matter. We shall see out the Christmas season here in London and then I am to accompany Watson to Cornwall. Young Dr. Vernet has agreed to purchase Watson's medical practice and he will arrive in London by the Dover boat-train on January second. Watson and I will celebrate my birthday with Mycroft here in London and then we shall leave for our holiday and my recuperation may begin.

Watson has purchased a lovely cottage by a bay near Poldhu in Cornwall with the down payment money for his medical practice. It is just the sort of place that he has always wanted to own, with walnut bookcases, a small wine cellar, and perhaps eventually a Springer Spaniel to accompany him on his walks and to lie by his chair at night. I in turn have transferred my most pressing cases to Inspector Lestrade, who in his later years has finally decided that my methods have something to recommend them after all and to freely admit it. He maintains a small private practice of his own now and he is willing to take the torch for a time from my hands. So it is that I am free again.

The lease on my cottage at Grimpen will end by Candlemas and I may resume residence there again if my health is not sufficiently improved by my visit with Watson to Cornwall. It will be good to see Sir Henry again and to hunt pheasants and grouse upon the moor. Perhaps, I was meant to be a country squire after all, but on a scale that allows me time for scholarship. I have acquired some fascinating early English Charters whereby towns were allowed to flourish, made up of freemen who owned the grazing land in common. It was the beginning of the breakdown of the strict feudal system. How sad it is that what began as the commons has now been taken up into the new feudalism of the rising industrial bourgeoisie! Where I wonder shall new charters be found to free the current slaves of industry of the capital markets? Ah well, one may speculate. I hope to write a manifesto of sorts someday on this topic. How strange it would be if I ended up as a Voltaire of the present age!

December 23, 1896
Whitechapel

How swiftly the seasons of the year rotate round us. Christmas is only two days away. The best use of the holiday spirit is to spread the benefits that the year has brought. I came over by hansom cab to visit the mission in the east-end of London here today. It is maintained by the St. Vincent de Paul Society. I find that the best preparation for Christmas is to be assured that some of the bounties of the year will be shared with others. I have always had a devotion to the fine wine that comes from the sunny slopes of Madeira. A local wine merchant gave me an excellent price on a case of amber bottles and I was also able to supply ten fine geese from a farm in Kent to the mission. These with some of the other fruits of the season brought by other hands should make it a warmer and brighter Christmas for those who come here for dinner on Christmas Day. Too often the poorer citizens of London only glimpse from afar the leavings of better set tables. These rely daily on a monotonous diet of stale fish and gin. One day of the year is not too often for sampling better fare, which please God, may someday be the rule should a more just and prosperous equity come to the foreground in these isles.

year ago today Watson and I spent our first visit together in many years to Baskerville Hall for a Christmas in a traditional fashion in an old English ancestral country house. It is a visit that will long take its place in my memory, one reserved for special joyful events. The great Devonshire Estate of the Baskervilles has prospered under the excellent managing skill of Sir Henry. On this special day a massive table had been installed in the great central hall for a feast not seen since the days of Sir Hugo Baskerville. Extra staff had been hired for the occasion and the huge ovens were busy for two days before the feast without intermission.

I can still recall the savory iced pike dressed in dill with onions, the roast suckling pig cooked with apples and chestnuts, and the several rib roasts of beef stuffed with garlic and slowly cooked over two kitchen fires. There was also a leg of lamb garnished with rosemary and mint and a bevy of fowl of all sorts and sizes, turkeys, pheasants, and geese. These were brought down by a small shooting party in previous days. Watson and I held our own with members of the local hunting club for game birds. Sir Henry's dogs led us into the frozen December fields and flushed out pheasants, partridges, and grouse. These were added to the domestic ducks and geese from the small lake located on the estate.

The table seated fifty persons and the local gentry of three counties had come to enjoy Christmas at Baskerville Hall. A string band regaled us with Christmas carols from the gallery throughout the meal and holly wreaths festooned the grim grey walls so that they seemed to spring to unwonted life. Two overhead chandeliers brought light to the gay and festive company below and a huge fire of scotch-fir burned in the huge fireplace until the last toasts had been made to the host and his good lady.

Later on Watson and I had sat up late in the library with Sir Henry reminiscing about the unrecorded cases in my unique dossier and in so doing examining the question of the value to humanity of the so-called mystery story beginning with Edgar

Allen Poe and brought to a high point of excellence by Wilkie Collins and by the Irish writer Joseph Sheridan Le Fanu. I can still recall the comfort afforded by the substantial fire that burned in the grate behind the unique andirons of twin stags at bay. The smoke from the Turkish mixture of Xanthi, Samsoun, and Latakia that I have favored since my Eastern journey curled upwards towards the ceiling with its elaborate carvings.

It seemed a long time until morning and we inhabited that strange leisure that comes at Christmas time when one year is ending and the next year has not begun. It is a time well-suited to reflection and this process is never more congenial than when one is surrounded by good friends before whom no pretence is ever necessary and the heart may unburden itself without giving offence to them or embarrassment to oneself.

The course of our conversation stirs even now in the ashes of memory. "Holmes has always taken me to task for surrounding his cases with romance," said Watson, "But surely the romance was usually present in the very facts themselves and I as a writer merely allowed the romance of circumstances to show through in my narrative of events. Besides who would care to read mere propositions from Euclid as Holmes advised? I flatter myself that I have helped to make the name of Sherlock Holmes by this good year of 1895 one that is on everyone's lips. What will he do next?"

"Take care, Sir Henry, or Watson will do the same for you, I warned our host. "I have recently caught him scribbling away at a tale that he calls, *The Hound of the Baskervilles.*"

"Well, I would never bring it forth without Sir Henry's permission," Watson protested.

"I should never think of withholding my consent since it might serve to discharge some measure of my debt of gratitude to the men who saved my life and by doing so has preserved the estate of Baskerville and saved it from a South American adventurer and usurper," interposed Sir Henry. "Besides, the horror that adds so much to the mystery story is no doubt inherent in the facts presented so that no one will accuse the good doctor here of producing another facile romance."

"Are we agreed then, gentlemen, that the mystery story owes its primary charm to atmosphere?" I inquired. "But if that is so then what becomes of the scientific reasoner who, if he is to be led by romance, will soon find his solutions biased in the direction that is dictated by the charm of the tale and not by the sheer naked truth of the solution. Surely a thing may be true and not simultaneously appealing to our hunger for the dramatic. The sense of the dramatic after all is produced by the surprise invoked in the reader who finds that his expectations may have been disappointed but not so violated as to produce a sense that the author has held something back that was essential to the solution. All essential facts then must be present in the story but unconnected until the solution is presented at last and the pattern emerges in a startling revelation of truth. If this is so then the best mystery story is the one that presents hitherto unglimpsed truth and atmosphere becomes a mere convention of the stagecraft of the amateur. Is a puzzle less compelling because it appears in the prosaic garb of the everyday unaccompanied by thunder and gothic castles? This is all that I have tried to explain to Dr. Watson when I have commented on his own style of composition."

Watson objected. "But surely it helps when an aura of nobility surrounds the facts; would Hamlet be equally compelling if he was not a Prince of Denmark? Humanity desires that it be represented by certain ideal types and not by the vague and boring character present in most people. Even history proceeds by means of the extremes in human personality. A well-balanced and sane man cannot move the masses. It takes a demagogue to command the excesses of loyalty that leads to wars and great social movements. So it is also that the mystery story must excite the passions of terror in order to reach the sublimity that we term mysterious."

I took note of his point. "I see that you are well up on the aesthetic doctrines of the poet Wordsworth who valued those great forms of tree and cavern in nature that call up the emotion of the sublime. But you must remember that my professional practice is designed to bring comfort in the form of truth to those who consult me and not necessarily to amuse and gratify your readers. That said I have no objection to the frisson produced by adventure. It is one of the remedies to the ennui of everyday life. Nay, I will go further still: a life without romance is unworthy of a human being.

Our aesthetic demands are not confined to canvass and manuscript. We demand that the true shall be beautiful and that the beautiful shall be true although they are not identical, Keats' opinion notwithstanding. To adopt an attitude of studious banality is to become inhuman. Art must permeate life if life is to be vital, meaningful, and even holy. It is no accident for instance that there has been no greater stimulus to art than religion. It is for this reason that most heresy begins with some form of iconoclasm. In the desire to rid itself of the image, the iconoclast reduces God to a pure idea without substance and impact upon the mind and the heart. This is why Christian orthodoxy always abjures those who desire to purge the flesh away from the virtues and to create a perfectionistic system of laws and ritual with no reference back to the human condition."

I continued, "As an example, let us consider the Protestant denial of the doctrine of the real presence of Jesus Christ in the species of the Holy Eucharist: what is left from that denial but a sterile reenactment of the Last Supper stripped of the very significance of the gift bestowed on that occasion to all of humanity throughout history? The institution of the greatest sacrament is a type of second incarnation, one no less wondrous than the first. If God can become man, then surely He may also substitute one species for another and alter bread and wine into his own sacred Body and Blood."

"But we were speaking of the mystery story in literature, were we not, gentlemen?" interjected Sir Henry.

"Yes, but in so doing we have now plunged into the question of the sublimity of truth and it is my contention that Christianity shows its truth by its ability to advance the ordinary and to add to truth first sublimity and then to go further still and to make the ordinary elements of life holy," I answered him. "This was never made clearer than when Our Lord assured us that many who are now first would be last. Jesus seems to enjoy upsetting premature certitudes. I am not at all sure that the presumption of preference in God is not the attitude that Jesus most abhors in the gospels. Openness to God requires humility based upon trust in God alone. The demands of faith are as extreme as they are then, not because faith is irrational, but because God desires that our trust shall be personal and not arrived at through simple human powers of induction and deduction. This is why the sacraments exceed our reason and turn ritual not into mere symbol, but into reality itself with the central words of consecration at mass of this is my body and this is my blood."

"So if I am to understand you correctly you are saying that the mystery genre depends upon atmosphere and the exaltation of the subject by an artificial aura of nobility, whereas truth is often quite humble and holiness humbler still," remarked Sir Henry.

"An excellent summation Sir Henry; I see that you have followed my argument closely. Let me then pose the next question of why does God appear to favor the ordinary and to take delight in the simple? Why for instance did Jesus choose a fisherman upon whom to build His Church? Why were his most intimate friends Martha, Mary, and Lazarus? Why so little time spent with the great and learned and so much spent with people whose understanding must have been entirely inadequate to the message that He hoped to convey? The answer is one of priorities. Love is not an intellectual exercise; or as the brilliant philosopher, Pascal once said so well, 'The heart has reasons that reason knows not of.' I will go so far as to say that Jesus was so negligent in his own definition of His Divine Personhood that it took the Catholic Church three hundred years to clarify its own belief under the guidance of the Holy Spirit. Why was this so? Was it not because Jesus may have shared with Watson his penchant for romance? How else shall we account for a religion that defines God the Father as love, not an idea, barely a substance, but instead as an activity—God as loving? Can anything more vital and less confined be conceived? Thus it is not surprising that God could become an infant in a manger, laid among the animals in a stable. It is what one would expect who knows God's penchant for the ordinary, which then becomes the Holy under the influence of the love of the God who is love."

"So are the gospels an example of the mystery genre?" Watson inquired.

"They are the account in the gospels of the *Mysterium Tremendum et Fascinans* of God and thus are mystery tales," I answered.

"But are they only stories for all of that?" asked Sir Henry.

"Dare we believe them? Does not their very craft betray them as fictions?"

I answered him, "Some would have it that the gospels are unworthy of belief based on the theory that such a great tension between expectation and actuality must be a fabrication, but I suggest to you that anything less startling and contradictory would be unworthy of God and would make faith unnecessary. God gives all and hence asks for much in return and jars us loose from our complacency."

"Must our understanding proceed so far into such subtleties though before we can simply celebrate Christmas?" asked Sir Henry.

"On the contrary, Sir Henry, it is more important that one feel and express love than that one be able to define it as we have just done. Therefore, whatever our beliefs may be, let us toast Our Lord's birth in Bethlehem and get us off to bed like all good folk, for I see that the fire is dying. The ashes lie pale upon the grate."

We all rose then for the toast.

"A Merry Christmas to us all and a blessing for those less favored than we have been this chill December night; may God be their refuge and their strength."

Thus did our Christmas celebration end that evening, a year past. Nor were the villagers left without provender on Christmas Day. Two huge tents had been set up on the grounds of the estate and many were the kegs of ale tapped that night with great loaves of bread, breaded flounder from the coast, a hearty venison stew, and a proper Christmas plum-pudding set aflame with brandy. A mime troupe was hired to amuse the children and treats were distributed carved by local craftsmen and paid for by Sir Henry.

All the tenants and townsfolk had prospered since that estimable gentleman's accession to the manor-house of the local shire. There followed several days of that joy that comes with good company and excellent conversation. Several houseguests stayed until the Twelfth Night celebrations and some until the Feast of the Epiphany, though we were obliged to return to London with Mycroft. Each evening the whole company was regaled by ghost stories serially told or readings from the poetry of Tennyson or

Browning. We would end each evening with glasses of Port or Madeira and an excellent cheese from Gloucester dotted with cranberries. Then up to bed to enjoy the dreamless sleep of the country where no sounds of traffic cause one to wake to the sound of a carriage wheel grating against the curb bringing home late revelers of the Christmas Season. The English, townsmen and countrymen alike, know as well as any people on earth how to celebrate Christmas. Life must admit of its seasons of largess as well as its times of thrift and fasting. Our feast this year as well though spent in Baker Street will not disappoint us I am sure and there is something to be said for Christmas in the town when all of the Church bells ring-out on the day commemorating Christ's birth for our salvation.

December 25, 1896
Christmas Day

oday Watson and I were joined by Mycroft for dinner at Baker Street. Mrs. Hudson outdid herself I must say. It has taken some years, but she has finally emerged as excellent a cook as anyone could enjoy. We had managed well with two geese with plum sauce and tapped a keg of excellent Yorkshire Ale sent down to London by Sherringford whose persistent gout prevented his undertaking the trip to London. We were however joined by Inspector Hopkins who has remained a bachelor all these years. He is truly wedded to the Yard. We all toasted Mrs. Hudson who joined us for dinner, although she was forever jumping up again to rush down to the kitchen with Watson who good fellow that he is had volunteered his services to serve as steward and the general factotum of our Christmas feast.

We all ate our fill and then sat by a warm coal fire and recalled cases from the past with their own unique features. How strange it is that from various crimes those of us in the realm of detection manage to distill a potent elixir of delight. But this pleasure is really that of the craftsman who should not be grudged the pleasure of a job well done. It is the chase after all that delights the best fox-hound and not the kill. Not upon reflection that my precious days have been spent in Baker Street engaged in detection alone. There have also been those many hours of quiet contemplation over various experiments with my chemical apparatus, the drama of creating various characters to sally forth into the London streets, and the inestimable company of my dear friend, Dr. Watson.

Mycroft left us at nine and I was in bed by ten under strict orders from Watson. The net result is that Baker Street is quiet tonight with only a single cab to be heard now and again bringing home the joyous revelers to break the stillness in my room. I did not cough so much today. I have these periodic times of respite and they are increasingly dear to me. I shall sleep peacefully tonight, thank God. Good night then and a Merry Christmas to us all.

December 30, 1896
London

I received an unusual post-Christmas letter from Sherringford today that I will transcribe here. His letters always inspire me with a certain degree of dread because they are never casual and usually they are indicative of some change or problem at the estate or some reservation towards whatever course my present mode of life betokens when seen from the august seat of his superior position.

My Dear Sherlock,

I am writing this to you on December 28th, the Feast Day of the Holy Innocents. You will recall that these were the children killed by order of King Herod in his efforts to kill the young Jesus shortly after His birth in Bethlehem. I returned to Sigerside after making my annual years-end obligatory appearance at the local Anglican Church vicarage in Sigerside Village to have high tea with the Vicar and his wife. I went into the library upon my return home and began turning over in my mind this whole question of the death of the world's innocents. I did so in the light of the assurance of Our Savior that unless each of us accepts the Kingdom of God as a little child, he shall never enter it. On its face this statement seems to demand that each of us retain or reacquire at least the dispositions of that age when we are most dependent upon others to supply our needs and wants. This has always been for me one of the hardest sayings of the gospels as it must be for any man who desires above all else to leave behind that season of supplications and refusals that is the chief burden of childhood dependence.

I do not consider myself to be exceptional in possessing the desire of some measure of independence in life and it has been a source of comfort and satisfaction to me that I have been able to acquire sufficient resources that I need appeal to no man for the essentials of shelter and sustenance. My needs are simple since I am not impressed with vulgar social displays. My wants are kept within reason and my wishes are met by simply calling my banker or my legal counsel and entrusting the matter to them. I am quite willing of course to adopt a supplicating posture before my God, but when I deal with my fellow men I prefer to be the master. I have seen enough of the insolence of office to know that when it comes to sheer arbitrariness and cupidity, those in power are without equal and that this type of man takes delight in lording it over others.

I am grateful that the accident of my station at birth has prevented me from having to go out into the world as you and Mycroft have done in order to procure my livelihood. It is a sign of this gratitude that I have always attempted to administer the Holmes estate so as to share its benefits with my younger brothers rather than to presume upon the privileges bestowed upon me by primogeniture by creating a reservoir of funds for my own superficial display of wealth. But that said I see the world becoming a most harsh and bitter place for those without the solace of property. A moment's reflection will reveal that the difference between an English gentleman and a mere denizen of our far-flung empire is one of capital as much as it is derived from superior education and breeding.

For this reason I have long practiced a thrift and economy in my personal expenditures. Still, I would not wish to imperil the salvation of my soul by purchasing earthly security here at the cost of enjoying heaven later. How then am I to interpret this gospel admonition about becoming like a little child? Does that station not invite a renewed risk of dependency? This I loathe above all else to do! You will recall that our childhood, after the death of our dear mother, was one that although not characterized by paternal harshness, still manifested the chilly and restrained nature of our father to his sons.

All of the joy of our house seemed to perish with her when she died and the last years of our father were a testimony to his desolation and desire to endure in silence what he found unendurable in the loss of his wife. We as his sons were left to our own devices as lads as we attempted to find a set of personal values and to achieve that practical knowledge that is necessary to face an indifferent world. Shall I then seek out now the childhood which I was denied in its natural time and season?

Perhaps if like you I had joined the Church of Rome I might by now have found in submission to the clergy the spiritual childhood to which Jesus referred, but I am still nominally in the Church of England and my position in the House of Lords for the region demands that well-established loyalty to the Queen as spiritual and temporal sovereign of her people. As part of this conviction as to the exigencies of my role I am asked to believe that the Queen of England is supreme over the Church in England. But what is the effect of this belief but to place Her Majesty upon the same footing in these isles as the Pope is over the rest of Christendom? Is England so special then that the Queen alone shall possess a merger of material and spiritual authority in a single hereditary dynasty? I see no evidence in the gospels for such an unusual disposition of power over the souls of Englishmen over against the rest of mankind. Shall I then reject her authority and plunge into the sea of heretical beliefs that prevail in the rest of Protestantism? I think not! Better to have an inadequate source of authority than to join those tiny sailing-craft skimming the waters of the great seas of doubt guided by the ignus fatui of individual biblical interpretation, which only pools the collective ignorance of the masses into temporary coalitions followed by new schisms. For the first time therefore the summons of Rome increasingly raises a clarion-call to my reason in religious matters. Yet I am an Englishman above all else, and a titled one at that, and less free than idle theological scholars who may seek the truth without the burden of my exterior obligations.

Not that my compromised position is unique. I realize that Mycroft is even more committed than I have been to the current government heretofore and to the course of present English history since he is engaged in helping to make it. But I detect in some of his recent correspondence to me a quickening of doubts about our policies in Africa. I do not envy him his place in great affairs of state. Indeed I begin to feel that a man's scope should be such that the majority of his time and efforts should be spent doing local good to those with whom he comes into daily face-to-face contact. In wider policy discussions it is far too easy to make broad assertions about other nations and peoples, even as regards places to which we have never personally traveled. Every atrocity takes its root in some premature generalization. There is a tendency for direct contact to result in compromise because one must gaze into another's eyes and perhaps hear the accents of one's own native tongue in another's voice and demeanor.

Distance and secrecy are the modes chosen by the tyrants of this world. By these means it is possible to deny the sovereign humanity of other men and women. It seems to me that the failure of empathy towards the sufferings of others is really evidence of a lack of imagination. We prefer to behave as though some sort of righteous armor protects us, that some sort of impenetrable membrane keeps us as separate cells of humanity rather than what we are: one common tissue knit by nerve and sinew with all men and women wherever they may reside. I have been as likely as others to feel this restricted zone of sympathy. Which of us after all actively seeks out suffering humanity as did the Good Samaritan among the many potential victims upon the road of life? Pray allow me to give a homely example of my current trend of thought so that I may make myself clearer.

Last year about this time I was riding about in the north pasture at Sigerside through the last of the fallen leaves of the beech trees there (that no doubt you recall) when my horse suddenly pulled up lame. I had to lead him home through the evening frost and by the time I had him stabled my boots were wet and my feet were quite frost-bitten. I had thought that I had recovered without any permanent injury to my feet, but this year I find that I possess a great sensitivity to cold in them. I seem at the least chill to feel that peculiar pain and burning of the feet characteristic of those that are similarly afflicted by neuropathy. Well, I find a similar sense of sensitivity and outrage lately in contemplating the events of the day as reported in the papers with their incessant catalogue of waste, violence, and pain. My mind is no more proof to impressions than my feet are to cold. I find that I have lost a sense of comfortable immunity to the human condition as a result. My own security profits me nothing when my imagination roams at large over the county and the condition of those within its borders. The very walls and gables of Sigerside seem to admit the same chill winds as those that moan about the grass-roofed cottages on the high moorlands that surround our own wooded parkland. Even the solace of my wine-cellar calls to mind the depths of the coal mines of Northumberland. Everywhere there are reminders of those who do not share the blessings that I formerly considered to set a bare minimum of a comfortable prosperity.

As painful as these reflections are, I am glad that I am feeling them now and that my conscience is showing me wherein I may have been remiss as a complacent Lord of England. I am happy to be able to seek a proper restitution in due season and not to find these matters assailing my conscience upon my death bed. That these doubts and trepidations should arise in me now should not occasion surprise in you, my brother. The usual burdens of age are beginning to descend upon me and I feel more than I once did the rigors of the Yorkshire winter. I find that do what I might I cannot dispel a chill lately that seems to invade my very bones. Nor do the superficial joys of Christmastide provide a remedy for my present discontent.

It has long been my opinion that much of the festivity that goes with Christmas is an effort to escape the natural trials of the dying season of the year, to hide beneath the façade of ivy and holly trimmings the sense of death that surrounds one in the very depths of winter when another year is ending and the coming year as one grows older seems less likely to beckon with elaborate promises than to add one more to our season of vain regrets.

Experience has taught me that extravagant hopes are seldom fulfilled. Instead one begins to realize that one's loyalty is increasingly directed toward that part of one's life that has already been lived. The small remnant of life that remains seems increasingly inadequate to produce a revolution in one's own character, let alone in the character of the world that surrounds us and that we perforce inhabit.

It is for this reason that even the senses begin to close in about us as if to protect us from the vast tracts of historical time that lie ahead after we shall pass on. They may form whole eons in which we will play no part. I feel increasingly that I have become a stranger even to myself. It was always my hope that I might preside over a dynasty and that the estate of Sigerside would become more than the frail barque of our patrimony alone and expand to embrace a multitude of descendents and beneficiaries of the land's largess. But by a hundred years after our death all real memory of us shall be lost. How swiftly even the twilight company of parents and children is drowned in eternal night that is the forgetfulness of those future generations who will not care to even name us, let alone remember us with fondness and affection!

Yet for all of my current lamentations at the rigors of time I am aware that we have been among the lucky ones of the human race. We have at least been allowed to live out the course of our lives in full measure and have been allowed to reach that age of penitence, regrets, and loss of illusions that is maturity. How many souls are snuffed out in anonymous labor camps maintained by one or another of the great dictatorships of the world!

What we term civilization seems but the veneer covering over the condition of the largest part of the world's inhabitants, the resources of which barely rise above the cost of their biological maintenance. I do not know whether this cold that seems to infuse my very bones is only the fear of death that one must feel with more acuity as one enters one's last decades or whether my soul itself is mourning all the generations since Adam. I am after all one to whom the final debt to life is no longer an abstract and distant prospect but a present reminder of inevitable mortality.

On another matter, I received last week a letter from an old acquaintance who is wintering in Mexico this year. His letter told me of the many atrocities committed against the local Indians by the cadres of the armed and mounted troops of the dictator, Porfirio Diaz. This man has just had himself re-elected by fiat as the continuing President of Mexico that is supposedly a free republic. In Mexico all opposition movements share a common fate. The work camps maintained in the Yucatan region are appalling places where the prisoners die like flies of Yellow Fever, Malaria, and Dysentery. Why should these people who are indigenous to what is now Mexico suffer such a fate? The Indians desire after all only that the government should honor their ancient communal land holdings rather than selling them off to American speculators who support the Diaz regime.

Nor are we as Englishmen untainted by these appalling acts of a distant government. Our own nation of England is deeply invested in Mexican assets. A third of all foreign investment in Mexico is of British origin. This man Diaz has seemed to reform the country by industrializing it but this has been achieved primarily by simply keeping the flow of receipts coming to foreign investors at the expense of the peonage of the people of his nation. What of the Mexican people? Have they no right to resist one man and those who support him? Why should they not recapture the benefits distributed to the cronies whom he favors? Why should these oligarchs hold such a disproportionate title to the land and its resources? Why should exterior investors take most of the patrimony of a foreign land?

The man of my acquaintance, disillusioned with what he has seen and heard there, is bringing his investment pounds home and I applaud his doing so. There is no nobility after all in stripping away the wherewithal of the poor. This whole business has made me wonder if we are as fair as we might be to our own tenants and laborers. We have always paid higher-wages and maintained lower rents, but is that enough if the entire system is wrong? Merely selling off the coal mining interests of course would only deprive our laborers of jobs or transfer our family interests to men who are unlikely to provide as well for the workers as we have been able to do. So it is that I am caught between the desire to do right and the economic realities of the time and place in which I live. I have no desire to be like King Herod and to oppress and slaughter the innocents. Yet do what I will, I can feel the ways that guilt can seek a man out. Even the comparatively just man must lament at the many who must labor in order to produce his own state of comfort and security. I see more clearly each day that there is no real security in life. The ice-floe of our days melts beneath us and the empty polar waters beckon. So it is that I have written to our managers in Northumberland to grant a Christmas bonus in food and apparel to the miners and the same to the crofters in Yorkshire. The estate receipts will be lessened next year as a result, but I feel better for making this decision, one which I hope that you and Mycroft will approve. It has been only after I drafted the letter to our managers that I seemed able to get any warmth from the fire of my own hearth.

I wish I had been able to join you and Mycroft at the Diogenes Club this year for Christmas or even to visit your own artistic domicile in Baker Street, but I could not face the rail journey and the prospect of having my back jogged about at the point crossings. My legs pain me lately as well and the prospect of slogging about in the dirty snow along Oxford Street and environs with the soot floating down over the foggy Thames made even the North Yorkshire Moors a preferable site for Christmas for me this year. Oh for a season in the south of Italy, but I have not been there since I made the grand tour as a youth. How pregnant with options the earth seemed to me then and how many years lay like a bright landscape before me! Ever since those youthful rambles I have been stretched out on this rack at Sigerside. The estate still exists and prospers thanks to my labors, but was it worth it at all? That is the question that haunts me this Christmastide. I should be most grateful for anything that you can offer to reassure me and restore me to peace.

Your devoted brother,
Sherringford

onight I am myself engaging in that melancholy task of balancing the year's achievements just as my brother Sherringford has done against the probable balance of remaining time that lies before me. A point must truly be reached in life when one must face the fact that it is too late to reconstruct one's entire character and when the sheer weight of the past begins to threaten to submerge one. I seem to hear the water slogging about in the bilge of the craft of my life and the vessel responds slowly to the helm. Each choice that I have made seemed inevitable at the time, but then I imagined that I could change things swiftly by coming about on an alternate course at will.

The strangest part of this present melancholy is that the year of 1896 has been the most productive year of my life as a consulting detective. I have been consulted on matters of the very deepest moment (as Watson would phrase it) by several great European powers. All of these matters have been brought to a successful conclusion, but still I am unsatisfied and why, because for the first time I realize that even public history is finally trivial. How quaint do the immense struggles and sacrifices made during The Thirty Years War of the 17th century appear to us now! How fatuous seem the issues and how unnecessary the slaughter that were then made in order to resolve them!

If it was only possible to forget, to sweep a wet cloth over the collective brain and to remove the thousand disappointments and regrets so that everything could assume again the enthusiastic perspective of youth, which imagines all things as possible because nothing has yet been tried, then some general prospect of redemption for the human race might be rationally entertained. Is it possible that one's personal regrets are only increased by the degree of one's success? Only those who have come a long way know how much still remains to be done to create a world of justice and equity. What did Beethoven feel as he stood before the blank sheets that would never see the notes of a new symphony? Yet Beethoven ended with his Ode to Joy.

Where is that joy in the life of Sherlock Holmes? I can hear the sounds of revelry outside in the streets tonight. Do those who are off to some fete or other puzzle their minds over the abstruse question of their place in history? No, their entire life is caught up into the immediate pleasure, not haunted by either past or future events. They may leave no record behind them, but their very loyalty to their present associates and associations will ensure that they are mourned for a time. My own career has been a succession of cases brought to me by clients most of whom I will never see again. It is as though my days were a series of discrete beads upon a string without wholeness, harmony, and integration into a whole. The end result of my life to date is without a cumulative summit, but perhaps I am premature in my judgment of my own accomplishments; there is after all the Moriarty matter still pending, which has hung fire all of these years since my return to London in 1894. But what if he has lost interest in our wager over time? After all he is still at large and able to amuse himself with science while I am the one dependent upon the very existence of the sordidness of crime for my bread and butter. Has he been laughing at me all this time? Which of us is still loitering above the abyss of the Reichenbach Falls?

But I must stop this melancholy reverie. Thank heaven that Watson has promised to come by later to see in the New Year. We will catch a late supper at Simpsons and then repair to the Criterion Bar to toast in the New Year at midnight with a plate of grilled oysters accompanied by a glass of hot whiskey toddy or two. Is that the familiar step upon the stair? It is indeed! Watson is before his time. Adieu then old journal, a better friend stands at the threshold to be greeted. "Cheers old fellow, try the settee, or shall we be off to Simpsons at once?"

January 1, 1897
London

A New Year begins today that may prove to be the most fateful of my career. Young Dr. Vernet arrives here tomorrow and I will likely be too busy to write extensively in this journal for some time to come. I hope that I will receive early news from professor Moriarty that will resolve our differences once and for all. Will he warn me before his plan goes into operation or will sudden and startling events be my first warning that the end I feared has come at last. Will the ruin of the nation descend upon us all like a thief in the night? However it turns out I know him too well to assume that he will act from impulse. He has never explained the details of his plan to me. All of our discussions have centered on the underlying justification or lack thereof for him to exact private vengeance on an entire nation. I have also been kept in the dark about his primary confederates if he has any.

Lately, I have even begun to wonder if the primary agent in this matter is someone of even greater power and resources than the Professor. After all most of his men have been apprehended and are in prison. There is someone else behind all of this whose plans may extend far beyond the initial threat posed by Professor Moriarty at the Falls of Reichenbach. The whole matter has an apocalyptic ring to it. I begin to feel that the primary force of civilization is not a function of wisdom or of insight but rather the fact that social change can only take place through the grinding inefficiency of procedural inertia. It is the delay inherent in the application of the laws that keeps dictators at bay.

I am not fond of global prescription for utopia. It is a peculiarity of apocalyptic literature that it compresses events. Is the revenge of Moriarty also to be accomplished at once or in stages? If I am able to read his design in the course of events, might I still avert the full measure of harm by catching his plan in its insipient and preparatory stages? Moriarty shares one definite characteristic with me. We are both dramatists at heart. We appreciate the wonder and the presence of an attentive audience. Like the magician we prefer to prepare our illusions well in advance so that when our secrets are at last revealed, the audience may first gasp and then applaud. But what is the audience for Professor Moriarty, unless it is confined to me? Does he play before the thronged gallery of hell? Or does he sit alone in the empty theater of his own great solitude? When the applause breaks out at last, will the applause come from his hands alone?

Perhaps he imagines that I will lend my own voice if only in protest with a final cry of despair as I witness what I could not prevent! Have I been foolish to leave him so long unmolested, trusting to my arguments rather than to try to have him placed in custody by the authorities? But to do so would have been an admission of defeat. I have relied from the first upon his great mind and upon his respect for eternal purposes guided by some overriding principle of conduct. I felt that if I could only lay before him both my postulates and my theorems, then he could deduce the rest alone at his leisure.

Perhaps I have been wrong. Perhaps there will always remain a gap between metaphysics and divine revelation that only an infused faith may ever bridge. If faith itself is a gift of grace, then perhaps Moriarty lies beyond the embrace of Christianity. But I have taken it as an axiom that God wishes that all persons may come to faith and that He will find a way to reach each soul in due season even in the case of a man like Professor Moriarty.

It is precisely here that my own latent doubts assail me. Does God stand behind history or is each event only a single note in some more extensive composition, so that even the pauses in the great symphony of being, when God seems most absent, only serve to further the design of the whole? As the events of history seem to rush with ever greater urgency upon us with an ever quicker succession of events are we entering the final movement of history before the Second Coming of Christ as prophesied? Will the evils of this present world mount up at the end so that God will appear to be most absent just before the long awaited return of the Son of Man? I think often of the lines of Milton from his poem about the blindness of Samson. It sums up my present mood.

"Oh dark, dark, dark amidst the blaze of noon, irrevocable darkness, total eclipse..."

Is that not an apt description of the age in which we all live? How long shall it be before some event of dark intent releases the storm that has been brewing in all of its pent up fury? How long before the manifold evils find a central locus in a particular individual to wreak ruin upon the earth? A great weariness seems to have descended upon the *fin de siècle* of the Victorian age. The easy paradoxes of my old friend Oscar Wilde seem no longer to wear the bright smartness that they once wore. Oscar should emerge soon from Reading Prison where he was sentenced after his fall to two years at hard labor. But to what life will he return when he is released? His very name invites exile from polite company. Whatever his sins may have been, they were not such rare events as to deserve the aura of scandal that they have born.

Societies that are becoming unsure of their own moorings often seek about for a symbolic scapegoat. Oscar always craved personal notoriety and it has proved in the end to be his undoing. Meanwhile that little beast, Lord Alfred Douglas, having sacrificed one of the great minds of his day, has gone unpunished. I met with Oscar during those terrible last days before his arrest and joined the voices of those of his friends who urged him to flee to France. I have never felt that he had any illusions regarding his immanent ruin. It was more that he could not imagine his life without public acclaim. He knew that to flee was to admit everything and he could not bear the shame of that admission. But I have also felt that there was something more in his peculiar conduct at the time.

Certain men imagine that they literally embody the spirit of an age. Perhaps Oscar Wilde is one of these. I always felt within him a desire to probe into the very depths of life, to walk a path between sainthood and ultimate moral destitution. If it is the nature of life to covet its own destruction, then his own life-course could not be complete until he had tasted the dregs of contempt and of disgrace.

What has been accomplished though by such a sacrifice? I dare to say that his disgrace will not mark the end of "the love that dare not speak its name." The ubiquity of certain practices will continue to exist at Eton and at Harrow and some will never lose a taste for what they have acquired so early in life. If the ranks of the barracks room and the ships of the fleet were purged of all who are no stranger to these practices, the prisons of England could not hope to hold them all. Though these may give evidence of our present moral darkness they are not as black as is our universal greed. England believes that it is in the vanguard of civilization, but to my mind it is brutes like Cecil Rhodes of Africa that should be picking with bleeding fingers at the oakum in Reading Jail.

had a somewhat unusual birthday present today. I received a card from young John Hector McFarland from Norwood. Readers of Watson's account entitled, "The Adventure of the Norwood Builder" will recall how that young man once sought my aid when he was accused of the murder of one Jonas Oldacre. I was able to free McFarland from suspicion and release him from arrest by discovering that the supposedly murdered man, a certain Jonas Oldacre, had secreted himself in his own dwelling in a hidden room to cast suspicion on young McFarland so that he would be hung for the supposed murder.

This man, Oldacre, struck me at the time as the perfect example of what I term, the petty villain. This type is so common that one encounters them in all walks of life. They have not the genius or strength to rise into positions of great power so their evil manifests itself more by causing chaos and inconvenience to all who have the misfortune to encounter them. There is a thread of sadism in their natures combined with a remarkable sensitivity to any perceived insult to their often exaggerated opinion of their own importance and dignity. To offend them is to risk their brooding displeasure, which will usually take precisely the underhanded and cowardly form that it took in the case of Jonas Oldacre towards young McFarland.

I can still recall the gaze of Oldacre's yellow eyes as they focused upon me when he heard that I had been instrumental in his undoing. It was not so much unnerving, for the threats that he made at the time were no worse than many have made in my regard, and yet here I stand to this day; but his threats left me feeling somehow attached to him as though a hideous leech had affixed itself to me and had made my blood unclean in the process. There are certain leaders of nations that carry a quality of character that can infect a whole people and cause an entire nation to subside into a common decay.

The mere thought that in his silent prison cell I was the focus of the thoughts of this vile man's hateful regard and frustrated malice seemed to convey a vague miasma of spiritual disease into the surrounding air. The thought of his diseased mind focusing all of its intent in the one direction of working me some harm in retribution for my part in the foiling his scheme against the innocent McFarland meant that at the very least I would be forced to be on my guard against speeding cabs and falling masonry upon his eventual release from prison.

It was then not unwelcome news to me to hear that Mr. Jonas Oldacre had succumbed to a case of pneumonia in prison and that he now lies buried under a plain white cross outside in the prison churchyard. Of course we are asked to pray for our enemies, so I suppose that I must include him in the list of my private suffrages for the dead along with Dr. Grimsby Roylott and not a few others, but he shall be included in the miscellaneous category and not by name. It may seem strange, but I am not sure that men like Jonas Oldacre: hard, petty, and merciless as his type so often is, do not number among the most satanic examples of evil existing among us.

There is something attractive in the very megalomania of the greater devils that is denied the petty demons among us and therefore they are more dangerous because they are less immediately repellant to our blighted moral senses. No Milton can add grandeur to a man who bears false witness against a young fellow like McFarland whose only crime was being born to the mother who had refused Oldacre's scaly hand in marriage in her youth. For such men as these, the pestiferous and noxious examples of ordinary human evil among us, a swift and blessed end is one of the unexpected advantages of the ravages of disease. To toast his demise would be to sully good brandy, but I did make a small notation of the fact of his demise for my files. It is a dusty book that contains these names and one that I only consult when absolutely necessary for the sake of the welfare of my own soul.

The primary indicator of being in the presence of evil is the feeling of heaviness or dread that evil communicates. Evil's signature voice is the sense of pointlessness and the uncanny; nothing positive is gained by its activity. The realm of evil is the gratuitous rejection of love and the relish entailed in that very act of rejection. The natural reaction of any normal being when encountering evil is first to be startled and then horrified. This is the great abyss that Jesus describes that separates the realm of the eternally saved from the realm of the eternally dead. Love simply makes no sense to evil which instead rejoices at the destruction that it creates all around it. For this reason and this reason alone hell is to be understood as irrevocable and irreversible, because the very means with which love would reach out to the damned would be that which are immediately doomed to be rejected. Hell accepts no imports alien to itself if I can use a commercial metaphor to convey my meaning here. A corollary of this is that the language of hell is non-translatable into the language of being, of exchange, of fairness, of the equitable, of sharing. Hell is a state of entire self-subsistence by beings, which by their very nature are ordained to receiving love so that they can share it and be transparent vehicles of grace to others.

Hell is utterly opaque; light can neither enter it nor can anything carry messages out and escape. It is in every way a prison house. If one might imagine ultimate congestion wherein the touch of another being is perceived not as joy but as fire because it calls into question the utter solitariness and feigned independence that evil claims for itself, one may then be said to possess an image of the condition of hell. In contrast one might imagine God as the ultimate impingement upon that solitude because God cannot be parceled out or fragmented into various spectra. Even the dimmest and most attenuated ray of light from God would be to hell's stygian blackness an intolerable affront to that central lie that it has made its own, one of absolute metaphysical independence from God.

But to return again to the ambiance of evil: when in its presence one does not deal with a substance but instead with a projected force, a gravitas as it were that would weigh down in sorrow all joy beneath its own insupportable shadow. How then can grace penetrate so impermeable a membrane as that which surrounds complete sin? For this reason the action of grace is reserved to God alone and its action is inherently miraculous for God alone loves where love is fundamentally absent. To find love by our own efforts is to imply that love can exist without its source, but to create out of nothingness is precisely what is denied us as created beings; thus God alone bestows forgiveness of sins and recreates within us what has been lost.

This is task is accomplished through the infusion of what the Catholic Church calls the bestowal of Sanctifying Grace that justifies the soul before God. If instances of Actual Grace stimulate our sense of awareness of the abyss of sin before we are completely enclosed within it, the mystery of Venial Sin and its difference from Mortal Sin is solved. Venial sin represents the guardian penumbra of our true nature speaking to us in time to avoid evil by withholding full consent of the will towards embracing actions that would kill charity, the infused gift of God that restores our true nature as children of God.

Even if an objectively evil act may still be committed a sense of nausea so encompasses it that it is recognized as alien to us and we repent as it were even in the very act of commission of the sin. Our soul is divided, somewhat alienated from its true nature, but not yet fully committed to its ultimate and final rejection. Temporary illusion may blind us to what we are doing so that the evil is hidden beneath an aura of proprietary goodness. We imagine that the thing we have partially chosen may still contain some balance of good that can be enjoyed without lasting harm to the soul. We choose evil then under the aspect of good, but even then its suffocating emptiness soon reveals its actual qualities of vacuity, pointlessness, and eventual ruin.

This is the mystery of evil to which no solution exists but repentance. We detect under the impulse of grace the mixture of being-nonbeing that is characteristic of evil done among us and see its results in the sorrow and harm to the innocent. It is important to recall that God alone is equal to the challenge posed by radical evil. This explains the crucifixion of our Lord and Savior Jesus Christ.

January 10, 1897
London

My comments in this journal of a few days ago started a train of reflections on my own safety which I will record here. Readers of the narratives of my friend and chronicler, Dr. Watson may have remarked that although my profession has often put me in peril of my life, my actual wounds have been slight over the course of my career. The alarm bell has been rung but the conflagration, beyond a few inconvenient wounds, has never broken out. Even my time with the dangerous Colonel Sebastian Moran was lacking in the incidents that made me anticipate at the time that I might never return safely to London. For this reason my often lamented decision to keep Watson in the dark about my supposed death at the Reichenbach Falls may be attributed less to what reason might have expected and more to my remarkable good fortune and the skill of Colonel Moran as a guide across those desolate regions of my pilgrimage. But can the same be said of my future time in London now that I have returned? My residence in Baker Street has never been a secret from the public or from my enemies, why then have I not been "done in" long ago by some enterprising thug?

The answer is a simple one. The world of crime is a community of sorts so that just as a naturalist could study a riverbank on the Nile and predict when the wildebeests will come down to the water to drink and how many crocodiles will gather to feed, so the criminal expert must know what is happening throughout the complex jungle of London's underworld. One of the reasons that Watson's narratives so often deal with unique and idiosyncratic events is that such crimes fall outside the usual communal patterns of the criminal class. It is not due to bravery but rather to my confidence in my own social diagnostics that has enabled me to avoid what might seem to be the all too predictable fate that I have courted as a consulting detective.

But I must admit that there was another key factor ensuring my survival. There is a hierarchy in the world of crime that is almost oriental in nature. It is not bragging for me to claim that my death by the hand of any criminal agent would be an event of almost universal interest across the criminal worlds of several nations. This fact alone meant that only a criminal version of the Shogun of Japan would be granted permission to kill me. For any common criminal to do so would be an act of the greatest effrontery, the presumption of which would ensure his death by the higher orders of the criminal demesne. My life therefore has occupied a sort of special preserve status to which I attribute my immunity from harm. I have not of course presumed upon that immunity but when it is combined with my own natural prudence and a certain degree of resourcefulness the result has been that I have remained year after year alive and well to pursue my calling unmolested by the everyday miscreant who knows his place in the rigid hierarchy of crime.

Still there have been men whom I have feared. The man whom I have chosen to call John Clay was one of these. If he was less greedy and cocksure he might with time have become another Professor Moriarty. He had the two first elements of the great criminal mind: imagination and daring. But he lacked the third element, patience. The greatest crimes are those that remain undiscovered. This is the one reason why most of our revered statesmen are not in jail. They pillage the public daily by their close association with the bankers. What is inflation for instance but a means of acting-out the role of the cut-purse, dipping into the pockets of an entire nation? What are called the iron laws of economics are really the result of deliberate machinations in more cases than the unconscious public ever realizes.

The average working man never has enough savings to invest so that he would notice this silent pillage. He lives from hand to mouth. The middle-class has whatever surplus might provide just such an opportunity of resistance to the pillage, but the habit of paying taxes dulls their natural indignation and breeds submission within its members. Only the truly wealthy notice what is happening, but for them the possibility of capital-gains on their assets induces them to turn a blind eye to the quiet pillaging that battens on the very substance of the lower orders of society. It takes a literary naturalist like Balzac or Zola to show the dynamic interchanges in society although Charles Dickens managed quite well in *Dombey and Son* and *Our Mutual Friend.*

But to return to the case of John Clay, his antecedents were such that his sentence in the case of *The Red-headed League* was only a brief one, but only on condition that upon his release he would quit England for good and leave for the colonies. His subsequent career in Australia was undoubtedly such that it might make an interesting narrative. Like many others he managed to make his fortune there that he thereafter took with him when he immigrated again to South Africa where his mining interests are now said to be quite extensive. He is rumored to be one of Cecil Rhodes' favorite companions. If there is honor among thieves it is only because the successful ones are respected by the same populace that ignores their depredations.

January 12, 1897
London

I received belated birthday greetings from Sherringford today. His health is still not quite up to the mark and he has never been good about remembering dates. I fear that the responsibilities of running the estate are beginning to exceed even his formidable capacities. Both Mycroft and I have advised him to take on a general estate manager, but he is used to doing things in his own unique way. Part of the problem lies in attempting to retain the coal mines on the borders of Northumberland and Yorkshire. I have long advised that we close up the pits and bring the men out who have labored so long in the bowels of the earth to add to the cottagers and yeoman farmers and sheepherders of Sigerside.

Coal is a dirty business. It is true that coal is a necessity of life in our present mode of living, but the mining of it is an inhuman and ghastly affair and I can well empathize with the miners who suffer from Black-Lung since my own lungs are the Achilles heel of my own constitution. These men must not be cast adrift of course in their dotage and whatever the value of this resource may be I trust that our generation shall be the last to require that so many men must die so that others may live comfortably by their coal fires. The burdens and risks of life should not be doled out with such inequality. Even the forces of will and of brain in those with executive abilities seem to me to disqualify them from possessing the simple nobility of the working folk of England. To say that one is a gentleman may not be a compliment after all when seen from the vantage point of God who is the succor and resource of the poor in spirit. Truly the first may be the last to enter the kingdom of heaven.

But regarding my elder brother, we have come in recent years to a better understanding of one another. He manifests the best parts of my father's spirit in his doggedness and willfulness and in his respect for tradition. Mycroft enlarges the latent trait of imagination a bit more; and I of course allow myself to weigh all data and reach an independent decision in virtually every case that comes before me. It is as though my comparative poverty compared to them has been my greatest resource. However my professional fees have increased lately and I am less dependent upon the estate for my livelihood. This increase may be attributed to the addition of an international practice to my usual caseload and by the sheer volume of cases that have come my way in the course of this last year.

It is indeed fortunate that I have been able to save and invest these funds, for the returns of this coming year promise to be spare indeed. I plan on joining Watson soon in Cornwall and then to go up to Devonshire to stay with Sir Henry for a bit as his guest. The January rains are as dismal as ever and the windows are only kept from fogging up by the continual wash of the rain down the windows. Mrs. Hudson is cooking a roast of some sort downstairs though and the smell of rosemary is providing some comfort as the incense of the meal climbs the seventeen steps to my own suite of rooms collectively referred to as 221B Baker Street.

It would be a comfort to me if Inspectors Gregson or Lestrade or even the comparatively young Stanley Hopkins would drop by with a minor case for me although I have sworn to Watson that I will decline any matter requiring any active investigation on my part. Which is more deadly to me I wonder, mental stimulation or mental starvation? Leisure has always been my bane; I thrive on the hearty fare of problems to solve. It is the curse of an active mind that it demands employment or it begins to feed upon its own substance. It seems to me that the affections and the affectations of mankind take the place of this peculiar hunger of mine, one lacking in the majority of my fellow human beings. I have long abjured the common affections as factors that bias the judgment. I try rather like the Zen Buddhists to abstract my own particular being into nothingness so that the thing in itself can appear in all of its clarity, the observed existing without an observer. But perhaps this conviction of mine is an illusion.

Is human subjectivity to be so despised? Can one solve human problems without being human oneself? There is a point beyond which imagination cannot go and actual experience is required. This experience demands personal involvement in the ebb and flow of life. It demands commitments and personal loyalties, even love. The uncommitted life is finally not worth living and commitment by necessity requires limitation to the particular and even to the unique. This is why adopting a merely statistical approach to life is always inadequate and why human sorrow is inevitable, because to be truly human is to accept as irrevocable the loss of what we love, what can never be replaced.

I do not know of a branch of knowledge that focuses above all else upon dissimilarities, but such a discipline should exist. Perhaps it could be called "uniqueology." When I first met Doctor John H. Watson I explained that my profession as a consulting detective was, as far as I knew then, unique, so perhaps my preferred subject matter is unique as well. I am not, as is the official police force, a mere conduit, a drain for the stream of crime, but rather the pursuer of the odd rivulet that escapes past the pipes, pumps, and flanges of the great waterworks of the city.

What have I to do with compounds; give me elements in all of their purity and irreducibility! Yet we live in a world of mixture and composition so to demand a premature simplicity is to miss much of life. A derivative existence is simply inadequate to pursue if one is to become a living soul. So it is that I have turned my back upon the reductive simplicity of the Zen Buddhist in his rejection of existence and his preference for the unity of Brahma and have chosen instead to view existence as divergent and in perpetual adaptation, with only the cross of Christ as our hope for the final reconciliation of this great diffused universe back to its origin in God.

𝕴 dined with Mycroft tonight and we discussed the situation that prevails at Sigerside. If Sherringford becomes unable to continue to bear the burdens of the estate, neither of us is free at the present time to shoulder the many responsibilities that are entailed in keeping such a large affair going. England is changing from a country of landed gentry to a nation of large industrial magnates. The old concept of *nobless oblige* is being supplanted by an aggressive spirit of international commerce and the colonial exploitation of India and Africa.

These economic changes have not made for a nobler product in our upper classes. Sherringford may be among the last members of a dying breed. His loyalty is to the small crofters and tenant farmers who exist as part of the land. These families for all of their hardships enjoy lives that are not without meaning and their loyalty to the estate is matched by the fact that there has never been an eviction from Sigerside. The children there receive an education and the sick are tended by a traveling practitioner from Whitby or in a local lying-in hospital endowed by the estate and further attached to care of the local vicarage. There are school-treats and nature-outings and a local grange has dances at harvest time. There is a common grain depot and food depository for the poor and none go hungry upon the moors of Sigerside in winter.

How different this is from the grim spectacle of life in the nearby metropolitan cities of Leeds, Manchester, Liverpool, and Birmingham. There one sees all manner of squalor and moral depravity. The lives of the elderly and of women and children are exploited and no questions are asked of those who batten daily upon the misery of others. Meanwhile wealth has all manner of means to hide its sources. The social fabric of England is becoming a great jungle. Fear of falling back into the seething masses causes each generation to attempt to climb the ladder of the class structure. No permanent immunity is granted though, even to the landed gentry. Though I have never been one to be impressed by outward social position or grand titles, this has been largely due to my own breeding and that I have been granted the luxury of insolence in regard to the great who call upon me and request my aid in some problem. They expect the usual deference due to their wealth and rank while to me they are merely another example of the human condition in operation. The same principles apply.

My profession of being the de facto court of last resort for those who seek my unique skills also allows me a degree of latitude with those who rely upon their wealth or illustrious forebears to put me in my place. If I were to imply that my discoveries are theirs for the asking, then I would be little more than a paid spy. I retain the freedom to walk away from even the most illustrious and impressive of clients if my conscience dictates that I should do so. Besides this reason for my often abrupt manner, the only way to get at the truth is to strip away the all-too-common play-acting and presumption of the upper classes so that what is essentially human within them may emerge.

I am not without my own personal pride though. Being raised by two such strong characters as my father and mother has left their traces upon my character. My father, though a democrat in spirit, was an aristocrat as regards his own person. His nature was to take charge and to demand to be heard in any setting whatsoever, as though he was a king and not a mere member of the minor landed gentry. My mother in turn believed in that highest of aristocracies, that of the artistic creators of the world. So is it any surprise that her sons think little of issuing directives and commands to their social and nominal superiors?

Art in the blood takes strange forms and often the artistic temperament creates its own form of art. Art is after all a thing above all else, the impulse toward the new in all things; it is innovative by nature. Yet a sense of tradition is also never absent and the greatest of artists must always be aware of the tradition that conditions and guides his own productions. The advantage of coming from a family with a certain rootedness in place and time is that there is a solid basis out of which innovation may emerge.

So I told Mycroft that it is my hope that we can at least retain the old manor-house at Sigerside and the immediate grounds of moor and stream and about one hundred acres that surround it. I should feel lost if I did not feel for all my cosmopolitanism that something of the past remained to me, one rooted in the soil of my forebears in Yorkshire and in France. It is not possible for each generation to begin again from scratch without descending mentally at the same time. The perfect mix is to grant the new generation sufficient freedom to pursue individual excellence, while still building upon a base of common memories and traditions. The branch requires a trunk to support it or it is just so much random vegetal growth.

January 15, 1897
London

More startling news! I received today a letter from Professor Moriarty, which I do not know how to weigh in terms of our ongoing battle of wits. He appears to wish to, as the barristers say, narrow the issues by making some concessions while retaining his primary cause of action. I shall let the letter speak for itself and then dismiss it from my conscious mind. It is always a capital mistake in both litigation and life to allow one's opponents to define the issues.

To the Very Reverend Mr. Holmes,

(It is addressed like this with either mockery or an attempt at humor, but which of the two it is, I cannot say).

It seemed to me the proper time to connect with you once again. We have come at last to the critical year of our wager reached in that little inn near the Falls of Reichenbach. How each of us has chosen to live since then is the best evidence of the wisdom of choices we have made. I am happy to say that my investments have prospered well. You really should look into the United Diamond Syndicate of South Africa. The dividends have paid for my breeding stables at Kings Pyland many times over. But to return our wager, I refer to it as a wager and not a contretemps for we have been both very well-bred in the manner of our discussions thus far. I must say that you really have acquitted yourself better than I might have expected in at least getting me to consider the religious experience as possessing some few elements of truth. But these elements are of the experiential order and are thus, I fear fatally biased ab initio. If God exists, at least the God that you would have me believe in, then that God, (please note that I do not say He for to do so is already an unpardonable anthropomorphism in my eyes) that God I say must be either radically other and outside of his creation or somehow co-extensive with it. I believe that the philosopher Baruch Spinoza was entirely too influenced by his own heritage in equating God with the mere sum total of all existing things; however superficially unorthodox his opinions first appeared. God, in order to be God and maintain that degree of sovereignty that the mere concept of the Godhead implies, must pre-exist all else that exists as mere contingent creation so that nothing at all may be predicated of God from within that creation. If that essential metaphysical gap is allowed to collapse, then the true majesty of God becomes a mere projection of our desires and our fears. Do you not see that?

In short there is an inverse relationship between the so-called mercy and tenderness of God for his chosen ones and the ultimate credibility of those assertions. It is not that God should be cruel of course, for what sense would it make for God to oppress created things, a product of his own industry? No, rather God should by all good sense be indifferent to His creation because it can add nothing to His inherent glory, so indifferent in fact that creation should have never taken place at all. In other words, the mere fact that things exist is the proof that God never made them!

The so-called problem of evil is actually based upon the absurd idea that things should happen as we wish them to happen. We invest our Gods with power so that we will receive from them what we are unable to attain by our own efforts. After that we devise all manner of conditions through which we can please them so that they will give us what we want. The whole thing is simply too childish to believe!

But, you will no doubt answer me that since we observe a world all about us creation must have taken place and we must fall down in wonder before what we see as the evidence of a benevolent God. But God is neither benevolent nor malevolent, because God does not exist! We are plunged into existence knowing only two things: first that we are surrounded by existing things, which are not mere imaginings derived from within ourselves (you see that I am not a solipsist) and second that we shall someday cease to be and that which fell upon us once as an unavoidable avalanche of impressions shall be succeeded by a great vacuum of all impressions whatsoever in death and that whatever allowed us to apprehend things, if predicated upon having a body, shall fail with that body as it molders into dust.

This raises the question of what having ever been in existence means. Let us imagine that a beam of light carries our image outward into the evidently unending regions of space. If light has some pre-determined absolute speed, then an observer on some receptive planet incalculable years hence might observe us as we are now and experience that observation as a present event to him. Of course in reality we would long since have ceased to be. Now then, which of these two positions is true? Do we exist then or do we exist now? And what if the witness to our being carried on that stream of light never reaches an observer, are we then eternal, existing always until some destination is reached when we will be observed once again as a fleeting impression in whatever mundane reality exists there?

Your position as far as I am able to understand it is this: that the fire of life may be transferred as an immortal soul between heaven and earth just as a flame may be transferred between two candles that host a single fire. I realize that I cannot disprove that thesis and as an image it is quite persuasive, but if that transfer is to take place, then who shall carry the flame? Let us return to my version of a quite aloof God, the only believable one. Why should such a God soil Himself with intercessions or interventions in our affairs?

I ask that you consider the unfathomable immensity of time. Imagine the horrible immobility of an unchanging God through the vast eons that preceded our own existence when mere physical concatenations existed, when neither tears were shed nor laughter rang. What God of tenderness and compassion could ever abide waiting for the eventual advent of man who as far as we know is the only intelligent agent of material being? What purpose is served by all the objects that occur in nature insofar as they do not aid the existence of a human mind? If religion is everything; then everything else nothing!

Or do you ask that I believe that man is himself an outside creation driven from heaven and plunged into the chains of change in this all too mutable world? Is all that we see only the cardboard facing of a stage for human actions? Did God create immense galaxies following their own courses only to startle our collective gaze as we perceive the sky? Why will you insist upon the particular human reality implied by religion and flee the general nature of the order of the cosmos in which we live with all of its brutality and indifference to our fate? Or are you convinced that this planet with all of its burgeoning life-forms is some Garden of Eden?

Ours is a world of tooth and claw. I tell you, Holmes, that if God exists at all, then we should all fear above all else that such a creator God would someday visit us. Far better it would be if we have been long since forgotten than that the great brute should ever come striding down amongst us through the Garden of our Eden to crush us beneath his steps! Nature shows us no mercy and thus neither does God show mercy. I therefore worship only the God who is in evidence here by adapting that same distant viewpoint towards all things that God shows to us daily in all things.

But again you will undoubtedly insist that God Himself is entangled like a fish in a net (this whole incarnation business) so much so that God has become man in Jesus Christ! Surely this is the most unaccountable mixing of categories. Why can you not see that the whole affair is mere rhetoric, a mere appeal to emotion? You would have me share your illness through this contagion of a vision of particularity and uniqueness, whereas I maintain that I am merely another chance mutation of the genus of the hominid apes. My thoughts are of a piece with all of the other thoughts that like a flash of lightening illuminate the earth only to vanish. Why should the synapses of my solitary brain be granted an eternal status? Surely I am the more humble of the two of us, Sherlock Holmes. I admit my own fatuity and purposelessness. Why cannot you do the same? In the name of God, why cannot you do the same?

Your most disobedient servant,
Professor James Moriarty

There it is; his final great appeal! I seem to detect a note of desperation here. It is unlike the Professor to admit so many contradictions to pass unnoticed. First, he insists upon a completely transcendent deity and then implies that God is Himself a prisoner of time waiting about for the advent of mankind. Though I cannot prove this, I believe that God may be able to view all of time just as we do fish in a fishbowl from all angles. What the fish perceive as the impenetrable walls of their glass prison and silvered ceiling may be from the point of view of eternity experienced as simultaneity or more accurately as a universal accessibility to God.

God does not, as John Calvin presumed was the case, foresee events and in doing so determine them; rather God sees all of existence in all of its ramifications while still allowing it to take that form that its intelligent free-agents may influence by their own actions. In saying this I imply that the world of creation is a living thing. God relates to the world without being subsumed by it; not as Spinoza assumed by being co-extensive with it. Nor is God immanent in the world as the pantheists claim; rather God is the active principle that sustains existing things while still allowing a type of selective liberty to intelligent beings. God is not then a great brute, as Moriarty asserts, but a brooding and one might even imply a maternal presence that nurtures His creation and delights in it. It is precisely here that Professor Moriarty betrays his own blighted view of fatherhood for a true father does not crush the spirit of his children but allows them to grow towards virtue and truth by guidance and patience, which are what the Old Testament calls wisdom and the Kabala refers to as the Shekinah or the glory of God.

Moriarty's opposition to faith thus reduces itself down to a

244

projection upon the world at large of his own unfortunate experience with his own brutal father and his early despair and contempt for his own twisted body and the malignant pride that it engendered within him. His contempt for God is really contempt for himself. God loves us from within our natures and by doing so draws us into His own nature. How may I convey this truth to a man who is so bound in his particular fears and hatreds? Therein my task lies before me!

January 18, 1897
London

A new business year has likewise begun and I went over our year's end receipts with our accountant at the bookshop today. I was able to report to Mycroft that our little bookselling enterprise continues to generate a modest but welcome profit. We have over the year developed a unique clientele. These consist of scholars for the most part who pursue any number of abstruse lines of inquiry. I have been able to employ some of my former Baker Street Irregulars as "book scouts" who go about the country seeking out certain unique publications at estate sales and library liquidations. Some of these volumes come to us in deplorable shape, so Mycroft and I have established a small book bindery in the East End to rebind many of these books. They return to us still somewhat tainted by the smell of mold and time, but we have given them a new lease on life so that they may continue their useful function.

A new lease on life is what I need myself. My old and persistent cough has returned and I have been sternly instructed by various specialists to leave London at once for the healthy air of Cornwall and Devonshire. I will stay with Watson until my own dwelling at Grimpen can be prepared for occupancy. The tenant who has lived there in recent years moved to Italy last summer and the cottage has remained empty ever since. If the mice and rats are to be kept at bay it must find a new tenant soon and what better tenant than a middle-aged detective with a stash of palimpsests and old English charters to be perused near at hand. So it is that I must forego the rest of the London season with its concerts and plays and become again a country gentleman in Grimpen. I shall conclude the case in which I am currently principally engaged and set off for the West Country district that I look upon as an alternate home to Baker Street. I have already wired Sir Henry of my plans and I am happy to say that the dear fellow answered immediately in the most flattering and amiable terms. Still I seemed to detect in his missive signs of an underlying uneasiness. He has yet to recover completely from the horrible experiences of a decade ago when he was menaced by the spectral legend of his family curse in the form of a devil-sent hound.

I am well acquainted with family curses. My own takes the form of recurrent bouts of lethargy when I find it impossible to act. It is as though the faculty of the will itself has been paralyzed. Perhaps my father suffered from a similar malaise. His neglect of his three sons may have been less of a sign of his indifference to our fate than it was a sign that he was lost in the corridors of his own mind after the loss of our dear mother. It was she who had once inspired all of his actions and his former remarkable optimism and the zest for life that he could remake the world in the image of his own aspirations.

In the last analysis the male sex is the servant sex. Life can proceed quite well without its men once their essential function in procreation has been served as the bees teach us. True manhood resides not in domination within the family but in being a servant to the life process, first to instigate life and then to preserve it by protecting one's wife and children. Wars are waged primarily by the unattached males in society whose youth has made them predators and not preservers of life. For this reason wars are unnatural things and must finally be eliminated if humans are to survive on this diminutive sphere. My fascination with bees is based upon my conviction that the bees alone have created a perfect society.

There is an economy at work in the hive of perfect cooperation and the procreative process is assigned to a single queen. She alone is the common mother of all. Her segregation is less a matter of power than it is one of trust. Is not our Queen Victoria similarly entrusted by the nation with its collective soul so that she may look to the good of all English men and women?

Whether she has proven worthy of that great trust is another matter and my own patriotic enthusiasm has waxed and waned through the years. Still, I see a certain virtue in monarchy because it removes the temptation to use public office for temporary enrichment at the public's expense.

Imagine if a democracy might vomit up some deranged charlatan to executive supremacy who through cunning and flattery could elaborate a national myth of innate supremacy and by gaining the confidence of the illiterate masses go on after coming to power to auction off the essential functions of government to private cronies and sycophants that minister to his need for adulation. Can anything more dreadful be conceived? England is to some extent immune from such a danger although America for all of its talk of separation of powers is not immune to the detrimental effects of popular enthusiasm. Tradition guards us to some extent from the power of the *nouveau riche* many of whom are vulgar landlords, mere vampires that prey upon the populace, like John Jacob Astor.

America, should it ever develop a cancerous regime led by such a man would require some jolt or shock to return it to sanity. Power is revealed as the hollow soul-destroying thing it is when a man has been led to pursue it from birth and finally agrees to be burdened by it through the course of a vainglorious career. In nature the queen bee must be segregated in order to endow her with those imaginary spiritual qualities that we deem appropriate in a monarch. All expansion of an apiary's hives requires a new queen. She must be segregated from the mass of the worker bees so that she can exercise her assigned function for the good of the whole hive. She alone is allowed freedom from material necessity. Similarly rulers of nations must be spared the struggle of existence, not so that they may thrive in luxury, but so that they may be liberated for the service of the citizens. However, to come to political power already committed to a course of excessive accumulation of wealth is automatically to be incapacitated for public service. Such a man will use the high office with which he has been entrusted in order to swell his own fortune and flatter his own vanity. He will likely be prey to every manner of delusional beliefs and convince himself that he alone can lead his nation to greatness and act as a sword of the almighty. Any nation has been prey to religious enthusiasms of the more hysterical sort such America has repeatedly been will provide fertile ground for such a man to prosper and gain the confidence of the resentful and the simple-minded in even a republic. Even a well-balanced nation, let alone one under the stress of rapid change, may succumb to madness.

January 21, 1897
London

At Watson's persistent urging I am off in a few days time to Cornwall to begin a period of indefinite rest. Finally I put up little resistance since I can feel the wellsprings of my energy at as low a level as I can ever recall. This factor combined with my usual January lethargy has quite laid me out. I am afraid that this Abbey Grange business must be my last substantial case for awhile. Even the effort to write in this journal threatens to exhaust this day's poor allotment of energy. Only now am I aware of the degree to which my life's activities have represented a drawing down of the body's equivalent of capital reserves. I begin this period fortunately with my financial condition assured for some years to come. My international cases have brought in munificent fees, our collector's book emporium has prospered, and receipts from Sigerside have shown the degree to which the international trade has picked up since the financial Panic of 1893. This means that I can now focus upon my health and recovery without those nagging cares that keep so many in the laboring classes working into even into advanced old age. For these there is no prospect of surplus; life is a daily affair of work until in sheer exhaustion they seek their only repose in death.

If I was not ill I would feel more of the guilt that any surplus engenders in the face of the contemplation of those without such resources. To the very poor the ordinary man is rich. It has always seemed to me that in a truly just society anything that exceeds our daily shelter and sustenance should overflow as rain does from leaves to nourish the roots of human-kind. Scarcity at all levels is the direct result of excess accumulation elsewhere.

So fearful though is the prospect of poverty that the reverse is the case and each social stratum deems essential the accumulation of that degree of wealth that will ensure that one does not tumble into the class that is just below it. Each class needs a buffer zone that is equivalent to its expectations of the wherewithal to purchase its future security and happiness. Thus social equity is never achieved.

Similarly, as the years ahead diminish and as lasting security becomes ever more a chimera in the face of the nearing prospect of death, our needs should diminish. But it is precisely these latter years that call forth and demonstrate the greatest parsimony in many people. Their desire instead is to remedy all of life's former deficits in their declining years and to re-double the effort to find whatever joys and pleasures life has heretofore failed to bestow upon them. There seems to be a certain odd relation in this drive for accumulation so that those who have enjoyed good fortune in life are unwilling to sacrifice and instead covet even more delights. The measure is always what is just out of their reach rather than the absolute scale that measures upwards from the bottom of extreme penury or an early death. Our expectations from life increase to the degree that they are gratified. It is to this fact that we can attribute the elusiveness of human well-being and satisfaction. To this perverse dynamic Jesus Christ opposes a contrary ethic—to seek no security, to live at risk of scarcity, of deprivation, and even of violence. So extreme is this ethic that not even Christianity has consistently imposed it upon Christendom. For this reason, Christians have always managed to accumulate sufficient resources to wage wars against other Christians. Armaments are the ultimate luxury.

If even barns are seen as superfluous to the man whose soul will that night be demanded of him, then how much more are castles, fortresses, bank vaults, and all of the other measures by which we measure our individual and collective security. I am not immune to this folly as this very entry shows. Sick as I am I imagine my recovery and that I shall have again the energy of that young fellow who first shook the hand of Dr. Watson when we were introduced by young Stamford so many years ago now. I will no doubt enter eternity still encumbered by the embarrassment of many excess worldly goods.

Perhaps only God can live without this gross hunger for security. The divine is known by its utter defenselessness before evil. How else can we account for the fact that evil exists in a world intended by God to be without it? Evil is the great spontaneity of created being. It is without any prior direct cause. The imperfect and contingent being can only create evil when it attempts to be like God who alone can engender the other Divine Persons of the Trinity. This is done not out of necessity or emanation, but by a purely gratuitous act of love. The Word of God, who is the Son of God, and the Holy Spirit as well, were each loved-into-being by God the Father. All merely created being exists to serve the Triune God and to reflect glory upon the Trinity by fulfilling its proper end. As the image of God, we are as insubstantial in ourselves as an image in a glass. A mirror remains empty without the original object to be reflected. All secondary and derivative images are equally insubstantial, even if they are multiplied into infinity. Only God has existence attributed of him as an essential predicate.

The surplus of worldly goods merely gives further evidence of our nothingness considered solely in ourselves. A man's riches are ultimately the measure of his lack of trust in God. Voluntary poverty, in contrast, is evidence that we desire to share all things just as Jesus did. Possessions are really a concession by God to our infirm nature. We only prove ourselves more infirm to the degree that we covet what we can never fully possess. God alone possesses nothing, for he distributes all of being to creation. Thus it is folly to ask where God is—he is in all things, yet not co-extensive with them, but is their source and origin. God is the remainder after all else has been subtracted. Yet that remainder is infinite and could re-institute all that exists in an instant by simply saying, "Let there be light."

Dr. Watson's Narrative Continues

After leaving Washington my overall impression was that the city is a great marble museum dedicated to the supposedly immortal ideas that its founders entertained regarding human liberty. The assumption seems to be that human beings when given full reign will naturally fall into socially useful and productive lives by allowing the masses to choose their own leaders. My experience of life has not born out these hopeful assumptions.

Liberty without education and some commitment to higher ideals is an ungoverned force that can wreak havoc until it is restrained. An example is the open-ended generosity advocated in the teachings of Jesus Christ. The divine mission as it is recorded could only have ended in one way. The gentle savior was caught between the twin evils two different images of a perfect world, one emanating from Rome and the other from Jerusalem. The prescription of Jesus: to render to Caesar the things that are Caesar's and to God (as filtered through the Sanhedrin) the things that are God's was at the time and is today as well an unworkable formula. It is not within the ambit of any individual to make that discernment.

Religion will always seek absolute power over any secular ruler that does not claim equal status by making himself a God. The ever-realistic Emperor Augustus realized this and tolerated the Jewish aspirations for some universal kingdom based in Jerusalem as a harmless illusion as long as it simmered and never came to a boil. In order to achieve that goal a Roman provincial procurator was appointed and even a king of sorts was allowed in the person of King Herod. The Jewish religious establishment meanwhile was kept in line by simply allowing endless debate between rival Jewish factions. The point was that the system was stabilized and nothing of note was ever going to happen ... until St. John the Baptist started in with his proclamation of an imminent advent of the long awaited but infinitely delayed Messiah. Nothing is more disruptive to the secular order than the expectation of some otherworldly fulfillment. It blinds people to the fact that there is nothing new under the sun. The writer of Ecclesiastes was correct when he said that all is vanity and a chase after the wind.

The final result of the mission of Jesus to date has been the creation of a centralized religious arbiter in the Roman Catholic Church that has kept hope alive while simultaneously keeping Europe nominally Christian. This civilizing force is about to come to an end. The odds that this comfortable arrangement would continue were never encouraging. Europe is essentially a backwater. The fate of the great Asian island floating between the world's oceans will always be in dispute. The surging populations of various regions cannot keep from spilling over the bulkheads in the stormy seas of contention. No system of recognized sovereignty has ever existed that cannot be supplanted by brute force. This means that politically speaking any document, even the sanguine and balanced document of the Constitution of the United States of America will someday fail when it encounters sufficient determination to either supplant it through force or to reduce it to a harmless idol.

Our time at the huge Biltmore Estate owned by one of the heirs of the fabulously wealthy Vanderbilt family in North Carolina only further dramatized the contrasts in the American economic structure that makes any talk of universal liberty and equality between citizens absurd. The vaunted three American transcendental goals of life, liberty, and the pursuit of happiness, wherein each man might be free of all hereditary impediments to prove his natural worth, had swiftly followed that great law of nature that separates any population into various social classes based upon their present income source and residual capital.

Industrial expansion follows its own laws. It is supported by the funds not expended upon simply procuring the necessities of existence. For this reason capitalism always requires capitalists, men with excess money who can obtain more money by paying wages rather than working for them. This fundamental distinction and the basis that it provides for the gap between classes are persistently ignored within the American ethos. Even land-ownership that always provided the basis for wealth in the England of the 18th century cannot hope to keep up with the productive promises of industry. A day may come when even industry may be dwarfed in this regard by a new technology beyond our present dreams of what is possible.

The actual American transcendental values are power not life, money not liberty, and the ability to control other people not happiness. Power and money are largely exchangeable and both imply an ability to control the labor of others, if not through chattel-slavery, then through control of the means for obtaining a living-wage or the extraction of rents or payments for basic services. The government that proposes to serve the common good in a democracy actually is the purveyor of promises and illusions. Statesmen for the most part work behind the scenes to enhance the power of the dominant classes in society.

This unpleasant background was easily forgotten during our short visit at the Biltmore Estate in North Carolina. Holmes and I were treated well during our time spent there and the tours through the lovely woodlands that surround it. Great enterprises require great fortunes to subsidize them. I reflected at the time that no social class has a monopoly on virtue or wisdom and I was once again confronted by the disconnection existing between any proposed economic or political system and its actual ability to avoid the results of venality, poor judgment, and the violent impulses of mankind. The results of the French Revolution may serve hereafter as a laboratory in this regard with the many successive governments it has engendered. Our horseback rides about the estate allowed us to witness how nature itself can be saved from exploitation when wealth is dedicated to preservation rather than to profit. It may be that the American aristocracy within a few generations may be the greatest force for civilization in the country.

The crass commercial classes in contrast may soon produce

strange fungus-like growths meant to cater to the ever-acquisitive and vulgar aims of the lower regions of the upper-class. Penury in turn spawns other social ills. Sorrow and brutality lead to crime and violence. It must be the aim of the nation to raise the general intellectual and artistic standards of the common folk through education. Finally, there is religion as a social force that all too often fails to be a unifying agent and merely sets a tone or provides a focus for the hatreds and fears of the society that uses it to justify its own baser instincts of envy.

The poor may be always with us, as Jesus once said, but we need not labor as hard as we do to make that statement a prophetic reality. All of this became more evident to me as we passed through towns and villages in the still war-ravaged south after leaving the Biltmore Estate. We traveled north again by a circuitous route through the mountains into Ohio and then Indiana. Our train soon left the great cities of the east behind us. We passed through Cleveland and Detroit and came at last to Chicago, that great sprawling city, which perhaps best represents the squalor and frenzy of the new American experiment. We did not tarry there long however but passed on to St. Louis where we changed trains and entered what a few years before had been the unspoiled plains of the western frontier.

At Council Bluffs we stood above the river and thought of the promises on that site made and broken to the Indians. It was there that we caught the train that was to take us northwards into the Dakotas. It was the desire of Sherlock Holmes that we should kneel and pay our respects at what should become a national shrine and place of mourning for all Americans, a place called Wounded Knee. This place of defeat for the proud remnants of the indigenous races of America has been characterized as a field of battle when it was in actuality a place of final decimation of a helpless people.

The pangs of the national conscience were beginning to gnaw at the conquerors and they needed one last purported victory to feed the imaginations of the people of the east who persisted in seeing the Indians as savages. For the cavalry the idea that the Indian nations had been inspired by a Paiute Prophet named Wovoka to dream of a final deliverance using a ghost-dance ritual from the invaders of their ancient lands was an intolerable affront. It was not that they credited these prayers for deliverance, to what they perceived as a heathen God, with any efficacy; it was that the Indian Nations dared to pray at all when the only true religion, one derived from across an ocean, had been shared with them. Faced with the prospect of conversion to Christianity what right had they to pray in the old fashion or even to exist for that matter when the imperative of national growth meant that they must be pushed aside along with the great bison that sustained them?

The net result was the ruthless slaughter of the old men and the women and children who no longer had warriors to protect them because they lay dead upon the plains that had been theirs since time immemorial. The now extended version of the original colonies was now styled America, a land where all men are created equal ... unless they are Indians, unless they are unconverted and unbaptized and thus still tainted with Original Sin. As our train sped north across the river towards the Rocky Mountains, I turned for the last time to those papers that had been entrusted to me by Sherlock Holmes, seeking in their revelations a memory of the years of our renewed partnership that began in 1894 when we were reunited in London. It has been a sustained partnership ever since, never again to be broken to this day, recalled now only in pages such as these and the all too short memory of the Victorian age that is now lost forever.

It was an era that at the time seemed solid and upright and as certain as any that human history has ever known. Its dark side was often hidden from our view and such was the natural desire of the men and women of the period to believe in progress that the many manifest injustices were allowed to ferment until they issued at last in a great war in the new century. Our desire to seek a universal peace through repeated conquests was to be thwarted by events that we could not turn aside. History is more often the legacy of defeats than of victories, but one must often grow old in illusions before one may realize this great truth and seek solace in resignation and the contemplation of God.

From the Journal of Sherlock Holmes

January 26, 1897
Enroute to Cornwall

Leaving Baker Street again for what may prove to be an indefinite period has not been easy for me to contemplate. Only the fact of the successful conclusion of so many of my cases during 1896 and the resultant inflow of capital has allowed me to face the future without misgivings. I have never been what I would term a prosperous man but I am at least for the present not what Sherringford would deem a blot upon the escutcheon of my noble forebears. Mycroft and I have hidden as far as possible our little commercial venture from him. I don't believe he could take the news that his brothers have gone in for a bit of trade. Even my professional fees seem to him an appalling source of income, though he takes comfort from the fact that I do not keep an office. This fact makes my consulting room into only a place from which I exercise what is from his point of view nothing worse than an eccentric hobby. Many a nobleman's son may spend his life touring the continent and visiting various spas without bringing disgrace upon his family, but to earn one's living through one's own efforts only serves to bring the family down in the social register. This is a well known class-based mandate of the present era, but should a more democratic ethos follow it will seem a bit strange. This prejudice against labor is less evident in America with its mania for commerce.

Leisure is generally frowned upon although it is the basis for culture. This very question came up last night as I sat with

Mycroft in the dining room of the Diogenes Club over a late dinner. We had the larger room quite to ourselves in the late evening, so discourse was permitted. Mycroft has been a member for such a long period that minor infractions are overlooked. It has been my experience that Mycroft grows more expansive after a good meal. On this occasion he treated me to his opinions on the German-Austrian question. I had just pointed out that wealth and leisure seemed an inadequate basis for any choice of rulers. This of course was directed at the institution of hereditary monarchy or its American equivalent. I have been listening to Watson and have begun to share some of his democratic sympathies.

"So would you choose the ruling class from the industrious bourgeoisie, Sherlock?" he asked me over cigars and brandy. "That is an interesting proposition, but how would you prevent members of that vulgar class from portioning out the national assets among their friends and associates. To rise in business is to make various alliances if one is to succeed. These loyalties would surely follow such a one into office. Even bankers and brokers of various sorts must 'play the game' as they say. You have only to observe the parceling out of offices after each presidential election in America if you would see the cost of the loss of a viable aristocracy to a nation. The entire American electoral process is redolent of a country bazaar or a cattle-auction. But you must not suppose that I would therefore swing to the opposite extreme and sanction autocratic rule such as that which prevails in Hohenzollern Germany or Hapsburg Austria, let alone the extensive Asiatic empire of the Romanoff's. What these nations gain in stability they forfeit in the human resentment and misery of their subject ethnicities. National aspirations are a natural desire of any cohesive linguistic or cultural group and its systematic frustration only sows the seeds of war. Not that fragmentation ensures peace. One need only witness the chronic unrest present in the Balkans to prove this. Ambition for more territory is as likely to arise among small states as among large ones and for this reason modern history has sanctioned the existence of even such polyglot and cumbersome empires as that maintained by the Hapsburgs. I would not admit this anywhere but in the silence of the Diogenes Club."

Here his voice was lowered to a whisper, "But that man, Emperor Franz Joseph, is a perfect idiot."

"Why do you say so?" I inquired.

"Well the man was a fool when he was young and he has not improved with age. It is clear for instance that Hungary is lost to the Austrian crown—why then not liberate them and the Croats and Serbs also for that matter. Set them all up as separate states. Why should the whole of Europe be drawn into the domestic politics of the Balkans? Allow the brush fires to blaze until these fractious Slavs reach a *modus vivendi* among themselves. Let them set their own borders through natural allegiance. People prefer the company of those who are like themselves. Tolerance and understanding are rare commodities. This business of the Balkans is a shadow that haunts Europe. I can tell you that Russia has been nosing about lately, asking Britain for an alliance in case of war with Germany. I have advised the Prime Minister to reject all such proposals. If Russia knows that it stands alone it will not meddle in the Balkans and if Russia leaves the Balkans alone then so must Austria also. But do you think that my advice will be welcome on the continent? No! My advice is to let Germany have its way as long as they stay to the natural border of the Rhine and as long as their navy does not threaten our islands."

I posed another question, "So you would direct any German desire for expansion eastwards, but is that not somewhat Machiavellian Mycroft? Who are we to decide the fate of other nations; after all what about the Polish desire for independence?"

He laughed at my poor grasp of the matter, "You misunderstand the relations between nations, Sherlock. Does it matter whether the Poles are dominated from the east or from the west? Shall Great Britain set the borders of Poland and Ukraine? It will be quite enough for us and for France to hold the rough line provided by the Rhine River. There is a gradual diminishment of civilization as our pointer moves in an eastward direction across Europe and into Asia until one reaches China where civilization emerges once again. We must remember that these regions have been the site of endless invasions and migrations over the centuries. In politics there is no original position; everything is in constant flux. To take an example, what is Islam but a vast ocean lapping at the shores of Christendom? The only good that Austria has ever done was to stop the Turks just short of Vienna. We must keep Austria's eyes focused towards the west when she seeks allies and towards the east when she fears the loss of her empire. I am trying to achieve, what may be my last effort for our government, to broker a peace between France and Austria. This will isolate Germany by focusing its security concerns simply maintaining its present southern and western borders. The result will be that its only open field for territorial expansion will be eastwards towards Russia. The Prussians will eventually want to move east in any case. Where is the German capital at present - Berlin! The whole of Germany is already leaking into the Baltic region and menacing St. Petersburg. It is merely a matter of time before Germany and Russia will be at war. The task of England and France then is to hold the line in the west so that Germany will not be tempted for any reason to enter into a two-front war, which of course would be the utmost folly."

"But France has always been our traditional enemy," I objected.

"Strange to hear you say so, since you are such a Francophile, Sherlock," he huffed. "I am not saying that I see eye to eye with the French on all matters, but we have managed rather well to parcel out Africa between us without going to war. Let us build then on a friendship of convenience and see if we can avoid being sucked into a general European defensive conflict that will only serve to diminish our present enviable supremacy over Germany in the race for colonies. That in any case has been my advice to Her Majesty and to her ministers."

He paused and refreshed our glasses with brandy before continuing with his most interesting presentation.

"Of course the real problem in diplomacy, once some degree of European stability will have been achieved, is to settle relations within the Near East. The Ottoman Empire is at present held together not by chains, but by nothing more than a frayed string. The whole tottering structure has been teetering for years, an ineffective and corrupt bureaucracy with a rotten center in the sultan. It has long been my opinion that political power is similar to those cyclonic storms that are called hurricanes or typhoons depending upon their point of origin. The center is a vacuum around which various forces swirl: the military generals, the scheming barons, or the various revolutionary factions. The Osmanlis of the Ottoman Empire implicitly recognized this image by establishing a sultanate as the center of power. The sultan is essentially a mindless center of organized depravity surrounded by a harem for his amusement. The bureaucracy ensures its own survival by seeing to it that the sultans are brought up in ignorance of everything but the arts of pointless indulgence with the result that power, which might gravitate towards the center if a man of insight or ambition were ever to occupy it, remains always at the periphery. Meanwhile the majesty of the sultanate is proven to the masses by celebrating in the person of the Sultan the luxury that the masses would wish for themselves with every sensual need gratified, every vagrant wish met, every whim catered to, and all to such a degree that it is reported that mere boredom finally is manifest in a loss of animal virility even for the Sultan who one would suppose would have enhanced it through constant exercise of the procreative faculty."

He smiled at this supposition, "It is not uncommon for the various candidates for the sultanate to meet an early death in the strange twilight world of intrigue that is waged between the various women of the harem, who are not wives in our sense at all, but are rather mere slaves fulfilling the most meretricious function of their sex, simply to amuse. Well then, when this ludicrous empire finally dissolves a power vacuum will occur of truly august magnitude. Who or what shall fill this gap and at what cost? That will be the great problem for the century that follows the period of the achievement of a general European stability. I do not envy the nation or nations that must address that problem, for what the Balkans are today the Near East will be tomorrow. It is a region of seething ethnicities and religious sects in contention all across the region east and south of the Caucasus. My own choice would be to aid the Persians to restore their empire as long as we can keep India. We need a strong force in the south to balance the aspirations of the Czar to control the Black Sea and the eastern Mediterranean. A renewed Persian Empire could keep peace between the warring factions of Asia Minor."

"But what of the Bedouin tribes of Arabia?" I inquired. "After all they control the access to Mecca."

Mycroft laughed disparagingly, "They are a people of shrines, tents, date palms, camels and wells…give them power, hah never! Why should what is nothing more than a mere caravan route be recognized as a nation? There are areas of the earth that are only desert regions to be divided up by various warlords. These areas can never be reduced to a nation-state model of governance. They are destined to pay tribute to an empire, which in turn will maintain some sort of order among them in return."

He paused for a moment and gazed into space before resuming, "The ancient Chinese realized this fact of geopolitics centuries ago and established an elaborate tributary system. It is in the nature of every great civilization to attract satellites from outside in the surrounding darkness. Trade is the greatest force for peace and trade must have a center around which to orbit. To assume a general ability to self-govern is to deny all that we know of human nature and of history. Even the Americans that strange mongrel people can barely manage to maintain a democracy; how then will these various tribal orders that dominate southern Asia be transformed so that they can maintain a European style of government? No, Sherlock, democracy I am afraid must remain for the minority of humanity, those who are best educated and most blessed with technical improvements and manufacturing ability. For the rest we may only pray that the less deplorable despots will gain the advantage in the incessant struggle for existence. The policy of Her Majesty's government must be to set up a balance of forces that can keep England and Western Europe at peace."

After another pause he summed up his thoughts in this way, "Think of diplomacy the way that a physicist thinks of vectors of force. By keeping a strong alliance with the French we push any tendency towards German aggression eastwards towards Russia and northwards along the Baltic. This drives the advocates of Polish nationalism southwards towards Rumania and Ukraine. The Poles will serve as a buffer against Russian aggression westwards into Central Europe, which in turn will preserve the Austro-Hungarian Empire. As an ally in achieving this policy a successful treaty should be signed with France and perhaps later on with Austria. We could use the power of Austria-Hungary against the Turks who may seek and alliance with Germany. There has been talk of extending a railroad line from Germany into Turkey. When the Turks find themselves blocked in the west they will in turn keep to their assigned role of opposing Russian expansion southwards into the Black Sea region and Mesopotamia. Greece and Egypt meanwhile will be our agents in the eastern Mediterranean. Further east still, by keeping good relations with Persia, we drive the Persians away from our Indian colonial possessions northwards against Russia and westwards to secure the barren Arab peninsula against the Ottoman threat of expansion. The Sultan will be effectively bottled up and must then abandon any aspirations to fight against the Bulgarians or the Greeks. They in turn will busy enough at home simply keeping domestic order, the first against the Tsigani and the second against the Macedonians. As for Palestine, our task there is simply to keep religious factionalism from rearing again its ugly head. I am opposed to any drift of the Jewish people back into Palestine."

I had not been aware that any policy in this regard by England was even contemplated. "And why is that?" I inquired. "Surely no more perfected title to land exists than that of the Jewish people to the land given to them by God."

Mycroft looked up in surprise, "I am surprised to hear you take such an obvious, but facile view of Divine Revelation Sherlock. The promises to Israel surely exceed a mere grant of real estate. The task of the Jewish people as shown by history is to be a great cosmopolitan force of civilization, to be dispersed into every corner of the earth and to bear with them the testimony of their remarkable adhesiveness to the Torah despite all the pressures to assimilate. Give the Jews a homeland and they are reduced to being merely another warring nation among nations. No Sherlock, the Jews must be kept out of Palestine at all costs in order to play their essential role in history, not merely to suffer, but to inspire and educate the world."

"But then they will continue to be persecuted as strangers in every place that they go. Surely history has taught us that," I replied.

Mycroft disagreed with my assessment, "Every race of

people is a stranger to every other race. The only difference is that the Jewish people never allow the collectivity of mankind to forget their specific sufferings; they have left a record of them. Every time they have been forced by a superior power out of their preferred place of residence they have read theological significance into the event. What if everyone did that? The present nations of Europe have been in constant movement and contention. It is the story of mankind to be dislodged and to return if they are able to do so. This is why every reader of the Bible assumes that it is talking about him. No other race of people has fully appreciated the utility of leaving a written record of their troubles behind with the added element of a God. The result is that we are still saddled with the Mosaic laws, whereas the Code of Hammurabi is a mere jurisprudential fossil. Why is this? Because the Jews never stop writing! Just look at the Talmud...has any more cohesive set of commentaries on a text ever been created by man. The Jewish people are in all truth God's chosen people by their sheer disproportionate influence upon human thought. No, it shall be the British policy to allow them to continue to do as they have always done by remaining dispersed. The renewal of a Jewish state in Palestine would merely act as an irritant to the Moslem tribes, from Arabia to central Asia. Why sow the seeds for such endless conflict? Please note, Sherlock, that all that I have said only addresses the political reality of the Jewish people, not their religious claims."

"I am afraid that from an Orthodox Jewish perspective the political and religious questions are identical," I observed dryly.

He smiled, "Well be that as it may, I am a serving minister in Her Majesty's government and I must operate within the constraints of that trust unless I am to resign my office. The final result of the approach that I have outlined above will be peace as far as the frontiers of China. By opposing force with force in one great balance of arms the result will be stalemate to the urge towards territorial expansionism into Central Asia by any European power. It may avert a general European war."

Mycroft yawned then and stretched his great frame.

"But I must tire you with these speculations on the very eve of your departure. It is time that you were home in bed at Baker

Street. Finish your brandy; it is too precious to waste. There's a good fellow. I will see that a cab is summoned for you. Write me from Devonshire and keep me informed on this Moriarty business and do please try and rest while you are there. You looked like the very devil when you arrived here tonight, but I trust that a good meal by the fireside has helped a bit. I would hear from Dr. Watson in Cornwall soon enough if I allowed you to leave London on your usual diet of boiled beef or fish and chips."

This ended what may be our last evening together for some time to come. Hearing him discourse in this way about world affairs I congratulated myself that as a private agent I need not think of the complex affairs of statecraft. It is a luxury to be spared making decisions that must by their very nature affect the lives and deaths of thousands. I doubt if I could sleep nights wondering what decision of mine might have doomed another person that I would never meet to endless rue over a lost husband, wife, or child.

My own moral system would come apart at the seams if I needed to act in the utter darkness of history and allow events to proceed as they will but deflected however partially by a decision made by me. It would be like standing atop a mountain and releasing a single rock, knowing that an avalanche would result. The control over our own lives diminishes in direct proportion to our power over the lives of others. Yet to abjure responsibility if one is called to assume it is a luxury equally to be condemned. I prefer to keep the scope of my actions close enough that the results are within the parameter of my vision. Blessed is the man who manages to live an entire lifetime without incurring blood-guilt upon his soul.

February 2, 1897
Cornwall

The first month of this fresh year has been more eventful than Watson hoped it would be. It began with a most interesting case at the Abbey Grange that delayed our departure for Cornwall. But we have arrived here in time for Saint Bridget's day, the feast of the Goddess Imbolg, or Candlemas as it is known in this region. Watson was particularly anxious that we be able to enjoy the festivities that accompany the holiday where the maiden of the coming year betokens the return of light and is in her own person an augury of spring.

I have brought along with me the old English Charters, which if properly interpreted according to a theory of my own may indicate that certain lands claimed by some of the richest barons in England were ceded to the people of the several counties before the sixteenth century. If this is so, then their successors in interest have a valid claim to this very day. The origins of property go back to feudal times and were based upon vows of loyalty and vassalage meant to secure an orderly society at a time when blind forces ruled the day.

How peculiar it is that our latter-day legal concept considers property to be a material thing without any immediate reference to the good to be served to the society by recognizing private ownership rather than common entitlement. The same society that serves as the basis for the recognition of the legitimate nature of a claim or its lack thereof is the *sine qua non* for property as an enforceable right to exist at all. This recognition is treated as a law of nature and the politically derived laws are treated as an outside party with only a marginal stake in any transactions that may occur.

There is a natural law right of course to the essentials of life and to some degree of ownership appertaining to one's personal needs, but that right is not to be construed to include the ownership of vast enterprises which are the fruit of the general progress of the technical knowledge of all mankind and the social adaptation by societies that create markets. I am often startled by the fundamentalism that gazes daily at the spectacle of unconscionable fortunes that now exist and assumes that they may be claimed by one man when the creation of such extreme wealth is clearly a product of the historical evolution of the society as a whole.

As such, these fortunes, to the degree of their superfluity, should be a possession of the commonwealth and shared for the general benefit of the nation. Mere accidents of distribution in an imperfectly organized economy must not be allowed to triumph above the common good or the very conditions that make wealth possible will be lost and a new dark age will be the inevitable result. The unjust nature of the present social distribution of assets may be easily calculated as proportional to the force that must be exerted to maintain it. It is no accident that nations that thrive on the depredation of weaker nations must maintain large standing armies in order to maintain their despotic rule. A free society needs little in the way of policing and abjures war as the last refuge of the greed of man or of the desperation of the oppressed.

Later—

Watson and I are quite settled in now, although work remains here to be done on my cottage and in finding Watson his desired domicile by the sea. As a respite from our researches we spent the day out upon the sea cliffs and in the nearby town of Tredannick Wollas with the vicar of the local Anglican Parish, a Mr. Roundhay. His name is descriptive of his person, for he is somewhat portly and possessed of a ruddy demeanor. His orthodoxy is unquestionable, but he has a certain degree of affection for the pagan remnants of Celtic lore in the region, and we have already had several most interesting discussions with him upon these topics. I even broached the topic with him of my pet theory that the ancient Cornish language contains certain common elements or roots traceable to the ancient Chaldean culture. The world of antiquity was not averse to odd cross-currents of trade and the commerce of ideas was more extensive than is generally realized or admitted. I do not know that it is possible to eliminate every remote influence upon even revealed doctrine. Indeed, if anything surprises me it is that any coherent body of belief is ever possible to attain at all, let alone that it might survive with any purity and consistency for two thousand years as in Christianity. This is due largely to the genius of Roman Catholic practice. While vigilance is necessary to prevent too great a drift in orthodox belief, the people must also be allowed to develop some degree of variety in their devotions if religion is not to be made so rigid and dry as to have no relationship to actual life. The mysteries of faith must often be clothed in aesthetic garb if they are to survive. It was the great error of the iconoclasts and later of the Calvinists that they denied the material aspect of man within their narrow creeds and by doing so came to rely instead upon a series of irrelevant abstractions rather than the living doctrines of Catholicism

After witnessing the local Candlemas procession we all retired to a pub for refreshment. The local mead made of honey from the moors is a favorite here. It was delightful to return to the comforts of village life after my recent years in the great metropolitan city of London. It is necessary to know and be part of a neighborhood such as a village provides if one is to know the perfect balance between solitude and social intercourse. I told Mr. Roundhay how we had progressed in our search. Watson and I have been able to provide the prospect of employment for several local artisans and furniture makers since our arrival.

I must say that my lungs have already improved sufficiently for me to take short walks above Poldhu Bay and among the sand dunes around the north point. There has been only one gale since our arrival, but it was followed by several days of sunlight and fresh breezes blowing up from the south. I fancied that that they carried with them the sweet scent of the Canary Islands and the Azores. I am already hungry for spring. Sir Henry has heard of our arrival in Cornwall and has asked that I visit him and his good wife as soon as I feel up to it. I look forward to telling Dr. Mortimer about the revelations I have received regarding the Druids from Mr. Roundhay. I must say that Cornwall has its particular haunted aspects. I do not suppose that any place may have a long history without its corresponding registry of specters. The past never really dies among a sedentary people where the force of tradition is a constant. But as I have often said to Watson, this world is big enough for us and no ghosts need apply.

March 16, 1897
Cornwall

I wonder now if the last line in my final entry may have been a premonition for the events of today, for a most interesting case has been laid before me involving a local family named Tregennis. It came to me through the agency of our friend, Mr.

Roundhay, who brought the afflicted brother to our door. It appears that an event both terrible and inexplicable has occurred during the night. Mr. Mortimer Tregennis has within the course of one night lost two brothers to madness and a sister to near death at the hands of an agency the nature of which only the most wild of speculations may be entertained. It is the doctrine of the Catholic Church that the devil is allowed a certain degree of liberty and that preternatural manifestations are indeed possible, but the suddenness and abruptness of the present visitation seems to me to be unique in its way and to suggest the presence of a human agency and not a diabolical one. Much to Watson's displeasure it appears that a new case has fallen upon my very doorstep. I can hardly refuse my aid under the circumstances. We must see if a solution may be obtained in this case by the exercise of reason before positing a cause beyond the natural dispensation of this world and invoking prayer and fasting or the intervention of a local priest and exorcist.

March 20, 1897
Cornwall

The aforementioned Tregennis affair has ended as swiftly as it began. The case has been one as startling and as unique in its nature as any that I have ever encountered. Certainly the pharmacopeia of nature appears to contain noxious agents of every variety. It has set me to speculating whether it is by just such a means that Moriarty will attempt to spread ruin among us. There can be no doubt that nature fell with mankind, not into sin but in relation to us antagonistic. How else are we to account for the poisons carried by spiders and snakes, the deadly varieties such as the Black Mamba of Africa that is said to be able to chase down a man in full flight? There are times when I think that the earth itself desires to shake us off from its back as a species and that it will take all of the ingenuity of mankind in the future to prevent it from doing so. Certainly I hope that our brief encounter with *Radix Pedis Diabolus* is the only time that I may ever encounter this dreadful substance. It was this that was used as a murder weapon against the peaceful family gathering on that dreadful night.

I have often asked myself from whence comes our innate fascination with deadly substances and agents? Why when life is so complex is death so simple to procure? Why should this reductive power exist? The disproportion of such noxious agents gives us a sense of power when they should only inspire loathing? Yet what is lovelier than the sheen of quicksilver, the compounds of which are more deadly than the metal itself? Then there is the case of the poisonous frogs of the Amazon, brightly colored to warn off predators, and the majestic spread-out hood of the king-cobra to awaken our fears. It is said that certain teeth have been found shed from a great shark that may have exceeded eighty feet in length. Equal sources of terror are the hurricanes and the volcanoes. These most fascinating spectacles awaken awe within us, but what they have in common is their power to destroy and to extinguish the complex processes of life.

Even the virulent microbes and the vile cancer have an obscure beauty in the sheer invasiveness of their operations. Perhaps this goes a long way toward explaining that desire to destroy that drives the brigands of this world. A man named Maxim has now invented a gun that fires repeatedly as though it were a veritable machine of destruction. Aim and accuracy become irrelevant to such a device. What is the point of warfare if mere superior arms can ensure victory? What becomes of courage, resource, fortitude, and will if mere technology is decisive in battle? How far has mankind regressed from its former chivalry!

The time cannot be too far distant when even civilians may become permissible targets for hostility in wars. Whole regions will lie despoiled of life and cursed by the sheer number of the dead. I hope that I may not live to see Englishmen behave in such a fashion. Will material progress only add to the innate brutality of mankind? If so we shall be hostages to the fear of destructive agents that may well escape our control. The end of the present affair has in any case allowed me to afford mercy to an outwardly criminal agent that may seem at variance with a strict respect for our English law. But the law in all matters must be tempered by the voice of the community. My ad hoc jury rendered judgment in the person of Watson and I have decreed the matter to be closed at last by our own form of summary judgment. I would not have

countenanced the revenge before it was exacted, but I refuse to aid
in the apprehension of the man who applied to the villain the same
means that had been used upon the woman that he loved.

April 7, 1897
Baskerville Hall

After concluding the strange case mentioned in my preceding
entry, which will remain unsolved as far as the local
populace is concerned, merely one more of those strange
occurrences that exist among a people who have never lost a sense
of dreadful certainty that the devil still moves among us. Watson
insisted that we move inland for a time to escape the last of the
spring gales. It is high time that I came to visit with Sir Henry after
his repeated requests made when he paid us a visit some weeks
ago on a business trip to Plymouth. He was quite insistent in his
importuning that we spend a month with him at Baskerville Hall
and see the improvements that he has made since my last visit.

The place has certainly lost much of its medieval
discomfort. Lady Beryl has decorated many of the rooms so that
the place is comfortable in a way that no mere masculine touch
could ever achieve. I plan on remaining here for the month of April
and will move back into my cottage at the end of the month.
Watson will return alone to Cornwall. It is one of the prerogatives
of age that it demands a zone, no matter how small, where one's
own preferences and particular daily schedule may be observed
without consulting another's comfort. I have always been as
irregular in my habits as Watson has been regular in his own. It is
no small measure of his virtues that he has managed for such a
large part of his life to exist in such close proximity to an inveterate
bachelor such as myself without losing all patience with me. Since
we have the run of Baskerville Hall at the present time, we have
been granted a period of expansiveness as broad as the moors
which lie all about us. I feel again some relief from my chronic
illness although Watson insists that I spend much of the afternoon
lying on a cot as though I were in Switzerland at the tuberculosis
spa at Davos. He has read a great deal on the various current
treatments for consumption and is in regular correspondence with

Dr. Moore Agar of Harley Street who knows as much about tuberculosis as any man in the world.

I know of no more insidious disease. It seems to toy with its victim, keeping death at bay for an indeterminate period and then suddenly grasping its victim in its claws for the final kill by a sudden hemorrhage. I hope to recover my full strength soon though because I may hear at any time from Professor Moriarty. If I do, I will require my full powers to be at my disposal. I am still somewhat haunted by the Tregennis affair since the revenge committed in that case cannot but remind me of the motivation of Professor Moriarty with regard to England.

The question of private action to remedy injustice is a vexed one at the best of times. The existence of the law is meant to represent the collective conscience of the community and to avoid the excesses that come into play when passions may ignite a chain of similar retribution on the one who seeks private revenge. The law by its august majesty breaks this chain by appearing to be impersonal. It is true that the judge is a human being, but his training is meant to dispel any personal feelings or prejudices that he may entertain in his capacity as a private individual. This same assurance is not present in the executive function of a head of state who may become a tyrant if not constrained by the population as a whole that in a democracy can at times be led astray by the same passions that lead them astray as individuals. It is the magnetic fascination of the demagogue that he can awaken the vile sentiments of the crowd to such a degree that the government at his hands ceases to have the force of law. If this occurs it may even take the hand of an assassin to rid the nation of a disease that has so conquered the usual defenses of the body politic that only this extreme remedy will suffice to bring it into health and balance again. This decision is not to be made lightly and it is more than probable that the benefit rendered will not be recognized for some time. Only history can judge the ultimate justification of such actions as Cassius and Brutus discovered in the matter of Julius Caesar. The chaos of the present assumes a different aspect years after the fact in question. History is replete with tyrants and they serve as examples of the fate that they invite.

I spent today in Sir Henry's excellent library before the fire. It is almost a pleasure to me to have been driven forth from London at this time of year into the countryside to watch the blooms appearing on the trees and to feel the spring in the air again. Part of having an illness like consumption is that it does not allow for hopes of an indefinite futurity by means of which most people avoid their mortal limits. It is rather like what Dr. Samuel Johnson once said about the prospect of being hung, that it concentrates the mind wonderfully. All extraneous factors fall away in the contemplation of one's immanent demise. It has been my habit over the years to think about the life of the great city of London with its many cross-currents and eddies as a great tidal-pool of life. Each person is engaged in pursuing some inner definition of happiness. It is when these trajectories collide that I am called in to discover how motivations and conflicts result in some mysterious outcome.

My first question is always whether by acting in the affair I can improve the situation, not only for my client but for all involved in the tangle before me. For this reason I often refuse to take on certain cases, which I am free to do for I am a bar of one. There is no license or degree that is a prerequisite to the exercise of my profession nor do I hang a shingle out or advertise my services. People find their own way to my door and they tell me of their problems. It is my business to be able to place data into new configurations and by doing so to arrive at what may be assumed to be the truth. This truth is not metaphysical in nature though, but is rather what may be termed practical truth or instrumental truth, truth that brings the participants clarity to guide future action.

I am not at all sure that the 19th century has left the need for metaphysical truths behind. We live now of course in a feverish age, one that is obsessed with pragmatic solutions and with power. The men who are most admired are those who have amassed great fortunes. I am not impressed by this excess however because the acquisition of such excessive wealth merely multiplies the responsibilities that must exceed the possibility of being guided, in the case of a single individual, by moral conduct and reflection. The chains of cause and effect become so attenuated that crimes are committed in one's name over which one has no control.

I on the other hand have the leisure to sift and weigh the actions that I can undertake in good conscience, a luxury that few men of power and wealth possess. My freedom is my fortune. I do not feel that I must reinvent the universe in my own image so as to justify the way that my own mind works as a man like Georg Hegel does in his *Phenomenology of Spirit*. I have written no *Social Statics* like Herbert Spencer. My writings consist of a few short monographs upon narrow and obscure topics. I do not include this journal of mine, which will no doubt be read by only my own eyes and perhaps those of Dr. Watson. My art will perish with me, for it is embodied only in the passing solution of puzzles the energies of which will soon be dispersed and defused in the larger currents of life.

I am resolved to be forgotten by history unless Watson's meager tales written for *The Strand Magazine* endure longer than I expect they will. There is a strain of romance and dare I say predictability in Watson's renditions of speech although his grasp of character is usually precise and his ability to conjure a scene is often quite impressive. But he will always insist upon entertaining the reader. His narrative eyes are always roaming the gallery and the pit to see if his readers are riveted upon the play. Thank heaven that I have been spared being a music-hall performer in this journal at least and can simply reflect at leisure the workings of my own mind. But then I have a passion for anonymity, just as Watson appears to covet his role as my Boswell.

There is always a measure of reflected glory in the disciple that the master abjures, for to seek glory would be to lose whatever was admirable and worth remembering in the subject. It is not that I am overly modest. I take pride enough in reaching my solutions, but it is enough that I reveal the results to one or two select friends and not to the great uncomprehending public at large. I have allowed Watson to publish a few of my little adventures while the vast majority of them have been filed away in my own records. No doubt Watson has spirited some of these away, to file with some records of his own that he keeps in a certain worn and ugly dispatch-box shoved under his bed that he refers to now and again when writing up his tales. When in doubt he asks my permission to publish them and I usually give my consent with the request that he alter names and certain locales that might embarrass those involved. My practice would soon dry up if my clients thought that this agency was a gossip bureau to supply a latter-day Thackeray.

Through the years we have reached a certain compromise. I allow Watson to make me celebrated beyond the select circles to which my practice is increasingly confined and Watson allows me to impose the ban of silence on the remaining majority of my cases. To be quite honest I have come to depend upon his courage, his loyalty, and his presence for my own mind to produce its greatest effects. The habit of anticipating the resistance of his own incomprehension has acted as a sort of governor to the engine of my own speculations. He is the anchor that keeps the light barque of my fancy from going adrift before the gale. I find that I cannot do without him and I dread nothing quite so much as his habit of wandering off into marriage. The fellow has been cursed by a domestic vein that quite baffles me. Can any sweetly smiling companion and soft voice replace a night spent crouched in a hedge awaiting the advent of a suspect? If I am a lean greyhound, then Watson has about him at times the air of a well-fed bulldog sleeping before the fire. But then to expect perfection in a friend just as to expect it in oneself is vanity and delusion.

April 14, 1897
Baskerville Hall

I woke suddenly in the night and seemed to hear again the sound of the ghostly hound of yore, but as I lit the candle at my bedside table I could hear only the crashing of the spring storm outside the windows in the trees. The ivy scraped the leaded panes like skeletal hands. I got up at once to add some coal to the cinders in the grate. The thin chime of the French clock on the mantel told me that four hours remained until dawn. I am not accustomed to splendor in my sleeping arrangements and I would gladly trade my curtained bed at the hall for my old bed at Baker

Street and trade the booming Devonshire gales for the familiar sound of a cab trotting down Baker Street before dawn to deliver milk from Suffolk. It is one of the plagues of an active mind that the slightest waking plunges it again into operation. I often labor to exhaustion the better to ensure against waking with only half of the night spent. I have brought with me a crate of books from our little bookshop and some documents that may promise equity to certain local yeoman farmers involving trusts and entailments. The point of course is to stay busy so that thoughts of Moriarty's plans will not eat the core out of each precious day. I know that nothing brings on my inveterate melancholy as much as the feeling of being disengaged and becoming a mere convalescent and not an active agent in life. Challenge is my meat and drink. There again above the booming gale is that sound. Ah well, nothing so awakens the imagination as an unsettled memory.

April 17, 1897
Baskerville Hall

I am feeling stronger and I have assured Sir Henry and Lady Beryl that I can get along quite well if I move into my cottage again. The habit of being cared for in adulthood is one that I can ill-afford to nurture. My early experience of living away from Yorkshire broke most of the ties that bind one to home and community and I have been selective in my choice of friends through the years since. Among men there is an innate competitiveness that makes of friendship, at least friendship on an equal basis, always a doubtful proposition. For this reason there is nothing quite as sad as the fate of a widower, one who has grown accustomed to the presence of one who takes notice of his health and habits. Suddenly he is bereft again as when he leaves the maternal home. I prefer to mourn but once in that direction. Beyond the general society of one's club, if one is sociably inclined, male friendships are usually based on finding a select audience before which one can boast of one's accomplishments in the great world. Most of such relations are beset with envy and contradiction and as such are best avoided. Women are allowed a degree of mutual affection in friendship, which between men is held to be compromising. There is a comfort in the general benevolence of strangers that may exceed most loves be they filial, fraternal, or romantic. I take as much comfort from a genial waiter at Simpsons or an elderly fellow devotee of Wagner who may tip his hat to me in the lobby between acts as from cultivating a select circle who burden each other with invitations to staid dinner parties. It is no pleasure to engage in the awkward business of explaining away a lost intimacy when interests change or one of the friends occupies a less favored station in life and out of embarrassment is forced to leave a set of formerly vital relations with a circle of friends behind. To share a common purpose outside of ourselves is preferable to friendships of choice among men. A soldier will give his life for a comrade, whereas friendships based upon mere pleasure in one another's company may fall before some mere triviality or misunderstanding. To know any human being too well is often to court disaster. The faculties of prejudice and a readiness to condemn the faults of others are never long in abeyance. To be granted a long life is to know a train of ruptured relations. This is not to say that the solitary bachelor or widower is to be envied, for he is often found dead in bed by his landlady when she brings up his breakfast one morning. My father solved this dilemma by dying alone on the moors where at least the earth and sky were there to minister to his dying strength. In my current illness, I find his example not one to be rejected out of hand. What man with a Viking spirit would wish to die while muffled in blankets and not out upon the empty sea or barren heath?

May 1, 1897
My Own Cottage on Grimpen Moor

oday is the First of May and the lads and lasses of Grimpen village will be dancing about the Maypole. Beltane is a pagan holiday to celebrate the renewal of earthly life and fertility. It is the day when an old bachelor such as I must wonder what legacy he will leave behind him when his own life ends. Of what use is a fire upon a lonely hearth. If the torch of life is not passed has one done one's duty to the life that one has received? Was all of the sacrifice and suffering of my unknown forebears endured simply so that it might come cascading down upon me, a final stagnant pool devoid of life? Where is that still rivulet within me that joined with another might allow the thread of life to continue even if only in a single representative, not that I might be preserved but so that life itself may continue?

But is human life dependent upon only me? If we are all sprung from the same primal parents, then human life is really one and as long as a new child is born anywhere in the world that child is in a sense my child and life has not been betrayed by my celibacy. Perhaps I am one of those eddies in the stream where it may pause for a moment in its great rush to the sea and reflect in its calmness on the distant heavens. Now and again a life must be lived with the full leisure to consider and weigh the human condition and perhaps pronounce upon it some sentence: that life is worth living after all, that life and the knowledge of life are not futile creations of a being born to vanity and extinction. I have sought out the well-springs of human knowledge and found much of wisdom and much of doubt within them. I have walked along, gazing at the dark reflection of night's stream and witnessed the day-spring of dawn. Through it all I have counted upon an endless stream of days to come so that when I found the solution at last to life's many conundrums, I might take up my sickle and seek the harvest of all my hopes with other men and women. But I am older now and my solitary track has left behind the dews of morn and my leaves are fading upon the bough. I have come to September in the life-course of man, when it is too late to plant and when the first harvest is already in the barns, reaped by other hands than mine. What remains then for me?

But these are not the proper thoughts for a spring day. I must enjoy by proxy the festivities as I tried to do before leaving the village today with a bouquet of flowers distributed by the children. I walked home afterwards with a lighter step than has been mine in recent months. Watson has returned to Cornwall, while I have remained in Devon. Baker Street is again the museum that it was during my long eastern sojourn. Mycroft stops by now and again to see that my rooms in Baker Street have an occasional tenant to imply that I am still in residence in case my movements are still followed and Mrs. Hudson sees that he is well-fed when he makes his periodic visitations. It is a novelty for the old fellow to have the solicitous care of a woman. He has grown more voluble with the years and I have heard from Mrs. Hudson that he enjoys sharing with her some of the thoughts that he now entertains of the foregone opportunities that exist in every life. She is also as lonely in her way and it is a pleasure to have at least one Holmes brother present now and again at Baker Street.

Watson meanwhile has returned as I have just said to the sea. He is quite settled in now to the rhythms known only by those who live close to the great oceans of the world. These shore-dwellers feel in the regular pulsation of the waves their closeness to the elemental heart of the earth. I possess my own barque, but it sails on the hollow dales of turf and rocky tor. The moors are like an isolated sea with waves of heather shaking in the winds of spring. My walks are easier for me now and I feel quite strong again. I did well though to leave London. The coal-smoke filled miasma of the city clearly does not agree with me. If I desire to live a full span of life, I will have to admit that my career there will be foreshortened. My beekeeping days may be closer than I would like to admit. So it is that I take life lately as it comes, adjusting my expectations to the exigencies of the times. It is one of the legacies of my readings in oriental philosophy that I ponder the sayings of the Chinese sage Lao Tsu who speaks of "The Way" that cannot be described; it can only be lived.

If I had remained all of my life in Yorkshire rather than pursuing my own fantastic visions, would my life long ago have achieved that rocklike permanence, that sense of inevitability that would justify itself even in my own eyes? What final presentation can ever be adequate to be a last testament of my one and only life? Perhaps if I had fled to France in the first blush of youth to find in the green fields of Brittany a comfortable exile, I would have known less doubt. Or what if I had gone to Germany and walked the streets of Tuebingen or Heidelberg with some of the greatest chemists of the day, would this have been a better life-choice?

Germany has now become the intellectual and musical center of the world. I might have spent my life as a violinist in Bamberg and joined the throngs of worshipers there at Wagner's shrine. I have reached that time of life when one's various phantom incarnations still beckon and ask to be made manifest, if only for a year, so that they may be said to have at least lived for a time in actuality. Is our destiny so written that some great underlying theme, some base-note of desire or ambition that would not be denied, has determined every circumstance so that each chance meeting, each minor articulation, has still carried the life-work forward to its inevitable end? Can I now by one last act complete that final movement of the great symphony and by doing so redeem the vanished hours of my greater powers? Can this be done even now in this latter-day exile upon the bleak moors of Devonshire?

Am I the complement of Professor Moriarty after all or are we both only two sides of but a single coin flung into the air and spinning slowly as it falls to earth? One side must be revealed at last as the victor, but shall it be mine? To have one event bear the result of the efforts of so many years is to court more than mere disappointment should I fail. It is to have each of my other possible incarnations laugh at me. It is to be mocked by possibilities that might have avoided this one particular hour in my own Garden of Gethsemani. Perhaps I should have taken my chance at the Falls of Reichenbach; by grasping the Professor in a grip of steel I might have precipitated us both backwards into the comfort of a definitive resolution for both of us in that seething abyss.

What later labors I would have spared myself! But no, I would abandon neither his salvation nor my own by such an act of comfortable despair. I risked everything so that I might convince even Moriarty as well as myself that there is some set purpose in our lives. If I could do so, I felt certain that I could resolve at once and forever the doubts and fears that have always plagued my own soul and I would also heal wounds of long-standing within me. A man is perhaps best known by those who oppose him. Our enemies show forth clearly the list of our various qualities. The way of opposition is the very nature of existence as the dialectical philosophers assert. Each of us, the Professor and I, has been father-haunted and mother- lost. We are both orphans in our way, as are all men and women born of the earth. Where is Ithaca that with welcome shores will receive the sea-borne wanderer at last?

But enough of this! Let me sit down to my dinner of hearty claret and oat bread in this my humble cottage. Perhaps a private domicile is the source of all of the comfort that a man may ever know. Let my phantom selves be put to rest as I sleep before the fire tonight. May the ticking of the cricket and the spring-song of the moorland frog be my lullaby! May I find peace at last in what surrounds me and allow my visions to fly into that infinite land of lost possibilities where all such phantoms must melt away at last!

May 12, 1897
Grimpen

The desire that is shared by both the Professor and by me, to attain the universal in our single concrete lives contains a great danger. What is our current battle but a great chess game of the mind with the universal at stake? There is something inhuman in this. It is after all the human condition to encounter limitations constantly. This has led many to conclude that it is pointless to even discuss the universals and thus to doubt the relevance of philosophy. But the temptation towards the universal meaning of things is always there. The proper task of philosophy then is to distinguish the true from the many false universal statements that become idols for mankind. Wisdom in the last analysis is found in the process of elimination of false absolutes through actual human experience in history. We learn by sifting through the ashes of the past for the occasional insight into how the particular manifests in a limited context the universal.

Watson has often described my method of solving the little problems that come before me as deductive reasoning, whereas in reality my method is to recognize the importance of details in the concrete situation. If I have one single maxim to give to the aspiring detective it would be to appreciate what is actually happening, a concept that the Buddhists term "mindfulness." This is the actual opposite of the course of deductive reasoning, which assumes that a generality exists, that can then be applied to the particular instance. My experience has taught me that it is the particular which must rule; change one fact and the entire pattern changes.

What separates me from the members of the official detective force is that the various inspectors usually rush to conclusions based upon a handful of pre-existing solutions that they carry about in their heads. Change one significant fact and the model becomes inapplicable. The result is that facts are trimmed by them so that the model can be imposed upon the unique situation at hand. This habit of mind often leads them astray. When I produce my own solution it is attributed to some unique magic that I possess rather than to my systematic pursuance of an alternative method, one that is suspicious of the tendency to assume the applicability of premature universals to the situation before us.

Watson has made much of my posture in my chair when listening to clients, one with my eyes closed and an expression of quiet or even boredom upon my face. What he is describing is my effort to rid myself of preconceptions and to listen to the facts before me as though they alone existed. There will be time enough later to apply various patterns to the facts at hand and see if sufficient similarity exists to imply resemblance or identity. The first task of the detective is not to seek a solution, but to resist the tendency to arrive at premature conclusions. So essential is this skill and so rare is its application that few detectives ever arrive at it. To this fact in no small part I owe my unique success.

What works for the detective would work in many other areas of life as well. There is no skill that is less diffused among the arbitrators of the fate of the world than that of resisting premature conclusions and the tendency to carry about any number of fixed ideas which they continually desire to impose upon their fellow men and women.

Not even the Church is immune from this fatal tendency. Human beings are not fungible commodities; what is fatal or ill-advised to one may lead another to a higher wisdom. What are wars after all but examples of this fatal tendency to compel obedience even to the employment of the force of arms to ensure consent? The identification of one's own convenient momentary position or conclusions with universal truth is to make of oneself a god. Time is the rack upon which humanity is stretched and it is time alone that will deliver us from our present discontents and partial insights. Individual faith embraces the universal but does not compel it in others. Therefore I can never hope to triumph over Professor Moriarty by imposing the Catholic faith upon him, but only by showing him in some measure his own fatal neglect of the concrete facts of his own life and its possible solution in Christianity. Conversion if it is to come must be motivated by forces that lie deep within a man and are nurtured by the quiet voice of God that is ever at his side.

May 17, 1897
Grimpen

The spring air has already seemed to bring back to me something of the vigor upon which I have always trusted to enable me to carry on my labors. I have always presumed upon life itself to supply me with what I have demanded of it, as though the universe itself were a collaborator in my efforts and affairs. It is a characteristic of certain personality types to imagine that they have been delegated the task of digesting the common experience of the human race. This type of person desires to abstract from the singularity so as to obtain the distance required from which to survey the passing scene of the multitude of human beings of all possible conditions that are alive at any one time on the planet. It is rather akin, this attitude, with that of the landed gentry to those denizens of farm and village that surround the estate. This of course is only a tiny microcosm of the conditions that prevail in other regions of the earth. Our perspectives are culture-bound entities and our aspirations are limited by our immediate experience of life and the traditions in which we have been raised. The earth is one single pulsing organism of amazing complexity and nothing happens that does not affect the whole in some way.

My own upbringing reveals the limitations of our sympathy. The deaths of the tenants and the village tradesmen once seemed as natural in the days of my youth as the falling of the leaves in autumn. There was little horror for me in the fresh mounds of the graves in the local churchyard. I will even go so far as to say that the headstones in the cemetery all leaning awry, moss covered, and forgotten were part of the joys of us local lads who would play at hide and seek among them. It was natural to us that the weathered faces of the elderly crofters and their wives with strange bewhiskered chins should pass beyond this lighted realm to death, to thread the darkened catacombs where their vanished souls abide. Now and again though, one of our little schoolmates would succumb to scarlet fever or typhoid and would never be seen again. For such as these death seemed an inappropriate invasion into our comfortable sense of our own natural immortality. Even now, my mates from my boyhood days seem still appareled in the celestial light of an eternal spring. Those whom I have not seen in many years but have later encountered in a London club seem as though they have assumed their present aspect of age as part of a harlequin show. They will remain always to my heart what they were once as children. True objectivity in one's views is diminished in direct proportion to the proximity of other's lives to our own. To deny their aging is to deny our own and to grant them a series of reprieves from death is to parole ourselves from the prison of our days and nights.

I do not now take the same comfort in my visits home that I once did. The ghosts of all my former selves still run along the paths through the Yorkshire moors where I spent my boyhood. I gaze upwards now into towering oaks whose upper branches were once for me the masts of sailing brigs scudding along under full-sail to meet in battle with pirates in the golden Caribbean Isles on the Spanish Main. I gaze upwards now on my visits home with heavy limbs prudently attached to the ground and wonder how the same tree, though older, seems smaller and less beckoning than once it was. But its changes are as nothing to those of its erstwhile inhabitant when like some chattering ape I once haunted branches that though thin seemed always able to bear my weight. I had no fear of falling although the tree itself seemed to sway beneath the winds that would come inland from the English Channel. What has become of that easy familiarity that made us one in a life that seemed able to span whole generations of mere men and women?

My own presumed immunity to life's vicissitudes was only an illusion after all. My youthful perspective was always one of history and not of the individual life. Is it fair then to suddenly find myself brought low from my eagle-like soaring and to find myself at last only one more lost denizen of the soil? Everything within me rebels against this realization! Like my father I would wish to hoist myself again into my saddle for one last gallop over heath and furze and seek out a high tor from whence I could observe the sweep of land and sky before surrendering to the common lot of man. I would shake my fist at the very providence that has decreed our shortened fate that time will inevitably deliver us to the soil from whence we have sprung.

It has always noticed that it is to the women that we must look if we are to be reconciled with our human limitations. A woman's body is by its very nature never entirely emancipated from the tidal rhythms of the earth. Her concern for her offspring, born through the rhythms and effort of her own being, is such that in her tears and sorrows, in her laughter and her joys, all things are reconciled and made one. Only men are allowed and even encouraged to imagine themselves proof to their origins and free to imagine kingdoms and empires, each offering willing obeisance to the governance of their own all encompassing will. This is the reason for the shock that comes upon the egoistic man when he realizes that he is not immune after all from the lot of all mankind and that the days and nights of his mortal drawing account will finally show a balance of zero.

It is only then that such men seek to flee their former friends who are already falling away into illness and death. Their very ills seem an impertinent reminder of one's own condition. Too late for escape! Like cattle once herded together at a slaughter-house he is now to be carried along with them, their frightened lowing is a mere echo of his own growing trepidation. Better finally to face death alone as though it was only one's own unique fate, one to be met with a desperate courage, rather than to feel part of a mindless herd of bewildered beasts. This is the moral stance of those whose claims upon life have always exceeded the limits granted to us by our common mortality. I am one of these men and perhaps Professor Moriarty is as well and this is the basis of our understanding.

I have quickly grown accustomed again to country living as though no intervening years had passed since I acquired this moorland cottage. I am obeying the doctors' orders as well as I can. I spend my days in research and reading and in the evenings I sit outside in my garden and look over the stone wall in the direction of Baskerville Hall and then turn my chair to the west to observe the setting sun. So peaceful is my existence here that I tend at times to forget that great issues still wait to be resolved that may pry me forth from this peaceful retreat and send me again into the great world.

This thought has made me wonder how it is possible for wars to summon forth multitudes of men to leave their homes and families and everything to which the normal loyalties and cares of life are affixed to form great amorphous masses rushing into the smoke of powder and the hail of steel. It makes me question whether famines storms or earthquakes are really unmitigated evils because they remind us of the precious quality of life whereas war represents the ultimate luxury for any society that engages in it; if all the nations of the earth could be reduced to a condition of absolute and abject penury, then from whence would come the armaments with which to wage wars? These voluntary purges arise not from need but from the unbridled desires of nations for honor, power, and possession.

As I reflect on our present age with the obtuse pageantry of its leaders and the common hunger for colonial possessions a chill runs through me. How long can it be before there is a great general European war? This absurd competition in every field of endeavor when coupled with inventions and industrial resources must change the very nature of war itself. The nations will be hard-pressed to maintain a reserve where non-combatants may continue the ordinary pursuits of living such as raising crops, providing transport for essential goods, and the equally essential pursuits of culture. There is apocalypse in the air, a desire for some overall solution to these problems, as though one age could resolve all things rather than simply contributing its tiny increment to life in its passing. We live in an age of false absolutes that are only held at bay by aging dynasties. I feel that a new dark age lies just over the horizon and I can do nothing to stop it. At best I can try and withdraw the tiny part that my own life represents and withhold my consent toward whatever is coming. I may however need to take a more active role. I am not ready to retire yet by any means although my present retreat is so satisfying that my old talk of Sussex as the site of my declining years seems unlikely to find fruition. It is not impossible of course that the process of letting go of my active life will happen by fits and starts and that a demanding public will repeatedly call me back to my old pursuit of the solution to crimes and puzzles.

I have often said that my mind rebels against stagnation, but is that not all too often what retirement represents for the average man or woman. Can death be far behind for anyone who lays aside all burdens of care and commitment? Rather, let me live until my final hour and die with manuscripts still open upon the table and books with markers scattered about the room and a client coming in the evening as previously arranged. I must say though that here is a zone of activity residing even in quiescence and this is my present occupation. The sun's rays lie golden over the bracken and moorland and already the white moths are flitting about like little stars. The mists are rising from the mire and the breeze carries the chill of night upon its shoulders.

I must go in soon and start a turf fire and light the candles before dusk. There is a smoked ham in the larder and a loaf of rustic bread and a great round cheese from the Cotswold's sent down by Sir Henry to eat so a late meal before bed beckons. My present needs are easily met and I am safe. Why is it then that I feel that a great storm threatens to close-in upon me, one that will send me forth towards greater demands than I have ever yet faced? I must use this precious time to good effect. It is those who first feel the change in the barometric pressure in their very being who must warn their fellow men and women when danger threatens.

From May to midsummer the months have passed and still there has been no definitive word from Professor Moriarty. I have endeavored to distract myself by pursuing my researches and by adhering to a strict regimen of healthy foods and rest I have striven to regain my health. Both methods have shown results, aided by the warm air of the surrounding moorlands and the clear summer nights. When the time for action comes, I must be well prepared. I feel my forces gathering within me for one last assault upon the battlements that have so long opposed me. I ride forth to do battle with my colors held high and my banners waving in the wind. If word shall come at last will it be as once before, a challenge to single combat to decide the issue? If so, I am prepared to sacrifice myself to save England. Oh friend Watson, where are you? Why are you not a witness to these, my glowing words? They are just such words as he would use to make of me a legend. If he could read however the trepidation of my heart and know how often I kneel in prayer with my lance abandoned upon the ground would he celebrate me so? If I am to prevail, it must be by marshalling the advantage of my noble cause and leaving the rest to God.

The perspective offered from the year's longest day is one of expansiveness and optimism. I can only hope that whatever his plans may be that the time for their execution will not be this winter when my energies are traditionally ebbing with the dying year. Of course it is Moriarty's contention that the role of England in the affairs of the world are also about to ebb away. I have asked myself which nation is best situated to take the laurel crown of victory from the brow of Britannia and quite honestly none presents itself. France is unlikely to wish for a repeat of the folly that led it to the gates of Moscow before being forced to retreat under Napoleon leading to his final defeat under Wellington at Waterloo. Spain ever since the defeat of the Spanish Armada by England under command of Lord Charles Howard of Effingham and Sir Francis Drake in 1588 lost its former position as the wealthiest nation in Europe, not that overall wealth is decisive as a measure of national power and resilience. Nor is the extent of land under national rule an adequate measure of military power otherwise Russia would certainly dominate the world. Russia is prevented from doing so because of the general backwardness of the country, inadequate industrial resources, and the challenges of its geographic isolation, and it has only recently been delivered from serfdom. This leaves only Germany and Austria-Hungary as contenders for continental hegemony. The latter is a polyglot empire troubled by fractious ethnic aspirations for sovereignty. This leaves only Germany as the only real threat to British supremacy.

Somehow I cannot imagine that the Professor's plan is military in nature. His comparative obscurity does not give him access to the rulers of nations therefore his vengeance would of necessity require a private party in order to finance the endeavor. It is unlikely that such an ambitious plan could involve a wide conspiracy because the probability of discovery is multiplied exponentially by the number of agents required for its prosecution. Taking all of these elements together and applying my usual methods I lean toward a model then of a close partnership wielding some yet to be determined agent of destruction that will disable the nation or lead it into war.

Again the military aspect is too complex to be arranged by private parties unless they have come into some manner of compromising letters that might lead to the outbreak of war as in Watson's tale, *The Adventure of the Second Stain* when the Prime Minister accompanied by the Right Honorable Trelawney Hope, the Secretary of State for European Affairs engaged me to find some possibly fatal papers that had evidently been stolen. It was a case where a wife's loyalty to her husband led her to trust in my discretion and the papers were safely returned by a ruse of my own devising. This case occurred in 1888 as I recall and was one of the first where my name began to circulate in the higher regions of government as a reliable resource. I have always attempted to hide my relations with Mycroft in order to prevent any suspicion that he was sharing secrets with his artistic and eccentric brother. After this case no such caution was necessary because I was a name in my own capacity as one that could be trusted in high affairs of state.

So there we have it as far as the present data will allow me to speculate: a close partnership, an unknown agent of destruction that will act quickly and that will be difficult to stop once it is in operation and one that will lead to secondary and cascading harms sufficient to disable the country leading to death and destruction of catastrophic proportions. I had no sooner made this summation when my wandering eye led me to my bookshelf where a copy of Daniel Defoe's excellent fictional account, *A Journal of the Plague Year* reposed in its worn leather binding originally published in 1722. It may have been entirely fortuitous, but this has happened many times before. There was my answer staring me in the face. Moriarty plans to unleash a plague upon England!

June 28, 1897
Grimpen

There is still no proposal for a final meeting from Professor Moriarty but I still receive an occasional message from him. Not a few are various scribbled notations of mathematics that he evidently considers to be self-explanatory. I have resisted getting into a course of regular correspondence with him because I believe that presence, the very means that God uses to communicate with us in prayer and in the sacraments, is essential to my case as well. As nearly as I can make out the argument of the Professor he is still engaged in attempting to locate God somewhere out there in space. For this reason he fails to grasp the nature of the Biblical text that is, in Christianity at least, the presumptive way that God has chosen to communicate with us. This implies some manner of subjectivity on the part of God and subjectivity need not be referred back to an object as its source. The communication in the Bible is religious in nature and takes as its subject a set of relations, historical accounts, prophetic utterances, and hymns of praise as well as other genres, some that are utterly unique as in the gospel narratives.

Therefore, the equations of Professor Moriarty, whatever they may reveal about physics have little or nothing to say as regards theology. I am not sure that this is not the primary problem existing between us that we are speaking about different things even at this late stage of our discussions or debates. How to bridge that fatal gap is the task that lies before me. Occasionally though he comes upon an insight of some significance and when he does I intend to transcribe them here. For instance, what am I to make of this statement?

The philosopher Zeno speculated that just as there is no ultimate scale of size because even at the furthest extreme of immensity something bigger could always be conceived, so also no matter how small something is we could imagine severing it into parts that would be smaller still. This means that the concept of infinity runs in both directions and any actual existing object must occupy a sort of middle-ground of size compared to all other conceivable objects. Therefore God if He exists must either be infinitely large or infinitely small unless we are to assume that God somehow pervades and included all conceivable objects; but of course this assertion inevitably takes us back to the metaphysical position of Spinoza. Unless you can come up with some other way that God can exist I am afraid that I will win our little wager.

Of course by phrasing the problem as he has done he has shown me his hidden card because he insists upon locating God in space and time and that has never been my concession. I maintain that theology is a science of relations not of substances. We do not know God directly unless He chooses to manifest Himself as such. Nor is God co-extensive with space and time no matter how large or small our coordinates may be. The appeal of God is not to our senses, but to the deepest ground of our being, that which sets a horizon to all of our experiences.

In a similar way Divine Grace is not a substance or some sort of imperial elixir to strengthen us in performing good deeds. It is also not something that changes human nature ontologically so that we become other than what we are. The "new birth" spoken of in the New Testament is *sui generis,* utterly unique and not to be understood except on its own terms; the closest we can come is to define it as the blending of two distinct natures through the indwelling presence of God that is always attempting to get closer to us and within us without obliterating or absorbing us or overwhelming us by its supreme power.

The presence of Divine Grace is known only indirectly through its effects. We believe it to be present in acts of faith, in prayer, and in acts performed due to charity in our hearts, but we cannot command it; at best we prepare the ground for its advent and believe the promises that assure us that it will come if we invite its presence into our lives. Anything beyond that is reducible to magic and a reduction of Spirit to our own summary demands that Spirit will serve us rather than our offering ourselves up in willing cooperation and service to Spirit.

Theological concepts are by their very nature a transcription of relations into terms that are meaningful to us by way of analogy, metaphor, and symbol; not to realize this is to do a sort of violence, not to God directly, but to our own understanding of God. Much of the division between religions is based upon a need to bracket off, as irrelevant to its particular truth, any cultural manifestations that serve as intermediary vehicles for the communication of divine reality that will be meaningful to us in our particular historical and cultural circumstances. Professor Moriarty is off somewhere in the jungle with a machete slashing away at the underbrush in search of truth, while I am trying to bring him back to what is really at stake in our discussion: our actual human existence which experiences the need of God in our very being. We need a God in order to account for our own existence as human beings. Morality is not something added on to life but rather something adhering to our inner sense and intuition of perfect justice and virtue. It is not that we create God though, for we experience a need for something more grounded than our contingent existence, some source of absolute truth on which we can rely, not simply now but for eternity.

July 1, 1897
Grimpen

I am still reflecting upon by conclusion that Professor Moriarty is preparing a noxious agent in order to destroy England. He will not be the first to have done so. Confidence in our mechanisms of survival both collective and individual can leave us open to invasion. To the romantic mind life appears to exhibit a malleability that will yield to the individual will so that we grow too confident of our own resources and defenses. It is an open question though whether even the powerful and the wealthy of this earth can escape from those larger dictates that we term history.

Democracy is always romantic in that it assumes that the many can always successfully evaluate the tenor of events and prospects clearly and choose wisely among candidates that have every reason to dissimulate and disguise their true motivations and policies so as to appeal to the broadest spectrum of the populace. Truth is always limited, whereas falsehood leaves wide-open the parameters for invention and duplicity. For this reason, I have little confidence in the progress of humankind even under democracy. Just as there are venomous animals that through a process of evolution have developed disabling venom, certain individuals have learned techniques of camouflage or other techniques that make them profoundly dangerous if they are encountered.

One of the worst of these is the political parasite that enters into the social-body and then through a process of cunning manages to use the mechanisms of the state in order to reproduce itself. The state in a sense becomes the host for the parasite and it will use it to sap its strength and corrupt its processes until nothing remains but a shell of the former healthy republic. This unpleasant prospect makes me uneasy even in my present comfortable circumstances. Yet I realize that I must act sometime in the near future due to the private knowledge that I now possess. I must emerge from my own quiet and natural existence spent here on the moors when the summons comes.

It will be asked by anyone who shares my disillusioned notion of history whether I can devise no comfort to offer if I were even allowed to give a warning, not simply in this instance, but as a general practice. It happens that I have, but it will be of less comfort to the individual than to the species as a whole. Nature is careless of the individual and only reckons its triumphs over centuries and millennia. History might be defined as that process that seeks a new equilibrium after and between various human errors. A rough balance is eventually restored after inequality and tyranny create enough dissatisfaction that wars break out. Thereafter death by war, disease, and famine is the great central clearinghouse in which the perennial account-book of humanity is balanced.

To consciously interfere with this ongoing process may be merely to spread the destruction over time rather than simply allowing what will eventually result if that balance is allowed to find its own proper level in one swift cataclysm followed by a period of peace. Just as an earthquake is only the greater for every year that the tectonic plates do not release the tension of their gradual movement in one great event, so a great and general war can usher-in a period as long as a century or more of prosperity and expansion in peaceful trade relations.

For this reason I place my hope in the minute and constant factors of life between such tragedies as those represented by the gentle pollination of the flowers by the bees, the rain clouds that move across the summer sky, the extinction of that which is exhausted with too much living, the emergence of a variety of new life-forms, the inevitability of change, and the certainty of death. In other words I allow this earth to enact its dramas of excess and depletion while trusting that if a fissure opens in the earth I will not be standing over it at the time. I desire the opportunity and ability to act as a witness of all that is, but I know that my own witness is neither essential nor adequate to the whole; yet I speak, I act, I hope, and dream of better things to come.

July 7, 1897
Grimpen

As I while away these long summer days sitting in my garden overgrown with vines and bracken among the flowers I have been reflecting upon my desire to find an orderly thread that could unite the diverse patterns of life that have found their way into my rooms at Baker Street. As a detective I have been forced to take human nature as I find it and to be acquainted with life's diverse passions and follies while seeking to avoid them in myself. I have tried to eliminate as far as possible the bias of premature and purely personal loyalties so that I can perceive a problem objectively. This requires that I think, not from within myself, but from the inside of persons who are often decidedly different than me. To act in this manner over an extended career might induce a sort of fugue in which all bearings are lost and a moral vertigo sets into the soul. For this reason some objective order must be posited for human life by religious teaching.

In contradistinction to this stringency of command though we have an assurance of the all-abiding mercy of God, which acts as a sort of universal solvent to penetrate into the various crevices of our sins. How to balance these seeming opposites is not the task of the moralist or of the detective since that ideal balance can only be achieved by God. Instead I have chosen the part of the realist who sifts motives into chains of cause and probable effect. This is not to say that I am never surprised. The deductive method must reconcile the common with the exception and when unable to do so it must suspend judgment until further data is available. I have often found that the more highly evolved personalities are always filled with surprises and contradictions. Many of my cases have placed me in the position of dispelling the confusion of troubled souls. It is my considered opinion that the human soul is not one but contains diverse chambers. I will even go so far as to say that the truly single-minded man or woman is so rare that as a detective I may omit even to assume his or her existence. Instead, I assume inner conflict as the basis of all human activity. Choices are often unmade as soon as they are made; we choose directions rather than discreet goals and very little in life is linear. The successful detective must accustom himself to curves and to changes of direction as he sifts what are so prematurely called clues. Each clue is both an indicator and a deception. Thus, I have developed my own method of pursuing what I once called "a three-pipe problem."

The first pipe is what reason tells me might have happened. Over the second pipe I try and find the more improbable courses leading to the same result. Over the third pipe I compare the various versions and seek a testable hypothesis. After that I try and see for myself by question and by direct experience with the parties involved at the very scene of the events what has actually occurred.

All actions leave traces behind them. The ultimate cause may be inferred by gathering the diverse threads of the result into one's hands.

No doubt the exact instant of divine creation could be arrived at by a proper measurement of each resulting action. I wonder, do all forces if sufficiently chaotic resolve themselves again into simplicity, just as the spokes of a whirling wheel disappear so that to the eye only empty space separates the hub from the rim of the wheel? What we term physical evil may from the proper vantage point appear as sublime goodness, but we are doomed to take the individual view that what harms me is an unmitigated evil.

But as a detective I am not allowed the scope of a blithe metaphysical optimism. Instead I adhere to the individual case even if it does not reflect a universal system. After all even systems do not abide in isolation but are part of a greater constellation of relations. This attunement to the particular may be my most significant trait as a detective, one that has allowed me to reach the truth when all off the collective wisdom of Scotland Yard's inspectors has taken another direction.

Whether this is instinct or method, I cannot say; but if even I cannot resolve the steps of my own analysis, then how can I blame poor Watson who so often fails to follow my line of reasoning? Perhaps because what we term reason is inadequate to grasp wholes in one simultaneous act of perception. The mind perceives in leaps and starts so that conviction is most often the advent to the mind of a unity between cognition and will. This is what is meant by the statement that to perceive the good is to do it. To perceive the truth then is a process of gradual unveiling so that deceptions fall away until at last what remains is compelling, unalterable, and integrated into a unity of the observer and the observed.

ord has just reached me from Robbie Ross of the release of Oscar Wilde from Reading Jail in May. The poor fellow has decided to settle down in Paris as an exile. If only he had done that before! Poor Oscar, I am afraid from the report I have received that his time in prison has quite destroyed him. I do hope that he doesn't resume relations with Bosey now that Oscar is free once again. It is clear to me that Oscar was a willing immolation on the pyre of Lord Alfred Douglas' hatred for his Father, the Marquis of Queensbury. Evidently Oscar felt that he must prove the sincerity and righteousness of his disordered attachment to that spoiled young man by allowing both father and son to manipulate him into inviting his own ruin by bringing the fatal libel suit. A better example could not be brought forward of the ruin of a man's offspring by the eccentricity, and perhaps madness, of a father (in this case the Marquis of Queensbury). The elder son died a suicide and the younger has become a byword as a young wretch catering to the peculiar appetites of a married man for the flesh of young men. Yet Oscar was once a model father to his own children, a kindly if abstracted husband, and as good company as any man I have ever known.

I have been allowed to see a copy of Oscar's long confession entitled *De Profundis*. It is truly a remarkable document. How strange that a man who began life so entranced with the trivialities of style and décor should have so plumbed the human condition in what may be his final work. I blame his early demise as a writer less upon him than upon the need of society to imagine that his vice is not widespread in England. Though natural law makes it clear that the procreative faculty should be reserved for its highest use, there is much about passion and the pairings it engenders that exceeds the most obvious use for the sexual faculty. To preserve that function seems guaranteed by nature itself in those who find what is most usual to square up with their own inner desires and dispositions. To condemn and to hold in contempt all other uses seems to grant too narrow an interpretation of what has been manifest in mankind throughout history in all places and times among a minority of individuals.

Still, I am willing to reserve my own private judgment on this contentious matter and to confirm in all ways my own opinions in this as in other matters pertaining to the Catholic faith to the teaching office of the Church. I have been fortunate in being granted a degree of immunity from that passion, which is so universal among humanity: to find one other person or alas for some people many persons, to assuage the essential loneliness of their souls by use of the body.

The entire sexual faculty has always appeared to me to entice one into a veritable quagmire, even in the temporal order. My plans and career have simply not allowed me the leisure to entertain, that which must inevitably if given free rein, be at the very least a distraction and in the most cases the utter ruin of the reasonable faculties and the destroyer of that leisure that I require in order to explore life in other areas. Surely Oscar's fate is the proof if any were needed of the costs imposed by a surrender of the will to mere appetites. Still, my knowledge of the man and his many talents and essentially kind soul keeps me from condemning him as so many have done.

Many men have structural fractures in their character so that it is impossible to isolate one aspect from the many that co-exist within them. Perhaps the soul is less one than it is a council of opposing impulses to the divided will. These conflicts are then manifest in all their days and nights throughout their lives and even at the end. It is not for any other man to sort these out and to decide which might have been controlling in that final hour when we all must render an accounting of our lives before God. Thus I do not judge him but only lament the early extinction of a great man of letters from among us.

July 18, 1897
Grimpen

It may not be amiss to touch upon the concept of love here. Perfect love is what our nature desires and demands just as we desire perfect knowledge and ideal beauty. Love may be termed the unqualified affirmation of a being in all of its unique individuality, an approbation of what is essential to the self, and a corresponding patience with all that adheres to the self through the accidents of life. Such perfect love also implies a corresponding recognition and desire to return love to its source, thus to love and to be loved exist in a corresponding relation. This creates a dynamic of interchange so that each participates in the very being of the other. Love that does not meet love in return exists in frustration of its own nature. Love that fears love's loss lives in terror of its own dissolution.

An exception to this normal course is termed *caritas*, the love that manifests in charity, the love of God. For instance the love of a father for his son, though held to be the very substance of the Divine Trinity, is seldom met with in this imperfect world. Fathers and sons are often divided by contrasting assessments and values. Sometimes the father imagines that the son is an inexact and unsatisfactory image or replica of himself and certain sons, feeling this disapprobation may exaggerate the differences with the father in order not feel overwhelmed by his superior strength and accomplishments. For this reason the son often turns to the mother and affirms within himself what he can share of her own characteristic qualities, while being deprived by nature itself from that total embodiment and identity of form and substance that exists between a mother and her daughter.

Similarly the daughter must find in her father love but not identity of form and substance with him. She may unfortunately later use her father as a standard measure applied to her husband forgetting the idealization felt by children for their parents upon whom they depend for their very existence. The generations of all men and women thus exist in a state of simultaneous affirmation and denial of love in their primal experiences with their parents: love offered and denied, love complete within and love kept at a distance, so that one must seek its fullness in another human being when they reach maturity. But no human being can achieve the perfect correspondence of lover and beloved that exists within the Godhead. Instead we live lives of fractured and incomplete love that often breeds out of love's substance pain and disappointment.

For this reason our lives are spent scattered among partially realized objects as candidates for our affection, admiration, and esteem. Marriage by its character of exclusivity offers eternity while denying it at the same time, for it is to a mortal creature after all that we are wed. Nor can a human being exist in such individual plentitude that sexual desire though squelched may be viewed as absent or unnecessary. If nothing else the mind covets sympathy and understanding. For these select beings there exists an area of subsumed desire in the form of a general love of the world, of sight and sound, of form and color, of music and silence. Perhaps the artistic mind knows and experiences love in the most refined form. Similarly the saints and benefactors, all healers of this troubled world, and the mystics adopt in a general approbation and a similarly sublimated sense of self what might be termed a love of the entire world. Whether love is to be general or specific seems the great choice of life for each man and woman.

July 23, 1897
Grimpen

Dr. Mortimer stopped by my cottage yesterday to break my isolation. As usual he brought with him some of his recent finds on his rambles out upon the moors. His belief in the existence of the fairy folk or pixies seems to be as strong as ever. He visited with Watson and me in Cornwall a few months ago during one of the visits of the great novelist, Dr. Arthur Conan Doyle, who is longtime associate and friend of Watson. Dr. Mortimer expatiated at length on that visit on his peculiar theories in their regard. We were all in a convivial mood that evening and while a spring gale from the sea lashed the windows we gave ourselves up to his strange discourse that I will try and reproduce here as best I may. After speaking at some length on the subject of fairies he took note of what may have been a slight attitude of amusement on our part.

"Ah you smile gentlemen," said he, "But is it likely that our present species of transitional anthropoid ape is the only intelligent life-form upon this planet? I beg you to consider the great span of time that must have existed before our arrival at a state of even the hunter-gatherer stage of our own development.

The period of our collective written history is of such a short duration that it would not be too much to say that even now we are still savages. Who can look at the life of the many tribes of persons from Australia or New Guinea or the Amazon region and not realize that a significant part of humanity still lives a comfortable animal-like existence. Then consider if you will that written human history leaps into being from sheer silence and illiteracy to the speculations of Thales, Anaximenes, Anaximander, Parmenides, Heraclitus, and Plato. Mankind it appears no sooner learns to write before it produces philosophers. Would one not expect a slower learning curve than this? Were we perhaps tutored by another race of beings? And how is it if philosophy is natural to man that the Amazon region has yet to produce its own Aristotle?"

"What answer would you propose then sir to your conundrum?" asked Dr. Conan Doyle with some interest.

"My answer is that evolution does not proceed apace through any given human population," Dr. Mortimer answered. "Even granted a similar cranial capacity and nervous system, humanity is not a univocal construct. There are men among us who are descending backwards retrogressively to assume the status of the great apes. These may soon show a greater kinship to the chimpanzees and the gibbons than to the higher hominids. If this process of atavism is real (and who observing our men in politics can doubt it) then could we not imagine an order of beings who may have long preceded us and from which we may have descended rather than evolved?"

He looked about him at our small circle for some sign of agreement or approbation before continuing with his unique hypothesis regarding the origin of the human mind. "The beings collectively referred to as the fairies of various types may be the survivors of the superior beings who, in their subtle state of intelligence and perfection of energy, once taught philosophy to their primitive students. Their characteristic faculties of speed, transparency, and evasiveness may be less an indication of their non-existence than of our inability to perceive them as they flit between dimensions that we cannot perceive, because we dwell on an inferior metaphysical plane. Their power of fluctuation between states of space and time may simply be due to an insight or invention that exists beyond our crude present capacities. Why when the existence of fairies is spoken of by countless cultures all around the world should we doubt that they exist? If a modern man of Victorian England were to appear among the denizens of a primitive tribe on some remote plateau and demonstrate any one of our current electrical devices and promptly leave again might not a legend of a great sorcerer join the collective memory of that remote tribe? Well gentlemen, we are that remote tribe and the fairy-folk are the evolved race that lives among us still."

He was silent for a time, but I could see that Dr. Conan Doyle seemed much impressed. We all sat smoking in silence for a time before Dr. Mortimer continued again with his discourse.

"Then we must consider the sheer antiquity of the earth. Why in all of that time should only one species have ascended to the level of even mankind? May we not be late arrivals upon the scene of wisdom? What of these tales of angels, of the jinn, and even of giants in the Hebrew and Arabic writings of antiquity? Can we honestly say that these are mere examples of folklore? But is not a dismissive attitude taken in their regard a classic example of presumption and intellectual temerity? How do we know what does not exist? It is surely quite enough to know what does exist. Even now we are discovering new species daily. Why not assume that the great saurian lizards may have been catalogued during their lifetimes by other intelligent beings?"

"If so then where are their records?" Dr. Watson interrupted. "Where is the legacy of their art and architecture?"

"Well as to that why should our crude monuments be the universal norm of civilizations past, Doctor Watson?" answered Dr. Mortimer in a nettled tone. "In a hundred thousand years the great sphinx may be reduced to so much sand. We judge what is ancient by our own propinquity to it in time. We may be like the amphibians, still only half-way out of the waters of our primeval birth into air. Who is to say what may someday be possible even for us if we do not sink again into a world of insensate and mundane temporality."

"An intriguing phrase, doctor," I said at the time, "But what do you mean by the term "insensate and mundane temporality?"

He answered, "Let me give you an example; the animal

world does not live in time as we do, Mr. Holmes. Our life in time is predicated upon a reflective sense of cause and effect; we understand the connections, while the animals do not, at least not in the sense of being able to consider the abstract relationship apart from its concrete constituents and manifestations in the particular instance. Animals live with an immediacy that we do not. The human way of thinking at its best consists in relationships of various sorts, which allow us to contextualize our thoughts in various ways and to transfer insights into new areas of application. There is a phase-change then between human thought and animal thought; to confuse them is to make a category error. Now then, imagine if there is a higher mode of functioning that is as different from our way of thinking as ours is from that of animals, might not certain advanced minds belonging to a higher life-form think in a manner so that its entire way of conceptualizing would become untranslatable to human thought except by the most arcane analogies?"

"Now you are surely being fanciful," Watson said. "We can only know what we think so that to posit such beings would, by that very act of positing their existence, imply a way of being that we can never hope to understand."

Dr. Mortimer rubbed his hands together at this, "Exactly, Dr. Watson, our comprehension would be confined to the sheer affirmation that they exist, but their mode of existing would exceed our capacities. This would hold true for all such beings insofar as their innate capacities exceed ours."

"Are you saying," Watson inquired, "That analogy would be inadequate in their regard as a mode of communication?"

Dr. Mortimer considered this before replying. "Analogy would be permissible as long as we realize that the two terms of the analogy are both our own and that we are reaching above our grasp to affix our line of reasoning to one of the terms of the proposition based upon our best visualization of what might be rather than our certain knowledge of what is. At best this is a pseudo-analogy of course in imagining their cognitive capacities and it may distort the actuality of the experience of higher-order beings than ours to speak in this way of them."

"But why should we imagine that such beings actually

exist?" asked Watson's friend.

Dr. Mortimer answered, "Now you come back to the point that I was trying to make. We may imagine that such beings exist for the same reason that Columbus might have imagined the existence of the Americas prior to his voyage there to find out: that what we know is all too little, there must be more! Why should we imagine ourselves as the very summit of conscious knowledge of the universe? Is such a boring and sterile assumption justified in any way? Yet that is precisely what the sterile skeptic must assert in order to forestall further thought. Such men exist in the decaying shadow of the sphinx and will remain there forever in the comfortable assurance that this world is only to be measured by their own intellectual lethargy."

"Still one must not be too credulous. Have you any actual data that fairies exist?" asked Dr. Watson, who was our host that evening in his new domicile.

Dr. Mortimer took on a mysterious air. "I have seen certain indications, gentlemen."

The wind beat against the windows that night as I recall and I must confess to a certain involuntary shudder as the blast shook the ivy leaves at our window.

"What do you think Holmes?" Watson then enquired of me.

I recall smiling in order to shake off the sense of the uncanny that is often induced by the writings of such men as the fabulist, Arthur Machen.

"Well gentlemen," said I. "My practice demands that I should be thoroughly grounded in the actual and the usual course of events. I will leave it to Dr. Mortimer to extend the horizons of our knowledge into these lofty areas. I am willing to entertain them as possibilities, ones that if they involve the fair folk, from all that I have read of them and their ways, I prefer not to encounter them while in this all too frail flesh and blood of a merely human animal."

Dr. Mortimer laughed, "Perhaps you are referring to the Scottish Kelpies or the German Kobold, or the Trolls of Norway or even our native Banshees. But after all shouldn't we expect some manner of resentment towards us? We have taken the high-roads and sunshine, while they are said to dwell in earth-mounds and underground chambers of feasting and delights. They are said to have gathered the treasures of the Spanish galleons wrecked on these shores."

"Of course money is of no use to them, for to desire a thing for them is to have it materialize at will. They may occupy an intermediate realm between God and us. He may use them for His purposes. Or equally possible is that they were not sufficiently evil to be demons and so ended up merely as tricksters to appear at cross-roads and other dreaded places by night and cause the drunkard to mend his ways. In any case this part of England, the barren stone-flung land reaching outwards into the sea is a place to test our limits and the foremost limit of the human mind is to speculate upon just such arcane matters as those we have discussed tonight."

I recall that the topics for discussion switched then to more prosaic matters, ones more conformable to entertain and not to frighten a man like me, one who lives alone in a cottage on the lonely moors of Devonshire.

July 25, 1897
Grimpen

The impulse that has given rise to Spiritualism is quite natural. There is nothing as bewildering as the seeming indifferent silence of the dead. It is one with the seeming neglect of God to directly address our untenable condition upon the earth. What more natural then than that we, while still living, might attempt to jar the memories of the recalcitrant dead and awaken them from their self-involved slumber in the earth, to communicate once again upon those questions that only perplex us more as we approach their condition? Yet necromancy is condemned as an impious practice and one ill-suited to the faith and trust demanded of the aspirant to true religion. A cynic would say that the practice is condemned because too frequent disappointment might give rise to despair. But a better explanation exists.

I asked a priest about this once and I recall that his answer was an interesting one. "The Church condemns the practice of necromancy," said he, "Not because it fears our disappointment but because what is beyond this life is incommunicable to our present perspective. Any answer received by the necromancer must then by its very nature be a lie and its source must then be the Father of Lies, the Devil. This is not to deny the validity of the occasional private revelation, which may come from God; but such revelations are not to be sought. The error of necromancy is similar to that of the Gnostics who presume to govern God by mere methodology. This would deny God's essential freedom. Ultimate reality is not subject to our manipulation but only our humble acceptance of its parameters, all of which have been instituted for our ultimate good."

I wish that I had explained the wisdom of this approach to Spiritualism to my recent visitors who called upon me two days ago. I had no wish though to take from them whatever ersatz religion, however inadequate it may be, affords them. It has always seemed to me better for a man to possess a proto-faith rather than no faith at all. God will surely lead all men to the truth in His own way and to do violence to that process through misguided zeal for a premature orthodoxy has quenched many a flickering candle.

July 31, 1897
Grimpen

J spent today's walk over the moor trying to clarify in my mind certain statements from the Nicean Creed should the Professor use them as a point of final resistance. It may be my own vanity but I felt that at our last meeting the advantage had shifted at last in my direction. I do not say that victory is at hand but I have at least forced the Professor to see the questions of faith from a different angle. For the Professor, a man who is accustomed to absolute proofs for every statement, to simply cast doubt upon his former premature certitude is to have a come a long way indeed.

The phrase from the creed that kept echoing in my mind today was that which states that the Son of God was "begotten not made." What this means of course is that the Second Person of the Trinity, without any diminishment to His own status as God was generated by the First Person of the Trinity, God the Father, but in such a way that no diminishment of the Father occurred in the process. It is not as though God is partitioned into two parts as one would slice up a pie. God's reality is primordial and thus the Son of God though begotten was not made as other things are made. The Second Person of the Trinity was not constructed as in the order of creation.

It is pointless to inquire whether all of the acts of God the Father whatsoever are simultaneous, because if God exists outside of time then sequential conceptions are meaningless. Instead creation is said to exist through the Son and with the Son. These imply that some sort of Divine Unity preceded creation and certainly did not occur as some remedial measure because a Savior figure needed. The Incarnation of Jesus then required the pre-existence of Jesus as the definitive Logos, the Word of God. At the same time the concept of redemption seems to imply as does the Lord's Prayer, the Paternoster, that creation is on its way back to God, and that a redeemed world will be caught up in the glory of God without being identical with God. Until then created being stands apart ontologically speaking in its essence from that of the Trinity.

Turning then to the Third Person of the Trinity, said to dwell in the soul of believers, we have an apparent problem. How can two diverse essences merge; or does the Holy Spirit merely exist as it were side by side within our humanity without actually interpenetrating it? Only Jesus contains both principles together in an undiminished fashion. Certainly the indwelling of the Holy Spirit within us is in no way analogous to the perfect Divine Union that exists between the human nature and the divine nature in the unique person of Jesus Christ. The union with God spoken of as sacramentally mediated must then be distinguished in some way from the Divine reality, yet still retain its suggestiveness and efficacy for our salvation.

I believe that the answer to this mystery lies in the order of causality. Whatever final destiny the believer shall enjoy as a child of God is entirely derivative from the presence of Christ within us through grace. This was what was meant by the assurance of Jesus to his followers that unless they ate of the flesh and drank of the blood of Jesus, they would not have life within them. That such a visceral act was proposed to an uncomprehending people has always been one of the primary scandals to those who wish to believe but are troubled by the apparently sanguinary act of Holy Communion, but in reality the idea makes perfect sense.

How better could Jesus communicate the absolute difference between the nature of God and that of all of the degrees and types of created mundane reality and also from the angels, as purely spiritual beings, and all of these from inanimate matter than by showing that our salvation and preservation depends utterly upon God's good pleasure to grant our salvation as a gift mediated sacramentally but intimately so that what was God becomes assimilated into us? We do not lay hold of immortality in the way of ordinary causation and instrumental control but instead by an act of supreme surrender by allowing God to come to us. This is the exact opposite of the practice of the many Gnostic cults, which imposed a practice with an automatic efficacy based not on an outside source but rather from the mere motions themselves. Part of the anger of Jesus at the reigning temple practices at Jerusalem was that over time these had assumed an autonomic character that completely forgot the purpose of the strictures of the law, which were to relate the Jewish community to God in a deeply personal and loving fashion.

All of the above shows why creedal statements are so important. Their intent is to safeguard and to formulate in however inadequate a form a set of essential relations. As such they are metaphysical statements and not subject to testing within the order of creation as though one were dealing with mere substances. For this reason any special or temporal view of succession must be eliminated when considering the relations that exist within the Divine Trinity. To say that Jesus the Christ was begotten of the Father does not entail the usual sense that what stems from something else must be in some way less than its origin or that the origin pre-existed it in time; nor does the fact that the Holy Spirit proceeds from the Father and the Son imply a derivative and hence inferior status to that of the Father and the Son. The reason that the Roman Catholic position on the question of the *Filioque Clause* is true and dispositive of the question is that it is precisely the intense union of the Father and the Beloved Son which generates the Holy Spirit. In this way the Holy Spirit can never be said to proceed from one or the other alone or to exist without them.

Any other approach would reduce Jesus in His Divinity to a mere suppliant of the Father and thus place him too close to the order of creation in respective dignity. If Jesus told his disciples that he would ask the Father to send the Holy Spirit upon them so that they would not remain orphans it is also true that Jesus said that he must go to the Father for this descent of the Holy Spirit to occur. The Holy Spirit only descends from the restored primal unity of the Father and the Son after the Ascension. The request of Jesus to send the Holy Spirit upon the Church was then not merely verbal but existential in nature. Anything less than this would reduce Jesus to the status of a mere messenger rather than being Himself Divine. Similarly the Holy Spirit is more than mere grace. The indwelling of God in the soul is more than a simple anodyne or specific to our mortality. God's indwelling in the human soul changes our very essence and by this means grants us an immortality which completely exceeds our capacity as physical beings. For this reason, the promised resurrection of the body is not a mere reconstitution of our former nature as embodied beings, but a reflection of the soul's glory and as such truly a new creation and a new birth.

Thus from a single creedal statement an entire set of theological relations is implied and thus the importance of the articles for our belief is shown. Revealed truths cannot be parceled out and considered in isolation, for each involves the others. This is the reason why heresy is so damaging to the integrity of the faith and why the Church has always fought so hard to maintain orthodoxy of belief. To allow any incursion of doubt or modification in these definitions is to risk the security of the faith and over time would allow the Church of God to capsize and to sink along with all of the fallacious versions of Christianity that no longer exist among us.

Time has weeded out the errors from the Catholic community through discussion and correction under the guidance of the Holy Spirit, which preserves the Church from error in matters of faith and morals. That many areas remain unaddressed and that many new issues continue to arise is the reason for the teaching authority of the Ordinary Magisterium of the Bishops of the Catholic Church in union with their head, the Holy Father the Pope, who occupies the place of St. Peter, the Apostle. These matters must be understood in their balanced relations through theological reflection and I do not know if the Professor will press me upon these distinctions, but I must be prepared for all eventualities by explaining why these distinctions matter and why the Church insists upon them in defined dogma.

August 8, 1897
Grimpen

My days that have been spent in intense theological speculation and reflection are at an end. At last I have received a communication from Professor Moriarty. I am summoned to Kings Pyland in two days time. At last the hour has come when I shall hear the proposed fate of all of England. Even to speak the words seems madness. I wonder if Moriarty has been leading me on all this time. Perhaps his threat was merely a means of insuring his own safety in the interim between 1891 and now - but no, if anything his threat merely increased the chances that I would have taken precipitate measures to oppose him. It would have been far more to his interest to have feigned reformation while carrying on his plot clandestinely.

Could it be that his threat to destroy England has been only a grim private act of revenge on his part to rob me of my peace of mind and to lead me by the nose across half of the world in pursuit of a synthesis that he will never share? Does he hate me to such a degree so that he would engage in such an elaborate hoax while merely laughing at me behind my back as I have tried to fathom his inscrutable intentions? Did he receive continual messages from Colonel Moran throughout our journey, updates on my elaborate labors and discomforts in Asia to aid him in his mirth?

Perhaps Professor Moriarty has been using my own nature against me, my fundamental belief that there is an answer for every question. But if that were the case, then I have surely been playing an equal game with him, because I know that he shares a common nature with me in that regard. If anything, his worldview is even more dependent upon reason than my own, for the atheist must explain away the very horizons of knowledge by declaring that all things are at least potentially knowable. The man of faith on the other hand uses reason to validate reason itself, but in doing so he realizes the limits of human rational discourse when it must confront the realm of revelation. The gross materialist, a school of thought to which fortunately Professor Moriarty does not belong, must go further still by reducing even thought processes to alterations in mere cellular functioning.

Human thought processes and consciousness rise above the mere material substratum that are its base. In this way its function is analogous to the role that Primordial Being that God alone possesses plays to actual existence. Man may reason about divine things from the known truths of existence that are indicative of the higher order of the Holy, which embraces all that exists. The order of ultimate causation however is always from above to below. God says, "Let there be light," and as a result there is light. No intermediary is required in creation. For God to will a thing is to see that thing accomplished. No means are required to obtain His ends.

This means of course that language when applied to divine creation when mundane causation is contingent and interdependent is inadequate to describe the true inner nature of God. All divine action, apart from necessity or what is called eternal law, is similar to the mystery of the Incarnation in its divine spontaneity. If God dwells as it is said in unspeakable light, then every communication of God to the created order requires a remarkable act of divine condescension to our limited view.

This in turn raises the question of why God should stoop to care for human beings. As Scripture says, "What is man that you should be mindful of him?" Professor Moriarty, as far as I can see, entertains a worldview that while not merely materialistic is not yet ready to embrace faith. He believes in man alone as the unique phenomenon that he is without tracing his origin to a supernatural source in God. Moriarty admits that man may embrace knowledge of relations with his cognitive apparatus and thus may attain limited truth, yet he denies that truth as such proceeds from the higher Truth of God. Human knowledge is by its very nature contingent upon the limits of reason. The philosophical idealists are correct in their assessment of these limits by reminding philosophical realists that reason has its limits and that our minds never escape from the fishbowl in which our reason swims. But the idealists are wrong in that they presume that the fishbowl admits of no intelligible relation or access to God. In the last analysis to be a philosophical idealist is to be drawn into the philosophical trap of solipsism where the human mind is confined to its own awareness of its perceptions with no relation to anything outside of itself. The human mind then becomes lost and isolated by being determined by its own constructions. If there is no independent outside reality upon which to ground reason and no divine mind to comprehend all things, then reason becomes mere mental gravitation drawing everything into itself and truth itself becomes illusory.

Any principle of verification requires something beyond the mind, some order of things that would exist even without an observer to describe them. Reason does not impose truth upon the world from outside in total independence; it engages with the world and formulates the order found there in various philosophical propositions. In this way our truth statements are not vain suppositions but rather descriptions of actual truth.

But what order of truth is describable? The answer is contingent truth, truth that still bears the limitations of being graspable by the human knowing apparatus. To all of this God stands apart in being able to will entire orders of being and by doing so to set them up. Yet having done so, is he thereafter bound by his own decision? Could God have willed that good be evil and evil good? Could God at once alter the moral rotation of the universe? It is precisely here that God differs from presumptuous Adam and Eve for God is Holy and the Holy cannot will evil.

Adam and Eve in their innocence could not know this prior to their sin. They imagined that to be like God knowing what is good and what is evil they might shake off the burden of human contingency and join God in what they imagined was his jealously guarded total freedom: free of love, free of holiness, free of even the law of His own nature as the Supreme Good! They imagined that to be free of limits was to know eternal happiness and to possess by right what the other tree offered, the gift of eternal life! But their eyes were opened as soon as they had made that fatal and irrevocable choice. They saw that they were naked as contingent beings as such metaphysically limited by their own nature. The things of God may not be usurped; they may only be bestowed as a vicarious gift in Christ and even then only as counseled by the wisdom of divine love by embracing charity towards one another. It is God's mercy that bestows upon us the gift of our limitations. We were exiled from paradise after Original Sin so that we might learn again the gift of being a contingent being, reminded once again that we are dust and unto dust we shall return. Even after being brought up short in this manner mankind remains proud, glorying in the tattered rags of our pretentions!

How much worse would we have been if having been given the premature gift of Eternal Life we were then in consequence plunged into hell, believing (as alas the devil evidently believes) that evil may be made good and good be made evil. This is the great abyss that separates those in heaven from those in hell that is spoken of in the gospels. The denizens of hell keep waiting for the great rotation to take place that will enthrone the evil principle into heaven and plunge God into humiliation by making heaven into hell.

Hell is the great period of waiting for what can never be! In the meantime the denizens of hell, deprived of all grace, gnaw upon one another with gnashing teeth, for in choosing evil absolutely they are deprived of any other choice. While we live, most of our sins, evil though they are, are merely indicative of this final choice to be made within the dark realm of death, when each of us shall be confronted with all that we have become in life.

We will then be asked by God as was Adam, "What will you have: all things in me or all things without me?"

This is the great test for which every moral choice that we ever make is a contingent rehearsal (yet no less important for all of that) for many will attempt to enter by the wide gate and choose to drag into eternity their residual belief in their own equality with God and find that they cannot have both God and themselves. If to repudiate even a single fully deliberate sin is difficult, how much more so will it be to repudiate an entire life-time of misplaced values at the moment of death!

For this reason there is a necessity for purgatory, a state in which on the very edge of eternal loss (but with the full intercession of the saints and angels and of the Blessed Virgin Mary, the Holy Mother of God) a man or woman may be drawn to turn back from the abyss and enter into the embrace of the Father, the Son, and the Holy Spirit by purging the damage done to the temporal order by their contingent actions; or failing to do so on one's own to have the debts of their lives cancelled by the infinite merits of Christ and his Mystical Body the Church through the Communion of Saints. To hope that each soul may be saved is not the equivalent of a bland universal assumption of automatic salvation for all of humankind, because to assume so would be to invalidate the fact of human freedom.

But to hope that all people may be saved is part of Christian charity and an act of faith that God's ultimate love might be universally efficacious throughout all of creation rather than to assume *a priori* that some corner of non-being reserved in hell enduring through eternity will fester as some quarter of smoldering and non-efficacious rebellion without hope for amelioration or change. In past ages the conviction that the majority of the human race was destined for damnation served the function of providing motivation for virtue and the assurance that the wicked would be punished may have comforted the victims of rampant injustice. A better end might be served by refusing to enlist God in our need for retribution. The teaching of the Catholic Church may perhaps admit a different model of the final judgment that sees God as the advocate and the devil as the prosecutor with the malefactor as the judge. The ultimate tragedy would be to refuse heaven with the prospect of acquittal already at hand out of the mere refusal to ask for forgiveness.

week has passed and I am home again and it is finished at last! I can hardly believe it. How may I hope to record here the course of that strange series of interviews between us? It requires powers that I do not possess. I can only give thanks. Professor Moriarty has given his word and his hand upon it that he will abandon his course of action and that he will do his best to disable the complex series of machinations that even now are beginning slowly to move into position to strike. It will take all of our joint efforts and Watson's as well if we are to prevent what even now will only with great difficulty be avoided: the outbreak of a plague such as this island has never known. I will do my best to set down what occurred between us in that fateful confrontation...

We met again as so often before in his vast library. He was sitting by the fire when I was shown into the room by his solitary servant. His stooped shoulders lent him an air of one who hovered over the flames of a feeble fire, seeking within them some way to warm his own aged form and to sustain its vital warmth. He seemed diminished in stature to me, more like a wraith with his dry cold skin and sunken eyes. Yet those eyes, when he turned to face me, were somehow different. Gone was that look of scorn and bitterness that I have always associated with his direct gaze. His thin lips had lost the scowl that they usually wore. He shook his head when he heard my name announced as though he did so in order to bring himself back from distant thoughts that had taken possession of him. He endeavored at first to rise and greet me, but in making that effort he seemed to sway and falter and was forced to retain the position in which I had found him. I rushed forward at once to help him back into his chair but he waved away my efforts as unnecessary. He passed a hand before his eyes though and asked me if I would mind pouring him some brandy, which I proceeded to do.

After taking some, his color returned somewhat and he thanked me before remarking, "I am subject to these occasional little attacks. My blood pressure tends to be below normal and I often find that the brain absorbs whatever little life force still resides within me. It may be folly in me to believe so, but I find that any long continued reflection deprives me of mobility. You have not been of help to me in that regard, Holmes. In our encounters over these last years you have laid before me problems that I have attempted to reconcile with my own long-held opinions. You have cast sand into a well-oiled apparatus with the result that it has finally quite broken down. Science will not thank you, but...” And here he paused for a considerable time before continuing, “I thank you. Your own conclusions now seem to me not a ploy to bend me to your will, but rather a corrective to a set of fundamental errors in my map of reality. It is the quality of universal paradigms that they tend to make conflicting data invisible to the theorist.”

“My own constructions, which I had always assumed to be the ultimate in objective clarity, appeared to me after our encounters to be suddenly tainted by the worst forms of bias and premature conclusions. I felt, not like a scientist, but like a petulant schoolboy who was determined to oppose insight through sheer stubbornness. Worse, you set me about studying again and at my time of life it is no easy matter to undertake new lines of research. Look if you will at that table over there. Where are the volumes of Spinoza, of Diderot, of Spencer, of Compte, or of Voltaire? What do you see instead? You see Thomas Aquinas, Blaise Pascal, John of the Cross, Teresa of Avila, and even Ignatius Loyola. You see the recent encyclicals of Pope Leo XIII and the Documents of the Councils of the Roman Church through the ages. You see the desert fathers. You see Cyril and Methodius and Simeon, called the New Theologian by the Greek Orthodox Church. All of this you have visited upon me to the degree that I have been, not only incommoded, but seriously hampered during a time when I had planned to be thoroughly occupied in other affairs. What have you to say for yourself in defense, Sherlock Holmes? Perhaps you can suggest a way out of my present difficulty for I admit that I am out of my depth.”

I paused, wondering if I was mistaken, for it appeared to me that Moriarty was actually engaged in an exercise of good humor.

At last I ventured this comment, “Well then Professor,

since you are so heavily burdened, something will have to be sacrificed."

"Precisely Holmes, you echo my very conclusion. But what shall I put aside? Perhaps I can skip Hildegard of Bingen or Julian of Norwich? I might cut short my readings of the Pseudo-Dionysius or Tertullian and skip Augustine's diatribes against Pelagius? But even that abridgement may not be enough to yield me sufficient time to reach perfect certainty..."

He paused before looking up as though the idea had just struck him, "Or should I perhaps defer my plans to celebrate the Diamond Jubilee of Queen Victoria by bringing her realm down about the old lady's ears as I had long anticipated doing. Well what do you say Holmes?"

I paused, still uncertain if he was toying with me. At last I said, "It did always appear to me to be a rather laborious undertaking," I remarked dryly. "Perhaps, as you say, that project might be indefinitely deferred."

He replied, "Yes well, I thought you might answer in that way. Unfortunately, I have waited until the last moment to abandon my project and I must tell you that certain gears of the vast machine are already in motion. One does not hope to bring about such a great result without preparation and my plans have begun to move now as if by a will of their own. A point comes where change requires an effort proportionate to all that has gone before. There is after all a momentum to events. I am afraid that my own energies are not sufficient to alter what has already begun. You see I have enlisted a rather formidable gentleman on the continent to assist me and he in turn has brought in other agents as far dispersed as Italy and the Malaysian archipelago. If this thing is to be stopped it will take a huge expenditure of energy."

"Are you asking me to take on the case Professor?" I asked quietly.

"I am attempting to avoid doing so, because the prospect of enlisting the aid of Sherlock Holmes to help me to turn aside a plan of my own devising is one that I never seriously entertained in all of my past life. But you have set me on a course that has caused a revolution greater even then the prospect of being your client as you well know sir."

He lifted himself then with a great effort from his chair and walked over to me and offered me his hand.

"I concede our game, Sherlock Holmes. It has been a long game between us, but you have check-mated me at last."

Startled, I took his cold hand in mine in silence and bowed to his gracious admission of a defeat, which was in fact a victory for us all and one that I could not claim for myself. He then proceeded to outline for me what his plan had entailed. I grew pale as he spoke, for I could see how great the task is that now lies before us. I must surely enlist Watson to aid us and Mycroft as well. It will take all of that remarkable courage and resoluteness that Watson possesses to help me in this dread hour.

I had heard of course of Baron Maupertuis, the Dutch banker and trader with the Far East. I have even read something of the Giant Bamboo Rats of China and Sumatra that are such a bane to the sugar cane owners of Indonesia. The dreaded plague known locally as the Black Formosa Corruption and by other even more dreadful names is familiar to me from my readings on tropical diseases. It would take a mind like that of Professor Moriarty to have devised a plan that could unite such a scourge into one mighty force to be unleashed upon an unsuspecting England. I could not doubt though that Professor Moriarty was sincere in his desire to turn the tide that he had set in motion for he laid a paper before me on the table.

"I would not have you underestimate the dangers that now lie before us and not least for me. We are not dealing with a man who brooks opposition easily. To come into any relation with him is to agree to continue until his purposes are satisfied. One does not depart until one is dismissed. In all of our dealings you have always presumed that I am the Napoleon of crime, but I assure you there are men upon this earth whose power, scope, and vindictiveness are far in excess of any threat that I ever posed or any malice that I intended. I am a scientist after all and science always imposes limits upon the mind. Ah, I see that you doubt my assessment, but it is not humility that makes me speak of having superiors in crime but fear. If you intend to oppose Baron Maupertuis you had best understand your man. Read this..."

The paper that he had placed before me contained an

article in an obscure journal of a society the name of which was unfamiliar to me. It was the quarterly publication of *"The Thanatos Society."* I looked up at the Professor in surprise. I opened it and read a few pages with increasing horror.

I looked up, "But if this man is as important as you say, then why did he come to you for this idea of introducing this strange disease into England?"

"Well he has his limits regarding pure intellect, but in power and in the grandiosity of his plans he has no equal. You will understand if you read further the designated article that lies before you."

It was clear that further speculation was pointless so I began to read. The article was entitled, *"A Neo-Malthusian Exercise on Population Dynamics."* It appeared to be a study of the effects of population growth occurring on a world-wide scale due to increases of production and distribution capacities induced by technological improvements. I will include a few pertinent quotations here:

{It cannot have escaped the notice of the members of this society that death is the most useful of agents to those who comprehend its role in nature. Selective death plays the same role in societies that pruning does to shrubs. It enhances growth elsewhere in the larger organism. Wars play this role in society by ridding nations of excess workers who might otherwise organize and oppose their masters.}

{The great problem today lies in the massive improvement of armaments, which destroy valuable property as well as persons. Persons are created at little cost due to the innate concupiscence of the human species, but property costs and losses are not so easily amortized or replaced.}

{At present an excess of people is required simply to rebuild the decimated structures that modern warfare techniques inevitably destroy. A point will soon be reached though where technological destruction exceeds all possibility of reconstruction, if science proceeds apace as it has hitherto done. If, in addition it is born in mind that every increase in population multiplies complexity in an exponential fashion, it will be seen that death, far from being opposed, must be fostered among us. But who is to

die, that is always the question.}

{True power is always defined by the power to put others to death. All other power is compromised if it is not backed up by this ultimate threat. Now the best means to foster death among the masses is to create that scarcity of resources that makes life a constant struggle among the superfluous masses simply to exist. From this scarcity there proceeds infant mortality, diseases, and the more brutal forms of labor that result in early exhaustion and death.}

{If world history is then to progress it must do so over the prostrate bodies of the many so that the few who remain may survive and prosper. A set limit must be determined beyond which population growth must not be allowed. Should a term of unfortunate peace allow population growth to expand inordinately then deliberate means must be found to restore the population balance through salubrious agents of death selectively employed.}

{No naïve concern as in prior social theory of procuring happiness for the masses should blind us to the imbalance of resources that would be the result of a more equal distribution of education, health, and prosperity among the mass of mankind. No society has prospered that has not been built upon the rule of a narrow plutocracy. Longer life only multiplies desires for those who are unworthy to entertain such fancies. Even mass sterilization cannot prevent the imbalance of input and output among the working classes. A point is always reached beyond which production surplus begins first to falter and then to decline. It is precisely at that time that death should be mandatory if efficiency is to prevail. As to the young of the poorer classes who continue to foist new offspring upon the land, these die in such numbers already from impure waters that little is to be feared by the sheer number of births. It is rather the fear that they may thrive that must concern all thinking men. Only the useful should be allowed to reach maturity. Since wars kill the sexually mature of even these select few, those of talent and intellect indiscriminately with the less endowed, war must be replaced by a more accurate and selective means for the elimination of excess persons from among the living...}

I could not continue reading. I dropped the paper from my hands.

The professor spoke, "Do you see now, Holmes, the man with whom we have to deal?"

"Yes," I answered simply. "But so we must!"

After that little more needed to be said. But will we be able to do so? That is the question that haunts me now. I can begin at once by informing Mycroft of the danger and Professor Moriarty has agreed to wire Colonel Sebastian Moran to see if the shipment of the giant rats that carry the disease may be stopped. Truly, dark days lie before us all. If the shipment cannot be prevented, its cargo must be intercepted. It is here that Watson's aid will be invaluable and I will summon him at once to be at my side. Before I parted from the Professor, I asked him if he might share with me the final point where he had ceased to travel along the course that he had formerly pursued.

He answered me by saying, "I can only answer you by drawing an analogy. I had arrived at a point in my mathematics where I noticed an unusual phenomenon whereby complex interactions may be best described by non-linear equations. I was led by this discovery to a new language in mathematics by observing certain irregularities in the motion of asteroids, which you will recall I had once described in a paper that you perhaps have read. It is now my opinion, though I cannot prove it, that chemical changes also occur by sudden changes that appear spontaneous and that energy emissions come in sudden jolts as it were from higher to lower states. To apply the analogy of this phenomenon to human thought; my own sudden reversal is similar to those spontaneous events that we observe in nature. Opposites are actually in rather close relation to each other. Wherever a bond exists in nature, even if that bond is one of repulsion and opposition, there is an underlying reality that unites both when considered from a higher point of view."

"Your prolonged opposition to me created the precise conditions for what might be termed a phase-change or a leap if you will into a new dimension of thought. It is not impossible that some future physicist or astronomer will be able to describe what I am only grasping by speculation and intuition. It is possible that being and nothingness are phase-changes analogous to that of a liquid to a gas. But, and here is the point, even changes of that magnitude would still require some higher order principle of origin or causality from which both would arise. The universe of possibilities cannot be confined to hypothetical universes blinking on and off in some underlying strata like a magic-lantern slide. There must be a source that embraces all conceivable possibilities before they can even be said to exist. What we have traditionally called God is that source, which holds not merely the lantern of what we see, but the shadow-lantern of nothingness that we do not see. Such a being would be the Lord of All Possible Worlds. The Hindus perhaps describe it better than we in the west are able to do. But there is no adequate vocabulary for the infinite, or if there is, God alone must teach it to us in another school than that which our own experience provides for us."

I was astounded at the depth and penetration of his reasoning and answered, "I am reassured that you have begun to entertain the possibility of a metaphysical God Professor, but why should that have caused you to abandon your plot of revenge?"

Professor Moriarty smiled, "Is it not sufficient that I have offered to do so. Just how unconditional must your victory be Mr. Sherlock Holmes? But since you ask, I will answer you as best I can. I still have a problem with the mechanics of salvation. I cannot see why God must suffer to undo any primal presumption that our so-called first parents may have committed in Eden. And I still find the idea of heaven to be distorted by various crude anthropomorphisms. I cannot for instance imagine the patience shown by God in allowing a molten earth to cool before the first one-celled organisms appeared and then waiting longer for a being to evolve that was capable of self-conscious thought. I cannot in other words merge revealed history with scientific history."

"Then you do not contemplate any immediate conversion to Rome," I replied.

He answered hesitantly, "Well not just yet, but you have opened a door to me where I did not believe one to be present. I have spent my life de-personalizing the universe so as to avoid bias. But, if I have read you aright, you seem to have been suggesting that we should, in religious matters at least, trust the furthest aspirations of our humanity. Our bias toward a fulfillment of our desires becomes then, not a source of error, but of interior guidance implanted within us by God. For the first time I have come to trust and not to deplore my own history as revealing a path to something greater than myself. There may be a certain felicity in being what is called a hard case. You have moved me by showing me an alternative hypothesis and I will not rest until I have followed your hints to the end. Until then, it only makes sense to call a halt to actions that no longer seem to me to be good, true, or beautiful. When no moral certitude exists, but a great risk of error does exist, the safer path is to allow time for greater clarity to emerge."

"Then my victory as you term it is not complete," I replied.

"Oh it is complete enough. I am an old man and a tired one. Though I am not sure about the nature of God, I am satisfied that He is not I. My dream of closure and completeness has been such that I felt that my own actions must be immune from any scrutiny but my own. You seem to understand me, Holmes. I am not accustomed to such transparency. Perhaps if there is a judgment of God, it lies in being completely understood by an absolute mind, that though it understands our every fault and failing, does not abandon us to our own limited views, but invites us instead to share His own perspective upon all things."

I do not know if I understood all that the Professor was saying to me at the end. The Professor's mind appears to move in several planes simultaneously, while I alas am only a poor Newtonian chemist after all, confined to relations of cause and effect in the science of deductive reasoning. I am no physicist or astronomer like the Professor. He is a man of multiple worlds, while I know only what a detective may know. I am one who measures footprints with an optical glass and pursues great devil-hounds across the moors of Devonshire, not one who charts the movements of the stars and galaxies. It was sufficient to be called into action at last and the rest must await further revelations.

It was necessary that come up to London. I am still mulling over some of the final comments made to me by Professor Moriarty before we parted. His comments surprised me at the time but I will set them down here for future reference when leisure may allow me time to consider them and to draw the requisite conclusions. As I prepared to return to Grimpen I was granted a final interview with the Professor. The subject of this man Baron Maupertuis came up again as was only natural because he appears to be the prime mover in the elaborate plot to bring down the empire.

Professor Moriarty came at once to the point. "You may consider this matter of the existence of an entire society devoted to the propagation of death as fanciful because of its very grotesqueness, Holmes, but I assure you that it exists. The men who are its members and contributors to its publications include some of the brightest stars in the intellectual firmament of our day as well as many highly placed political figures. Their fundamental assumption is that life is not an irrevocable gift but rather is a contingent privilege to be granted or withheld according to a utility calculus. It would seem at first blush that systematic atheism would make human life more sacred because if this life is all that we have then it should be preserved at all costs even among the weak, the inferior, or the disabled, but these men do not take this view. Their conviction is rather that for life to advance it must be confined to those who through innate capacity or endurance are most likely to thrive and to prosper in a highly competitive environment. All others are a form of inertia holding back human progress and as such should be eliminated. Of course all of this would be mere bluster if it was confined to empty political discourse, but many men of science and what may be called applied ethics have joined the Thanatos Society as well. Many modern philosophers have given intellectual respectability to what would otherwise be mere fulminations of various cranks and crackpots. But it is the scientists from whom we have most to fear as I know because I am one myself. I understand these men and their Faustian desire for knowledge irrespective of its potential abuse. There have been rumors in certain advanced circles that mass and energy are so intimately related that one can be transformed into the other under certain conditions."

He was fell into silence for a time. I should have thought that he was busy assembling his thoughts if I did not know that no such process was necessary for the Professor; his thoughts were always ready to hand as were the words to express them. It seemed to me instead that he was debating whether to take me into his confidence, as though he were about to take an irrevocable step.

At last he began again to speak.

"What I am going to tell you now I cannot prove and for a scientist to speak of what he cannot prove is mere intellectual folly. Yet I am certain that what I have intuited is correct. You have perhaps read of the experiments of Ernest Rutherford? Ah, excellent! It is always so much easier to speak with you than with the commonality of men since you make it a point to stay current with fields besides your own. You will recall then that Rutherford has written extensively upon the structure of the atom and the potential energy contained in the bonds which hold the atom together. This energy is of a magnitude that exceeds any mere chemical combustion reaction. If it could be released in a focal way an explosion would be produced beyond anything that we can currently imagine. A weapon might therefore be produced that could devastate whole cities in an instant. A weapon applying this principle would cause a degree of general destruction such that great masses of people could be eliminated in an eye blink. Do you see how such a weapon would appeal to men who are already sworn to the policy of elimination of masses of their fellow human beings just as many of the men in charge of famine relief at the time of the Great Irish Famine of the 1840's delighted in the decimation visited upon the troublesome and rebellious Irish? Could not such a weapon be used to clear whole regions for later resettlement by favored racial or national groups? If even the English possessed such a weapon now would they not use it to clear away the present inhabitants of the Sudan so that its resources could be added to our present holdings in Africa? Such immense power is simply too great to be entrusted to the short-term and opportunistic designs of men, yet the accelerating pace of technological discoveries will no doubt find a way to liberate this great force in the century that is just now dawning upon us. I will not live to see this, nor may you, but it is coming I assure you. I fear for those who will then forever after be destined to live in the shadow of imminent and ever-present destruction."

Again he paused and again I waited for him to resume in his own due course. "But there is something that I fear still more, though had I not become prey to your own peculiar ministrations in our recent war of the mind I might not have realized it. I fear that this habitual sense that life may be determined by the will of another will also be distributed generally among the population. The agents of death will include those who tend the aged. These agents of death will include mothers who will slay infants in their wombs if conditions seem to mandate that choice. The agents of death will include those who employ workers in industries where they will be exposed to noxious substances or other hazards to life and limb. All of these will share a common belief that the death or dismemberment of others can be tolerated if only it makes their own lives easier or more secure. The increase in the sheer size of the human population in the coming age will be met with an ever greater readiness of some to exterminate others because human life when viewed as mere biological mass becomes but one more cheap resource to the ever more industrialized mass of mankind. The individual will be regarded as nothing, a mere cipher. He or she will not to be regarded first in his unique and irreplaceable nature, but as an alien fragment broken off and severable from some larger entity. For this reason I have yielded to your arguments that life must be preserved, although I do not as yet share your Catholic faith. You have at least convinced me that we live in a world of incommensurables: that a thing is itself and not something else and that the uniqueness of even the most seemingly trivial objects must be cherished and preserved. The manifoldness of the world must never blind us to the singular. If the singular is lost then so will the multitude be compromised in due course; it is as though, to apply my statement just now about the power contained within atoms, the fissure of an atom might spread into a general conflagration. In social terms a similar fragmentation or fission, one based on race or ethnicity will cause a general war between nations to break out by their striving to preserve their cultural identity and exclusiveness to the detriment of other nations. Of course this fear of mine yields a corollary of great value, which might be considered a principle of general ethics: that the unique must never be sacrificed absent an overriding need and that overriding need must be carefully reviewed lest it yield merely an apparent pragmatic good. Convenience will be the face of evil in the coming age. All manner of atrocities will be countenanced because they are convenient to someone with the power to decide who shall live and who shall die."

I could not forbear asking him why having come so far in his assessment of life's prospects considered from the perspective of history he could not yet take the final step of faith. He took some time before answering me, which showed me that his reservations were not due to mere prejudice or pride on his part.

"The issue for me is evidentiary in nature. The Christian message seems to me to be an instance of special pleading by a community attempting to prevent defections in the course of persecution. When it became evident to the early converts to what became Christianity that their expectation of an immanent return of Christ to redeem his faithful ones was being indefinitely prolonged the early enthusiasm of many converts quite naturally began to wane. Until that time there was far less emphasis upon a universal community of believers. A convert was part of a local community of those who had adopted this new way of life. There was charity of course between the churches as is shown by the collection for the relief of the Christians at Jerusalem mentioned in the letters of St. Paul. The Church at Jerusalem was being hard-pressed by the wider Jewish community, which had not embraced Jesus as the messiah, but this inter-communal unity of the separate churches was largely incidental and extraordinary considering the means of communication available and the great distances involved. Instead it was the periodic visitations of St. Paul and Barnabas that had sustained the unity of these early assemblies of believers. It was Paul who would renew their hope and conviction when disruptions would occur. But soon the number of the dead began to exceed the number of the living. The present condition of the dead would naturally become a matter of renewed speculation among the remnant of the community who were still alive. Those who had "fallen asleep" included those early believers who had thought that they would be spared the experience of dying because Jesus was expected to return to render judgment, yet they were now dead."

"Early messianic beliefs of restoration and subsequent glorification in an earthly kingdom were gradually yielding to a new conception of Jesus less as a human brother and more as a God who had reassumed his former status at the Ascension. It was only now that the gospel accounts began to be written. Can it be a mere accident that many of the words attributed to Jesus are precisely those that would reassure a community on the verge of abandoning the faith? Jesus tells his followers that they must hate father, mother, and indeed even their very selves if they wish to be his disciples. Were these the actual words addressed by Jesus in his lifetime to a Jewish audience or are they not rather the words that the evangelists were now placing in His mouth to address the crisis of a later day and the concerns of another audience during a later period of Church history? It was only now that the Jews begin to be demonized as the primary opposition to the mission of Jesus, whereas before it was the Jews to whom Jesus had appealed in His ministry, just as John the Baptist had before Him. The entire Christian message as embodied in the gospels begins now to revolve about the axis of rejection and the essentialness of the Crucifixion as the final dramatization and enactment of the rejection by the Jews of Jesus as the messiah. As the locus of belief shifted from Judea to the outer regions of the Roman Empire it must have seemed necessary to denigrate the persons and community where Christianity originated. This would also explain the triumph of the Romans in the sacking of Jerusalem when God would have been expected to intervene. Community solidarity now required that some meaning should be found in their sufferings. Can it be a mere accident that the leader should share precisely the experience of His later followers? But which experience is primordial and necessary and which is accidental to history? By binding the two together suffering becomes the *sine qua non* of Christian experience; the Christian life must include suffering!

From this suffering a further elaboration comes about, which is that suffering is analogous to the pain of the animals in the ancient temple sacrifices and Jesus ceases to be a teacher and a prophet and becomes instead a victim as the Lamb of God. Only in the later gospel of St. John does Jesus regain His full dignity as the pre-existent word of God, the Logos."

He paused before continuing to see if I had been capable of following him thus far. His next discourse was even more interesting. "You see, Holmes, that the faith that you would have me accept is not severable from the ordinary course of historical development. But let us not stop here in our historical consideration. Let us proceed to the time of the conversion of the Emperor Constantine in the 4th century. It is only now that the early victim Church assumes a central role in history, one of triumphalism and conquest. The early beleaguered communities are now knit together into the Universal Church of Rome victorious and triumphant! What does it matter now if the Second Coming of Christ is indefinitely deferred? The present life of the Church is quite adequate to those who find a place within its orbit. The clergy assume posts of honor and rejection and contempt are visited instead upon those who once constituted the opposition to the spread of the Christian faith. Enthusiasm for the return of Jesus is naturally proportionately diminished as liturgical celebration and other ceremonial institutional norms integrate the Christian life with the demands of secular rule. In later centuries the lands are appropriated by monasteries and the bishops become analogous to princes who rule over territories. Kings become anointed rulers who embody not Christian teachings as much as they embody Christendom, which is now a civilization based upon power and property for the few and patience by the many who are allotted a life characterized by the words that were written to a different audience centuries ago when all Christians were persecuted alike, both those of high station and those of low station in life. The dawning hegemony of the Catholic faith in Europe now yields to the feudal ages and to the brutality of the crusades. The early proclamation of immaterialism and simplicity of Jesus and his followers yield to a defensive attitude of ever more clearly defined dogmatic statements in order to define the indefinable and even to delve into the intimate relations and assignments of labor prevailing within the Holy Trinity. Fear takes the place of confidence and the freely offered gift of redemption becomes hedged about with layers of obscurity and abstruse observances accompanied by uncertainty regarding salvation in the individual case. This results in various schisms and excommunications and finally leads to the upwelling and chaos of the Protestant effort at reformation. Where is the liberating spirit of life in all of this? It seems to me that the entire process is rather what one would expect of historical development from the point of view of those that advocate the pursuit of power as the ultimate end pursued by mankind, even if no God existed. Surely your own reflections must have revealed something that might help me as I struggle with these reflections and the limitations that they reveal in the very structure to which you would have me look to sustain my nascent faith."

Professor Moriarty paused again to regain his strength before continuing with his exposition, "But let us pass on a thousand years in Church history and what do we find. You have only to look at the conquistadors of Spanish America, Holmes. It was the alliance between the Spanish throne and the Church that caused the subjugation and extermination of their supposed brothers and sisters in Christ, the Indian converts. Could this have happened if European believers actually saw in the suffering of these people a parallel to the sufferings of Christ? How could they not? The answer is simple: the function of religion had changed while the words of the gospels had not, so the gospels were simply ignored by those who claimed to be carrying it to the new mission territories. Meanwhile the Protestants, aghast at the power of the Universal Church, attempted to recreate the tiny splintered churches that had been addressed by St. Paul and by a renewed millenarianism the Protestants tried to recapture the enthusiasm of those who had once anticipated an early return of Christ. Thus we have the fractured Christianity of today, one that is divided between the claims of an infallible papacy, one trying to regain a triumphalism that was already waning after the 13th century, and the rebels who have only succeeded in creating a hodge-podge of various revivalisms, no one of which can gain sufficient members to mount a real and effective challenge to the pretentions of Rome. I ask you now this question: where is Jesus in all of this? Can we ever hope to find Him as a point of objective knowledge? And if He cannot be found, then what is left to us but the empty and acrid plain of a individualistic and entirely subjective faith, a faith without any basis except that which proceeds from the sheer desire of the heart of man that there be some answer to our endless seeking. Are we then, from a historical point of view, not transported back to the condition of Abraham and Moses and the first seekers after God in the desert? Are we not just as lost as the Hebrew tribes that once wandered the wastes of the Sinai Peninsula? Tell me Holmes…where is this God that you speak of to be found!"

His desperation impressed me at once because any more casual approach to human existence is unworthy of a religious solution. The effort to posit a divine and supernatural being demands nothing less than that we should risk everything to attain communication with it as the great spiritual writers have shown. A purely utilitarian religion is worse than atheism. God cannot be reduced to merely one other subject to be explored by sociology. Even theology falls afoul of its own subject matter because a cup cannot hold the ocean. To approach God one must feel the desperation inherent in the awareness of death as absolute extinction and that in dying the world is utterly eclipsed for us in order to assess what is at stake in either affirming or disaffirming a God to sustain not simply a memory of us but our very being so that a resurrection is possible. Only Christianity takes as its ultimate symbol that in the crucifixion of Jesus God himself is eclipsed by death only to rise again. It was from this perspective that I dared to answer the appeal of the Professor.

"God is on the Cross, Professor, where alone He is always to be found," I answered quietly. "Now you begin to comprehend what it was for Jesus, while hanging from the Cross, when those whom he desired to save made it a condition for their belief that He should come down from that Cross. The Cross is the eternal question that hovers over the entire earth. Why should God the Father allow, not simply the suffering of mankind, but that of His

Beloved Son as well? Is evil such that the Cross alone may suffice to redeem it? Why does Christ not simply descend and keep everybody happy? But then what becomes of the dark and absurd pointlessness of so much of human life? If God does not enter into the entirety of human perplexity and powerlessness, then the Incarnation becomes only a partial gesture of good will on the part of God and not the definitive answer to all men and women in all times and places and conditions of life that it in fact is. It is because I take all of this seriously that I have come to you expecting nothing less than conversion of heart and mind and that you share my own conviction the Jesus is Lord precisely because no aspect of our human existence is foreign to Him including that we must all die."

Professor Moriarty looked bitterly at me, "I have surrendered on the practical issue at hand, is that not enough?" he said with cold deliberation.

"You may have surrendered to me but I have been playing for higher stakes," I answered.

"Then why have you not stepped aside and allowed me work my little scheme against England?" he smiled grimly.

My answer was brief and pointed. "I have never prevented you from working your will in that matter...it is you who must decide! If I wished only to prevent you from committing further crimes, then you would not have left the Reichenbach Falls alive so many years ago. I knew you see that you would be there and with Colonel Moran at your side and that it was quite possible for one or the other of us to demand the life of the other."

"And I knew as much as well," he answered.

"So here we are," I said quietly as I took out the gun that had reposed in my pocket and lay it on the table between us.

"What am I to do with that?" inquired the Professor.

I answered him with cool deliberation, "Well any number of possibilities is suggested by the presence of a single loaded revolver in any situation; the question of such lethal force readily at hand is dispositive for many in this world when confronted with a challenge of opposition that places everything that they believe at stake."

"I scorn to use force against you, Holmes," he answered quietly.

"As do I also," I answered taking up the revolver and replacing it again in my pocket.

"So what becomes of the higher stakes for which you have been playing, Holmes?"

"That does not depend upon me and never has. There will always be any number of alternative explanations for Christian failures and any number of false doctrines that will attempt to make Christianity eminently reasonable and faith inevitable. Each of these is only the clamor of the crowd that asked that Jesus come down from the Cross so that they would believe in Him, individually and collectively. Yet Jesus remained on the Cross and died and the eternal question to date has received only that answer to the problem of evil—that it requires the death of God to restore creation and to return all things to the embrace of God the Father."

"So we are back to doctrine and dogma after all," Moriarty smiled. "And no doubt you will tell me that I must accept these on the teaching authority of the Roman Catholic Church; there is no doubt though that you can recognize a circular argument when you see one. The Roman Catholic Church derives its authority from Jesus Christ, but the only Jesus Christ that we have is that presented by that same Church. Perhaps, my dear Sherlock Holmes, you should quit while you are ahead."

I smiled at this suggestion. "I do not wish to seem ungrateful for your concession as regards England Professor, which I trust is subject to no condition subsequent as to your personal conversion, but since the ultimate issue between us is still before us and since I trust that you would not have proceeded thus far if I had not piqued your interest, allow me to proceed. It is true that the Roman Catholic Church proposes itself as the definitive source of the Christian faith, but that proposal is addressed not only to those who are outside of the Church but to those within it as well. Indeed the witness of the Catholic Church is primarily to them. The Jesus Christ of the Catholic Church is the product of the collective reflection of the community of believers upon their own experience in the light of the life, death, and resurrection of Jesus Christ, which began first with those who knew Him and heard His witness from His own lips while He lived among them. The Church is itself incarnational in that the Third Person of the Trinity abides within the Church in order to guide, vivify, and enlighten it. For the Mystical Body of the Church is itself the living witness to Christ and the only source of discernment for what is true concerning the life, mission, and ongoing activity of Jesus. This is why it is a misunderstanding to refer to even Sacred Scripture as though it were a separate source of authority, severable from the life of the Catholic Church out of which it rose. The authority of Holy Scripture derives from the selective process of recognition of the early Church, which recognized some literature as orthodox and thus worthy of inclusion in the Canon of Scripture while rejecting other writings as containing error and unworthy of inclusion. By what power could this sifting process proceed but from within the Church's own memory of Jesus and its reflective experience upon the meaning of Jesus, which the community had received and has promulgated to this very day?"

"So you admit that the argument is circular and self-referential. Yet you still persist and insist that the flaw is not fatal. Why and from whence then can the basis for certainty in faith be found?" asked the Professor

I answered, "I do not admit that the argument is circular in the usual sense, because in the last analysis the pursuit of faith is not a matter for argument and contention, but rather of insight and subsequent conviction. Argument as a prelude is not useless, but it does not pertain to the initial experience of faith but to the later clarification of subsidiary issues on theological matters. This was why Jesus asked His disciples, "But you...who do you say that I am?" Has any more ironic statement ever been made? God at the beginning announces through Moses that though nameless as an object, the nature of God is simply to be. God cannot be objectified. The word Yahweh means simply 'I am that I am.' Only of God can this phrase be predicated. Now Jesus stands before the Apostles and asks them to in effect decide upon the measure of the divinity that may be made manifest among them. Jesus does not announce but instead questions as though He were asking them what they as free individuals will allow Him to be for them. Not that God's essence is determined by His creatures, for God would remain God even had no creation ever occurred. But in the definitive revelation of Jesus we have as it were God pleading with man to reverse the sin of Eden by asking us to consent to allow Him to be God-for-us, by trusting Him, by having faith, by determining just how far God may break into history. It is all up to us you see. The sin of Eden was for man and woman to imagine that they could be God, their own source of being. The question posed to those who would now attain to the fullness of human dignity in Christ is whether they are prepared to attain a greater dignity than that promised to Adam and Eve as the mere image of God. By embodying Christ to the world by allowing God to live within us both individually and collectively, we attain the status of Children of God. This is the significance of the Sacramental Presence of Jesus in Holy Communion and of the assurance that unless we take and eat of the Body and Blood of Christ in Holy Communion we shall not have life within us. The mission of Jesus you see was not merely redemptive but ontological in nature. It was to do sin one better by taking fallen human nature and exalting it to a status beyond our wildest ambition to be like God knowing good and evil. We are allowed to encounter evil just as Jesus did in allowing it to work its way among us and yet not to touch us if we are in Christ. This is what is meant by the symbolic language that those who believe in Jesus could handle serpents yet remain unharmed. *Evil is defeated by its utter non-being in the face of God who alone is.* To take Christ within us in Holy Communion then is not a mere symbol but an actual participation in the same uncreated essence of the divinity by God's own invitation and not by our own willfulness as it was in the eating of the Tree of the Knowledge of Good and Evil in the Garden of Eden. Now we are invited to eat from the Tree of Life in the Center of the Garden and to attain the full stature of man and woman in union with Christ. *It makes all the difference how we respond, for God only allows Himself to be God to us by our own consent.*"

"And if we withhold that consent?" queried the Professor.

"Then we are left with the world precisely as it has always been and we are at the mercy of each other, we who historically have shown each other little mercy but only fear and retribution. It is not you see that God's judgment is to be feared, but rather it is we ourselves who are able to cast one another into hell through our own rejection of the image of God within us. The reason finally that God must reveal Himself to man is that absent revelation we would never deduce God as He is but only our own image of God seen in the imperfect glass of our conceptions. This is why the life of Jesus frustrates any image that we might initially entertain of that which was proper to the Son of God and why Jesus became a servant and not a master, a poor man and not a rich man, and died rejected and alone on a cross. So you see Professor that the argument is not circular but open-ended and thus not an argument at all but rather an invitation, an invitation upon which the very essence of being human depends. What we believe Christ to be determines what we shall become...all of history and the course that it will take collectively and individually depends upon our answer."

"And what then becomes of heaven as a reward for virtuous living?" he hinted smiling.

As usual he came right to the point. I answered, "Heaven cannot be conceived absent union with God in that status to which God invites us to share in His own divine life; that is why any testimony as to the nature of heaven is inadequate for one who does not yet experience it. To be in heaven is to require no explanation for we will then see Him as He is. In the Old Testament it is stated that no one can see God and live and from that evocation many have concluded that God is terrible. This is our own fear speaking, the same fear that Adam felt when he hid himself from God because he realized that he was naked. But God has always known us as we are, but it is we who have not known God as He is...until Jesus showed us. Jesus says as much to Philip when he says, "Have I been so long among you Philip and you still do not know me? He who sees me sees the Father. How can you ask that I show you the Father? Do you not believe that I am in the Father and the Father is in me?"

Professor Moriarty shook his head. "Well, Holmes, you may succeed after all in your game of high stakes. I have never seen it played better. But then if you are right it is more than a game that we have been playing."

"Much more," I answered quietly.

That was all that was said between us and I departed for my home in Grimpen soon after. I was astonished to have heard him speak as he had done that day. Was this the man who I had once been convinced was the source of most that is evil and all that is undetected in London? Yet I was convinced that he could not speak as he had if he was not convinced and in earnest in all that he had said to me, even as I was equally serious in all that I had said to him. Truly if such a transformation from base denial was possible to Professor Moriarty, then there must be hope for all men if they will only use that divine faculty of the intellect that is present to some degree in all humans to discern the right and to know the difference between good and evil, a choice made once and for all at that hour when men and women became human beings by the choice in Eden made by our first parents Adam and Eve. Let it suffice for me to close this most important entry in this journal by saying here that I rose and left him soon after this discourse between us and for the first time shook his hand in parting with true and mutual affection and esteem as a brother in Christ.

September 1, 1897
London

I leave today to return to Grimpen. The past two weeks I have spent in London. I have had several meetings with Mycroft. The government has been put on alert, but no mention has been made to alert the general public, which would only create panic in our seaports that a plague-laden ship might arrive at any moment. Import trade from the east would come to a standstill. If the plague has already arrived, there would have been reports already of strange deaths. So we may still have time to prevent the incursion of the agent of death among us.

Professor Moriarty has left the timing of the event in the hands of Baron Maupertuis and his agents in the Far East. The most likely point of entry is somewhere on our east coast, perhaps in Norfolk or Essex. This would allow the contagion to reach London swiftly, before precautions might be taken against the spread of the disease. There is however another school of thought.

Perhaps the disease will arrive in the western ports so that it may announce its presence gradually as its spreads eastward. This would only increase the terror as the disease marches across Wales and into the more heavily populated midlands. Terror is in many ways superior to slaughter as a weapon, for it is only when the country distorts its own internal operations in anticipation of disaster in order to fight the agent that the greatest costs will be incurred. All traveling will by necessity be restricted, internal trade patterns will be altered, and fear itself will cause the very life-blood of commerce and daily life to freeze.

The balance of a national economy is a precarious thing. It takes little change, if that change is something entirely new, to create havoc in any system with many independent factors and determinants and once the damage is done it is often impossible to restore equilibrium for years. Then there is the entire question of war and peace in Europe. If it is decided that the outbreak of this disease is part of a deliberate plan, there is the possibility that hostilities will break out between Germany and England. Even France might be suspected as the real agent provocateur. Then there is the whole question of an Italian connection. Baron Maupertuis may even hide his role in the plot by having the plague reach the continent as well. Perhaps Trieste would be a likely target. The plague might also appear in Odessa as well or in Alexandria. But once the deliberate hand of Baron Maupertuis is suspected the game will be up. He will become the focus of an investigation so that thereafter he will not dare to make the investments from which he no doubt hopes to prosper. That very point was raised at once by Professor Moriarty when he disclosed the details of the plot to me. It appears that the Professor was to be paid a set fee for originating the idea, but the real profits were to be obtained by Baron Maupertuis through making strategic investments in anticipation of the economic consequences that would follow the plague's introduction among the populace of England. A nation in turmoil will both under-value and over-value key assets and advance knowledge will allow profits to be made in either direction.

The very idea of deliberate collusion between the private sector and the machinery of government has hitherto seemed to be an impossibility for the simple reason that mutual envy and suspicion makes of the private sector its own police force. Capital competition ensures that no private agent can attain the monopolistic power of any given sector of the economy. But from what Professor Moriarty told me, this man, Baron Maupertuis is no ordinary individual but a force that has over years insinuated his private interests with various rulers and statesmen so that he is implicated in the internal operations of several nations. He has not confined his business interests to a single industry but has instead diffused his noxious presence through virtually every sector of the economy of nation after nation. He places his loyalty nowhere but in himself. At the same time he has managed to portray himself as e benefactor of mankind by purchasing strings of newspapers so that what he says soon finds a responsive echo in public opinion. Nothing is so easily swayed as the mind of a mob or the prejudices of a nation when they are carefully wooed by a man who understands the fears and hopes of the body-politic. Baron Maupertuis is just such a man.

Even the underlying anxieties of the age have combined to enable him in his schemes. The doddering empires of Europe have outlived their usefulness and a new spirit of nationalism is growing every day. Revolution is in the air and socialistic ardor pervades both the unions of working men and women and the drawing-rooms of the idealistic and cultivated artists and philosophers. The various atrocities attendant upon colonial rule are becoming ever more widely known and outrage is the order of the day. This will not however deter a man like Baron Maupertuis who knows how to direct even the forces of social conscience in ways that will benefit him and those with whom he associates.

What a dreadful man he must be to hope to profit from so much suffering! But then his type is common and well-known among many international investors. King Leopold of Belgium is just such a man with his holdings in the Congo region from whence alarming reports are beginning to emerge. These men see only numbers upon a balance sheet and not the human suffering involved at the remote points of production. Nor are the English investors and imperial magnates uninvolved in the darkness of such trade. One need think only of the influence of Cecil Rhodes on domestic policy in England and the misfortunes that he has brought to the tribes of Africa through his trade in diamonds and gold. No, I fear that Baron Maupertuis is only an extreme example of what is becoming a general imperialist trend among the great nations of the world. His uniqueness is to be found only in his willingness to practice his techniques in the very midst of the European heartland rather than upon those distant coasts of Africa or the Far East.

Even America is not immune from the technique, even if it is not quite as deliberate there in all instances. Have not smallpox, measles, and consumption cleared the path before the American settlers of the west? We send our diseases before us in the vanguard of conquest. Neither age nor sex is spared an early death. Professor Moriarty based his entire plan as a mirror-image of the philosophy of Trevelyan, who saw in the typhus and starvation of the Irish famine, a way to rid Ireland of the fractious Irish people. The implements of war become crude and costly when nature may do the work of armies.

Professor Moriarty has pledged his full cooperation in all efforts to stop this engine of destruction in time. Colonel Sebastian Moran has been enlisted to attempt to discover the point of origin of the shipments of the giant rats and the probable destination of any ship or ships carrying them. He has many contacts in the east and if any man may discover what is afoot there, it is he. For my own part, I have the full cooperation of the British government at my disposal, although the danger was at first deemed by some to be fanciful. It is a characteristic of the bureaucratic mind that it does not entertain new prospects until the danger has actually emerged, after which it goes into a state of spasmodic contractions or seizures and spends immense resources where they are least needed and most ineffective. In this way the damage is not contained but spread into new areas of the national life.

Mycroft has had a ship placed at my disposal in the west, ready to sail from Cardiff to intercept any suspicious vessel, and a similar vessel lies at my disposal in Scarborough, should the attack come from the channel. Even Scotland has not been ruled out completely, but since the cost of maintaining two ships and crews in constant readiness is not inexpensive, this was all that Mycroft was able to obtain for me, at least until there is some sign that a plague-carrying ship has landed, which unfortunately may be too late because by then the disease will already be among us and spreading. A general interdict of commerce is of course out of the question on what many regard as mere speculation and unfounded rumor. Only Mycroft's word has obtained the little assistance that has been forthcoming. This is more of a courtesy than a sign of confidence that the nation is actually in danger. Ah well, we must be grateful for small favors. It will do no good for me to remain in London. There is always the possibility that Moriarty will receive some communication from the Baron. I have a plan then to return to Grimpen and to await developments there. If I hear anything of note, I shall cable Watson in Cornwall and he will be instantly at my side.

September 4, 1897
Grimpen

I have taken up my post of observation at Grimpen, but I am prepared to move swiftly when the time comes. I must do something at present to quiet my nerves. Waiting has never been easy for me. I am much more at ease when the view halloa has been given and I am in full pursuit of my quarry. But I must make do as best I can. So it is that I turn again to this old familiar journal of mine. It may be a strange thing but my interactions with the Professor have persuaded me to doubt the wisdom of the established order.

I am not yet an anarchist or a revolutionary by any means, but I find myself to be at one with those who demand some manner of change. The great reigning houses of Europe seem in this modern age to be not merely antiquated but ridiculous. Of what practical merit are these stuffy and posturing dukes, barons, and viscounts in a world that seems to be leaving such pageantry behind? Are the great decisions that must soon be made to be assigned to mere children trained up from youth to hunt, ride horseback, and dance a quadrille? What do these know of life with its endless struggles and manifold deprivations? By what logical order can the rule of mere peacocks supplant that of eagles?

Yet even the eagles must yield in their course also if the sparrows of the earth are to be fed. Social justice must arise and do so soon if there is not to be some vast European conflagration. Already a generation is rising up that embraces despair and death rather than life. Disappointment is breeding first discontent, then desperation, and finally violence. Each generation is born, lives, and descends again into the earth with no real advance made against early illness, pinched poverty, and the squalor bred of congested living-quarters. In nation after nation the cry of bread and freedom is to be heard. It only takes a Moriarty to give to these great masses a purpose and a voice. But I have now threatened to derail all of that, at least in England as regards this particular scheme. Professor Moriarty has trusted me and has agreed to surrender his long-planned design. But what have I to offer him but hope that the weak and downtrodden of the world, if they shall wait upon the Lord, will not be disappointed. Has their promised deliverance ever yet come to hand? Where has that charter of the rights of all mankind been written and proclaimed abroad? Instead all is struggle; all is opposition and betrayal. No sooner is a new set of leaders in place than they are converted to that same desire to cement their own position, which characterized their predecessors. The fulfillment of promises is endlessly deferred. An age of revolution and of desperate remedies may soon eclipse all that has been achieved of graciousness and beauty.

How many a Robespierre waits in the wings for his cue to take the stage? So it is that I am pursuing my researches into early English charters, seeking that model of good governance through equality that may, if it shall take root here in England, be spread by our far-flung fleets of ships and commercial interests to the entire world. Here in the intersection of production, commerce, and distribution a system may be formed that will raise, not only the few but the many, beyond the darkness of what has always been the human condition for the vast mass of human beings upon the earth. What I propose will take the labor of years to formulate, but to that end I intend to dedicate my final years. Until all of mankind buzzes with the efficiency of a great beehive, I shall not rest.

I recall asking Mycroft once at the Diogenes Club about the unequal distribution of the world's resources. His answer was a classic one in its justification of the present economic order. "It must be so Sherlock," said he. "Evidently you imagine that a surplus, if distributed to sufficient poor people would have the salutary effect of expanding the industrious middle-classes. What would that effect produce but a tidal wave of expenditure for worthless gewgaws? Do not suppose that any surplus would be wisely invested; it would not. The masses are incapable of both wisdom and the judgment inherent in good taste. In addition they lack the restraint to confine expenditure to the necessary elements of the good life. I assure you that every vice would be exercised by those whose only virtues have heretofore been those of necessary thrift and industry imposed by the strictures of scarcity in their lives. Take away that scarcity and their motivation vanishes. The demand for gin would go up first, then the number of cheap music halls would double, and last there would be an increase in socially acquired diseases."

"No, Sherlock, I am afraid that without a stable class structure a breed of temporary idols would arise admired not for any useful talent they may possess or any contribution that they might make to the social order but simply because the great sloshing about of money may have rewarded them for some trivial contribution to alleviate the boredom of the now sated populace in your new economic order. There must always be the rulers and the ruled if a society is to remain stable and to prosper. The key is to reward production and innovation and to prevent excess wherever it develops in the veins of the social organism in order to prevent thrombosis. This is achieved by the electric shock of an alternating current between expansion of the economy and recession. Expansions, if indefinitely prolonged, create illusory market conditions stimulated by greed. Recessions if continued too long cause the economy to seize up as those with money refuse to invest due to excess of fearful prudence. Yet in moderation each economic cycle counterbalances the other and creates balanced growth over time."

"You must strive to be more realistic, Sherlock. Human nature must be herded about if its worst elements are to be kept in check. Only imagine the general expansion of markets if each man's desires were to be met! By thus burning the candle at both ends the resources of the earth would soon be exhausted, extensive though they are. Life is only kept in check by nature's refusal to cater to our every wish and desire. Alter this balance and what have you but a cancer of the entire human race running amok on this island earth swimming in the firmament of space."

"Desire grows faster than fulfillment; there is the fundamental tenet of economy. This means that some measure of scarcity is inevitable. The human race will swiftly breed itself into oblivion if disease and starvation were absent. The wealthier nations of the world merely export misery to those quarters of the earth that are unable to command higher wages. Plenty at home is always purchased by misery abroad. The economy of England rests upon the bodies of the Chinese that supply us with tea and the workers in the Indian cotton trade that supply us with clothing. Even our domestic fleet of servants exists to make our lives of grace and leisure possible. What Mayfair hostess is able to bake a crumpet without aid or set a proper table? Would you give all these things up simply to procure some slight tightening of the gaps between the social classes? Where should we be if every servant needed half-a crown before seeing that your hat is properly dusted or that you were provided with sandals and a towel in the Turkish bath?"

I did not know how best to answer him. Perhaps a balance of our respective views can be reached by the economists and political scientists of the coming age. The ills of the present system are all too evident so that some change seems to be demanded by the seething multitude of our struggling fellow men and women. But these feverish thoughts no doubt stem from my own personal impatience. I have yet to learn that the salvation promised by God cannot escape the crosses of scarcity, age, suffering, and death.

Shall I succeed where Christ failed? Is it for me to devise a system that will produce peace and avoid evil when God Himself could do no more than to take that evil upon His own shoulders and bear the stripes of its malice? Would my system not lead soon to a race of new governors as unjust and dedicated to self-glorification as that of those whom they would supplant? Would I not be better advised to embrace the charity of the moment and to dish out soup to the aged in a Salvation Army soup kitchen?

It is part of the burden of my intense rationality that I tend to simplify all things and to imagine a general solution when none presents itself. My desire has always been to put myself out of business by preventing the very problems that are my bread and butter. Perhaps every historian wishes for history to end in his own lifetime, to exist at the summit of human development so as to miss nothing. But what if I must leave life at a time when all seems about to erupt into a chaos unknown to European man since the dark ages? What new Charlemagne will then stand fast against the new hoards of men that are arising today in nation after nation, driven by a single idea of revolution? One book in my father's library explored this idea prophetically and rather well. It was written by one Fyodor Dostoyevsky and published in 1872. It explored the decay and diffusion of the romantic ideals of the reformers of 1848 when the notions of social change moved from France to Russia, a land singularly unprepared to embrace higher notions. Brutality is not altered in a single generation. The Russians will only be changed by religion or by force. No people have been better designed to bear pain then the inhabitants of that frozen and bitter land.

September 8, 1897
Grimpen

I received by post today a letter from Professor Moriarty, which shows the state of his present convictions and the considerations which may have led to my prevailing in our duel of the minds. It is an extract from Moriarty's diary and appears to be a rough sketch for a future scientific paper. It is undated except for the notation of the year as 1897.

Extract from the Diary of Prof. James Moriarty, Ph.D, 1897

Sherlock Holmes has quite confounded me lately with his usual sophistries so it may be as well here to set down what a mathematician might conclude about the origin and nature of the universe. To perform a thought experiment: Let us assume that the origin of the universe was not due to a continuous process but instead due to a singular event. Let us assume as well that prior to this event there was nothing, complete metaphysical absence, with the exception of God whose own existence must be posited to exist in some separate realm about which we can say nothing.

Now then, that nothingness might as it were spontaneously change its valence and become something appears to violate the primal metaphysical intuition that from nothing, nothing can as it were arise *sua sponte*. Absolute Nothingness has no content or properties that could leave it with a potential or the pregnancy to allow anything to emerge. But from Absolute Being it would be no great thing to create lesser categories of contingent being at will. To assume absolute nothingness as the source of being is to turn a negative into a positive, but that a being whose very nature is to exist might multiply its own essence or any lesser degree of being does not contradict logic.

But perhaps our error here is to even speak about nothingness as a noun rather than as a verb or an adjective. Absolute nothingness is an abstraction that would entail the negation of the ontological status of everything that actually exists. We are not simply describing a change of form into something else but rather the absolute extinction of all being so that nothing would remain, which of course is impossible. But it is even more absurd to arbitrarily assign that negation back in time so that being emerges from nothingness as though that nothingness had the quality to create while remaining itself non-existent.

However, if that was possible then the moment of creation could then be imagined as one of pure and perfect act without opposition or contradiction. The question then arises whether all events are present in compressed and summary form from the moment of creation and thus theoretically predictable if the initial state could be known completely; or is it possible that forces only develop over time in an indeterminate manner as the universe decays?

If the latter is true, then God created an indeterminate universe and truth becomes only a measure of what has thus far occurred and not a statement of the forces which may someday appear. Even time might conceivably reverse its onward course as matter loses momentum so that universal gravitation reverses cause and effects. An outside observer would then see causes and events running in reverse. The natural termination of this would be to proceed backwards to the moment of creation and then vanish again into nothingness. But this tends to violate all that we know of thermodynamics and the conservation of energy. Matter is dispersed as it loses energy, but it does not become non-being.

However, what if all things were to run metaphysically in reverse? Would the laws of thermodynamics still hold? Science is always prospective, looking toward results for future confirmation. The entire enterprise is imbedded in matter and energy graphed over time. How then can science account for singular events such as creation ex nihilo? Of what use is a simplicity that precedes all known forces?

There appear in addition to be all manner of uncertainties, which provide insuperable gaps in our measurement of events. The foremost of these is the difficulty of assessing the initial state of any system in position and momentum. Time is forever hurrying us along. Subdivide as we will, we cannot reach a fine enough mesh through which to sift all conceivable events. The very act of observation in time distorts events by freezing them into immobility at the moment of recording our data. But if all measurement is an approximation and if atoms are forever scooting about the table of the universe like billiard balls, then it is only the initial state that can represent pure simplicity, for only it is pure and undefiled by later motion. But we cannot get back to the initial state because we are ourselves a product of a later era after simplicity has been degraded into the categories of being that we know.

Science is really only a temporary exposure of a passing scene, to use a photographic analogy. Even mathematics expresses truths that are merely empirical the certainty of which cannot be proven to exist independently of the mathematics that we use to describe them. An example is the lack of a theorem that will predict in advance when a further prime number will occur. We recognize it when we see it, but we cannot predict its occurrence. Thus knowledge is forever coming up against these absolute walls and this stickiness of events that clog and impede not merely our relative progress, but set an absolute limit to certitude.

Thus faith of some sort would appear to be the only way to

achieve certainty even in science. This makes the demand of faith made upon religious believers far more rational than such demands would otherwise appear to be. No intuition can proceed indefinitely without periodic confirmation by events if it would be scientific, but what if complete knowledge must be delayed until the final unveiling by God. Has God from mere caprice planted the realm of knowledge with minefields of the fundamentally unknowable?

Or is God constrained by his own rules? A truly contingent universe is by definition unknowable even by God, for to know it would be to violate the very indeterminacy of that world. This opens up the very real possibility that God may have created a world without anticipating evil except as a mere possibility. God may have been as surprised by the resistance that He encountered in creation as we are when we encounter a stile placed in our way in an apparently open field.

Why then considering the risk did God create anything at all? Or is all created being contingent after all? As unthinkable as it first appear, could something come spontaneously from nothing? Might a causeless cause suddenly just happen? Can a more simple but paradoxical idea be entertained than this? But such an initial violation of our primary sense of order must invalidate all subsequent sense of measurement and reason. Thus we return to the logic of faith, for if such an absurdity as a purely contingent universe without an absolute being as its source might be entertained, how much more reasonable is the supposition of a derivative universe stemming from an absolute being that is God.

Having established the intellectual respectability of believing in God there still remains of course the question of the significance of human knowledge and assent to truth: from whence comes this desire for perfect knowledge that bedevils at least the more intelligent members of the human species? Why should a short-lived ape trouble itself and waste its few and fleeting days on purely speculative knowledge that only adds complexity and detracts from the daily struggle for mere subsistence and amusement? This problem of the human race applies with even greater poignancy to the individual mind. Is the individual qua knower merely a link in a chain of previous knowledge? Of what significance is my individual realization and assent to truth? Should I forget all that I have once known through senile dementia, then what happens to my immortal soul now tied to an inconsequent body? Or do I possess multiple souls, one for each age and succeeding disposition of my mind? Am I the same stable boy that I once was? Who or what shall I be tomorrow? Should the innocent boy be damned for the later malefactions of the adult man? Should we only be judged by the testimony of our finer hours or those dispositions towards eternity and God prevailing at the moment of death?

And why should God care after all for our obedience, comprehension, and praise? If a thousand worms were to worship me as I walked about my garden would it add to my pleasure or stature? If God presumably knows all things, then our admission or denial of our own subservient status should be irrelevant; unless that is that God takes pleasure in the mere sharing of goodness with contingent beings. Created reality is a messy business when laid alongside the perfection of uninterrupted non-time, non-space, non-mass, non-energy. Nothingness would seem in its simplicity to be superior because unflawed. But can an aesthetic of nothingness be said to make sense since nothingness by definition has no qualities to be attributed and assessed for value? Even an imperfect universe would reflect in some manner the glory of its source. Perhaps God desires that we play some role in the completion of his work, to span the gaps as best we may and lay girders over the abyss of time that lies before us.

In the last analysis all thought seems to be bedeviled by circularities. We set off in one direction and end up coming up behind ourselves. Our very fear of contradiction blinds us to the source of our bewilderment, which may be imposed by the mind itself. Perhaps some abnormal particle of excess tissue growth or some calcification of the vesicles blocks the human mind from seeing the world as an illuminated whole without the ponderous limping along of reasoning from propositions to conclusions. But why after all should a pound or so of grey matter in the cranium be able to mirror the universe? We are like children making shadows on the wall with finger-play. Who is more the fool then, the simple believer or the doubting professor; and who could tell whom why he should or should not believe?

If the scientist is inevitably frustrated in his quest for a reductive principle or formula that will explain all subsequent manifestations, then how much more is the man frustrated who would account for human thought with all of its aspirations on its own terms? It is precisely here that all so-called humanisms fail because they would close human thought in upon itself as its own object, whereas it is the specific character of the human to seek transcendence from the human condition. Human thought is oriented to explanations that have no immediate survival value. In fact the human thought processes have a tendency to disclose even dangerous knowledge, which is to say knowledge that may so dispel our illusions that they bring about depression or fear in the seeker. It is for this reason that all advanced thought tends to abstract from the human or at least to attempt to do so for we forget at our peril that it is human flesh that is doing the thinking. A moment of reflection should be adequate to show that the mind may become lost within itself. We cannot abstract from those languages and primal categories of experience which allow us to sift data and to express conclusions.

I have spent my life as a scientist using mathematics, assuming always that mathematics possesses a reality that is as immune from the human as possible. I now realize that this assumption has no real basis except in a feigned humility. Would it not be more honest to admit that my desire for perfect knowledge and simplicity is a desire to make myself a god at least insofar as I might view all phenomena from outside, thus assuring complete objectivity. But there is no getting outside because all of our observations are made from within the very cosmos that we are trying to describe! The result is that all true science should begin with a confession of our underlying compulsion to attain total knowledge.

The reason that I have refused to take my own advice heretofore is that it has seemed so patently absurd to me that the vastness of the universe should allow itself to be comprehended by a miniscule ape-like creature like ourselves. My contempt for my own person and species has then been projected outwards by assuming that God could not possibly care enough for humankind to create a universe for us to muddle about in. But that scorn of my own being and of the being of others is less an attitude based on humility than on my own pride. How dare God care for me!

Such is my fear of such a great love that I would prefer to invalidate my own thought processes to ensure that the universe is entirely self-contained and explicable from within its own material processes without a point of origin outside of itself to which it is oriented in however imperfect a fashion for my own convenience. I would force the universe either to cater to my every whim as though I was God or alternatively I would make of my own desire for happiness and immortality mere illusions. Both of these solutions are petulant in the extreme! Both stem from my desire to be like God knowing good and evil instead of accepting this one and only universe on its own terms although enlightened by such communications as God has chosen to make known from time to time in the obscure texts of revealed religious truth that address our condition as human.

It therefore seems more intellectually honest for me at this moment to admit my needs frankly and to deal with my terror before the certainty of my own eventual extinction as a thinking being. What subsequent honesty is of any use if I fail to admit my need for something beyond myself to save me and to preserve me? The more complete my knowledge becomes the more in need I perceive myself to be for a basis in something beyond my own cognitive apparatus. To presume the non-existence of God is thus to arrive at a conclusion prior to the data; data that would in any case fall far short of proving its penultimate hypothesis. If even a general explanation of all material processes eludes us, then how can we speak of what may precede and be the origin of all known phenomena.

My present position is similar to an object that has lost all former momentum on its pre-established course but has not yet received sufficient impetus to instigate a new momentum in a different direction, which is to say that I am not yet a convert to Catholicism. I have resolved any metaphysical reservations that might have stood in the way of my belief in God, but I still find the Christian God far too domestic for my tastes. Why should the august creator of the universe consent to be worshiped by inane hymns sung in the cracked voices of elderly men and women who find a solace in their infirmities by imagining that God will restore in a heavenly kingdom the very youth that they once spent in sinful pursuits?

Then there is the sheer diversity of beliefs that afflict mankind as regards the nature and number of deities. Is this not evidence that God is a creation of man just as art and culture are? Finally, there is the question of history: why if the Christian God promises to create a different order of things at the Second Coming of Christ why has He allowed the present flawed and perilous order to persist for so long? Why should souls be imperiled by the delay of that promised return? Even the Holy Roman Catholic Church has known a less than uniform vision of itself and has suffered schisms, crusades, inquisitions, and is now so reduced in influence that its temporal rule is reduced to the few kilometers of the Vatican.

If certainty cannot be found in science, still less is it possible in tracing a course and purpose for history. The individual is lost in a world of conflicting claims, each demanding faith to close the loop. Will a final triumph between these contending religious doctrines be a matter of accident or of will and if the latter then is not an earnest skeptic as honorable as any man? At least he does not use force or stratagems to convert others to his way of thinking.

Yet, I am of all men the least comfortable existing in a perennial state of disbelief. I consider the uncommitted life the recourse of cautious and lazy souls of which I trust I am not one. It therefore seems to me to profess a provisional belief that opens the possibility of confirmation over time as more courageous than to hang fire while others are firing all about me and advancing across the field of battle. Better to join the general fusillade even though all of us may be shooting into the mist at mere shadows. Would it not be better to be in error with some of the greatest minds that this world has ever produced with Pascal, Aquinas, and Dante than to join the nameless company of the voluptuaries, the dullards, and the inert souls for whom the question of God is put off from day to day until in their death throes they mutter a despairing prayer hoping that something will hear them and respond?

Do these men and women live better lives in their pursuit of wealth and pleasure and their hope that from day to day death will stay the hand that must extinguish them utterly? What false courage is shown by the stoic whose attitude will soon be mocked by the foul decay of his members? His noble brow will soon be covered with mold as bronze is by verdigris. Is it dishonor to join one's hopes with those who do not spurn even this flawed and fleeting world, but hope beyond death to find a love denied them here? No, if the virtue in not believing is only supported by the continuance of an open question, I prefer to err with those who have made the great gamble of belief.

September 10, 1897
Grimpen

I was quite pleased by the extracts from the Professor's Diary. Though some of his scientific speculations seem to be in advance of the current body of opinion in physics, I cannot say that he is wrong. That my own arguments have moved such a titanic intellect is indeed gratifying. If he could only know what I have thus far revealed only to my own soul: that my arguments were at first conceived simply to quiet my own questing soul.

It still seems strange to me that God has placed the fate of his own creation, at least on this earth, in our hands. God's confidence in us seems to have been long since shown to be overly generous by the course of history. But then who can say how much time may still remain to us before the return of the glorified Savior? We may be still at that stage that has yet to realize the full promise of the Holy Spirit. We may reach a day and hour when the miracles performed by St. Peter in the Acts of the Apostles become the measure of a renewed faith and appear everywhere. Certainly the New Testament writings contemplate the transformation of souls under the impulse of grace so that we might truly be recognizable and acclaimed as the Sons and Daughters of God.

I have often reflected on the short and transitory presence of Jesus among us (although in his sacramental presence He has never actually left us). So much was yet to come of salvation history under the ministrations of the Church by sacramental aid and inspiration. The teachings of Jesus had barely penetrated His native Judea where in fact they had been authoritatively rejected by the very priests who had been commissioned to safeguard authentic prophecy when Jesus ascended to the Father. The whole Christian movement should have been extinguished according to our ordinary expectations: first by the death of Jesus and later by the defeat of the Jewish nation and the destruction of Jerusalem by the Roman legions. Defeat, loss, and rejection—what great movement has ever had such strange antecedents? It may be said though that these are the very indicia of the Christian truth. The Cross of Christ has become the symbol of these as nation after nation and empire and after empire yielded to the appeal of the gentle teacher of Galilee who went to his crucifixion as a lamb is led to the slaughter.

Beyond His sacramental presence all has been left in our hands. We are commissioned as were the Apostles to be the salt of the earth, to quicken a new birth of charity among men, and to transform the world unto one worthy of the return of Jesus at the end of this age. Each believer is signed and commissioned by his Confirmation and sealed with the Holy Spirit of God to become a saint and to join the communion of others so sealed in the One Holy Catholic and Apostolic Church. Belief in God is not then an end but a beginning. Each soul is placed in the very position of Jesus in the desert during his fast of forty days and forty nights. It is said that after this great fast Jesus was hungry and on the cross he said the words, "I thirst." God appeals to us to achieve His designs.

We are not asked though to enter the desert alone as Jesus was, as the sinless Savior. He was never, until the last Agony in the Garden of Gethsemani deprived of the inner presence of the Father. During His final agony He was as it were cast into the shadow of the sin of the world and in His fear and terror first glimpsed the fate of man without grace and without God. The nameless suffering of our death loomed up before Him so that even as God he prayed that this cup might pass him by. So much is not asked of us; we are not the universal Son of Man as Jesus was. The believer is strengthened by the sacramental presence of Jesus in the bread and wine of Holy Communion so that he or she may never know the hunger or thirst that went with Christ's exile among us. Thus we are, because of Christ living in us, commissioned to do what in ourselves we could never attempt to do—to act as God would act among men—with the same mercy and with the same all embracing love.

A concept so daring makes the mind turn in vertigo about itself, yet each age witnesses the truth and the realization of the command that disciples of Jesus should love one another. The Litany of the Saints is nothing other than the proof of this unlooked for success and triumph over all the normal expectations that accompany most efforts of voluntary reformation out of our own fragile resources in this most intractable world. The saints are the sole lights that stand like stars against the unfathomed darkness and abyss of history; our final destiny, if we so choose, is to be found among them in the Kingdom of Heaven after we die.

September 12, 1897
Grimpen

In the last analysis human effort is not up to dealing with its own darkness. It is just possible that the entire purpose of this brief and tragic interlude of life, which so tries the heart and sinew of even the greatest of men and women, is simply to wean us of the desire to define existence on our own terms. The inflexible rules of cause and effect acted out against the shifting tapestry of time are such that much can be irrevocably lost, for instance by the hasty word that flies to the heart, the arrows of misplaced desire, and the snares that lie in wait about our feet. Each can lead us to the very threshold of everlasting darkness. Who can say when time itself will cease for us and all our plans and aspirations come at once to a cessation that will never resume its chaotic and headlong course? The brief issues of each day are a prelude to eternity.

For this reason an admonitory voice should whisper at our

supine ear always—take care, take care! Life forces us to take our definitive position finally, to sink our roots deeply and to set our feet in stone never to be moved. To put off that decision day by day imagining an infinite horizon and time to sport with dark spirits in the last twilight of a summer day may find us all too soon plunged into an unending winter and the eclipse of a night that shall never witness a returning sun.

September 14, 1897
Grimpen

The origin of Christianity took place at a time when the tide of expectation that God would soon intervene definitively in human affairs was at its height. The coming of the Messiah was also to witness the final triumph of Israel and the direct rule of God on earth. Now almost two millennia have passed and the world is passing more and more into human control with each passing year. Our existence is increasingly becoming a matter of our own engineering so that human nature itself is becoming understood to be a human construction. How distant seem the minute prescriptions and proscriptions of the era of Moses, which promised to set up an ideal human society around the laws of the Torah. Just how free man is to resolve the increasingly complex ethical questions presented by our own ingenuity is the great conundrum that the future now presents to every level of social organization.

The delay of the Second Coming of Christ (a delay from the point of view of our own natural desire to witness and inherit the final fruition of the plan of God for His creation) calls to mind the words of Jesus that much would be expected from those to whom much had been entrusted. It begins to appear that God desires to penetrate history through our own actions and that the easy solution of immanent messianic age will not save us from this assigned labor. If by Original Sin man and woman desired to become like God knowing good and evil, God appears to have allowed us the full measure of that presumptuous choice. We must with the gift of the Holy Spirit enter into the labors of God. We must become as Jesus and fulfill in our own bodies what is lacking in the suffering of Christ as St. Paul once said. God will not be hurried and history may be entrusted to us for an indefinite time to come.

This world must be enough for us and the love that we receive and share through the Holy Sacraments must be a sufficient foretaste of heaven. Messianic hope must be content to remain hope and the light of faith must be adequate to light our way in the darkness that surrounds us. If we are to know love it must come from each other through the mandate of charity. The writings of Pascal describe our perilous position poised as a mortal being and cast out into infinite space while stretched along the rack of time. How comforting is that end that will wind the separate threads of creation around the great spool of God! But God insists that the weaver of the cloth of eternity that must provide our wedding garment must be largely our own task to accomplish.

It seems at times too much for us; how glad we would be to return the fruit of the Tree of the Knowledge of Good and Evil uneaten! But these matters were decided in a manner and condition that we legatees of history can never regain. The Cross of Christ shows that even God has become subject to that primal choice, the one that has determined the extent of the responsibility of the human race for its own fate. We are aided but not supplanted by God in our governance of the world. So it is that step by step through all the long and weary days of life until we die we must press on into that untold world that is taking shape around us, largely as the fruit of our own actions. Will God intervene before whatever final disaster we bring upon ourselves is made fully manifest or will mankind succeed in becoming subject to the dictates of divine grace at last and turn aside from cataclysmic folly? Over the course of one obscure lifetime it is enough for a single man to turn the gristmill for one more revolution and then to see the crushed grain fall through his fingers like the sand of an indifferent and unmeasured sea.

357

September 17, 1897
Grimpen

There is no more time for these far-flung speculations to be exchanged between the Professor and me for the time of action has arrived in the present crisis and the work of a mere consulting detective is at hand! The game is afoot at last! We have received word from Colonel Sebastian Moran. A single ship with its deadly cargo aboard has set sail from an obscure island off the coast of Sumatra, the Dutch freighter Friesland. Only a single ship has been traced thus far. Can it be that the threat will come from a single vessel rather than an armada? I thought this strange at first and requested that Professor Moriarty write back to Colonel Moran for details and confirmation. The response was that so great is the dread of this creature that no willing crews can be found who will sail upon a ship with them aboard. They are seen by the natives as possessed of the spirits of demons; no doubt a legacy traceable to the disease of which they are the usual vector. In the region of Sumatra and Borneo entire fields are often burned to kill the animals and their cries from out of the flames seem an unearthly screaming of more than a mere rat.

There are also certain advantages to be gained by using a single vessel from a strategic point of view. The disease, when it reaches England, will fan out slowly from a single point and thus escape notice until it is well established among us and may spread to domestic rats as well, after which it will be hard to contain. It is in the nature of evil to seek through a small and narrow channel to establish a secure foothold. It does not announce itself with a blare of trumpets. It prefers quiet infestation and only reveals itself through a vague sense of unease in its presence. It moves among us like a canker in a fruit or dry rot in healthy wood. It follows the inner channels of our soul, creating the environment that is most conducive to further decay.

So will it be with this bamboo rat that often carries in its blood the microbe of the Black Formosa Corruption. It will move about among us until the deaths begin to mount and the health authorities at last take notice that something strange is afoot. By then the real plague will begin, the plague of fear in which each person must fear the other as a source of contagion. Social intercourse will stop then and the links that form human community will break down. Gradually people will become isolated and from isolation is bred a spirit of unimaginative self-interest.

Private property serves this same function amongst us. What is mine cannot be yours. It is the various fears in life born of self-interest that breed violence; just as violence, once it has its hold upon us, begets more violence. Disease is thus not merely an example of a physical evil, but of a moral evil as well, for it leads people to shun each other.

In just this manner the leper was once isolated as unclean, not that the others who did not suffer from the disease were morally cleaner, but simply because in its fear the society of the Jewish civilization needed a focus for the sense of sin that lies within us all. The leper serves the function of allowing evil to become manifest so that we may pretend to deal with it; but the real evil lies within us where it hides from sight. It is the hidden evils that do the most harm. Therefore the wise man may expect to find the larger evils where false honors are bestowed to men and women of wealth, power, and beauty. Our idols house our demons, while those whom we scorn may well be angels in disguise.

But to return to this ship, the Friesland; it is a Dutch ship and surely that is a significant fact. The hand of Baron Maupertuis may be observed here. It is he who controls the Greater Netherland-Sumatra Company and it is he who is the active agent for Moriarty's plan. No ship's manifest was available upon loading that Colonel Moran has been able to discover. The ship set forth from an uncommon port of call. It is a phantom vessel then. It will move among smugglers and forgo docking for supplies at established ports on its way here. This will make its progress towards England difficult to trace. For this reason the ship may arrive at any time and we must use a form of dead reckoning to measure its progress.

I have alerted Mycroft and he has instructed the various British customs agents by wire to keep their eyes open for any sign of a lone Dutch freighter between here and the South China Sea. The threat of this vessel moves in its own shadowy cloud of obscurity, yet we know that it exists, and we know that the ultimate destination is England. When the time comes we must be prepared to act swiftly upon any intelligence that we may receive.

September 21, 1897
Grimpen

There is word at last on the agent of our proposed doom. My own plans in response must spring into motion, but be coordinated in such a manner that the threat is contained while not losing from my trap's embrace those who have designed and forwarded this elaborate assault upon the British Empire. A ship that meets the description of the Friesland has been reported from various ports in Africa. It is only a matter of weeks or at most a month before the ship will be off our own shores, the shores of fair Albion my home.

I believe the time has now come for me to summon Watson to leave whatever his local medical labors may be or to abandon his effort of writing-up my cases of the past few years at his comfortable Cornish retreat. It is time that he join me now at once in what may prove to be one of the most interesting and dangerous investigations that we have ever undertaken together. His courage has never failed me in the past and he would surely never forgive me if I did not at least afford him the opportunity to be at my side from the beginning in this Moriarty/Maupertuis affair. I will telegraph him today and we will see if two old hounds may run our quarry to ground at last.

Book Nineteen

The Circle Closes

From the Journal of Sherlock Holmes

March 1, 1899

We are off and the shores of America have vanished like a dream in our foaming wake. I had often wondered prior to my arrival there whether America is primarily a place or rather primarily an idea. America has for so many been a means to shake off all prior history with its memories and limitations. Yet from its beginnings as a Puritan colony it has carried the baggage of the old world with it. The very idea of colonial rule implies subservience to the mother country. Indeed it can be said that America only became itself with the declaration of independence from England. Never before in the world's history had a society made the dignity of the individual the very basis for all governmental legitimacy.

The idea of a private realm impervious to inquiry or invasion is even now held as suspect by the very government that was instituted to protect these freedoms. The growth of extensive capital enterprises that style themselves recently as "legal persons" threatens to impose new types and means of servitude upon mere human beings who are now seen as merely a labor pool to ensure profits. How long can it be before some manner of general rebellion crowns the manifold discontents the nation? Will this be manifest as in a revolution or will it show itself in a struggle with other nations for empire? That is the question that will no doubt occupy the remainder of my life as I widen the sphere of my investigation to embrace the underpinnings of civilization. Along with this question there is the parallel one of what role shall the man of insight and conscience play against the backdrop provided by great events that in combination together exceeds the strength of the individual to transform by the exercise of his unaided will.

I should feel better penning here a definitive conclusion to our efforts in America if my mission such as it was had not been transformed in the course of its very execution. We came to America to urge the Americans to build a canal through one of the Central American nations so as to prevent Baron Maupertuis from preempting them in this endeavor. The nation that does this will open the eastern regions to trade and alter at once and forever the current balance that exists among the European nations in their greedy search for domination of the less developed regions of the world. Yet, why do I term them thus? Through what virtue did we Europeans inherit the revelation made to Israel? Was the penetration of Christianity into Europe due to anything more than our proximity to the Levant? Surely our general history since that fortuitous acquaintance reveals little to our credit. When have we ceased to make war upon one another, Christian nations all?

Not content that our secular arms have been raised, theology itself is one convoluted bone of contention. Even if the oft disputed question of indulgences may have been a misuse of a doctrine to fill the coffers of Rome and if the Lutheran teaching "salvation by faith alone" causes some souls to neglect the requisite interior penitence in reliance thereon the results have been no worse than the harm caused by the splintering of Christendom due to the so-called Protestant Reformation. The pursuit of certainty as regards salvation is to probe into the eternal mysteries.

Roman Catholicism in contrast has always taken mankind as it finds it and allows God's mercy to sort out human souls, while the more businesslike Protestant mind desires absolute certitude about salvation because of a basic mistrust of God that is a legacy of the sin in Eden. I was surprised in our journey among the Americans to see how the American desire for material rewards and progress infected the spiritual realm. Many of the sects anticipate a millennial rule in an earthly kingdom not much different in its way from the expectations of the Jewish people at the time of Christ. It appears that the mind of man, always loathe to abandon its present pleasures and unable to await the final disclosure of our ultimate reward in God's own time, is always engaged like a suburban sketch artist making caricatures of the last day and the final judgment and transforming these images into one or another heretical formulation of Christianity, each a form of Gnosticism. The freedom of religion promised in the American constitution places no limit upon the luxuriant growth of this spiritual vegetation with the result that the entire fabric of the nation is interwoven with the weeds and briars or theological error. The only point of unity in all of this appears to be a national consensus that the original inhabitants of this land may be killed and despoiled at will by the mere fact that the invaders are nominally Christian.

But to return to my own state of mind as we head westward towards Asia, I am conscious at present of my own limitations with poignancy that is new to me. I have met many great men in these last two years and sensed in each of them that for all that they have achieved, it is all too little to meet their aspirations of success. Life finally becomes little more than a gesture made in a particular direction. Is this enough to provide a basis for divine judgment? If we are wanting even in our own estimation, can we be assured of anything other than that God desires to build on our own sorry foundations? Yet God treats us each with respect as befits a child of God. Divine pity must exceed divine umbrage or else why create anything at all. If God delighted in being offended then why nurture a world that seems beset by disproportion in all of its facets even those most orderly and inorganic.

To take only a single instance, immense planets composed of methane and ammonia crystals dwarf this planet and even here earthquakes topple our most august monuments to the ground. Everything about us manifests a lack of stability and inveterate change. The great 17th century author, Sir Thomas Browne, assures us that the numbers of the dead far outnumber the living and who will say at what point the numbers were in exact equality? The anticipated return of Christ far exceeds even the most sober anticipations of the first century of Christianity, yet the churches are full and the supplications for the dead are no less ardent and confident in faith for all of that. Though we probe abysses of time and space and find them all devoid of even a tracing of our own significance still we believe that the God behind all things cares and is concerned with our fate and destiny. We cannot imagine that in the entirety of this unfathomable universe we alone are awake to notice and to record in our various configurations from cave paintings to the writings of the sages what we have hitherto noted and observed.

If the species seems diminished as our knowledge increases, then how much smaller does my own sole life appear to be? Of what use are these, my confessions, when set against the record of better minds and a community willing to acknowledge the immediate appeal of their pronouncements? But then I recall that even the great St. Augustine died not in triumph although he had written, *The City of God* and many other great works of polemics, but perished with the barbarians lapping like a sea at the gates. How many have been the efforts to write a coda to the unspooling of fate and time? I think of Thomas Aquinas, Baruch Spinoza, John Calvin, Georg Hegel, Immanuel Kant, Ludwig Feuerbach, and Soren Kierkegaard as only a few of the minds that have wrestled with the great perennial problems that have beset me here and turned my attention from what I might have enjoyed such as a walk on the moors with a playful hound at my heels or to play an evening game of billiards with my friends and to finish my evening repast with a glass of port with my feet toasting by the fire before retiring to a dreamless sleep. Instead I am far from home and still tossed by an unquiet sea.

Who am I then to dream of success in my various quests? Am I to triumph or even leave a small subscript to the age in which fate has placed me? Even Baron Maupertuis must fall someday of his own accord. No doubt he will live for some years though and who may say what harm he will accomplish. But I have maimed him. He has been hobbled at least as they say on the racing circuit and will need to consider that I am watching him. If my powers are diminished they are far from negligible and I am wiser for having experienced frustration and only partial success in my quest to the new world of America. Now I am off to Asia by way of that homeland of elaborate artifice that is the Empire of Nippon. It is a matter of regret that time has not allowed me the opportunity to consult with many of the experts in Japanese art and culture prior to a brief stopover there on my way home to England.

Since the American Admiral Perry forced trade upon these aloof and involuted isles a series of visits have allowed the Japanese to study western technology. The speed with which they have adopted our industrial techniques is already causing fear in various quarters. A navy that had once been confined to sampans is now an iron-clad fleet. I fear that an aggression that slumbers in the councils of the various clans that divide state functions among them may soon result in an exhibition of the desire of Japan to play a role in the international order of nation-states. I advised President McKinley that in Japan he will find no mere opportunity to extend colonial rule as in the Philippines. There is a labyrinthine intricacy in the politics of these people that requires years of study to penetrate. To call it by the name of duplicity is to imply a cowardice that is foreign to this people. Instead what is present is a sleight-of-hand whereby any statement is balanced by sophistication and reserved understanding based upon engrained training and feudal roles that have existed for centuries among the fir trees and volcanic slopes of Japan. Even the Koreans and the Chinese cannot understand the enigma of Japan although the former contributed its racial stock to settle the islands and the latter contributed the seeds of its writing and religion.

The Japanese are geniuses at the art of adaptation and ornamentation. If I were to choose one word to describe them it would be "refinement." Politics, worship, and art are one. No simple act but finds its reflection in ceremony; from this national characteristic comes the religion of Shinto with its reverence for the spirit world of the Kami, a word that has no western equivalent. The individual is always acting against a background of the honorable past to which he must bear tribute. A host of unseen observers watch over his conduct. Actions bear consequences that can unbalance a more perfect world that parallels our own yet exceeds it and to which we are oriented in sign and gesture as well as in substance.

Shinto appears to an outsider to be a primitive animism with an overlay of Buddhist beliefs with all the moral rigidity of the Confucian ideal of right government. Such a formidable combination requires an intense study as we tunnel into the fertile ground of Japanese culture. However I fear that the pride of the existing powers is too confirmed in complacency to undertake the effort required. The result will be a costly one no matter what the period of delay will be. The east will first gather its strength, taking every advantage of the pride and contumacy of the western trading nations. The strike when it comes will be as sudden as the strike of the cobra and as silent.

March 4, 1899

The great Pacific Ocean has embraced us. Already America seems a distant dream, America with its quiet provincialisms and its quaint conviction that it is destined to dominate the world through sheer energy if not by virtue of its culture, which to date is confined to the cities of Boston and New York and in the south to Charleston and Savannah. The rest of America is empty prairies of wheat or corn and the processing centers for agricultural commerce like Chicago and New Orleans. The thing that I remember most about Washington is the marble and the muddy streets threaded by pompous gentlemen in top hats who never cease in their campaigning for re-election. I think that after six years few men in the Senate have anything new to say or insights to contribute to the progress of the republic. Vested personal interests will always tend to the defeat of democracy if allowed to fester in office. Flushing out the serpent's den periodically is advisable.

But why should I be thinking of America since I am unlikely to return there? My health has improved sufficiently that I can contemplate a few more years of professional practice before retirement. Mycroft has the situation well in hand at home as evidenced by his private correspondence to me and my absence has left no decided deficit. Still, I long to return home; it is too late to imagine embracing the life of a Tibetan Monk or even becoming a missionary. I might have become a Jesuit in my younger years, but then obedience to a superior is hard for an independent spirit such as mine. Besides, in the true missionary compassion for those to whom one seeks to spread the faith must reign supreme as in the case of St. Francis Xavier in Goa on the Indian sub-continent or St. Isaac Jogues and his companions martyred while carrying the gospel message among the Huron and the Iroquois Indians in what was then French America. I am afraid that I am more like Voltaire, an intellectual opportunist rather than a systematic thinker like Thomas Aquinas or Immanuel Kant. Give me a problem with borders and I can devise a probable solution, but always with a remainder set in reserve to account for contingencies. Mine is the art of imperfection; I always keep an ace in reserve. It is that habit that has made me formidable when dealing with the underworld. Perhaps Colonel Sebastian Moran and I are more similar than we appear to be. This may account for his evident affection for me whenever he is operating without instructions to gun me down like a tiger. I look forward to our reunion in a few short weeks in the Malay Archipelago that is now his home. But will I encounter the same man that was my reluctant companion over my extensive travels in the quest for religious truth by observing its actual effects among various believing communities?

March 5, 1899

It is only now that I realize the implications of what I have been about during this last year. The whole thing began as an effort to defeat the schemes of Baron Maupertuis but he was defeated by his own boundless desire for power, not by me. In any case I was converted from the task itself as I recognized that history is not malleable. Every position reached in diplomacy sets in train a set of counter-responses like pieces of glass in a kaleidoscope forming a new collective pattern distorted by the mirrors within the tube. History simply emerges in various patterns and plays itself out by various means to reach a lower state of energy. It takes good men a long time to realize this and when they do it often destroys them. Still, we must do our best to contain the uncontainable. To align one's own personal conscience with the right, that is the task to be embraced. How strange it is that nations have yet to attain civilization and adherence to the rule of law. Suspicion, duplicity, and brutality rule the day. This is why we must not be surprised that heads of state have blood on their hands.

We ask the citizens to obey the laws because we can compel them to do so, while nations remain free to make wars and pillage restrained only by nations or alliances that are more powerful. Threat and counter-threat all made by gentlemen in frock-coats who later adjourn to various clubs and laugh over their drinks while young men wait in the wings to serve the needs of slaughter should they be demanded. Meanwhile we deny women a voice and a vote because we fear that they might demand restraint and peace would then ensue. Why is it, I wonder, that winged victory must always be portrayed wearing a woman's form as though it was she who desired that the fruit of her loins be slaughtered to supplement the career aspirations of the officer corps—corps and corpses they go together.

Watson and I are soon to visit that martial nation of Japan built largely upon the Bushido Code. How strange it is that the cultivators of such delicate poetry as the haiku, a people of exquisite gardens and Shinto shrines should, since their unfortunate awakening by Admiral Dewey, have embraced with such reported enthusiasm the western implements of war! President McKinley has given me a letter of introduction to the American ambassador there. The way is already prepared for us. We will not be merely two middle-aged Englishmen adrift upon the waters of the orient but representatives of uncertain status and power and perhaps be treated as such by a people that recognizes status before all else. I shall have tales to tell Colonel Moran who is another who reduces everything to questions of power and predation.

March 6, 1899

I have just been re-reading my last letter from Mycroft. In it he requests that I engage in some of the same distant diplomacy that he requested of me in my travels through the Sudan so many years ago. The new stage of empire has moved from Africa to Asia, and particularly to China. The Manchu Dynasty is fragmenting and the nations of Europe, like so many jackals or hyenas are drawing in, each hoping for a choice piece of

China. America will no doubt retain the Philippines as the perfect staging-area for its own overseas fleet with Japan as the only perceived threat. There are the Russians of course to be reckoned with as well, but Russia is currently obsessed with the Balkans and with its relations with the French. The English government meanwhile desires to placate Japan as a local threat in the Pacific without alienating the Russians.

My assignment is rather vague. I am to "assess the situation there." It is not a task that I relish. I prefer what may be called the definitive solution to a problem and then to move on while diplomacy is a never-ending cycle of threats and secretive proposals. The whole thing is too much like a seduction rather than a deduction. I think that Mycroft agrees with me, that a source of reliable private information is necessary and he trusts my observations precisely because I am an outsider. In any case he has made the request so I must comply if only out of fraternal loyalty.

Watson, as ever the good and loyal Englishman, might resent my growing disillusionment with our homeland so I will reserve news of this communiqué for now. We both leave America without regrets. It is strange how swiftly the Americans have forgotten that they were once themselves a colony; now they fancy that they can take their place among the ancient nations of Europe with a legacy of petty wars to obtain territory and commercial influence. The vigor of that little man Theodore Roosevelt is alarming. He is forever climbing mountains and shooting buffalo. I trust that he can exhaust his energies in some posting to the west where he can pursue sage-hares and not siphon his way into power through attaining higher government office.

Not that he is the worst of those who covet the American Presidency. Worst of all are the commercial types who would turn America into a great humming factory of steel and armaments. There are also types who see public office as little more than some sort of personal encomium where they can reign in king-like splendor and allow their own personal pet ideas to distort an entire nation by being reduced to executive practice if the Congress allows them to proceed unhindered. It is the people who most covet power who should never be allowed to obtain it. The Japanese for instance by report show every sign of desiring to emulate the Europeans since their protective isolation has been breached. From a localized threat to China and the Korean peninsula they may just break out some day into open field running. But then they are said to be an artistic people and an imperative for ceremony and a stable emperor may contain their nationalist aspirations.

Imperial rule is after all a messy business; one must not be afraid to act the part of the brute. To kill with style is the essence of the Bushido code, a study of which I am currently making. The Japanese have raised duplicity to a form of art and even the assassins there must bow before they strike. It will always be a mistake to judge the Japanese mind by western standards; they are a people of infinite patience as befits a nation that is convinced that their ruler is a descendant of the Sun Goddess. It is civilization rather than the resort to arms that alone can ensure a stable empire and when a civilization's ideas decline no force of arms are sufficient to sustain it. At first the legions will choose who is to be Caesar and when necessity arises they will kill him, while at the frontier the barbarians with hungry eyes for plunder are massing for the slaughter and divestment of supremacy.

March 7, 1899

Watson still keeps his physician's eye upon me and is assuring that I eat well. He would have preferred no doubt that we winter in California, but I hunger for England and hope to be home by late summer. We will witness the blossoming of the cherry trees in Japan and see what we can there, but I do not fancy tarrying long in the malarial zones of Indochina or the Malay Peninsula once spring is well advanced. I prefer to clear Ceylon by May and to make for Suez after crossing the Indian Ocean.

I hope to see Cairo once again before crossing to Montpellier or to Marseilles. Then it's away home by rail to Dover and to London. I am amazed at my recovery from my bout with the deadly tubercular bacillus but then I have been well feted in America. I wonder if the Americans fully realize the spiritual burden that has been placed upon them by we jaundiced

Europeans in deferring to their independence. The rest of North America that remains with England and recognizes our sovereignty may be a better repository for civilization than that bumptious republic to the south. The American Constitution and the Declaration of Independence that provided a preliminary justification for their temerity in breaking free from England represent the very essence of those principles of the eighteenth century derived from reason rather than from religious enthusiasm. How odd that a nation that so long embraced slaughter and slavery still speaks of the rights of man! In the United States the pursuit of power and of commercial advantage will always rule the day. In America for the first time mankind has imagined that it can conduct its affairs without first consulting the mandates of religion for its first principles; the very appellation of superstition to the Christian faith, which had hitherto obliquely guided all public policies shows the degree of the deviation onto a new course taken by the intrepid but foolish mind of man. This will never be more evident than when religion is hijacked to provide a moral veneer for naked conquest and exploitation.

Once this path is taken it is perhaps inevitable that a nation like America might attempt to found a democracy or a more disengaged and aristocratic republic resting upon engineered consent of a supine and ignorant base of voters to pursue evil ends. To seek a point of unity in a racially and linguistically uniform nation might be theoretically possible, but to attempt as the Americans are doing to obtain consent from so many diverse parties seems the very height of presumption. The two hitherto enabling factors that have allowed them to do so to some degree were the seemingly endless expanses of the frontier regions and the desire of most of the immigrants to make a clean break with their past. European History largely consists of bad memories, of wrongs that still draw about them the present loyalty of the young who hope in acts of vengeance to obtain some post-hoc vindication for the dead bones that dwell in premature graves. The young are sacrificed in every generation to extend the undeserved life-span of their sires.

But in America the long beleaguered denizens of nation after nation has imagined for their progeny a new beginning, one untainted by the sorry legacy of their prior history in the lands from which they have come. Now, one hundred years after its founding, the brave citizens of an overriding idea are beginning to realize that the frontiers of the great land-mass of the North American continent have been attained and surpassed, and the history that they thought to escape is now been marred by a self-engendered great civil war and a subsequent decline into the rule of the wealthy beneficiaries of trusts and corporations. What has ensued is an immense productive engine dominated by the heirs of the great Protestant infusion that founded New England and the Mid-Atlantic States. The working men and women who are now immigrating to America are largely derived from the Catholic countries of Europe. Protestant hegemony in America is natural since one of the primary tenets of the Calvinist Reformers was the narrow exclusivity of the saved. The easy assumption is that the vulgar working masses are to be exploited in this life and damned in the next. It is no accident that the former slave states of the Confederacy are the most obsessed with precisely this variety of religion—long on hysterical display and short on basic decency.

Over one hundred years since its founding there has yet to be a Catholic President in America, because the very essence of Catholicism is to retain its roots through the Apostolic Succession and the preservation of the deposit of faith. The universal outlook of the Catholic mind can never provide the self-regarding focus of a nation bent upon material progress and ever-renewed conquests of new territory. The Protestant mind however, taking its very birth in an act of rebellion against established authority, rejoices in severance like the waves in a pool ever extending outwards from an initial impulse. This dream of new beginnings besets most of the people Watson and I have met in our travels. In the last analysis Americans are running from that very emptiness that was a precondition for its expansion; indeed it was the very basis for the intoxication of the European mind when it first realized that it could turn its aggressive and acquisitive ways away from internecine strife by annexing other lands.

America is now entering the twentieth century as merely one more colonial power and by doing so betraying that very set of ideals that led to its own creation. At the present moment the invading troops of America are engaged in disabling and disarming their erstwhile allies among the population of the Philippine islands the better to impose colonial rule there and to supplant one tyranny with another. The population is largely Catholic, but it is reported that President McKinley has determined to announce that America will retain these islands as a protectorate in order to introduce Christianity among them! I doubt that he will be the last to use religion to advance expansionist claims. His memory is most likely to be invoked by some later dreamer over maps.

Perhaps the greatest malice of what may be termed the American heresy is that it possesses a short memory; it always imagines that it is new and has no need to express gratitude to the forebears of its derivative share of civilization without whose loyalty to the true faith their own effort to elaborate a new covenant from scratch would even lack the terms that its uses to define itself. In a similar manner the American mind imagines itself as a point of origin rather than having built its first edifice upon ideas derived from Greece and from Rome. The effervescent froth of thought that appears in Ralph Waldo Emerson and Walt Whitman represents America's effort to devise its own national mythos from scratch. These intoxicating effusions are not without literary merit, but their optimism is predicated upon forgetting all that has gone before in human history. The human brain itself is a legacy recorded in anatomical tissue. If the evolutionary scientist Charles Darwin is correct, all the experience and adaptation that has gone before our species is contained within the human brain as the memory of struggle with mastodons, of desert wanderings across the frigid Mongolian plateau, and the fetid swamps of ancient jungles. A frightened primate screams within us when we meet disaster and a well-fed lizard lazy on a log smiles within us after parting of a banquet; from whence comes then this new pretence that the human spirit can be renewed by the mere expedient of crossing the Atlantic Ocean?

Alas, I fear that the Americans have caught up with themselves and when they most imagine themselves to be the guardians of liberty they will be most likely to act the part of Nero and Caligula and to oppress the citizens of other nations. The Europeans meanwhile remain as they have always been—divided, suspicious, and greedy. What is called our sophistication and good taste as a species is merely a veneer that has now been further gilded by our pretence to objectivity. Science is nothing of the sort. Science represents no less than the Faustian bargain that mankind has always found to be irresistible as it proclaims its independence from nature. The aptly named pragmatism of America is nothing less than the proclamation of its metaphysical despair. Cut off from its roots in history mankind possesses no impulse towards humility. It is only when we witness the mess that we make of all things that we even imagine looking beyond our exile for the God that we have long since abandoned forcing Him to seek us out.

March 8, 1899

The ocean air though cold and bracing is not without its own salubrious effects. The consumptive patient is actually being destroyed by his body's own efforts to mount an effective defense against the tubercular microbe. Over time excess tissues proliferate in the lungs creating scarification. When these tissues rupture hemorrhages occur and it is not uncommon for the victims to drown in their own blood if they do not first succumb to the exhaustion and wasting effects of the disease.

The inner urgency that I remember feeling in the atmosphere approaching the year 1896 drove me nearly to a state of frenzy. What I felt then was a typical symptom of the disease and not merely a result of the stress that I felt as my affair with Professor Moriarty reached its tipping point. My present attitude as we sail towards the orient after leaving San Francisco is precisely the opposite from the attitude that has prevailed within me in recent years. It is not mere lethargy but rather resignation. I feel that life's events are far more resistant than I had once imagined them to be. Ordinary notions of linear causality break down before what might be called a multi-determinant set of factors, each exerting its separate force to alter any desired outcome. This makes social engineering well-nigh impossible. In practice when applied to the international arena this realization means that catastrophic events, those that can benefit no nation or ensure the ordinary processes of world peace and international trade, such as a general European War if one ever occurs may still come upon us. Recently there has been talk in various quarters of an international peace conference in order to prevent that dreadful possibility. If it is usual for the nations of the world to define the future order of nations using the model provided by the Peace of Westphalia of 1648 that terminated the Thirty Years War and The Congress of Vienna that arranged affairs after the ravages of Napoleon's conquests, then it should in theory be possible to identify legitimate national interests and zones of influence and to reach agreement to prevent war based upon other factors than the ultimate resort to arms. The relative strength of nations can be calculated and assessed so that bargaining might better negotiate outcomes without the usual toll assessed by warfare upon all the contending parties. Even the victor after all must mourn the dead whose bodies paved the road to victory and pay for reconstruction of friend and foe alike. Circles of mutual dependency are such that complete hegemony is a fruitless affair. The administrative process becomes overwhelming when applied to the resentful and defeated population of a vanquished foe.

I often wonder if wars actually have as much to do with weeding out the excess males in a society on both sides as they do with the stated reasons for the conflict. If we view any given population from a merely procreative angle, there will be an excess of male contenders at any given moment for that portion of the female sex that is actually physically capable of bearing children. Warfare equalizes that equation. The difficulties attendant upon a rough equality of numbers between the sexes will be complicated in any case by the short period of fertility of the human female when set against her total span of life. There is a further difficulty posed by the related phenomenon of the decrease in numbers of women who die in childbirth, which further decreases the ratio of fertile females to males so that over time the latter tend to predominate absent some similar affliction that pertains to them alone. As societies become more civilized and educated the natural recklessness of young men may cause them to suffer injuries, but these will usually stop short of death. Although maimed and less productive they will remain to live and to seek out those females who will consent to bear them young. Nations, most of which are governed by older men, deal with this situation by arranging these occasional periodic blood-lettings whereby the superfluous males are sacrificed to some preposterous national idea accompanied by much flag-waving and by large amounts of rhetoric all dealing with notions of pride and national honor as though the two were equivalent concepts. Humility seems far more honorable to me than pride, which is far usually numbered among the seven deadly sins.

Jesus said that the peacemakers would be blessed and be called the Children of God. The desire to achieve some work of noble note still exists within me, something more than merely returning to my practice as a consulting detective upon essentially private matters. The retirement of Professor Moriarty leaves England without its sole single focus for crime. The result is that my thoughts have assumed an international flavor rather than my former contentment in solving those little puzzles that my friend Watson has turned into a pastime for the British reading public.

Would Watson's avid readers be as inclined to read of my personal eccentric habits if there was no reassuring background of Baker Street and its domestic comforts including my violin, the ever present whisky on the side-board, and my collection of pipes upon the mantel. Even the thought of these reminds me how long we have been divorced from those regions and habits that were once no small part of my definition of myself. It is not too much to say that my knowledge of London was once as intimate as that if any man living. What am I now since I have become virtually another version of Marco Polo? My former duties were extensive, but at least they were confined to what a detective might contemplate; while to be a philosopher at large was dictated only by my unique wager with Professor Moriarty. The habit of philosophy is a fatal one and once one begins it is difficult to return to the comforts of a prosaic acceptance of the way that things actually are. Realism is universally understood as defined by an attitude of resignation in its proponent. From this point of view philosophers are seldom realists when seen against a worldly perspective of values. It is the specific province of the true philosopher to question and to disturb the complacent ever since

Socrates upset the good citizens of Athens.

The public peace appears to require a supine populace so that those who do actually influence the course of events may proceed to do so undisturbed by doubts and moral qualms. The forces of assimilation soon reduce all new ideas to sterile orthodoxy. One needs to look no further than Leviticus to discover how ritual can prevail over the substance of moral thought. It takes a prophet such as Isaiah to inspire by image and sheer poetry. Therefore philosophers, the prophets of any culture usually die young by either being ignored or worse still actively opposed or even put to death. There are a set number of professions that oppose dictatorial rule and among them are philosophers and even lawyers.

Nations and entire social orders exalt the rhetoric of peace but practice the arts of war as focused upon those few individuals who actually see what is happening around them. My recent exposure to the art of politics in America merely confirms this insight. But if the political order must of necessity be banal and mendacious then where is mankind to look for hope when it acts collectively? The temptation for the thinking man is thus to withdraw into a private life where he can retain his sanity, to find a company of the like-minded and there to erect a wall of isolation to contain the light and prevent its diminishment and diffusion into the surrounding darkness. This temptation must be resisted and risks must be run in order to be true to one's values.

As I approach Japan I wonder whether I should search for its spirit among the diplomats and heirs to the Shogun rulers or whether in some Zen Buddhist or Shinto shrine to seek out men whose views may be more congenial to my present dispositions. My assignment is after all a rather vague one. Mycroft asks that I access the situation the better to enlighten him upon my return. After all, with the exception of a few artists who have been fascinated by oriental art and pottery the habits of the Japanese mind are as veiled as ever they were prior to the opening of western trade by the commercial interests of the empire builders. But then profits rather than prophets have always guided the course of human events. Now that my dawning recovery has opened again for me the paths of life the question of how I should spend the years ahead is posed for me in a way that I had not hitherto anticipated. My life had been constrained by the dangers that I courted perhaps to avoid those very questions that now present themselves to me and to all thinking men once it becomes evident that merely daring to encounter death's embrace is not adequate to avoid the slow increments of age.

Caution becomes natural to the aged man when the vitality of our early sap wanes and our limbs sense that autumn is near. Mankind has always included certain tree-worshipers because the longevity and sturdiness of our wooded-brethren promise the immortality that our own human flesh denies to us. The oldest living things are the trees. Many of the great Sequoias and Redwoods of California were living when the Roman legions conquered the ancient Britons. The Japanese take great pride in their gardens and shrines in which trees play no small role. This may open a common topic of conversation between us when we make landfall in Japan.

In contemplation of their Bonsai gardens I may discern the role of that new life that I feel being thrust upon me. How to combine now the roles of detective, chemist, diplomat, and my role as a semi-official courier of British good-will that now seems to be expected of me. This is the great question of the present point of my life and one that haunts me with doubts and perplexities. It is no easy thing to set aside the habits of a lifetime. The role of the uneasy dreamer may have been appropriate to my youth, but it now appears to have been the height of post-romantic self-indulgence and I have much for which to answer at the final judgment.

March 9, 1899

The air grows colder as we approach the Japanese islands and rain obscures the pounding seas. I had not realized the sheer size of the Pacific Ocean. Our progress is so slight each day that I feel that we have been long becalmed in these leaden waters. Watson has displayed his usual invaluable gift of allowing me my little silences. He is a man easily amused by the humble comforts of life aboard ship. The table is replete with various fish dishes and the cook knows the proper way to prepare the iced oysters that we brought along. The ship's library is well stocked and as a parting gift Mr. Sutro, the famous builder of the Sutro Tunnel on the Comstock Silver Lode in Nevada and the proprietor of the great elegant hotel at Cliff House presented us with some very fine California vintages of both Port and Sherry. The American embassy in San Francisco presented us with the President's compliments and supplied us with letters of introduction before we left that may be of use to us as we tour Japan, China, and the East Indies.

We can expect to meet courtesy in any case, because towards foreign powers the Japanese are as outwardly courteous as they may be secretly duplicitous and resentful. Open insult is not to be anticipated. Open displays of power will be delayed until the Japanese feel sufficiently powerful that they can clarify their ambitions. Even to use the word nation is perhaps a misnomer as applied to Japan. This intensive and complex feudal society is governed by a set of expectations that bridge the realms of law and religion. Obligations are inter-generational and points of honor are so refined as to constitute a sort of poetry of circumstance. It takes just such figurative language to convey eastern truths to the western mind.

Most western diplomats will not adopt such refined perceptions towards them with the result that the Japanese can weave silken threads about the opposing nations while allowing then to bask in their own notions of superiority until the critical hour arrives. There is great danger here. However, I must see the process in actual operation if I am to advise Mycroft wisely upon my return to England. His position is one that is highly compromised at the present time by his convictions that match my own in many respects. This race for colonies abroad to feed industry at home can no longer masquerade under the guise of missionary work or the spreading of the benefits of civilization. Our collective presumptions are only matched by our cupidity. Material progress feeds not our security but our fears. Each day our fleets expand their circumference until they span the globe and everywhere we encourage mistrust in the populations that we encounter.

It is no lasting answer to the internecine conflicts of various tribes and regions to unite them in opposition to us. Those who remain at home obsess over maps as though these brightly colored regions could be altered at will to merge in an extended regional supremacy under British rule, just as the extensive Siberian taiga is ruled by Russia with its capital at St. Petersburg westward looking to Europe for guidance. Russia is our great tutor in the follies of empire. What has the Ukrainian to do with the oriental Yakut? Why should the Caspian region look north to Moscow for its rulers? Why should the Orthodox Christian rule the believer of the prophet of Islam? When will this extensive and unworkable effort at a universal government first dissolve into its natural constitutive regions? These are the questions posed in light of the current China question.

Now that the African question is well nigh settled it is to the orient that all eyes are turned. Will the Chinese submit as easily as the fractured tribes of Africa that for so long glutted the market for slaves from the Amazon regions to the Carolinas? I fear not, but how to supply Mycroft with the hard data that will tamp down the smoking fires of British ambitions? To contain them may serve to put off the day of a regional lesson of resistance that will at least be less costly than the direct conflict of well-armed European powers that will pose a threat to the domestic populations of Europe. We need to encounter limitations short of catastrophe to reverse by slow degrees the long-established tide of victory.

March 10, 1899

I must devote today's entry to my friend Watson. He has been rather quiet since our departure, pacing the deck and showing all the signs of one who has left something precious behind. I have no doubt that it is Irene who is the cause of his much constrained lamentations. I tried to bring him out today on the matter.

"You seem overly quiet my dear fellow," I began.

"Well this voyage does appear to be an interminable one, Holmes," he answered in his most laconic manner.

"Well, I have read that the Pacific Ocean is somewhat extensive."

"We might have returned by way of New York on the train with Miss Adler [he still prefers to use her maiden name] rather than taking the long way round through the Indian Ocean and leaving her with that threadbare theater ensemble."

"I had no idea that you felt so strongly about the matter. You did not suggest that course at the time," I admonished him.

He made no response to this.

"Silent? It may help if I tell you that I am not unaffected by the demands that have determined our present course. I was quite ready to return home by the shortest route."

"You seem to prefer a life of travel," he said grudgingly.

I objected to this. "On the contrary; you of all men should know how lazy I am when at home in Baker Street. It is only when I am well-launched upon a course of action that I prefer to see it through to the end. I do not anticipate being this close again to the orient."

He conceded my point, "I understand, but in any case I thought you were under orders."

"You mean from Mycroft? Mycroft does not give orders; he gives indications. We are to assess. No one can compress more meaning into a single infinitive."

"Very well, so we are to assess. How long do you anticipate that this assessment will take?

"It is not a question of time, but of accuracy; great and compelling interests are at stake. You may not realize it, my dear fellow, but we stand on the threshold of a great re-ordering of the political structure of the world. The Americans are forcing the issue."

"You mean revolution?" he inquired with concern.

I chose to correct that automatic and too easy assumption, "Oh nothing so limited. I fear that events are afoot that may require a century or more to sort themselves out. History when set upon a new course is like the movement of glaciers: extensive and slow. What we will soon witness if I am not much mistaken is the end of the later renaissance period. We are closer my dear friend to the beginning than to the end and what we have called modernism is, in point of fact, only the last throes of a dying civilization."

"You alarm me."

"On the contrary you are skeptical; admit it. You are the one fixed point in a changing age. You desire comfort and will affirm any faith that promises it. Your attitude is the antithesis of what Jesus announced when he spoke of kindling a fire, of setting close relatives against each other, of bringing not peace but a sword! Oh, he was not speaking of violence, but of the degree of change that is demanded when an old era ends. The effort to retain power beyond its legitimate end can result in more destruction than we may readily imagine. It is that fear that haunts me day and night. It is that fear that motivates our present journey to the east. We go not for the needs of the present hour but to resolve questions that only the coming decades will pose. They cannot be anticipated or formulated in their exact parameters now, but we may at least begin to develop the categories of thought that may contain them. This is no doubt what Mycroft with his superior intellect means when he asks us to make an assessment."

"And then may we return to Baker Street?" he asked plaintively.

"Yes and to the west-end theaters, where no doubt we shall have the opportunity to again be present at one of those performances of Miss Irene Adler, she whom you once referred to as of dubious and questionable memory."

"She is an angel," he opined in a most dreamy fashion.

"Well, she is at the least a proper model for one of those Pre-Raphaelite paintings of Mr. Dante Gabriel Rossetti," I suggested.

"She is more refined than any of his models," he commented with some umbrage.

I was somewhat amused to see how the old fires of romance still burned within him. "Yes, but take care old friend. I know of her power over the mind and heart. I have fled from her for that very reason, lest seeking to possess her I should possess nothing else, not even my own soul. There are women whose love can eclipse all the rest of existence for a man. We pass among them daily: wise, intelligent, beautiful, and the source of new life. How should we survive as men if we did not diminish them? The

Moslems so fear their women that they wrap them up in black attire. If they did not do so there would be no end of duels for their favors. So unsatisfied is the Moslem desire for woman that the mind of the believer imagines paradise, not as the celestial discourse with God, but as a garden party served by available virgins. Definitely a mere aperitif to a more sophisticated theology, but it motivates them to daily prayer and to acts of charity and gives them a sense of brotherhood so who is to complain?"

"You mock me in describing her in this fashion," he said.

This pained me, "On the contrary I affirm your excellent taste and I share your preferences; but I must warn you, knowing you as I do that where the heart prevails the force of reason is often inadequate to follow and restrain. But, the sun is declining there beyond the clouds that deck the horizon and the chill of night descends. Perhaps we should dress for dinner and enjoy the stimulating conversation of our fellow passengers over a whisky and soda. We shall see her again."

We adjourned then to our staterooms. It was only upon reflection later when writing these words that I realized that I too missed Irene and that my desire to return to London was greater than I had supposed. It was all too true however that fortunate circumstance had provided me with an opportunity to observe the oriental regions at close-hand, that region of imperial contention between the various self-appointed paragons of civilization in their quest for trade and commerce, a race that America had now decided to join.

March 15, 1899

We have made landfall in the islands of Japan. My initial impressions are almost too many and too complex to record here. What I have been left with is an abiding impression of quiet ant-like order and activity. Everyone seems to know precisely what he intends to do and is busy accomplishing it in the most courteous and decorous way possible. The contrast with the noise and squalor of our European cities is discouraging. How is it that we imagine that it is we who should be colonizing and civilizing them? The written language here is derived from the Chinese characters and is astonishing in its visual complexity. This means that literacy is reserved for a minority of the population while the rest depend upon an elaborate and long-standing sense of tradition and family loyalty to sustain them and to direct their hopes and aspirations.

As to where the country is headed I can only say that it will soon be a force to be reckoned with in the councils of nations. At present the culture is an inharmonious mixture of western customs overlaid upon a feudal society. The effect is often amusing in its visual incongruities as top-hats appear in combination with kimonos. The signs of rapid growth in various industries are present everywhere from steel production to ship-building. The Japanese are busy rapidly arming themselves, but whether this is being done to resist further incursions upon their long-established customs and way of life or as a prelude to foreign adventures I cannot say.

Watson and I are ensconced at the British Embassy. As usual Mycroft's name opens all doors. My own poor reputation as a solver of puzzles avails us not at all insofar as anyone has even heard of me beyond the confines of England and France. The best that I can hope for is that a stray issue of the Strand Magazine has found its way to the orient and even then most people assume that my clients are primarily made up of governesses and others among the working classes. There seems to be an abiding conviction in those who have heard of me that most of my cases involve snakes.

I am afraid that Watson has systematically undermined my future economic potential by implying that I am a brain without a body who can afford to eat every night at Simpsons and to turn down cases that fail to intrigue my own overly refined tastes for the piquant and the obscure. I am not after all maintained under pension of the government and the remissions from Sherringford are not what they once were. When I return to England I may be in the same position as the Dickens character, Mr. Micawber, hoping that something will turn up.

When I said as much to Watson he reminded me of the little bookshop, of my holdings in various railroad stocks, and that I own my home in Devon free and clear, and by this means managed to cheer me up. In any case we are currently being fêted like princes. The Japanese seem unable to decide whether food is an artistic production or a means of subsistence. Seafood, vegetables, rice, and endless enamel cups of sake are the staples. Beef is a rarity here although pork abounds. For the rest I am continually chilled in the houses that appear ill-heated and overly exposed to the elements when we go out of the British compound to make calls on various local dignitaries.

An ability to maintain a stoic calm in the face of deprivation appears to be a characteristic of the people along with an excessive sense of honor in even the smallest of interactions. Humor is present but usually induced by what most Englishmen would consider remote causes and small incongruities, which they find quite amusing. They seem impervious to many of our own conceptions of propriety, while I am assured that we must be constantly on guard not to offend them by our own behavior that often seems loud and callous to them. They seem to thrive on indirection and pointing in particular is universally abhorred. All in all I shall be happy to be under way to more tropical climes and to leave these frigid shores. I realize more everyday that I am an incorrigible Englishman. Oh for a cold joint of mutton and a savory Yorkshire pork pie and best of all some good British gin and a hot lemon drink before my own hearth fire!

March 21, 1899

I am sitting above the city of Kyoto on a lushly wooded terrace and gazing out upon the surrounding well cultivated countryside. I have received a new missive from Mycroft that I cannot say pleases me. I have been re-directed. Mycroft asks now that I return only after making an excursion to Istanbul where I am to meet with the Russian ambassador to the Sultan's court there. The Ottoman Empire along with Persia and Russia dominate Asia. Whereas China I am coming to understand since my arrival in Japan is viewed not as an empire but as an unclaimed region ripe for invasion.

Mycroft desires that I "make a general appreciation of the situation wherever I go." He evidently thinks that the world is my oyster and that I possess boundless energy. I might of course plead renewed illness and Watson already disapproves of my recent peripatetic existence, but I had rather finish with what I have begun in the way of world reformation once and for all while opportunity offers. After that I will ensconce myself again at Baskerville Hall where Sir Henry's library is at my disposal and concoct a general solution to the world's ills distilled from a review of each nation's foundational documents. I hope to be the Sir Walter Scott of the dawning century. What a luxury it would be to prescribe social remedies without considering the vagaries of cultures and of human nature. Will a real science of human affairs ever be possible? If it is not we may finally perish at our own hands as we evolve the means to do so.

I tell Watson that the natural desire of any man of insight is to escape, to create a realm of grace and light and civilization while the "ignorant armies clash by night," to quote the poet and essayist Matthew Arnold. If it were not for the deaths of the innocent this course might be generally advised as the most moral one that could be chosen, but alas to be aware is to act for the man or woman with an ethical base. So it is that I must complete my course in practical politics when my own desires would lead me in quite another direction to embrace mysticism and to wander the moors by the side of Dr. Mortimer in various fanciful discussions. There is a fellow in England of the name of Gilbert Keith Chesterton who is much of my own mind in these matters. I must look him up when I return home.

March 25, 1899

I am now in the new capital city of Tokyo. I would like to jot down a few notes here on the Japanese governmental system insofar as I understand it and contrast it with the other absolute monarch the Czar of Russia. Both rulers combine absolute power in the secular sense with a centralized place as a mystical figure in a religious role. The Emperor of Japan of course is not a mere figurehead or dynastic ruler; he is viewed as a lineal descendent of the Sun Goddess. His priestly function in the system of religious observance called Shinto was held to be of such importance that much of his governing power was delegated to various clans, each of which specialized in a specialized court function. The net result is a seamless web wherein ritual and law are co-extensive.

The people in turn occupy a remarkably peaceful and loyal strata based upon honor and obedience. Revolution among them is inconceivable although various clan wars do erupt from time to time. The Fugiwara clan has been historically the most important and it is not too much to say that the Emperors prior to Emperor Jinto were in many cases virtual ideological palace prisoners who were so controlled by their role that their lives became one long alteration between sensual pleasures and their obligations to uphold a virtually static society. All of this was upset by Admiral Perry of the United States who insisted upon opening Japan to trade with the outside world.

Compared to the Emperor of Japan the Czar is allowed great freedom. Upon his accession to the throne he had already married a German princess, Alix a woman of his own choice. He is allowed to travel and to maintain various estates rather than bring confined to one centralized compound where most of his functions are exercised. Like any western monarch he is a head of state and governs by laws of a sort although without a parliament to check and balance his decisions. Instead he is dependent upon an apparatus of local governors and an extensive police force that has insinuated itself into every aspect of Russian life. It is this faceless because multiplex institution that Mycroft most fears as his letter to me of a few days ago specifies. Absolute power creates various hangers-on who can act in secret for the simple reason that absolute power cannot be effectively exercised by a single man. The religious functions of the Czar are largely symbolic. They do add a patina of God's blessings though to what might otherwise be resented by the people. There is evidence though that the Russian people are growing restive under the sway of the Czar and his administrative state and this also Mycroft wishes me to assess. A revolution would be unfortunate because the results would be unpredictable. A known threat is much easier.

The Ottoman situation can be summed up briefly as a case where concubines and eunuchs run an empire where sensuality has been raised to a principle of governance. The harem is a secret realm that no one can understand who is not privy to its daily workings. It can only be judged from outside from whence it appears not so much religious as an example of decadence and indulgence. An autocracy imposed upon an essentially tribal base cannot long endure, at least in the present age. The Turks lost their hold on Europe at the siege of Vienna. It is the one thing that Christian civilization owes to the Austrians, that and maybe preventing the Roman Catholic Church from being an exclusively French church by holding out during the Thirty Years War. That having been said the Austrian Empire is not much healthier than that of the Turkish sultans. When old Franz Joseph dies the whole thing may come unglued. It is at present an unnatural conglomeration of divergent linguistic and cultural groups.

In point of fact that is the entire problem with diplomacy; there are simply too many variables to be harmonized. My ability as a detective was based on one key fact, the triggering event had already occurred. All that I needed to do was to reconstruct what had already happened, but the event itself was set in stone and thus unchanging. Now in Mycroft's world everything is in flux. He must not only keep every causative factor in play, weigh it, and trace its probable effects, but he must also know that on the morrow everything begins again. Even from his God-like post at the Diogenes Club with its various comforting amenities he is exhausted by evening through sheer mental effort. It is for this reason that he asks me to play my own role of observer on the actual scene of what for him are merely political forces in play. How does one weigh a qualitative fact or that pervading atmosphere of scent that events give off? It takes the quivering nostrils of an old hound like me to do them justice.

March 28, 1899

Some thoughts regarding the economies of newly discovered regions...
There is an inherent logic to the migration of capital in a mobile world that will inevitably undermine local land-based economies. Capital can always move faster and more readily then people or productive facilities. A corollary of this is that national

borders are an unnatural phenomenon from the point of view of capitalism and trade patterns will sooner or later tend to undermine localities, first within nations, and later on between nations. Whole regions of the earth will be subject to exterior colonization by nations with superior military power and that power will reflect the relative strength of the economies of those nations that care to exploit other regions of the earth.

It will make little sense to abduct people from those regions and transport them to the home country when they can be enslaved where they are, just as the Spanish in Peru were content to work the natives to death in the silver mines in their native land. The mark of slavery is that it is employed to serve a need that may have nothing whatsoever to do with what is necessary or advantageous to the people where the resources are located. The Peruvian Indians managed quite well leaving the gold and silver where it was. Their culture saw value elsewhere and they had every right to pursue their own interests without being forced by violence or artificially induced scarcity to exchange their goals as a society to feed the demands of an outside power.

The ability to evict an outside predator demands a singleness of purpose that many more innocent societies do not possess, just as women have been effectively placed in a subservient position by virtue of their inherent physiology that subjects them to physical attacks and sexual violence. The virtues of the victim are often the very means that the aggressor uses to subdue them. That which is most personal and intimate to an indigenous people or to an individual provides the point of vulnerability that opens a path to exploitation. What one fears most to lose is what the aggressive power is most anxious to obtain, because its loss is irreparable; the spirit of an individual or of a people once it is crushed sometimes never recovers. Whole fertile regions of the globe are turned into wastelands and the corrupting power simply moves along to its next station of destruction. Justifiable revenge when it comes can be terrible. I fear that the western powers will realize this too late in their relations with the east.

We are again underway. My abiding impressions of Japan are of necessity glancing, idiosyncratic, and incomplete. The culture of the nation is so intricate and detailed, so guarded and secretive, and so dependent upon ritual and symbol that most statesmen and naval assessments are bound to be erroneous. This is what I will seek to convey to Mycroft. I will advise against any alliance opposing them because it will only strengthen Japanese ambitions in the Pacific region. For all of our mistrust of Russian intentions in Persia we must not forget that Russia is also the key to restrain German ambitions. If Russia is compromised then it will be up to us to secure the Balkans, a task that would be unduly costly and would require an expeditionary force along the coast of Bulgaria or the coastline of the Ottoman Turks. The peace of Europe can only be maintained by a stalemate between the contending colonial powers. The rest will depend upon the stability of the border regions and the ambitions of various ethnic groups striving towards independent statehood. The very idea of the nation-state will be the hobgoblin of the next century. This is the only justification for empires: they are strong and stable enough to curtail regional conflicts unless, and upon this unless much depends, the empires choose to use regional disputes as a primer to ignite a big-power conflagration.

It is precisely here that the power of personalities can come into play. History is moved by the way that individuals can read the trend of events and cause them to deviate in a direction that is consonant with their ideology and desires. It is virtually impossible for the peacemakers to interdict these selfish processes for the simple reason that to suppress one demagogue is automatically to favor his opposing demagogue. Few leaders recognize the benefits of achieving a stable balance of discontents between contending parties. This is why trying to achieve directly and unilaterally any proposed ideal state of international affairs is a virtual invitation to war.

To live virtuously and wisely is to accept the world as it is and to intervene only insofar as the inner disposition of self-effacing charity permits. To mobilize the masses is always to risk that a stampede of unreason will intervene before anything good can be accomplished. Fortunately the dull round of prosaic pleasures and partial satisfactions deflects most people from heroic aspirations. We are saved by the virtue of a general lethargy among the peoples of the world. My recommendation for peace is the prescription of a general soporific to be administered in generous doses.

April 3, 1899

I shared my last entries with Watson and he took exception to what he perceives as my cynicism in world affairs and the historical outlook for progress.

"I fear that your recent illness has given you a fatalistic view of life," he concluded.

"Perhaps you favor the views of Mr. Kipling then?" I suggested.

"I favor individual courage and the rule of duty," he replied with some asperity. "Where would the world be without its inspirational figures like Gordon of Khartoum?"

I disagreed, "Yet the world is actually sustained by the multitudes of unknown figures simply performing their dull daily tasks of raising grain, loading ships, and driving locomotives. The world is sustained by the sinew of labor going about its assigned tasks without question or complaint. I am mistrustful of movements that reduce the daily human drama of existence to abstractions, even when those abstractions are religious in nature."

Watson considered this for a time before replying, "I still say that the world needs its heroes to inspire action."

"Perhaps it does; heroes are entertaining if nothing else. They encapsulate our hidden desires and suggest untold possibilities, but I fear that they are far more likely to advance the case of mischief than to usher in the millennium. I take great comfort from the fact that Jesus spent thirty years laboring at a humble trade and only three years confronting the Roman occupation and trying to raise the consciousness of the Jews from a dream of national glory to a universal mission of charity for all people. The proportion is correct."

Watson greeted this observation with some asperity. "You say this now, but have we not just finished a two-year escapade that has forced us both to dabble in world politics in order to defeat Baron Maupertuis and address the aspirations of American empire building?"

"Precisely," I answered, "And for that very reason I hope to return to England and adopt a quiet life of scholarship and meditation if I am allowed by events to do so. I am weary of the company of the great, Watson. I hunger for days spent digging up artifacts on the moors with Dr. Mortimer and playing chess with Sir Henry before a roaring fire after a dinner of venison and partridge. The pleasures of the chase are wonderful, but even the most avid foxhound is happy at the end of the day to return to his kennel and dream of plunging horses and foxes leading the pack a merry chase. What would life be without its comforts?"

"You intend then to return then to Baker Street?" he inquired.

"Well I must still keep *au current* with the criminal world. Even the sharpest sword is likely to exhibit oxidation if not in use. My recovery promises me the longevity that both of us doubted would be my lot only a short year ago. Your ministrations have been as ever invaluable, my dear fellow; but what of your own intentions, will you retire to Cornwall when we return?"

"I prefer to remain at your side," he said with the old loyalty.

"You say that even despite all my cynicism? That is kind of you, old fellow. I must warn you though; I am not entirely at my own disposal."

"What do you mean?" he inquired with a puzzled expression.

"I am afraid that my reputation as a person to consult in political realms may not be easily extinguished. There will be calls made upon me by various foreign potentates, particularly if Mycroft chooses to relinquish his unnamed post as the arbiter of British policy. I can hardly refuse appeals made by the inner circle at home, however much I deplore the machinations of politicians."

"But your restored health will suffer in consequence,

Holmes!" he objected.

"I intend to follow your recommendations and take things by degrees," I promised.

"Well then, perhaps all will be sustainable, but you must resist your former habits of excessive labors and poor diet not to mention," he paused but his meaning was all too clear.

"Fear not, my good fellow, my decadent period is behind me ... the follies of youth."

"You will keep me informed to the degree that you can?" he insisted.

"You will be always at my side when danger threatens. As for the councils of state however I may be sworn to confidentiality. I hope you will forgive me if I am compelled to preserve various secrets even from you."

He spoke grudgingly, "It will make my task as your chronicler more difficult. I will be proceeding at times with only partial knowledge and there is always the possibility that I will go off on a false scent." He said this with a rueful expression.

I answered at once to reassure him. "We must of course trust to our old confidence and our mutual respect to smooth out any misunderstandings or misapprehensions that arise."

"So you promise that no repetition of the Reichenbach affair and its sequel will occur?" he said smiling.

"Ah Watson, I shall always reproach myself for keeping you so long in the dark at that time, but what was I do? It was after all a most complex affair. It may take you several volumes to explain it to your loyal readers, if you care to undertake the task."

"As I shall with your permission when we return to England," he replied with energy.

"Then I beg you to hold the manuscript back until it can do no harm or prejudice my efforts in the realm an international consultancy when we return."

"I promise," he said. "It shall remain in my strong-box until you give your permission to publish."

"Excellent, Watson, more adventures lie ahead for us. In a matter of days we shall be off the Malay Archipelago and we will have time with our old nemesis, Colonel Sebastian Moran. But it is growing cold here on deck and I think we had best prepare for dinner. I shall meet you in the ship's bar for a brandy and conversation with our good captain."

April 4, 1899

The problems of nations are a subset of the problems existing between individuals in relationship. Most of my cases involved human passions in some way. In nations passions are reduced to policies that appear bleached-out and objective, but they are none the less vicious and primitive for all of that. I will go so far as to say that it is precisely this aura of being commanded by some powerful defensive imperative held to be entirely justified and beyond criticism that betrays the inner and primitive impulses that although diffused throughout the entire populace are no less subjective in their orientation and purpose. Similarly, one of the illusions of diplomacy is that what goes on between diplomats and even heads of state is not personal and that somehow the ordinary personality of the office-holders can be left behind in discussions.

Character in all of our affairs is a constant and will eventually become manifest. I have been consulted on occasion by persons of high office and it has been my habit not to confirm them in whatever illusions they hold regarding their own superiority to the general human condition. I make it a point to receive solicitations in my own chambers where the advantage is mine and where I am free to decline my services if that should be prove to be necessary or advantageous. Other than a general courtesy I prefer to reveal nothing to the client as the story unfolds lest I bias the presentation to meet what the client judges to be most important. My most salient clues emerge most often from some trivial detail that the client initially feels is unworthy of note, but which later proves decisive to the outcome of the case.

We have sailed past the coast of the Philippines where we could see on occasion signs of the conflict being waged there by American troops engaged in subduing the efforts of their recent allies against Spain as they strove to emerge as a sovereign state rather than as what I fear they will now become, the advance staging area for American commercial interests in the Pacific region. As one of the weakest of the colonial powers Spain was a natural target for any avid successor to its former colonial supremacy.

I regret to say that what has been called the American Civil War was in reality a war of conquest by the powerful commercial interests of the northern states against the agrarian south. Industrialism demands cheap raw materials and the imperative of mindless profit will use violence to acquire sources of those raw materials. It should come as no surprise then that the war waged between the American states to weld them into a commercial union would not prove sufficient to feed the insatiable maw of industry and eventually other wars of conquest would follow. Of course Americans have always believed that their republic was founded on various transcendent principles rather than a mere desire for conquest and expansion. Subsequent experience in the period called reconstruction has not been particularly successful; brutality and terror still keep the post-war population of former African slaves in a state of terror and subjugation, the federal laws notwithstanding.

The European states are not similarly burdened, because they have emerged through almost two millennia of conflict and shifting borders with intact ethnic conclaves. Regional identity remains intact even in the face of wars of annexation. One need only think of the Alsace-Lorraine region or of the often shifting claims over Bohemia to see my point. The European conscience is permanently compromised by its failure to embody Christian principles where national boundaries are at stake so that imperialism there is a natural outgrowth of greed and competition. But from America one might have wished for something better; alas, it is not to be. America will remain a divided land both racially and regionally.

Our swift vessel soon left the Philippine islands behind and with that region the outer outpost of progress as well. We are now entering the Indonesian island chain that is claimed by the ever-enterprising Dutch. The people of the Netherlands have a genius for commercialism second only to the English. Even in the realm of ideas the Dutch have refused to raise artificial barriers. For this reason the Jewish philosopher Baruch Spinoza was at home there where the inquisition could not reach his body and where his books might find an audience. Of course the freedom of ideas does not necessarily restrain the desire for foreign conquest and as a result these pristine islands now fly the Dutch flag. Of course our present goal is Malaya where we hope to enjoy the hospitality of the man who acted as my guide and guardian through the years from 1891 to 1893. This he did under orders from Professor Moriarty who wanted me to return alive and well to engage with him in an intensive battle of the minds over certain basic questions of life and of death.

As our time together over many regions continued I began to suspect that Colonel Sebastian Moran was developing a grudging respect for the effete city-dweller that he once thought me to be. I learned to ride camels, to endure hunger and thirst, and to stomach various partially preserved and dried meats of uncertain origin and provenance. He acted as my host later on in the hilly cliff regions of the Principality of Monaco under far better circumstances when I was on my way to Rome and my fortuitous reunion with Irene Adler. Since then other than a few meetings in London I had not seen him.

I wonder if he has changed greatly. The sun of the tropic regions is brutal to those of Caucasian descent. He is not a man who will welcome easily the changes that come on with age. Yet I cannot imagine him in any state of decrepitude. Some men seem predestined to perpetual vitality and to deprive them of the fullness of their functions is to kill them. These men are by nature immune to the joys of contemplation and the solace of art; they live at a visceral level like beasts of prey, magnificent and subject only to the imperative of survival. They are proof to all delicacy of feeling and sympathy for them is an invitation to be duped. Such a man may be a valuable ally in regions where civilization has yet to arrive, but they are the very death of nations if they ever are placed in positions of power and control.

Yet in spite of these reservations I have always perceived in the Colonel a reserve of wry humor that in him is a saving grace. He is able to enjoy the humor of his own base and brutal impulses and he is not without a sense of honor and loyalty to ideas and the persons who are capable of realizing them. Professor Moriarty saw these qualities in him and relied on them in making Colonel Moran his second-in-command. I in turn saw the Colonel as immanently redeemable and was instrumental in helping him out of several rather embarrassing entanglements in London. I have always been of the opinion that the quality of mercy is not strained and I would rather error on the side of leniency than to condemn a man when there is still room for repentance and restitution. Of course there is in this attitude a risk that others may be harmed. I will admit that there are some individuals where the flame of humanity burns sufficiently low as to be to all intents and purposes non-existent and they must be subdued if not destroyed the better to safeguard the innocent.

Watson's accounts include a few of these and of my manner of dealing with them. There is a mystery in the human heart that some among us appear beyond redemption, but as to who these are no man can say with absolute certainty. There will as a result always be a divergence between practical morality and the ideal that is most pronounced when we condemn not merely a man's actions but the man himself and if necessary put an end to him to save others. Unfortunately most deaths wrought by our own hands upon each other are not the result of individual assessment, but rather the direct result of our habit of seeing each other as adherents to doctrines that we despise or nations that oppose our own self-interest or national loyalty. In war we congratulate ourselves when we should condemn our actions. In our victory is our shame.

It is strange but we presume that people who have played any significant role in our lives are preserved as long as we ourselves are among the living as though an invisible chain of prior meetings and shared experience guarantees not only that they will be alive and hence assessable to us on demand, but that they will remain as we last saw them although we ourselves may have known alterations with age and experience. I fully expected Colonel Sebastian Moran to be as hearty and as resilient as he appeared at our last meeting and I was surprised to hear upon our landing that he was unable to come down to greet our boat and was confined to the plantation where his carriage would convey us.

My thoughts immediately referenced an inventory of his various vices any one of which might be supposed to have a decided effect upon the health of an ordinary man, but then the Colonel was not an ordinary man. I could recall every sinew in those tanned forearms and his face although lined and dried as an old buffalo hide was for all of that full and massive, his hair like the mane of an old lion, and his teeth white and tenacious in a firm mouth.

Imagine then my dismay to see him confined to a cane chair, beset with various malaria induced agues, and weakened by the cancer that was soon to take him forth from among us. With his customary reticence he had not written to me during the past two years so that I was ill-prepared to come suddenly upon him in his present state. I am happy to say that his spirit, for all of that, was undiminished; but still so great is our sense that the physical presence should convey what we know of the other person that it was like coming upon a great fire when it has dwindled into only ash and embers.

His voice was firm but fainter than of old as he rose and greeted me. "So Holmes, you hardly thought to confront a wizened elf when you landed, did you? It is my little joke upon you. You must allow me the pleasure of witnessing your surprise, the great deductive reasoner, finally at a loss for words. Your years at London hospitals should have prepared you to encounter cadavers."

He subsided into a fit of coughing before continuing, "You on the contrary look splendid. It pays to have a physician in residence I see. Dr. Watson, you are a wonder worker! I expected to see an emaciated consumptive disembark and contemplated that the two of us would sit in the sun wagering as to which of us would be the first to keel over and be buried back in the fetid cane-break yonder. Now I shall rest alone. Ah well, you see how this damn sickness has affected me; I am turning sentimental."

I went up to him and grasped the hand stretched out to me, one now bereft of its former strength and substance. For lack of anything immediate to say to him I said, "I bear greetings to you from the Professor."

"And how is that old star-gazing reprobate? Is it really true that he has come over to your way of thinking? I always warned him of the fatal consequences of speaking to a philosopher."

"His stables have become renowned throughout England and he continues to teach at Exeter. He has sent a remittance in care of me that can be cashed at the Bank in Kuala Lumpur."

"A gratuity for old services, quite generous of him I am sure but of no earthy use to me now; I am a dying man. My one comfort is that this is the land of teak and mahogany so I will not face the prospect of eternity ill-provided for lack of a proper casket to house my old bones. Ah, he has been more than generous! This will add silver handles to the whole affair and the local Muslim potentates and princes will be much impressed. We Britons must appear before the natives in our complete panoply of splendor to keep control in these distant regions; cannon alone are insufficient. We have to keep the brutes believing that they will profit from association with us."

"Yet you have always despised imperial rule Colonel," I objected, anxious as I was to allow him to cover his embarrassment at his present state by resuming our former relations of thrust and parry.

"You are quite right, Holmes. But then I had heard that you have become a diplomat and a servant to empire. Are you not come fresh from America, the newest of the imperial nations?"

"Well my mission there was altered by my own conscience. I advised that America keep confined within its two oceans. I said as much to President McKinley.”

He chuckled grimly, “And you were no doubt rebuffed. Like most Americans he no doubt thinks of himself as a bastion of light in a darkened world. The Americans will always veil their conquests in protestations of benevolence and progress. They are a people addicted to romance as applied to themselves and utter cynicism towards the aspirations of anyone else. It is part of their genius; it keeps their conscience at bay.”

“How strange to hear you mention the word conscience!” I interjected smiling.”

He continued, “Oh I have my code. I have always enjoyed playing the game and what is a game without rules?”

“Yes, but you don’t mind cheating on occasion,” I chided him.

“Part of the game my dear fellow; I do so only to keep the dealer on his guard. I consider God the dealer of his universe and I demand that he show all of his cards. It is only fair.”

I followed up on this observation of his. “But then where would mystery reside if the dealer was so obvious. Make the game too obvious and all the challenge goes with it. Would you ever enjoy shooting a lion that refused to charge?”

“Work not your magic on me, Holmes. Save it for the Professor who enjoys the charm of your dialectics. With me the senses are supreme. Did I tell you that I am contemplating joining the Moslems in anticipation of the virgins of paradise?”

“I should have thought that you had already obtained enough of that sort of thing in this life, Colonel,” I objected smiling.

“True, but virgins are a rare commodity even in these regions. Women out here look like their mothers by the time they reach thirty. A complete set of teeth is a rarity. No, the Moslems have the right idea of paradise. Some transcendent beatific vision may impress the followers of Dante Gabriel Rossetti who are content to contemplate a painted effigy of flesh, but as for me...” he subsided again into a fit of coughing.

I took up for him at this juncture, “Yes well, we shall have plenty of time during our visit to discuss the finer points of these celestial delights. I see that the sun is setting and the mists are rising and we have not yet been assigned quarters."

He looked up at me with just a tinge of gratitude for my tact. "Quite right, you see how remiss I have become with so few white men as guests. We shall dine later. It pleases me to see others enjoying what I can no longer share. Don't ask me what we shall be serving; just know that you will fund nothing like it in England. I haven't seen a cheese in years."

He forthwith clapped his hands and his majordomo appeared and led us to our rooms in the spacious mansion that will be our home for the next few days before we resume our voyage.

April 19, 1899

We are now quite settled in here at the edge of the jungle where sugar-cane fields are supplanting the virgin forest. The great house does not border the fields, but stands on raised pedestals by a sapphire-blue bay and is surrounded on all sides by the beauty of the great hardwood trees and interlaced vines. This has the advantage of making the house and its surrounding park impregnable to attack from the landward side, but it has the disadvantage of making the great beasts and reptiles our near acquaintances. An occasional melancholy orangutan condescends to emerge from the jungle for a treat, which amuses the Colonel greatly.

Ever since *The Adventure of the Speckled Band* I have harbored a mistrust and loathing for poisonous serpents. It has come therefore as an unwelcome surprise to discover that the denizens of these regions have perforce become used to living in daily familiarity with cobras and kraits. Colonel Moran has adopted an ingenious method of dealing with them by domesticating and raising Mongooses that consider it great sport to kill and eat these deadly snakes. This still leaves the neophyte awake though at night as the deadly mosquitoes' shrill buzz surrounds the netting around the beds and the sound of great water buffalo and elephants resound as limbs are broken and trees uprooted by their nightly gambols. The result is that I sleep little and wake each day with the dawn when the jungle birds start in and I cannot return to sleep. I am grateful that our visit will be of short duration.

I have avoided speaking to the Colonel about his health and have tried to keep our conversation to topics that he would find interesting. Today we spoke of Persia, which along with China promises to be the region around which various international tensions will be manifested in the coming years. This was a topic dear to the Colonel and his observations were both interesting and useful to my own conceptions.

"The world is shrinking, Holmes," he said one day shortly after our arrival. "The great powers are running out of regions to incorporate into their extensive trading webs. Eventually it will all lead to war."

"You think so?" I commented.

"Of course, how can it do otherwise?"

"Well I had rather hoped that some compromise might be reached, some agreement to share the relative advantages of..."

"Bah, compromise! You evidently do not understand the role of bluff and bluster in world affairs. Each nation must in effect believe in its own superiority and invincibility, and as parity of power comes closer the need to prove superiority by arms will increase until sooner of later some triggering event will occur. After it gets going such wars must continue until all opposition is neutralized. It is the law of progress applied to arms."

"But that would be unbearably costly to all parties," I objected.

"What is cost when survival is at stake and ultimate beliefs are being questioned? We are totalistic creatures Holmes; it has been the secret of our survival as a species. Other animals quit when the opposing force retreats; only man pursues his enemies to the very last survivor. We burn, we pillage, and we kill regardless of sex or age. We leave no smoldering wick of resistance to kindle again into flame."

"You don't allow much room for the role of reason and diplomacy." I commented.

He smiled grimly as of old, "Diplomacy is simply the ordering through contract of what has already been decided by the relative ability to deploy force. It all comes down to power, Holmes, although relative cunning plays a role as well. We must not forget the power derived from a fearsome appearance. Threats will always be effective against the habit of comfort and good living by providing an impulse to appeasement, but sooner or later power depends upon the will to actually use it. The world is not governed by morality or noble ideas. These are only assembled after the fact to bless carnage as somehow motivated by the will to protect the women and the children at home by killing the women and the children of the opposing nation or tribe. China of course is the great prize and Indo-China next door."

"And Persia, where does Persia fit into your scheme?" I inquired, knowing as I did from past experience how pointless it was to dispute his pet ideas.

"Persia is the key to central Asia and the gateway into India from the north," he replied complacently. Russia and China in turn will always be threats to the keystone of the British Imperial Crown, which is India. For this reason England will be forced to keep Russia weak without actually attacking that immense empire. Russia combines two opposing qualities: it is too big to ignore, but no one actually wants to live there. England can achieve its aims by forcing Russia to choose between an alliance with France and an alliance with Germany and then make sure that England weighs in as the third member of whatever resulting alliance is eventually formed."

I found this observation amusing, so I pressed him further. "But what about the Pacific provinces of Russia; you surely don't suggest that the British should station a fleet of ships in the Pacific to spread the Russian defensive forces to protect India?"

He sniffed, "Of course not. England will make Japan its proxy in the Pacific, if the Americans don't get there first. The Japanese have been waiting to test their new navy on someone; it is only a matter of time. Russia is the most likely target."

"Why? I asked.

"Because Port Arthur is too distant for the Russian fleet to maintain it properly and still keep a presence on the Baltic Sea. The Germans could bottle them up in an instant. Not that anyone wants what the Russians have to sell. What Germany fears most is a two-front war and the line from the Baltic to the Carpathians would open Germany to an attack from the east."

"You seem to see the world as a sphere containing certain key areas prone to conflict," I observed.

He subsided into silence considering this thesis.

"You are right, Holmes. The natural condition of humankind is to be at war somewhere and with somebody. The struggle for trade and resources form the key and for this reason a strong navy is essential to any nation aspiring to be a great power. The problem with Russia is that all of its greatest rivers flow north into the Arctic regions; this makes effective trade extremely difficult. As for resources, well there is always the possibility that oil reserves will be discovered and the Ukraine region is valuable for the grain it can produce. The biggest problem of Russia is its lack of population concentration sufficient to build an industrial base and the appalling lack of education of its former serfs."

"And what of the other nations, what are their relative weaknesses?" I enquired.

He smiled, "The Italians love life too much to fight. The French value display over efficiency. And the Germans have no imagination to adjust their goals once a plan is formed.

"And what of your own countrymen," I pressed on, "What problem do the British have?"

"The British suffer from a habit of fixed ideas," the Colonel answered, "Once they own something they believe it will be theirs forever. For instance, they still think they can control the Americans."

"And the Americans themselves," I finished, "What is their national problem?"

He smiled, "It is difficult to say when they have so many, but if I must choose it would be their collective addiction to thinking too well of themselves. No people are more insensitive to their own faults than the Americans. It will take something really dreadful to bring them face to face with their own history and the ultimate limitations of what they believe to be their infinite prospects. Not even a great Civil War was sufficient. They are a democracy after all. Someday the ignorant masses will elect a government that mirrors so perfectly their own national ethos that he will lead them into the quicksand of their own endless aspirations. They will wake up too late to their folly and by then ...

oh well that will be long after we are both gone."

I spoke up in order to prevent his usual afternoon lapse into melancholy. "Well since I am fresh from Japan does America have anything to fear from that quarter? You surely do not imagine that the United States will simply sit still and watch while Japan becomes a local oriental hegemon."

He looked up, interested again by my question. "I grant your point, but no one understands the Americans, including the Americans themselves. They are a peculiar people, sentimental and realistic simultaneously. They are a young nation with short historical perspective. They have yet to learn what other nations know—that wars are inevitable, but never glorious; they are simply a cost of doing business. What will always make the Americans dangerous is that they feel that somehow victory is owed to them, because they are impressed by their own virtues. It makes them cherish war as some sort of national valediction."

I whispered, "Don't tell that to Watson. He is quite fond of the Americans. He is possessed by something of the spirit of the revivalists and has never surrendered the thought that a better world is attainable."

The Colonel smiled at this. "Yes and he has always had a devotion to you and remained blind to your many faults as well. The Professor and I are your only real friends, because even knowing you as we do we see your value. You have always had a penchant for anarchy and follow your own will. You are impatient with forms and in your own way you are a brigand. The world has little patience with you and the Professor, men who assume that they can afford a private conscience. It kills such men. Why do you think that your Jesus was crucified? Jesus was never a real threat to the Romans, why the man was a pacifist at heart! His problem was his desire to sell the Jewish people a God who hated war and loved all people. Such ideas could not be allowed to stand. People are jealous of their gods and one who has no national loyalty is pointless. Worse still, such a God is a threat to national survival. That is why prayer is always guided by the national interest and why the troops are blessed as they go forth to kill. The only real universal faiths are those that turn their backs on the survival imperative completely like the Buddhists by saying that in this world we all end up losing, because we must suffer and die at last. Shall I give you a quote from your own gospels to prove my point?

'The man who would save his life will lose it; but the man who loses his life for my sake will find it.'

"Can any more uncompromising position ever have been made? Even the Buddha with his first noble truth that all is suffering is pale in comparison."

"I am surprised to hear you speaking in this way," I commented.

"How else should a man speak who knows that he is dying?" he replied quietly lapsing into silence.

A short time later Watson joined us and the conversation that we had been having turned to other topics.

April 22, 1899

It was a few days later that we spoke again and perhaps for the last time of the enduring questions that must perplex all thinking men and women; the great why and wherefore of human life. Of course Colonel Moran, long the purveyor of death to some of the greatest predators had as a consequence come to imagine that we can make peace with death by being its servant. I sought to disabuse him of this idea by saying, "You have done marvels with your estate Colonel. You have enabled many people here to survive and prosper. Land that was formerly desolate and non-productive has become an enclave of flowers and useful vegetation. You are to be congratulated on your industry and imagination."

He waved my compliments aside, "The land is the constant and it should be the task of various species to adapt to the opportunities that it affords to them in its native state. The rich variety of animals and plants sets its own balance without any human intervention. When we intervene we apply human concepts of profit and selection that are poor substitutes for the iron laws of nature that unconsciously create more beauty than the greatest of artists could ever conceive and execute by human agency. You betray an English provincial attitude that insists on seeing the world as a country estate. Perhaps I should be admitted among the ladies of our dear England for my garden," he muttered scornfully. "I assure you that even weakened as I am I prefer whores to horticulture."

He was as moody now as ever during our travels, but I made a further attempt at civility. "Is it so imperative then to forswear the gentler feelings, the products of civilized life? Why do you take such pride in the inhuman elements?"

He answered me without hesitation, "I like to place my bets on the winning numbers that is why. Look all about you, Holmes. Within five years of my death this place will have been looted, the schools I founded will be abandoned, and the natives will have reverted to throwing spears at each other. Death and dissolution are the great laws of being; everything else is governed by chance. The wheel of destiny spins and your number of choice does not come up again. Order and beauty are the exception set against the sovereign order of dissolution and the re-circulation of energy. Why can't I make you see this? You continually insist upon some naïve churchman's ideal of angels singing and scrubbed faces on a Sunday morning followed by crumpets and tea with the vicar."

I was somewhat nettled at this characterization of my religious beliefs, "I emphasize the positive aspects of life because you take such pride in losses and bloodshed, my dear Colonel. It is as though you prefer a game where the odds are always against you. You crave the prospect of defeat the way that other men wish each other for good luck. Isn't this because you don't want to appear foolish if everything just happens to work out after all?" I suggested quietly.

He sniffed scornfully at my diagnosis of his habit of mind. "Sheer clerical humbug; I should have left you on that mountainside in Abyssinia when we were surrounded by brigands and I took the leader out before his first demand was completed. Just how far would you have managed I wonder with your philosophy derived from a Soho garden party," he added with some bitterness.

I disagreed at once, "You underrate the power of ideas. The most savage tribes of central Asia were captivated and subdued by the poetry of the Koran. Ideas, my dear Colonel, govern the world and where ideas stop miracles begin. Divine Grace insinuates itself between cause and effect in ways that we can little imagine. There is an intricate tuning of the symphony of events that incorporates all discord into a greater harmony."

"And how do you know this, Holmes? Is this not the final result of Plato's delusions that have haunted every subsequent philosophy ever since? Look at the things themselves in all of their static uniqueness, alone and unconnected! Order is the great delusion of the intellect and the curse of language imposed on a mute set of sense data."

I brought him up short at this, "And do you really believe that you are just as illusory as these formal constructs of thought that you disparage? Can you deny that there is a conscious entity present in you behind whatever is perceived, one that is involved and aware, purposeful and ordained to an end beyond being a simple mold to receive and to record impressions that are distilled from the melee of impinging events? You deny any transcendent purpose for human life, but how does it come about then that we seek what can never be found? From whence is derived our metaphysical hunger? Think of only the simplest of our pleasures and ask how it is that the universe affords us the smell of a flower or the taste of chocolate or the bouquet of a fine vintage of wine? It is not that the world is devoid of meaning and significance for us, but that it is so charged with various goods and delights that we cannot number them? Why should living give us any joys at all if we are only epiphenomena of mindless physical changes in an insensate world?"

He was silent for a time before answering in a croaking voice. "The universe only toys with us the better to betray us in the end. I tell you I am dying. All of the delights that you speak of will exist for others but not for me. Death is the great negation of all our hopes."

I spoke gently but firmly in answer, "Would you have the world begin and end with you Colonel? Of course they will enjoy what you have enjoyed and like you they will part with them in due season the better to enjoy greater delights those prepared by the very agency that has given us these preliminary proofs of its generosity, an aperitif of what shall surely follow."

"But your proof Holmes; where is your proof?" he asked in

desperation. "This insistence on faith is the great cover-up of a failed mission."

"To demand proof is to pose the wrong question Colonel. Life is designed to show us the alternatives to one great choice for eternity. We must finally commit to one or the other great assessments of all things and we will be constituted by that choice."

"And if we conclude then that we are nothing?" he proposed, not without a sense of trepidation.

"Then we shall spend eternity seeking to make that great negation real. Nothing shall then persuade us that love is possible. It is not a winning bet, my dear friend. Why not leave the doorway open to surprise, since as you say you are going to die and become nothing. What point is there in striking an attitude for some statue of stoic grandeur lost as we are in the jungle that you exalt? A little humility at this critical time can still purchase much."

"Was this the sort of magic you worked on the Professor?" he asked.

"Perhaps it was, but what if this entire world is magical after all? Does it not take even more presumption and confidence to deny the remote possibility offered by eternal life than to affirm it? If you are really a man of strict reason then it should not be too much to generalize from a set of data to a possible if remote conclusion; or are you really so determined that you must be disappointed at last when you may be one last spin of the wheel of chance from the winning number? Is this the Colonel Moran, the master of the roulette wheel at Monte Carlo?"

He was again silent before saying, "I will think about it. In any case I will probably have some months still to mull it over. Would you care to stay and witness the outcome?"

"Well that is between you and God, Colonel. My presence would only distract you from that essential dialogue. Anything that I have said is not mine and to defeat me is not to win. Take what I have said not as 'my magic' but as simply an option presented by human existence itself. Make your own assessment and then choose."

"And if I choose wrong?" he inquired hesitantly.

"Oh well, I trust that God makes allowances in that grim

hour for futile gestures of fear and pride, shows us his wounds, and enlists compassion for others if not for ourselves. We may be saved at last less because we are overly merciful towards ourselves than because we desire eternal happiness for others. We may be judged for our best impulses in our most fortunate hours in preference to our habitual sins. Hope achieves what all else would deny."

April 27, 1899

Our ship picked us up again as our boarding vessel motored out to it from the extended loading-dock that was not the least of Colonel Moran's accomplishments. It just managed to clear the reef so that various small trading-craft could load and unload their goods. Our own ship home to England having a deep keel needed to keep well-off in the clear green waters.

I sat with Watson in the stern and gazed back over the waves at the frail form of the Colonel as he waved to us, leaning for support on his Samoan valet's arm. I would gladly have remained longer with him, but I knew that it would have been embarrassing to the Colonel for me to witness his final decline. His own stern dignity demanded that he face what life remained to him alone. Women are accustomed to face the pangs of childbirth in company, but there is an abstemious and ascetic quality in men that desires to veil anything that reminds them of our animal nature. We prefer to steel ourselves, turn our faces to the wall, and expire in silence.

In our last days together we did not have recourse to our conversation regarding the last things. Instead the Colonel amused himself by telling Watson tales of India and the high frontier regions of Afghanistan, and of the more embarrassing interludes of our journey together between the years of 1891 and 1892. Watson is the ideal listener and he has never outgrown a young lad's joy in tales of far-off places and romantic adventures. There is a joy in the merely physical that gives way to philosophical joys as we age. Watson always insisted on making me a figure of romantic conjecture and speculation in spite if my protestations. Now here he was in the presence of a true figure of romance in Colonel

Sebastian Moran and rather than take copious notes he merely nodded his head like one who has also known the nearness of death on the long and dusty road across the Punjab region to Afghanistan.

We are now resting on the great heaving bosom of the Indian Ocean with only the Island of Ceylon before us before we near the great Arabic Peninsula. I look forward to hearing from Mycroft care of the British governor in Kandy. My ideas regarding my own future are still rather formless. The cases that once brought me such delight seem to me now rather puerile and elementary, mere puzzles that yield swiftly to anyone who can observe accurately and suspend premature judgments long enough for reason to assemble chains of cause and effect with imagination to give shape and cohesion to the whole mystery. For the first time I am more motivated by the significance and innate value of the solution rather than by the process of de-mystification and the aesthetic pleasure of simply reaching an accurate conclusion. This new propensity cannot fail to alter the types of cases that will be adequate to motivate me and to fire my waning energies as I adapt to a new career.

April 30, 1899

As we approach the Arabic Peninsula I find myself spending more time on deck gazing out towards Africa. Now and again strange fishing craft appear on the horizon and vanish as swiftly as we press onwards like the albatross with folded wings as they haul in their catch or fall away to our stern crossing each other's paths. The foamy wake leaves our trail across the sea and is soon erased by the heaving cross-swell. I turn to this journal seeking some final point of unity in what I call my faith and all that I can find there is the difficulty of maintaining faith apart from the Christian community that serves to convey and then to embrace and embody the teachings that for me are like a sextant or compass, the navigational tools for a directed life.

The concept of a life lived in visceral communion with sheer impulses, the way that many people do in fact live, causes me alarm and a vertiginous spell comes upon me. Yet when I peel away the concentric layers of history seeking the original Jesus event I come only to the primary accounts of the earliest Christian literature that is already a selection if not a re-working of whatever Jesus actually did and said. Thereafter, as layer after layer of subsequent theological elaboration in Church documents purport to solve the problems and answer the questions of each succeeding age until in the present day Jesus falls away in the same way that our ship's wake falls away behind me. I wonder whether I shall only arrive at the final formula governing a life when I have no life left with which to embody that ultimate conclusion in actual actions to make this a better world?

And I must confess that all of this thought still remains on the individual level and within the cultural coordinates of a nominally Christian ambiance. But what if I must now apply secular counsels to problems that will affect the lives of thousands; in this case will the gospel admonitions not seem to diminish to the vanishing point in terms of providing a proper answer to the complexity of the questions posed? Is it possible to remain a Christian and simultaneously address the imperatives of statecraft with war and peace in the balance?

May 1, 1899

The ship is still keeping well off the coast in the security that only the oceans can provide from predatory man, not that we carry jewels or spices aboard. Our cargo is confined to those persons whose business forces them to traverse these blue waters in search of fortune and power. Few people realize the blessings conferred by obscurity. Would it really be so bad after all to grow old and die in my old rooms at Baker Street and be carried out at last feet first? I can summon up the scene clearly enough.

"Who is it that who is dead?" a passing figure will ask.

An idle bystander will exclaim, "Oh it be that there detective feller what was said to be able to solve any problem as was presented to him. Personally, I always had me doubts. A lot can be managed with skillful editing and they does like selling copies of their magazine, them folks at The Strand. He did know how to dress the part though coming out of that very door wearin' all sorts of disguises. I used to watch him and me a-standing right there by the lamp post and him letting on like he was all secretive and unobserved. As for me I trusts my safety to the blokes at Scotland Yard what knows a thing or two about detection and not to him there with all his wigs and whiskers."

But then Watson always resents it when I speak so disparagingly of his case reports. He is determined that I shall live up to my image in the press and will not cease badgering me when I speak of retiring. I would like to do so though and find a place where I could think the best of my fellow creatures by the simple expedient of possessing nothing that they want. I would gladly take the vows of a Cistercian Monk and wake in the night to chant matins and lauds in choir or sharing my sole possession, the praise and thanksgiving that should accompany our every hour. Then I could greet death as just another wayfarer on the uncertain road of life and ask nothing but mercy for my soul. Instead I am tied to the cross of expectations that I can adjust the fate of nations and answer questions posed by the various ways that we pursue our versions of disappointment and dismay on this short day of frost and sun. Ah well, our lives are not our own and we must make the best of things as they are. As for Doctor John H. Watson, since I owe so much of what I am to his fertile authorial mind I must not disappoint the poor fellow, and so for the thousandth time I proclaim, "the game is afoot..."

[Note: Not to unduly try the patience of the reader I omit the next journal entries on our voyage and resume the narrative with the following encoded letter that played a decisive role in what was soon to come.]

Letter of Mycroft Holmes, Dated March 19, 1899,
delivered at Cairo May 25, 1899
to be held for Sherlock Holmes

Dear Sherlock—

You must allow me to express my admiration and appreciation of the manner in which you managed to discharge your mission in America. You did so without the application of the purely mechanical reflexes of the trained diplomat. The reports that I have received indicate that your opposite numbers in America were impressed to be dealing with that rarest of specimens, an honest man of conscience.

Having said this I must also add that nothing so alarms men of affairs as meeting just such men because they are unpredictable and diplomacy depends upon the careful execution of certain well-practiced gestures much as in a dance. This sense of alarm was noticed however in Whitehall and was found to be quite a refreshing change with the result that Her Majesty's government may have further use for you in the near future.

I therefore beg that you will not refuse outright any proposed commission that may be forwarded to you in Cairo for consideration before you return to England and we can discuss the matter fully. I only mention this now because I desire that you give the matter some consideration in the following weeks and so that we may devise a proper excuse if you decide to refuse the commission. Without desiring to unduly influence you in what may be a state of exhaustion and hesitation after your recent labors it may help if I place before you some of my own candid conclusions as to the present course of history and the critical issues that lie before us as a nation.

Humanity's cultural evolution is reaching a stage where the various dynastic wars of the past will be succeeded by wars of ideologies. We have already seen how costly these can be from the Napoleonic Wars, although in many ways even these were a case of dynastic conflict in disguise. We may always be suspicious over claims of liberation that depend upon force to succeed. Nations must determine for themselves the degree of flexibility in domestic laws and in the degree that various freedoms are subject to oversight and limitations. The mass of the citizens will always be subject to being misled by vacuous promises and appeals to various collective delusions. Amusement will tend to predominate over prudence and the labors incident to progress.

Popular demagogues will always be able to purchase trust by proposing various excesses and by a manner calculated to awaken passions and to appeal to latent fears and desires in the masses. The pursuit of power will always appeal most to those who should never be entrusted with it. Men like Immanuel Kant assume that the species has a capacity for philosophy and imagine that what is the sole possession of genius is the norm for a species still mired in its simian origins. The representatives of nations chatter at each other suspended in trees by their tails.

So where does that leave men of humility and perspective who desire peace and that the conditions precedent to civilization may be maintained? These must strive to arrange the allocation of power so that it is neither tested by revolution nor allowed to assume that a premature universal enlightenment has been reached by our benighted species so that anarchy can prevail. However a greater danger still is posed by the government of secret and select groups who only masquerade as populists while serving private interests. You can play a role in this balance by helping to avoid the probable historical drift of the next century into an era of unparalleled barbarity.

I believe that Russia is the key. What is needed is someone who can understand the various domestic forces at play in that convoluted and archaic autocracy and I believe that you are the only man who I can trust to use your skills as a detective in that frozen and inscrutable land mass that reaches from Europe to the Pacific Ocean. You must sift the various layers of Russian society with all of the precision of the fractional distillation of petroleum and then assemble from these various conflicting forces a sense of what policies are likely to prevail and which actors will play a decisive role in international events.

I wish that I could tell you how to manage this august assignment. What it will demand though is clear: you must be there personally to observe and to question various dignitaries and then report back to me by coded missives. Will you do so? The stakes will involve the lives and welfare of millions. To one such as you to whom much has been entrusted much will be required. I beg you to think on these things and then to graciously receive my next communication with your assent and usual facility in solving questions that are of the utmost moment to England and the world.

Your devoted brother,
Mycroft

Telegram to White Hall

To Mycroft Holmes:
The donkey kicks against the goad but will respond to gentle persuasion. Definitive answer will follow from Odessa.
Sherlock Holmes

May 15, 1899
The Bosporus

The crossing from Alexandria *en route* to the Black Sea came as a surprise to Watson. We have arrived at our first destination on our deferred route home to England in answer to Mycroft's summons sent to me in Cairo. The entire world at present is divided into various contentious regions, each with their own national sense of why this particular landmass should be their own. Nowhere is this truer than in the Balkans.

The Black Sea region has the destabilizing characteristic of providing the only viable warm seaport for the Russian Empire at Odessa. This means that like a huge snow-mass on a mountain Russian power will always be exerted downwards into and around the Black Sea through the Ukraine. The difference in religion will mean that Russia will favor Bulgaria and Serbia and will mistrust the Turks who dominate the Ottoman Empire. The desire to annex the entire region will only be thwarted by the opposition of the other great powers, England, France, and Germany.

I do not include Austria-Hungary because as is becoming evident daily the effort of the Hapsburg Dynasty to retain its grip on the disparate peoples of the empire is becoming too costly to maintain. The whole calcified structure is broken by a multitude of fissures and only threats of force will hold the delicate balance together. Austria-Hungary has become a by-word for tyrannical rule and has been since the time of Prince Metternich. The grace and artistry of Vienna covers a reality of blood and sorrow.

This is the situation that greets us as we enter the narrow waters of the Bosporus on our way to Odessa. My assignment is to assess the situation there. In reality this means to get a sort of intuitive grasp of the state of seriousness that stands behind various nations as they press up against each other, grinding together like geologic plates. No one can determine what decisions may emerge from the contending polities. Decisions when they come may supersede all prior calculations. This means that it is imperative to set up alliances that have the effect of creating a stalemate between contending blocks of nations.

As crude and mindless as this may sound, it is as close as greedy mankind has come to a strategy for achieving a sustained peace. It is pointless to speak of principles of equity and fair-play when dealing with raw power. Ethics does not apply here for the very reason that each party believes that it is defending what is its own against an aggressor. In the absence of an all-powerful international arbiter this will always be the case. National power obeys certain laws of probability, but there will always be an uncertainty coefficient where personalities can play a decisive role. For this reason I am being asked to meet with no less of a personage than Czar Nickolas Romanoff that is being arranged. I have received a further communication from London asking me to use my skill at character assessment to obtain a reading of the one man whose actions may determine whether Europe will remain at peace or be plunged into war, to the possible extinction of civilization. It is not a task that I relish, but it is also a task that I may not refuse.

May 18, 1899
The Black Sea

The Catholic Church in its teachings regarding sin and individual salvation ventures forth into the public realm of politics and commerce only when necessary. Recent Papal Encyclicals have taken a hard line towards secret societies, particular those that go under the name of freemasonry. The Church is suspicious of any transnational movements of radical democratic sympathies, particularly if they claim as the freemasonic movement does that the lodges represent a society of craftsmen traceable back to Egypt that possesses special spiritual insights akin to the heresy of Gnosticism. Mystery as a category is assigned to Christianity alone because in its wisdom the Church realizes the persuasive power of cultic practices when belief is severed from practices of open inquiry and research. It is only a small step from the hitherto unknown to the ontologically inexpressible mystery of God, to which only Catholicism has access.

Any politics that does not rest in mere pragmatism must seek some deeper source for its persuasiveness and credibility. It is a truism to point out that climate and landscape affect our expectations in life. It is no accident for instance that the Polynesian people are a gentle and hospitable population because nature has generously provided them with warmth and sustenance and their remote location makes attack from neighbors a rarity. In contrast the fierce suspiciousness and bloodthirsty tribes that make up the southern Slavic regions stems from the mountainous and uncompromising demands made upon the native people that inhabit the lands from Serbia to Bulgaria.

What then are we to expect of the character of a people that is subjected to the intractable expanses of Russia from manifesting a degree of feudal ties that condemn people living in states of destitution to living in local proximity to the rich estates of the grand dukes and subjected to the domination of local judges and corrupt bureaucrats that serve the Russian aristocrats? Add to this the sheer rigor of the Russian winter, the inadequate roads, and the prevalence of illiteracy and disease, and it comes as no surprise that the Russian character is one of domestic terror and the ever present scourge of vodka. The only force of amelioration is the Russian Orthodox Church with its dark mysticism and its elaborate liturgy and music. From all of these it may be possible to deduce something of the Russian soul, the composite identity and aspirations of the people. When all of this has been accomplished, then and only then, can we begin to assess the political direction of a Russia is likely to pursue.

It may be helpful here to ask why empiricism found such ready roots in the minds of the English Philosophers and why Pragmatism is the natural bent of the philosophical mind in America. The answer is that the English and the Americans have been conditioned by industrialism and trade to focus on the material plane of existence. No philosophical issue can be raised in either place without thinking of the impact that the answer will have on daily commercial relations. Compare this with the Germanic mind of a figure like Immanuel Kant, one seeking some universal ontology and metaphysics. On his repetitive perambulations through the little town of Konigsberg his mind was forced in upon its own operations; the practical and the commercial did not enter into his philosophy. No one cares to ask about the price exacted by anyone using Kant's categorical imperative because cost is irrelevant to an absolute ethical mandate. The Germans are geniuses when dealing with abstractions, but virtual dunces politically speaking. But if one wishes to study politics in all their refinement one must go to France. The French are experts in drawing minor diplomatic distinctions. France in the 19th century has tried virtually every form of government, while at the level of village and region the lives of the people are virtually unchanged.

The mystique of national character is such that even works of literature are virtually untranslatable because the same actions and classes differ between various countries—a French courtesan is an entirely different creature from a British trollop. Seen against a larger stage this is why the various plans of conquest are so unfeasible; no rival power can govern a people with a different cultural bias. This is why the need to subjugate finally becomes the urge to exterminate.

One need only think of the policy of the Americans towards that strange mystical people that had lived for years scattered across the vast American prairie lands and forests. The conquerors tried in vain to explain to them the concept of borders and private ownership of limited resources like land when migration between regions was natural to them and the land was an environment not a possession. The result was that the Americans attempted to obliterate the language, religion, and customs of tribe after tribe only managing to kill them in the process and worse to destroy their very souls. No sadder spectacle exists than the photographs of the great Indian chiefs like Sitting Bull brought finally into captivity and subjugation.

This sense of the difference between peoples is the necessary background for any political opinions I will express to the Czar. Among the first of these problems is the difficulty of grafting loyalty onto a new Czar and Czarina by the mass of the Russian people. The present Czar is a virtual twin of his cousin who is destined to assume the reigning power in England and his wife is a Danish Princess with relations among the ruling houses of Germany. How can such a man not only act as the temporal ruler of such a vast empire but act as its spiritual leader as well? The suspicions that might be engendered could be fatal should the royal couple appear to stray from the mystic ties to the Russian soil. The Russians are essentially an Asiatic people and no amount of intercourse with Europe will be adequate I fear to bridge that essential gap between regions.

May 19, 1899
Moldavia

As the regions formerly settled by the Roman legions gives way to the lands settled by various wandering Asiatic groups the physiognomy and culture show distinctive changes. I find myself thinking back to an intriguing comment made by Colonel Sebastian Moran before our recent departure from the Malayan archipelago. I hinted that I was about to undertake certain diplomatic actions at the behest of the government. He smiled at this and remarked. "In the affairs of nations there are no principles; there are only actions and consequences. One can never be sure of the results of any particular policy until it is put into effect."

I remarked at the time that this observation was not encouraging to one about to venture into that confused realm. He shook his head before expanding on his initial apothegm on world affairs.

"Your bias towards moral solutions will not serve you well in what you are about to undertake. The higher the level and the more complex and varied the result that may be obtained the more any set policy is bound to betray you. The sword must be cunningly concealed beneath a veneer of civility and respect without in any way diminishing your own dignity. You must appear candid without being naïve, humble without being obsequious, so that your opposite number is left guessing what you actually meant in even your most considered statements. Above all else avoid taking any fixed position that will curtail your ability to pivot and adjust to any change in circumstances. Do not feel compelled to speak before it is necessary. Feel out your opponent by using his anxiety to allow him room to betray his intentions. Courtesy invites disclosure. Most men are in a hurry to get their own position firmly on the table under the impression that they can define the essential issues unilaterally. This is seldom the case among equals and you must behave as though your power is equal to an opponent even if his actual power exceeds your own."

He continued, "Do not neglect the advantage conveyed by symbols of office; men set their initial expectations according to points of reference in clothes and bearing. At the same time many a fool has been led to underestimate an opponent when he begins by holding him in contempt. He may appear less masterful in manner and less imposing in carriage and demeanor. The strike when it comes will therefore be entirely unexpected and defeat follows. This is particularly true when dealing with women; the fair sex is particularly skilled at the arts of deception and the man is defeated before he even realizes that a contest of relative power was even being waged. Never forget that even in seduction what for a man is a game can be a question of survival for a woman. She ceases to see love as a game while she is still dealing with ardent and enflamed boys her own age. It is when she reaches the age of active courtship that her entire future is at stake and she must not be led astray by illusions. It is not fair of course, these life and death struggles; but the welfare of the species depends upon the outcome."

I pointed out that he surprised me with his sagacity and intimate knowledge of affairs. His answer was brief. "I have learned much from reading memoirs and collections of letters from men like Talleyrand and Casanova and Madame de Stael."

May 25, 1899
Odessa

e have just arrived in the port city of Odessa, one of the most habitable of the cities of the empire ruled over by the Czar. It is here if anywhere that a sense of comfort can supplant the arduous spirituality of the Russians. Here palm trees make their appearance and white beaches invite frivolity. Tea houses line the waterfront but it is to none of these that we will repair today but to the Czar's dacha where a private interview has been arranged for us with the sovereign. So much I discovered in a missive sent by a liveried messenger shortly after we made landfall. The short layover of our vessel precludes our staying for a week to sample the charms of this resort town and the hospitality of our host country. I fear that this encounter must not only be a swift one, but held in utmost secrecy.

It is precisely my unofficial status that makes me an invaluable present asset to the government of England. I can feel the uncertainty and hesitation that prevails at the home office. How will the Russians respond to the current tensions building in this region of the world? The Turks are beginning to flex their muscles, fearful that their empire is slipping into obsolescence. The Balkan region is as always contentious and unstable. Worst of all the Austrians are lately inflamed with a desire to emulate the other great powers by expanding their influence into the Southern Slavic regions and Italy. It is too late for them to acquire colonial acquisitions so nothing is left for the Austrian Empire but to extend the borders of their own influence here at home in Europe.

Already the Hungarians have managed to obtain a semi-independent status in the dual monarchy of Austria Hungary. Why then should Serbia, Dalmatia, and Bosnia languish under Germanic rule, particularly while Russia sees itself as the protector of the Southern Slavs? But does Russia speak with a single voice? The Czar for all of his power is no doubt influenced by contending voices among his royal advisors. Besides there is parliamentary pressure building at home. Many Russians are demanding that a Duma be established and a constitution be granted to the Russian people. Is this anything other than an invitation to the various

Balkan regions to revolt and seek national status? These crumbling empires are held together by four factors: a centralized civil service, an oppressive secret police, the network of petty nobility on their country estates, and of course the Roman Catholic in the case of Austria and in Russia the Orthodox faith. These contending groups control these absolute monarchs every bit as much as the Royal Families control them. None of these feudal influences are amenable to the development of a healthy merchant class or to the industrial order of more modern states.

Russia in particular is at least a half century behind Germany, France, and England in industrial development. This has not escaped the more cosmopolitan minds of Russia. The result is that the Russians are forced to appear more unified and confident than they in fact are. They must pose before the court of public opinion as the center of Christendom and the guardian of the Slavic people. To puncture that pretense or to challenge it will force the Russians into conflicts that they cannot sustain. If there is anything worse than hegemonic pretentions between nations it is the danger of unmasking their hidden national weaknesses. This pattern invites aggression and is a natural prelude to war. I think it beyond question that a general European War would be a disaster to our current international progress and prosperity and could even undermine civilization. Therefore I must flatter Russian vanity while not encouraging them to undertake any sudden moves. Beyond this I must simply listen and hope that I can obtain the trust of Czar Nicholas Romanoff.

May 27, 1899
Odessa

Watson and I were picked up at our seaside hotel today and taken for tea at the dacha. The terrace overlooks the sea and with the appending gardens the entire scene was lovely. The Czar was dressed in his white military uniform, while the Czarina and the Grand Duchesses wore long white dresses. The family was swiftly dismissed and their place was taken by various officials, silent men in frock coats, each evidently desirous of appearing important yet simultaneously desiring to avoid drawing attention to himself by making any overt comment. This made the meeting more like a formal dance than a forthright airing of views.

The Czar did most of the talking. I paid more attention to his manner than to what he said as is my professional habit as a detective. He is evidently a man who prefers domestic joys to governing. He appears too gentle for the position that life has assigned to him. There is nothing of Ivan the terrible in him with the result that others, feeling the vacuum that surrounds him, may be encouraged to be terrible in his stead.

The Czarina Alexandra made, I am sorry to say, an unfavorable impression upon me. She is undoubtedly a great beauty, but there is something of premature age and care already written upon her face. Her eyes are sorrowful and except when gazing on her children she seldom smiles. I had the feeling that prefers that the family should be left alone and that she shows impatience with courtiers as she does with outside guests. I had the distinct impression that she exercises a subtle and powerful influence over her husband's mind and that the influence she has is regarded with jealousy by the men who surround their King.

Towards me she appeared proud and even haughty. I am not overly impressed by royalty and although I am willing to grant them their prerogatives, I do not consider them to be above the common station of humankind marked with mortality and beset by sin. I avoided though any sign of insolence, but I am sure that she realized that she was being closely observed by me and that her insecurities had been noticed. I do not think that I will be invited back soon, a circumstance that is to my liking. I have no desire to be on constant call for such missions. I prefer that professional diplomats fulfill their assigned functions and leave me to the domestic mysteries presented in our home islands. Still, I have read some recent papers by Charcot and by Freud discussing hysteria and while I am not a professional alienist I think I can say with confidence that the Czarina would not be ill-advised to consult a discreet medical opinion at some future date.

After tea was served from a great silver samovar we were served English style cucumber sandwiches and some small pies of meat and cheese called pirogues. We all sat about one great table with the Czar at one end and Watson and me at the other. I explained that Doctor Watson is more than my friend; he is an essential adjunct and counterbalance to my own judgment and the guardian of my health. This seemed to set any suspicions to rest as to his role. My own irregular status already precluded any revelation of actual state secrets, so it really made little difference what Watson might hear and retain of our meeting. The company seemed as perplexed by us as we were of them.

I will nevertheless attempt to set down as well as I can recall it the Czar's words for later reference when I speak to Mycroft. The key point though is what I observed of his manner. He does not appear to me to be a born autocrat. He may be little more than what might be called "a fool of fortune," a man exalted by history to assume a role for which he is quite unequipped in intelligence and strength of character.

He is not alone in this attribute. Our own Queen Victoria in her religiosity, her perpetual mourning for Albert her spouse, and her eternal widow's garb have cast a pall over the triumphs of the British Empire and may be a sign of clouds on the horizon. Her offspring fill the royal thrones of Europe while she is little more than a dwarf-like figure surrounded by obsequious men like Balfour who will never have the confidence that she once reposed in Disraeli. Of course all of this is Mycroft's domain. I take refuge in what remains of my commoner status and my obscurity and doff my hat and bow when her carriage sweeps by majestically down Pall Mall on the way to Buckingham Palace.

The Czar began his address in this manner. "We welcome you, Mr. Holmes, to Odessa. It was good of you to interrupt your travels at our request and we trust that you are comfortable in the lodgings that we have arranged for your visit."

I assured him that we were quite comfortable and found his city charming. He warmed to this and I saw the boy in him kindle to life.

"I much prefer it to Petersburg. My family is quite happy here. Some of our happiest days have been spent aboard the royal yacht or bathing in the sea. I have been told that you are lately from California in America. Does it resemble this?"

"We departed from the northern city of San Francisco

where bathing is ill-advised due to sharks, Your Majesty," I answered.

"That is unfortunate. I have heard that the city is beautiful though, a jewel in its setting by the bay. Your mention of sharks though is apropos. I wish to speak to you about the sharks that at present circle Russia. Are you aware of our construction of a railroad across Siberia?"

I was loathed to mention that I had received no specific training to prepare me for my assigned role as a spontaneous diplomat, but my own sense for the times was sufficient to tell me that Russia is attempting a policy of rapid industrialization and railroad building, so I answered in the affirmative. The Czar looked at some of his aids and nodded as though my answer demonstrated that I was indeed worthy of the frankness that he was displaying in his manner of address to me.

"It is essential that we should be able to secure our eastern frontier and to move troops there if pressures are applied by Japan. The enterprise has been costly though. We have had to make reductions in other areas, not least in our naval maintenance. This of course means that the vessels that we do possess must be allowed access to certain areas of strategic importance, because we simply do not have sufficient vessels to garrison the Baltic Sea, the Black Sea, and the Pacific simultaneously. I am being quite frank with you, Mr. Holmes, because I have received a communiqué from your brother, Mycroft Holmes, who has assured me that what I say to you will be treated as quite unofficial. Our contact with him was arranged In London. It is however essential that someone with influence will explain to your government that to weaken Russia is to invite a European conflict."

He said this with such deep earnestness that I was much impressed by his manner. I was even more surprised when he promptly dismissed his aides and those cabinet officers who were present so that we could speak alone. I could see that this did not please them and that some of them may have doubted the wisdom of his candor towards me.

After they had left and we were quite alone he said, "It is not my desire to court opposition, Mr. Holmes, but I am the Czar and I must do as I think best. I will not fuel the fires of rumor by being misquoted therefore what I will now say to you shall be between ourselves alone. Russia at present fulfills two functions for continental Europe. First, it preserves the eastern border of the European states from aggression from either France or Germany and in this way Russia keeps both nations from engaging in an open conflict with each other. If however we are forced to declare an open allegiance to one or the other of them it will raise the level of alarm in the non-allied party and lead to a race to increase arms. Russia must seek support from England if it is to fulfill its second function, which is also to contain the spread of Islamic influence. Your own India would not be safe from Persia if we did not apply pressure from the north. Yet, England mistrusts us and does what it can to weaken us. We are, as I have just said, surrounded by sharks and England mistakenly sees us as the most likely aggressor. Now your brother has intimated through our ambassador in London that he is sympathetic to our position and would be willing to use his influence to modify British policy as regards Russia. Will you in turn express to your brother our appreciation for the clarity of his vision and assure him that Russia desires peace?"

He looked at me earnestly before continuing as follows, "We are already sufficiently engaged in simply retaining our outlying provinces and feeding our people. We have neither the resources nor the desire for war. In addition, my own position is a delicate one. There are many factions in Russia and I must mediate between them. If the monarchy was ever to fall, chaos would result and the temptation to invade Russia would plunge all of Europe into war, because it would imbalance the delicate equilibrium between the other colonial powers. For this reason we are about to propose an international conference on disarmament. This will allow us to build our railroad to the east and secure Siberia as far as the Kamchatka Peninsula and incidentally to prevent the United States from acquiring control of trade with China and Japan to the exclusion of the other nations. A peaceful world will lead to general prosperity, while any de-stabilization leading to war will put progress backwards for a century or more. Ours is the hour where peace and prosperity are possible for all nations as long as no single nation attempts to take the lion's share of world trade and influence."

I do not think he could possibly have made a clearer case in seeking my aid, but it struck me at once that his own admission of Russia's weakness might inadvertently invite the very aggression that he feared if it was generally known. It is a sad truth that maintaining fear between the great powers is a better source of international equilibrium than the mutual benefits promised by peace. Man does not live by bread alone, but by the feeling of supremacy and glory that over-lordship provides. Once our basic needs are met we turn to whatever enhances our pride as John Milton said so well in his great epic poem, *Paradise Lost:* Better to rule in hell than to serve in heaven.

It was strange for me to look over at this man, the supreme overlord to the largest landmass of any nation on earth and to realize how essentially fragile as a man he actually was. Suddenly my own position in life seemed infinitely preferable to his. I had often told Watson how dreadful it is to bear the burdens of history, to answerable before God for the lives of millions. What greater luxury can be imagined than to live an obscure life, one that demands little more than a comfortable drawing-room and the leisure for a serene walk in the country before dinner followed by a book and sleep? This man would never know this blessing, born as he was to either triumph or to ruin. Truly Jesus was right when he said, "Blessed are the meek for they shall inherit the earth."

After in essence presenting his case Czar Nicholas asked me if I thought that Mycroft's counsel would find willing ears in the government of England. I told him that Mycroft's word had often determined British policy in the past, but that his position was unofficial in every sense. I explained that as an advocate he was always in the posture of making an appeal not in rendering a decision.

He was thoughtful upon hearing this and then said sadly that those who must make decisions are curtailed by the surrounding situation so that what looks like freedom is often a choice between two or even more equally unpalatable options. I assured him that I would do my best to accurately relay the information that he had confided to me. He expressed his thanks and Watson and I were conveyed back to our hotel. A fete was to be provided for us later under a great pavilion by the sea.

I have decided to return to England by rail rather than to face the further inconveniences of sea travel. It has been some time since I traversed Eastern Europe and I think it may help my mission to sample opinions along the way by listening to the conversations in our hotels. This plan will put us home in England when the last of the late spring rains will have abated and everything there will be blooming. My plans for the summer are still somewhat vague, but both Watson and I are badly in need of a rest after our exertions. I hope to visit Sir Henry and I may even look in on Professor Moriarty and perhaps get some leads on the best horses running in the Wessex Cup.

Ah, to be home again! The very name of England is sweet to me after such a long absence. To smell again the green fields, the heather, and to hear the gulls and curlews crying along the channel ports; best of all will it be to sit in a proper country pub and hear native English voices again with a pint of stout or cider before me and some proper roast beef, custard, and port. And let me not forget my books, a good winged-armchair with neither obligation nor summons to fill a role in the troubled councils of the great and powerful. But will fate be so generous as to allow me this latitude to simply live unmolested and serene, the proud possessor of a private life?

June 1, 1899
Vienna

We left our vessel behind us in Odessa and traveled by rail through Bucharest and Budapest to Vienna. The lush green of the Carpathians was lovely as our train wound through the mountains and traversed the valleys with their farms and vineyards. It is so difficult to convey a sense of place when it precisely the unexpected and incongruent scene that is most memorable. The ordinary is most congenial though and without it we could not find that sense of predictable rewards that we seek. If a cake should overwhelm us with salt or bitterness rather than the sweetness and savor we expect it might be memorable but certainly not fulfilling. In just this manner we covet the mundane and prefer our actual adventures when they occur at one remove. We gasp and weep at the theater or opera but are quite content in our secure box seats with the security that our carriage will deposit us later at our own domicile where a warm bed and a nightcap of golden sherry awaits us. I will therefore not cram my own journal with the picturesque details that Watson so favors, convinced as he is that no word he has written will go without the ardent perusal of a grateful public. Suffice it to say here that a rural landscape has extraordinary charm for one like me who has been too long an exile upon the great blue expanse of the ocean. It may do no harm to reflect the passing joys of my homecoming in this journal because like most of humankind I will no sooner be settled in again at home than boredom will make me long for distant and obscure destinations and I will lament the very comforts that I now covet.

Our passage through the region dominated by the Carpathian Mountains was too swift to obtain any accurate impressions of the political climate that prevails there. In any case the political passions would no doubt be hidden beneath deep veils of sullen discontent rather than by signs of open rebellion. The latter demonstrations would be put down swiftly by the Austrian police authorities who are no less efficient than the Czar's Cossack troops at maintaining civil order and ensuring the servile docility of the masses.

I was not prepared though for Watson and I to be shadowed by an official-looking figure from the train station in Vienna to our hotel, by a man who must have imagined that his crude tactics would escape my notice. No doubt the American clothes that we purchased during the course of our journey were sufficiently noticeable to draw the attention of the local authorities. It would not bode well for our mission if the Austrians should become aware of what was discussed in our meeting with the Russian Czar. Perhaps this was why Czar Nicholas dismissed even his own officials before going into details with us. Spies and double agents are able to penetrate into even the inner circles of governments. It is this general transparency which allows rumors to acquire the aura of truth and add to the risks that armed conflict will break out in some obscure corner of the world and then spread into a general conflict.

The absence of any higher tribunal in international affairs, one designed to forestall impetuous military action, makes even any partial mobilization of enemy troops sufficiently alarming to be tantamount to a full-fledged cross-border attack. This means that to maintain readiness for instant measures of defense is as aggressive as a cannonade into opposing troops. It takes extraordinary patience and forbearance to sit still and continue with diplomatic initiatives when opposing troops are already marching towards the front. There is an accidental quality about the manner that war can begin that should not be present in any undertaking that can entail the deaths of thousands before a mistaken conclusion can be theoretically remedied. Once the machinery of war is in actual operation reconsideration and redeployment, let alone retreat, becomes impossible.

As to our recent "guardian angel" I decided that the best course was to ignore his presence and to endeavor as far as possible to give the appearance of a comical British tourist, one much impressed by Austrian grandeur and sampling with gusto the rich cuisine available. The Austrians presume that any dish is enhanced by sufficient gravy and heavy cream and lots of paprika. One must stick to a diet of fish if one is to have any hope of not adding an inch or two to one's girth.

While we were in Vienna Watson and I visited the parks of the great baroque palaces by day although we were not admitted to the ranks of the illustrious personages who arrived in heavy and ornate carriages at dusk dressed in all manner of finery and excess for various evening entertainments. Three days were adequate for us to sample the glories of the Austrian Empire at close hand and to sense the depth of the underlying atmosphere of indulgence coupled by fear that an entire way of life is about to perish. The days of Prince Metternich are no more. Austria exists in an afterglow of supremacy and now exists within the nimbus of Germany's rising military might. Austria dare not move without assurances that Germany will stand by any secret alliance that may exist. Treaties of course are only indicators of intentions, rather than an iron-clad guarantee of compliance if the hour of decisive action finally arrives. No one can say whether the Austrians will ever trust German assurances. The most that may be said is that if Germany imposes objections the Austrian troops will not march. This in turn means that the key to European peace or war on the continent remains ultimately in German hands.

The great weakness of Germany is its own ambitions. These may lead it into a conflict that it cannot maintain without bringing ruin to the Hohenzollern Dynasty and to his people. The Austrians have a similar weakness, the fear of losing international status. It is their remarkable clumsiness in dealing with their subject peoples that may doom the Hapsburg Dynasty. The Austrians have been so long convinced of their own superiority that they forget that the various mongrel factions that surround them have a vigor based on living in mountain regions with few comforts. One need only compare these ill-equipped but courageous legions to the pampered officer corps and drunken regimental culture of the Austrians to see what will happen if the Austrians presume too much. Austrian presumption and German greed if combined might result in war. These are the impressions that I will share with Mycroft upon my return.

Of course the political tension between centers of power is a constant element in world affairs. It is not this tension that worries the men who rely on Mycroft for advice; it is the prospect of a realignment of forces that worries them. Wars, like the shifting of tectonic plates in the earth that cause earthquakes, occur when tensions are suddenly released before new alignments of nations are securely in place that can release the tension slowly and systematically over time. War is the attempt to speed this process up in anticipation of a quick victory purchased by force of arms. Any unequal bargaining power at the eventual peace conference sows the seeds for later conflict. Humankind has never managed to translate the suffering and damage of entailed in warfare into an alternative and less costly method to settle upheavals. The only successful wars are the short and brutal repressions whereby a superior power maintains a gross advantage over a subject people over time—this is the definition of colonial rule. As for the prospect of revolution carried on within any dominant power by a subset of the citizens, history shows that even the greatest tyrants usually manage to retain their control over the citizens unless they lead their nation into utter ruin and destitution or they are dethroned by an outside force of liberation.

June 6, 1899
Paris

Beloved France! Watson and I both heaved a great sigh of relief as we left Austria behind in the mountain passes of the Vorarlberg followed by a brief exposure to lovely Lake Constance, to Stuttgart, Freiberg, and then on to Strasbourg. We did not delay there but pressed on to Paris arriving at the Gare d' lest in the hours of darkness. We were too elated to sleep in any case. We sent our baggage ahead to our hotel and had an early breakfast along the Seine. We drank our morning coffee with a brandy and then watched as the light of the rising sun illumined the stately boulevards and made the street lights pale to invisibility in this most lovely city in the world.

Later—

We bathed and then slept until tea time when we ventured forth to the British Embassy to give a brief report that would be forwarded to Mycroft at the Home Office. Afterwards we had a most exquisite dinner and then went to the opera for an excellent rendition of Verdi. It is now almost midnight and I am exhausted. It would not do to arrive home ill. For this reason I do not intend to press on immediately to London, but will spend a few days at Quimper on the Brittany Peninsula and then cross over from St. Malo to Plymouth in Cornwall. I have telegraphed Sir Henry and he will be there with his private carriage to meet us there and accompany us to Baskerville Hall. Mycroft will simply have to be patient. It will help to have a few days in quiet and familiar surroundings to put my observations in order so that when I do make my final report it will be accurate and seasoned by reflection.

I find that I think best, now that I have been forced to give up my inveterate pipe-smoking, when I am breathing the fresh air out on the open moors of Devonshire. It is also useful to have certain volumes on hand to guide my thoughts. Among these are Edward Gibbon's magnificent work, *The Decline and Fall of the Roman Empire.* This author has the ability to encompass great events in a prose so stately and sonorous that the sordid elements of history resemble the great elemental forces of the ocean. Accidental elements are reduced to seeming inevitability without depriving human agents of freedom and at least some measure of discretion to arrange their affairs. Nobility exists side by side with venality and squalid passions across times and places on an epic stage. Whether God takes equal note of this rhythm in the affairs of men and nations is an open question.

June 9, 1899
Biarritz

Watson suggested that we might do better than Quimper if we are to take a brief seaside holiday, so we have opted instead for Biarritz. It is a pity that Colonel Sebastian Moran is not here to advise us on the fine points of roulette. We are surrounded here by the rich and the self-indulgent. These are the classes that imagine that wars will better their situation. These men own the stock in great commercial enterprises, above all in the lucrative armaments trade. They leave the lower-middle classes to pay the taxes necessary to amortize the war-debts and occasionally they offer their sons to die in battle, while to these aristocrats the luxury of patriotism is supplemented by the profits that make their way of life possible. This is a cosmopolitan crowd, all mingling together and sharing the sea-air and promenade before dinner. We took a table to ourselves at dinner and drew little notice. The local oysters were excellent and we each ordered a bottle of Chablis.

The smoke in the casino later was somewhat oppressive so we adjourned early to our sitting room. The air was still so I took a lamp out onto the balcony and read until I grew sleepy. I would be quite content to remain here a month, but I have no desire to return to England a pauper. As it is I hope that a remittance will be awaiting me from Sherringford with the mid-year rents from the estate in Yorkshire. These will have to suffice until I can take on a case or two to replenish funds.

June 12, 1899
St. Malo

As our journey comes to an end in this last year of the 19th century the search for certainty is everywhere. There seems though to be neither the leisure nor the appetite for either the all-encompassing faith of the past or the equally all-encompassing belief in unaided human reason to explain our collective existence. Instead economics rules the day with its twin imperatives of headlong production and ever-increasing consumption. Time has itself been distorted in the process. Any activity that does not involve production or consumption is viewed as wasteful and somehow unpatriotic. This has naturally weakened the respect owed to purely academic activity and to the habit of intelligent assessment of the human condition.

Religion itself has been distorted and co-opted by this economic approach to reality. By speaking of the Bible under the overarching canopy of being, "the word of God," the origin of scripture as distilled from within the early Jewish and Greek communities of believers that grew to accept this collection of testimonials has been lost and what were originally separate books have come to be viewed, not as an anthology, but as a single unified text. It is within the province of the theologian in contrast to the exegete to act as an intermediary between revelation and actual human experience so that the first has something authoritatively to say to the second.

This process is not on-directional however; human experience was present in the composition of the texts that we hold to contain revelation. To deny this historical fact is to imagine that the divine reality and the intentionality maintained by God towards the human race, His Divine Love for us, takes no account of human realities in its transmission and expectations. A purely detached theology therefore, one divorced from cultural practices and the increasing awareness of our nature and capacities over time must distort the very object of its inquiry by providing an unacceptable and arrogant picture of God frozen in time and according to a presumed perfect original vision. This in turn leads to a simplistic and easily assimilated world-view that can be adapted to serve the most venal of earthly ends while returning a handy profit to various persons and groups who can use the language of scripture to secure their own political power over others. The interpenetration of religion and politics is therefore more to be feared than the simple incursion of men like Baron Maupertuis who rely upon purely material advantage in their business activities without any hypocritical admixture of references to God to grease their depredations.

I am afraid that Watson and I are likely to be at loose ends for a bit after returning to England. The world seems smaller to those who are travelers. It seems after a time as though there is no particular reason to be in one place rather than another. The constant stream of strange faces and strange languages makes one feel like a universal alien. For one like me who for so many years confined my voyages to the various sections of London and its outlying districts to have spent so much time without a domicile has been both exhilarating and distressing. It used to be adventurous enough for me to wander between the settee and the bookcase where I keep my commonplace books for easy reference. The world came willingly to London with various raw materials and the factories in Manchester, Leeds, and Liverpool sent out finished goods to the world. Now there seems to be competition everywhere.

Tariffs are being raised in country after country as excess factory capacity dumps goods on the market faster than they can be purchased by the ever more impoverished workers fearful of another economic contraction like that of 1893. This only increases the level of international anxiety and tension. Worst of all there has been a natural tendency to augment national wealth by adopting the mercantilist philosophy of Spain in the 16th century and to rush into the extraction of wealth through enforced concessions imposed upon regions with mineral wealth in gold and diamonds. This is particularly evident in the British interests in South Africa.

At home essentials like coal have never been more

expensive and as a family my brothers and I would be profiting from our former holdings in the coal mines of Northumberland. Our withdrawal has not changed the position of the miners, but it is at least a relief that as a family we no longer take a share in the labor of others. Industrialism with its effect on craftsmanship has distorted the lives of so many people and I am afraid it can only get worse with time. The political establishment has fallen under the spell of precisely those figures that are the cause of so much misery in the majority of the population. Various would-be reformers have sold their souls to self-interested business magnates who know no particular loyalty to any country but whose interests span the entire globe.

I am no better prepared to oppose these evils than the mass of my fellow countrymen. Only the prospect of my possible imminent death from consumption and this dangerous plot of Baron Maupertuis with its ramifications could have forced me to depart to such an extreme degree from my usual sedentary characteristics. Now the question is whether I can manage to settle in again to the placid routine of my former consultancy. My hope is that I can make my report to Mycroft and never hear again of the sordid affairs prevailing between nations. One of the advantages of the remote moors is the sense of isolation that they give one. It is quite enough if the weather allows me to take a brisk walk through the maze of stone huts and monoliths each day or to trace a path around the various bogs and marshlands while holding a one-sided conversation with the local waterfowl. These pleasures of solitude are lost in the noisy bazaars of Singapore and Cairo and even in America no town is without the peculiar urgency that makes the American character so restless. I want none of that now. I would be content to know well some fifty square kilometers of land. I hope to spend some time with old friends like Doctor Mortimer and Sir Henry Baskerville and leave to others the paths of glory that as the poet Thomas Gray says lead but to the grave.

Even our time at Biarritz was cloying. The rich often seem in their frenzy for pleasure to be as lost as the impoverished wretches of Whitechapel. These two ends of the social spectrum are alike in their discontent though the causes are different. Against the spectra of material resources we have nature where our fellow animal and floral creatures manage to keep the balance of all things without endangering that whereon their own existence depends. Compare this to mankind with its incursions on to land and sea changing both in order to give reality to our ideas and overweening designs.

How long will the earth endure us? Perhaps the earthquakes are like the quivering skin of a horse in order to shake off the flies that encumber it. Watson has gone down to purchase our cross-channel tickets to Plymouth and I am resting here at our inn. If time allows prior to sailing we will take a carriage along the shore to view Mont San Michel, the picturesque monastery that has been so often the subject of oil-paintings in all times and weathers. It is difficult not to imagine that past ages manifested a grace and dignity that humanity will never again reach. Why should any nation take pride in its power to use implements of destruction? To act in this manner is to exalt the pyromaniac over the artist. What fools most rulers are. I am glad to be free of their company. Ah, here is Watson back. We can manage a last excursion in *la belle France*!

June 14, 1899
Baskerville Hall

Home at last! As our ship came into port I was able to spot Sir Henry on the wharf wearing his great wool cloak and a white scarf to set his figure off from the crowd. He greeted us with all of the abandon of old friends among whom any restraint is a mere affectation. We shall spend the night in Plymouth and proceed to the hall tomorrow. He was surprised to see me looking so well after our long journey. He looks every inch the prosperous country squire, no longer the lean youth who met us in London over ten years ago when the treacherous hound was still alive to menace his life and perhaps cut short all of his prospects to carry on his uncle's reforms in the county. Sir Henry is now active in every way in local affairs and Lady Beryl as well; this means that the yeoman farmers have prospered as a result. A school and hospital have been built and Dr. Mortimer has been placed in charge of a local museum to display the various artifacts that he has unearthed and catalogued from that picturesque region. Sir Henry assures me that the good doctor is all afire to show me his latest treasures.

Plymouth seemed remarkably sleepy and provincial as we stepped off the gangplank and my feet felt the solid grasp of my native soil. Can it really be the case that we English manage to rule a significant part of the globe when so much of England differs little from the colonized regions? What is the basis for this tribute from our empire? Are we the bearers of the glories of Anglo-Saxon civilization or are we merely brutes with a navy? I have no trouble feeling only contempt for the recent American bid for colonial rule because they are so clumsy about it. Americans must trot out such transparent justifications for their greed. It is all about spreading democracy and such nonsense. In contrast we as Englishmen simply expect to rule the world as if it was an imperative of the natural law that we should do so. If anyone asks us why we possess that right we simply look annoyed at the impertinence of the question and answer, "Why because we are Englishmen of course!"

In my early days I felt a similar awe in the contemplation of the virtues of our beloved Queen Victoria. Englishmen answer any trepidation that they may feel by referring any moral doubts to the abstraction of service to queen and country. We feel that we owe nothing to the world as such. This is hardly a Christian attitude, but it is our customary outlook nevertheless.

Meanwhile, at the county level a Cornishman looks dubiously at those folks over in Devonshire. We value our lords and ladies unlike what an Englishman calls "that revolutionary rabble in France." We are not averse to reform, but we loathe all revolutionary tendencies as poor form and a prelude to anarchy. To know one's place in the social order is a comfort for us and prevents the omnipresent dissatisfaction that keeps the Americans restless and ever on the move westward. Sir Henry is noble but unaffected in manner and the result is that he is something of a hero in these parts and his fame has spread beyond his county to the surrounding regions. He is often called away for sessions in the House of Lords, but he prefers the routine of estate and village to the noise and squalor of London. He goes up to Bath occasionally with Lady Beryl to take the waters and for a bit of genteel company, but he is not overly impressed by titles. A boor is always boring to him. He is not averse to reading progressive plays by the like of George Bernard Shaw or Henrik Ibsen, but he prefers sentimental books like Oliver Goldsmith's, *The Vicar of Wakefield*. He reads a bit of Montaigne though now and again, but finds him at times to be a little too frank in his revelations.

Yet Sir Henry is decorous without being stuffy and humorous without being prone to music-hall drolleries. I enjoy his company because he can walk with me for a mile in silent enjoyment of the scenery without either of us finding the silence to be awkward. We share a friendship without the taint of competitiveness. I don't chivy him as I do Watson and I would not do so with the dear doctor if we were not so damnably earnest at times. Still, I would not have Watson any different than he is. My affection for him is so well-worn and comfortable that I can almost always anticipate his responses and he has a remarkable way of drawing from me my very best efforts. The simple act of imagining how to explain a set of facts to Watson helps me to set everything in order and often leads to the solution of the little problems that come to me from time to time for solution.

We enjoyed the hospitality afforded to us at our hotel and made a fine meal of local haddock and Cornish pies. Over our port later I filled in Sir Henry about the highlights of our American journey and described our impressions of Japan and Malaya. I did not mention our detour to Odessa or our meeting with the Czar. There will be time to discuss these matters later and I must respect the confidences that are to be shared with Mycroft alone. I can sense the excitement in the air here over the current crisis with the Boers in Africa and I am sorry to say that it is no different from the atmosphere that pervaded the American populace over the recent set-to (I can hardly call it a war) with the Spanish. The naval victories were so one-sided that it was as though the Americans simply stripped away these former possessions of Spain rather than fought for them. I fear that the Americans may too easily become enamored of war forgetting the recent slaughter entailed in their conflict with the Confederacy of the Southern States. What for the British is a cost of empire is a fetish for the Americans. The British learned, in the Crimean War and those conflicts along the

Afghan frontier, that any armed conflict is a bloody business. Many a brash young cadet is now a crippled old pensioner still feeling the effect of wounds from decades of campaigns to police the colonies.

Even Sir Henry bears various scars from unfortunate encounters in Saskatchewan and Manitoba. There was also a skirmish with a wolverine and of course he received a proper going-over by the infamous and spectral hound before Watson and I were able to dispatch it with our revolvers. So it was with a sense of pleasure that we arrived at Baskerville Hall after a ride over the bumpy moorland track and reached the smooth stretch of road leading through the park to the great doors and stately columns of the front portico of Baskerville Hall. We were greeted with great joy by Lady Beryl and quickly installed by Perkins in our accustomed rooms. I have taken some time to write this before tea-time and I see that it is now time that I dressed for the evening and repaired to the library, so adieu for now.

June 16, 1899
Baskerville Hall

I have wired Mycroft that we are again inhabitants of this blessed isle that my commission was successful and that I have much of interest to relate to him. He wired back that he is grateful for our safe return but that he is anxious to receive our report, so Watson and I will cut short our stay here and take the train tomorrow for London via Exeter. Mycroft asks that I meet him not at Whitehall but at the Diogenes Club. The existence and nature of my mission is clearly of an entirely private variety and his choice of the location of my report to him is clearly a deliberate one. Mycroft more than most men understands the delicacy of his official position in all its potential ramifications and how it may compromise his private values and beliefs. If the tension becomes too great a withdrawal may be the only course open to him as a man of conscience. There is a reason that so many politicians are rogues; it is because they have no real self to be compromised. A man must know who he is before he ventures into the political realm. This is why I have never attempted that perilous passage; I prefer to maintain the highest latitude and scope to make my own decisions. We are not led by the best of men but rather by those that the reigning powers select in advance to play their various parts on the political stage. Democracy is a pageant performed for the masses by demagogues and party hacks and the latter far outnumber the former. For this reason Plato did not favor consulting the collective ignorance and prejudices of the masses in order to determine the course of their governance. If all men and women were equal in possessing wisdom and restraint there would be no need to govern them. A society allows the wealthy to exist among us not in deference to their wisdom and virtue but rather in order to demonstrate the folly of excessive indulgence and the countless ways that they in turn would work their own misery if they were similarly endowed with riches and had the means to do so. The great mass of humankind is at least useful and in being so they are happy after a fashion.

June 17, 1899
London

I have met with Mycroft and I want to record as much as I can recall of our extensive discussion while it is as fresh as possible in my mind. I took a cab from Baker Street directly to the Diogenes Club upon arriving in London and was admitted as so often before by the saturnine individual who acts the part of Cerberus at the gates of Hades, but in this case his function is to keep intruders at bay. The Diogenes Club caters to a unique type of man, one that values the amenities that a town-club can afford while not relishing or even taking note of each other as they pass each other in the hallways or to take down a well-thumbed book from the walnut bookshelves and then to resume their places in the deep leather armchairs of the reading-room. A grunt in passing represents the outer penumbra of social intercourse allowed and expected, and even this brief sign of recognition is reserved for men of long-standing familiarity in that outer world that exists beyond the silent confines of the club.

I was ushered into one of the private rooms where converse is permitted and there I found the bulky form of Mycroft in a chair before the fire reading with the usual dyspeptic expression on his great furrowed face. He hoisted himself up with an effort and crossed over to me with one ham-like hand extended. His all-comprehending gaze took me in at a glance and he looked pleased with the result. He motioned me to a seat by the fire and settled into his own again. Still no word had passed between us. Mycroft's mind is always dedicated to the essential. Everything is allocated to its own particular file and folder. I sat back and waited while he brought me fully up into his purview and took no offense that his welcome was less effusive than one might have expected after my long absence.

His speech was as sudden when it came as the arrival of a great storm, "You look a good ten years younger than when you departed London, Sherlock. Travel evidently agrees with you. You make me wish that I was not so rooted in place like a great oak tree. Still even oaks... but I will come to that later. What is important now is that you tell me what your impressions were of the Americans, the Japanese, and the Russians. I echo what you always told your clients when they similarly related a set of circumstances, to spare no detail. A point of no immediate importance to you may carry great significance to me when it is translated into the obscure language of diplomacy. One misconstrued phrase in a treaty has been known to cost the lives of thousands if it leads to armed conflict."

I nodded in assent and he continued, "But let me begin first by setting before you the posture of England at the present hour to better frame our discussion. We are at an end of the period of unquestioned British supremacy represented by the reign of our Queen and Empress Victoria. England is now menaced in a manner and degree that we never supposed was possible during the last fifty years. We can no longer allow the continental powers to arrange their own relations through wars and threats of war. England will have all that it can manage to hold the empire together once its figure-head Victoria dies. That old woman cannot endure much longer and I am sorry to say that the men who currently form the government are unaware that mere spit and polish will likely soon be measured up against that rough but competent army fielded by the Boers in the Orange Free State and Natal in southern Africa."

"Wars are no longer a matter of the gallant cavalry charge, the smart infantry advance, and the skillful cannonade; there is or soon will be the massing of an entire industrial order of the composite productive capacity of the nation ranged against the entire industrial capacity of the enemy with deaths reckoned in tens of thousands. Peace is the new imperative, but we may need to exercise a credible threat of force in order to attain that peace. Among the great nations of the world there are no friends only allies and these will always be speculative and of questionable value until the decisive hour for deployment arrives..."

His voice trailed off, but at last he came to himself again, "Ahem, but that is enough from me. I am more anxious than you can well imagine for you to take me into the realm of your own perceptions. In these fractious times personalities may prove to be dispositive and you have encountered some of the men who will be key players in whatever new drama may emerge in the first years of the new century. The ticking over from one century to another of course has no immediate significance; it is a mere way of reckoning time, but we tend to impose meaning onto artificial eras rather than admitting that one conflict only sets the stage for others in an ongoing balance or lack thereof of contending forces."

He fell silent then and the ball was passed to me. He closed his eyes to manifest his desire that my voice alone would now receive his entire attention. I therefore marshaled my thoughts and began the following discourse that I will record here for future reference.

"Perhaps, I should begin by informing you that in my opinion the Americans fully intend to build a canal through the central isthmus of the Americas. I don't think it will matter which party is foremost in power. The Democrats and the Republicans are alike in favoring a new aggressive posture in world affairs. I also think it exceedingly unlikely that the Americans will withdraw from the Philippines. They are taking to colonialism like a duck to water. The Americans consider the entire Pacific region to be their natural realm. America also has its eyes on China. This latter ambition will of course be opposed by the Japanese, but not immediately. The Japanese prefer first to annex Korea and leave China for a later day. Any aggression directed towards Manchuria of course will put Japan at odds with the Russians. Russia is currently engaged in extending its eastern railroad to reach beyond the Urals to the distant Pacific Ocean. This of course will make Port Arthur and Vladivostok citadels of the greatest importance. A railroad without ports on the Pacific would entail a journey over tundra to no purpose. The expense of the railroad will mean that the Russians will have fewer resources available to guard their western and southern borders. The effort to open Siberia with its mineral resources to further exploration and exploitation is a great gamble. I suspect that the Russians will have cause to regret this decision. Russia is simply too large and sparsely populated to be both a European and an Asiatic power."

Mycroft interrupted at this point. "Your observations are of the greatest importance, Sherlock. I have tried repeatedly to persuade Lord Salisbury on this very point, that we are overestimating the Russians. England is of the opinion that Russia threatens India and Persia so our government favors strengthening the Japanese position in the Pacific as a counterbalance and to keep the Russians off guard."

"I also think that policy would be a mistake," I said agreeing with Mycroft. "The meeting requested by Czar Nicholas was meant to impress me and to reach your ears. His Majesty desires to maintain close relations with England. He gave me no impression that he has any designs on India."

Mycroft again interposed, "India is the gem of the Empire and our government will run no risks of losing it. And then there is this whole pending Africa question to complicate matters."

I noted that Mycroft looked troubled, even anxious, which on his usually placid features was alarming.

"The Africa question; is there trouble again in the Sudan?"I asked him.

He looked at me with the greatest seriousness. "We intend to displace the farmers of the Dutch Free-state at any cost and annex their holdings. It is an action of pure greed on our part, but we will mask it as an act of pacification of an unruly group that dares to question our right to continental hegemony and deprive those Afrikaners who favor England of their rights. It has come to this, that we use the loyalty and patriotism of the young to enrich the old. It is all about the vested capital interests that are never satisfied. This has been going on in one form or another of course for a long time. Perhaps it is only my own tolerance for humbug that is faltering, or maybe I am running short of countervailing considerations to swing the great balance of equity that exists in my own conscience to favor England. To entertain such reservations when facing blatant venality is fortunately my right and that of the individual conscience of any Englishman, but in my sensitive position any reluctance to proceed with main speed would be seen as tantamount to treason. This is why we are meeting in private today. "

He paused again before looking at me directly and saying in the clearest possible terms, "Sherlock, I fear that I will soon need to resign my position or forfeit my own honor."

This did not come as a total shock to me so I said at once, "Would that eventuality be so terrible then? You have served well and faithfully and…"

He held up a trembling hand, "No Sherlock, I am afraid that you don't understand. My position is not one that I am free to resign without consequences. I would most certainly be killed."

All at once certain depths of iniquity seemed to open before me.

"But certainly your many contacts and connections … they wouldn't dare," I said with trepidation.

"I assure you they would," Mycroft answered.

I was silent for some time before saying with deadly seriousness, "But you forget, they would then need to deal with me. I would leave no stone unturned."

There was then no further sound in the room than the ticking of the clock upon the mantel and the shifting of the logs in the fireplace. Mycroft sat slumped in his chair and at first I feared that he had not heard me.

At last he spoke, "Thank you for that assurance and I did not doubt that you would proceed in this fashion, but I am afraid that you do not yet understand the true depth of complexity in international affairs. There are linkages among men of power that transcend nations. Everything is a balance maintained day by day while the masses circulate like so many unknowing cattle in a pasture. These are sent to slaughter now and again on various fields of battle and historians make of it all a grand spectacle, but behind it all the old order prevails and soon it is a case of business as usual. Did you know that in your absence Baron Maupertuis addressed a council of British and American bankers and was given a standing ovation?"

"What, the very man who planned to kill hundreds of thousands of our population?" I exclaimed.

Mycroft nodded, "The same man; he has already absorbed his losses and has negotiated a loan so that he can turn his gaze elsewhere ... towards diamond mines. Canals are after all rather plebian affairs. He has proved quite ready to turn the whole prospect over to the Americans. The Spanish War shifted the balance in the Americans favor. They are just learning to play the great game, you see."

"Then why was I even sent to America?" I inquired in bewilderment.

Mycroft shrugged, "It was a contingency. Your presence there was not without use in any case. Baron Maupertuis feared an emerging North Atlantic alliance between England and America. Your presence in Washington was like the movement of a major piece in chess. It put a halt to his machinations. This turned his gaze towards Africa. You must understand, Sherlock; yesterday's enemy is today's friend ... and vice-versa. Holding grudges simply costs nations too much in lost trade."

"Well, it is all a dirty business," I said in disgust.

Mycroft smiled, "You have spent too much time in monastic contemplation, brother. The masses of mankind are quite ready to turn their gaze away from the real workings of the world. Give them only the pittance necessary for survival and a few amusements and they are satisfied. This leaves the wealthy free to proceed unhindered."

I shook my head. "In any case I am well out of it. I hope now to spend my time in Devonshire unearthing any Chaldean artifacts that I can locate there. Did I tell you my theory of ..."

Mycroft grasped my sleeve. "Wait, Sherlock, I am afraid that you do not realize your own position. You are already being carefully watched. Baron Maupertuis is not a man who forgives past slights. I am afraid that the die is cast and that your proposed retirement must be indefinitely deferred. You have been grasped by one of the arms of the kraken and now you must either kill it or we shall certainly both perish."

June 18, 1899

have interrupted my last journal entry because its essence is best grasped through the lens of my later discussion with Watson. As is my usual custom I find that explaining matters to the good doctor helps me to clarify my own impressions. Needless to say I was appalled by Mycroft's words. I had imagined that when I had at last returned to England that I would be my own man once again and have time and opportunity to pursue those thousand and one items of personal interest that are no small part of the joy of living. My travels through America had left me with a rather nasty impression of the course that the world was taking.

Both Rousseau and Chateaubriand had imagined for America a new version of the redemption hitherto promised only by the cross Christ. Here on this new continent primeval mankind existed in its natural state. The noble and indigenous inhabitants of the land were imagined to be immune from sin and provided for by all of the bounties of nature with abundance so that there was no need to acquire those habits of private property that are the bane of mankind in the regions where Christianity took root. Imagine a continent devoid of bankers and immune from the burdens of taxation. The wild inhabitants could pursue every avenue of development rooted in the benevolent heart of man without those obnoxious incursions of debt, investment, and the petty-fogging machinations of various committees. Above all they would be free from the laws that so oppress us. Imagine thousands of square miles without governors, lawyers, or magistrates!

Of course this romance was all wishful thinking. The lives of the first inhabitants of that vast continent were just as likely to kill members of rival tribes as the Arabs or the Hottentots. Our species is a savage one. The treatment meted out by the Huron and the Iroquois to the Jesuit missionaries, Isaac Jogues and his companions, chills the blood. But the vision of a new beginning did at least promise a new start for any peace-loving Europeans who might desire to shake off the burdens of history. The American Republic is after all only just over one hundred years old and only recently delivered from a civil war; America is already in many respects indistinguishable from the greedy and acquisitive nations from which the new inhabitants migrated. Already a native aristocracy is in place who will with time lead their fellow citizens by the nose into debt and ruin. Chattel slavery may have been defeated but wage slavery still remains. Tell the laborers who are tied to their looms breathing cotton fibers all day in Lowell, Massachusetts or the coal miners in West Virginia that they are free. They had just as well spared themselves the hardships of the voyage to those far-off shores. Even the Australian convicts have fared better than many Americans raising sheep in the open air rather than being confined to a factory.

But I have digressed here. The point is that having been obliged by my own sense of duty to visit America and then Japan, having listened to the Czar as he recounted the woes of Russia, and finally having made my report to Mycroft I had imagined that I could now return to Baker Street and that Watson and I, no longer the young fellows that we once were, could give ourselves up to those comforts that add charm and interest to advancing age. I had imagined myself dropping by the bookstore where some of my own small capital is invested. I would be greeted warmly by the current round of sales-clerks and could withdraw to my accustomed table and armchair in the private quarters there to sit by a small coal-fire and pursue whatever my current interests might be. Watson and I could resume our devotion to Covent Garden and divide our time between opera and theater. I hear good things of this playwright, George Bernard Shaw. Evidently he is quite an amusing fellow.

Instead of this blissful scenario I am now to be plunged back into danger and the inconveniences attendant upon the maintenance of vigilance whenever I am not at home. Worse still I must now worry about Mycroft who is far too stout to be able to defend himself from any blackguards or roughs who might set about him with cudgels. Watson as an old campaigner will of course be of undoubted use to me at such a time. He is as ever the soldier of old. His experiences in Afghanistan have left a lasting impression upon him.

When I left Mycroft at the Diogenes Club I proceeded immediately to Baker Street where I climbed the well-remembered seventeen steps to our old door. The scene that greeted me brought tears to my eyes as the memories flooded in. There as of old were all of the various impedimenta out of which we weave our lives. There was my old arm-chair, my chemical apparatus, the whisky, the gasogene, and there was the Persian slipper with my tobacco (a lost indulgence). There were my old pipes and the violin that brought me comfort in the old days, and above all else there was the settee and the old cane-backed chair where Watson was accustomed to read his sea-tales of a winter's evening and dream of tropical islands.

I hung my old hunting cap on its peg by the door and sat down by Watson who was toasting some bread over the fire and drinking his Indian black tea from Darjeeling (ghastly stuff). I much prefer the Chinese Jasmine. As I remained silent and meditative Watson finally spoke up, "Well, I trust that Mycroft is well."

I continued silent.

"Holmes?"

"I am sorry by dear fellow but I have been much perplexed by our interview."

"Really, how so?" he inquired.

"Well not to bandy about the bush it appears that Baron Maupertuis has not descended as I had hoped into financial ruin. He has risen like the Phoenix and has surrounded himself with a coterie of British Bankers who are willing to overlook any past differences that they are aware of ... Mycroft did not go into details."

"They are willing to lend him funds?"

"They are willing to give him what all men of that sort use to build their fortunes; they have extended to him a line of unlimited credit."

"But how will he use it?"

"He has turned his sights towards Africa, a zone that lends

itself to vast speculations.”

“Does he intend any further harm to these islands?”

“No, the Moriarty affair is evidently quite forgotten.”

“Well then...”

“But I am afraid that this amnesty does not extend to us. We have crossed him Watson and he has not forgotten any little inconvenience that we have visited upon him.”

Watson was silent for a bit and then looked up with the old steely glint in his eye that I always found to be so reassuring in times of trouble. “Well, then we shall be ready for whatever comes.”

“Good old Watson, you are the one fixed point in a changing age. But it will not be easy. You see before we were fighting in full union and with the support of the English government. Now the tide has turned and we, my dear friend, have been left at high tide stranded. We are now an inconvenience, an embarrassment to the powers that be.”

“But we succeeded in thwarting the affair of the plague that was to be introduced into these isles by Baron Maupertuis! They can’t have forgotten.”

“Oh but they have. You see Watson, we have been playing a more dangerous game than even we suspected. This was a matter of the affairs of state. Have you never wondered at the men who can send countless young lads to their deaths and still sleep well in their beds at night? Men of power take no note of human costs; lives are reckoned in units like chips in a casino, red, green, blue, 10, 100, 1000 francs; do you see? The chips are placed on the board and when the croupier pulls away the losses more chips are sent for.”

Watson looked down grimly at his leg which still ached at times from his old wound.

“But this is not warfare,” he commented quietly.

“Oh is it not? To men such as these the campaign of the pursuit of power never ends. Money, land, acquisitions, sales, war, re-building after wars; there you have a summary of the course of history and all the while there is this parallel world, the one recorded in the novels of George Gissing, the dark world where children labor in factories and where women weep at all the losses that must pave the way to glory. Life itself is a struggle just to stay alive and the majority labor so that the few may thrive."

We sat still listening to the wind that had come up suddenly outside our windows. I had noticed a strange mugginess in the air that afternoon and now the distant rumble of thunder could be heard out towards Hampstead Heath.

At last Watson spoke up, "You think that events may prove too much for us?"

"I think that they shall try the temper of our steel," I answered.

"What have we to apprehend?" he asked.

I smiled grimly, "Well, if nothing else there is the inconvenience involved in continual apprehension. You spoke of returning to Cornwall and I had thought to return to my little house in Devonshire and now we may be called upon at any hour..."

There was a pause.

"Holmes?"

"Our return has not been unnoticed, Watson. Here is the evidence that a path of retirement has escaped us. Even now I see mail here upon the table from potential clients. We must lay low and bide our time. It would be well if we appear to be unaware of any threats to our safety. This will allow the cat to toy with us a bit before pouncing."

"Why may we not take the offensive?"

"Because what we fight is hydra-headed, lop off one head and another will surely take its place. No, Watson, we must play the game and await the proper hour. Then we will strike with all the force at our command."

"But you imply that Mycroft will not be of aid to us as he usually is."

"I will explain. This country is about to go to war in southern Africa against the Boer farmers in order to annex their lands and provide investment opportunities for Maupertuis and men just like him. Mycroft, more power to him, will of course voice his opposition and as a result he will of course be cashiered. One does not oppose what others, more highly placed, regard as a necessity of state. "

"What? After all his years of service; this is his treatment!" Watson objected with spirit.

"Tush, Watson, would you expect them to be grateful? He has been of use to them in their careers and that is all. He will not even receive the usual public honors attendant upon his services; no knighthood let alone a peerage will await him. The secrecy of his position makes such a display unnecessary and worse still inconvenient to the men who have always treated his ideas as their own. His value to the government was always that no one knew that Mycroft even existed. Even his compatriots at the Diogenes Club imagine that he is no more than an eccentric gentleman of independent means who likes his whisky of an evening and a good meal of beef and Yorkshire pudding and that stew of limp and boiled vegetables that is an English specialite."

"Then what will happen to him?" Watson inquired.

I answered him at once, "Oh Mycroft will be pensioned off like most merely competent men are and after that his very existence will cease being an asset and become a liability to the very government he has served for so long. When Mycroft resigns he will be watched and when the right moment comes ... a runaway hansom cab, a knife in the ribs outside his lodgings, an air-gun; who can say? There are only the questions of where and by what means he will be dispatched. It will all be very neat and clean as such assassinations always are."

Watson was appalled. "Then we must protect him."

"But only if we are still here to aid him; we are more expendable still you see. If Mycroft is in danger; we are only the more expendable; I as an eccentric detective and you as an old soldier with a penchant for writing lurid tales for the Strand Magazine."

"But there are still your friends at Scotland Yard..." Watson objected. "They will not stand by and allow such a thing."

I smiled, "Well there is more than one inspector who will not be sorry to lay a wreath upon my grave. I am still viewed by some at the Yard as an amateur upstart. Your stories in the Strand have made them look rather feeble to the reading public."

"Well we have Inspector Stanley Hopkins at least." He assured me.

I assented, "Yes, we do have him and he is not without friends at the Yard. And there are still the older men who have since retired, Gregson and Lestrade and we have one other asset as well."

"What is that?"

I smiled, "We have a certain gentleman in Devonshire who will be quite willing to advise us in such matters bearing on life and death, the very topics of his former specialty and vocation."

"And who is that?" he asked with some premonitory sense of my answer.

"My dear friend, surely you can guess; our hidden asset is none other than Professor Moriarty, the former Napoleon of Crime."

June 24, 1899

I am happy that I have not yet lost the ability to leave Watson with that expression of utter bewilderment that always amuses me. All of his air of military precision and that self-assurance and infallibility that goes with being a physician leaves him and he is left like a great trout gasping on the shores of incomprehension.

"Really Holmes, don't tell me that we must throw our lot in with Moriarty again!" he expostulated.

"That's right you never did quite believe in Moriarty's reformation, did you? Evidently you do not appreciate the attractions of pure physics. Crime is a vulgar pursuit after all. I managed to awaken the Professor to the true majesty underlying creation that can only be truly apprehended and then appreciated by the man of faith."

"If that is so, then of what use can the Professor be to us in matters of practical defense? What becomes of the command, thou shalt not kill?"

"My blushes, Watson, do you not see that in spite of his reformation his memory has remained unimpaired. In Moriarty we have a man whose very name once caused the most vicious of cutthroats to quail in terror. He is a master of organizational dynamics as well as the dynamics of an asteroid. He knows the language of power that we humble artisans, you a doctor, and I a detective, do not possess. He will advise us before we set off for Holland."

Watson was again nonplussed. "Holland? Why we have only just arrived back in England; why should we set off again so soon?"

"Oh, didn't I mention it? I thought that I had made it clear when I described our peril."

"You said that we have much to fear from Baron Maupertuis, so why are we going to Holland of all places where he casts such a shadow?"

"Well Watson, he is least likely to make an attempt upon us on his own doorstep. But that is not the reason that we are going. We have been appointed as unofficial observers at the World Disarmament Council that was proposed last year by Czar Nicholas. It convened in May and is in mid-session at this very hour. Its proceedings may very well last for another month and we may be able to exercise a salutary but indirect effect upon it. Mycroft would go, but his own health will not permit it. We are again to be his eyes and voice."

"Then time is of the essence since the conference is already underway, so where does Moriarty come in?"

"I have a copy of the agenda of the conference and some notes from our delegates to guide us. I have been given permission to share these with Professor Moriarty and to get his opinion."

Watson shook his head. "These are dangerous waters, Holmes. What if Moriarty should contact his old confederates if any are left and return to crime?"

"Ah well, one must take chances when much is at stake. This conference bids fair to being a great opportunity for the nations of Europe to collectively come to their senses. I do not think that many people realize the full extent of the damage that can be inflicted on the battlefield and to cities and villages by modern arms. The Krupp factories alone in Germany have designs for cannon that dwarf the imagination. Then there is talk of bombs being dropped from dirigibles. It is all quite horrifying. You recall the havoc wrought among the crack Sudanese troops at Omdurman last year by mechanized guns. It was a complete slaughter. Are we prepared to witness such scenes enacted on European soil? No, the impending sense of war must be stopped and the Czar's proposal is both timely and essential to that end no matter what the chances are for its success."

"Then why are we needed?" he asked. "If we have no vote in the proceedings, then what use are we as mere reporters?"

"Because, my dear fellow, the nations are possessed by a sort of madness. There is a blind belief in the essential superiority of our troops because of a long legacy of European peace, one broken only briefly in 1871 when France and Germany went to war. The border conflicts were mere skirmishes. They have tended to favor the British troops in particular in India although we were soundly bloodied in the Crimean War, a messy affair. The leadership there was appalling. We also have the disadvantage of some remarkably pig-headed men in the current cabinet. I cannot say that I am fond of Balfour. We may not be able to exercise power for a sustained peace directly, but we can make an informed assessment at the conference and then work from behind the scenes until Mycroft is forced to resign."

Watson was silent for a bit and he looked deeply troubled.

"But see here Holmes, your language is becoming deeply disturbing to one who once served his country on the frontiers of the empire."

"Ah you raise the question of patriotism. You were never quite reconciled to my refusal of a knighthood. I made every effort to spare Her Majesty any embarrassment on that occasion."

Watson protested, "Nevertheless it was a sleight at least if not an insult."

"Well s surely it is up to me whether I cared to have a "sir" affixed to my name. I will be no man's lackey or a woman's either. What I do I do because I think it is right and that is an end to it! You must have noticed my occasional cavalier attitude towards great men. I assure you, Watson, power does not impress me because I know by what shoddy means it is often acquired. If you had been present at my latest interview with Mycroft you would have heard how he is coming round at last to my views. I will tell you in confidence that his resignation is uncertain in time but imminent in any case and when it does occur Mycroft will join you and me in danger and expendability. We must move now while we may, because a time is coming when like the proverbial fox we must find a secure cover and go to ground. Your old fiction of my retirement to the Sussex Downs will have to be trotted out again while we establish our real quarters elsewhere."

I could see the chagrin upon his face when he asked, "And my own house in Cornwall; what is to become of it?"

The poor fellow looked so crestfallen, that I was stirred to the heart. I offered some words of reassurance. "Well we must not get ahead of ourselves. It may be possible for us to devise a way that you do not share the evil effects of proximity with the Holmes brothers. We might devise a falling out or simply a gradual diminishment in our relations for public consumption. It already strains credulity that two gentlemen could share lodgings on and off again over a lifetime without getting on each other's nerves in the process or implying an improper relation. You might tell your readers that I started in again with my cocaine addiction, or took to dressing up as my grandmother on occasion, or some similar hereditary madness. The whole thing just became too much for you and we had to part."

"Oh come now Holmes, what would then become of the public's admiration for England's greatest detective to say nothing of what little literary reputation I might possess?" he protested.

"The intelligent ones will see through our little ruse and as for the rest... Well, you know, my dear fellow, that it is not the first time that we have 'had them on.' You need only recall our shifting about of dates for some cases, references to non-existent persons, and innumerable instances of hiding the ball; scarcely cricket, old fellow, not strictly above the mark."

"But out and out deception ... really I must draw the line here, Holmes, if you are not pulling my leg by even making the suggestion."

I persisted only half in jest, "Well, you could simply write-up some of our older cases in preference to our more recent engagements and save the rest up for one final grand unveiling. How would that be? Ah, I can see that my suggestion intrigues you. There is a hidden Tolstoy in you, Watson. Give the fellow a free rein I say."

Of course I hesitated before suggesting the most obvious course, which was simply to continue to hide behind the man, under whose name, Watson's many tales had been published. And there we left the matter. Now the good doctor and I are off again to Devonshire. I have wired the Professor at Kings Pyland and he has wired back that he would be most happy to see us. So there it is. Our leisure is deferred and we are again called to the unrewarding tasks that fall to men of honor and probity to assume from time to time with only God's good pleasure as our only witness and reward.

June 21, 1899
Kings Pyland, Devonshire

We took the early train down to Devon from Paddington Station, changed trains at Exeter, and came on to Kings Pyland where we are ensconced in the guest house with an excellent view over the heaving swell of Dartmoor. The Professor insisted upon taking us over to the stables while his head groom and trainer showed off his latest breeding acquisitions, thoroughbreds all. The Professor seemed actually disappointed that our stay here is to be so short. I believe that Watson and I may be part of a very select few who are allowed the privilege of visiting the stables and the estate. Of course the Professor is as much occupied as ever with his research papers, but he does enjoy congenial company, particularly company where he need not maintain the pretense that he has ever been other than what his neighbors think he is, the complete country gentleman with the eccentric hobby of pursuing arcane and abstruse mathematics.

When I explained the nature of our visit he suggested that we first enjoy the comforts of his board and wine cellar and then we would spend the evening in a leisurely discussion as of old. This was acceptable to both Watson and to me as well because we were weary from our journey and sorely in need of refreshment and rest. I must say that the Professor looked well. Evidently the air of Devonshire is good for him and virtuous activities are their own remedy after a life spent in criminal pursuits. We dined on several pheasants cooked in Cointreau and brandy with a crème brulee afterwards for dessert. After this sumptuous meal we took our port to the library. The servant attending us was soon dismissed and we got down to business.

"I trust that you met with success in America, Holmes. Did you by any chance meet Professor William James the psychologist and philosopher while you were there? No? Ah that was a misfortune. He may be the only man in America who I would care to meet. The generality of Americans with the exception of a few clever inventors have yet to make any significant contributions to world culture."

"Their economy is thriving though," Watson remarked.

The Professor took a balanced view to this observation. "Well it would be remarkable if their economy did not show signs of prosperity. After all with an entire stolen continent, one neither mined nor farmed, opportunities for riches were abundant. Watch though, the Americans will make quite a mess of it given sufficient time. Give them another hundred years and the whole place will be dustbin. The ungoverned desire for acquisitions and profits is the distinguishing characteristic of most Americans and contributes to their barbarian ethos. But in this they are not alone. Their type is here as well. What is the news of Baron Maupertuis?"

I looked surprised, "I had hopes that you might inform us."

The Professor scoffed at this, "I inform you? I am quite isolated here and by design. When I switched my loyalties in answer to your victorious conclusion to our famous wager I broke off all contact with the Baron. You may recall that I managed to convince him that his own organization had broken down and that any failure of our scheme must be left at his door. I was quite huffy and indignant at the time. With a man like that it is imperative that one immediately seize the high-ground and keep it thereafter. I even had the temerity to demand that my final remittance should be paid as my consulting fees are not suspended in the case of failure. I led the Baron to suppose that I still have assassins on hand to take care of collections from those who delay or prevaricate."

The Professor laughed quietly but with some of his old sinister demeanor. "It was all a bluff of course. I am afraid that my enforcers are serving long sentences at nearby Princeton Prison on the moors. The exception of course is Colonel Moran, but he has retired as you know. Were you able to visit him?"

I reluctantly informed the Professor that his old comrade was gravely ill and dying and was surprised to see that he was much moved at the news, which was more evidence of his reformation.

At last he said, "Ah that is bad news indeed. I must write him at once."

I dared to advise a contrary course, "I think that to do so would give him pain. He is not a man who covets sympathy."

"But I owe him so much, as do you also, Mr. Sherlock Holmes. You know how essential he can be in a tight spot. I doubt if you would have returned safely from the Red Sea coast or from the Sudan without him."

"You will serve him best by remembering him as he was," I insisted.

He gazed off into space and then replied at last.

"Let it be so then. We are all of us soon to be rushed from the stage in any case. I spend my days in the writing of monographs and in corresponding with various scientists. There is no time to be wasted on sentiment where it is neither useful nor welcome."

I returned the conversation to our reason for the visit. "In any case Watson and I have come here to consult you on a matter of the very deepest moment. I trust that you are still on retainer in light of our shared past."

He answered, "Well as you see I am quite comfortably fixed here and the university has been so kind as to grant me a stipend for life. How can be of service to you?"

I proceeded to explain that Watson and I would be traveling within days across the channel to attend the Hague Conference on Disarmament that had been suggested by the Russian Czar the previous year when the invitations were sent."

"Well I hope that you do not imagine that the delegates are there because of their actual enthusiasm for peace," remarked the Professor.

"Why else would they come?" Watson inquired.

The Professor laughed, "Why in order not to appear to be the aggressor should war soon break out. Nations like individuals prefer to be well-stocked in the order of self-justification. In the case of nations it helps when it becomes necessary to whip up public sentiments for war; then when the boys start coming home without limbs the same high-sounding rhetoric stokes the fires of revenge."

"Then why did the Czar suggest this conference in the first place?" Watson persisted.

The Professor answered at once, "In order to hide the fact that Russia is slipping into being a second or third-rate power of course. Russia is badly in need of friends at the present time. Russia has held on far too long to the three things that most truly characterize it: a serf economy rather than an industrialized one producing a skilled middle-class, an inefficient rural bureaucracy that stifles free inquiry, and a benighted aristocracy of idle and ignorant petty landholders. Add to this a miserable climate, poor roads, and a habit of surviving on borscht, dumplings, and vodka and a certain nervous debility that seems endemic and you have the best portrayal of the Russian existence and why it will always lag behind Europe. Russia is a region in any case, not a people. Everything beyond the Urals and south-east of the Caspian Sea should have been cast adrift long ago."

I told the Professor, "But the Russians are currently in the process of building a railroad to the Pacific Ocean."

The Professor laughed again, "Are they now? A capital mistake, but one characteristic of its empire mentality; the Russians refuse to admit their current position in the world so they are determined to keep up a false front. You must not think that the gesture of building a railroad is being misconstrued by England, France, and Germany. I would not care to ride on it in any case, a jolting passage from nowhere to an even more remote nowhere."

"I noticed that you did not mention Austria-Hungary," I remarked.

"Ah there is another empire that is falling apart piece by piece and throwing off fragments left and right. Nothing so invites wars as the death-throes of an empire in decline. As the periphery disintegrates the center attempts to tighten its hold, which only increases the spirit of rebellion among all the indigenous elements that are or have become over time disaffiliated with the governing regime. Besides Austria is governed by a coterie of hot-heads and by Franz Joseph who should long since have retired to some hunting-lodge and abdicated in favor of his young heir Franz Ferdinand.”

“So your reading is that Russia has made a mistake in calling the conference at all,” I summed up the tenor of the Professor’s prior remarks.

“Oh as a gesture it may have been well-intended, but I fear that it will have precisely the opposite effect to the one intended. It will broadcast to Germany that Russia is drifting into obsolescence and this in turn will draw England into the mix.”

“Really, how so?” I inquired.

“Well, surely it is obvious. Germany and France will always be opposed so they cancel each other out. War will only occur when one national block will perceive that it has an advantage or is itself about to be attacked. The origin lies in the Germany/France rivalry. Now then, which nations will ally their interests with Germany; that is the question? The Germans when they cease to philosophize are remarkably short-sighted.”

Watson piped up, “Austria will go with Germany.”

“Bravo Doctor,” smiled the Professor.

“And England will go with France,” Watson went on.

“Ah, but we must presume that England will try and remain outside any continental dispute if possible, so we must put England aside for now,” corrected the Professor. “Who will support France if England is not included?”

“I suppose the Russians,” Watson replied.

“And why do you suppose so?” asked the Professor as though he was still in a classroom.

“Russia has always admired the French and in polite society the French language is still in vogue among those with pretensions to culture.”

“Purely an aesthetic preference; we must not forget that Napoleon savaged Russia before being driven back from Moscow.”

“Well then am I wrong?” asked Watson.

"Not at all, Doctor, but the reason for the alliance is the key point. The reason that Russia must conclude an alliance with France is that no one else is available! The Russians are desperate. Germany would be a likely candidate, but in that case the Germans would lose their own natural alliance with Austria-Hungary, because the Austrians have eyes on Balkan expansion and Russia favors Slavic independence, so Russia would be forced to intervene if Austria should be so misguided as to exert itself to discipline any independence movements in that area. So let us assume that we have a Russian-French alliance opposing Germany and Austria. What will the unaffiliated nations be forced to do?"

Watson hesitated to risk any more comments, so I spoke up. "You have already disposed of the main contenders and are holding back on committing England, so I can only imagine that you are talking about Italy."

"Precisely, bravo to the world-wanderer," exclaimed the Professor who poured himself another glass of port. "Italy is the wild-card. The Italians have been hoping to prove their mettle now that they are one unified nation with a monarchy. Italy will be feeling its oats and will be courted by the two alliances, to mix metaphors. If Italy joins Germany and Austria it will put huge pressure on the Balkans and the bulwark will buckle and when it does war will break out. Unless possibly..."

"Now you have come to the very reason why both Doctor Watson and I have come to see you, Professor," I interjected. "We hope to preserve the peace in the interests of England. Were you about to suggest that England could sustain the peace by throwing its lot in with a Russian-French alliance to discourage Germanic aggression?"

"I was thinking along those very lines. No doubt you are here at the request of Mycroft," smiled the Professor. "I have long been aware that you have been drawn into the circle of your middle brother. I hesitate to aid you now, because Mycroft and I were early rivals; but in light of our current relations I will make an exception and give you my best advice. If you wish to keep the peace you must influence Italy to stay neutral or to ally itself with Russia rather than draw England into the stew. Even this of course might lead the Austrians to make a desperate move because patriots in the Balkans are looking for any sign of weakness in Austria to break away. But Germany will never fight a three-front war. Any added threat from the south from Italy would be sufficient cause for Germany to rein in Austrian escapades or ultimatums in the Balkans."

"But why to go round the entire table, should England not throw in with Germany and Austria and demand immediate Balkan pacification by aiding Austria in its domination there?" I inquired.

The Professor answered, "The answer is surely obvious. That would put England at odds with France that would fear complete encirclement by hostile powers; besides the French have still not forgiven us for Waterloo. In any case England does not think the fate of the Balkans is our problem and we are already more friendly to the French than we used to be. After all they are only just across the channel from us. Germany will not look with a friendly eye to any aid we might be willing to offer the Austrians because Germany has two obsessions: to build up its navy and to get a stronger influence in Africa where it lags behind England and France in colonies."

"So how can England maintain the peace?" I inquired.

"Certainly not through any direct action," the Professor replied. "However it might do so by concluding an alliance with Russia on condition that Russia shall use its influence to clap a lid on the seething cauldron of the Balkan independence movements. There is your answer to Mycroft. England must support Russia, but on this very specific condition that Russia must keep its own house in good order and manage the hotheads in Serbia and Bulgaria. This may be enough, but for good measure you must keep Italy from joining the German-Austrian alliance by pointing out that Italy is still unprepared for what will happen if a general European War breaks out. Your task will not be an easy one there of course."

"And why is that?" I inquired, anxious that the Professor should speak his whole mind on these essential questions.

"Well simply look at a map," he suggested impatiently. "Italy and Austria are natural rivals. Austria is landlocked and Trieste is a bone of contention between them. You must not forget that Austria and Italy are at still at odds over the Southern Tyrol. Italy will therefore desire an alliance with Austria to secure its northern border and allow it to make its own bid for African colonies, which are just beckoning like ripe fruit across the Mediterranean Sea: Libya and Abyssinia. Italy may request just such a dance, but proud Austria will refuse. Of course there are one or two other key factors; for instance there are various upstart nations that can play a distant role."

"And they are...?" Watson inquired.

"The Americans and the Japanese of course, these two could throw the whole of our careful calculations into disarray. That is why I said at the outset that Russia would do well to forget any ideas that it has of holding onto the Pacific region. Let the Americans and the Japanese decide between them the fate of that area of the world."

"You are forgetting China," I suggested quietly.

The Professor looked up sharply, "I am not forgetting it, but China's fate is a question that will not be resolved in the next hundred years. If peace is sustained in Europe; only then China can be shared."

"The Chinese may object," Watson remarked quietly.

The Professor stated his conviction, "There is no real China apart from its decaying dynasty. China is held together only by its rivers. It is a region not a nation."

"But what if it should become a nation?" Watson asked.

"Then it may be the nations of Europe that will be colonized by it instead," said the Professor ominously. "But that is a question for another day."

June 23, 1899
Kings Pyland

The next day we resumed our discussion after Watson and I took advantage of the lovely June weather by taking a stroll around the grounds of the Moriarty estate. The rhododendrons we in full bloom and the horses were allowed to graze freely in the pasture lands that had been reclaimed out of the desolate moorland with its abrupt valleys and coverts. Watson was in one of his quiet and thoughtful moods and I inquired what might be troubling him. It took him a while to formulate the source of his trouble but he said at last, "Well Holmes it seems to me that both you and Moriarty have fallen into speaking of war as though it is a mere chess game. Where is the dust and noise? Where are the whistling and explosion of projectiles, the cries of pain and dismay as one realizes that one has been wounded or has just lost a beloved comrade in arms? Surely these considerations should be paramount and not simply a balance of forces discussed by men of middle age over a table littered with maps and logistical reports!"

"Well we must point out your concerns to the Professor and obtain his opinion regarding the impact of just such factors on the decision to go to war. Certainly no war has ever been put to a plebiscite before being declared. The people are presented with a fait accompli and are then asked to rally round to the cause."

"Yes Holmes and that is the trouble. Where is the democracy in battle?"

"You forget the essence of the state's sovereign power to command regarding its own survival, its capacity to frame laws and to tax, and many other matters that are beyond any need to consult the citizenry. War is merely an extreme example of the lack of freedom in the individual to determine his own fate."

"Well it is all a cold-blooded business," Watson said in disgust.

"As it must be if wars are ever to be waged," I replied.

"Then perhaps they shouldn't be waged."

"I quite agree my dear fellow but as long as greed and the rule of economic scarcity prevail in this troubled world, wars are inevitable. Our task is to sustain the peace by so aligning the major players that the costs will appear to be prohibitive. It is self-interest that makes wars feasible and it is self-interest and fear that will prevent them. It is all a matter of maintaining a balance of terror that to initiate proceedings will entail a high probability of one's own destruction. We must find a way forward by peaceful means to secure mutual prosperity while not exhausting the limited resources at our common disposal. That by the way is the function of treaties and these in turn are the function of imagination and skillful drafting. The rest is simply to obtain consent after the inevitable bargaining and posturing. So much of politics is selling the result at home after the fact. We are a sanguinary species and a wise compromise is never as palatable as the promise of victory in battle. Convert the spirit and the results will follow. Have you ever noticed how many of the skulls dug up on these very moors by our archeologist friend, Doctor Mortimer, show the results of violence? The species has only had marginal inroads made upon it by civilization and by religious teachings. Give us another hundred years and perhaps...”

Watson looked up at me in horror. “One hundred years Holmes! If what you say is true of humankind and our technical progress is allowed full sway why then we are talking of the deaths of millions in the coming century!”

“Yes, Watson,” I replied sorrowfully, “I’m afraid that we are talking of a slaughter beyond our present imagination’s ability to conceive. Why do you think that I desire to return to the bleak Aran Islands monastery to spend my final years in prayers and reparation for all that surrounds us? If this is all that we have yet to make of our redemption after two thousand years will we ever see a third millennium?”

We had a luncheon of cold mutton and cucumber sandwiches before adjourning to the library to continue the discussion of the previous day. Watson still seemed subdued and he left it to me to summarize our conclusions of the morning for Professor Moriarty.

“My friend Doctor Watson has been so good as to point out the distance that is maintained between those who take us to war and the ultimate results that must be borne by the actual participants. He has himself seen the costs of battle. I must ask you Professor how we may make these costs evident to the men at the council on disarmament.”

“I am afraid that will be difficult,” answered the Professor. “You must see the whole thing from the perspective of the relative freedom of the participants. It is not the actual nations in their totality that will be present. Instead those who will be attending will be drawn from that class of men that can listen for hours to heartfelt and inspiring rhetoric about peace while keeping in mind that any concessions will be interpreted by their opposing parties as signs of secret military weakness thus lessening their relative bargaining power I other arenas. Arms are merely the last resort of power but it is power itself that is the goal. Power is the ability to obtain consent with a minimum of force exerted or relative inconvenience suffered in order to obtain that consent."

We took some time to absorb this insight. But I was impressed once again by how fortunate I was to have emerged the victor in the wager made with Professor Moriarty so many years ago on the brink of the Reichenbach Falls.

"You will be dealing with mere functionaries Gentlemen. The actual play is being written in the various capitols, in St. Petersburg, in Paris, in Vienna, and in Berlin. The whole thing will be decided by telegraph."

"So nothing will emerge from the conference?" Watson inquired.

The Professor trained his shrewd and serpentine eyes upon him.

"There will be some progress made in details but I am afraid that the ultimate result will not lessen the prospects for war. The only thing that can prevent war is to make it absolutely infeasible and we have yet to acquire weapons of sufficient horror and general destructive power to remove forever the temptation that one might emerge from war with a marginal power advantage over other nations no matter how dearly that advantage has been obtained and at what cost in the future to quality of life and the future prospects for the survival of the species."

"This is all rather cold comfort Professor," I said.

"Well you must both bear in by the conditions that prevail at the present time. If I may take my study of asteroids as an example: in order to calculate any directional movement you must first ascertain the state of the initial position of the object to be moved, its location and its directional velocity. This must be your guiding principle gentleman in political action as well: simply ask yourselves what each nation would desire if its will was not opposed. Each nation will try and emerge from the conference as from a war with those prospects diminished or compromised as little as possible. But I am weary, gentlemen, and you must excuse me if as an aged professor I keep to my normal schedule of sleep and waking. We can take all of this up tomorrow."

We terminated our discussion on that note. I am afraid that we must get back to London the day after tomorrow and then cross the channel as soon as possible. It is interesting that the question of Baron Maupertuis did not proceed further. The Professor merely intimated that we should keep alert and on guard. Evidently we are at least safe for the present as long as Mycroft remains at his present post with its power and influence. However, when that protective barrier is dismantled the question remains what measures the Baron will take. These issues are still veiled and the answers perhaps unobtainable. We may all of us need to vanish into obscurity for a time and remain untraceable until a more propitious hour or until we can obtain relief from some unexpected quarter.

June 24, 1899
Kings Pyland

The next evening we found ourselves in a position to profit again from the thoughts of Professor Moriarty. We asked few questions relying instead upon the systemic features of the brain of the Professor. He began at once so as to complete his discourse before the wine that we had enjoyed at dinner betrayed any discernible effect on his remarkable powers.

"Have you ever considered the many ways in which politics and religion interpenetrate, gentlemen? No? Then perhaps you will allow me a little presentation on the matter. The first thing to note is that nations as we know them today are constructions rather than natural entities. At any given moment a group of people will claim some part of the earth's surface as their own and then proceed to recognize some structure of relations and laws as the manifest framework for their common will. The problem arises when some governing structure and the people it represents claims a geographical area hitherto occupied by another group and its governing structure; the number of the justifications for such an adverse claim are legion. Usually there is some period when the frontiers were more confused that can be appealed to in order to portray an invasion as in reality a restoration of prior rights of possession."

"A unique example of this rationale finds its basis in the Old Testament. No more elaborate and poetic excuse for repeated invasions has ever been composed. The Jewish people admit in Deuteronomy that the nomadic people from which the Jewish people owe their identity descend from a father who was 'a wandering Aramean,' a phrase used even today in the Passover Haggadah. This people in exile, similar in many ways to the Roma or gypsies of Eastern Europe, goes to the trouble of developing an entire metaphysical justification for their appropriation of the lands of other people. Compare this approach to conquest to the Germanic tribes that sacked the Roman Empire: these tribes simply went where they chose and took what they were able to carry back with them into the forests. There you have the two models for conquest: one claiming moral justification and the other simply appealing to the ungovernable use of force."

"Now then, as regards this peace conference that you plan to attend, no nation voluntarily surrenders their sense that they are completely justified in holding onto what they already possess and no nation accepts that its current measure of influence and power is entirely adequate to its future needs. This means that the use of war to preserve what one has and to gain what one does not yet possess will always be the primary temptation to mankind. This means that the conference is based upon something entirely foreign to human nature and is therefore unlikely to succeed in achieving its stated purpose. But this does not mean that you should not attend. By going you will witness precisely that bargaining process that occurs after every war at the peace conference that follows an armistice. You will witness the posturing and the duplicity, the grandstanding and the high-flown rhetoric, the appeals to ideals coupled with blatant self-interest that always characterizes these affairs. It will be an education to you and disillusion you from maintaining romantic ideas of human solidarity."

"As to religion, the same elements are often operative. No religion is satisfied to exist without proselytizing its views through various missionaries and foisting its ceremonials upon unwilling recipients of their largess for the souls of others who will be most certainly damned if they do not embrace those very beliefs telling them among other things of a danger that they had no prior suspicion they might suffer had those missionaries not arrived to tell them so."

The Professor chuckled, "I know that you will consider this comparison unfair to religion, let alone that the conquering power of the state usually has religion as its handmaiden; but you must grant me that historical experience supports my views on the matter."

I corrected him at once, "You are forgetting that the Jewish people in that same Old Testament stated that their victory was meant to benefit all of the nations of the earth and that the primary message of the gospels is not damnation but the good news of salvation and a sharing in the very life of God."

He answered, "Religious genius to be sure, Holmes, but you must admit that these promises seem as remote today as they have ever been, at least when world history is placed upon the table. The prospects of conquest have never been greater and even the Americans may throw in their lot with the imperial powers if the Boxers of China should get out of hand supporting the dynasty against foreign encroachments. America has significant Pacific aspirations. Since the acquisition of Alaska in 1867 the Americans and the Russians have become neighbors. How long will it be before they reach a separate entente and understanding and agree to divide the world between them? Just watch if the Japanese and the Russians have a falling-out and see which country will generously step in to broker a peace conference between them like some governess with unruly children at her feet. Europe has much to fear from just such friendly gestures and you can bet that American interests will benefit from the exchange."

"But I have no wish to depress you unduly; after all you still see your mission as being a knight of the woeful countenance, Holmes, and the world will always require such men, just as it will also require men like me who have learned by experience to accept that whatever power God possesses in the celestial regions, that power of prevention is not active here on earth and that nothing will prevent us from destroying ourselves with the highest of motives to justify that destruction."

That concluded our discussion and Watson and I retired to our rooms soon afterwards.

June 25, 1899
Diogenes Club London

We are again comfortably lodged at the Diogenes club. I gave a quick summary of our discussions with the Professor to Mycroft and he seemed pleased with the results of our consultation. We agreed to table further discussion pending our observations at the conference. We left Kings Pyland this morning after thanking Professor Moriarty for his counsel.

As a piece of parting advice the Professor said, "I doubt that Mycroft will believe that our rivalry, from my side at least is at an end, but I have a word of advice to give to him. I did not choose Baron Maupertuis at random. He is a most dangerous man. You once called me "the Napoleon of Crime," Holmes. Well this man is far worse because he manages his depredations with the full support and agency of the great powers. You will not be able to defeat him by force of law, because he generally keeps well within its borders when he is not actively engaged in changing the laws themselves. It is not too much to say that in some countries his will has the force of the laws because his influence has so inundated the high offices and tribunals that those who occupy roles and positions of power follow his bidding as if it was the source of practical wisdom and prudence in all things. He has been honored by some of the greatest universities on the continent and it will not surprise me if he is has asked to address the Hague Peace Convention though he owns a controlling interest in many companies that manufacture weapons of great destructive power. He will appear there as an angel of light although he receives whatever marching orders that he deigns to adopt as his own from the very prince of darkness. It will be of interest to you to observe him when he is in his element. Try and avoid a direct meeting though. Follow the advice of St. Philip Neri. He was once asked by an admiring acolyte how he dealt with the devil whenever he appeared. St. Philip Neri was renowned for both his holiness and his humor as you know. The saint said, "Whenever I am sure that it is the devil... I run away as quickly as I can! My advice to Mycroft and to you as well is to take the greatest care possible, for you can little imagine what you are dealing with in him."

On the train later I asked Watson for his reflections on the past three days. His answer was sensible and balanced as always, "Well Holmes it appears that we have our work set out for us and that discretion must trump valor if we hope to survive."

"Well, Watson, you are always the soul of brevity and conciseness; but this is unfortunate because you also prefer action and we may be forced to work from behind the scenes if our efforts are to bear any fruit. I am not even sure what our position is to be."

"Surely it is obvious, Holmes. First, we must keep on guard from any menaces unleashed by Baron Maupertuis. Second, we must aid your brother to avert the pending conflict in southern Africa. Third, we should see what we may do to fulfill our mission from the Czar to influence the British government to support the Czar's efforts to thwart Austrian expansion into the Balkans. Have I missed anything?"

"That certainly appears to be our position, my dear fellow, but you have sidestepped the preliminary question of how any of this strenuous activity conforms with the instinct of men of our age to seek comfort, good company, and to read quietly by their fire at night before retiring to prayer and peaceful slumber. The instinct to maintain a private life may be indefinitely deferred or even permanently abandoned, but if we proceed on our present course of conduct they will no longer be available, as each of us hoped."

"Well the excitements of the chase were always welcome to both of us in the past," he answered.

"Yes, but we usually managed to bring clarity to the problem and to set things right, but in the case presented by these international affairs things seem to simply merge into one long chain of misjudgments and malfeasances. Matters never reach a head, or if they do it is precisely at the moment when all human agencies seem powerless to decide matters and to attain the general good. Social forces simply unfold in response to other forces many of which are beyond alteration or diminishment and to avoid disaster is impossible. We are present Watson at a scene of compounding evils that dwarf the imagination and defeat all hope of reason to address them."

"Well Holmes surely that is the very definition of evil," Watson concluded.

We both fell silent then gazing out at the rich fields of England and the pasturing flocks of sheep. Neither of us was prepared at the moment to specify the outer limits of our endurance or even of our willingness to set our own lives aside to pursue the greater good of humanity and civilization. Perhaps the most troubling element was the probability that our efforts would not only go without thanks, but that we might be perceived as acting contrary to the narrow confines of the British national interest. We might even be called upon to undertake actions that might be construed as treasonable. The pursuit of short-term interests is not merely an individual failing; nations also are blinded by a sense of relative advantage to seek to shoulder other nations aside and grab whatever they want. I have rather strong convictions on these matters, a privilege accorded to one who is ultimately not answerable for the subsistence and welfare of a wife and family. My cases have often involved a degree of danger and difficulty beyond what most men would wish to invite or tolerate no matter how stimulating the thrill of the chase might be. But can I in good conscience invite Watson to share this particular adventure with all its complications and incalculable permutations? Surely the good doctor has sacrificed enough through the many years when we have faced similar dangers together. I thought of the many times that I had taken him from his hearth and home even in the later years when we did not share a common domicile. A sense of fatality attends some masculine relationships. I thought for instance of Percy Shelley's poem, *Julian and Maddalo,* describing his relations with Lord Byron. Both of them died young, although under different circumstances. Perhaps it is not an unqualified benefit to know Sherlock Holmes. I carry about with me my own fatality.

I have loved only two people outside of my family circle where affection is presumed if not always present. I need hardly state them here but I do so in case this manuscript is ever read. One of them is of course the woman, Irene Adler and the second is Dr. John Hamish Watson, friend and comrade.

As proof of the above mentioned sentiments and hesitations in my journal, a letter awaited me upon my return to the Diogenes Club addressed to Sherlock Holmes as a confidential communication with a note from the Professor to accompany it. The note stated....

As per our agreement I am writing you to let you know that Baron Maupertuis is still in communication with me. I regard his communications as tests to see whether my sympathies are still with him in his audacious schemes. My answers are short and non-committal. I desire that he should regard me as a man caught up in my own affairs and with neither the time nor the energy to aid him further in his schemes. He may have been inebriated at the time that he wrote the following. I leave you to assign what significance is to be afforded to the following transcription.

Dear Professor Moriarty:
I am writing to you to ascertain your opinion regarding the feasibility of certain long-term plans of mine that still reside at the stage of rumination. I like to think that my plans will always be in advance of any existing stasis point between nations. I prefer to regard the masses of human beings, those great ignorant hoards, as mere productive assets rather than as active agents pursuing their own interests. It saves so much trouble to cut to the bone in these matters and eliminate the embroidery of ordinary forms of political discourse. What all types of government existing at the present day omit is the realization that humanity as a concept is already largely irrelevant. The mass of humanity is superfluous.
Slavery in one form or another is the natural condition for the majority of the human race and it is good that this is so. Most slavery is of course voluntary to a degree. Men become captives to their own ideas, while women are content to be loved and provided for adequately so they can pursue their little fads and fashions. Knowledge and affection are the twin illusions that turn the wheel of history. This insistence upon the existence of a

rational or a kindly universe denies the fact that you as a scientist will appreciate that we live upon the skin of a planet of boiling and molten rock. All life-forms are a mere excrescence upon the skin of an insignificant sphere orbiting a minor star. From whence then comes this talk of nations and empires while slavery is the norm and not the exception? I suggest that they take their origin in this need to formulate and find order in what exists only for itself—a universe of facts and relations with no underlying teleology. There is no directionality in the universe—simply a little more matter here or a little more energy to be expended there. This means from an economic point of view that these balances can shift if sufficient force is applied. I take that as the first axiom of my system and policy. For instance it might be possible for the dull consciousness of the masses to be corralled and led to the most absurd conclusions by a systematic effort exerted towards misinforming them in a convincing manner so as to obtain high political office.

The formula is a simple one: Information + artificially induced credibility = power over others. These techniques are already being practiced by others. Take America for instance, that nation of manifold illusions, I pose to you a hypothetical case where a superficially appealing ignoramus is to obtain the office of the Presidency. Could he not thereafter be used by a cabal of intelligent investors to advance their own ends? Or if you wish another hypothetical could not those same investors obtain a religious monopoly by simply purchasing the primary locus of religious authority? What do you suppose Italy would accept for the former Papal States? A man who could thus possess Rome could by means of careful and selective attention to those in the hierarchy alter the balance of consciences among the faithful. There is no absurdity so egregious that Catholics will not believe it if it is rendered with sufficient authority from Rome. Why has this investment opportunity been so long overlooked?

I tell you I learned enough from the late lamented Cardinal Tosca to open my eyes to the value of marshaling religion and government into a single unit and then acquiring both on the open market existing between nations. The minds of the masses are infinitely malleable if properly approached.

Imagine for instance if the universally unpopular prohibition against adultery could be exchanged by granting an indulgence to be granted to every act of fornication. Think of the increase in the numbers of the human race if the full measure of human fertility could be exercised at will—no shortage of cannon fodder for wars—no lack of slaves to be paid a pitiful wage guaranteeing mere subsistence—and with no ridiculous prattle about human dignity.

Since it is pointless to try and extirpate religions why not simply purchase them lock, stock, and barrel by controlling their administrative apparatus? You may ask what has continued to make Catholicism so successful, particularly after the period of the Protestant Reformation in the 16th century, after which other varieties of Christian practice became available inherently less demanding to the believer. Why continue to fast and to abstain and to filter one's direct and personalized experience of God through a cumbersome organization presided over by a celibate superstructure? Why when a single act of honestly professed belief could ensure salvation would anyone choose to retain belief in a tradition that left one perpetually uncertain of meriting salvation and either being rewarded beyond one's wildest dreams or plunged into unending torments with no hope of reform or amelioration? Yet this is the product that Catholicism as successfully managed to use to keep even kings in terror so that in their final hours they evict their mistress from their bed and send for a priest before commissioning an endless string of masses to be said to ransom them from Purgatory.

Surely the wise investor can foresee that a new business opportunity is presented now that a facile atheism has supplied any number of non-believers prepared to run the risk of leaving the Catholic Church and who find the alternatives to be either absurd or unpalatable. As the churches empty the real estate that they occupy can be purchased and turned to other uses. Once people become willing to accept that life has no inherent meaning they will become easily reconciled to enjoying the pleasures of youth without the hindrance of the scruples of those who are beyond enjoying those pleasures themselves. Shortening the pain and disgust that come with advancing age by willingly relinquishing a life that is as burdensome to witness as it is to tolerate will also become natural. This practical approach to life will give people what they want for as long as they want it while gradually weaning people from the breast of eternal satisfaction by providing certitude that at least they need no longer fear eternal punishment for simply being human.

I rather think of myself as a benefactor to mankind in this regard. If called to a deathbed I would simply inform the sufferer that his miniscule life made little difference for good or for ill to the majority of the human race, that all memory of him will soon evaporate like morning dew, and that his goods and wealth will swiftly be transmuted to other uses by his heirs. He will neither witness the gradual acceptance that turns initial grief to eventual rejoicing, nor feel the loss of what was once his alone. The power of even emperors is soon forgotten and even dynasties pass away. If religions pass away, the same is true of kingdoms and their disputed territories.

This same logic applies to nation-states, even those that make a great noise about human freedom. Promises and plunder are compatible and can be combined side-by-side into a single administration. One need only find a President willing to sell-out the nation to the highest bidders, foreign or domestic, while keeping up the pretence of populism, flattering the masses that a new Golden age is at hand. Debt rules the affairs of nations as well as the affairs of individuals; the great task is to be the general creditor of mankind and then to foreclose on that debt. God alone has possessed that power until now; die in God's displeasure and be condemned to hell. Offend an all-powerful ruler and be sent to a prison camp.

It is not necessary to imprison everyone of course; after all some work must still be done to be gathered in by the chosen ones who will profit from the system and therefore have no desire to overthrow it. It is sufficient to maintain control that the citizen never know for certain what law he may inadvertently have violated. Fear is the great motivator of mankind. I for one would be more merciful than the deity and let the masses work off the debt they owe for existing in servility while throwing them a bone now and again of hope for an illusory escape for good behavior.

The great prior owners of mankind have hitherto needed to make some small provision for the superfluous mouths that needed to be housed and fed. Advanced mechanization will eliminate that necessity. Private capital will make the subjugation of the desperate masses both practicable and inexpensive. The easiest course is to provide them with the means for their own self-destruction by various intoxicating substances, a measure devised by the English towards the Chinese in the Opium Wars of 1839-1842. Until this intriguing possibility arises history will have to play out its little games of wars and revolutions, both of which are blessed by both nations and by religions.

England has had the good sense to combine the two sources of power and to vest control over both in a single sovereign, while the Catholics attempt to maintain a single empire over the consciences of mankind by a nominally celibate man in Rome. I think I could manage things better and would be happy to have your advice and counsel when the opportunity arises. Until then I play the game as we all must. History must continue until the engineering of all mankind becomes technologically feasible. It is as always a question of bringing the right people together while keeping the masses in the dark until it is too late.

This process may be easier than you suppose. There is no man so stupid or vacuous that he will not be adored if he tells the people what they wish to hear. Ignorance always desires an echo. You may not be aware that I have been in attendance at the great peace conference at The Hague. It opened on May 18, 1899, the Czar's birthday, which was appropriate since he called for it, no doubt as a gesture of Slavic goodwill. The Russians as you know are quite bottled-up in Asia. A general European war would be quite fatal to them, so naturally they desire that the western nations will agree to arbitration before an international tribunal rather than being forced to defend a thousand mile front in case of a war. It would take months merely to mobilize the Russian troops. The next war will go to the most expeditious army. Logistics and speed of deployment are essential. Of course wars are nasty and costly affairs. Everything has to be rebuilt afterwards at great cost to the victor. Then there is the matter of converting ex-soldiers to laborers in time of peace.

You see why I thought I would attend the conference. It will be amusing to be among so many pacifist and idealistic fools and to hear them prattling away about the brotherhood of man. I thought of opening a booth and passing out free copies of The World as Will and Idea, but thought better of it. There is no way to stamp out nationalist sympathies that stir at the first bugle-call. The mothers weep while the fathers regret that their days of adventure are behind them and the young men of course die. This leaves many untilled wombs at home. It is alas the story of mankind and yet we do love it so.

Fortunately there are profits to be made in arms sales. Nothing so stimulates the preparations of war than the desire to secure a permanent peace. The longer a general bloodletting is postponed the more inevitable it becomes. The best way to prosper under the prevailing condition of world politics is to talk much of peace while investing in the producers of armaments. It is essential to maintain an image of popular concern in order to keep the torches and pitchforks of the peasants at bay while reinforcing the walls of the castle against the inevitable backlash in case they realize in their dull but instinctive way that they have been betrayed into our hands.

It is above all else essential to control the news apparatus that shapes public opinion and to enlist popular figures in support of our interests. As for the secret societies and communist brotherhoods, their tactics betray their interests because they frighten the populace. We must learn from their failures and when we must be brutal we must leave the impression that we are merely sustaining law and order. Never underestimate the value of having a team of barristers on hand; they are worth every penny that they cost. Nothing is as valuable to us as a well-publicized lawsuit that makes it appear that it is waged by fanatics against sound business sense. Even so small a matter as wage increases should be portrayed as an impediment to trade and a stimulus to eventual unemployment. The peasants do love their jobs and we can work them to death before they will risk losing them. Above all else we must make work appear noble, particularly when it comes closest to being so automatic and boring that even a horse would shake its head if we employed it to accomplish the same task.

Please take these recommendations to heart. There is always something of the idealist in scientists and this concerns me. The only truths that matter are those that will turn a profit and towards that end falsehood if popularly believed is even more useful. Do not be led astray by a vain search for verifiable data; the task is to create the data and then use it to support a chosen strategy. When you are herding sheep it is important that the sheepdog is sufficiently frightening that its authority will not be questioned. We must be willing to learn from those other great herders of mankind, the priests. These men have kept the consciences of believers in thrall for nearly two-thousand years by offering heaven and threatening their parishioners with hell. By pretending to possess hidden knowledge they are able to adapt a position in any given case between these two poles of absolute pleasure and unendurable pain without fulfilling the one or inflicting the other.

Now and again of course they forget themselves and lose control by taking their message too seriously. When that happens they wage a crusade or start burning scholars or witches at the stake and it leaves a nasty taste in the populace so that when some measure sanity returns the churchmen will retract their claws for awhile. But it is far better to stick to the tried and true methods that I have just mentioned. We must learn from them the art of sustaining a careful balance between hope and terror. I will not require from you any more stratagems for overt violence, since our one little venture in that direction was clumsy and ill-timed and I am willing to confess that I learned from it. There have been rumors that Sherlock Holmes, the private inquiry agent, may have played a role in that singular defeat. I was not pleased to hear this and I must say that being on the spot you might easily have done better to have prevented his interference. But I realize that you do not have the physical resources that were once at your disposal. I hardly expected you to engage personally in eliminating him and for that reason I have been willing to overlook a failure… once.

I don't at the present time require any further services

from you, but I hesitate to sever all ties because one never knows what the future will bring and you do have an excellent mental apparatus I am told. Science is always stumbling upon new sources of power and profit and men like me will always find ways to put theories into practice where profits beckon. Let me know any thoughts that you have on these matters should anything interesting come up, Professor. That is all for now.

Remember that I regard you as my obedient servant,

Baron Alphonse Maupertuis

June 28, 1899
En Route to the Netherlands

Receipt of the above included letter put wind in our sails. I began to realize the very real and present danger posed by entrusting large capital to the hands of a few unscrupulous men with utter disregard for the general condition of mankind. A compact of sorts appeared to have been concluded that would align the laws and the governing structures of entire nations to serve the private interests of the ultra-wealthy. At least the dynasties of feudal times maintained some belief in a watchful deity that would ultimately judge their actions and reward them accordingly. This was less likely now as the decay of Christianity proceeded apace. The formalized structures within the Church betrayed in many respects a process creating a monopoly of power and control over the masses of human beings whose only function was to hear and to obey or pay the consequences. The scriptural grounding for these distinctions that had divided Christianity appeared to be based upon a selective reading and interpretation of scripture the tendentious nature of which was everyday more evident.

Meanwhile these same governing structures appeared to manifest certain common organizational diseases embodied in the very administrative practices that they traditionally employed. Private interests and personal pathologies were everywhere evident in private fiefdoms allowing for undue influence to be employed in Church affairs while showing all the effects of interpersonal struggles for power and prestige. Even the language

484

of theology was frozen into categories derived from the philosophy of another era. The customary metaphors employed were mired in the very history that had traditionally employed them so that the terminology was inadequate to meet the needs of the present hour let alone to guide the geopolitical realities of the day. This left only the nation-state to govern the world where the Catholic faith taught that the Second Person of the Holy Trinity would someday return to usher in the Kingdom of God.

I write this aboard the boat taking us again away from England. I trust that we may meet again with Czar Nicholas if he is still present at the conference. If he is not, then we shall meet with whoever he has entrusted to speak for him. The events of the new century will no doubt affect so many diverse interests that no one geographical locus or political system will be able to determine the course of world events. Floating about between the various capitals seeking clarity of intent in various nationalist aspirations will be a vain pursuit and most critical communications will be unavailable to us from the moment that Mycroft steps down from his exalted post. We are reaching the point where world events will escape any singular point of analysis. Only the sense of our shared humanity will be able to set the parameters of future conduct so as to provide for the needs of all people and secure a lasting peace.

June 29, 1899
Hotel d'Anglais, The Hague

Our boat brought us into port and for the first time both Watson and I appeared in disguise; nothing elaborate of course, merely a bit of facial hair. It has long been my belief that the most effective disguise is the one that causes one to disappear unnoticed into a crowd. The primary goal must be to approximate the average rather than to accurately represent any particular character. It is surprising how many people of great depth and virtue may live an entire life and never be noticed, while various fools and cads draw great attention to themselves with the resulting influence and acclaim of the servile populace behind them. It is fortunate that the coming of age rather than bringing notice tends to render us invisible to the extent that we lose the beauty that is meant to draw attention and thereby ensure the survival of the species. All of which is a roundabout way of saying that two more middle-aged gentlemen on a boat-train are quite inconsequential. It is in this guise that we will attend the conference tomorrow. We will enter the hall when matters are already well underway. Our papers are all in order and once we are past the door with its security personnel we shall find a place in some obscure corner and listen to the speeches. If the groups adjourn to small meetings we may filter about as best we can. I think that is an adequate summation of our strategy. We are off now to dinner. The Dutch know well how to cook and I have been longing for some fine Gouda, some rye bread, and a hearty Schwartz-beer.

July 1, 1899
After a Day at the Conference

I am writing this in the evening after a most tiring day. It is remarkable how much verbiage can obscure any real content. Indeed it is only now that I realize that the question of disarmament, the announced purpose of the conference, was never directly addressed by any of the speakers. Instead the direction appears to be to better define the permissible limits of potential belligerents such as the treatment to be afforded to prisoners of war, innovations that are bound to be viewed with outrage or distain by those who consider that war should forbid nothing. But then the world has never faced such new techniques of slaughter as the possible bombing of cities from the air. Such weapons are by their very nature indiscriminate in their choice of targets and as such should of course be forbidden among all nations with the pretence of civilization. The entire atmosphere of the conference strikes me as unreal. The posturing and preening, the assumption of earnestness combined with a refusal to undertake even the slightest compromise before being assured that little inroads will actually be made on each nation's coveted sovereignty.

What are nations after all? Why does any free man or woman bow to the inroads of various groups of men who have managed to use the inefficient and yet intricate means by which they assume power over the lives and fortunes of citizens of the commonwealth of mankind? Would the world not do better to jettison all laws and governance and try whether Thomas Hobbes was correct in assuming that in a state of nature our lives would truly be nasty, brutish, and short? The various indigenous peoples of the world, those living in small groups, seem to be able to create certain organic patterns of leadership where everyone is heard and compromise ensures the survival of the tribe.

A quick assessment of the lives of working men will reveal that the lives of the great mass of humankind are already nasty, brutish, and short. Would even tribal warfare, confined by necessity to the comparatively small harm that can be wrought by sword and spear, compare to the prospect of industrialized weapons produced by nations that can summon the great economic power that they possess to turn factories into the dark smithies of death by forging bombs and cannons for mass-produced slaughter?

I would say as much if I were allowed to speak here, but our role is not official and our own safety depends upon not revealing our presence. Baron Maupertuis may well have lost our trail in the course of our various perambulations about the globe. His revenge will only be stimulated if we should emerge from hiding. I think that both Watson and I would prefer to provoke an actual confrontation if by doing so we might regain our freedom to walk the streets of day and night without the necessity of looking over our shoulders, but we must consider Mycroft's position. He is less easy to conceal. To add insult to injury the very man that I so dread was allowed to address the conference today. I was able to receive a transcription of the speech by feigning to be somewhat deaf and applying to the equivalent of a master of ceremonies. I paste the transcript here into my journal.

Speech of the Honorable and August Baron Maupertuis

Distinguished delegates...

I appear before you today not as a man of entrusted office still less as one entrusted by God with the right to rule in his name. I am only a man of business and of the noble profession of banking. To men such as my humble self is entrusted the blood supply of money that if stopped in its flow must have the same effect as does a stroke or apoplexy producing similar signs of paralysis in the world economy as in an individual. Money is the sole recognized medium of exchange in a world based upon mistrust and fear between nations. But my dear sirs, what is to count as money between nations?

Surely you are aware that each nation has its own domestic requirements to expand or to contract credit, to raise sufficient funds through taxation to ensure that its government shall function, and to promote the general welfare of its citizens by stimulating trade and manufacturing. In this realm each nation is free to act the part of the profligate and the spendthrift and if its tendrils have woven their way into the fabric of other nations through fraud, extortion, or ill-considered international loans then the fall of one economy may by contagion be the ruin of all. How then shall the great nations of the world devise means to discipline malefactors without a readiness of arms to do so? Take away the salutary medium of armed conflict and sloth and lethargy shall rule the day. I do not speak here as an advocate of war, but as a realist who understands that only the ever-present threat of war can deter its actual eruption among us and the misfortune attendant upon that event.

I do not say that you have gathered here in vain by seeking peace through disarmament, nor do I wish to impugn the high and exalted motives of the Czar of Russia whose foresight has gathered us here at this critical hour in the world's development, but gentlemen we must not presume that all men share his virtues and laudable intentions! My many years of service to my stockholders and depositors alike have shown me that discretion is the better part of valor and what can be less discrete than to adopt a general policy of disarmament in a dangerous world? Only a balance of fear will contain aggression and to that end I submit that any nation that will not bear its fair share in the common burden should be marked by you as an outcast!

Show me a peacemaker and I will show you one who

desires to shift the burdens of national defense to others. What is such a nation but one that has grown decadent, effeminate, and one that has lost the great will to survive and to thrive that are the glory of our species? It is our honor as men to bear the burdens of conquest so that the weak, the crippled, the feeble-minded, and yes even the lazy and unprofitable members of society shall not be neglected. Money is the very means whereby generous impulses can become manifest among us. Who dares to speak against money by libeling it by such terms as serving mammon or dealing in filthy lucre? If so condemn me for the making of money has been my vocation and my sacred calling before God!

Where would the nations be if there was no centralized and organized system of exchange to sustain them, no capital reserves to energize industry and spur invention, no means of filtering out the noxious products of folly and inefficiency? Statesmen that most of you are, could you hope to survive without the financiers whose triumphs you may later claim as your own before the scrutiny of the voters who have placed you where you are? Is it to leadership alone that you owe your success? If you return to your seats of government with only the assurance that each of you has agreed to be weaker and less able to go to battle if need be, how will you be received? Take the path of peace and excellence shall falter, take the path of peace and glorious ambitions shall be replaced by degeneration and decay and the world will become one great hospital to cater to invalids and imbeciles. We must purge the herd occasionally by salutary wars so that the mass of the able and industrious may thrive.

Read the Old Testament and you will see how even the great God Jehovah favors war or else the tale of Jericho is a lie. Look to the great Iliad by Homer and you will hear celebrated the glories of war. Would you invite slavery? Do you wish to place your citizens in chains? Disarm and you shall ensure servitude to that one nation among you that is still willing to sacrifice so that it shall be reckoned supreme in the councils of nations and take its place at the head of the table rather than to grovel at its foot.

I tell you gentlemen that even gathered as you are in the cause of peace you would be better advised to better discern the common requirements of war so that when you take arms to defend your just claims you may fight openly and not as cowards. It is not arms you must abjure but savagery. Turn your thoughts towards these smaller but achievable goals and you will have better served your people at home while putting each other on notice that you are not to be trifled with and that should due cause arise you will not hesitate to rise up in righteous anger to defend what is your by right and reason even if it be to death!

At that the entire hall burst into spontaneous cheers. It was as though a great burden had been lifted from their shoulders. Here was an honest man at last, one proud of his fortune, one worthy to stand tall in the council of nations, one able to slice away the fat at home, and to act as a model to the less prosperous nations that now realized why they owed subservience to those nations stronger than they were. War appeared again in all its splendor and they recalled, these fattened and powdered men, and how they themselves once dreamt in youth heroic dreams of conquest and of glory.

I must tell Mycroft that he can little imagine the positive response of the various delegates and deputies to this speech. It had all the cunning of the serpent in the garden and in its course no one seemed to remark that any mass investment in arms would make Baron Maupertuis and the other arms dealers and manufacturers richer year by year, while the anxieties of nations would only increase as the scale of possible ruin was multiplied beyond all calculation.

July 7, 1899
The Hague Conference

The speech of Baron Maupertuis proved to be a turning point. Talk of disarmament was replaced by various rules for the conduct of war. These rules are in their way excellent and should have been long in place but alas it is war itself that must be left behind as a legacy of our animal origins in jungle and in swamp. Surely we are above this now or else let us reduce every great painting, sculpture, and all music and literature to dust.

So far Watson and I have eluded detection and I hesitate to try our luck much farther. For this reason I have booked passage home but not directly; instead Watson and I will proceed southwards to Paris. It is there that I hope to visit the Russian embassy when the conference has been concluded in order to ascertain Russian intentions and only then to return to London and report fully our impressions and conclusions to Mycroft. After that we shall need to arrive at a plan of sorts, pray God one that will not leave us the sole option of remaining constantly on guard and alert for attempts on our lives.

My years as a detective has taught me much about the innately criminal mind, one that savors the suffering of others with the same gusto as a wine connoisseur distinguishes between different vintages. It is no surprise that such persons often find their way to high office since political power allows them to graduate from local evils to embrace harms that will affect the lives of thousands. Often these men carry about with them some absurd pet idea that they wish to see in operation. They are no longer confined to merely sensual disturbances, but turn instead to various plans of reform that can uproot the security of an entire country and even plunge it into war. The astonishing thing is that they often manage to seduce entire sectors of the populace who see in such men qualities of leadership rather than of megalomania. History bears witness to this type some of whom even begin with a modicum of insight and virtue and only end, after a gradual process of degeneration, into a state of delusion, folly, and ruin; but by then their legacy is often smoldering ruins and famine.

July 18, 1899
En Route to Paris

Our time at The Hague peace conference was limited by our discretion. There was little more to learn after the first week there and we did not choose to remain and to draw too much attention to ourselves. In order to ensure our safety we took the expedient of changing our hotel daily while in Holland as an added precaution and traveled second-class to Brussels before switching to first-class accommodations in an express train from there to Paris. I fancied from time to time that we were followed by a little man in a black cloak but a note delivered to me aboard the train told me that he had been sent over by Scotland Yard at Mycroft's request to keep us in view whenever we left the security of our hotel.

After switching trains at Brussels we went to the dining car and have just finished a late luncheon there. I hope to rest during the afternoon. I feel only too keenly the stress of recent days and my own disappointment at the turn that the conference took. It appears now that the coming century will witness a series of crises, any one of which may result in a general European war. There is no hope then but to follow the analysis of Professor Moriarty and to adjust the tension between various blocks of nations so as to produce a stalemate of sorts. The problem of course is that this approach merely makes any ultimate breakdown in the stalemate both universal and catastrophic in scope. It would seem that the collective conscience of civilized man could readily devise a more sensible solution that would benefit all parties. One need only think of the vast expenditures in arms, the potential disruption in world trade with its attendant losses, let alone the priceless impending losses of the young lives involved in a war between the great powers to marshal sufficient evidence and incentives for a policy of peace.

How then is one to explain this luxury of competing national vanities? Why keep the world at such a heightened level of risk? Surely all other business should be set aside until this collective dilemma is faced. Each nation is a de facto hostage of the nations that are least trusted. It would seem then that this tension should be dissipated by reaching agreements so that where trust is absent actual exchange and resolution should prevail. Isn't it precisely this settlement process that resolves even the most incandescent of civil legal disputes? Why not apply similar resolution techniques in the case of international disagreements? Our steam engines have escape valves to prevent explosions, so where is the equivalent to bleed off rancor and to dampen tempers when diplomacy fails? Or is diplomacy really nothing more than the cold and calculated exchange of threats and counter-threats?

Force and the proximity of its deployment trump all rational arguments and spiritual concerns even among nominally Christian nations; how much more must these arguments fail then where religions differ and cultures are opposed! As an example the Japanese hold their emperor to be far more than a head of state; he is a god or at least the progeny of the sun goddess. As such the emperor is the source of all ethical imperatives and the Japanese have devised an elaborate system to preserve their sense of honor. Can we conclude alliances with them on the same basis as we would proceed with a European nation? Yet even that possibility has been considered according to Mycroft. As our national reach has been extended we have come into intimate proximity with nations that formerly were of little consequence to our national security. It has reached the point where Britons believe that all of the world must pour its riches into our coffers. From what source comes this sense of universal entitlement in a nation? Are we Englishmen more virtuous, more politically able, we who have yet to sensibly resolve the problems posed by nearby Ireland?

During all of the time that Watson and I spent in America I felt the sense of emulation of the Americans for the British ideal of empire. Does that nation of farmers intend to supplant us once their navy equals ours? And what may be said of the plans of the Germans? Bismarck did the diffused principalities and states that shared a common language no favor by fusing them under Prussian rule. Italy has followed the same policy when it deprived the Popes of their temporal possessions by seizing the Papal States and then united the fractious and opposing regions of the peninsula into a single nation with a common sovereign. Among many nations peace at home is only attained by focusing on enemies abroad. Is this the purpose of war to bleed off our inherent and inescapable animosities? Do we enjoy killing for its own sake? Do we escape a sense of our own mortality by visiting life's ultimate divestment upon others? Is this merely a larger version of Isadora Persano's passion for dueling? If so then all comparison of costs and benefits to be attained is pointless: the human race makes war because we love it. War is merely a central modality of life like eating and sleeping and as such it will always be with us.

Word has just come to us that the peace conference has finally reached its termination. The documents that will embody the agreed upon terms will be circulated widely and it only makes sense to allow Mycroft to reach his own conclusions before receiving my summary report and tentative conclusions. I am happy to be installed here in the city of light and to set aside here my dark meditations of recent days. We are quite comfortably installed in a four-star hotel not far from the British Embassy. I intend soon to report our whereabouts here once we are settled in since Mycroft will be anxious about us. A coded dispatch will assure him that all is well. I will also give a partial assessment there of our impressions regarding the conference, which I thought likely to stay in session for another month. Its general direction was taken early and what remains will likely be confined to details. In any case we are well out of it.

I intend to give both Watson and myself some well-deserved leisure here. We will tour the new additions not the least of which is the great church called *Sacre Coeur* that now towers over Montmartre. Paris has the advantage that when one is there every element of culture, refinement and grace is simultaneously present. This then is precisely the place where Watson and I can burrow in and pursue by other means whatever effect we can produce on the critical events that lie ahead as we enter a new century.

It is amazing how the French have cycled through the various options in the forms of governance since the revolution of 1789. Compared to them we British are rather stodgy. We seem to have evolved in our class system a sort of national consent. Everyone knows just which grade of humanity he is entitled to look down upon by virtue of the class to which he himself belongs. Beyond an occasional fortunate marriage, or perhaps by writing some noteworthy novels like Mr. H. G. Wells, generation after generation keeps its relative position.

One of the reasons that I chose my particular vocation as a consulting detective was that I would be *sui generis* if possible. It is not that I scorn competition for advancement but rather that if the truth be told intermittent periods of sloth are my prevailing vice. I used to be quite content in my younger years to lie about in a dressing gown while playing various odd pieces or parts of pieces on my violin. It used to quite disgust Watson who was then all spit and polish and ready for reveille. It used to amuse me to scandalize him, poor fellow. All of that cocaine twaddle that he has written about was largely an exaggeration. My use of the drug was merely an occasional effort to wake myself up and one that I swiftly outgrew as my practice increased and more interesting problems came my way.

During my early years I largely subsisted on occasional remittances from Sherringford who had no desire that his wastrel brother should disgrace the family name by ceasing to live like a gentleman. I could have gone home of course to Sigerside and assumed some inconsequent tasks upon the estate, but I had no desire to walk about the bogs and heather flushing coveys of quail and scaring poachers away. It is a great pity that I cannot get those ill-used years back. I subsisted then largely on self-pity as so many young people do. I had imagined great and enduring exploits then where I would play a singular and heroic role; strangely enough my imagination in those far-off days had concocted something very like the business that I am now occupied with as I attempt to play some signal role in the destiny of nations. Imagine my surprise if I had been told then what a sordid business it all is! Now I hunger for that most unattainable of luxuries, a private life. Watson once thought to make me famous, whereas I cannot imagine a more gracious destiny than to be forgotten and to merge unmourned into the line of the silent, humble procession of the nameless dead.

August 2, 1899
Paris

Since the signal benefactor of my early days after our father's death was my brother, Sherringford, as mentioned in my last entry I am in duty bound to record here my impressions of his current posture toward the changing economy of England. He is rather confined now to his home in

Yorkshire and has given up most of his former occupations. The estate is doing well though and remittances continue to Mycroft and to me. I must visit him soon. It will be a great loss to him when the present queen passes because Sherringford in many ways is the ideal representative of the old order in England under Queen Victoria. Here in the ever more modern city of Paris, this cauldron of ideas, I can see that the new century will be dominated by machines and much of grace and beauty will be lost in consequence of that trend. Even the luxury of a proper prose sentence as in the rather self-indulgent novels of Henry James will undoubtedly be lost. The new authors will be expected to get to the point quickly rather than to explore various nuances of meaning in leisurely prose. Men like Carlyle, Newman, Ruskin, and Pater will be supplanted by a staccato firing squad of men targeting the simplest declarative sentences with neither nuance nor suggestiveness.

In music there is already a movement in Schoenberg's compositions towards atonality and I must admit that much of the drama of Wagner lies in his lack of melodic elements. I am not pleased by this trend. In musical composition even the excess and saturation of Wagner is preferable to various experiments that seek harmony in discord. Melody is not to be scorned merely to give a sense of creative improvisation. I feel that the great axis of the world is shifting and that as a result all things are to that degree out of balance. Various sculptors already indicate this same trend towards structures separated from both nature and humanity. There we find simplicity of line and a general continuity and flow that refuses to condescend to actually embody a definite form; it is as though any generality or hint may suffice as a subject while the particular is abjured. Even the eye is expected to leap over all barriers of doubt to reach a hasty conclusion. Can political discourse fail to follow this same trend where virtually anything can be asserted without fear of contradiction or correction by reference to a generally accepted standard of verification and good taste?

Expositions may cause provincials to gawk in wonder at these trends, but I remain unimpressed. I long for the comparative lucidity of the Middle Ages when God at least was secure in his heaven and we knew where to look for Him should we desire to do so. Now we appear to proceed towards the merely human ends of power, speed, comfort, and stimulation of the nerves. Surely these new standards if they are made into ends in themselves will provide no gateway to ultimate meaning and civilization will falter as a result. As a seeker of ultimate answers I naturally lament the increasing elaboration of the problems posed by our own existence with no ready answer in a common faith forthcoming. We are living in an age with satisfaction indefinitely deferred. If we do go to war it will in the last analysis be a mere exercise of will without any overriding object, a pointless demonstration that we and not God can be the end of all of our endeavors.

August 3, 1899
Paris

We spent today at the British Embassy where we were graciously received. We were led through various high-ceilinged rooms to an immense office and then through that to a more comfortable but less imposing sitting-room with a cheerful fire. There we were served a selection of French pastries and cheeses with a stimulating sauterne before any questions were posed to us. When we met with the ambassador he listened patiently to the impressions that I have recorded here at greater length. It struck me that he was meeting with us as a courtesy and that he cared little for anything that we might report. At last he spoke up in turn.

"Her Majesty's government had of course very little in the way of expectations from the conference. The whole idea simply presumed too much. It shows a want of good judgment on the part of the Czar to have ever proposed it. This is not a time to display weakness. The Americans for instance were quite in favor of provoking a war with us over some obscure border dispute between Venezuela and British Guiana. The Americans are fond lately of trotting out some obscure Presidential diatribe that they call 'the Monroe Doctrine' whenever any matter treads too closely on what they regard as their own doorstep."

"We sent a sensible but firm reply to their threatened

action and they prudently elected to fight Spain instead of us. What if we had shown them the white feather, eh? We should have been put to the expense and inconvenience of sending ships to pummel Boston, New York, Baltimore, and Charleston ... a lot of beastly fuss, but we would have had to do it you see to maintain credibility. Too bad that the southern states didn't win their dust-up with that fanatic Lincoln," he added shaking his head. "Ask any New York Irish immigrant if he cared to save the union; Lincoln was a lone idealist and the northern manufacturers and bankers found him convenient to their ends."

He confided in us further, "The whole problem for us is that since the war with Spain the Americans have the bit between their teeth good and proper. They need a bit of a thrashing, but it would be awkward if we were put to the expense of doing it. We have quite enough to do to keep the French and the Germans in line over here. As for Russia, well, what can one say about that beastly place? Everything east of the Danube is barely civilized. Russia isn't even worth the trouble to colonize it. The only use it has for England is to trot it out to the Germans who fear it as posing the threat of a two-front war. The Germans fear encirclement by hostile powers; but a stable alliance is another thing. It would make for peace. This alone is good cause for us to placate the Czar while avoiding anything like a too strict alliance that might embolden them to take the initiative and attack Ottomans. There you have our current international posture in a nutshell, Mr. Holmes, which I need not tell you must be kept in strictest confidence. So you can see for the Czar to talk of disarmament would be as good as surrendering the whole world to the beastly Yankees or even to the Japanese. By the way it is surprising how fast those people are coming along in development, quick as monkeys at picking up a trick. The reports are that they are well on the way to developing a rather neat and proper navy too. These are the keynotes for us to play in the coming years and no mistake about it, if the European powers are not fall behind in the coming struggle for economic supremacy."

I pointed out to him that he had not mentioned the French, at which he chuckled and favored us with this observation, "Oh the Frogs are alright. We maintain a quite cordial attitude lately towards them as they do to us. After all London is more vulnerable to attack than Paris if we were to come to blows. The French fear the Germans though and they depend upon us to help in case a repeat of 1871 was to be launched. Beyond that we have agreed to bury old grievances. I am quite happy to be stationed here. The French know the good things of life. I don't know how I should adjust if I was to be recalled home or sent somewhere else abroad. I would probably take my pension early. The food alone is reason to stay, no suet puddings and crusty pies here. The language is a bit tough, all those extra letters, but thank God most of them speak a nasal but adequate English if they try. The ladies here are willing and there is a bonus in that too, so all in all I have learned to manage quite well. As for what they talk about in their cafes, whether it should be philosophy or revolution; it is no business of mine. Well, gentlemen, many thanks for your report and let us know here if we can be of any use to you while you are in Paris. I have assigned a man at your brother's request to see to your safety and take you about by automobile."

I put a few last questions to him and pretended while he had been speaking to write down a few notes, but the whole thing seemed to me a preposterous charade. There is no neat and clean solution to international affairs in my opinion, but only a sustained dance of death. What is my place in all of this? It is coming on three years now since I became enmeshed in world politics and I am already sick of it. I feel as though it is a case of 1896 all over again, which brought on my former collapse. Worst of all, I knew that what I was hearing from our host today was a balanced assessment of the conditions of only that present hour; things might change at any moment.

I was surprised though at the candor shown to us by the ambassador. He clearly viewed us as persons "in the know;" but his blithe acceptance of the necessity of war bid fair to putting me in one of my dour moods. Shall I spend my last years trying to turn the tide of war if all about me great forces are determined on a contrary course and purpose? Shall I hope to succeed where even the Czar of all the Russian people has failed? I still rankle when I think of the favorable reception accorded at the conference to the words of Baron Maupertuis. I could see that Watson noticed with concern how silent I was when the promised automobile deposited us outside our hotel. I am perturbed by troubled thoughts of the future just when I most anticipated a period of rest and recuperation. I am reminded of the melancholy of our early years together when I put Watson through the wringer as he adjusted to my artistic temper with all its variations. Ah well, I usually manage to pull out of my moods in due course; but Watson will definitely be with me for the duration and that is as always a comfort.

August 7, 1899
Paris

𝕴 had a dream of the coming war last night. I have been much oppressed today with a sense of the futility of attempting a solution to the present trend of events. Perhaps a bloody purging that will involve the slaughter of unimaginable proportions of each nation's population is precisely what will awaken the human race to the realization that our ultimate survival is in our own hands. The lure of a misplaced patriotism will turn our green fields into mass burial mounds for those who serve at the front. Each willing participant must be presumed to covet the opportunity to throw his poor twig upon the fire of national destruction and to watch it catch fire and blaze.

Is the domestic arena of life with its subtle joys and sorrows worth preserving without being sacrificed to these causes that always present themselves as worth dying to preserve? What if our enemies should thoroughly trounce us and march their troops through our streets in victory would our slavery be any worse than what we already owe to the rich among us pinioned as we are to mortgages, liens, taxes, assessments, requisitions, and interest payments while all the while we are hoping that we can manage by some means to reserve enough in a pension fund so that when all of our creditors finish wringing the final drops of sweat and toil out of us we may maintain our poor aged bag of bones in warmth and safety until that blessed day when the commissionaire discovers that we have not collected our mail in several days and are presumably dead?

Is it surprising that the young men rush off to war where

they hope they can defy death for a few glorious moments in a cavalry charge before falling with their noble friends before machine gun fire? At least they will have the comfort of being mourned at home as heroes by their mothers and sisters or perhaps by a sweetheart who will turn pale for a moment at the dreadful news that she will never see her erstwhile lover again? Who after all mourns the man who having outlived his friends finally succumbs to gout or palsy and dies snoring in his chair before a fire? Such men as these are lucky if their domestic servants refrain from slowly poisoning them with arsenic in their tea in order to pilfer their few belongings. Even those men who are fortunate enough to find the love of a good woman must watch as her charms fade and perhaps wake one day to find her even a greater scarecrow than the face looking back at him from the mirror. Will he envy the dead and wish that he had died young in order to escape becoming a stranger even to himself?

Many men come to loathe this aspect of their visage as they gaze into a mirror or feel their diminished powers. How many more feel appalled when they realize that our age-mates form a ghastly parade, a *danse macabre* with the tomb as its only terminus? Better far it would be for a great wind or hurricane to pluck us up *en masse* and send us whirling upwards into the sullen sky or be ripped asunder by its force to fertilize a field so that at least the wildflowers might prosper by our demise. Besides, a swift look about us will reveal that the loins of the young are never idle; our successors already hunger for the ground that we occupy and covet our custody of the earth. Napoleon's troops had scarcely withdrawn like a receding tide before everything was just as before in the lands he had decimated by his advance. Will it not be the same when the great guns have thundered and the shrapnel and grapeshot have festooned the trees with flesh? Is death less to be dreaded than embraced since we evidently long for it more than life? Having once realized that death must come to us in time our only remaining agency is to receive it bravely and to offer our bodies for sale in that charnel marketplace that we call the field of battle. Only then and in those circumstances are we allowed to shake our fists at fate and to perish with a brave sneer upon our lips.

atson has just read my last entry and with grave disapproval of my sentiments. His comments were, "You have been using yourself up again too freely and the usual black reaction has consequently come upon you."

He prescribed a walk in the Luxembourg Gardens where among nursemaids and their young charges I managed to find again the thread of hope that must sustain us if we are to escape the ever present inroads of disillusionment and despair. The separation that exists between statesmen and the people whose lives their policies may plunge into ruin is astonishing. The mass of humankind live as mere children while the world whirls past them like eddies of fallen leaves. It takes an extraordinary degree of submission to fate that is little short of heroic at times to persist in seeing life as joyful. The wonder is that every day does not witness some storming of the Bastille by the indignant hoards of the insulted and injured. Wars are merely an extension of this same attitude when the outrage and frustration of life is directed outward towards some enemy rather than towards the actual source of our domestic oppression.

Compare this willing acquiescence to death present in the young with the attitude of an average elderly gentleman who generally views any interruption of his routine as at the very least an act of impertinence if not as an affront to his dignity. Such men do not obey orders. This is why only young men are sent off to war, because only they will consent to go. For them war is a great adventure, a confirmation of what they wish to believe about themselves: that they are gallant, fearless, noble, and immune from death. Why after all should they doubt that they will return unscathed? They feel the strong run of the blood in their arteries and sense the strength of bone and sinew in their young flesh. What enemy may hope to confront them surrounded as they are with equally gallant and confident comrades? Of course the opposing force feels precisely the same.

Meanwhile, at home old men, who once served in various regiments, still recall that they emerged from the fire and smoke of battle sobered and with a renewed vigor and a deeper sense of the value of all things for having once fought and survived. Women will think of how grand their betrothed looked on the eve of his departure and will reflect that they believed then that their love and prayers would erect an impregnable cordon of security around the man that they loved. And so it goes and history records the outcome in substance, but not detail.

The surest sign of my age is that all of this seems so unreal to me. I am astonished at my own loyalty to the era in which I have spent my life. What wearies me now was once accepted as the best way forward in life. In the past I would doff my hat with the others when Queen Victoria's coach passed by me in the street. Now I ask, "Who is this woman that her offspring should govern without opposition the royal houses of Europe?" Whatever conflict ultimately emerges will be largely a family fracas. Do they speak for the hidden aspirations of their people or merely embody in real life the march of leaden toy soldiers across a counterpane? Perhaps these leaders of the nation should be confined to some asylum where they can issue various orders and decrees to the empty air. Would their people fail to thrive if they merely continued matters as they are and went about their peaceful routines as before?

The ordinary life of the ordinary man and woman contains their aggressions and limits the harms that they can do to each other. One need only cry, "murder," and the surviving women will go screaming out into the night and the gendarmes will be called, while on a battle field deaths occur to the beating of a metronome and draw little interest even from those who will soon share the same fate. Death is reduced to a product on some factory line with the laborers bent over their tasks. Surely death may accomplish its own timely tasks unaided by our ingenuity. To stand back from life is immediately to be struck by these incongruities. For this reason I have tried to maintain some buffer zone of music or of art in the hours that are my own. Even when on a case I knew when to disengage my energies the better to have the force to act at the critical moment. But now when each day is only a reprieve from the destruction of all of Europe where can a source for such repose be found?

have recovered my equanimity, as I usually do given sufficient time and Watson's ministrations. We went up today to Montmartre and stood outside on the marble steps of *Sacre Coeur* looking out over the great city of Paris. All was peace and serenity. We saw children with balloons and later on a procession of nuns. This region of the city was formerly reserved to artists and to the *demi monde*. Now it is made holy and sublime by the great edifice rearing above our heads.

I am partial to the Pre-Raphaelite painters. For all of their lushness and color the spiritual element is also not absent. I am impatient with painters who reduce everything to an ideal. I am a believer in the value of the tragic flaw. What would our lives be without pain or beauty without any trace of sin? I have always treasured that passage of scripture that assures us that where sin abounds there grace super-abounds. Something must always be left over for Christ to accomplish lest we imagine that we are the sole determiners of our own salvation. I would however preserve all innocence from despoliation if I could manage it. Some things once lost may be healed but never returned to their springtime freshness. Watson once wrote of me that I was acquainted with every horror of the century. I would scarcely care to know as much now if I could choose a different course in life. The final years of any man's life should be a time of purging. Who would retain every legacy of sorrow that he has witnessed?

Most crimes after all are sordid affairs. Few criminal acts would be worthy of Shakespeare and it has been these cases alone that once appealed to me, because they revealed something of the tenor and tension of all human life, the great perennials of existence. I always told Watson that the art of detection should be as elegant and refined as a mathematical theorem. The criminals I admired were always unique in their way, always ready to advance their peculiar avocation to new heights.

If Dr. Grimsby Roylott had been content to simply murder by some ordinary means his step-daughter Julia Stoner and her sister Helen with a little cyanide in the soup I should have simply referred the matter to Scotland Yard. It was the hiss of the swamp adder that made the whole thing piquant and unique. What better evidence of fateful nemesis was there than to have the serpent wind itself about the villain in triumph, to be discovered by us when we entered the room after driving it back upon the very man who had nurtured it.

Would Watson's tales in the Strand Magazine have reached the audience that they have without just such subtle artistic touches as these to awaken a proper dense of horror? Take away the sense of divine retribution and these accounts cease to be morality tales and become only mundane overnight entries on a police blotter. Anything that is truly moral invokes both gods and devil; without them the human would be merely the daily casualties of precarious animal life. Perhaps this is what makes death *en mass* so frustrating for me, all meaning vanishes and heroism shares the same fate as cowardice. The killer has no real relation to his victim. There is nothing left to solve; no moral to be deduced. The casualty is merely felled by some anonymous mass of metal, has picked the victim off by chance to kill. No need of any Sherlock Holmes is present or even of mourners or an undertaker. The surrounding fields are one great grave or a ruined city with each victim erased in a common sepulcher.

August 10, 1899
Paris

Today we called at last upon the Russian Embassy on our own initiative the better to share our impressions, while they might do some good before the conference at The Hague is adjourned. We were led through well-appointed white chambers to a quiet office where we waited while our credentials were circulated through various channels. The officious young man who admitted us was soon replaced by an elderly official who with profuse apologies took us from the small and chill room where we had been waiting to a great marble room where we were introduced to the Russian ambassador. His welcome to us indicated that some degree of hope had been placed in our ability to advance the Russian cause.

This should not have surprised me since the Czar himself had condescended to the degree of making a personal appeal in Odessa. I could only hope that this private correspondence would not be given an interpretation should the facts of if its existence come to light that would reflect poorly on Mycroft. By proceeding beyond normal diplomatic channels it might not be too much to say we were all skirting dangerous ground (treason no less). At these high levels the drafts of treaties and even or ordinary correspondence can cause national embarrassment if their existence comes to light. If it appeared that we were engaged in pursuing a course in opposition to what various men in power thought was in the best interests of England (again I emphasize as those interests appear to them) then we would be "for it" or "in the soup" as those who favor the use of slang say. How far am I justified in putting Watson at risk I wonder? While the words of the ambassador are fresh in my mind I will jot them down.

"Please forgive our negligence, Mr. Holmes," he began. "Our reports were that you were in Holland at the conference and we little thought to find you here in Paris. The man who admitted you has been reprimanded."

"Nonsense sir," I replied. "Any fault in the matter was ours by calling on you so unceremoniously. It is good of you to see us on such short notice. I hope that we do not take you from more important duties."

"There is no more important issue than the one at The Hague. Even now we hope for some concessions towards disarmament. We are anxious to hear your impressions, Mr. Holmes."

"Then I fear that I must disappoint you. I have discussed the matter at some length with my friend and colleague, Dr. Watson here, and his impressions correspond with my own."

The elderly gentleman looked somewhat crestfallen at this news but he replied, "Nevertheless we would be happy to hear any conclusions that you may have reached."

"Before I speak I must know just how far what I shall have to say will be disseminated," I said cautiously.

"I can assure you that the only recipient will be the Czar."

"Very well then, I trust that you understand that I am not

acting in an official capacity and that even my brother is only indirectly involved at the Czar's request because I have no desire to place him in danger; I consider this to be merely a private consultation."

"We quite understand; please proceed."

"I must then ask you some questions as well the better to frame my comments."

"I have been instructed to be very frank as to our position."

"Then sir I must tell you that you must not expect that England will conclude an alliance with you. England gives every indication of wishing to play an independent hand. You are perhaps aware that war was contemplated with France as recently as last year and all of Europe is aware of your nation's special affection for France. If we were willing to engage in a naval dispute with a nation only across the channel then why would we offer Russia any guarantee in the Balkans. The Ottoman Turks are in a position to threaten Egypt and the Suez Canal and we have no desire to lose them to the Germans. If England appears to favor you then we will force the Turks to turn to Germany for protection."

"You may assure your brother that we have no intentions to attack the Sultan."

"Are you denying your ambitions in the Black Sea?"

"I don't know what you mean by ambitions sir. Our concerns, you will agree that 'concerns" is a far better word, are that Russian warships shall be allowed free access through the Bosporus to protect Odessa and Baku. We also owe something to the Christian Armenians if any steps are taken against them by the Turks. Beyond these concerns our sole desire is to support the Slavic movements in opposition to Austrian aggression in Serbia and Bosnia. There I have as you say laid our cards on the table."

"I appreciate your candor but you in turn must understand our own reluctance to do anything to provoke a Balkan war. The ongoing state of tension in Morocco is quite enough to destabilize the relations between the great colonial powers; we do not intend to alarm the Italian government by sending a fleet past them to enlarge our presence in the eastern Mediterranean which we would have to do in order to be effective if we concluded an alliance with Russia.”

“We are not seeking an alliance but only various guarantees so that we need not bear the burden alone.”

“And what is that burden, sir?”

“Surely England must appreciate our fears that a German-Austrian alliance would not only menace the Balkans but could result in war along our entire western border. We simply must have aid to contain this potential aggression.”

“Surely the Russian forces are formidable enough to forestall any such extensive moves by the Germans or Austrians,” I commented.

“Alas sir, they are not!” cried the Ambassador.

“Dear me that is not good news. But are you right? After all we must not forget your great victory against Napoleon as celebrated in Tolstoy’s great novel.”

“A different Russia sir and you must not forget the price that we paid. It is not a price that we care to pay again one hundred years later!” the old man said with sorrow. “Surely England could spare some small inconvenience when the stakes are so great.”

I tried to place myself in Mycroft’s position before making a reply. At last I said, “You are forgetting the delicacy of our relations with Germany. Any aid to you would appear to the Germans a confirmation of their own fears of encirclement by a hostile alliance. This will only lead the war contingent to increase the drive for Germany to arm itself against this fancied threat. Then what becomes of the Czar’s invitation to disarm? It will be interpreted as a cunning ruse to put the Germans to sleep while the Czar prepares for war against its natural ally, Austria.”

The room fell silent at my last words. For the first time I began to grasp the full complexity of the puzzle that lay before us. The entire matter is based on fear. Of what use is a nominal common Christianity between the European nations to forestall the use of force at the least provocation? Now more than ever before I saw how the analysis of Professor Moriarty was correct. War was inevitable; the only question was how the pieces would be aligned and what the triggering event would be.

I decided to press whatever grim advantage I possessed by

reminding the ambassador of one last key factor. "Then sir, there is the question of Persia."

"Persia?" he answered as if awakening from sleep.

"England fears that Russia contemplates a southern expansion into Persia by way of a trek through the Pashtun tribes of Afghanistan."

"We have no desires in Persia."

"Ah but you must understand that India is the crown jewel of the British Empire. How are we to understand this building of a railroad across Siberia but as a commitment to strengthening Russian power along its eastern and southern frontiers? This in turn would threaten India."

"I do not believe that your countrymen understand how vulnerable we are to Japanese aggression. Already the Korean Peninsula is virtually a Japanese protectorate. How long can it be before Port Arthur is threatened?"

"Well surely China has more to fear from the Japanese," I replied.

"We have reports that I am not at liberty to disclose that would indicate otherwise. Will England at least use its influence to help us contain Japanese expansion?"

I looked over at Watson for aid at this point and he spoke up.

"It is a matter of logistics sir. If it would be costly to increase our presence in the Mediterranean it would be even more of an expanse to send warships to Hong Kong or Shanghai. As an old soldier sir I can assure you that it always comes down in the end to pounds sterling. It costs money to keep an army in the field supplied and ready."

The old man spoke quietly, "This is why we invited the nations to consider disarming"

"Then how will those in power justify the expenses already undertaken. To disarm is to invite attack. The least change is noticed and the odds are calculated anew," Watson replied.

I was surprised at his ability to say much in a phrase, but then I have often been guilty of underestimating him. His rhetorical trick of pretending ignorance so that my own gifts might shine brighter may have made his stories popular but that simple ruse does not reflect his own occasional intuitive grasp of the truth.

We had been speaking at some length but to little purpose. In any case I was not authorized to come to any agreement with the Russians but only to explain how delicate Mycroft's position was. At last the Ambassador made a final appeal.

"I appreciate all that you have told us, Mr. Holmes. Your reputation is indeed a well-deserved one. I will in turn take a risk and tell you that you must not be under any illusion that the dynasty is securely in place. The Czar has many enemies. Even his own security forces are implicated in various revolutionary movements. His Imperial Highness is like a man balancing atop a stack of books to reach the top shelf and likely to fall. It may be England alone that can help him to keep his balance."

As Watson and I left I was only more convinced that the world is in the grasp of complex forces that elude any solution that adopts some univocal tactic expecting easy and automatic success. Such solutions are magnets to the simple-minded. In actuality for every force there is a series of counter-forces in play that will nullify any proposed action or worse increase the very danger that was designed to be prevented or obviated by that method. How many public figures stand before an admiring crowd of their ill-informed supporters promising them a new world! The reality is that with the adoption of the idea of unequal trade, with interest charged for the use of capital, the profit motive was introduced into world economies many of which were formerly confined to simple bargains where each item to be exchanged was essentially equivalent in value.

Fair trade thrives on seeking a fair balance between an excess in one place and a corresponding but different surplus in other place of roughly equal value. The level of exchange in this scenario is one of equilibrium of power remaining after the exchange has been made. Compare this to economies based upon colonial rule where one nation claims the right to demand unequal trades based ultimately upon the threat posed by force and conquest. The capital flows in this case are not only unequal but superlatively so because they reduce the standard of living in the colonized nation and doom the population to an ever-increasing penury and relative deprivation, while simultaneously unjustly enriching the colonial power that grows fat on its victim's labor and resources. Add to this the effect of unjust credit policies that ensure that the debts incurred by the colonized nation can never be repaid and the full malice of this system of international affairs becomes evident.

I begin to fear that until all of mankind is on its knees in supplication to God that peace will never come. It is as though each of us adds our tiny increment to the sum total of fear and mistrust that keeps the world balancing over an abyss or universal ruin. How long will it be before our human ingenuity discovers the ultimate secrets of nature that govern the primal forces of life and death? Each life-enhancing leap has a corresponding misuse hidden in its pocket. Only a general and universal conversion of the nations of the earth will be adequate to deal with the temptation for each nation to press its advantage and to try the measure of tolerance of its neighbors and by doing so to ensure our own destruction in the resulting wars.

August 11, 1899
Paris

After the meeting with the ambassador it was even more evident to me that the cause of peace is an elusive one as long as any marginal advantage is perceived by those who are in power to take their nation to war. When two additional factors are added the inevitability of conflict only increases. First there is the profit motive from the sale of arms. Second is the conversion of the technical improvements of manufacturing so as to produce weapons of ever greater destructive capacity. Combine these elements with the motive of unbridled greed and the desire for domination of one people by another and the formula of history with all of its varied atrocities is explained and its perpetuation of future evil secured. Absent a mass conversion to the great religious insights of humankind the minority with power will always be able to use the bewildered masses as cannon-fodder while their rulers remain unscathed and alive. Revolution is no answer to this problem because revolution entails the very violence that its advocates condemn and in the ordinary case lead to nothing more than a substitution of regimes with the new one as venal and acquisitive as its predecessor.

What is the answer then but to flee from the wrath to come if one is able somehow to manage this? Most people cannot escape the bloodlettings of history and must share the fate of the vanquished as a witness to choosing the course of pacifism and inadequate defenses; or alternatively they must join the victor and be allocated a small share of the spoils as a reward for their abdication of moral sensibility. The latter must accept their share of guilt for the blood that has been shed proportionate to one's complicity or approval of the result.

These reflections explain the rationale for the withdrawal to the desert of the earliest monks and desert fathers. These gave up any immediate expectation of the second coming of the Son of Man in His glory and placed all their hopes in whatever reward might be theirs after death when each would present his own testimony of fasting, abstinence, and penance. Ours is a voluptuous age however, one that is awash in velvet and plush couches and our succeeding heirs will no doubt be even more concerned with their comfort and luxury usually purchased by the slavery of others.

These considerations of the benefits accruing to, "the good life," will make the sacrificial life of the early Christians appear as folly rather than a sign of supreme wisdom. To lose confidence in what seems so self-evident in its appeal and availability will appear in contrast as ultimate folly. Yet it is precisely this temptation to ease and to freedom from care each day that seems to beckon me. I long to withdraw to some quiet place and to leave all of these impossible questions to answer themselves; but to do so when I have any chance to avert catastrophe is to bear a share of the guilt for what is to come. There in a nutshell is my present dilemma.

oday Watson and I paid a visit to the great palace at Versailles of King Louis XIV who reigned until 1715 and was called "the sun king." As a monument to human vanity this palace is unsurpassed. The luxury embodied within its walls is extended until it manages to defeat its own purposes through sheer excess. I much prefer my humble and smoky rooms in Baker Street to sitting on a gilded throne giving audiences to various lackeys. I was happy to return to Paris by a late train after wandering through the gardens and graveled walks. To shake off the impressions of the day Watson and I walked about in the cramped and smelly district of the left bank of the Seine so beloved by artists and by melancholy poets.

Perhaps it is only the artists and the poets who may truly be said to have lived by exploring life in all of its ramifications as well as those despondent valleys of the spirit that only they know. Their sympathies and perceptions exceed the measure of their own consciousness, while their sensibility aspires to the universal. We saw a great many of these as well as of students of both sexes in berets and of various young women displaying their charms and offering their favors to various middle-aged patrons. These artists of the boudoir no doubt learn to take delight in their own mastery of sensation, but long experience no doubt blunts even the residual pleasure that must be presumed still to exist when imperiled by the need to solicit ever more business to make do when their charms have fled with the years.. The profit motive wherever it appears brings ruin. Perhaps the kept mistress fares better, but she must live in fear of being replaced in due season just as does her peripatetic sister of the streets. Youth in Paris becomes a cyclic commodity and thereby forfeits all of its charm and uniqueness. The end result is boredom all round such sordid transactions, a sad state of affairs.

The only exception is the grand passion where one woman emerges from the throng to bewitch, beckon, and enslave the heart. Even I have known the power exerted by this force as Watson has explained. By doing so he no doubt tickled the ears of his readers and perhaps gave the occasional spinster grounds to suppose that I might be swayed to adopt the common course and to marry someday. That I have not done so has been largely due to lack of leisure for domestic life. My practice has seldom failed to produce clients in abundance and the between times were spent in research or in unrecorded consultations by various befuddled inspectors who would drop by for a whisky and soda and leave me a five pound note for the privilege of receiving a few hints towards the solution to a crime. Add up the years and here I am wondering what course to take during my remaining allotment of life.

I could of course join those elderly gentlemen, a type that one meets again and again on the continent, as they wander from spa to resort to metropolis. They start the year in Monte Carlo or Nice. Spring finds them moving from Avignon to Arles or along the coast to Montpellier. By May they are in Paris or Trieste. They spend the summer in Biarritz or San Sebastian for the fresh sea air and by autumn they are again at some spa in the mountains or settled in for the winter in San Marco or Naples. They travel alone or with some companion of a certain age whose charms have been weathered into a veneer of restraint and respectability. This set samples the comforts and cuisine that ample means afford to those who are fortunate enough to turn a mere competency into moderate wealth. It is an empty life though for one like me who hungers for ultimate answers to the deeper questions of existence.

I might of course take the Byronic course and offer myself up on the altar of some fruitless cause or other. I could see that I was found dead before the obstreperous Turk or like Gordon of Khartoum remain too long wherever Englishmen are not wanted, but even this seems a waste of the forces still at my disposal. All of which is to say that I am bewildered and at odds with myself. The result is a general restlessness that distresses the good doctor who looks to me to say where we shall go next when our Paris sojourn has ended.

My most obvious and immediate duty is to report to Mycroft in detail my impressions of the conference and to discuss our meeting with the Russian ambassador here in Paris. Of course the present situational report is only applicable to the present moment; change any factor and the entire constellation of power must be altered in order to accommodate that change. This requires a system of communications that would be instantaneous as well as one that could keep track of the probable weight to be assigned to each variable. Of course this is impossible at present because stated intentions may contradict or overestimate actual intentions. There is simply no way to find certainty in these matters. Risk of death is also in the nature of the game. For this reason it would be advantageous to have a set of buffers in place to restore balance and find points of compromise when crisis threatens.

Each nation prefers to keep all of its options open even if that increases the likelihood of war; there is the sticking point in all negotiations. To press the issue is always to risk that desperate counter-measures will be taken by one's opponent. Wars might be thought of as merely a long series of reprisals for disappointed hopes. Each side believes that reason and virtue favors its position. Patriotic sentiment then drives the men into the field and the rest is slaughter until mutual exhaustion favors peace. But when the losses become great enough so as to become insupportable anything less than victory becomes unacceptable and thus the war goes on. This means that the only ultimate limit to a major conflict's duration is the willingness of the losing party to use its last resources to continue fighting rather than to save its remaining resources and manpower to serve the function of seed-corn and enable it to recover after peace is finally reached.

In times of war all subsidiary issues tend to fade into insignificance. This accounts for the triumph of savagery over civilization and even over the survival of whatever is most precious at home. The last of all wars according to this logic will leave only a wasteland from which it is impossible for all parties to ever recover.

e shall leave Paris soon. Watson and I have enjoyed our Paris sojourn and are ready to seek respite elsewhere. I discussed the matter with Watson earlier today.

"I am as ever at your disposal of course, Holmes, but I sense that we have more or less run the table and have no immediate point of entry into what is essentially a closed-game where outside counsel is not appreciated," he said after hearing my solicitation of his views on our joint experience.

I agreed, "It certainly appears so to me but then we have to consider that even our intermeddling has not gone completely unnoticed."

"There is that to be considered. Are we now to go into hiding then?"

"Well if we do I can hardly continue my practice when my clients cannot find me," I smiled ruefully.

"You have enough money put away to get by of course," Watson commented.

"Yes, but Watson, I have no desire to hang up my sword and buckler as yet," I insisted.

"And as your faithful Sancho Panza I am to come along reluctantly while you seek out new windmills I suppose," he said with a gracious smile.

"Ah but these windmills are well-armed as you know," I cautioned him.

"They are indeed giants," he admitted. But we have finally stripped evil down to its current manifestations and they are legion. We cannot invite all of the interested parties to Baker Street as of old and work our magic. I fear that we have found our limits at last. It would appear that we stand on neutral ground and are therefore free to pursue our own interests at last."

I considered this point before replying, "Well we can at least lower our gun-sights and pursue smaller game. But even then we must hang out a shingle. No, Watson, it appears that we are about to be put out to pasture and if so the question is shall we continue as of old or shall we each pursue our long deferred interests as though we lived in a better world and selfish leisure was an option. You at least have made a difference by your medical ministrations, while I feel that my *summum bonum* is still before me. I feel the burdens of bachelorhood in a way that I have not felt them before. Where is my legacy to life, Watson? The torch has not been passed. I cannot find that most basic of all human gifts: not to change the world or forswear its ills but to at least allow a new generation to grapple with the old perennial problems. Was it pride after all rather than generosity that I thought I could sum up all things? Look about us. What do you see but unreflective life pursuing its mindless course? Look further and see with what grace other men accept their inevitable limits. See how they fall as gracefully as leaves from the autumn trees having known their summer days and are now willing to let go and die when the winds rise to leave the barren bough behind."

"But your bough is not barren," Watson protested. "You have been and are the greatest detective of your age!"

"Thanks to you old fellow, thanks to you who have made me a legend beyond my deserts; you always knew how best to display the magician so that the audience would not see the hidden wire or the rabbit up my sleeve. Tell me are you current with your tales?"

"Well, there are quite a number of cases that I have yet to write up," he admitted.

Here was my opening, "Then I propose that you do so and add to them the tale of these last years when together we sought to alter the affairs of states and of nations. Return to Cornwall for a time until I need my old Boswell once again."

"And what will you do?" he inquired with a dubious look.

"Oh I will lead the hounds a merry chase. I shall leave England, but you must keep up the pretence that I am still in practice until ... well let us say 1903, when you may tell the readers that I have retired to that mythical Sussex Bee Farm at last. By then I will hopefully have completed my mission."

"Will you share news of your adventure with me?" he asked.

"Of course old fellow, in due time; but for now you must

allow me to absent myself for a time from the felicity of sharing your company until the time is right. I hope to draw the hounds so you must give the impression that we have drifted into separate channels of life."

"But what if Baron Maupertuis catches up with you? I must be there as of old!" he insisted.

I was touched as always by his devotion. "Dear old Watson... But surely you must see that we are like an old music-hall team and far easier to trace together than apart. We must change our coloration a bit for a time the better to blend in to a newer world. All of your readers know of your loyalty to me and for that reason they will imagine that I am still in England. Your sacrifice will enable me to act abroad unobserved. The magician always misdirects the attention of the audience so his sleight-of-hand is not observed. I am afraid that I know no other way to proceed."

He was silent and I could see that he doubted my sincerity, but at last he reached out his hand and took mine in both of his. "I have never refused you anything and I will not do so now, but I shall be at your disposal night or day should you ever require me." To the affirmation of such a noble heart there was no answer to be made, so I made none and we walked together side by side down the *Champs- Elysees* towards the *Arc de Triomphe* in silence. My way forward is as uncertain as the times and as the condition of the human race that only flatters itself that it has reached the height of civilization when perhaps its darkest age lies ahead.

August 31, 1899
Paris

My last entry sounds grim and final upon re-reading; it is as though we were to part immediately and perhaps forever. A friendship such as we have shared is not so easily severed, even when done for the best of reasons, and with complete understanding on both sides. Watson will therefore accompany me until we return to England. He will go on to Baskerville Hall to inform Sir Henry of my present plan regarding the disposition of our affairs regarding Baron Maupertuis.

Meanwhile I will confer with Mycroft before going on to Yorkshire to visit Sherringford.

It is a relief to have at least some sort of plan in place. I only wish that the world was as certain regarding the next steps to take. The number of factors in play is such that even Nostradamus could not foretell the future. Each nation has its own set of aspirations to annex adjacent territory and within each nation racial and linguistic minorities desire their own homeland. This is not so very different from the *causus belli* of the war between the American states. There seems to be no way to prevent the human spirit from desiring that it should be answerable only to those who share the same individual characteristics.

Of course foreign occupation is intolerable when the majority does not share these same features. For instance, the mountainous region of the Balkans is particularly volatile. Bulgaria has its eyes upon Macedonia and Serbia bristles under Austrian rule. There are undoubtedly portions of the earth that should remain in quarantine because of their propensity to create the spark that might ignite the flame that could soon become a general conflagration. It is for precisely this reason that the great powers must act as containment vessels by being unconditionally pledged to sustaining a general peace that benefits all parties.

But alas that is not the case. The great colonial powers use regional conflicts to justify their own "interventions." The entire idea of separate "spheres of interest" tends to legitimate greed and seed aggression. It is like putting cats in a bag and shaking it. I fear that only a common threat to the whole of mankind from some outside source can ever really unite us. One might have thought that our common mortality and the way that various plagues can span vast regions of the earth would provide that threat, but armies are accustomed to carrying pestilence as their companion-in-arms along with famine and waste among the non-combatant population of women and children. It is the latter who suffer most. Women may on occasion urge their men to war, but children do not look kindly upon the loss of the source of their security.

A father is his children's great link to life itself in this cold and incomprehensible world. Children are conditioned to find the world a paradise and their sorrow cannot be easily compassed when it first dawns upon them that this expectation will not be met. Who can say what would happen if even one generation could be spared the knowledge of these past atrocities, if the link of the great tragedy of mankind could be broken? Only sever one link of sorrow and even Original Sin might be muted in its effects. The great bane of history lies in its continuity. The old wounds are never given time to heal. Human solidarity is nowhere to be found. Even religions aspire to a severance from the world, either by the forming of monastic institutions or through individualized prayer and meditation, as though Christianity was a solitary affair between the soul and God rather than in union within the Mystical Body of Christ.

Silence becomes the great refuge for those desiring peace; although music can bridge the gap between persons as nothing else can. The charm of music is that it is devoid of ideas. It touches some common thread in our natures and allows our thoughts to proceed unhindered. In this music is akin to dreams; the spirit is liberated from the mandate of linear cogitation to embrace realms beyond both space and time. Our perceptions are grounded in the concrete and for that reason limited; only intuition can bridge forms so as to create a hint of perfect unity that is not a sum of various parts but is so infused by a common life that all demarcations vanish.

Such a universal perception, if we could apprehend it, would be so total and enveloping that it would be completely non-contradictory and yet too wonderful to be obvious. The reason that no evil can be predicated of God is that pure being is not subject to even an imagined antithesis. This gives the lie to any residual Manichean tendencies in Christianity: God admits no rival. Evil can gain no foothold there but only demonstrate its own essential emptiness. Its effects are less substantial than they are impediments like dust gathering in an unused room. Ah, but apart from metaphysics those impediments may seem very substantial indeed...

September 1, 1899
Paris

Word came to the consulate from Mycroft. The situation in South Africa grows worse each day and the possible war promises to be brutal. How can it not be when the combatants are farmers fighting for their land? I append a transcription of Mycroft's note:

My Dear Sherlock:

War can no longer be avoided. You may suspend all efforts to ensure peace. I doubt that other nations will get involved, but no one can say for sure. I do ask that you return at once so that we may discuss the options we outlined at our last meeting. I may be joining you soon in your gypsy perambulations.

In sorrow,
Mycroft

September 3, 1899
Paris

After receiving his note I took a day over what was definitely what I used to call a three-pipe problem. The world appears to be entering one of those periods when the earth seems to shift on its axis. I found a seat along the Seine near the great gothic cathedral of Notre Dame and attempted to use my old methods in order to shed some light on current events. My first task was to set down clearly a few guiding principles. I will list them here:

1. Power is never a constant; it is always either increasing or decreasing. For this reason history never stands still.

2. As power decays it creates a vacuum that is soon filled by various contending factions that have been poised to supplant the former dominant power or hegemon.

3. To take any established position is to be open to attack; it is far better to sail with the present order until its hour of obsolescence arrives at which point action must often be swift and uncompromising.

4. The probable direction of change is always potentially readable, but to do so the mind must be ready to reject the organic unity of what is generally accepted by the masses. This requires imagination and the ability to visualize a new state of affairs that has yet to come into existence.

5. To conceive the likely parameters of a new order is to discover that one is quite alone.

6. However, power during times of transition flows in the direction determined by insight coupled with determined action.

7. Filling in the gaps later is a matter of accurate timing, of adequate resources skillfully deployed, and care that nothing of importance has been overlooked that can cause a reversal and reconstitution of the old order.

Applying these principles it became clear to me at once that the whole of Europe is engaged in a process of collective suicide. Any generalized war that could emerge would be one where no group of nations has a clear enough advantage to procure a swift and total victory. Instead resources between the contending alliances would be depleted until some outside power would perhaps emerge and intervene to dictate the terms of peace. Any country that could avoid becoming engaged in the coming struggle would emerge unscathed and be in a position to profit from the aftermath. The exhausted contestants would be in no position to resist that latter incursion. Suddenly it dawned upon me that I had stumbled upon a conclusion that was in its way as predictable as the flow of heat through metal or any other physical process. Personalities are always subsidiary to physical conditions; when the conditions are right some group of men are certain to read them. Men are called forth to war by the conditions that prevail and not vice versa.

But if history is in any way predictable, how are we to explain a man like Napoleon who acted as though he was a force of destiny? It would appear that he was making history of any man ever did, but if that is so then why did his genius forsake him at his most critical hour as he tried to take Moscow? The answer is simple; he pressed beyond the borders of the conditions that had hitherto sustained him. His prior victories created their own historical vacuum and Wellington and the remnants of the old order stepped in to fill it. Overreaching brings on retribution. This is the way of the world.

The charm of the Beatitudes lies in the way that they give the lie to human nature; they proclaim that among the blessed will be found those persons that all of our usual conceptions would view as unfortunate. The result is that there is little competition as to who will best manifest the virtues recommended by Jesus. There is always room for another saint in heaven. I thought back then to the story of the Tower of Babel. We are so constituted under the sway of Original Sin that we can, only by the aid of grace, willingly turn aside from whatever seems to increase our power to procure our own delights. As our technical power increases we will construct marvels that will cast the fruits of all prior empires into the shade. The people will flow like a slow but resistless river towards whatever utopia exceeds their own dull imaginations. Various false Messiahs will arise and before they are supplanted they will drag millions into death. God alone knows where it will all end. The general trend though is readable enough; it leads to destruction, but by how many steps?

This year I turned forty-five years old. If my present recovery from consumption holds against any new infection, should the illness be only slumbering, then I may have many years of life still ahead of me. I believe that it is time to surrender what are really little more than parlor games. I blush at the thought of the wonder that Watson perennially elicits by his tales. He has turned my little gifts of sleight-of-hand into miracles of observation and deduction. A new path beckons. Beginning in 1896 and continuing until the present hour I have been routinely consulted by heads of state, but to what end? Can I explain to them the principles that I have just outlined? Shall I become the 20th century's equivalent of John the Baptist urging a new brood of vipers to repent? Am I not in the same position as the man who wished to warn his brothers of what awaited them after death, one who was told by God that if they did not obey Moses and the Prophets then they would not listen even if someone was to rise from the dead? History must go the along the same path that was foretold and in the end there will be wars and rumors of wars and great wonders leading to disaster. Perhaps then God will intervene to save those who may still profess the faith. They will bear testimony to the beatitudes and in them will be the earth's sole comfort and for their sake God may stay the destruction that we have wrought upon the earth.

September 14, 1899
London

We are home again! The efforts of Mycroft have been of no avail. The course of escalation towards war achieved through the machinations of Alfred Milner has finally born fruit. Kruger has been backed into a corner and the British government has received an ultimatum, which Her Majesty's Government will no doubt reject. Open hostilities may break out at any moment. For the first time in years Mycroft has been denied access to the deliberations that are going on between the Prime Minister (acting as Foreign Secretary as well) Lord Salisbury and Joseph Chamberlain the Colonial Secretary and the rest. England fears being put to rout by the farmers from the Orange Free State that we hold in contempt. I fear that the ultimate cost may be more than we expect.

The present expectation is that by taking a firm hand we could gradually annex the Orange Free State. The British already control the Cape Colony and Natal. Colonization of the whole of South Africa would ensure the vote to the present British settlers in the regions that are not yet under British control. Of course with our control of the Suez Canal the alternate route to India is somewhat lessened in importance if not yet superfluous, but where gold and diamonds are concerned the freedom of transportation issue was perhaps always a mere pretence as a reason for war.

England is evidently determined to control most of Africa and the Germans of course feel proportionately threatened. The Kaiser is not a patient man and these actions cannot but raise resentment in Berlin. I feel the temperature of the world rising. A decisive conflict is not inconceivable. How it is that our little island imagines that it can dictate to the great world is beyond me. I have always felt that precise observation and reason must ultimately prevail, but in world affairs there is the incorrigible influence of mere power to be considered. Power of course cannot be strictly defined beyond simply getting one's way in any conflict or negotiation. Dominate or be dominated appears to be the rule in diplomacy, all else is mere ceremony and pretence.

One might assume that voices of peace would come forth from various religious communities, but even there power and domination rear their demonic heads. Young men will be sent peremptorily to their deaths over a war that will primarily favor private interests. I recognize Alfred Milner as the prime fomenter of the coming struggle, although much of this knowledge has been gathered from sources that I dare not mention even here. The memory of Mycroft's past services seem to be wiped out overnight and with his tenure displaced perfect folly prevails. As a last measure Mycroft asked me if I thought that a direct appeal to the Queen might avoid what is coming, but I advised him to refrain. Events finally reach a posture from which they cannot be averted by outside actions and we are outside now, the both of us. A new age is dawning that augurs ill for the coming century. The example of America's successful wars of aggression in the case of Mexico from 1846-1848 and with Spain over the Spanish Colonies in 1898 are too recent to be forgotten. They appear to have shown the advantages to be gained by summary invasion. The great manufacturing nations of the world are busy reducing the remainder of the world to mere sources of raw materials and enforced consumption. Nothing is so anathema to the current international ethos and structure than movements for independence and freedom. This makes even the democracies tyrannical in the final analysis. I marvel most at the Americans who are never more adamant about talking about freedom than when they are denying it to others. But I am a son of England and I thought (more fool I) that our own sense of propriety would always supplant mere pecuniary gain.

Stripped of any suggestion of superior morality our claims to rule, whether in India or in Africa, are the mere assertion of superior force and as such my own loyalty as a man of honor can no longer be compelled by blind patriotism. This forces me to a reassessment that I never thought to make in these years of maturity with their natural desire for repose. I had thought to concentrate my forces upon contemplation of the eternal mysteries. Instead I feel that I must commit myself to causes infused by politics and by commercial interests. I find myself thinking of my intense struggle with Baron Maupertuis and wondering if I might better have followed the advice of the redoubtable Colonel Sebastian Moran when confronting a charging tiger, "Shoot quickly and never turn and run."

I recall asking him once if he was ever tempted to allow a wounded tiger to escape. His answer was a memorable one. "The tiger," said he "Knows only the logic of death. He kills because it is his nature. To wound a tiger is to preempt any other distraction from that inherent logic and therefore one's course is set and one must become a tiger as well. Nothing less than death can bring the affair to its natural termination. Peace can only occur when one party or the other is utterly defeated and for this reason tigers should be avoided at all costs. But if you encounter a tiger in the bush one or the other of you must surely die."

September 21, 1899
London

I met Mycroft again today at the Diogenes Club. Watson has left for Cornwall to see to his affairs there and I am alone once more. I am rather at loose ends for now. If war breaks out in South Africa, which now seems all but certain, resistance on the home-front will become impossible. War or radical political change always arouses some latent impulse within the general body politic, as though some nerve in the spinal column had been stimulated with an electric current. Patriotic zeal then carries all before it; the time for reasoned argument is past. Similarly when a tyrant captures the loyalty of the public mind only some outside force can restore order such as defeat in war or economic collapse. No nation however powerful can hope to prevail against the conscience of the world.

Dictatorships are violent, but are usually of short duration. Those who wish to resemble Caligula of Rome eventually share his fate. This is of little comfort though to the victims whose lives are shortened and whose fortunes are lost until a new equilibrium emerges in world affairs. Most such regimes fall in a palace revolt. How many emperors who set out from Rome never returned to assume their comfortable place on their throne? They died at the hands of the legions that they commanded who installed one of their own as the new Caesar.

Eventually Rome itself fell. No civilization lasts long. The duration of Christianity as both a world religion and as the basis for European identity is no guarantee that it will always remain. Jesus promised to be with us until the end of the age, but He also asked his disciples this haunting question, "When the Son of Man returns will he find faith on earth?"

God, in the Incarnation of Jesus Christ, effectively placed the fate of the world into our hands. The power of the Catholic Church is in its celebration of the victimhood of God at our hands. The Crucifixion and Death of Jesus represent that abdication of divine power. Evil is not defeated with its own weapons. Triumph is not to be obtained by our own efforts. The worship of the Holy Mass sometimes gives the impression that we as sinners implore God's mercy as though that mercy had not already been shown. In reality this equation should be reversed because God has always shown us mercy or we would long since have crumbled into ashes or ceased to exist. The directionality is actually that God implores that we find it in our collective hearts to have mercy on each other and in that way repay the mercy already shown to us by God.

To say that God is love and that he who abides in love abides in God and God in him removes all speculation as to causes and effects. God abjures our categories of time and space. God cannot be found out there somewhere. God's reality and even His being are evident when certain conditions make him PRESENT AMONG US. The name Yahweh has a circular significance, I AM THAT I AM. God's essence is not defined prior to His actions. Instead what is involved is a process of recognition and discernment. WHEN WE FIND LOVE, WE FIND GOD and WHEN WE GIVE LOVE GOD EXISTS WITHIN US. These are truths that the world does not know, but Jesus brings us this comfort even in his rejection and his seeming defeat on Calvary as he told his disciples and that every crucifix proclaims:

BEHOLD, I HAVE OVERCOME THE WORLD.

Book Twenty

Stand with Me
Upon the Terrace

Note from Dr. Watson

I now must tell the faithful readers of this narrative that the alternating accounts of this immense book having circled round to find a common nexus as the new century began ceased with these last entries in the journal that mark the end of the common passage of the twin narratives present in this multi-volume presentation of the events that took place between 1891 and 1899. My own reading of Holmes' Journal on our trip to America came to an end as we crossed the great American continent. Now all that remains is to give an account of that final period of the epic journey that took us both across the western states of America and thereafter home to England by way of Japan.

Having included here the final notations of the journal entrusted to me when Holmes heard that I was working on this extensive and final account of his life, Book 20 will both revive my memories of that memorable visit to America and set the stage for any later sequel, one best prepared by another hand than mine, to cover in detail the thoughts and actions of Sherlock Holmes after the year of his retirement from work as a consulting detective, which occurred in the year 1903.

During the composition of this extensive work I have kept Sherlock Holmes continually aware by correspondence and by occasional brief meetings of my project and he has given me a free hand to share with the world the events that terminated just prior to his retirement. Sherlock Holmes essentially retired from his private practice as a consulting detective in before taking up a more public role in world affairs that has lasted from the year 1903 to the present day. As part of that permission and pursuant to my desire to bring my own narrative to a conclusion (since my health and energies are failing) by laying before the reader all that I possess in memory and documentation, Holmes recently sent me the remainder of his journal. It spanned the years after we set sail for Japan from San Francisco and terminates just before the outbreak of the Boer War that began on October 11, 1899. This final Book 20 will serve as a memorial coda to this immense symphonic work celebrating the life of my dear friend, Sherlock Holmes.

o account of the doings of my friend Sherlock Holmes can ever be complete within a single cover. But I am still, as Holmes claimed that I am an aesthete at heart and given to form and summation. So I will state boldly here that the theme of my narrative has been one of an Odyssey and a homecoming, not merely for Holmes and for me, but for the entire human race. The desire for closure and completion though is frustrated by the times in which we live. As to the future course of this present terrible war, which still rages as I conclude this manuscript, I can only say that all of the many contenders seem to be reaching the limits of their endurance. I do not say their human endurance, because when one is speaking only of nations all sense of a proper humanity is exhausted within the first few months of the beginning of a war. It will take scholars of some distant age to place this war in its proper historical context. Like most wars this one will be seen as a product of the end of an era, in this case the era which began with the idea of the sovereignty of the nation-state which emerged at the Peace of Westphalia of 1649, which put an end to The Thirty Years War. Our present war will be no doubt be seen as the war to end the era of I imperial empires and what shall follow will I hope will be an era of sustained peace among the nations of the world.

So fractious though is the human race that only a global tyranny can impose peace against various internecine squabbles. No one idea seems capable of uniting all of mankind. The alternative of course is a balkanization of the human race into various states and principalities, some so tiny and lacking in power that war, though a constant in human experience, will be confined to local flare-ups that can be quickly extinguished by the greater community of nations that find the prospects of peace to better serve the majority of mankind. Such a global order of peace will yield a better life for all.

National prosperity though always yields way to the desire for permanence and groups coalesce around ethnic groups or other points of shared interests and make the fatal decision to rely upon the accumulation of arms to resist predation by others. Universal poverty of course is no better, for it instigates want and envy and the desire to steal what another possesses. A uniform distribution of goods would seem best to forestall both penury and excess, which alike breed the desire for war. This middle course may be the best hope for peace insofar as the material order is concerned.

But wars are also motivated by the desire to impose meaning structures upon others. The only remedy for this is that truth should never be a mere matter of faith, but of objective proof so that debate and experimentation may replace the blind loyalties and excessive confidence regarding what cannot be proven. Since so much of life lies beyond proof, the very religions that offer mankind transcendence also appear, in the short term at least, to guarantee that perennial conflict will occur among men. How strange it is that men will blow each other into eternity by weapons as the final means to test their respective views of an afterlife! But if mankind cannot escape warfare and if the genius of the human mind will continue to develop more efficient modes of killing, can any hope exist for the survival of the human race?

For this reason I have elected to place my only hope upon God as I understand him. I have vowed to do no harm to those who do not share my beliefs. To do this seems to be the very definition of the type of man heralded by the angels at the Nativity of Jesus that we celebrate every Christmas. The angels at the time of that event proclaimed: *Glory to God in the highest and on earth peace to men of good will.*

Christ's Vicar on Earth, Pope Benedict XV, attempted to show the faltering nations of Europe a way out of this mass suicide. From the very beginning of hostilities the Pope has sought to bring the nations together and to mediate a sensible peace, but he would not be heard by the quarreling factions of a shattered Europe. Thus the madness unleashed by the various empires in their efforts to sustain their own pride and prosperity must now run its course. There seems to be a momentum to history that exceeds human control because the decisions made are various and collective and based upon prior definitions of what is negotiable and what is not.

Such is the pride of man in his own collective undoing. We are all hostages to the very weapons that were meant to purchase security. Alas, the only true security is to submit to the peace that comes by submission of our wills, both individual and collective, to the will of God. That will is that men should live at peace with one another. Sherlock Holmes once said that the scandal of the cross is the very means of its efficacy and reality. If the origin of human consciousness lies in the desire to become like God and to dictate out of recalcitrant reality how things should proceed, then the action of God in making Himself subject to human contingency, helpless before Pontius Pilate, is the very reversal of that Original Sin. If the first, Adam in a sense chooses a world that opposes God simply so that in triumphing against Him he can prove himself a god; while in the second Adam, God Himself becomes man so that He can show wherein true human nature has always resided. Contingent beings are meant to glorify God. Reality, which seems so antithetic to our desires, may be revealed as a world in prior bondage to the devil, but not hopeless for all of that.

The history of salvation exceeds human history because human history was preceded at least ontologically speaking by the fall of the angels. The world of creation was already biased towards evil prior to our advent upon the scene. In some peculiar way the fate of humanity is the ground of contention between God and the devil. In turn our fate will determine that of all the lesser elements of creation. Nowhere has this been more clearly revealed than in the mystery of the Incarnation, when God took on the nature and being of mankind in the person of Jesus. The course of history demonstrates again and again the folly of seeking to manage our own affairs apart from God, while God demonstrates in the drama of the cross what Divine Love must suffer as the price of evil. Thus man is asked to have pity upon God! Far from being able to will a better world, God makes Himself subject to the world precisely as it is, as our own primal choice and creation. If this seems to reverse the entire metaphysical order of thing perhaps it is only because we persist in viewing God from our own ideas of greatness, power, and glory as the origin of the world that we see about us in its fallen state. The world takes the shape of our conceptions. When we speak of God as the Holy of Holies, only then do we consider how far the activity of love can alter our image of God and defeat our desire that God should be alien, volcanic, majestic, just the sort of God who speaks in lightening and not in the tiny whispering sound of his actual passing among us. The Cross of Christ then is not a mere historical happening, but the sign under which all things exist, so that redemption renews the entire universe, one no longer subject to any power but that of God, a process in which we are still engaged but whose finality is now determined and whose triumph has already been achieved. History, insofar as it does not cooperate with the action of God under the Cross of Christ, is merely the last few volleys fired by the defeated army of the devil before the silence of victory which is always peace.

Turning then to this present war, I will summon forth the scene where Holmes asked me to stand with him upon the terrace after the defeat of the German agent, Von Bork in 1914. As usual I was taken to task for my dogged adherence to the literal when Holmes spoke of an east wind coming upon England. At the time Holmes took the view urged upon us by those patriots who always believe that such great efforts as those that war calls forth must lead to a better world, despite centuries of unremitting slaughter that have failed to usher in a world of lasting peace. It is now my considered view that these self-purges of our species, this reduction of intelligent beings to so much dung to clog our fields is the single greatest demonstration of the pointlessness of evil. Warfare attempts to erect a spurious immortality of the few at the cost of the many. What victory is anything but a reshuffling of the inconstant borders of nations? Is any race of men so alien to my sympathies that his death can reaffirm the loyalty in me bred of a mere accident of birth within an opposing race, nation, or culture? If men were sent naked into battle, how swiftly would a confusion of arms result: who is friend and who is foe? In the misery of maiming and death only our common frailty as human beings would be affirmed.

Surely death does not so tarry that it must be rushed ahead by such arbitrary means. Rather, let us cherish life and advance it by all possible means; another man's survival is my own by proxy. Instead in age after age we are mesmerized by illusory goals as though mere strenuousness and pain were the guarantee that what is sought in war is worthy of honor and sacrifice. Particularly in this present war I am not sure that any sensible military options or objectives now remain. Each new assault of man against mechanized death only further gluts the vast graveyard of the great wound that stretches across France and into Belgium. Flesh was not made for such vile usages.

The generals on both sides seem to have lost all sense of proportion. There is no strategy or tactic that can make it possible for war and mankind to co-exist in the new world that our own adaptations and inventions have visited upon us. Instead, what is left is only the slaughter of the young to salve the egos of the old and to preserve a decrepit order among nations, the justifications of which, in the light of these dreadful events, can never again be given credence. It will take more years than are likely to be granted to me and a wiser mind than I possess to place this war in some context in the bloody record of human history. I am not sure that all of the governments concerned have not been permanently discredited by this massive resort to arms. They should all make a pilgrimage to Rome and lay their swords at the feet of the Vicar of Christ with a pledge never to take up war again.

Instead what will no doubt emerge from this world conflict is an exhausted and bitter peace that will only sow the seeds for further wars. But this is for the future era to decide and I am, as are all those who have survived as soldiers, part of an era now gone by. The wisdom born of much thought and disappointed hopes does nothing to work a change in human nature; all still wear the mark of Cain, which was meant to preserve that first murderer's life from vengeance. The trail of bloodshed that should have been extinguished with the first murderer has instead been the most salient fact of human history. If there should be a final conflict at Armageddon only God shall work a victory and by a means that only God may comprehend, perhaps by removing once and for all the sword from our hands.

We cannot choose the historical era in which we will live our one and only life, nor choose the circumstances into which we are plunged at our birth. Our very identity is forged by historical circumstances so that each of us is the product of a personal and collective history, only part of which is our own doing and responsibility. It is natural to wonder what will follow our departure from this life, what wondrous new inventions will swirl about over one's insensate grave, what progress or regress will be made by mankind as the last remnants of our physical being filter into the soil until even our dust is no longer dignified by a particular identity. To the extent that a man dies in the full extent and capability to exercise his powers, death must always seem premature. Only the disappointed and the despairing welcome death as the definitive solution of a problem that they could never successfully formulate let alone reach an adequate solution.

So it is that I speculate that the era during which I have lived is not a beginning but the end of a savage epoch of our evolution as a species. I believe that the present war will be only one of a series of conflicts that will continue until mankind ceases to seek a point of advantage over other men, whether enforced by military might or by unjust economic advantage based upon ownership of the means of production. The new social units to be formed in a better world will be neither nation-states nor corporations but extended units of cooperation based upon principles of information, freedom, and consent. Only this form of life will be able to abandon coercion and force with all their attendant violence. Only agreement and cooperation among men will allow for the efficient use of limited resources for the survival of all people.

To depend solely upon the occasional saint or the martyr in order to resist mass evils will be inadequate in a world with a vastly expanded population in which various groups will claim to possess absolute truth and right on their side. Perhaps the progenitor of a society of adhesiveness, as the American poet Walt Whitman termed it, will be provided by the ease of travel and communication provided by various new technical developments.

This free exchange will make traditional property arrangements obsolete, because they are insufficiently adaptable to the future needs of all of humankind. Capital must be allowed to flow freely to where it is most needed by the total social fabric, much as repair-cells in the body migrate to a wound in the body in order to heal the wound and prevent infection; rescue and recourse should go where they are most needed. If I am correct in my bold projections, then I am sorry that my own life has been spent in such a tragic era during which so much of waste and oppression have reigned supreme

On the other hand the time that is coming may only refine the means by which some men will extract the labor and the very means of life from others. A new and darker age of intrusiveness and control may be coming upon the earth and if these are successful then not the greatest tyrants of Imperial Roman rule will exceed what is to come. Nero and Caligula will then be remembered more for their moderation than their greed and folly. When man has cast off once and for all the guidance provided by divine revelation and the remnant of eternal law that the philosophers have termed natural law so that man spurns all sense of limitation and begins to design the world according to his own imagination and seemingly limitless power, the world will truly bear the stamp of mankind, just as hell bears the stamp of angelic rebellion and pride. What hybrid devices and ideas will then come upon the earth? What monsters will biology not devise? Not even the imagination of Mr. H. G. Wells or Mr. Jules Verne will encompass then this world of man's own devising, which as an echo of his own emptiness will distort all things.

I pity the poor beasts to be crowded out by masses of humanity, most reduced to slavery because they are no longer seen as children of an Eternal Father in heaven. God asked that we subdue the earth but not that we destroy it or reduce it to our own uses alone. All things were created as good by God and all are to be preserved as a sacred trust and legacy. Man cannot exist alone without the other animals shoved into such proximity that all civility fails. Such proximity will lead to wars and to a final struggle to dominate the world's remaining resources. Mankind will then fragment into pieces along every fissure-line of race and class and nation.

The Universal Catholic Church guided by the Pope as heir to St. Peter who was entrusted with the Keys to the Kingdom of Heaven has been reduced to occasional pleas to the diverse religions and peoples of the earth to return to God, the One Father of all human life. History, now cast adrift from God, plunges into realms unglimpsed by the cultures that once sustained religion. History now proceeds like a comet into the endless abyss of unfathomed space. I sit daily in my chair and ask myself those most poignant words of Jesus on the way to His crucifixion: *"the Son of Man goes the way that is foretold of Him; but when He returns will He find faith upon the earth?"*

The question posed by individual faith requires that we dare to answer the question posed by Jesus, *"But you, who do you say that I am?"* By these words Jesus appears ironically to place the question of God's very existence up to our discretion. If the sin in Eden was that man asked to be like God knowing good and evil, then God appears to have granted our collective demand. God appears at times to have vacated the universe so that it wears an aspect of callous disregard for all that is human within us. We face what appears to be a vast unconsciousness, one characterized by mere activity and events without any higher purpose and therefore without consequence or meaning. Deprived of a point of origin we are alike deprived of a terminus and a conclusion. Existence lies against us then not as a parameter to curtail our imaginings and desires, but instead opens outward into fathomless space and time in which we are lost.

The very earth is dwarfed first by constellations and these by galaxies and these in turn are mocked by the infinitely small which for all we know may open into ever smaller versions of the cosmos that to us is infinitely large. We may occupy but a single stair step along an infinite ascent or descent! If this terrifies the mind, well so it should, for what mind can ever grasp such things! If the Incarnation of God seems absurd let us only recall the helpless dilemma posed by the human condition if we remove God from consideration. Faith is the only alternative to doubting all relevance and purpose to the human condition as such. God comes to us because after Original Sin we could not come to Him.

So it is that we must grasp at Divine Grace whenever it becomes manifest to us. So let us live in the tiny web of relations and affections that form the fragile stage of our individuality. Let us not spurn our transient affections and our futile impact upon even this tiny earth that sustains us, for God has condescended to take notice of us and to allow us to affirm our place in eternity, which like a great wave shall soon break upon us at our individual deaths when all shall be revealed as it is in the sight of God.

Now this account is complete and the reader has learned what I was able to learn of the true story of the great spiritual duel between Sherlock Holmes and Professor Moriarty that took place between the years 1891 and 1897. What I learned during the years that followed that momentous year of 1897 (when I first heard that Professor Moriarty had not perished at the Falls of Reichenbach) regarding human life and destiny gave me an invaluable insight into the extraordinary mind of my companion and friend.

I learned that Professor Moriarty, once considered to be the very Napoleon of crime, was in fact a seeker after truth similar in his way to Holmes. Both men had long sought that underlying dynamic of the universe that would explain all things. It was this desire to probe into the essential character of events, not the least part of which was revealed by the conclusion that what Professor Moriarty represented was what might be termed "principled evil."

It was this conclusion that led Holmes to give Professor Moriarty time to seek and to find what Holmes had himself discovered by other means. Each man has his own path to find God. The fruit of faith does not always hang upon the lower boughs of existence. Many follow an obscure course to reach a common end. For Professor Moriarty it took the possibility that his bitterness and revenge might be brought to the very edge of completion before he would decide to reverse his course and to aid Holmes in his efforts to avert a great catastrophe that would have brought untold suffering to many and have inflicted a blow upon England of incalculable dimensions.

Although his technical conversion to Catholicism was anything but complete, the Professor that I learned to know was a changed man by 1897 and was well on his way to the reassessment of life that is termed "conversion of heart and mind." In the end, as the years passed, the Professor became first a deist, then a moralist, and finally he came to embrace in his last illness, as all truly wounded men must, the conclusion that it is only in the Suffering Servant, the one spoken of by the prophet Isaiah long ago, that our many and various wounds are to be healed. We are healed finally by the One who bore all things for our sake. The last years of Professor Moriarty were spent among his beloved horses. He seemed to find in those great beasts a tenderness and strength, recalled from his youth, when as a stable-boy they alone received in their brute power and incomprehension the silent confidences of the secret pain of his heart.

Professor Moriarty is dead now as I write these words in 1918. He succumbed at last to the constitutional maladies that were a legacy of his blighted early youth in Ireland. Holmes was with him in the last days of his illness along with the local Canon of the Parish of Grimpen. In that quiet and select company Professor Moriarty received the final comforts of the Church into which he had been baptized so many years ago in Ireland by his devout mother, who through all of her sufferings had never abandoned her faith in God. This was her only comfort in bearing what she had long endured from a brutal husband.

Professor James Moriarty died with the Holy Oil of Extreme Unction signed upon his forehead after making a good confession of the evils of his past life and receiving the Holy Viaticum that seals the soul in the life and death of Jesus the Christ from whom all salvation comes. Holmes said that when the great change came upon him, those sunken eyes seemed to widen to embrace eternity and his face took on a look of wonder and of peace, wonder as of a man who sees Darien or as an avid astronomer when a new planet swims within his ken to paraphrase the immortal words of the English poet John Keats.

During the fateful years of 1897 through 1899, Holmes was also forced to deal with another type of man in the person of Roger Baskerville, a man who manifested a type of evil based upon the desire to dominate the world and to play with it for some obscure pleasure derived from evil's very self. He manifested that peculiar blend of selfishness, pride, and twisted wonder, as of a snake sliding silently amid the vines and branches of Eden while seeking out the first woman so that he might tempt her.

But to a woman also was entrusted the consent to the coming New Covenant in Jesus. There is an arresting symmetry in the human story and it centers upon the role of woman as the sole minister of life and death, for it is she who accepts the seed of humanity. It is she who nurtures and brings to birth both good and evil. From her comes all mortal flesh from Adam to the present day. From her comes the first humanly transmitted evil when Eve carried the deadly fruit to Adam and from her consent came salvation for the human race in the birth of Jesus.

There is a degree of wisdom in woman that exceeds that of her mate. Eve was made from Adam's rib as a mirror image of the begetting of the Eternal Word, who is the Beloved, begotten from God himself before all of creation according to revelation. Eve and her sisters exist as God's most perfect creation. The Virgin Mary is spoken of as the Mother of God. She is honored in the Catholic Church as the Mediatrix of all Graces. God acts through woman then to channel to all men and women the fruits of salvation, so that what began with a woman ends also with a woman.

In his prosaic way Roger Baskerville was the snake to Lady Beryl as a new Eve whom he first deceived when she was only a young girl in Costa Rica. She came to England still believing in his virtue and hoping, as perhaps only a woman can ever hope, that his evil might, under the influence of her love, be turned into goodness. She never abandoned him, though he had long since abandoned her.

Roger Baskerville may have acquired the disease that led to his madness in an evil den in Costa Rica, a victim of excesses in keeping with his own vile nature. The British Counsel confirmed his death at sea and his few final possessions were shipped back to Grimpen for internment in his stead in the family graveyard upon the Baskerville estate. Though he probably died in sin, he was given some memorial of a Christian sort in the end and both Lady Beryl and Sir Henry stood by the grave as the coffin containing all that was left of what had been his was lowered into the sodden ground on that bleak late January day.

At the final moment, for so Sir Henry confided later to Holmes and to me, a wind arose from the south and brought the scent of far-off Spain across the barrenness of the late autumn moors. Sir Henry and Lady Beryl (who was now definitively no longer to be called Mrs. Stapleton) were wed a week later in the parish church of Grimpen. They departed for a wedding trip to the south of France and to Italy where they spent the winter, wed at last in the eyes of God and of the Church, as they had long since been wed in their respect and devotion toward each other. The Baskerville Curse was ended at last. No cries of the spectral hound would echo again across the barren moors to strike fear into the hearts of all who heard it. What had begun with Sir Hugo Baskerville ended with Roger Baskerville who now lay in the distant sea and not in the soil of his forefathers where they slept while the yellow leaves descended from the last trees and the dark cypresses bore mute witness to the dead that lay there noble and iniquitous alike.

Regarding that other estate upon the moors, Sigerside, located on the North Yorkshire Moors, some final words must be said. Sherringford Holmes died on the estate in 1914, just before the outbreak of the current war that fall. He was able to live his life entirely during one of those great periods of peace that occur now and again in the march of conflict between nations. He was a deeply civilized man and represented the feudal system of England at its best. He felt a loyalty to his tenants that far exceeded what most employers feel for their workers in a capitalist system. With his passing, the Holmes estate descended upon Mycroft by right of primogeniture.

Holmes second brother, Mycroft, left his post with the government during the Second Boer War of 1899 to 1901. He had disagreed with the policy of the British internment of women and children in the inadequately supplied camps prepared to house these non-combatants. It will be recalled how many civilians met their death in those camps through malnutrition and disease. As Mycroft had no natural replacement, one who possessed his unique gifts, his office died with his resignation. Perhaps had he been present in office to give his invaluable advice, England would have taken a stronger stand in the second peace conference of 1907 that preceded the Great War of 1914. A progressive trend of disarmament might have brought Germany around before declaring war on Russia after the partial mobilization of the Russian army ordered by the Czar in 1914, while there was still time to back away from the coming conflagration. But who can say whether any merely rational considerations can interfere with the evident passion of mankind to destroy itself?

After the bloody battle of Omdurman in the Sudan and the slaughter dished out upon the forces of the Khalifa of Khartoum by Lord Kitchener, Mycroft Holmes could never again believe that the British Empire was a force for civilization in the world. He could not therefore in good conscience have remained in office. Perhaps he was influenced by his brother in this regard, for when Holmes returned to England in 1899 he devoted what time remained from his busy practice to labor in the cause of peace and justice among nations and for the restoration of the commons to the small farmers of England.

Mycroft was too accustomed to trips to London to assume the usual rural duties of a country squire after the death of Sherringford so the Holmes estate was broken up among the families who had for so long worked the land. The coal mine interests of the family had been long since sold and the hospital set up to treat the former miners was financed by a trust fund that was endowed with the proceeds of the sale of the mines. There were to be no new generations to occupy the Holmes' estate. Mycroft and Sherlock were to be the last of their direct line.

The old house and lands of the Estate of Sigerside proper (now reduced to about one hundred acres) were to remain for the use of Mycroft and Sherlock during their life-times. Should no descendant from a collateral line exist, then the property would be ceded to a monastic foundation of the order of Cistercians of the Strict Observance, often referred to as the Trappists after their first foundation at La Trapp in France. The sound of Gregorian Chant will perhaps echo across the moors at some future day and masses will be said in perpetuity for those who rest there in the family crypt and cemetery.

Mycroft is still alive in this desperate year of 1918. He has lost weight in recent years with the duties imposed upon him at Sigerside where he now visits. He did not wish to remain alone there though, and by one of those strange twists of fate, he decided years ago to marry Mrs. Hudson, a woman who had labored as a landlady far beyond her child-bearing years, but who was both amiable and patient and just the sort of woman to accompany an old bachelor to Yorkshire. Her labors there have quite transformed Sigerside, which is now as comfortable as Baker Street always was. Sherlock Holmes continues to pay her rent as he has always done at 221B, for a woman should always have some money of her own. Mrs. Hudson's own rooms, located at 221A Baker Street, have since been leased to a retired diva of the stage who divides her time between London, where she likes to visit a few time each year with an old friend and her own villa in the eternal city of Rome.

As for myself, I still remain in Cornwall. I meet Holmes occasionally in our old rooms in Baker Street when I come up to London or accompany him up to Sigerside to visit with Mycroft and his good wife. I see less of Holmes now, but we remain as always the best of friends as my readers who have read my story, *"The Last Bow,"* will bear witness. That story deals with the Von Bork affair of 1914, which tale must be placed with this larger work as my final efforts as a writer to celebrate the career of my friend Sherlock Holmes.

I have provided this brief summary in case my health should fail suddenly. I am reconciled to the prospect of death, but for all of that the pulse of life still beats strong within me, and the sea is as ever my one great companion. The final entries in the Journal of Sherlock Holmes recorded the course of his new mission after our return from America, one waged upon an international stage. What Mycroft could not accomplish through official channels the two brothers sought to manage through private action using the proceeds of the Holmes legacy and the yearly income provided by various investments to maintain that independence that is essential if one is to escape the various ways that the arms of commerce reach out to subjugate the spirit and enslave the body. The trend of the new century will undoubtedly be directed towards the consolidation of power as the last remnants of colonial rule struggle for their independence. The outcome of that struggle between the silenced multitudes of the earth and their masters will perhaps remain undecided and pose an eternal struggle.

Dr. Watson's Narrative Continues

It is one of the few prerogatives of age that those of us who have been fortunate enough to reach advanced years may allow our minds to wander over the entire course of human existence. When I first began this narrative I was divided in my mind. On the one hand I thought that the public might benefit from having an extended exposition by his own hand of the unique and probing theological investigations of Sherlock Holmes, but on the other hand I was also seeking to create an all-embracing appraisal of the forces that have led up to the present great war of the European powers. Then there was the consideration of writing my own book of Lamentations for a vanished era, which despite its many faults, has contributed something to world civilization. The result has been the valedictory address that the reader now holds in his hands.

I wonder if I am not unlike those public speakers who in a darkened hall continue to address the darkness, never having noticed that their audience has trickled away in twos and threes to go outside and smoke. The theater of history has grown noticeably colder since I began to write and the hour is late indeed for the human race. For this reason I have allowed myself to linger over an era that may have produced better men and women and higher ideals than this present age. Things seem to be spinning with great rapidity out of their natural orbits. Men such as that mad German, Friedrich Nietzsche, have noticed that there is more and more night coming on all the time. As the demands placed upon human nature have increased, our ability to meet those challenges while retaining our dignity as human beings has decreased. I have little confidence anymore that better men will arise to lead us from the ruin of these days. So it is that I have continued to write, perhaps fearing that when I have once laid aside my pen, that a deep and abiding silence will envelope me. Will that silence be the silence of death? Thus it is that I press on, ever seeking closure upon a time and season of our lives that has already been both sealed and superseded by greater events. It only remains for me now to record here the course of our journey to San Francisco where we embarked for the port of Yokohama on our voyage home to England by the western route rather than returning to New York.

Holmes' health was quite restored by then so he was able to undertake this final excursion across America; then after the voyage home to resume his consulting practice in London. I close then with this coda of our journey to San Francisco and our visit along the way to the site of Wounded Knee in the Dakotas, a place that Holmes had always desired to visit. We stood together on a bleak and wintery day at this singular location among the great ocean-like space of the Great Plains of that land of so many great ambitions. Wounded Knee is part of the great Sioux or Lakota reservation called Pine Ridge in the Dakota Territory, which by right of conquest has been annexed to the expanded colonies that by their own proclamation now call themselves the United States of America.

That this process of conquest and expansion claims to be legitimate is based upon only one thing, the failure of a more legitimate claimant to be able to resist and to contest that claim. What this means of course is that no title can be perfected in the occupied lands even should they be occupied for an indefinite period, for it is a fundamental principle of the common law that a thief cannot perfect title against a protesting rightful claimant to the land in question. It is for this reason that the American government in the course of the systematic and pervasive duplicity practiced against the Indigenous Tribes has relied upon a supposed bargained-for-exchange under the treaty laws authorized by the U.S. Constitution. The problem from the beginning of course was the lack of adequate contractual consideration on the part of the European emigrants followed by a series of broken promises that clearly breached the terms of the Fort

Laramie Treaty.

No decent court of equity could ever find that the benefits conferred upon the American Indians by the emigrant European populations or their representatives colonial or otherwise have adequately repaid the Indian tribes for the virtual vacating under duress of an entire continent. If the various treaties had been executed in good faith by nations of roughly equal bargaining power and with full disclosure and bilateral compliance, then the surviving Indian populations would be among the wealthier and more prosperous citizens of the American nation. This is particularly so considering their diminished numbers on American soil through the twin agents of violence and disease. Since this is patently not the case and since the Indian people existed at the time of our visitation and still exist today in abject poverty and physical deprivation, it is clear that some dreadful and widespread inequity has been visited upon them to wrongfully deprive them of their lands. Until this situation of remedied, the government of the United States has no more standing before any principled people adhering to a rule of law, which is the foundation for all civilization, than any other marauding and pillaging force in the long history of the world.

When we reached San Francisco Holmes and I submitted a letter to President William McKinley that included among other things the following statement:

It lies within the power of the President to convene a committee of settlement in the U.S. Congress to address the Indian question and to restore land when it remains still under Federal Control and to institute proper proceedings of reclamation under eminent domain when these lands have been ceded to private parties. The existing overly generous railroad concessions may be simply rescinded as having been made without justification under the existing treaties and the railroads should be given the choice of consenting to some remuneration or face the nationalization of the rail system. The railroads can fulfill their present function without the added inducement of resources stolen from the Indian tribes through which these railroads pass.

In this way some measure of delayed justice may be rendered to the American Indians. Failing this America has no right to sit in the councils of world nations. America must then seek its peers among the great barbarian invaders such as Genghis Khan. Neither rhetoric nor form of law may alter what history will testify to in the coming generations. Nor will America be spared in due season a just retribution for its collective crimes. Any nation that takes the rule of force as its preferred method of obtaining title to land has only that rule to sustain it when met by a superior force. That force may come at some later day, perhaps wielded by the emissaries of the collective conscience of mankind. At some distant hour when principle shall be reduced to practice in the intercourse of sovereign states and nations the great correction to the present injustice may come. Until that blessed hour each holder of the office that you currently occupy and each sitting Congress only adds its own complicity to what was wrong when this policy of conquest was instituted, is wrong now, and shall continue to be wrong until this terrible injustice is made whole.

I have quoted above from this letter sent to President McKinley based upon Holmes' own rather extensive study of Early English Charters and the Common Law. Holmes was something of an authority upon the common law, feudal rights, and Magna Carta; he knew his Blackstone as well as any barrister in the realm. Thus it was no whim of his that dictated this letter, but a principled argument to a sovereign to re-consider its own position *sua sponte* and to rule that it lacked any jurisdiction or power (to use the sacred language of the law) to clothe its crimes in rectitude; or if it did so, to leave itself open to the collective contempt that is justified towards all such usurpations of right and justice. Holmes and I received no reply and we expected none. It is sufficient that the indictment was rendered by the one man whom I felt was best able to do so, for Holmes remains in my mind the best and wisest man that I have ever known.

Our path to Wounded Knee was circuitous. Our train left behind the great city of Chicago after traveling across the lush green fields of Ohio and Indiana. We had left the lands behind of the Cherokee, the Huron and the Iroquois. We now entered the lands of the great tribes of the plains, the Lakota, the Cheyenne, the Arapaho, and the Pawnee. The lush forests of eastern Missouri were soon left behind and we came to Council Bluffs in Nebraska. The great and endless prairie regions stretched out before us and our train conveyed us past the poor farms of the immigrants, these held hostage by the railroads that transported the grain that they raised so that men in Chicago might grow rich on the commodity exchange markets.

The Indians who had been removed to reservations were now consolidated and settled upon the cold dry lands of South Dakota at a placed called Pine Ridge. It was there that we were headed so that Holmes might fulfill a private vow and come to Wounded Knee, that last site of conflict with the defeated inhabitants of the Great Plains of America. If it seems strange that a British subject would feel so implicated in the slaughter of the women and children by the Hotchkiss Guns of the Seventh Calvary under General Forsyth, I must state here that Holmes always felt responsible to some degree for the bloody Battle of Omdurman in the Sudan. Whatever their beliefs, the Moslem forces had been defending their own land.

What right had the British to be there at all? What right has any distant nation to the lands of people that the colonizers through most of Christian history did not even know existed? What right had this new America to its newly acquired colony in the Philippines? Was not America's worldwide trading aspiration a reflection of England, the same England against which the Americans of 1776 had revolted when they themselves were an oppressed colony subject to taxation without representation? The famed Declaration of Independence, which spoke so eloquently of the rights of man, in practice had only served to inaugurate an era of depredation and servitude for the Indian people, while African slavery supported an entire economy in the southern states.

Holmes now desired to perform an act of public penance for evils past, even if what had been done was irrevocable by 1899. The buffalo, the foundation of the Indian way of life were gone by that time with their bones bleaching on the prairie. Sitting Bull and Crazy Horse and so many other great chiefs were dead and the ill-clothed and starving survivors had been slaughtered by the army in a final frenzy of revenge at the Indian presumption of daring to exist on the lands now claimed by America.

It has seemed only appropriate that I end this book that embraces the decline of nations, the betrayal of Christian ideals, and the struggle for a universal faith by going back in detail to the last days that we spent in America at the close of the century. With our essential business completed in the East we were free now to cross the Great Plains and to witness the last vestiges of resistance of the original inhabitants of that splendid continent. We came at last to Grand Rapids, South Dakota. It was there that we obtained horses and guides to proceed with our journey. Irene Adler chose to accompany us. We hired some Crow Indian guides to accompany us on the way and we ventured forth into the bitter snowy land of the Dakota frontier.

I have never been to the Russian Steppes, but I imagine that they look similar to the landscape that we encountered during the following days as we moved from small settlement to settlement on those now sparsely inhabited plains. Each day I awoke to the same haunting sense of vacancy. In the stillness perhaps I was awaiting the thunder of the hoofs of the great bison herds that were now no more. The legacy of the ages had been squandered for mere tongues and buffalo hides by the white traders armed with Winchester rifles. I could not but think that so much wanton waste, if it were a harbinger of things to come, foretold the wasting of the continent at the hands of the intrusive new claimants to the land.

Much was spoken in the east of the American juggernaut as a civilizing influence. Is civilization then mere rapacity? To spread railroads and great cities over pristine and balanced regions ... is that civilization? If that is so then the locusts of old, which were once called one of the seven plagues of Egypt, must be seen as the very symbol of the American advance across the Mississippi River under the pretence of a right granted by the Louisiana Purchase from a France desperate for money after the revolution. The processes of justification for expansion that Holmes and I had witnessed at close hand in 1898 have merely increased since the time of President McKinley. Whatever means that the man that we had met managed to summon up in order to justify these policies of acquisition the ultimate legacy is clear. American supremacy will become a curse and the final retribution of God will be proportionate to the evils inflicted due to the proud mindset of the conqueror as in every other empire that history has ever known.

That curse was not long delayed in the case of William McKinley. He was shot dead before his term of office was over by a man who had intended his action to be seen as the action of a liberator. Instead the assassination was universally loathed and provided the justification for even greater oppression of the farmers and the working masses in the sprawling cities, ugly make-do affairs that were now sprouting up all over America. Meanwhile the arrogant isolation policies represented by the American tariffs and the refusal to accept silver as a supplement to the prevailing gold standard led to the banking collapse of 1907 and the resulting economic depression as trade came to a standstill.

After his assassination the late President was to leave to his successor, Theodore Roosevelt, the task of the building of the great trans-oceanic canal across Panama. We had been present at the moment when the Americans, having pushed the Indians aside, turned their rapacious gaze upon China. The policy of keeping China open to trade with all nations was not a voluntary one. The Chinese tried in the course of the Boxer Rebellion that took place between 1899 and 1901 in support of the Qing Dynasty to repel the great tides of foreign trade lapping at their doors and destroying their ancient civilization in the process.

China was like a great enamel box forced open by a gang of thieves, each one demanding equal access to the spoils within. It is an open question whether the canal as time passes will open a flood-gate for further American incursions on that fabled land of Cathay? Perhaps a time will come when America will maintain garrisons around the world to guard its various commercial interests, just as the cavalry once maintained forts on the Indian frontier. But perhaps I am being fanciful. No nation escapes nemesis forever. The extension of empires always leads to their downfall. The Americans will learn the brutal lesson that the nations of Europe are learning at this present hour as the war enters this new year of 1918 and hopefully winds down to its disgraceful and tragic end. Each year the generals promised victory with one more last great assault upon the entrenched lines of the enemy. Desperation becomes more desperate in order to redeem those who have already fallen with ever new waves of young men to be plowed into the soil of France like so much humus until the dead rest in strata upon the dead.

The fields of battle have come to be places beyond the remedy of tears, beyond all conceptions of human atrocity. The mind of man must invent new terms for what we are witnessing daily as the war grinds on. Can any intelligent mind or conscience bear the insupportable weight of the tears that have been shed at home? What charts with tiny boxes that represent armies can symbolize the men with feet frozen in mud, no sleep, no decent food, all stumbling through the mire into the clatter of the guns that mow them down like so much wheat?

Was the slaughter at Wounded Knee a prophecy of this, now that America has joined the fray? America was settled primarily from the nations that are now making war upon each other. Perhaps the Paiute Prophet Wovoka was correct when he instituted the Ghost Dance Religion among the despairing Indian tribes in the late 1880's. Wovoka spoke of a vision that he had had of the land rolling up like a blanket carrying before it the white men while behind that great wave came the buffalo and the lost people, slain to defend their lands. That great wave has clearly arisen, but not in America. It rose up in 1914 on the fields of Belgium and France, in Russia and Italy and in the Ottoman lands at Gallipoli and in the course of the Arab Revolt. It is a wave that has carried away an entire generation, young men who might have contributed great ideas, marvelous poetry, or new technologies, all have been silenced in that great wave of death. Were these lost men any different than the Indian warriors? Was not the slaughter of the buffalo an early image of the wanton contempt for life that has come to dominate our way of thinking? Shall power and glory for the few mean the desolation and loss of the many with no hope that justice will finally prevail and Christian ideals be realized at last?

Perhaps man is a herd animal after all. If so, then why not

follow the good shepherd, the Prince of Peace, rather than these demi-gods, these emperors whose claims lead only to a great wasteland and an everlasting shame. There can be no unity but that inspired by grace and freedom. Empires built on the monopolization of resources are always devil's spawn. Now as the great empires lie bleeding together in the sacrifice of their most precious resource, their youth, the devil's laughter may be heard in the stutter of the machine-guns, the booms of the howitzers, and the despairing cries of the wounded and dying. No giant rats carrying the dark contagion of a rare disease could have brought as much destruction as that which is now raging over what once had been rich and fertile fields now poisoned with nitrates from the shells, littered with the rusting hulks of burned-out vehicles, imprisoned forever in a sea of mud and the rotting corpses of the unburied dead.

All of that carnage lay ahead in 1899 when we went to the site of the Wounded Knee massacre. The world of the white man as the new century was about to dawn seemed superb in the triumphs of the new civilization of electric lights, railroads, transoceanic cables, automobiles, and telephones. What had the Indians to compare with all of this? They must pass with their visions, with their vast empty spaces, with their ability to live in their own way as they had always done. Contact alone had meant inevitable conquest. It was destiny that they must step aside. Such was the comforting cant of the time that we were bringing the Red Man and the Red Woman to God. But they had always known Him. They had called him Waken Tanka in their great wanderings, the long exodus that had spread the Asiatic migrants throughout a continent to the very tip of Tierra del Fuego. They had differentiated by tribe and language, but retained a sensitiveness that made them well-adapted to their place, in unity with it and viewed as sacred and charged with spirit and energy. Their sacred books were written in the memory of their people. God was as close to them as the wind over the prairies, as the storm clouds that hovered over the great Rocky Mountains. They could not imagine their way of life passing, so that when it did pass, it was easy for them to believe that God would not suffer so great a wrong to remain unavenged. God would cause the land itself to rise up and push them back, these men whom the most courageous of their warriors could not repulse.

But by 1899 the great chiefs were dead. The buffalo had perished and their bleached bones littered the plains that we crossed on day after day with its bitter cold and distant horizons. It took us a week to get to Wounded Knee. We were met there by a representative of the Pine Ridge Agency. I think he was suspicious as to our motives in coming there, but we carried a letter from the Secretary of State that requested that every effort be made to accommodate our wishes. There is something in the bureaucratic individual that turns him from a tyrant into a vassal when met by any evidence of superior authority. The man whose first greetings to us had been brusque was now virtually climbing over himself in order to aid us in our "official mission." I recall his words well to this day because of the impression they made upon me at that time.

"I should not advise you going over to Wounded Knee. There is nothing to see there you know. There is a mass-grave where the frozen bodies were laid out, but most of the men who were there have been assigned to other commands. There is nothing to learn here. There is no one to talk to about what happened, unless you speak the language of the Sioux and nobody does. These people don't talk much anyhow. Never turn your back on them; not even the women-folk. They'd plunge a knife in your back quick as look at you. No Mr. Holmes, you had best leave Wounded Knee alone. Now if you want to see something, you should go up north to the gold diggings in the Black Hills. Fortunes are being made up there. Money brings in the comforts. You could find suitable rooms and food. There ain't much here to eat and that's the truth. I haven't been paid in a month. The Indians have even been eating their dogs. I get shipments now and again from Saint Louis, but it's damn poor quality, lot of moldy corn meal and dried horsemeat, some sorghum and molasses. Most of the Indian brats have been shipped out to the mission schools. Nobody left here but the old, the toothless, and the sick. You wouldn't know it, but a mere ten years ago we were still scared of these people. That's what did it you know, fear, that and revenge for what they done to General Custer and his men of the 7th cavalry up in Montana. Folks hereabouts have a long memory. Anyway, there ain't much left now of what was once here. You'd be looking out at nothing."

"That nothing sir is precisely what we came to witness," answered Holmes solemnly.

The agent shook his head and his quick, little eyes looked at Holmes as though he suspected him of some sort of mental imbalance. At last he spoke again, "Well nothing is what you will see here and that's a fact because there wasn't much here to begin with and what was of value we burned. They won't be dancing any more ghost dances again, not in our lifetime anyway. The Indians know their place at last. They never had any real chance at all if you want to know the truth of it, not against seasoned troops fresh from fighting a civil war. Just too dumb to know it, that's all. They could have all been alive, could have taken up plowing, made something of this land. Just you watch and see what these farmers from Sweden or Poland make of this country in the next twenty years. Guess I won't see it though. I've applied for a transfer down to Oklahoma. I can't take the cold up here. It comes right through the walls. I don't know how those poor beggars manage with a few flea-ridden blankets. I've asked for more blankets, but the army quartermaster says there ain't any money in Washington. So what can I do, I ask you? Maybe if you have ties to Washington you would be so good as to write a letter about me. If you do, I hope you won't forget to mention that I gave you some coffee squeezing. It's the last I had. Oh, and mention my transfer request if you will." He looked down then, "Can't stand this place! The wind comes in every day. I get to thinking I hear things in the wind. I imagine things. It ain't healthy for any white man to be assigned up here away from civilization. No one as is still alive looks at you. I might as well be the ghost that those ghost dancers was trying to summon up as be a living man."

We did not tarry long over the bitter chicory that he called coffee but parted from him then with the one local man that he provided to guide us to the immediate site. We left the representative of the American victors standing in the doorway shaking his head after us in the lean-to and adjoining sheds that he referred to as his official residence. We mounted our horses and rode on through the bleak sage and grasses under a leaden sky that threatened us each instant with a renewed fall of snow. I kept thinking as our horses' hooves rang on the frozen ground of what Holmes had said in parting. I was not certain of his meaning. Is it possible to see "nothingness?" Is not nothingness the most mystical of all metaphysical insights? Somehow the mind of man is aware that all that exists around us is contingent; in other words it might not have been. But can anything that has been ever become nothing? If the physical laws of conservation of mass and energy are true, then nothing is ever really lost; it can only be transformed into something else.

But no, something can be lost; in fact the experience of loss is more familiar to us as human beings than creation. Even to write a single sentence is to be aware that one might have written something else. The unexpressed thought often vanishes forever. Where for instance is the form that was once my wife, Mary? Where were all the men, women, and children of Wounded Knee? To change form is to negate whatever once was and surely that is the deprivation of what was; and if what was had roots penetrating down into one's very soul, then what remains but nothingness at the center of one's surviving being. We are not merely allotted a location in space and in time; something within us presumes that what has been must be preserved somehow in its very essence as it was and not as something else. If we are not ghosts, we must have left some imprint upon the ether, some deflection of matter to be carried onwards like a wave that bears witness that we were once here. Perhaps that is what all of human conflict is about, all struggle, all ambition: to leave some witness, some marker that we were here and that this great world of light and shadow was once ours alone to preserve or to alter and to redirect.

Perhaps eternity is right here among us but unseen. Everywhere there may be ghosts seeking to reclaim the earth as they knew it! What opera house exists without the unheard echo of some vanished diva whose shrill voice is still present high among the darkened boxes now silent of applause? What battlefield does not contain the sound of the clash of distant arms as a witness to the dead? Nothingness! When will the buffalo return?

Then there is the opposite of nothingness, which the philosophers term pure Being, that which exists and is sustained by nothing other than itself. The greatest synthesis in all of human thought occurred when the philosophers first intuited and dared to describe uncreated primordial being. This was later identified with the historically revealed God of the Hebrews, Yahweh, a word best translated as the phrase - I am that I am. Even God comes to us through experience of course. There is always the mediating world of objectively existing but contingent being summoned forth out of nothingness by God. This is the world that we observe all about us accessible through perception and reason. They constitute a world that we come to understand in some vague and incomplete manner, but never in totality. Only the mind of God may will and know in the absolute sense, unconstrained by any limits beyond those which He imposes upon Himself as dictated by His own nature, which nature is itself beyond all judgment from any outside source. All of which is to say that God is not answerable to any lesser order of being, since He Himself is the source not only of being, but of all categories by which being is to be judged. His Being is not confused into parts, knows no inner conflict, and as such is its own abiding standard of perfection. It cannot vary from itself or choose to be other than what it is.

This is however the exact opposite of the arbitrary will that men associate with power and its exercise. It may not be too much to say that God is the victim of His own goodness. This is what is meant when it is said that God's ways are not our ways and that as high as the heavens are above the earth so high are God's ways above our ways. Even to conceive of God too clearly is itself a great act of temerity, even sacrilege, the temerity of creating an idol as an image of God. If God is beyond all our images, so also He is beyond our conceptions of what is appropriate to Him. We are confined to what may be termed objectivity. Our concern is limited by the world of objective things and relations, which even in their fallen state still bear some residual glory trailing from God's initial intentions for them. How much of what remains to us from that initial intention present in the creative act deserves our praise is celebrated by the poets and the mystics. But there are also the great pessimists who make a virtue of despair and court disillusionment. The truly objective man is the one who neither denies the world's evils nor is overcome by them, even when they seem to partake of irremediable misfortune and desolation as at Wounded Knee.

These were my thoughts as we plodded on, even as Holmes had plodded on by camel over the great deserts of Persia, of Arabia, and of the Sudan. We had wrapped-up our heads in woolen scarves against the cold. I could only see Holmes' piercing eyes from time to time when he would turn in his saddle now and again to see that Miss Adler and I were alright. I must say that she bore up magnificently. Indeed her only concern was that the rigors of this excursion would not cause a recurrence of Holmes' chronic illness. The horizon was already shrunken for us because the snow had begun to fall again and our vision was limited with few signs to guide our progress. It was as though all about us lay shifting curtains of mist and only the path before us lay open as though it was bidding us to come and see that place, which in all of America bears the most eloquent if silent witness to the great crime of conquest and theft that is the basis for its existences as a nation.

The wind that had previously been still began to rise as we approached the actual place, one barely identifiable as a place where people had once lived. Our surroundings seemed to cry out through the sage and the few low and skeletal trees. It was here that the women and children had sought shelter after the first blasts of the Hotchkiss Guns had mown down the few armed men who were present. The panic-stricken remnant died wherever they sought shelter in various hiding places along the river and the children without mothers were summoned out only to be killed as well.

Few signs of the conflict remained. Only a lance with feathers marked the spot and it had been uprooted, broken, and thrown down. No sign of resistance was allowed to remain standing, no insignia of an unconquered people, who would live as long as one of their children remained alive, was allowed at that desolate shrine. We un-wrapped our heads then and stood bare-headed while the bitter wind ripped at our clothing and brought tears to our wind-stung eyes.

Our guide wandered off a few paces and put his horse between him and the wind. The snow was all about us now. It landed upon the flanks of our horses like so many summer flies. It landed upon the mantels of buffalo hide that we wore over our shoulders. It rested upon the land as though to soften the bleak stones and the thin soil out of which some Congressman imagined that the Indians, un-accustomed to farming, could coax crops, using the feeble labor of the aged and the infirm. If the false treaties that had provided the quasi-legal basis for all of this had been written honestly they would have said something like: "And

In return for all of this grandeur and beauty, we the people of the United States condemn you to nothingness. We condemn you to give up your language, your religion, your clothing, your family ties, and even your very names. We condemn you to become like us and only insofar as you become like us will we consent to see you at all."

The snow was now becoming alarming. We could see nothing of the way that we had come. How had we managed to arrive at such a place? How would we ever find our way back again to the comfort of what we had known only this morning, where our fire had been warm and the sun shown out on the plains like a land leading to a distant Eden far to the south and west? I was about to turn to Holmes in alarm when he spoke quietly.

"Do not be afraid, Watson. We are guarded by those whom we have come here to remember. He walked over to his horse then and reaching into the saddlebag took out a parchment upon which many lines had been written. He walked back to where I stood together with Irene and began to speak in a strange chant-like voice these words that he had culled from their native sources:

"Do you see me Father? I have come so far? Look where my horse dies. Do you see it Father? Look where my children cry. They have no food. My arrows lie broken. Do you see me Father? My gun has no more bullets. Do you see me Father? Where are the great bison herds? They will come no more. Where is the fire in my lodge? It has long gone out. Where is my sacred pipe? It smokes no more. The spirits are scattered? Where are the old ones now who could give me counsel? They are no more. Where is my wife? She died in the first winter snow. Where are my children? They have taken them to a strange place. Do you hear me Father? Do you listen only to the wind? Come then Waken Tanka. Come then Waken Tanka. Come then Waken Tanka. If you come, all will return. I see them coming. I see them coming. I see them coming. Come back oh warriors! Come back my children. Return to the land you knew. Come!" He folded the paper then and placed it back in his saddlebag and bowed his head in silence.

After a time Holmes said, "It is still illegal for the Lakota to chant the Ghost Dance to the four winds while casting the earth into the air. The earth is too frozen now to bear witness in any case. It has therefore remained for me to do so, and may the Lakota people forgive my temerity in doing so, but I make no claim upon this place, and I ask pardon for those who came to see and remained to steal. Mere penance and contrition are only gestures after all; it is God alone who re-unites all things. At Eden all was lost. Now our faith says that all has been restored in Jesus Christ. The Ghost Dancers still await their savior, but He will surely come and perhaps these people who have been made last shall then be first. The Ghost Dance ends as does the great book of the Apocalypse of Saint John: 'I am the Alpha and the Omega, the beginning and the End.'"

The snow that had barred our way only minutes ago began gradually to cease and eventually the path appeared again with only our few footprints in the snow as we wound our way back to the trail and rode away never to return. We three witnesses that stood there on that day so many years ago as I write this at the great neglected shrine of America are still alive. Places like this that are treated by some as places of victory and honor are for others places of defeat and shame. Wounded Knee is still neglected because it calls to the mind of Americans memories not of triumph and valor, but of brute ignorance and of racial contempt. More than that Wounded Knee speaks only of an anti-climax to the wars against the Native people of America, a final "dusting up" in the words of Lord Kitchener at the Battle of Omdurman in Sudan, of the victors over the dead.

But the dead people like the buffalo upon the plains exist still in the sacred ground of memory, even as the heirs of the victors would re-write that history to serve their need for other conquests. They have become ghosts. It is these spirits that blow in the wind on a summer day, when the daisies arise from the soil and the prairie grasses blow like one great and waving sea beneath an endless sky bowed over them like an embracing providence. It is they that mourn in November when the ground becomes hard with frost. It is they that speak in the bitter January winds that scour the land. They say always, "We died unjustly and we died too soon."

And what of those who came with nothing and took everything? Where are their spirits now? Are they doomed to a long purgatory of reflection? Must they gather here yearly throughout eternity at Wounded Knee to see at last what they have done while their progeny still confirmed in pride and arrogance, reach out to ever new shores with power and the desire to dominate other peoples in other lands? It is not that the Americans are worse in this regard than the British, the French, the Germans, or the Russians, but that America once promised a new creed, a new chance to break with all that had gone before, to allow God to walk among men. But they looked at the Red Man and saw only a devil, a pagan, and lost souls where they should have seen men and women who already knew God, but by another name. God was as familiar to them as he was to Plato or Aristotle or Confucius or Buddha. God alone determines the final measure of his salvation and the extent of his grace. If Jesus died for all men and women, then he is the means of salvation for all. It may be better to worship a God unknown than to claim to know him and act as Christians have often done. The last shall be first in the Kingdom of Heaven.

So it was that Holmes ended his journey to the east by going to the west. He took with him the two people who on this earth meant the most to him, Irene Adler and myself. We stood together in the swirling snow at that bitter place where a people had finally lost whatever little hope still remained to them. But the message of the Ghost Dance still continues, I realized. What were the whirling dervishes of snow that day but the ghost dancers crying out in the wind in defiance? What was it but their voices calling for the Great Spirit to restore to them all that had been lost and to remove from them the bitter scourge of the victors whose momentary triumph only portends an ultimate defeat? When the last day comes and all is made manifest in the light of God, they will have their vindication. Then the land will indeed roll up like a blanket and behind it will come the buffalo again and the great warriors who were lost and the women and the children will rejoice as after a successful hunt. There will be dancing again and full tummies and the children will lie warm beneath their buffalo robes at night. Such was the promise of the Ghost Dance vision; if that vision is not true, then neither is the hope of Israel, nor the promises of Mohammed to the faithful of Islam, nor the Beatific Vision of my own Catholic faith.

God is a God of the living and not of the dead. The Spirit of God blows where it wills and none shall say to it: here you must remain or you belong to us or you are bound to us alone. Rather it is we who are bound to God and under such terms and conditions as He alone decides, he who alone is all good, all holy, and far beyond our furthest conceptions of mercy and justice.

In the end no one may protest on the Last Day that he or she has been treated in any way other than they deserve. Such a man or woman in accepting justice from the hand of God must meet the precondition of all mercy: that condition is that we rely upon God who alone cancels all our debts and restores all things. After all who may say whose debt is greater? To the one to whom much has been forgiven much love will be demanded and shown in return to God. For this reason there is more rejoicing in heaven over the repentance of the sinner than for those who had no need to repent. All of heaven bends over the earth to save what has been lost, to comfort the sorrowing, and to restore hope to the broken hearted, just such hearts as were broken at Wounded Knee.

I felt at the time that I had received a premonition of that final day. As suddenly as the snows had come, they drifted away again. At first there was only a lightening of the surrounding grey. It began to glow with a pale yellow tinge and then suddenly the sky burst forth in radiant blue and the last flakes of snow glittered in the late afternoon sun streaming out of the far west from the great mountains that we would soon cross in order to reach the Pacific Ocean. We found that we stood upon a small hill above the flowing water of Wounded Knee Creek. The trees stood peacefully along its shores bare but clear and crystalline in their frost in the slanting light. I waited for a sign from Holmes that we could leave. At last he placed his old hunting cap again upon his head and we mounted our horses and simply rode away.

To bear witness need not be a lengthy affair. It is enough to speak the truth, simply and plainly. Neither does contrition require long lamentations, nor does faith require endless efforts at conceptual refinement. We are told that if we do not approach Jesus and His heaven as a little child we shall never enter it. A child accepts what it is given as a pure gift and not as a rightful claim. The door of Eden has always stood open to the innocent of heart because they never really left Eden. Theirs is the narrow gate that need never be barred against invasion, for it is few who find it since the majority is always seeking elsewhere for happiness. The narrow gate requires divestment of attachments; not because they are evil in themselves, but because many have lost the source of that value by being grasping everything too tightly, as if God was always seeking to take things away from us rather than to bestow them upon us in His generosity. Much must be surrendered, before we can enter into the presence of God. We come to heaven with only the lamp-oil of the wise Virgins of Israel. The most proud and self-assured of Christians will need to tarry longest among those waiting outside until the last farthing is paid and the lamps burn brightly once again to welcome the Bridegroom, who alone may welcome us into his home where we will dwell together forever.

We were soon traveling on by rail again to the west. After leaving the Dakotas we transferred trains at North Platte in the State of Nebraska. The great inter-continental railroad would carry us westward through the Rocky Mountains to Nevada, and over the Sierra Nevada Mountains to California. We were traveling across a bleak snow-covered landscape as we entered Colorado but our accommodations were comfortable. Our spirits revived as we caught our first glimpse of the mountains that divide the continent of North America. Soon we were among the great peaks. Yawning chasms opened at our sides and we were able to appreciate the engineering marvel that had cost the lives of so many, especially the Chinese workers who had been brought into the country as a source of low-cost labor. The building of the great railroads spelled the death-knell for the plains Indians. The west could now provide grain, gold, silver, and other essentials to feed the appetite of eastern industry. The west also provided the terminus for the migrating pilgrims of the Mormon faith that had first taken root in the State of New York. The eponymous city that grew up near the Great Salt Lake of Utah was designed to be the New Jerusalem of a faith claiming to be derived from a newly discovered scripture.

As we approached Salt Lake City, I thought of my first acquaintance with the Mormon faith at the time of the adventure that I entitled, *"A Study in Scarlet."* This was the first of the books through which I attempted to record the unique gifts and personality of my friend, Sherlock Holmes, just as this present account to be completed at last in the year 1918 will probably be the last. How strange it seems to me that we should be passing the site where the Mormon pilgrims had come to rest at last and where the group known as the avenging angels took their inspiration. One of these would end up in London and write the word "Rache" in German upon a wall there, a word meaning revenge.

The present narrative is in many ways the epitaph of the extended story that began with my first tale. It concludes, not with a story of revenge, but with the laying down of the sword of vengeance by Professor Moriarty. My theme has been that even the one who has been most tried and vexed by evil should not choose to do evil in return. For this reason we made our pilgrimage to the site of Wounded Knee and not to the site of the Mountain Meadow Massacre which will forever stain the history of that nascent religion. That massacre had been inflicted, not upon the Indians, but upon American settlers by other America settlers. The victims were those regarded as gentiles by the secret Mormon society called the Danites or the Avenging Angels. Fanaticism and religious persecution had been visited upon the Mormons as well and had eventually driven them into exile. In fact their presence in what became the state of Utah, formerly referred to as Deseret, was due to the rejection of the claims made by their founder Joseph Smith. Whether his audacious assertions were made in earnest or were merely one more instance of the methods whereby religion has been used to seduce followers and to confuse minds will perhaps never be resolved. In any case religious reprisal is never the right of man, but the sole prerogative of God. If this truth were ever grasped, then all wars would surely cease.

As we came down from the mountains to the valley of the Great Salt Lake I could not but think about America and its aspirations to make all things new. It is not strange that a nation that had inaugurated democracy in politics might also wish to create a revolution in Christianity by forming for itself a new religion under the auspices of a new and native-born prophet; but whereas democracy stems from the essential natural rights of man to govern the temporal order for the common good and is thus based on natural law, there is no similar right to create a new religion to meet the unique needs of the American people. The various instances of odd Pentecostal out-pouring referred to as The Great Awakening shared these same characteristics.

The best indicator of truth in religion lies in its continuity with the past. With the single exception of Abraham, who walked familiarly with God, no prophet can claim to have been the sole source for new religious truth. God does not move backwards in his dealing with mankind to correct prior errors. Even the new law of Charity celebrated by St. Paul as the basis for Christian hope did not abolish the Torah and the witness of the prophets but instead fulfilled them. The Catholic Church established by the Holy Spirit at Pentecost received the entire message as to the relations of God with man. For this reason all subsequent dogma and liturgical practice must refer back to the time of the Apostles through the sacrament of Holy Orders and Apostolic Succession to claim validation by the Holy Spirit. Tradition in the Catholic Church is the sign of the indwelling presence of the Holy Spirit that alone confirms the Church in its ancient faith and strengthens hope its hope and mission to the world. Therefore the concept of reformation when it is applied to the Catholic Church is actually a misnomer. The living Church cannot err in its deposit of faith for it is dependent not upon man but upon the voice of God living within us as members of the single corporate body of the Church. Public revelation ended with the death of the last Apostle and all subsequent formulations of the faith must be in accord with the writings and the living tradition that prevailed at that period of Church history.

For this reason, subsequent Church practices, even such rooted institutions as monasticism, may change over time, while the substance of the faith remains unaltered. Any attempt to as it were graft onto the great tree of faith a new off-shoot in the form of a new and altered essential revelation must then we condemned, not in its motives, but simply because it does not coincide with the truths revealed by Jesus during his life on earth which are complete, eternal, and unchangeable and completely adequate for our salvation. Anything not contained within that public revelation, which ended with the death of the last apostle, remains within the mystery of God and shall only be known on the Last Day.

The Catholic Church in its humility resists all attempts to accommodate the faith to flatter the temporary temper or prejudice of changing times and places. Its message is universal and enduring and requires neither augmentation nor amendment. For this reason all attempts to supersede revelation through assuming some new intervention by God are precluded by the prior truth of God, which is unalterable. It is the firm belief of the One Holy Catholic and Apostolic Church that the birth, life, and death of Jesus Christ while he lived among us and after His resurrection provided the definitive and actual means by which and through which all of humankind are to be re-united with God. The fundamental destiny for all of mankind was brought about by the perfect adherence of Jesus to the will of the Father. By this means and through our incorporation into Christ by one Baptism the entire human race is renewed and brought together in One Body. The Church does not despise prophecy, but all supposed prophesies after the death of the last Apostle (what are termed private revelations) must adhere to the substance of the faith as already taught and believed from the beginning.

For this reason, the writings of the Koran and those

contained in the writings of Joseph Smith may be valued insofar as they urge men and women to charity and enhance the natural virtues, but they are misleading and in formal error to the degree that they propose an alternative revelation that is incompatible with what has been taught and believed from the beginning by the One Church of God. Jesus Christ as the Second Person of the Holy Trinity completed all things by His life, death, and resurrection. The Church may grow over time in its appreciation of the faith, but that does not create new dogma. Its progress is in depth rather than in breadth of understanding. Its true growth is horizontal, by reaching out to all of mankind with its essential message. For this reason the Church wishes to confirm the stirrings of the Holy Spirit, wherever actual grace may be operative, but it adheres to its mission to preserve the truth from diminishment or amendment until the return of Jesus Christ on the last day.

Any temptation to create a new version of the eternal truth has been the spring of all heresies from the beginning. Only the steady anchor of the chair of St. Peter has been able to preserve the great ship of the Church and keep her on course in spite of all cross-currents and storms by various enthusiasts and their erstwhile followers. As our train came to Salt Lake City, we were able therefore to admire the vision of Brigham Young as a purely human phenomenon and the vision that had led the beleaguered pilgrims of that faith that followed the intricate and creative teachings of Joseph Smith to a land the startling beauty of which seemed to augur a new vision for Christian thought. If one were looking for a land the very nature of which seemed to recall the deserts of Palestine and of Sinai, one could not wish for a better place to start a new religion than Utah. That it is not the function of the Catholic Church, preserving as given what no man can create on his own initiative.

Yet to weaken or destroy even a misguided faith in others wherever it is to be found, can be an uncharitable act. God judges the sincerity of the heart of the believer more than the strict coherence of his or her mind or the accuracy of one's honestly held beliefs. One may proclaim the adherence for a lifetime to the one true faith and yet never live according to the tenets of that faith. For this reason the Catholic Church can only speak to those who will be able to hear its voice and receive its sacraments in return with all that they promise. It is not the function of the Church to besiege or to uproot. The action of grace is gentle and partakes of the love of God, who we believe knows best how to draw all men and women, and indeed all of creation, to Himself.

After we left Utah our train pushed onwards towards the dry and jagged mountains of Nevada, we left the Great Salt Lake shimmering in the sunlight of a late winter day. We knew that we would soon be in California by the time of the Spring Equinox and I could feel already the call of the great Pacific Ocean in my blood. We would be staying at the great hotel called Cliff House when we arrived in San Francisco. It was built by that most extraordinary man, Adolph Sutro, the builder of the famous Sutro Tunnel that had drained the mines of the Comstock Silver Lode at Virginia City since it was completed in 1878. The Comstock Lode had by now fallen upon evil days and was currently in borrasca which means that only low-yielding ore was coming up out of the mines. The great bonanza days were past. The Sutro Tunnel created over such great obstacles of resistance by both nature and by man in spite of opposition by the entrenched interests of the Ralston Ring, was now more of a curiosity and a memorial to the spirit of its builder than it was an aid to the extraction of rich ore from the mines.

Sun Mountain appeared to have been emptied at last of its treasury of riches and the town of Virginia City that had once drawn miners and poets from around the world to celebrate its glory was now only a shadow of its former self. Our visit there was to be a brief one. We took a stagecoach up the mountainside from Carson City and passed though Gold Canyon and the ruined mining camps sitting lower down on Sun Mountain until we reached Virginia City. We went to Mass the following day at St. Mary's and looked eastward from the graveyard there over the dry and shining plain towards the distant mountains of central Nevada, reaching eastwards from us now towards the America that we had just left behind us. Irene Adler gave an impromptu vocal concert that evening at the Opera House as a benefit for the mining widows and their children. We were all invited to be guests later at the home of Mr. McKay who was one of the last of the Silver Kings of Virginia City.

After we returned to Carson City our train labored up the steep sides of the high Sierras towards Lake Tahoe ending at the Truckee station where we again disembarked to spend a few days gazing down at those chill and lovely waters that sit in a great bowl high in the embrace of the Sierra Nevada range. Lake Tahoe cast a certain spell over my companion as it must to all who see it for the first time nestled in the surrounding mountains timbered by the great Ponderosa pines. Its name means "big water" in the local Indian tongue. Its superb clarity is such that the refractive index is in the violet range, which accounts for its extraordinary blue. As we first looked down upon it from our train as we approached the Truckee it did my heart good to see that Holmes had recovered his spirits since leaving Washington D.C. His keen grey eyes gazed down upon the waves that caressed the surface of the mirror-like waters below with signs of serenity as if some great deliverance had taken place within him.

We alighted from our train and promptly hired a carriage to take us to a rustic lodge on the North Shore of the great lake. There we remained for several days. It was like a renewal of our time together on the coast of New England when we wandered along the scenic Ocean Walk at Newport. It is of the nature of old friendships they may easily tolerate silence. In the presence of such beauty we found that speech was superfluous. We saw what lay before us and that was enough. The gentle murmur of the water of the lake was conducive to reflection and to contemplation.

On our third day at the lodge I found Holmes by the shore sitting on a log and reading from his copy of the Chinese classic, "the I-Ching." He smiled at my approach.

"You have caught me in the midst of my oriental studies, Watson. I find that chance suggestions may stimulate reflection and to that end the I-Ching is an invaluable tool. Today I am reading from the fourth hexagram, the Meng hexagram, which represents the folly of youth or difficulty at the beginning. The situation presented is that of the student seeking a teacher. The image is of the seeker after truth who is the pilgrim. It is in this

571

sense an image also for all detectives seeking for clues to solve the great mystery that is life. The book of the I-Ching is a guide for the man seeking wisdom and virtue. Its mechanism is its sixty-four hexagrams, each with a separate meaning and branching associations. Each hexagram consists of two primary trigrams, one above and one below. In this case the two trigrams are: Ken above meaning a mountain or keeping still and K'an below meaning water or the abyss. It is rather an image in its way of my position so many years ago at the Reichenbach Falls and in many ways of our position here today at Lake Tahoe."

He paused to see if I had followed his thoughts before murmuring, "Ah, those were the days when I thought that I could do all things. Youth has not yet encountered opposition so it imagines that anything is possible. In the Meng hexagram there is a tension between the fourth and the sixth lines. In the fourth line the advice is when danger threatens one must act precipitately to remove oneself from the danger, while in the sixth line rescue comes from an unexpected quarter. Had I followed the dictates of the fourth line and shot Moriarty down at Reichenbach in order to extricate myself from the threat he posed, I would have been shot in turn by Colonel Moran, who unbeknownst to me at the time, was waiting at the top of the falls with an airgun. When the Colonel perceived that the Professor and I delayed coming to grips on the edge of the waterfall, he concluded rightly that we had reached some sort of agreement. We then adjourned to a nearby inn, the site where we elaborated our great wager and the Colonel quietly withdrew. By following the course that is contained in line six, although I was not acquainted with the I-Ching at the time, I opened up the possibility for an unexpected outcome, which was my rescue from the situation by Professor Moriarty himself. His hesitation opened new possibilities for both of us. He was no more anxious to dispose of me than I was of him. Each of us posed an essential question that only the other could answer. By means of our mutual wager he opened to me a chance to journey eastward and inward as every man must to discover what he will choose and who he will become in the end. We will never know how much what happens to us in life is the product of chance or how much what happens is really simply divine grace in disguise or perhaps what is called 'the providential design of the universe.'"

As Holmes spoke I thought how we two might have been two monks sitting by a temple wall beside a lake in the high mountains of Tibet. Holmes continued in this fashion, "Much will always remain hidden of the ways of God with man. The various religions of the world are by necessity adapted to our cultural needs and our customary perceptions. We only see now, as scripture says said, *in a glass darkly.'* There will always be a mythological and thus naive aspect to any expression of religious dogma, for it must be expressed in the language of perception and of concepts and God is beyond both. This means that all religions, even in their highest and most formal proclamations, fall infinitely short of being able to describe and embody their most sacred beliefs."

"All creeds are an approximation adapted to our human capacities. The cryptic quality of the I-Ching is thus its guarantee of applicability to the general human condition, because it always relies upon analogy more than naked assertion. The best use of the language of religion must be evocative rather than definitive. This is why dogma must be supplemented by ritual. Ritual or liturgy must take over where dogma leaves off. It is only by enactment that we realize the deepest truth of what we believe. This is the role that the Holy Mass and the Sacraments serve in the Catholic Church."

"Faith demands action. It is by prayer and sacrifice that we enter substantially into God. Therefore, when the mind is exhausted by the doctrines of the Church, it must turn to the Rituale Romanum or to the Hours of the Divine Office where it will find the presence of the communal dialogue with God that it desires. The Chinese sage turns for such guidance to the I-Ching."

I was not sure that the two were in any way comparable in dignity, but I did not interrupt Holmes' discourse. After a brief pause for reflection he continued, "The days of my youthful folly are over now, fled with the days that have now gone up like smoke. My days of reading examples of Bildungsroman are over. It is too late in any case now to begin again with a clean slate and to develop into an entirely different Sherlock Holmes. The frame for my life perhaps already existed before the paint was even mixed upon the palette and before my first tentative brushstrokes. Every man lives his life within a context so that his freedom is always conditioned. Yet freedom is still a reality for all of that. In the end we must, as the I-Ching says, cross the great water. All of life is a preparation for the hour of our death when God shall meet us at last face to face and we will be asked to choose our abode for eternity in the light of all that we have made of ourselves. We pray that we may be spared the rigors of that hour. It is the hour that Jesus knew in the Garden of Gethsemani before his own crucifixion. It is the hour of the temptation of Adam in the Garden of Eden. Will we in turn say as Jesus did in speaking to the Father, 'Not my will but Thine be done?' when the great question is put to us by God?"

"And what is that question, Holmes?" I asked him quietly.

"The question of whether, in the face of all of our experience, of what we have made of ourselves in the dialogue of grace and freedom, we are willing to live in and for God alone, or if we would prefer to go our own way and make gods of ourselves. After death the fullness of being descends upon us as an irrevocable gift, the full implications of being an immortal, spiritual being must be faced at last. We are no longer guarded by the merciful cordon of time and place those twin shields which allowed us to act, yet to amend that act by future action when we err. At death what we will be hardens instantly into an irrevocable disposition. What we are becomes eternally evident. Nothing remains hidden. We may no longer hide behind the duplicity of the body and the incomplete knowledge of the resulting chain of events. In eternity each action and motion of the will is known in its furthest possible manifestations."

"That seems a gift that many would prefer to refuse," I commented.

"Without the comfort of the intervention of the saints on our behalf it would be intolerable," Holmes commented. "At last we are given the fullness of what we chose when we desired 'to be like God, knowing the difference between good and evil.' In the light of this total illumination of mind and heart it is possible for us to see at last that time, with its attendant phenomena of suffering and death, was always really the mercy of God bestowed upon us.

It has always been so. Had our initial choice been visited upon us in Eden, we too might have gone the way of the devil, who having chosen evil could not thereafter repent of it because of the very perfection of his angelic nature. You see it was always the intention of the Evil One to wish to be a sort of Fourth member of the Trinity, but through the exercise of a power other than that of love. Satan, the Prince of the Fallen Angels, hates God for His nature as love itself. The devil, unlike God, would have compelled obedience and obeisance from creation not merely invited it. The devil takes hostages by giving rewards. In this he is the father of the marketplace mentality. God, in contrast, asks for our love, irrespective of any advantage accruing to ourselves except that which is inherent in possessing Truth itself. Truth is self-validating and needs no reward. This is why evil (and the hell to which evil leads) is a cheap tinsel replica of the Beatific Vision where we shall see God as He truly is in all His simplicity."

Holmes paused to let that sink in before adding, "Please note that point, Watson! Our proper destiny is to see God as he is, not as (in our own evil manner) we conceive Him to be. Jesus said that. 'He who sees me also sees the Father.' Jesus also took our doubts into consideration when He praised those believers who would not be scandalized by His claim to divinity. What this means is that God's nature is one of true innocence, innocence that does not depend upon ignorance of evil in order to be preserved as is the case with children. God's innocence is different in its very simplicity, which knows neither differentiation nor diffusion. God simply is, as His name implies, Yahweh - I am that am."

Again Holmes paused before continuing, "God is One and there is no other. Therefore to see God demands the choice of God alone in which all things cohere. Evil in contrast abides in multiplicity and division. The devil thereby attempts to simply outbid God for our souls. This is the very nature of his empty promises, for behind the glittering kingdom of evil is the great and final emptiness of hell. I like to think of hell as a huge embassy reception hall where everyone is engaged in self-reflection, chattering away, thinking that everyone is very impressed with their attire and accomplishments, while in reality everyone is looking at mirrors that line the room, thinking of how great and beautiful they are, and resenting it that no one is paying them any attention at all."

"Here is another analogy: Hell is this eternal posing before an indifferent audience while awaiting the final revelation of the illustrious Guest of Honor, who is Satan himself, a being whose nature, now turned horrifying beyond belief, would reveal (should he ever appear) to each of his minions their own deficient idea of perfection, now grown ugly and deformed, because these traits are no longer a means to seek out love and to find God."

"As a final humiliation our bodies are to be re-united with our souls at the Last Judgment when the eternally lost are to be reminded that they are only men and women after all, poor fragments of their initial wholeness in God; that would be the hour of wailing and gnashing of teeth, not in contrition but in realization!"

"Christianity teaches clearly that men and women need love to attain full humanity. Each sex is severed from the other so that our very natures might remind us that love requires more than just ourselves. We are born incomplete and in anguish so that love may beckon to us and we to love. Our sufferings are the pathway back to God and we know as Christians that God Himself has embraced our sufferings and made them His own."

"Even after the resurrection, Jesus did not spurn the nail marks in his hands or the wound in his side. God has taken upon himself the humility of what time and circumstance bestows upon us. God has made Himself a victim of history and made himself subject to our choices, as Jesus proved when he said to his Apostles, 'But you, who do you, say that I am?' and Peter answered Him, "You are the Christ, the Son of the Living God!" Jesus then tells Peter that this revelation, this faith just announced by Peter, coming as a revelation from God the Father, is the rock upon which Jesus would build His Church and 'the gates of Hell would not prevail against it.'"

"This is the faith that you and I follow Watson, these many centuries later, the faith that has been proclaimed by all of St. Peter's successors ever since still lives. It is grounded upon that same rock of conviction, that Jesus is the Christ, the Son of the Living God."

Sherlock Holmes sat there looking out over the water toward the distant mountains with his keen grey eyes as though he wished that even then the sky would open and all be made clear and clean as the edges of the lake were with its granite boulders or the white snow-capped ridges on the other side of the lake shining before us in the sun. I shall always remember that day as being one of great peace and triumph after our long struggle to understand and even to affect the history of our time.

What had been our longest case was drawing to an end, though there were to be many adventures ahead for us both still. On that day at Lake Tahoe I realized that Holmes had at last completed the circle of his long speculations and that his quest had bestowed upon him the gift of a faith that could endure all future trials and the dangers that were to come as the world entered a new century, the challenges of which would exceed all that had ever gone before in human history. We had each done his best to address the needs of the times in which we had found ourselves, yet I knew that Holmes must often feel as I did that as William Shakespeare said in his play, '*The Tempest*,'

We are such stuff as dreams are made on and our little life is rounded with a sleep.

I clasped Holmes' hand before leaving him there, sitting in the sun that streamed down over the mountains. It would soon sink below the horizon made of the tall peaks on the opposite shore and leave the lake like a great silvered disk, reflecting back the glory of the pale blue winter sky and night would come.

On the following day we returned to Truckee Junction and by slow degrees descended from the high Sierra range into the rich green hills of the great central valley of California where San Francisco lay slumbering above the golden waters of the bay.

On the train Holmes gave Irene and I a brief lecture about the man who was to be our host during our last week to be spent in America.

"You have heard no doubt of the tales of the legendary Comstock Lode, perhaps the greatest silver strike that the world has ever known. The center of the lode was Virginia City which stands upon the eastern slope of Sun Mountain where we have just paid a visit. The light of the rising sun illuminates the dry sage country and low hills to the east where the silver was to be ultimately shipped after passing through the Carson City Mint. The Comstock vein was called 'a true fissure vein,' running into the earth to a depth of over 2000 feet. Each foot of soil though was mixed with clay and scalding volcanic waters tinged with sulfur compounds, but accompanying these there were rich quantities of a blue material that represents some of the richest silver-bearing ore ever found.

The claims on the Comstock Lode consist of adjoining mines with colorful names, each slicing vertically into the earth hoping to follow the ore body downwards as it weaves from side to side, now favoring one mine and then another. The Comstock Lode is not the story of a few men or of a few mines. It is a tale of fortunes made and lost, of successive waves of bonanza, each of which brought a fortune to whichever group ruled the lode at that time. It is also the story of the city of San Francisco and above all of the Bank of California with its director, William Ralston, and his Virginia City agent, William Sharon, the man who built the first railroad up Sun Mountain and the one who opposed Adolph Sutro's innovative idea to build a great tunnel to drain and to ventilate the mines. Getting air down to the miners and the water draining from the seams out of the mines was no small task. The heat at the bottom and in the remote drifts was often near 120 degrees with the men working almost naked. Accidents when they occurred such as the one in the Yellow-Jacket mine were both terrible and costly affairs so that the plan for a tunnel was both sensible and humane. The problem was that it would take ore from the stamp-mills up in Virginia City controlled by William Sharon and the investors from San Francisco who controlled the lode and profited from every ton of ore extracted."

"Adolph Sutro's story is the story of one man pitted against some of the richest and most powerful men of California and Nevada. I first heard about him from our friend, Thomas Reed, the Speaker of the U.S. House of Representatives. I told him how much I desired to meet this man before leaving America. Mr. Reed offered to act as a go-between with the result that we have a most splendid week ahead of us. We will be meeting a man who may be the most extraordinary engineer now living in California, a man of great visions. His most recent exploit has been to build an affordable street-car line so that the less fortunate citizens of San Francisco can access Cliff House where he has built an intricate complex of salt-water pools for the bathing recreation of the citizens of San Francisco."

"Every age contains a few men of supreme genius who benefit the majority by their inventions and constructions. Adolph Sutro is one of the great men of our age. Such men seem to belong almost to another species. Their belief in themselves and in their vision is such that no obstacle is allowed to pose anything but a stepping stone to the achievement of their final designs. It takes a certain degree of ruthlessness in order to create a new world. Many men died in the course of building the great tunnel linking the Carson River stamping mills to reduce the ore to the lower levels of the mines at Virginia City. Great men must carry before God a legacy of both life and death. For this reason it is a fearful thing I believe to aspire to greatness. It is one of the reasons that I wish to spend some time with this man. The last two years have involved my own attempt to have an effect upon the course of history, to have some effect upon the great tidal sweep of the present age, rather than merely to solve those humble problems brought to my door at Baker Street. I believe that I know now how fortunate is the man or woman who lives in obscurity and whose life plays only a transient role among those whom he or she affects by their one short life. To take any decided position in this world and to pursue it requires a degree of confidence that tends to feed self-idolatry, which I need not tell you is a most dangerous spiritual condition to be in. For this reason it would be well for all men of power and influence to recall daily the words of Jesus,

'What does it profit a man if he should gain the whole world and lose his immortal soul?'"

"Against such strong opposition the tunnel was delayed year by year. New investors came and went and the shares of mining stock rose and fell on the San Francisco exchange. Many times people wrote off the lode as finished and then a new strike in some remote drift would be struck and the whole game was on again. At last the tunnel was completed as Sutro had promised, but by then the shares were owned by many people and Adolph Sutro had moved on to other things. He became the Mayor of San Francisco and later built the great luxury hotel at the Golden Gate, an emblem of the city. This is the man that we are now going to see as his honored guests."

We were met at the station by Adolph Sutro's personal carriage which took us through the bustling streets of the thriving city of San Francisco to the western-most part of the city, Pacific Heights, where the former Mayor of San Francisco had erected the exquisite mansion called "Sutro Heights" that stood just above the bluff on which Cliff House and its recreational facilities had been built. It was there that he received us at the gate so that we could walk together through his garden of statuary to the house missing no element of what he clearly intended as a tribute to the promise of the west. The marble statuary provided a classical setting among the lawns overlooking the Pacific Ocean. As we drove up he was smoking a cigar and gazing out towards the great hotel where he had reserved rooms for us during our stay as his guests. How shall I describe him? How can I convey the remarkable force of intellect combined with the great body of the man once called, "the honest miner?" His enthusiasms were still immense and varied as they had been when he envisioned a town at the base of the tunnel that would become a model community. He rushed over immediately to greet us as the carriage drove up to the private drive that meandered its way through the grounds to his new home.

"Gentlemen, welcome to San Francisco!" he exclaimed as we alighted. "When I first heard from Thomas Reed that you were in America, I hoped to travel east to meet you before you returned to England. I assure you that I have followed your exploits for years, Mr. Holmes. You will find in my library a complete record of your published cases by the hand of your excellent friend here that I assume is Dr. Watson. I hope that you will be able to refresh and restore yourself after your journey while you are here until you depart for your Pacific voyage. Until then please consider my home, Sutro Heights, as your own. I have placed you in one of the tower suites at Cliff House across the avenue. Your rooms over-look the Golden Gate and you may swim in the salt-water pools at the baths at your leisure. I trust that you will do me the honor to dine with myself and my family in the evenings and join me here for breakfast whenever you wish and of course my library is at your disposal as well should you wish."

"I have also arranged for comfortable accommodations for you, dear lady, at Cliff House," he said greeting Irene Adler and kissing her hand. "Please consider all the facilities at Cliff House, many of which are designed to cater to feminine beauty and comfort, with my compliments during the entire period of your performances here in our fair city by the bay. I hope in the next week to introduce you to our director of the opera and to our orchestra conductor."

He rubbed his hands together briskly before continuing, "Now, if you will join me, we shall go up to the house where you may refresh yourselves after your long journey. I have had a meal prepared and you must meet my family. Your luggage will meanwhile be conveyed to your rooms at Cliff House so that all will be in readiness there for your arrival after lunch."

The days that followed were such as to erase from our minds the impressions that remained from our time in the east as well as the desolation of winter still lingering on the Great Plains. Spring seemed to be in advance of itself in California. I do not believe I have ever been among a people who showed forth such energy; hope and optimism seemed to be the very fabric of each day. Although the waves of discovery of gold and silver had passed, a new source of wealth had taken its place, one more lasting because it was rooted in the living processes of the land and climate, rather than what might be extracted from its heart.

The benign setting of California combined with the rich soil found there was such that all manner of produce could be grown. Gold and silver are in the last analysis dead things, mere bargaining chips used to bridge the gap of trade. In the end trade is based upon essential goods rather than upon money or metallic specie. For this reason California was a land that promised prosperity and grace, just as the sunlight that never seemed to be absent promised ever renewed life to the flowering earth. The sense of abundance had entered into the spirit of the people that residing there. There was an ease and expansiveness in all that they achieved, a sense that whatever was lost in life might be swiftly regained with sufficient effort. I found myself asking why such a favored place would wish to be admitted to the union of the other states rather than being its own country. The Sierra Nevada Mountains seemed to me an adequate wall to hold at bay the pretentions of the eastern aristocrats, the great railroad barons, and even the edifice of English common law. Here, it seemed to me a new legal structure might emerge that would support a true common-wealth among its residents, one secure and adequate in itself to meet every human need.

I found the place so thrilling that while Holmes and Mr. Sutro began their discussions each day I would take the street-cars each day down to the docks where fishermen brought in their daily harvest from the sea: cod, halibut, and tuna. Great crabs and abalone were boiled in large pots on the docks before being sold, wrapped in newspaper, and to be taken home or packed in ice for transport to the many fine restaurants that lined the bay. The water would lap at the shore as I sat upon a terrace sipping the local steam beer where I could be entertained by the fierce life of the city going on all about me. The terraces were bedecked with fresh flowers and each establishment overlooked picturesque Alcatraz Island and the green hills of Marin County across the water threaded by all manner of ships and pleasure craft.

I was often left to my own devices because Holmes was occupied in his discussions with Mr. Sutro and Irene was busy with the ladies of San Francisco who had invited her to innumerable formal teas to introduce the famous actress to the local cognoscenti. We would all gather together again in the late afternoons to take a short swim at the Sutro Baths or to walk along the beach below Cliff House. The sun would already have begun its long declination then and the color of the sea would change and enter that strange mood that prevails while the sun seems to draw all things into itself as its incandescent light burns downward towards sunset.

It may have been a mere fancy of mine, but I seemed to feel that same draw as of ancient tides in my very blood as I gazed into the molten disk of the sun and heard the sea lions barking on the rocks below the baths. The air changes just at sunset and the wind, which might have proceeded all day from the west seems to reverse itself suddenly and come from the east carrying the smell of dry grasses and the warmth of the sun-soaked land. The waves change then to a lovely shade of jade as they rise up as if to block the last light streaming upwards from the sun just submerging itself below the horizon. It as though the waves are living things, frightened horses rushing upon the sands where tiny birds called sandpipers run about like little children playing with the waves.

It was always a pleasure for me then to see Irene walking along the beach beneath a lovely parasol, which the wind threatened momentarily to snatch from her grasp. Holmes would be walking by her side, filling his healed lungs with great mouthfuls of fresh sea air untainted by the fogs of London. My prayers for his recovery had been answered. My friend seemed again to be the hearty fellow that I had met so many years ago when all of life seemed to lie before us both filled with adventure and mystery.

My own physical wounds, acquired in the Afghan Campaign, healed in the Baker Street of 1878 after I first met Sherlock Holmes and settled in at Baker Street. But there are still wounds to the soul that remain even after the body is again intact. I found in Sherlock Holmes over the years of our partnership more than just a friend. He seemed to possess some rare instinct for truth and a hunger for clarity that is all too rare in this confusing world. Yet I always knew that he suffered as well from the intense expectations with which he faced the world. He demanded in his way more than this life can ever give of certitude and of peace. For this reason he often sought refuge in the illusions of perfect clarity and the power of the drug cocaine that had once threatened to eclipse his early promise. It was due to my constant vigilance and often expressed disapproval that he at last turned from that chimera of the senses and accepted the limits that are perhaps our only guarantee of real happiness in life.

Yet true happiness is neither freedom from pain nor ease in

living. A life devoid of challenges and one that is unwilling to accept the inevitability of contradiction and paradox is as illusory as any drug- induced state of bliss. To attain heaven one must risk at times offending God. I will go so far as to say that the one who fears God so much that he cannot love God will never find God. The hunger for truth demands daring and a willingness to test the margins of what is knowable. An easy exposition is likely to be overly simplified and as such to be well off the mark. This is why generalizations are so pernicious.

To find happiness in solitude or in the pursuit of wisdom as embodied in literature and philosophy is to engage in a dialog with persons long since dead but who are no less human for all of that. Together they form an interminable conversation that draws the best minds of each age together so that the printed page is a gateway across time and space into the very souls of some of the most stimulating people who have ever lived. After all there is more loneliness in mere social display than in reading poetry. To learn how to read a text as though it opens horizons of meaning beyond the literal and bare denotation of the sentence is to truly master the art of reading.

I think that Holmes believed in the end that a theology that is so blinded by God's grandeur that the human element disappears is not Christian. The most faithful steward of orthodoxy is not the one lacking in all imagination who is so convinced of the unchangeable and multitudinous perfections of God that he is convinced that God is frozen and finally unaware of even the petitions of prayer sent up before His august and adamantine throne of glory. Many people worship their idea of God rather than God as He has dared to show Himself. Traditions that are a prison are ones from which the Holy Spirit has been evicted. I prefer to think that God adapts Himself to our capacities to receive Him and that grace like a flexible membrane is so close to us that it is at times indistinguishable from our own better impulses. This is why all proofs of God are likely to lose their direct object in proportion to the supposed accuracy of the reflections contained in our synopsis.

To the earliest Christians the message of the gospel had yet to be refined into the neat affirmations of a creed or the equally complex critique of faith that is theology. These were phenomena of a later day and meant to address problems and doubts that only the later centuries of Christendom's triumph would present. The first message was no doubt so astonishing when seen against the backdrop of the power of ancient Rome that people no doubt embraced what they could not yet have defended using these tools of a later day. They only knew that death no longer posed an absolute border to their existence, because Jesus of Nazareth had managed to die a horrible death on a cross and return to explain that the love and generosity that he had spoken of during his life now had eternal significance. Alternative sorts of scattered communities began to embrace this strange conception after His ascension and base their entire way of life upon it. If asked they would have referenced their own practices to the gift of the same spirit that had animated Jesus in life that now impelled them to face even a martyr's death as in the case of Stephen.

The life of Jesus as the Christ now clearly appeared as a ministry and not the set of delusional variations from the refined Judaic practices recognized by the Sanhedrin that had motivated the Jewish leaders to call for his death. By the time of the Gospel of St. John the overlay of concepts was already sufficiently refined that it was fully acceptable to a refined Greek-speaking audience to employ references to Jesus as the Logos or Word of God as a perfectly acceptable and comprehensible title for the preacher from Galilee.

This is not to say that these appellations are wrong, but it is to say that how Jesus and his teaching are received often says more about the needs of the community that receives and proclaims that message than it does about the primary message of Jesus, which is to love. The non-definable God of Abraham eventually comes to bristle with definitions and attributions so as to live up to the role demanded of Him. This process is not surprising considering the role that religion plays in human life, but it is rather odd that so few people seem to notice it or to trace it to its source in our own need for clarity about what we will never fully understand.

To say that I found happiness during that precious week in San Francisco before sailing would be inaccurate, because what I found was more akin to timelessness, a foretaste of eternity. I was with the people I esteemed and in a place that made me feel young once more and ready to embrace new things. As our short week in San Francisco drew to a close I lamented that this way of life might not be indefinitely prolonged, but our passage was already booked and there were men in Yokohama who expected our arrival. They hoped to learn of the methods of England's great criminal expert from his own lips. From Japan we were to travel to Hong Kong and then by way of the Indonesian Island chain and Malaya to Ceylon and at last through the Suez Canal to Montpellier where we would take the train to Calais. After that there would be the familiar boat-train to Dover and then home to London. But that long journey was still before us and there was still time to savor our present comfortable situation: to drink American whiskey in the walnut-paneled bar of Cliff House while gazing out the windows at the sea cliffs with the ever present chanting of the sea lions before returning to our rooms to get ready for a late dinner at the Sutro Mansion with our host.

He had already shown us his magnificent library, one said to be the largest privately-owned library in the world. After selling his interests in the great tunnel he had built, Mr. Sutro began a period of wandering over Europe collecting books as he went. Books were for him precious objects, each containing a unique world, the labor and insight of the men and women who have left some record in our common intellect of their experience and wisdom. I would say that Mr. Sutro was one of those men who might be called preservationists. He had spent the years since 1878 building a complex monument that celebrated the best things of our present life: physical culture and great ideas.

There had never been anything like the interlocking salt-water pools of the Sutro Baths with their glorious views of the ocean through the crystal palace of its windows. Though his own health and vigor were just beginning to fail after a life-time of labor, I could still feel the spirit of the man reaching out to a world that vast as it was could not contain his spirit and his hunger for life. What is the life of a man if it does not leave something behind to show that he has lived? All of the great benefactors of the earth, the poets, the scientists, the prophets, have this desire not merely to know the truth but to be caught up in it so that what they have discovered and communicated bears some slight imprint of their individual mind and spirit. If reality stands against us as brute objectivity, it is also true that how that objective truth is formulated shows some element of our own unique being. Even the majestic and risen savior-figure of Jesus Christ is best expressed for us as filtered through the letters of St. Paul who never saw Jesus in familiar flesh while He lived.

The voice of the risen Jesus at that stupendous meeting on the road to Damascus, the Christ of the gentiles, seemed at first to exceed even what St. Peter was willing to accept at first. Does this mean that what God is to each of us is conditioned by what we are able and willing to accept of God's grandeur? Does God adapt Himself to our needs so that each man inherits the God that he deserves? Do we create the world in our own image after all? Is that part of the residual power claimed by Adam's sin: to be like God knowing good and evil? Does God allow us to go that far before reminding us that we are creatures at last?

Jesus once said, *"Blessed is the man who finds no scandal in me."* Perhaps that refers to those who look for a different image of God or possess a different expectation of what salvation would mean for each man and woman rather than the individualized approach that Jesus took to each person who asked something of Him. Each encounter with Jesus is as though no other soul was present at that moment of most profound intimacy—God in the Garden of Eden asking Adam where he had gone.

The disciples of Jesus were often all too eager to decide who had a right to approach Him. Those who are quite satisfied that they know what is best for God turn aside from the way proffered by Jesus and gaze upon the humble man from Galilee before turning away in scorn of that humanity. These religionists are those who are scandalized by Jesus and by being so they turn away from the blessing, the only true blessing that God can ever give, the blessing of His very self in the One Divine Word, the Beloved Second Person of the Trinity, the one who asks what the petitioner seeks from Him—the one who says to each believer, *"But you, who do you say that I am?"*

Similarly, each man has only his one-self to give to this world and by doing so he gives whatever he possesses. He leaves his own small word, brought forth from deep within himself. It may be the words of a Shakespeare, it may be the formulas of a Newton, or it may be only the cultivated land of the farmer who has left in the tilled soil some sign of the plow held in his gnarled hands, some caring husbandry for his herds, some sign that he was once among the inhabitants of the earth.

Just so it was with Adolph Sutro, a son of Israel; after he left Germany. He built his great tunnel on Sun Mountain and later Cliff House and the adjacent Sutro Baths both finished in 1896. His desire was to place his wealth and energy to use in order to stall that inevitable erosion that brings all of us to nothing in the end through the processes of change and the forgetfulness of time. Our host was secretly ailing during our visit, but his indomitable spirit was still unvanquished—his benefaction to the city that he loved soon perished as well; a few years after our departure for Japan the magnificent Cliff House Hotel burned in a fire on September 7, 1907.

I recall as I stood on the shore in those last days of our sojourn to America I wondered how long these great achievements would last. How long I wondered would Cliff House stand like some great castle transported from the Rhineland to California? How long would the Sutro Tunnel bring forth the last remnants of Comstock silver from Sun Mountain, that famed site that was already sinking into itself as if to fill again the vacuum left by its rifled treasures? How long would the new and wondrous city of San Francisco itself stand beside its golden gate to the orient with its busy markets and its grand Palace Hotel that had been the dream of Mr. Sutro's rival, William Ralston, who ran the Bank of California? The Palace Hotel burned in the fire caused by the great San Francisco earthquake that occurred in the early morning hours of April 18, 1906 and the structure was later demolished.

If everything must pass, as all things surely do, then new people need to dream again and gather up what has been scattered, even as Adolph Sutro had done in collecting his great library and bringing it home to San Francisco in building Cliff

House and his elegant marble mansion, Sutro Heights, by the mighty Pacific Ocean. Thoughts of the possible immorality or long duration of our achievements possess us all. It is when my thoughts are most focused on just such hopes that I recall the words of Sir Thomas Browne from his great essay on immortality, *Hydriotaphia or Urn Burial* from which I cull these lines...

There is nothing strictly immortal, but immortality. Whatever hath no beginning may be confident of no end; - all others have a dependent being and within the reach of destruction; - which is the peculiar of that necessary essence that cannot destroy itself; - and the highest strain of omnipotency, to be so powerfully constituted as not to suffer even from the power of itself. But the sufficiency of Christian immortality frustrates all earthly glory, and the quality of either state after death, makes a folly of posthumous memory. But man is a noble animal, splendid in ashes, and pompous in the grave, solemnizing nativities and deaths with equal luster, nor omitting ceremonies of bravery in the infamy of his nature. Life is a pure flame, and we live by an invisible sun within us. Oblivion is not to be hired. The greater part must be content to be as though they had not been, to be found in the register of God, not in the record of man. Since our longest sun sets at right descensions, and makes but winter arches and therefore it cannot be long before we lie down in darkness, and have our light in ashes; since the brother of death daily haunts us with dying mementoes, and time that grows old in itself, bids us hope no long duration; - diuturnity is a dream and folly of expectation.

As a doctor I have witnessed these words both spoken and fulfilled as souls beneath my care have passed beyond my poor ability to recall them. As a doctor I can neither create life nor prolong it when the time allotted by God for its departure is near at hand. To preserve memory is the task of the author and sometimes by the reader's gracious consent dead words live again in print and in that hope the author takes up his pen and writes.

ou are being thoughtful again Watson," said Holmes to me that day. "You are in many ways as inscrutable as the sphinx," he added smiling and coming over to sit beside me. We sat together side by side overlooking the sea, which broke in silver ripples visible to the very margin of the clouds that still lingered far out at sea.

"Am I Holmes," I replied. "If I am so then I am likely to remain so for I have no Boswell to record my thoughts unless I do it myself."

Holmes nodded, "Then perhaps you will do so someday. In your desire to celebrate my own small gifts, I fear that you have neglected your own. Jesus told his friends that no disciple is better than his master; but of what use is it to point the way if that way is never taken at all? We do not know what we can accomplish until we try. Even Our Lord assured his followers that what he had done during his short sojourn upon the earth would be done by others also because they would receive the gift of His Holy Spirit and He would be present within them thereafter, sacramentally."

"We are all of us present to one another. The entire human race is as it were one individual, the one Adam created so long ago in paradise. For this reason, the immortality of one is for the benefit of all. Each of us has it within him or her to extend the borders of this single humanity so that it embraces a wider reach. To be created in the image and likeness of God is to be ourselves creators. The care of the entire earth is entrusted to us. The primal unity symbolized by marriage may create more god-like beings among us to cherish what we have left for them and to carry on after we pass. Every child of the earth is the child of us all in the last analysis so that each of us is completed or diminished by what others do and have done. That is the anodyne for our personal failings. All things will be completed in due time even if the hands that achieve this fruition of the earth are not ours."

Holmes sighed, "I told as much to our new friend, Adolph Sutro, the other day. He is not in good health Watson. Indeed, I doubt that he will long survive the date of our departure. We have had the rare privilege of meeting a truly remarkable man at the height of his many achievements."

"He must be very proud of all that he has done,"

I remarked.

"On the contrary Watson, he is a man in a state of great desperation," replied Sherlock Holmes.

"You surprise me, Holmes! Few men have accomplished as much in their lives as he has."

"Ah, but the standard that each of us maintains and later applies to those achievements comes from within ourselves, my dear fellow. Men such as Adolph Sutro must always have some new project in hand. When you are in the library tonight with our host, just look about you at the full extent of his mostly unread books many still unpacked. Adjoining the library there is a room filled with boxes only recently received from Europe."

"Mr. Sutro stood before me yesterday, Watson, and raised his hands above his head like a titan reaching for the skies, and then allowed his hands to fall, the very hands that once worked a pick alongside his men who were building the great tunnel into the base of Sun Mountain. It was a gesture of despair. He kept muttering to himself a single word repeated over and over again: 'Time, time, time.'"

"His troubled manner distressed me, so I asked that he come to the window and look out to where Cliff House stood shining in the spring sunshine with the entire ocean at its base, reaching out towards China and the Indies beyond. I felt for a moment like the devil that once stood with Jesus and showed him the whole world and its kingdoms with all of their glory. It is the world that will open to men like President McKinley or that mad fellow Theodore Roosevelt, if the Americans ever succeed in beating Baron Maupertuis in building a canal across the isthmus of Central America. It is the world that each of us leaves when we die, little knowing how long our personal empires will survive. I asked Mr. Sutro if what he saw before him was not enough for any man."

"What answer did he make?" I asked quietly.

"The same answer made by every great man who has ever considered the question, my dear Watson. He made the same answer as Andrew Marvel made when he said, *'Had we world enough and time, this coyness lady were no crime ... But at my back I always hear, time's winged chariot hurrying near; and yonder all before us lie deserts of vast eternity.'*"

"Mr. Sutro turned to me then and gave the same answer from a different poet, William Shakespeare, whom he quoted in part, *'That time of year thou mayst in me behold when yellow leaves, or none, or few do hang upon those boughs which shake against the cold, bare ruined choirs where late the sweet birds sang.'*"

"After quoting those lines Mr. Sutro shrugged in testimony to the same answer reached in the Book of Ecclesiastes: *'All things are vanity and a chase after wind.'*" I must confess to sharing his sentiments from time to time, Watson. I suppose that all men do; all thinking men that is. As for the rest there is always some project before them, some delight to be enjoyed or something to conquer and death catches them unaware."

I considered this for a time, wondering how much this dissatisfaction mirrored the desperation that had once set Sherlock Holmes forth on his own long journey of discovery in search of God in 1891 or the despair that I had felt at the death of my wife that resulted in my going out to the leper colony at Carville Louisiana in 1892 when I thought that Holmes was dead.

"What answer did you make to him then, Holmes?" I asked after some minutes spent in silence between us.

Holmes shrugged, "What answer can ever be made to the honest pain of such a formidable man? I could only hold up to him the mirror of his own minor achievements and my own dissatisfaction. To this I added three small quotations. The first came from Robert Browning who says that, *'A man's reach must exceed his grasp else what's a heaven for.'* The second is from the gospels when Jesus says to Martha, *'Martha, Martha, you are busy about many things but Mary has chosen the better part and she shall not be deprived of it.'*

"And what was the third quotation?" I asked since he had hesitated to proceed further.

"Oh, something from the Jesuit poet, Gerard Manley Hopkins," Holmes replied. It is begins, *'Margaret, are grieving over golden grove unleaving?'*"

"I am not familiar with it," I confessed.

"Ah, that is a pity since it is one of the poet's best. In the poem Hopkins suggests that young Margaret's sorrow is not for the loss of grove or bird or sunlight but the knowledge that is within us all that we must someday die. But there is comfort there as well. It is a difficult task, Watson, for even the Christian to accept that God's demands of us are as little as they really are. We each dream of recreating the entire world anew in our own image through some magnificent labor or by some unaccountable stroke of good luck. Mankind desires immortality, but only on its own terms. We each desire to achieve a name that shall be proof to oblivion. Even that excellent Christian philosopher, Soren Kierkegaard, had difficulty understanding and accepting human limitations. To Kierkegaard there was a disproportion between risking an eternal happiness or unhappiness based upon any historical event whatsoever, because nothing that takes place on earth can have eternal consequences. He thus proposed a new ontological argument to prove the existence of God. Kierkegaard proposed that God must exist, because God alone can satisfy our desire for the infinite. Our own need becomes the measure of its fulfillment otherwise our human longing for completion is absurd. Of course there are various peasant cultures around the world that manage to accept the limitations of the hard life that they often lead without the consolation of philosophy or the blind assurance of faith. Cultures such as these feel quite close to the lives of the animals that surround them daily and upon which animals their own existence often depends. It always struck me as the most troublesome aspect of many Christian persuasions that their own certainty of salvation could see no inequity in the corresponding belief that members of just such primitive communities were doomed to eternal punishment because they were deficient in a profession of faith promulgated in a geographical part of the world of which they were blissfully ignorant."

Holmes considered for time before continuing, "The problem with the argument of Kierkegaard, although I have found it to be personally quite persuasive, is that mankind remains the center in this argument for the existence of God. The argument from our own inner perplexity and disappointment is leveraged to summon forth a metaphysical source of solace. God must exist because we demand that He solve our problems for us. In contrast to this argument a truly authentic faith follows the example of Job in Holy Scripture, a man who makes no demands at all upon God even in misfortune. He bears in mind the wonderful fact that we exist at all, that we receive without prior petition this momentary existence in the shadow of our mortality. What did we ever do that we should have been summoned forth from nothingness to debate the very existence of God? What strange guidance leads the one-celled zygote along the path to maturity so that it may one day face another similar being and debate such huge questions? What temerity it is that man presumes to judge whether his species is the height and summit of all things!"

Holmes paused here in order for the full impact of his discourse to have its effect upon me before continuing with this question, "Is it not because of our faculty of knowing that we dare to debate the very grounds for our existence? Gnosticism is in the last analysis the fundamental heresy. We demand that God make sense to us on our own terms and to serve our own ends. We design for ourselves the contours of paradise. We presume to decide who shall merit eternal life so that God will validate our conceptions. If faith is so difficult to attain by our own efforts and above all else an undeserved gift from God, then why do so many Christians speak with such conviction of the most peripheral aspects of a belief system that is not self-evident?"

"One does not need to turn further than the gospels to see all of these presumptuous theses denied. In the gospel accounts we see that God himself does not hesitate to enter into the concrete events of people's lives and the circumstantial elements of our all too mundane existence. God makes His own being historical in the person of Jesus. God plunges into the temporal and the actual. Salvation for all humankind is not a proclamation from on high, but an actual acting-out in the world of the mission of Jesus that began at His Baptism by John in the Jordan River, later in His ministry upon the roads of Galilee, and finally in His crucifixion and death on the hill of Golgotha outside of Jerusalem. God uses the particular to show that we are living in a real world and not a world of mere ideas. Christianity is a religion of actuality and not of mere phantoms of the brain. In that sense Christianity leaves philosophy behind. Although it is true that all creation awaits the revelation of the Children of God at the Second Coming, that awaiting is not for some breakthrough of Platonic forms or ideas, but for an actual re-creation of the world by a returned Jesus, a state of being referred t as the Kingdom of God. This is why orthodox belief adheres to the dogma of the Resurrection of the Body and not the mere transmigration of souls into a spiritual kingdom.”

“Each human body is historical and unique; it is not to be subsumed someday into some general cauldron of merged identities where the historical becomes of negligible significance. The Communion of Saints is then a real community and though we are One Body in the Church, still that body is one of many members, each with his or her own unique presence and worth to the whole. We are what we do. Our lives are an exercise in individual response to the promptings of grace. Our sins are as real as are our acts of virtue and each is conserved and reserved to be redeemed by the merits of Christ and the forgiveness of God through the sacramental action of His Church.”

“All earthly events are pregnant with eternal consequences. We live in a world where life and death are suspended before us and we are asked to choose with every action of our lives how ee shall spend eternity. The earth is at our disposal from the plowed field to the mines that gut the surface of the earth. God has placed His own desire for our universal salvation as entrustment. Even the Church itself is placed in our keeping. The history of the Roman Catholic Church is replete with the misuse of that gift, yet Jesus the Christ remains upon our altars at Mass and the stream of grace and life bestowed upon us through the Holy Spirit has never ceased.”

“The Catholic faith endures and shall endure until the end of time. It is the faith that opens the door of salvation to believer and infidel alike, for only God knows the final manner of his announcement to the soul in its final hour. The answer to time is not properly contained within the temporal, yet this does not imply that the temporal is insignificant. Time structures what eternity shall be for us. It is in the most minute and trivial actions of our lives that we nurture the dispositions that open or close our hearts to the life of God.”

“Christianity dignifies the ephemeral. If God can have a

history in the person of Jesus, then who are we to feel that history is too small to contain us? Is one lifetime too short for us while thirty-three years was adequate for Jesus to save the world? How many Sutro tunnels must be built, how many Cliff Houses, how many hours spent bending over books that are too numerous for his shelves to contain, so that many are still lying in boxes? How many more cases for that matter must there be for one Sherlock Holmes of Baker Street? You see, Watson, I understand Mr. Sutro because we are both drawn from the same type of man, one who must press the very borders of the earth for testimony to the truth, and even then we would desire to place another question or assume a new task at the end of our lives. We are both the type of men who never understood that only one thing is necessary."

"And what is that?" I enquired.

"You have read my long confession as recorded in my journal and still you ask me that question, old fellow. You must know by now that I am the last man to rest easy as Martha's sister Mary once did at the feet of Jesus. I am not even like Martha, who was busy serving the guests. My life has been a quest for knowledge, only to find myself standing here on a foreign shore with a few trunks awaiting passage on a ship about to sail for England by way of Japan and wondering what I shall do when I return home to England."

"Shall I return once again to Baker Street or shall I retire as before to Devonshire and dig up more Celtic artifacts with Dr. Mortimer? Or should I remain here and seek solace in my remaining years in the arms of Irene? Oh yes, I have considered that possibility if she will still have me. You see my problem, old friend. It has always been the same; it is the problem of making the correct choice among the many life histories that might have been ours, which chain of events will we activate, knowing that each chain of events implies a unique identity for our very selves."

"Who finally is Sherlock Holmes to be? So rather than making one total choice, I have preferred to make all choices severally, to attempt to be the universal man who, having no life of his own, studies instead to solve the questions presented by the lives of others! My life is one long series of observations and deductions. I feel as though I was just beginning life and lo the end is already in sight. Shall I scramble about now and assemble a life at random that will be presentable to God as an actual human life? Or shall I take my own advice and rest secure in the inadequacy of any history on its own merits to justify this one human life that is my own? Will God be satisfied when even I am not? Shall God admit me to the Kingdom of Heaven when I long tarry at the gate, asking for still another day or hour at least to formulate the words that may adequately describe God, who already knows Himself and has no need for my grand synthesis honoring His many attributes? If even the exalted Seraphim chant only, 'Holy, Holy, Holy is the Lord God of Hosts,' why should I wish for a clearer formulation before I will so much as grant my assent to faith and believe, I who am only dust and ashes?"

I was the sole witness of this startling confession by the one man who I had long felt had an answer for any problem that I could ever pose. It brought home to me the awful responsibility that each of us faces alone: 'Who shall, I ever be?'

Holmes sighed after a time and threw up his hands, "Well so it is, old fellow. Perhaps now I understand why even the great St. Thomas Aquinas could look at his great Summa Theologica, and say in the end that it was only straw. I am left with only this, the admonition of God to the Israelites: *'Hear oh Israel, the Lord your God is One; this is what the Lord your God requires of you, that you act justly, that you love tenderly, and that you walk humbly with your God.'"*

He fell silent then and I asked him no more questions that day for there was nothing further for me to ask. I never felt that I understood him better or admired him more than at that hour. Adolph Sutro died before the century that had witnessed his spectacular achievements had passed. He was thus spared the knowledge of how short a time personal empires can endure. What we gather is soon scattered so that all that remains of even the greatest among us is the tangential repercussions of our actions that soon join the general current of the passing ages of humankind.

Lest I prolong my own curtain call past the endurance of my public, I must soon conclude this strange narrative of the life of Sherlock Holmes. I doubt that it shall see the light of day until each of us has passed that final gate that awaits all flesh. By then it will be too late to amend what I have written here, though I doubt that I would have anything to add. It has been my policy throughout to error rather by excess than by omission and I trust that the patient reader has not been lacking in indulgence if he has come this far in my narrative. But such is the mind of an old man that he will always find in that huge repository of memory, that sea of opportunities missed, some final incident to record or wisdom to impart.

I am just such an old man now living as I have done for many years by Poldhu Bay in Cornwall, in my little cottage, one built in the 1890's with the proceeds from my Kensington medical practice. I have lived here as my primary residence since 1903 when Holmes withdrew from his singular practice as England's first and greatest consulting detective. I may not mention his present whereabouts even here without placing him in danger, but I desire the reader to know that he continues hale and healthy into this year 1918 when this account is being completed. The malady of his youth that had once threatened to cut short his valuable life troubles him no more.

I recall that on our last day we left Cliff House to join Irene prior to breakfast for a brief walk along the beach that lay just south of the great hotel. The time of our parting was to be soon and we were both loathe to part with that dear lady, who was to remain in San Francisco for some time to come, as another lovely ornament of that fair city. Holmes had been assured by Mr. Sutro that he would take her under his patronage so that we might depart with the assurance that she would be quite safe and would prosper in the renewed career that would soon bring joy to the many who would hear her marvelous voice upon the stage.

Our ship was scheduled to depart in the evening and we were to board at three o'clock that afternoon. Mr. Sutro had invited us to breakfast with him at Sutro Heights. So it was that we found ourselves walking through the park that surrounds the great house just as the mists of the night were lifting. It was to be another lovely California morning with the scent of the early flowers of spring in the air. The breeze would be fresh from the ocean carrying with it the scent of that special realm which always quickens the blood within me. So lovely was the day that any hint of melancholy at our departure was overcome by our anticipation of the journey that lay ahead for us both.

Already I imagined myself wandering through some oriental markets where I might find carvings of jade in the intricate boxes of the Chinese or those marvelous cabinets made of teak which I hoped to purchase in Ceylon and have packed for me aboard the ship to enhance the furnishings of my cottage in Cornwall. Sherlock Holmes in turn was looking forward to visiting various Shinto Shrines and talking with some of the Zen monks in Japan and the Buddhist Monks in Ceylon. I could tell that Irene already felt the pain of our imminent departure, so both Holmes and I attempted to cheer her up with the prospect of her coming triumphs upon the stage. We felt that we were leaving her with good friends in the Sutro family, so that she would not be alone after our departure.

Our breakfast was an extraordinary affair served with iced shrimp, an excellent quiche, and plump beef sausages seasoned with sage and parsley. Mr. Sutro seemed as sorry to see us depart as was Irene. I believe that he had found in Sherlock Holmes the sympathetic ear that he had long sought. It was as though he hoped that Holmes might give him that final measure of esteem, that approval and sense of completion without which no man, however accomplished he may be, can leave this world with the sense that he has lived well and completed his life-task with honor. Even with the evidence of his success all about him, I could not but feel that this titan of a man still lacked something, and for that reason had asked that we join him, one last time, on this our final day in San Francisco. After breakfast, his daughter Emma volunteered to take Irene around the conservatory while we three gentlemen retired to the library where we partook of an excellent California Amontiado and sat before the morning fire, as the sunlight, shining through the French windows illumined the dust motes in the air.

Mr. Sutro looked weary to me that morning, more so than he had looked in recent days. I had noticed certain signs as a physician of the illness that was to claim him within the year.

"I shall be sorry to see you depart gentlemen," he confessed from deep within his great chair as the sun illumined his intelligent and noble face. "I have spent my life in a struggle so that my foes were my familiars and I have had precious little time for my friends or indeed for my family. I am afraid that I left my children to raise themselves. I was more of a father to the tunnel project than to them and I fear that several of my children resent me now for that abdication of responsibility. But you see so much was at stake. I had planned a town to be called after myself, the town of Sutro, to be built on the Carson River. It was to be a model city with every resource for the young and later plenty of jobs to be found in the stamping mills along the river. But when the machinations of the California Bank, of men like William Ralston and Bill Sharon, finally ceased it was already 1878 and the great silver vein, which had seemed inexhaustible, was already virtually played out. Of course I could not be sure of that; mining is an uncertain business. I only knew that I needed a change and San Francisco provided it."

"The Comstock Lode is now only a shadow of what it once was. Some have blamed me for selling my interests and moving to San Francisco just after the tunnel was completed, but you see I was trying to give my children what they had missed and to be a father to them at last. But I found that my years of travel back and forth to Europe to secure financing for the tunnel had made me an inveterate wanderer, so that I could not cease from travel. I imagined that my declining years would be spent here in this very mansion and that I would have time to read some at least of these many volumes that lie about you on these shelves. Instead I feel that I shall be carried out soon upon an ebbing tide so that these volumes will outlive me and all that I have gathered will be scattered among my children. Will they someday appreciate why I did what I have done? I wonder if I have given them enough affection so that they in turn will wish to preserve what is in its way a great legacy."

"I am Jewish as you know and the Jews of Europe were forbidden for centuries to own land, to engage in commerce, or to practice the professions. They were exiled from the guilds in the middle ages. Only in our day have these shackles been removed. Can you be surprised then that I have tried to overcome those long restraints and in our age of comparative freedom to fight the modern tyrants wherever I found them nested in their dens? I have been blessed in my enemies. They called out the best that was in me."

"Perhaps you also, Mr. Holmes, have been blessed by having an opponent worthy of your steel. Ah, I see that you understand me. I thrive best under opposition, or at least I have until this present hour when I see death approaching at last, not as some distant specter, but as my immediate future. Even then I would do battle with it, but death you see is not an external enemy; it emerges as it were from deep within our own being. We gestate death throughout our lives as a mother does a child. Death, if this metaphor is to be exact, is like a birth. Our soul must emerge at last from its tenement of clay and stand alone with just what it has made of itself, for I do not doubt that each man is free to choose his own life's course."

"Although I believe that I have chosen well for the most part, I do have my regrets now, as all men must. But strange as it may be to say, it is my victories that mock me most. Do not be surprised that I say this. You have many years yet to live, both of you. You cannot know what it is to have known great victories and to know how long they have taken, how much of life was wasted in futile effort against the immense inertia that opposes all human progress and insight and how ever-present are the forces of dissolution and decay that may reduce the works of a lifetime in a moment to ashes. Even the Egyptian pyramids, which have lasted longer than any other human creation or the Great Wall of China that rivals them in antiquity, mock the men who conceived and built them. How much more must the great destroyers of history come to lament that they have left only rubble in their train! Even ideas, which seem of all things to be the most immortal, are supplanted by other ideas. All prior formulations appear quaint in light of the new sciences. Books begin to mold before the ink has even dried upon their pages. Where then is immortality to be found? Or is it that man must accept and even love the fact that he must die, so that the land may not be burdened by the usages of yesterday and the mind may not be stifled by the conceptions of antiquated brains. Perhaps my children will know better how to use what I have left as a legacy to them. If nothing else they will live, for that is what I fear I did not sufficiently do. I built Cliff House and the great pools of the Sutro Baths that have just opened so that I might see others enjoy in their youth what in my age and illness I cannot. When I hear the laughter of the children as they dive and swim like the seals on the cliffs below, I feel happy at last."

"And is that not enough?" asked Holmes with a smile. "How few men attain such happiness or know that they can bestow it upon others."

Mr. Sutro gazed at him with pleading eyes. "But how long shall I be even a witness to that joy, Mr. Holmes? The grave already yawns before me."

Sherlock Holmes got up and went to the French windows, which he opened wide. He stood there in the morning sun breathing the fresh morning air. Mr. Sutro watched him with a puzzled expression upon his face.

Without turning Holmes spoke, "I am one familiar with the grave. I lost my mother as a lad and watched as my father descended into a realm of solitude and could not admit even his own sons to share his grief. He had begun life as a great idealist in the manner of Rousseau. He was one of the few members of his class who welcomed the ideas that lay behind the Napoleonic Wars. He was only a child born after the time of the French Revolution, but the liberal sympathies of his youthful admiration for liberty, equality, and fraternity took root within his very soul and remained within him after he came to manhood, so that by 1848 he was to be found in Paris where he met and married my mother."

Holmes smiled briefly before continuing, "It is one of the paradoxes of men who entertain extreme ideas that they often reverse themselves as they age. The easy confidence of his youth grew into a profound pessimism in my father as he aged. He no longer felt that education could work the redemption of human nature. He came to fear the commoners of his own county of Yorkshire and became convinced that rebellion and unionization might be at hand among the coal miners of the region. This led him to embrace Tory principles and to abandon the Whig convictions of his young manhood. He came at last to loathe the policies of the liberals and to lament the few freedoms granted to the Scots, the Welsh, and the Irish. He turned at last into a man of stone as barren and bleak as the cold moors of our estate in Yorkshire."

"It was as though he blamed God for robbing him of our dear mother, the sole joy of his life, though it is God alone who understands the true evil of death. That evil does not abide in the mere recycling of the elements of which we are made, for that much of death pervades all of life. It is rather the second death that we must fear, the death that comes from an attachment to life without regard to its origin in God. After all, what are our bodies but engines of destruction of what we consume and then recreate in our own image. It might be justly said that the earth in turn consumes us in the end, so that it might bestow life again upon other forms. But what then is preserved of us? Are our thoughts, our memories, our monuments so swiftly turned to other uses that no trace of our forming hand remains?"

"But even these are not really us? We are rather more akin to light speeding forth and away from a dying star so that it may continue through the vast regions of space long after the birthing star may have burned itself into oblivion. Yet at the head of that traveling beam of light the star would appear again to be intact in its timeless origin. If then we may imagine ourselves in a sort of mental experiment at the very earliest manifestation of light and moving together with it at great speed, then time as we know it would cease. All things would be coterminous with the primal event of creation."

"What then is time as we know it, but simply being left behind by that light that contains the essential us? We lie now, as it were, in the stagnant pool of past events, slipping ever deeper into the slough of what has been and is now no more. The present universe itself is an engine burning itself out and leaving only ashes behind. In my talks with the great Professor Moriarty we often discussed such just things as metaphors of eternity..."

Holmes turned again to face us. "Why then have we been left behind in this state of exile? Is it not so that we may gaze outward into the immensities of space that still record events as does a boat upon the waters when a wave has passed, rocking in the motion of that passing event? We are witnesses to the passing event of creation, which like a boat upon the distant sea, leaves only these testimonies as a vestige of its passing. All that we now know is encased within time and space, which are only the detritus of this decay."

Holmes returned from the window and sat down beside us by the fire, "So you see, gentlemen, how true the statement is that even in life we are in the midst of death. This then is what it means to live in contingent being, knowing all things in but a limited way. We sift through the ashes of matter and look for God, yet God is not to be found. What is left to us then but only ourselves and our brief affections and the warmth of the human heart? These are all we know of love, so that when they and life itself are taken away, we imagine ourselves eternally bereft. This is the appalling nature of death, that it takes our loves away. Our friends vanish one by one until we would wish gladly to have preceded them to the grave rather than to know the emptiness that they have left behind. "

"I have spent my life in the shadow of the disease of consumption that plays with its host as does a cat with a mouse. It forced me early on to ask myself the eternal questions and to walk along the very precipice of human thought. A few years ago I stood by the bedside of Mr. Nietzsche. He is another who dared to ask the unfathomable questions. It drove the poor fellow quite mad in the end, so that his mind became like ashes. He could not find God in the great darkness, yet he longed still to find him so that he could voice man's complaint to the author of our being."

"What is that complaint?" asked Mr. Sutro from where he sat bundled up before the fire.

Holmes walked back and closed the windows behind him and drew the drapes against the morning sun, before joining us again where we sat by the morning fire.

"Yes, there is still a bit of a chill coming up from the bay, but to answer your question, the complaint of man was uttered by the one man who called himself by the title, the Son of Man, in order to show his solidarity with all of humankind, Jesus of Nazareth. The complaint was uttered from the Cross in the prospect of His imminent death when all seemed lost. It is the cry of sinful man before his God. It is the cry of lost Adam echoing down through the ages since Eden. That cry is *'My God, My God, why hast thou forsaken me!'* It is not really a question you see, but a cry of desperation to be saved from what we have ourselves done with God; we have put Him away from us. It is not an act of despair and pride, but of horror and lamentation as man realizes that he can never be like God knowing good and evil. It is the cry of immanent repentance and it has called forth from the bosom of eternity a response, that God Himself would someday bridge the infinite gulf of our being and seek out man and woman where we lie adrift upon the ice-flow of time. It is that barren ice-flow where even now we their children wait, clinging still to the ice and beset by angry seas, awaiting the redemption of our flesh on the last day, when the dead shall rise again and all will be made whole and complete."

When I heard Holmes speak these words of comfort distilled from his reflections regarding the ultimate meaning of each human life in relation to God I could not help but reflect how little considerations of personal sin and accountability enter into the great sweep of history. Would Genghis Khan have been deterred from his conquests by the voice of conscience reminding him that the Lord of the entire universe: almighty God the creator of all things had commanded, *thou shalt not steal?* History like a great and mindless juggernaut, although it is presumably within the control of human agency, does not pause or alter its course in the pursuit of moral ends. It had long been clear to me that most of the ills of mankind were inflicted upon mankind by itself, which of course means by individuals granted power by groups and constituencies that serve to profit from precisely the scourges that we collectively call the problem of evil. But that problem is selectively allocated by the strong so that it rests securely on the shoulders of those groups least able to bear that dreadful burden.

Death is all about us each day, so ordinary in fact that unless that death or its prospect is our own we give it little thought. This made me impatient with those who have achieved much in life who in their final days are surprised that they are prevented by time's great scythe of death from further impressing their unique personality on the age and nation where fate has placed them. Who are these fortunate ones to complain? What of the great voiceless masses who are born to live and die condemned to the bare struggle to obtain the means of keeping body and soul together? What history do they leave but only their collective anguish largely invisible to those persons who determine the fate that will be theirs by their own privileged decisions as though they themselves were gods?

olmes was silent for a time and we all sat looking at the fire ticking to ashes in the grate. After a considerable pause he continued and his voice seemed to come from far away, from those remote regions of Tibet that he had visited, from the valleys of Persia, from the deserts of Abyssinia, all of which he had traversed between 1891 and 1892 seeking what he now confided to us.

"We must all pass that narrow gate, gentlemen, the august gate of death," said Holmes. "But a gate it remains and every gate is a way of entry to something new. Does any man return to the womb that bore him? Could a witness from without speak to the babe who swims there in warmth and comfort, nourished by the placenta, and speak of this outside realm of air, of sights, of sounds, and activity; would its blandishments persuade this nascent being to forfeit its present comforts willingly? Just so I have long imagined the heirs of eternity must find it impossible to speak to us of the results of their second birth."

"We still exist shackled to time and to space even as does the babe in the waters of the womb. Only when we are freed at last will we see how all of our limits, imposed by God, were for our benefit and nourishment. We live our lives in a sort of sleep. One third of our lives we spend in the insensibility of actual sleep. Why then should we fear death anymore than we fear the night that precedes the morning? Death then is not the end but a victory which precedes the bestowal of the only lasting laurel. It is not for us to question life and death or the unique status granted us upon the earth. We may no more turn back than a man who has been caught in a fast-running stream that will take him wherever that stream wends its sinuous way."

"Faced with this fate the Buddhist doctrine advises the believers to cease the struggle, for everything is an illusion and that illusion feeds on precisely the desire that wishes to control the shape and direction of our destiny. Every religion attempts to clothe in reason what we encounter each day yet the shape and character of that dim castle in the mist that is eternity exceed all of our descriptions. It is not for us to descry its battlements. We turn to some faith or other, because not to believe requires that we accept the pointless dissolution of all that is at the moment of death. Faith is the natural course for each man and for each woman. It takes an extraordinary insolence or pride to state with certainty that nothing lies beyond us here."

Again I must pause here in my memory of that occasion to comment. We sat in a library that contained among its other treasures all the great writings of the world bearing upon the question of God and human destiny. One needed only to walk a few paces and there were the Bible, the Koran, the Talmud, the Upanishads, the writings and sayings of Siddhartha Gautama, called the Buddha, the sayings of Confucius and Lao Tsu, the myths of Greece and of Rome, and countless others. Why among so many presentations tempered and refined at later dates by philosophy and celebrated by art and sculpture, each with adherents in the millions in age after age, should one choose one of these systems of belief over the others?

I felt have felt at times that every religion falls short of solving the essential human problem, which as always seemed to center upon what should be done and why should one do it. As a soldier I was trained to embrace duty as my highest function, but what that duty was depended upon policies and ends that were not for me to determine or decide. As a doctor my function was clearer, first to do no harm, and second to use the state of the medical arts to restore health if possible so that my ministrations would eventually no longer be necessary. As the assistant to Sherlock Holmes my function appeared to be to enable him to exercise his gifts at the highest level possible and later to share with the world the unique moral insights that solving crime often reveal. But any source of sensible morality and that morality stemming from religious convictions often seemed to me to be ill-fitting if not opposed to one another. This observation was always more salient for me in the religion of Christianity that claimed the majority of adherents in England and did so much to divide the population of the British Isles into opposing camps.

Many prelates counsel patience in adversity when its presence should motivate us to make this a better world. Christian beliefs seem at times to imply that God thrives on punishing his creation for not being exactly God-like, an attribute that can be predicated of God alone. I am not offended as a doctor when someone comes to me with a disease, so it has always seemed strange to me that various purveyors of Godliness give the impression that God is astonished at human sinfulness and that He is as chary with His grace as a miser is with his money.

Even the idea of atonement or satisfaction for sin seems to involve God in a mindless visitation of pain on the innocent. If this conviction is accurate in reading the mind of God, then no greater act of virtue could be imagined than torturing people who have done no wrong and the sadist would be the highest example of humanity. The term, "the economy of salvation," has always sent chills along my spine because it casts God as a banker and keeper of accounts rather like some of the tiny twisted men I used to encounter hurrying along Oxford Street of an evening, muffled up against the cold and carrying bulging briefcases, nasty spectacled men worn out by scanning documents by inadequate lighting for fear of missing an entry. The economy of salvation might better be called the economy of salivation for those theological wolves that have enumerated various sins in carefully wrought taxonomies as though they had spent time in the jungle of human malfeasance noting them down by genus and species without ever having sinned themselves. These men live in a world that has not been contaminated or qualified by human necessities or colored by passion. Their only sin has been the fear that for all of their intense efforts they may have missed an occasion where God's greater capacity for the scrutiny of motives and the weighing of intentions has discerned something that they might have missed in their taxonomy. They fear in consequence that the error will be attributed to them instead of to the sinner.

I prefer to see it the other way round: that it is we who demand strictness in judgment and suffering as recompense and revenge and that only God is able to bear the weight of that demand in order to reveal its essential wrong-headedness. The mercy of God cancels what no satisfaction can ever achieve. It does not deny what has happened, but tries whenever possible to set things moving once again. God in this model is not unchangeable, because God is in constant motion; a stable perfection if applied to God is idolatry.

Many eastern religions in my estimation come closer to the mark in this regard. They use dogma to defeat dogma by diffusing our mental energy between two incompatible statements as in the practice of meditating on the Zen Koans in Japan. A rigid fundamentalism in contrast reduces God to what can be accurately described by us as human beings. I submit that a proper reading of the Holy Scriptures is resistant to just this premature moral certainty because it wraps us around the text and the text around our understanding of it. When this inadequate approach occurs then God, as God actually is, disappears to be supplanted by our own interpretation. We construct a God in our own image to suit our preferences and we determine the measure of justice we feel is appropriate for God to apply.

Sherlock Holmes turned then to our host, "Mr. Sutro, you are a man of great resource and determination, as am I also. My life has been spent as a wanderer and a man who dared to question all that he has ever received. Was the totality of that struggle necessary to confirm what I might have accepted as a mere child and nourished thereafter without doubts and fears? Yet I have felt impelled to probe into things the better to understand them and to justify my confidence that they were in fact true. Though one may lament the days that are no more, with their comforts lost and many opportunities missed, we all must reconcile ourselves to the fact that just as everything falls away from us finally we will like Adam and Eve eventually stand naked at last before God. The folly of humankind has always been that we shun that divine and loving gaze, for God does not mock us in our nakedness. Rather, he sees within us what He put there originally.

He sees in us the image of God. He sees Himself in us and in doing so he loves us, for what God has made is good, indeed it is very good. For this reason the blessed woman Julian of Norwich said that it was revealed to her that all will be very well despite our fears. It is this assurance that we all require at the end of our lives. You may have heard of any little reputation that I have as a detective. Let me assure you then that I believe that all will be very well. No promise of God will fail. God will always remember Israel and all of the Sons and Daughters of Israel. You are part of us, though we may not be part of you. The branches would not exist without the root, although the root may not acknowledge the branches. Israel's waiting shall not be in vain. A history of so much suffering, of so many wanderings without end, of your unique and perennial witness must finally be honored and fulfilled. The restoration of Israel lies before us still and when that day comes and the Messiah is unveiled in His splendor, then all differences that have divided us shall be healed and we shall each of us find our place in the Kingdom of God, for God does not reject the man or woman who has sincerely sought to find Him."

The room was silent for a time before Mr. Sutro shook his head and spoke. "Well all of that may be true, Mr. Holmes, and it is gracious of you to say so, but I was never one to wait upon heaven. I have done my best to build a life for my family and for San Francisco that will shine in the days to come, but I can already feel that things are slipping away from us here in California. We are being pulled back into involvement with the eastern states. Congress tells us what we may do here in this golden land. The Comstock Lode was drained to restore the finances of an eastern war. If those riches had remained here, California would have been among the richest nations of the world."

"On the other hand you are now part of what appears to be an expanding empire," said Holmes with an ironic expression on his face.

"Bah empires," Mr. Sutro muttered scornfully, "That is not what I came to America to find."

"What did you desire then when you came here?" Holmes inquired.

"I desired the freedom to do as I have done, to be

measured, not as a Jew, but as a man. I desired to find a nation, the laws of which would yield only to reason and not merely to the power of one's place or station in life. But more than this, I wanted to possess land. I began here in San Francisco as a simple tobacconist, although I did run the family linen business in Germany before I came here. But when I heard about what was happening on the Comstock Lode I had to see it for myself. The whole thing was a great mess. It all grew up by accident. The mines were like mushrooms growing on a tree stump. The whole thing needed coordination and a common purpose. So it was that I came up with the idea of the tunnel and the city on the Carson River that I wished to bear my name of Sutro. But there were always men like Ralston and Sharon and their cronies who opposed me. They desired to suck the mines of Nevada dry to finance the building of San Francisco."

"And was that ambition so wrong, since you in turn have ended your own career by making this new and glorious city your home?" Holmes inquired.

Mr. Sutro smiled bitterly before answering, "Perhaps not, but you see they used stock-jobbing and manipulation to serve the ends of the Bank of California while my tunnel was at least real. I know that people like William Ralston feared that when it was completed I would rule the Comstock as they had done and William Sharon feared that his railroad and stamping mills would fall into ruin. The mills would relocate to the Carson River with the completion of the tunnel. But if they had listened to me from the start, they would have seen that the tunnel would have saved miners' lives and would have drained the seepage of waters, which was the curse of the mines. It rotted the timbers shoring up the shafts. They fought me; and why? Because I was Sutro! So I built it anyway, though it cost me the better part of my life to do so, and I was forced to leave my wife and children alone in the care of a dear friend."

He shook his head sadly, "When at last I sought a home life, my wife had grown bitter and my children had become strangers to me. Even now they do not understand me. But look about you, was it not worth it? I have shown all of San Francisco what a modern city can do for its people. I tried in my years as mayor to share my vision and met with only the scorn of small-minded pigmies. But I built Cliff House and the Baths to show them. And now I have retired here at Sutro Heights and now and now..."

He fell into silence. Both Holmes and I stared at him in commiseration. I could feel the great force that still remained within him, which was dying for lack of fuel like a candle in a votive cup flickering into the darkness.

At last he shook his head. "What was I saying gentlemen?"

"You were speaking of your career on the Comstock Lode and as the former Mayor of San Francisco," I reminded him.

His eyes brightened. "Yes of course. What I was about to say is that I still have plans for my library. A library is more than a collection of mere random volumes. In the last analysis a library is an organic creation of the man who assembles it. His choices of the volumes to be included are a mirror of his preoccupations and interests over time. For this reason each library is unique. By its nature it must exceed the reading capacity of its founder, just as a man's vision must exceed his present situation. No man can saturate the earth with his presence or influence, the best that he can do is to point in the direction that he would follow if time allowed him to exceed the limits of his own single life. What you see before you, gentlemen, is only part of the whole. Much remains to be catalogued. Many valuable volumes still repose in their crates from Europe. Yet each represents a unique moment when I held it in these rough hands and allowed my eyes for a moment to peruse the contents that would require hours, days, even weeks to fully assimilate and place in its proper order in my mind."

"I once dreamed that my own brain could hold the output of the countless great creations that encompass what we know to date of the human experience. There was a time when I imagined that my own powers of assimilation would so grow with the years that I could drink their contents in just as a bee drinks the nectar from the flowers in my gardens, pausing for only a short instant before flying on to another flower."

"Instead I find that my eyesight and mental capacities have diminished with the years until the words run off my mind just as quicksilver runs off a tilted table to scatter into tiny balls about the room. I finally have the time to read some of these volumes and find that I cannot summon adequate concentration to assimilate their contents and retain what I have learned. Still I want to bring men here to San Francisco, great men, wise men, leaders in their fields. They can stay at Cliff House and we will walk in the afternoons in the garden and look out over the sea and we will discuss how to build a better world. We will find a way to bring pleasure and happiness to the working men and women of San Francisco in their leisure hours. We will bring painters and sculptors and make California a truly promised land and a model for the world. The world still has hope, you see; but the people are always unwise in their choice of whom to follow. They do not follow the builders, the creators. No, they follow instead the men of arms and conquest, men who are always mere brigands. The end and the result is that all empires fall into ruin. We might have elected wise men on the Comstock Lode, but instead we elected self-contented scoundrels like Stewart and Sharon to carry our needs to Congress. We sent them back east as Senators to Washington where they were wined and dined and soon they became just like all the other easterners profiting by the silver that was produced here by honest miners." This last was interrupted by a fit of coughing.

After he recovered his breath he continued in a melancholy voice, "If I only had a few more years I would do what I could to make all the lands west of the Rocky Mountains into a separate republic and rid us forever from the railroad barons who are sucking the life out of the farmers of the west. I would protect what we have here and forget about foreign wars. Even old Andrew Carnegie, the steel baron, could see at last that peace and not steel is the foundation of the world. He became a builder of libraries."

Mr. Sutro lay back in his chair and sighed with satisfaction, "There can still be honor in possessing riches you see if one gives something back to the society that made it all possible. But the people are so foolish. They believe in the men who will lie to them. They always believe the lies of those who would take everything from them, while they scorn their true benefactors."

Then he said fiercely, "But even that realization would not have changed my course of actions. I have been a creator in my way. I had no choice. I saw the tunnel whole and entire in my mind long before it existed. No obstacle could cause me to abandon my plan. Is it that way with all creators I wonder?"

He paused to take a sip of the Amontiado from the Napa Valley that he favored before continuing, "Perhaps creators always press on no matter what the cost. Could God have allowed Adam and Eve to be happy in their newly found independence and knowledge of good and evil without condemnation of pain and exile, or was it rather that having so chosen they found the burden excessive and begged God to take them back to their former innocence. Perhaps pain is actually a gift, for it gives us something with which to struggle. Knowledge always has its price! It is struggle that makes us men and women. It makes us worthy of being created in the image and likeness of God."

This last was said with conviction, but then a doubt crossed his face. "But is even God subject to some higher rule of his own ordination, I wonder? If even God cannot repeat the past and seek a different outcome, how much less may we. Our entire lives and even our greatest victories finally lie about us like so much straw. All is cast in stone, for we can never return to our former state to alter or amend, can we gentlemen? What has been done hardens into the mortar that seals our days and nights. Though so much changes about us what has been remains. It is conserved in history, the vast edifice of time. Yet we press on and on and suddenly time ceases for us and we ourselves return at last to our primal elements. The vase is shattered to be sure, but does it not remain somewhere in the conservation of forms that is the past? Can our record ever be augmented in some other realm? Or does time itself stand upon the night-table of God, for mere idle reading matter as of a journal long since discontinued?"

Holmes and I had remained silent during this great summation of his life's work by a man we both admired. I could not help reflecting that if such a man as this must finally face the inadequacy or even futility of his days, then what hope of futurity remained for the average run of mankind. Mr. Sutro gazed sadly into the fire which had dwindled to a few small flames in the glowing embers of which lay the ashes, now ghostly in the morning light. At last he bestirred himself and rose.

"You must pardon the melancholy musings of an old man, gentlemen. I must not detain you further. Shall we see whether Miss Adler and my daughter are finished with their tour among my flowers? You will need to return to Cliff House and pick up your luggage. My carriage shall call for you at 2:30 and take you to your ship."

We arose from our chairs and walked with him out of the library and into the long hallway where we passed through several passages to the conservatory, which was empty. We could see through the windows though that Irene and Emma had sought out the late morning sun and were wandering below the trees in the spacious park. The tree-tops swayed in the fresh ocean breeze and we could see the sails of several ships below us catching the wind and the bathers on the beach far below the mansion. As we joined the ladies on the lawn, Holmes walked over to Irene and took her arm and together the two of them preceded the rest of us as we walked through the park towards the gate where we had arrived a week ago. Outside of the park the city was alive with wagons and with strollers who bowed or tipped their hats to Mr. Sutro where he stood in the gateway leaning upon his daughter for support. It was the last that we would see of our gracious host who stood there that morning surrounded by the works of his industrious life, one of the last noble symbols of America. I prayed that he might find peace at last. How great are the burdens of such extraordinary men who ask more of life than merely to sit by their own hearth in the evening beyond the reach of fame.

I had come at last to share Holmes' belief in the precious gift of living a commonplace life. There is nothing more ordinary than the entry of souls into the Kingdom of God. The stars of heaven are not more numerous than those whose lives of quiet virtue and the ready acceptance of daily grace ensures their eventual salvation. For those who choose or are burdened with the harder path of great questions and speculations, may this account of mine bring them some resolution and solace.

Sherlock Holmes and I had attempted for a time to alter the history of a great nation, but in any democracy the preservation of the rights of its citizens must be the fruit of the efforts of the entire people and if the people are sleeping, they must be awakened. Democracy must be re-discovered and affirmed again by each successive generation or the nation will descend into a new tyranny, perhaps one worse than the one that prevailed at its origin under the rule of an English King. Turmoil and privation are not always the worst social evils to be feared if freedom is at stake. Worse still is a comfort that lulls to sleep the higher aspirations of the citizens. The wealth of America may someday be its source of ruination. Americans have been spared from many of the natural means by which other nations have been tutored in adversity. Americans have found it convenient to build a nation upon an involuntary legacy wrested from the native people between its two oceans. Can such actions fail to bring nemesis upon this favored nation at some distant date? Can such a short memory or its origins suffice to build a culture contributing something beyond mere manufacturing and consumption? Will each new arrival on these shores lose the best of what they brought here and be reduced to the lowest common denominator of human greed and arrogance? It is a dangerous thing for a nation to be spawned by an idea. Noble ideas are subject to later appropriation by private interests and even the best of them are subject to dilution over time. Men often drown in their abstractions and concepts. For that reason, the heart of freedom lies not in its proclamation but in its exercise. Delegated power can soon be usurped by overweening commercial interests and the dull mass of mankind cannot be relied upon to purify ideals that have grown stale and meaningless through long repetition without the substance to back them up.

I recall that Sherlock Holmes once said, "It is not only the rich man who will find it easier for a camel to pass through the eye of a needle than to enter the kingdom of heaven; the same may be said of the men of power and influence." There is no greater temptation for a man than that of justifying his own life and believing that he deserves the Kingdom of Heaven as a reward for his own efforts. Such a man makes pointless and vain the sacrifice of Christ on the cross for the sins of men and women. Even the devil shines in the devil's own estimation. That is the devil's curse. It is the legacy of us all to be stripped of everything in the end, even of our very flesh.

Of what value then is the ego? To see oneself before God is to realize that all of our being is derivative; it is a gift and that gift is a grace and nothing more. This is what the Roman Catholic Church means when it says that even virtues are of no merit in the eternal order unless they are performed under the impulse and indeed within the very life of God as mediated through grace. All that is done without love and in love profits not the soul for it is done for our own vanity and pride so that we need not turn to God to complete our works. This attitude of serene independence is Original Sin all over again: desiring glory so that we may become like God, knowing good and evil. In ourselves we are the origin of nothing. The best that can be said of us is that we cooperate with the graces bestowed upon us. The poor man, the obscure man, the humble man, he is the one who sees his proper place is the order of the universe and in the face of his fellow men and women. He knows that it is only in relation to others that he may be said to exist at all. Therefore he dares not raise his eyes to God but says ever and again these ancient words of the prayer called the Confiteor:

'I confess to almighty God and to you, my brothers and sisters, that I have greatly sinned in my thoughts and in my words, in what I have done and in what I have failed to do, through my fault, through my fault, through my most grievous fault; therefore I ask blessed Mary ever-Virgin, all the Angels and Saints, and you my brothers and sisters, to pray for me to the Lord Our God.

Reflecting back now on the many battles of the mind between Sherlock Holmes and Professor Moriarty as recorded here; no proof is ever really adequate for us to affirm the existence of God with our entire being because even to demand such proof is redolent of Original Sin. God need not submit Himself to our proofs. He has already come to be among us as one of us; surely that is enough! To face our own actual death when we have existed all of our lives in its shadow, this is when the soul shall meet its greatest test; it must stand before God and only in God to see itself as it truly is.

If it should see first itself and prefer itself to God so that

God is eclipsed by the tiny point of fading light of its earthly pride that remains, then the soul shall perish in the whirlpool of its own nothingness, cascading down into that place reserved out of the mercy of God for the devil and his angels, where alone they can revel in their self-created meaning. Yes, even that place of darkness is due to the mercy of God, for where would the soul go if even hell did not deign to receive it? Is it not better to rest in a pool of fire, than to fall forever and without witness into one's own eternal solitude? Supernatural faith, one not derived from human experience asks that we risk everything and turn from all partial goods in order to achieve a supreme good the Beatific Vision of God.

Sherlock Holmes once summed up this up in one of our discussions at that time. He said, "This complete commitment of our entire lives to God is an uneven contest from the start. There is no objectivity possible when faced with such a choice. Our very being as being is at stake. This is what the philosopher Soren Kierkegaard meant when he said that truth is subjectivity, not that we constitute our own truth, for that would be to lose our souls in pursuit of self as God, but rather that God must be for us our all in all. We must realize this truth in our very bones! Jesus said this most clearly when He said,

> *'The man who wishes to save his life will lose it. But the man who loses his life for my sake will find it.'*

A statement like this would be completely devoid of sense if applied to an ordinary man; this is why the Church proclaims in all confidence that Jesus is Lord as its primary basis and foundation."

When I first heard these words from Sherlock Holmes, I remember finding this a hard saying, for like most men I wished to think well of myself and to imagine that I existed in some way in my own right. I wished my own share of earthly remembrance as the friend of the great detective. My own life would no doubt have been as predictable as that of any medical man of my era had I never become acquainted with Sherlock Holmes. My own innate nature has always been to believe that others are wiser then I am and to assume a maturity and virtue in my compatriots until circumstances dictate a contrary belief. Like many who have lived their lives in the Victorian age I had hoped also to see the progress of mankind, tied inevitably to the fortunes of the British Empire.

The new age of machines and technical progress seems to me now though to augur not a golden age to come in the twentieth century, but an age of the loss of what it means to be truly human at all. We are becoming strangers to ourselves. But when the ashes of this Great War, which now besets the nations of Europe shall settle at last, perhaps a new age will dawn after all. Surely such great slaughter as that which we have witnessed during these years must teach finally and forever to all mankind the vanity of resort to arms in general warfare between nations.

Life will go on of course in any case. Each separate human life is set into a niche in time as fleeting as a shuttle, and each of us must act out an eternal destiny against the background of the issues and conflicts of his particular time in history. We grasp at the few and feeble joys of our declining hours as our particular sun nears its horizon. The great courtroom of life is silent, awaiting our summation and we rise to address the great judge of us all. All of our carefully drafted briefs fall from our hands though, for suddenly we realize that no life can stand on its own without the support of the intercession of the great body of all mankind, above all in the living body of the Catholic Church, consciously animated by the heart of Christ.

For this reason I dare to say that no man may write his own epitaph, least of all me. Have I done so at last in writing this long account of our adventures? In any case, to write of another as I have tried to do in my recounting here of the life of Sherlock Holmes is not to judge but rather to record the mere data of a life. In spite of Holmes' occasional humor at my expense and his admonitions that I should strive for pure objectivity, I know that I have attempted to portray Holmes in the truest of lights and with the least deflection possible caused by my own values. As to my honesty regarding my own biases, I confess them here. I prefer a greater measure of illusion in my life than Holmes could ever accept. His own boundless curiosity combined with a need for clarity drove him to explore the darker regions of the heart of man and to plumb the depths of our fallen world. More than most men he carried death at his side due to his lung condition and his refusal to curtail the excessive demands made upon his own physical and spiritual resources. Knowing him was to receive by a process of absorption and diffusion some tincture of his own essence.

Perhaps over the course of our many years together I was able to share something with him as well. Our partnership grew with time to a point where even Holmes' great intellect seemed to require my own stolid reactions as a weight or counterbalance, a governor to his own wild speculations. He was among those men who have wished to recreate the world in their own image and he might have fallen into the very evils that he deplored if I had not been present to remind him, by my own mediocrity, that all flesh is as grass and that he, who had so long scorned his own physical being was only a man after all.

I like to think that as his friend and physician that I served him in this way. What would my own life would have been without him is a question that I may never answer. It is the dull life that reaches a premature exhaustion of its resources. With Holmes I always felt that there was always some new adventure before us. To live as though one had just begun the adventure that is life was part of his particular aura. He was of that spirit that we attribute to the knights of old, always sallying forth to encounter giants. If the world is always inventing itself anew, then who can with ease surrender and pass out of time's onward march but only he whose loyalty to what has been exceeds the reality of the present hour. For these reasons I doubted that Holmes would ever really retire as that term is usually understood. The public would in any case not stand for it. As long as there remained some problem to be solved and he could be reached, he would be consulted.

For this reason he has on numerous occasions requested that I use my pen to throw the public off his track, to buy him time for those particular areas of research and activity that he has made his own. The results of these may have a greater impact upon our world and the course of history than is yet apparent. Of these efforts of these latter days this present account is only one, though it may be the last recorded by one whose energies have been bowed down by the trials that are now upon us. So it is that I have endeavored to do justice here at least to the decade of the 1890's as Holmes and I lived it. Our journey together to the America of 1898-1899 had spanned the continent from the great summer houses of Newport, Rhode Island to the abject poverty of Wounded Knee in the Dakotas. At the end we stood upon the further shore of the continent and gazed westward from Cliff House to where the great Pacific Ocean stretched outward towards the Far East that beckoned us onwards.

The reach of the Americans had already extended to its furthest margins, so that it appeared that nothing could contain the American aspiration to be the Babylon of its day and age. I thought then of all of the kingdoms of the earth and their inevitable passing, of the vanity of power, and the absurdity of glory. I saw England, my England and the England of Sherlock Holmes, grown decrepit like our Queen and burdened with the superfluities of empire. Like all wanderers upon the earth I had begun to feel that I was in exile and had no longer a home even in England. I seemed to feel already that the final conflict had begun upon the earth, the conflict that would draw the pity of heaven at last to end it, like the weeping of the skies in the early morning when the dew descends. I seemed as I recall, even in the last years of the preceding century, to hear the trumpets of that last morning, as I seem to hear now the roar of cannons and the senseless stutter of the guns of war in far off France. How long I wonder shall it be before the dove comes to us at last bearing the eternal branch of a lasting peace.

The pressure of the coming generations demands that the aged must die. The world must be surrendered at last to the heirs of all things; but they too will grow old in due course. Even to share an era is to be contemporaries and of one age when seen against the vast abyss of all that has been and all that yet may be. The baby shares one atmosphere with the grandmother. It is the great relationships that endure: marriage, parent-and child, teacher and pupil, priest and acolyte, master and apprentice, man and woman. We do not really exist without a social context. The greatest difficulty is experienced by those who imagine that it must be their own efforts that must remake the world—one in their own image; this frustration is often only augmented by success in life. But those who mourn also, imagining their supply of days to be unlimited, have put off too long life's necessary commitments.

Those who mourn are always weighing options, but never make a beginning for fear of falling short. The truth is that to both the great and the small, what one does not achieve must fall to another to complete. Even mortal enemies may in time see their enmity buried by the love that bridges all divisions. The great genetic pool of mankind is constantly shuffled so that within seven generations one becomes a stranger even to one's nearest kinfolk. The progression of the denominator is geometric as follows: 2, 4, 8, 16, 32, 64, 128. If each generation is separated by roughly twenty-five years, then in more than one century all personal resemblance to our forebears is diluted and lost. Thus, there are no real dynasties. All are finally the progeny of all. To leave life is to have another take our place; to leave is but to begin again elsewhere...

My thoughts on that last day were again interrupted by Sherlock Holmes. So deep in thought had I been that I did not realize that we had entered Cliff House and climbed to the high tower from which we could see the city to our east with its great docks where our ship lay at rest, building steam in its great boilers to carry us away to Japan.

Holmes broke into my thoughts as he had long been in the habit of doing during the course of our long friendship. "Brooding still as I see Watson," said he smiling. "I have often thought that in you the waters run very deep indeed. If you have developed over the years a certain strain of pawky humor you have developed also a certain grim philosophical strain. Perhaps you have spent too many years with me, your melancholy and introspective friend. But as Captain Ahab once said to his first-mate Starbuck on the ship Pequod, 'It is a mild looking sky and a mild looking day.' We shall soon be out upon the great ocean. Our task is not yet done Watson. Many voyages lie before us. Let us tarry no longer. Goodbyes are saddest when they are prolonged." He drew me to his side then and pointed through the window to where our ship lay alongside the docks and recited from Tennyson's great poem, Ulysses:

There lies the port, the vessel puffs its sails, there gloom the dark broad seas. Come my friends, t'is not too late to seek a newer world. Push off, and sitting well in order smite the sounding furrows; for my purpose holds to sail beyond the sunset and the baths of all the western stars until I die. It may be that the gulfs will wash us down: it may be we will touch the happy isles and see the great Achilles whom we knew. Though much is taken, much abides; and though we are not now that strength which in old days moved earth and heaven, that which we are, we are; one equal temper of heroic hearts, made weak by time and fate, but strong in will, to strive, to seek, to find, and not to yield.

So saying, he clasped my hand and side by side we left the tower to seek out Irene who awaited us below in the sunshine. It was there that we wished her a fond farewell. How long the time might be before either of us saw her again, neither of us knew at the time. We left her then and sought out at last the vessel that would carry us home by the westerly route to England.

The gaslights begin to dim at last upon the scene. My tale has already continued longer than I thought it ever would, but the habit of prolonged curtain calls grows over time with anyone whose life has been lived partially before an admiring public. This work has been written over several years and contains the sum and substance of the spiritual journey of my dear friend, Sherlock Holmes, whose life has influenced so many of my own life's choices, the man whom I will ever regard as the best and wisest man whom I have ever known. No more shall I write of hansom cabs splashing through the rain to draw up at our door. No more shall I write of the winded client gasping for breath before our hearth while the winds whip down Baker Street as Sherlock Holmes asks him to "try the settee" and to endeavor to relate as best he may the string of events that led him to consult us on what was always a very grave matter. My public must rest content with those tales that have already been brought before them in order to demonstrate my friend's unique gifts. I doubt that I shall live long enough to add more. My rough notes must suffice to give a hint at cases whose full exploration will never see paper.

As my final image of those busy years that are now fled

forever into the past I return in my mind to the casting off of our vessel from the docks of San Francisco. I can record here that as our vessel passed out to sea, we could both observe the tall and stately figure of Irene Adler where she stood upon the balcony that ran around the tower at the top of Cliff House. She stood there, proud and erect in the light from the setting sun, waving to us as our ship passed out through the rocky promontory of the Golden Gate. Holmes raised his hand to salute her and a short time later the land was gone and there was only the foaming wake of the ship that was to carry us home to England and to the cases that were still ahead for us both, enough cases to fill the years ahead with the prospect of future adventures of the mind and heart. Farewell.

Epilogue

s so often in life, I find that I have no sooner determined to make an end when I am drawn forth again into a new beginning. But repetition is the characteristic folly of old men. I must plead in my defense that such an extended narrative as the one presented here requires more than the usual tying together of strings and final explanations, lest the reader remain unsatisfied. I must therefore say before I bid a final adieu to you oh most patient reader that I had hoped that I might continue this narrative into the period subsequent to Holmes' retirement in 1903. There is also the matter of Mycroft's retirement from his government station, which came at the time of the second Boer War with its disgraceful use of concentration camps for the non-combatants. Mycroft had seen this brutal policy coming, on with the new reliance upon unbridled force, after the negligence shown in caring for the wounded by the troops under Kitchener at the Battle of Omdurman.

England was not alone in the atrocities committed in this new phase of warfare. The same brutality was displayed by the Americans in the Philippines in the process of subduing the local patriots there. The loss of civilians to disease due to imprisonment was appalling to English sensibilities at home.. The conduct of the Boer War against the Dutch farmers of the Transvaal cost an overwhelming number of British lives as well and the entire belated campaign with its many defeats left a sour taste towards English expansionism among the nations of continental Europe. Mycroft was spared any personal involvement in that deplorable war of greed. He played no direct role in military deployments. However the nation was soon to sorely miss his wise counsel, but once he left he continued to refuse any offers to return on a piecemeal basis. Instead he retreated into the great silence of The Diogenes Club where he had long known that he would find refuge when the folly of the age became too great for him to bear any longer. The world is being thrown perhaps too much together. The experiment of Holmes to see beneath the multifold languages and cultures of the earth in order to find one common human sense of community, one united in the One Body of Christ, still eludes human history and perhaps it always will. Still it was a brave search, and had he not made it I doubt that the England that still struggles to survive in this year of 1918 would have survived. The Black Formosa Corruption might have ravished our shores had it not been for the final victory of Sherlock Holmes over Professor Moriarty. This victory extended to the nefarious and far-reaching plans of Baron Maupertuis as well. His great financial empire came finally to lie in ruins. There is no love lost among the ambitious men of the world. Ruthless men finally meet their likeness in those who gather about them even among their subordinates. There is no lasting progress to be made in the world without a measure of trust between men and among nations.

As to the great canal project, the Americans managed to complete it after all. It was built through the Isthmus of Panama after that nation was separated from Columbia through American intervention, in a continuance of the new imperial policies begun under President William McKinley. The great landmass that once separated the Atlantic and the Pacific was breached by the design of man. One by one the borders between the regions of the world were falling. But is mankind prepared for such contiguous relations between regions with little prior experience in the intercourse of ideas and commerce? If even internecine feuds still exist, how then may peace be maintained when the weapons that we will no doubt develop will traverse the entrenched borders our defenses. Behind what citadels will security then exist?

But I am an old man and an old soldier and have no answers to these questions beyond a great weariness of war and the preparations for more wars. I have come to see the value of all things that limit a universal access of one human being to another. Human limitations of time, space, language, and custom create a zone of sympathy among those fitted to be neighbors. All further aspirants had best remain well afield. It is asking too much of human nature, absent a shared belief and union in the universal charity of the Church, to make the world into one common assemblage. It is even folly to expect too much from the various sects practicing a form of Christianity; the history of our religion bears witness to this.

I find that age is already allowing me to merge with the silent and inanimate world all about me to which my body will soon be joined in death. I take comfort in sitting daily by the sea, knowing that its great and sonorous song will be unaltered by my passing. To that foretaste of eternity I entrust my soul. Most men desire some enduring monument to give their lives meaning and significance, but I have come lately to see the value of anonymity and insignificance. Most fame in the historical sense is really compiled far more from deeds of infamy than of virtue. Since whatever significance our lives really have must exist not in the memory of men but rather in the mind of God who alone can reconstitute and restore our lives on the last day it is my wish that my own small contribution shall be soon effaced as is a sand-sculpture before the advancing sea.

If these words of mine endure let them endure for whatever use they may have in the lives of others, they may at least perpetuate an era seen here, as all past eras tend to be seen, through the veil of romance. In touching upon romance, I will also record here a summary of the unique role that Irene Adler continued to play in both of our lives after we left America. By the year 1907 I admitted to myself that I was likely to reside permanently in Cornwall. When I told Holmes of my plans to remain there he shook his head and chaffed me in his own barbed but good-natured way. "The habits of our youth are hardest to break, old fellow. You have a fatal affinity to married life, which may someday take you again from my side as my dearest and most essential companion. But then marriage is a sacrament and it would be blasphemy to mock or contravene it. Still, I will miss your daily company."

"Have you no plans of your own then in that direction," I inquired.

He turned away for a moment and then faced me once again.

"Well as to that we must allow your readers the latitude for speculation. What is the interest in life after all if every mystery is to be revealed?"

He would say no more at the time, so neither shall I speak here of the years after 1903 when we had both returned to England. I am happy to report however that Irene Adler is still very much alive although she has long since retired from the stage. She resides now in Rome. Sir Henry and Lady Beryl are also alive, although Sir Henry is prey to various ailments, an unfortunate legacy from his wild adventures in Canada as a young man, and that he is confined now to a wheel chair. Professor Moriarty was able to meet his one surviving brother during the Professor's final illness. Holmes judged at last that neither man would be harmed by learning of the existence and survival of the other. There are wounds that only a common blood can ever heal.

Colonel Sebastian Moran passed on some years ago, a victim of his life of excesses, though it is said that he was visited during his last days by a Jesuit missionary who may have heard his extraordinary confession in his final hours. The Moriarty Breeding-Stable at Kings Pyland is now a riding school administered by the Moriarty Trust, which has also established a scholarship program at Exeter University for young men of poor backgrounds who show promise in applied mathematics.

The Holmes Estate at Sigerside continues to exist to this day, even after the death of Holmes' eldest brother, Sherringford, who labored until his last day to preserve the Holmes' patrimony intact. It is still managed by Mycroft and his wife, the former Mrs. Hudson of Baker Street. His indulgence in the pleasures of the table are now confined to a hearty soup at night and a single glass of port, but he does not complain to that dear and patient lady, whom I shall ever remember fondly for her endurance of the two men who would insist upon clattering down the seventeen steps to hail hansom cabs at all hours of the day and night during their residence at 221B Baker Street.

After the death of Roger Baskerville, Holmes courteously informed Isadora Persano through Dr. Blackwell that he need no longer fear any harm from his old associate. We heard nothing back from him at the time, but several years later Holmes had the occasion to consult Dr. Blackwell upon another matter. Holmes took on the opportunity before leaving to ask if the doctor knew anything of the fate of his former patient. Dr. Blackwell explained that Mr. Persano had died in the asylum the previous year. The man had never quite recovered that serene confidence that had once allowed him to act as an arbiter of life and death in his unusual profession as a duelist. Perhaps the number of ghosts that pursued him had mounted until even his adamantine conscience was overcome at last by them. He had managed to elude his own terror of death by courting it as his own familiar, but the devils that we conjure forth are not as easily returned to that dark realm where they abide, only waiting their opportunity to seep into our mortal realm again.

This was perhaps a lesson learned by Dr. Mortimer as well. His fascination with Celtic lore never left him. He became a haunter of the dark, wandering over the moonlit moors in search of the fairy folk. He had become convinced over time that the ancient inhabitants of Devonshire and Cornwall still lived among us as spirit beings somewhere between heaven and hell. What had begun as a mild eccentricity grew at last into an obsession. He had made many transcriptions of certain runic phrases the meaning of which was as indecipherable as the texts that perpetuated them were unintelligible. It was not long before he developed his own theory that they might be called forth at midnight in certain rock-strewn circles that are common in the southwest of England. Be that as it may, he disappeared one day and was never seen again. Whether he was a victim of one of the lesser known bogs of the region or of some darker fate will never be known for sure. Who can say where those portals may lie that may transport someone to the shadow side of reality? Perhaps, there are certain matters that had best be left alone by the impetuous seekers among us.

William McKinley died at the hand of an assassin and Theodore Roosevelt, whom we had met in Newport, was destined to take the steps to see to this key project of canal. It was finally completed and opened to commercial passages on August 15, 1914. The railroad in Costa Rica was sold at a loss to a third party. Baron

Maupertuis managed to sell off his shares in the Greater Dutch Canal Company at a great financial loss to him but a greater loss still to the few remaining investors who had once trusted that a financial titan like the Baron was infallible. That great financier is dead now and his once great empire in the East Indies has been dispersed among countless distant relatives united only by their good fortune at the Baron's passing.

The way of the powerful of the earth is to leave behind only monuments to human greed and the hunger of their successors in wealth for endless new acquisitions. The entire earth has been spanned at last and knit by communications networks of ever greater sophistication. The America once referred to as part of "the new world" is entering into its own period of obsolescence, one always preceded by reaching an apogee of power and confidence often symbolized by a single man who in his own person symbolizes the populace that has blindly exalted him and in doing so augmented his power. When Holmes and I visited the Hapsburg palace in Vienna on our trip across Europe in 1899 we both remarked on our joint impression that the furnishings there, elaborate as they were, seemed vulgar in their superfluity and excess. How different from the prophet from Galilee who once said, *"Foxes have dens, and the birds of the air have nests, but the Son of Man has nowhere to lay his head."* Jesus left only His Holy Spirit as a legacy and the question posed on that third day after His crucifixion when Mary Magdalene reported to Peter and John that when the women came to the garden they found an empty tomb.

Documents Found Among the Papers of
Dr. John H. Watson
Last Will and Testament of
Sigurd Holmes

The following contains my last will and testament as regards my estate at Sigerside and all other property real or personal in my name to be disposed of as follows:

My wife Violet having come to me by marriage and having predeceased me dying intestate left me with merely her good wishes for her sons and such requests as I her husband, knowing her mind know best how to interpret. She was a woman who in conformance with the emotional character of her race was guided more by affinity than by reason. I am sorry to say that in my youth I shared her enthusiasms and that of her age. The revolution in France raised hopes in many that the condition of mankind could be elevated by education and in one lamentable experiment I put the same theories to a test by paying for the training of the son of a groom.

The death of the father left the lad on my hands and as a salutary impetus to the dreamy lethargy of my own sons I gave this young whelp, Moriarty, an education befitting a gentleman's son. That he later turned these gifts to no good end I have observed and that he will go from bad to worse I do not doubt. I have come to a belief in taints of the blood and I fear to say that my own sons are no exception to that iron law of nature. What they might have gained from me has been so diminished by intense emotionalism that each in turn has proven to be a disappointment to their father.

The first, Sherringford, has absorbed the greater part of my own plans for the estate and thankful I am that primogeniture will ensure that most of the estate shall be under his guidance and care. But what he has learned from me is obviated by a lack of hardness and resolution perhaps induced by the loss of his mother at a time when he was still much attached to her.

The second, Mycroft, is no doubt bright but he is much occupied with eating and can barely sit a horse. I can think of no line of work or profession that will accommodate such self-indulgence and for which he might be prepared. For this reason I desire that an allowance be made for him of seven hundred pounds per annum from the gross revenues of the estate and paid over to him by Sherringford for his maintenance, which stipend will no doubt make many a grocer and butcher rich.

As for my third son, Sherlock, a strange dreamy lad whose talents and nature quite elude my comprehension, I desire that he be spared the usual squalid end of dreamers, poets, and assorted mystics. I desire therefore that he be made the permanent ward of his brother Sherringford, that he receive the sum of fifty pounds per month during his life for his maintenance and education, and that the doors of Sigerside may always remain open to him as a place of asylum and sanctuary from whatever folly or the fruits thereof may follow him in life.

As to the servants I leave forty pounds to each of those servants who are in personal service to me at the time of my death and an additional sum of one hundred pounds to be shared among the superintendants of the coal-mining and estate interests in Yorkshire and Northumberland on a per capita basis. I desire a bonus of five pounds to be paid to each coal miner employed at the time of my death.

I further direct that I be buried without ceremony at that spot where I have breathed my last if it be on my own land here at Sigerside. If perchance I should die elsewhere then let me rest in the family crypt.

I have no more to say except that I quit life gladly. It is all a damn poor show to my way of thinking and a fools game altogether.

Signed...
Sigurd Holmes
November 12, 1866

Affixed with the Seal of Sigurd Holmes as Justice of the Peace for Sigerside and duly witnessed by the signatories below.

Letter of Mycroft Holmes to the Home Secretary in the Year of 1914

My Lord,

I trust that all memory of the days when I had the honor to be an advisor to the British government has not been effaced since my retirement from active service. The recent outbreak of hostilities on the continent is such that all civilized men must apprehend this event with dismay. It is imperative that the conflict be contained lest it become a repetition of the Thirty Years War of the 17th century.

To that end I urge that this country address its primary effort on the Turkish front. An early defeat of the Ottoman Empire will safeguard the Bosporus and open the door to an invasion of

Austria, which will also strengthen the Russian Front against the Germans. Since this conflict originated with the question of Serbian security we will reinforce our Russian allies on the eastern front and the German forces will have to abandon the ill-advised wheeling maneuver through Belgium and France of which you are no doubt aware through our agents on the continent. The Germans will have no choice but to move to the east and the French can no doubt bear the burden of its own defense while we secure the east.

I am sure that it is immaterial to the British interests whether Germany or France controls Alsace and Lorraine. But it is a matter of supreme consequence which nation may be in a better position after the war to exert pressure upon Persia and the Arab lands in the years to come after this present conflict ends.

As you will recall, during my time in office I asked that my brother Sherlock assess the situation in the Sudan. Even at that time I realized that British interests were centered upon the Suez region. Little has changed since that time. I will be happy to meet with Your Lordships and representatives of the Parliament to explain these views in more detail should you wish.

Until then I remain Your Lordships' Humble Servant,
Mycroft Holmes

Posted from Sigerside Halt, Yorkshire
September 1, 1914

Why Adopt a Theological Approach to Sherlock Holmes

It is no small task to take the DNA provided by the creation of another artist and then to unwind it strand by strand in order to locate certain genes that seem out of place, to isolate them, and then to graft into the surrounding structure elements that seem to follow logically so as to eliminate gaps or inconsistencies that were present, whether by oversight or design, in the original framework. The novels and stories by Sir Arthur Conan Doyle featuring Sherlock Holmes are essentially morality tales. Holmes admits that it is the outré and the original case that intrigues him. The more odd and outlandish the circumstances presented the more likely that Sherlock Holmes would stir from his usual dreamy lethargy and suddenly be transformed into an avid foxhound prepared to plunge into thicket and underbrush hot on the scent of some buried villainy. This was the initial impetus of my own effort to probe the character, not merely of Sherlock Holmes, but of the characters who were closest to him in life and to explore the wider stage that forms the setting for these supposedly quite comfortable tales.

However cozy and nostalgic the world of Sherlock Holmes appears at times there is a brooding darkness of chaos just below the surface. If his clients share one common set of characteristics it is that of bewilderment, desolation, and the need born of desperation to appeal to Sherlock Holmes as a final measure in order to restore their lives to some sort of normality. Reading these tales serves the same purpose for many readers; which of us would not wish to run one of our own most persistent dilemmas by Holmes in hope for a definitive if sometimes belated solution. The desire for a sensible and cohesive worldview is something that we all wish that we possessed to the degree that Sherlock Holmes sometimes demonstrates.

However it is my belief that such rare qualities of wisdom and balance, whenever they are found in life, are the result and final element of character formation and of a life-experience most present in those persons who do not quail from an intimate acquaintance and even familiarity with evil. This is not to say that evil should ever be rashly courted though. Each of us has both a guardian angel and a resident devil assigned to us. It is those who imagine that evil has somehow passed them by through some inherent quality that they possess who are most likely to be wound-up from head to toe in the spider's web.

Please allow me then to anticipate the objections of the disgruntled reader who may say that he enjoyed my overall treatment quite well, but that the catechetical passages were somewhat excessive. Alas, I knew only one way to tell my tale. It occurs to me that many writers must have felt this same sense that their book might have taken a different course or used a different format, but one must say what one must say as best one can. Finally the book simply stands alone and naked as Adam and Eve were in the Garden of Eden and the snake of disapproving criticism must simply hiss if it wishes to do so or perhaps forgive whatever were the author's worst offenses.

The epigraphs drawn from the original stories with which each volume begins demonstrate that both Sherlock Holmes and his creator were deeply interested in religion and what philosophers refer to as "the problem of evil." As I stated in the introduction that accompanies each volume, the mystery story originated in an effort to dramatize the miraculous stories of the Bible for a popular audience through various "mystery plays." There is no greater mystery for each of us then the question of our own nature. Amidst the fascination that we all feel for "murder mysteries" one essential key may lie in the fact that human life is sometimes prematurely terminated by a human agent. I would suggest that all lives, even those most fully lived and complete are prematurely terminated in that we die at the very summit of our wisdom and experience. It is precisely when we are "finally ready for heaven" that we die and the majority of us are not yet ready for that great transmutation.

This book that you have just read is my effort to add a postscript to the writer of the Book of Ecclesiastes who concluded that all things are vanity. The New Testament adds to this observation in these words of Jesus that must haunt all men and women: *"What shall it profit a man if he should gain the whole world and lose his immortal soul?"*

What mystery exceeds this question of whether we may have a valid and reliable hope for futurity after we die? It is a feeble life that can contemplate its own eternal oblivion with equanimity. Though we may hold ourselves in contempt, might we not wish to live on at least to observe one more revolution of the seasons with the various attempts of men and of women to deal with the human condition? Is our allotted time really adequate to our need to frame a cohesive picture? Why does one read if not to expand the parameters of our daily round and to fill our hearts at the wellspring of the collective history of the human race? How much may still be written to add to that universal archive? Even one day more might bring the insight that will unite the whole or to at least extend the horizons of our inquiry further. Even those who are without faith might wish for at least a hint of what may come after death. Can any human life be understood on its own terms?

In order to attempt an answer questions such as these and amidst the many suppositions given by other writers I have attempted to chart a course for one fictional detective of venerable memory by imagining what he might have thought, even if his thoughts and those of the other characters as well have been my own thoughts. I do not claim to be without bias and a fixed-position, but perhaps seeing the scope of what mine is, my readers may care to do what each man and woman must finally do: adopt a final position towards one's own path to eternity.

This search for a final position is not confined to individuals alone. The progress of the collective human intellect and the struggle to improve the physical condition of humankind, while combating disease and economic scarcity, has been the occupation of both nations and individuals throughout history. It seemed to me quite natural to speculate how two titanic intellects in opposition might be used to clarify through a sustained dialectical process this struggle to reach a final position regarding the nature and destiny of the human race.

History was bound to play a role in this exploratory process. The search for a cohesive and predictive model of history had puzzled great minds such as Giovanni Vico, Oswald Spengler, Arnold Toynbee, and Christopher Dawson and their search for a pattern brought into play the question of how texts of various sorts play a role in history. One key question presents itself in all hermeneutical inquiries: do texts emerge from history or is history created by the process of formulating the text? In the interplay of idea and event, which of these takes the lead in the dance?

Philosophy in its very essence is a historical phenomenon. Each age asks certain key questions and the mindset of each generation is in many ways unique. There are also major groundswell waves that can span centuries. So fundamental are these major perceptual influences that they often play a greater role in the arts than local or national or linguistic influences. One of these comprehensive cultural movements has been existential phenomenology, the predominant continental school of philosophy throughout the last century. In many ways these distinct philosophical movements shared a common dominator - that how we live is more important than what we believe. To prior centuries this concept would have been held to be highly suspect. The belief in the univocal human soul and its ultimate destination in either heaven or hell were unable to deal with the conflicted and fragmented aspects of human experience. Through most of European history belief systems particularly those that were nominally Christian provided the foundational structures not only of religion but of national identity as well. Sovereignty was based upon the existence of a sovereign who was usually an anointed king or queen. The first example of an international tribunal with universal authority was the Roman Catholic Church as presided over by the Pope. Protestantism in contrast arose from questions that had not been asked because within the ambit of orthodoxy they were simply inconceivable and were therefore meaningless even had anyone had the temerity to pose them. Conditions must be appropriate before certain questions can be seriously entertained.

Protestantism was more than a religious movement; it was economic, political, and philosophical as well. Despite its early emphasis on getting back to primitive Christian praxis by using Holy Scripture as a vehicle, the protestant mindset is always future oriented and locally based. Protestant belief is non-hierarchical to its core and for that reason led directly to what has been called the Enlightenment in the late 18th century. The fact that the great thinkers of that later period were either deists or atheists was a logical result of the breakdown of authority of the Roman Catholic Church and the feudal order that had governed Europe since the middle ages.

The 19th century that provides the background for the battles between Holmes and Moriarty was an age of expansion and of doubt. The prior so-called "age of reason" that formed the ethos of the 18th century died in apollonian splendor with the advent of "the Romantic period" of 1789-1832. This period evolved its own ideas for a renewed golden age by assuming that unbridled freedom would always lead inevitably to the triumph of virtue if uncontaminated by the historical residue of the past. After the death of George Gordon Lord Byron fighting for Greek independence and the accession to the English throne of Queen Victoria this ethos changed. The course of history thereafter could be traced from the influence of that tiny figure and her progeny. A new collective basis for social cohesion even in Europe let alone in the wider world has yet to emerge. Instead the emphasis has been placed on industrial expansion and colonial acquisition in ever more varied forms between nations. The wars of the 20th century were an attempt to force a solution of this problem.

After peace was reached in 1945 Europe was in ruins and America was left as the single most powerful and influential force in world history. It was a burden that it could not sustain because its own intellectual roots were not sufficiently deep to provide an ideological basis for the world beyond a shallow pragmatism feeding production and consumption, the so-called American Dream. This meant that Europe, the traditional core of what is termed Western Civilization was the only place to look for an overriding philosophical synthesis. That post-war synthesis was existential phenomenology. Even the later work of Ludwig Wittgenstein, one of the founders of the school of Logical-Positivism was moving in this direction. The central insight of phenomenology was that the various categories of thought can determine results and for that very reason philosophy should try whenever possible to get back to the things observed, the phenomena prior to anything that could be said about them. In essence phenomenology is a theory about how to reject theory. It places critical commentary in a process of infinite regress.

Similarly existentialism said that there is no central basis out of which history moves and individuals exist—we form ourselves and we determine history by what we do rather than what we are. The human condition in other words is entirely open—there is no source of ultimate truth or purpose. (This was essentially the way that Professor Moriarty in this book looked at the world). In this sense Sherlock Holmes (and the even more traditionalist Dr. John Watson) is fighting a retrograde action from the start of the book in order to salvage Christian and especially Catholic beliefs in an age that was perishing around him and about to enter that period of dislocation and slaughter that has been the 20th century.

Politics in the widest possible sense plays an immense role in *The Confessions of Sherlock Holmes* because one of my purposes in writing the book has been to give certain hints regarding the course that I believe human events are about to take. The trans-cultural period of what has been called "Modernism," (of which existential phenomenology is a sub-set) reached its high point in the 1920's just prior to the Second World War. It was followed by what has been called "Post-modernism" stemming from the writers that have been influential during my own lifetime from the 1970's until the present day. If I could choose a single characteristic of this period to sum up both of these two great cultural movements it would be the failure of any theory to gain universal consensus. Much human communication consists of incommensurable discourses. Instead, the overriding characteristic of Modernism/Postmodernism has been an obsession with methodology, a close-examination of each realm of thought and of its foundational texts ultimately yielding inconclusive results. In other words we are now at a point of a new beginning faced with a vacuous intellectual desert littered with the remains (now fully deconstructed) of whatever has preceded us. The whole world currently exists at ground-zero waiting for the bomb to drop with nation after nation engaged in fighting yesterday's battles.

This was precisely the position of Adam and Eve after the Original Sin had been committed, with one murder at least already accomplished when Cain slew Abel. If Abel had been "more able" things might have been the other way round. As this first dysfunctional family was packing up their RV to hit the road and say goodbye to Eden with the prospect of a life symbolized by a mansion in Florida in the far distant future the bewildered couple might have turned to God and hypothetically said:

"All right, we made a big mistake, so what do we do now?!!"

The answer of God (if I may be so bold as to suggest it) was this:

"Well my children, this was exactly what I wanted to spare you from ever encountering, the fact is that good and evil are now your responsibility, knowing good and evil is a matter of encountering them and that you will now have to do so if you are ever able to find redemption. I will give you one hint though—you will not be able to do it alone, although part of your new status in regard to all created things is that you will try. I will keep talking to you however for you are still my beloved children and when you are ready I will be waiting to see what you have learned."

This of course was undoubtedly not what Adam and Eve wished to hear and like the petulant children that they now were they probably said something like this in reply.

"Well that's just great!! Why didn't you tell us what we would be facing instead of just giving commands? Who do you think you are, God? ... Well can you at least give us some final advice, some parting gift ... something?!!

What answer can God make to such a request? I suggest in my little mini-tale that He answered:

"My dear children you have just entered the realm of history, my advice to you is ... to get busy."

"The Confessions of Sherlock Holmes" represents my way of staying busy. This has been my motivation in writing this book and my readers must never forget that mine is a fictional account and that not every thought expressed here may be orthodox and free of theological error. It is the advantage of the fictional form that even errors may be explored and supported by reason and rhetoric and for this reason Plato mistrusted artists.

I thank you for reading it. May it be of some use after all, or as my humble hero Sherlock Holmes once said, echoing Gustave Flaubert in his letter to George Sand as quoted in one of the original tales by Sir Arthur Conan Doyle,

"The man is nothing, the work is everything."

Thomas Mengert possesses a Masters Degree in English Literature with a special expertise in the complex works of the Irish author, James Joyce. His background in humanities and philosophy are combined in this probing novel. As a final Sherlockian synthesis, The Confessions of Sherlock Holmes is Mengert's attempt to understand the true depths of the best known detective in world literature, a hero to his many fans who find in his character and habits of mind an endless fascination.